Evil Hammering at the Door

by

Clive N. Ramkeesoon

RoseDog❧Books

PITTSBURGH, PENNSYLVANIA 15238

RoseDog Books
585 Alpha Drive
Suite 103
Pittsburgh, PA 15238
Visit our website at *www.rosedogbookstore.com*

ISBN: 978-1-4809-6977-3
eISBN: 978-1-4809-6954-4

For my dearest Lee, Sari, April and Joan. C.

Prologue

In a flash, the noonday sun vanished turning day into night. Like some foul slithering creature, a cold eerie darkness engulfed the planet emitting its stench. As a hush fell upon the earth, a soul-shattering howl of anguish split the night. The infernal wail echoed throughout the firmament startling the inhabitants on other planets and deafening the ears of human beings.

Men cowered in fear jabbering like monkeys sick with terror. The earth spun drunkenly on its axis and its sudden clumsy rotation wreaked havoc on the world's weather patterns. No sun shone. Bolts of lightening flashed in the darkness. Night switched into day for seconds only. Men held their collective breath and gasped in dread at each thunderclap.

Clouds of darkness eddied and swirled over the poisonous effluvium of the bog. A huge macabre presence lay enshrouded within its putrid miasma. It billowed like smoke seeming to be insubstantial and congealed into a solid impregnable mass. Then, like a giant foreskin, it peeled itself back to reveal the gargantuan head of Satan.

The archfiend lay spread-eagled on the smoldering bog, dazed by his fall. He howled his despair throughout the caverns and corridors of space, shocked at his tragic sentence. The darkness eddied and swirled in its aura of filth and corruption as he seethed with rage, humiliated at being cast into outer darkness and booted out of his privileged post at the very right hand of God. His anger congealed into an icy hatred inciting his determination for revenge. Being powerless against the Creator, he declared war on His Creation and hurled his minions of death and darkness into every corner of the globe.

Part 1

Chapter 1

South Korea
In the tiny township of Hamyang, lost in the depths of rural South Korea, a few of the basketball teams from the south were in transit to a national tournament in Seoul. The town fathers had invited them to use the town's facilities and park as their boot camp, and one team was spending its leisure time hurling a Frisbee at one another in the local park bordering an abandoned woodland area. The players were tall and muscular, all approaching seven feet. The captain was even taller, well over seven feet and more muscular and powerfully built than any of his teammates. When he moved his muscles seemed to come alive. They squirmed and slithered like snakes under his skin. With prince-like features, an upright stance and regal bearing, he seemed the type of man who was born to lead, to be in charge. The tone of command was in his voice. He would have been earmarked for greatness but for two major flaws in his character. The first was his lust for women, all women. The second was his inability to keep his hands to himself. He, and each of his four member team, sweating and shirtless in the warm fall weather, were racing around and leaping like streaks of quicksilver to catch the disk-like object as it careened through the air. Caught by the blustering wind, it would veer sharply upwards or downwards, before shooting off at a sharp angle. The players, in their different colored shorts, dazzled the eye with their speed and physicality. In the peak of physical condition, they raced frenziedly up, down and across the field, displaying their agility and athleticism.

The Confucian principle of a rank-based hierarchy that underpins all Korean society can be seen at work even in their game. The captain hurled the Frisbee first to his vice-captain who flung it down to the next in line and the Frisbee was chucked to each team member in a descending order of rank until it landed in the hands of the lowest ranked player wearing red shorts. As with a wolf pack in which the Alpha male dominates, pack members fit tightly into a hierarchy of rank. All follow their leader's dictates and the smallest breach of etiquette is ruthlessly punished. In the same way, the team captain dominates, and all members follow his lead on pain of severe censure.

The captain's face bore deep parallel scars on his left cheek as though it had been gouged by the claws of a bear, or far more likely, by an irate lady. Like his team mates, he was proud of his lithe, supple and streamlined body, resembling a predator in his swift aggressive movements. His scars, like neon signs, lit up his face. They drew all eyes so that women kept their distance spurned him on sight and exposed him to a life of suspicion, embarrassment and shame. Being a social outcast drove him wild with rage and robbed him of 'the milk of human kindness'. He became a man without mercy or compassion waiting for the opportunity to vomit his hatred on any unsuspecting female who fell into his grasp. For him, Nirvana would be to die throttling a beautiful woman to death in either of his hands.

In her graduation year at high school, Serena had taken an evening off from her studies to see an early movie, *The Sound of Music*, and to give herself a couple hours of relaxation before going to workout under the keen eye of her Sensei at his dojo. The truth was that although put off by the sub titles, she had enjoyed the music and applauded the courage and determination of the Von Trapp family in escaping their Nazi pursuers. As she stood on the sidewalk before the theater entrance waiting for her father to fetch her as prearranged, patrons of the movie kept streaming out of the theater chatting to each other.

On looking at the diminutive school girl waiting on the curb, few would have noticed the toned muscles of her arms sprouting from her sleeveless tank top, or those of her legs below the mini skirt she wore. Even fewer would believe that one so vulnerable in appearance could have completed the arduous regimen of exercises required to attain the third level of the karate black belt. They could hardly be aware that she ran for an hour on her treadmill before her father–himself a black belt of a higher rank–supervised her practice of the unending series of kata, the two hundred pushups and the one thousand sit ups she completed each morning. Then, three times a week, she undertook grueling workouts with her Sensei, going through her kata, training to empty her mind of all thought in order to act superhumanly fast in response to any physical act that threatened her person.

"Thought slows reaction time," her Sensei would warn. "Empty your mind! Empty it of all thought." While she found it an easy concept to understand, it took weeks to put into practice. There was also the training of breaking boards, and later tiles, with hands, feet and head.

"Come on, you've only broken five out of eight. Concentrate!" He would warn. "Your aim is a bit off, and so is your speed. There's still the punching bag and the dummy to attack." His criticism would force her to try harder, and he never stopped pushing. Although exhausting, it pleased her. She knew that the considerable progress she had made was due mainly to his insistence that she keep trying regardless of her fatigue. Like her father he was relentless in trying to make her an exceptional person.

"That's very good! I like that!" He would sometimes say while she performed one or other of her routines, "your hand and foot movements are getting faster. But, they need to be faster still. I want to see a blur of motion." While she listened to his advice of criticism she kept pressing her thumb against her index finger. Finally, she had mastered the deceptive feint, striking first with one limb of her body to draw the opponent's attention then striking hard with another limb at a spot where the blow was unexpected. Although the whole point of the training was aimed at confounding the opponent, and protecting oneself, her Sensei had repeatedly stated: "the martial art should be used as a last resort and only after an individual has been physically threatened."

John decided to go to the gym to practice his squash game. He thought he would use the hours of waiting for the movie to finish, before going to fetch Serena. His thought processes like his speech would emerge in verbal flurries like raindrops in gusts of wind. Once on the court, he began 'ghosting.' With racquet in hand, he raced from the "T" at the center to the front left corner, played a stroke at a non-existent ball, and still facing forward, sped backward to the "T." He immediately repeated the same action, this time to the right corner of the back court where he played another stroke at an invisible ball before returning to the "T." The non-stop repetition of this action for ten minutes to the four corners of the court was a means of increasing his fitness level and encouraging his smoother and swifter flow over the court. When exhausted and sweating profusely, he rested for a few minutes. It was then that he realized he had lost track of the time. When he looked at his watch, he knew that no matter how fast he drove, he'd be late. "Oh damn!" He shouted, rushing to his car, still in his gym outfit. While driving he held the wheel with one hand while nibbling at the other.

Serena waited a good fifteen minutes, recalling the images of the film while trying to ward off worries over her father's failure to appear. She knew that punctuality was one of his virtues and not being parked opposite the theater entrance, as he had promised, meant that some problem must have delayed him and prevented his arrival. In her mind, he was a younger, more intelligent and kindlier Polonius, often dishing out advice to his daughter about the virtues of punctuality and responsibility. But to be fair, she knew that few could guard against a flat tire or a clogged traffic route. Since it was a warm evening of late fall, just bright enough outside, she decided to take a short cut to her home through the park and abandoned woodland only a few blocks away from the theater.

Whenever Serena set herself a goal, no matter the degree of difficulty, she became single-minded in her purpose and commitment. She would permit no problem, no obstacle to stand in her way. Her latest project was to undertake a new regimen of exercises. She would then ask her dad to guide or supervise her in her new enterprise. She knew he would agree since he had always encouraged her to spread her wings; to be a better individual.

"Are you planning to repeat the whole series of kata that I already supervised this morning?"

"No Dad. Those exercises were strictly for my karate training. Now I want to work and build on my flexibility, my agility and especially my strength."

"What particular exercises do you have in mind?" He asked while chewing at his fingertips.

"I'll be doing multiple sets of curls and presses with lightweight dumbbells. That's for my arms and upper body. For my middle, my thighs and legs I'll do stomach crunches and lunges."

"You know that pushing yourself to such extremes when you already have attained the third level of the black belt will act as a character booster?"

"I suppose." She then smiled and shot a look of admiration at her dad. "There's a certain gentleman I know with far more than three notches on his belt. He hasn't stopped pushing himself. It's his example I'm determined to follow." Her dad remained silent feeling proud to learn that he was passing on to his daughter the principle that big dividends are gained by hard work. He then followed Serena into their gym where he watched her push herself to the limit of her endurance.

By the time she reached the wooded area, she had already begun to drink in the heady scent of the warm earth mingled with the pine scented air, marveling at the way the trees-some still dressed in their summer greenery, others in their autumn foliage–stood out against a sky of cerulean blue. The musical trill, chirp and whistle of birdsong was so gay and melodious that she sat on a nearby log to listen. She thought she could discern the beautiful notes of a lark warbling its song to the heavens. She then thought she heard a crow or was it a jay? The confusion of sounds from the variety of birds trilling, cawing, chirping or whistling at the same time, made it impossible to be sure, especially since many of them were hidden high among the leafy branches. Some of the trees grew so closely together and were intertwined in such a way that their leaves and branches carved out jagged blue ribbons of sky.

The scene before her was unexpected. An occasional oak, elm and maple was scattered among the stands of pine and fir. As she listened and looked among the lower branches, she caught sight of a few Black-tailed Godwits, and a couple of endangered Black-faced Spoonbills, their long black beaks standing out from their perfectly white plumage. They had to be migrants from the Song Do tidal flats in Inchon, making her wonder what they were doing so far south. Still listening to the birdsong and watching a Siberian Chipmunk scamper away at her approach, she caught sight of a few waxwings, their silky plumage and red wing-tips easy to spot amidst the green leaves. She couldn't help remembering, some six months ago today, that some of those deciduous trees stretched their bony arms against a heavily overcast sky creating a sense of loneliness and desolation. Today, the bright sky and the stretches of green, blue and gaily dressed autumn foliage dispelled that dismal impression.

Despite the distraction, she was worried, wondering what could have happened to make her dad fail to keep his promise. It was so unlike him. He was a man who could always be relied upon, especially about punctuality. "You must remember that the person you are supposed to meet has organized his other commitments to be available at the appointed time. Your being late shows a total lack of consideration and respect," he would preach. "It's very rude." With this advice in mind, she thought it would be a good idea to lecture him about the virtue of punctuality when she got home. The thought had her smiling as she imagined the unlikely scene of a daughter reprimanding her father, thereby upending Korean protocol.

On leaving the woodland, she was again surprised by what she saw in the adjoining park. It was occupied by a bunch of half-naked men in their different colored shorts hurling their Frisbee at each other and racing around to catch it. She looked on for a few moments and could soon see that the team leader was the tallest and most muscular of the players, while the lowest ranked member was the shortest and least powerfully built. They reminded her of a bunch of feral animals honing their predatory skills. After a few moments as she stood watching, the Frisbee landed at her feet and suddenly, the huge team leader stood menacingly before her.

"Where is Serena, John? Why isn't she with you? Leesa, her mother asked her father. When she saw him nibbling at his nails, the embarrassment and distress on his face, even before he spoke, she knew that something was wrong. "What happened?" She whispered, her face already turning pale. Head bowed and tongue-tied, John didn't know what to say; how to break the news. But as always, he decided on the truth.

"I was practicing on the squash court, using up the time it would take to fetch Serena. I hurried to get there, but I was late, arriving after the movie was over."

"*You* were late John. You who make such a virtue of punctuality?" A note of hysteria had crept into her accusation. "Why weren't you waiting for her before the movie was over?"

"I misjudged the time, leaving the gym late. When I reached the theater, she wasn't on the curb as we had arranged." Anxiety had him biting his nails.

The man who stood sneering down at Serena was a mountain of muscle, one cheek scarred with four parallel gouges. He bowed in greeting, making steady contact with the cold, marbled eyes of a serpent. His mouth was set in a cruel snarl and the malevolence etched on the surface of his opaque eyes alarmed her making her wary. He seemed about to strike when, in a flash, he extended his hand, palm open as for a handshake. She only bowed in return, refusing to respond to his insolent gesture, it being inappropriate for a man to offer his hand to a woman.

"Gal, so you refuse to be friendly," he shouted. "Fellas, this gal figures she's better than us," he shouted to his team. "Is that what you figured?" He questioned her insolently. Serena noted that he kept referring to her as 'gal' instead of 'woman.' And each time he used the term he curled his lip as though he considered the word derogatory and demeaning. His whole attitude of hostility directed at her who was innocent of wrongdoing suggested that he was basically angry at all women perhaps as a result of being disfigured by one. At her refusal to answer, he extended his arm behind him, palm downward, and moving his fingers in a scratching motion, summoned his teammates. "Come!" He commanded. "She's an intruder refusing to be friendly. She figures that her stylish outfit and expensive perfume sets her apart. Such a sophisticated gal no doubt sees us as scum; it's beneath her dignity to extend a hand in friendship." Listening to his ironic remarks, Serena knew that she was in trouble especially when suddenly confronted by five half-naked, sweating males. She realized that her fate rested in the hands of the team leader. Still, through her growing alarm, she managed to keep her cool. Appealing to his better nature, she spoke to him politely:

"Sir, may I please pass?" When he didn't respond, she again addressed him: "Sir, I have no quarrel with you. Will you please let me cross the field? My parents live close by on the other side." Again there was no answer as Scarface, looked at Red shorts and jabbing his index finger, he pointed at her with a scowl. "Get her!" He commanded.

At Red's approach, Serena began to back away slowly, suddenly recalling the exchange of words she had had with her Sensei.

"Many people consider karate an exercise in self assertion, seeing it as a skill that gives them an excuse for violence," he had said. "I prefer to think of it as a discipline that shapes and sharpens both the physical and mental faculties."

"Suppose you are physically threatened?" She had asked.

"Even then, you should use your mental astuteness to sidestep a physical confrontation. That's what your training is all about; using your mental faculties to avoid violence."

"Are you saying that we should never use the violence you teach us here?

"Only as a last resort," he had replied, well aware of the irony in his answer.

"So what did you do?" Leesa whispered to her husband, John.

"I waited, as people were still leaving the theater, expecting to see her. She wasn't among them."

"Didn't any of the theater employees see her?" His wife again asked, on the verge of tears.

"Yes, after I described Serena's appearance, the tank top and skirt she was wearing, one of the employees had seen ..."

"And?" She cut him off with eager expectation on her face.

"She saw Serena on the sidewalk. But somewhat later, when she again looked, Serena was no longer there."

"Could she have walked off since you weren't where you were supposed to be?" Leesa questioned intent on flogging her husband for his lateness. "It's fairly close through the woodland and park. And biting your fingers won't help."

"That's a possibility I hadn't considered." He replied in a chastened voice.

Despite the rigorous physical training Serena had undertaken to develop her flexibility, agility and strength; despite the fact that she had broken countless boards and tiles with head, feet and hands, she had never confronted anyone in physical combat. She had certainly not come to grips with anyone possessing the evident muscle, athleticism and physical prowess of her five male assailants. She couldn't help wondering whether she could prevail against such daunting odds.

On hearing Scarface's command, Serena realized she was in imminent danger of attack. She felt the fear of defeat by these five goons; the fear of being subjected to the evil will of their leader. Such thinking forced upon her the realization that she was no more than an ordinary teenager confronted by five stalwart thugs. Her two fingers were already rubbing against each other. Then, becoming ashamed of the fear mounting within her, she decided to try reason once again.

"Sir," she said while retreating, "I have not provoked any of you. I am an innocent bystander." No one took any notice of her words and Red pants kept advancing. I must try to avoid any physical conflict, she said to herself intent on eliminating her growing fear.

"Gentlemen, shouldn't you be protecting an unescorted lady?" She shouted, but her words again fell on deaf ears. She realized that Scarface had an insatiable greed for self gratification especially where women were concerned. He would always want the upper hand, obsessed with the craving of being in charge. The image suddenly came to her of a pig enjoying itself as it rooted in mud. Although she was retreating, Red pants was closing the distance between them. She then tried a final warning.

"Stop where you are Red pants! Don't force me to hurt you!" But she knew by the fixed scowl on his face that the time for averting a conflict had passed. Being physically threatened, she'd have to treat this confrontation as a 'last resort.' She would have no alternative but to protect herself. The scowling set of his features, borrowed from his leader, showed his determination to appease his superior; perhaps to justify his leader's reliance on him, the lowest ranked team member. More important, she thought, he was pleased to be chosen, since he would win bonus points from his leader by crushing her, his puny female victim. Serena used her training in deception to appear what she was not. Red pants rushed at the timid and helpless looking girl whom he saw as no match for his size, strength and muscle. One quick blow from his powerful fist would certainly be enough, he thought. But he'd have to be careful only to stun and not kill her. He felt lucky. Such a diminutive opponent was no match for him.

Meanwhile, Serena knew that she couldn't let him get too close, if she didn't want to become jelly in his powerful hands. She kept retreating. Red pants so badly wanted to showcase his fighting ability to his Captain and team that he completely failed to consider whatever skills his opponent might have. He made a sudden lunge at Serena throwing a series of wicked punches targeting her head. To his surprise, the target had suddenly disappeared from where it had been. Red's face became twisted and ugly with rage at being made to look ridiculous in front of his mates. He again rushed forward lashing out at Serena, both fists flying. She escaped the brunt of his attack by blocking his punches, but he landed a few solid body blows. She was dazed momentarily, and Red succeeded to connect a powerful right hook to her midsection followed by a furious blow to her temple. She was hurt, almost fell but recovered quickly. Since she couldn't keep him at bay, she acted quickly. When Red reached for her with both arms outstretched, she darted into his embrace, grabbed both his ears and with all her strength jerked his head forward to clash with a vicious head-butt that smashed at his nose. Her Sensei had taught her that the thick frontal arc of the skull is the strongest bone in the body. There was a grisly crunch of bone just prior to his high pitched scream. Blood poured from his nostrils, flowing into his mouth and down his chin. He stood paralyzed for an instant. She finished him off with a powerful knee to his groin. His legs buckled and he sank to the ground screaming in pain, his face contorted in agony. One hand covered his nose, the other protected his genitals.

"The employee knew nothing more. She was cleaning up the theater, making it ready for the next show."

"Oh my God! John, you should have been there earlier? How could you be playing squash instead of waiting for Serena? A mixture of loathing, confusion and grief had crept into his wife's accusation. Anger and exasperation flashed from her eyes although she avoided looking fixedly at her husband.

"The truth of the matter is that I came at once to get you," he said sheepishly. "Now we need to go and report the incident."

He drove to the station where they found that the police had already been notified. Someone fitting Serena's description had been reported at the local hospital. The officer couldn't say if the individual was their daughter nor did she know the extent of her injury. They then drove to the hospital. On the way, Leesa held her husband's hand leaning her head on his shoulder, needing his touch to sustain her. Yet, all the while, she chastised him for being the cause of their daughter's misfortune. To mollify his wife and to assuage his guilt, he raised her hand to his lips from time to time, but was too ashamed to reply. Imagine playing squash and forgetting your daughter, he thought guiltily, chiding himself. Please God, let any injury she may have be superficial! Please let any injury be superficial!

Scarface was aghast and embarrassed to see one of his teammate demolished so effectively by this slip of a girl. Anger flushed his face, his scars became even redder and his eyes grew bloodshot with frustration. His body became hunched like that of an attacking predator reminding Serena of a rabid dog or wolf. It was evident that he loved violence perhaps even feeling a fleeting sense of admiration for the frail looking girl who had so rapidly vanquished her opponent. But while he might admire her courage, speed and agility, there seemed to be no room in his make up for forgiveness or compassion.

"She really thinks she's better than us," he growled. "Well, let's see how much better." With a smirk, he turned to the next member of his pack in seniority.

"Grab the bitch!" He hissed, dispatching Blue shorts to do his bidding. Immediately, the minion rushed towards Serena. But on hearing the loud moaning of his teammate, and seeing him writhing on the ground, Blue became more cautious in his approach. As he advanced, Serena tried to prevent further violence and shouted:

"Sir, I have no quarrel with you. Leave me alone unless you want the same treatment as your buddy. He paid no attention and kept advancing, but cautiously.

Serena ducked when he feinted with a left but he quickly changed direction and with his right fist hooked her with a stunning blow to her kidney. She only partially blocked the unexpected punch and its power knocked her down. She took a couple of deeply indrawn breaths and sprang to her feet. Before Blue could react, she aimed a chop at his neck. He knocked her hand away sidestepped the rapid kicks that followed and landed two hard punches to either of her biceps trying to immobilize her. The blows had little effect on muscles that when flexed became granite hard. She darted in and stamped with her pointed heel on his ankle. The sudden sharp pain forced him to hop onto his other foot and threw him off balance. He swiftly tried to right himself but Serena had already attacked. She administered a series of swift kicks to the center of his chest that knocked him backwards and threw him rolling in the dust. She rushed forward about to jam her foot on his throat just as Scarface ordered his other more senior colleague to "get her." She had to back off swiftly from Blue when suddenly confronted by Green pants. He advanced cautiously not wanting to suffer the same fate as his mates. When she stood her ground instead of retreating or advancing as she had done previously, her apparent lack of fear puzzled him, stalled his advance. He quickly recovered then darted forward taking her by surprise. He snapped a flurry of stinging punches to Serena's head and torso. The powerful blows knocked her to the ground again stunning her momentarily. Surprised and delighted at his instant victory, Green hesitated, turning to glance at his Captain for approval. The pause permitted Serena to recover. She somersaulted backwards to her feet and attacked Green in a flash. Taken by surprise, Green stuck out an arm to repel the attack. Serena chopped down on the arm above the wrist with all her strength. The bone snapped and Green stood screaming in pain and shock. It was at that moment that the two remaining members of the wolf pack descended on her.

Scarface and his team mate grabbed Serena. They twisted her arms up behind her back until they heard them crack. The intense pain forced her to bend forward bringing tears to her eyes.

Scarface then stood before her, his face purple with rage at the way the frail-looking teenager had so thoroughly destroyed three members of his team. He stared at his captive, perhaps confusing her face with the woman who had disfigured him. "Now bitch, you're going to pay," he hissed. Something snapped inside him, and he suddenly struck her with a blinding right to the jaw and a wicked left to her temple. Then, in a blur, he booted her in the stomach, forcing the wind from her body and knocking her backwards to the ground.

She fell in a semi-conscious state. Several more kicks pummeled her body as hot hands clamped over her mouth, gagging her when she began screaming. Through the semi-darkness of approaching unconsciousness, she felt hands rifling her body as an arctic numbness froze her insides. She seemed to remember vaguely retreating from a number of advancing males so she must have made a desperate bid to escape. Then, faced with the inevitable, she tried to remain aloof in her mind, wanting desperately to preserve her dignity; prevent the corruption of her essence. She forced herself not to think of the defilement, but how do you preserve your dignity, resist submission while your body is being violated and fouled by corruption? She felt like a boxer battered into submission by her opponent but refusing to go down. While her captors ripped off her clothes, she was overwhelmed by a sense of deep humiliation. She wanted to believe that she was a civilized, sophisticated human being that set her apart, made her different from her barbarous aggressors. A blow to her head sent her mercifully into darkness and she ceased to struggle. She lay like a rag doll, incapable of offering even a token resistance to her violators.

Chapter 2

The matron in the hospital's rape center was explaining about the new patient to a nurse who had just come on duty: "She's been comatose for several days, curled into the fetal position."

"Have her wounds been dressed and a vaginal swab taken?"

"Yes. That was done as soon as she arrived. We've also had a doctor apply stitches where necessary. It seems she was beaten, gang raped and left for dead. Only a pack of predatory animals disguised as humans could have orchestrated such an attack on a helpless girl."

"They must have worked her over severely for her to be still comatose after so much time! Good God! I would never have believed that human beings could stoop to such evil?"

"They gave her a thorough mauling," Matron replied, before continuing. "On arrival, one of her blackened eyes was large, staring and empty, except for the glazed look it bore."

"Her other eye is still swollen shut and blood keeps leaking from one nostril on to the stitches that look like obscene insects crawling across her lips," the nurse pointed out.

As they approached her bed, both could see some of the blue bruises turning yellow blooming on her face and no doubt over her body. They could also hear the moan rising from her throat that formed a part of her breathing. Her passive state suggested that she had surrendered to the enemy in whatever battle she had been fighting.

"If she recovers from her coma, we'll take her statement and pass it on to the police," Matron stated.

The news of Serena's gang rape spread like wildfire through the township of Hamyang. It was especially noteworthy as a topic for conversation and prolonged discussion since it had the all the ingredients that made for the juiciest gossip—illicit sex, criminal conduct, and the violation of innocence. While the rural townships of Korea were long thought to be devoid of violent crimes, Father Murphy knew better. Every day the pale priest left his church with a heavy heart after hearing the wickedness and wrongdoing confessed to him again and again and again. Indeed, the accumulation of sin so sorely grieved the priest that he thought it necessary in his sermons to call attention to the growing menace of evil afflicting the individuals and families of his flock.

My God, how could I be playing squash when I should have been waiting for Serena? John kept chastising himself while sucking at his finger nails and waiting in the hospital to see his daughter. He was bowed down with sorrow and shame for causing Serena's catastrophe. As he sat in a waiting room at the side of a ward, he considered that like him, most people detested hospitals. He knew that, if truth be told, they had to be dragged there, often against their will, to visit an ailing relative or friend, after a sudden illness or accident.

Like him, they distrusted the smell, the silence, the sanitized sterility. They found it depressing to walk the corridors of wards and catch glimpses of bedridden patients, some silent, others immobilized by pain or disease. Like him, they viewed a hospital as the destination of the suffering, the diseased and the dying. The truth was that some patients would never leave, for it was a place where life ended. Few, he thought, regarded it, as he was now doing, as a place where life begins; where countless babies were born and where brilliant minds, skilled hands and dedicated personnel eliminated pain, cured disease and prevented death.

Standing at Serena's bedside, John felt a surge of rage as he bit his nails. His daughter lay comatose on the bed. With her jet black hair cascading over the white pillow, her face was almost as drained of color as the pillow on which she lay. He wanted to tear to pieces the scum who had fouled his daughter. He felt intense pain for the torment and distress Serena was experiencing. Yet, he was powerless to rid her of her anguish. However, as her parents, he and his wife could shower her with their love. That was his only comforting thought.

Apart from that, he was overwhelmed by his helplessness. If only it were possible, he would willingly bear her pain.

It was with very reluctant steps that Leesa first made her way towards the room in the hospital that had been converted into a chapel. Once inside, she seemed to have entered a different world. Apart from the shelves stacked with sheets, pillowcases and blankets on either side of the room, there was an altar with a crucifix at the far end and lighted candles on either side. The scent of fresh linen and burning wax in the secluded room overpowered the hospital smell of disinfectant mingled with unwashed bedding and bodies prevailing elsewhere.

The atmosphere of silence and serenity imposed a sense of calm upon her muddled thoughts as she wondered in consternation if she could pray, and then, whom she should first pray for. She clasped her hands, rested them on the back of the chair in front of her, her forehead leaning on her fingers, while her coal black hair flowed down her back and shoulders. The sadness stamped on her attractive features made her even more beautiful. She was still seated instead of on her knees, for though she wanted to pray, she didn't know how or where to begin.

In struggling to decide, she cast her mind back to her days as a pre-schooler. She remembered waking at night, still sleepy-eyed, intent on slithering in between her sleeping parents. She'd hold on to her father, Yong Sang, then press both feet against her mother's side straining her legs to shove her off the mat. On the floor, Kim would sit for a long while in silent contemplation, no doubt angry over her daughter's jealousy but barely able to keep her self-control intact.

"What are you doing on the floor so rapt in thought?" Yong Sang, rising from the sleeping mat, asked his wife.

"Leesa kicked me off and I was just thinking it was 'deja vu,' as I remembered a similar scene."

"Where, and with whom?" John asked curious about her statement.

"Oh, it was one of the case files we studied in Psyche," she lied unable to make eye contact with her husband. "The daughter kept wedging herself between her parents, shoving her father off the mat." Then she added: "in that scenario, the daughter had bonded with her mother."

"He must have been a neglectful or indifferent father! Did it happen a lot?" He asked offhandedly.

"He was a devoted father, and yes, it happened pretty much all the time."

"Children can be mean little wretches! Especially those who would treat a devoted father so cruelly, don't you think?"

"I suppose so!"

"So what did her parents do?"

"They bought a bigger mat."

The continued practice of her daughter's alienation of her, irritated Kim, but she too solved the problem by purchasing a larger mat. That didn't help. Leesa continued to shove her mother away from her father. On looking back, Leesa thought that her mother, Kim must have considered her a malicious bitch, but she remembered that although Kim's face often grew red with anger, she managed, with great effort, to control her temper, showing only the love she felt for her daughter.

When the effect of the drugs wore off, the pain within her was like a wildfire raging out of control. Its heat was intense, searing the tissues of her body. The flashbacks of a fight against several men, who committed violent sexual acts against her, haunted her imagination, terrifying her. Her face and body were puffed up with swellings, the insides of her thighs were badly bruised and her genitals were raw and blazing like an inferno. An unknown woman took turns helping the nurses tend to her needs. "Only God," she heard the woman say, "can deliver us from such an evil attack."

Serena had not always been ailing. As a healthy twelve year old, she spent a great deal of time working on her drawing and painting while studying her favorite subject, art.

"Yuk Lin, I'm thinking seriously of letting Serena skip the eleventh grade and go directly into your class after reading her last project report. You won't believe some of what I'm going to read to you."

"If you think she's up to the high standard I set, go ahead," Yuk Lin answered, chuckling at the intended humor of her immodest reply.

"The essay she handed in on Greek art is nothing short of astonishing. She divided it into its three periods–the Archaic, the Classical and the Hellenistic eras."

"It would be surprising if she pointed out the special qualities of each period."

"She went further, citing specific examples and giving reasons for her preferences."

"Really? Sure you aren't exaggerating a bit?"

"Not at all! In her view of the archaic artists, she chose the *Lady of Auxerre*, depicting a Greek goddess with right hand on her torso and left stiffly at her side. She considered 'the stone figure was too solidly built like the ugly sculptured figures of Egypt and Mesopotamia that inspired it. The frontal facing square shouldered stance was unnatural, too rigid and stylized.' Further, she considered 'the waist was too narrow, the hair too stiff, and the fingers too disproportionately long.' Since 'the silly smile glued on her face was conventional rather than natural,' she found that the statue bore little resemblance to a natural human figure."

"Lee, are you sure Serena is a preteen using such cynical yet cryptic and precise criticism?"

"I'm sure."

"Was she less analytic, less sure of herself and her material in her criticism of the Classical period?"

"Quite the contrary. The 'repetitive devotion to deities' she found tiring, but thought 'their idealization of the human figure a beautiful and significant change from archaic convention. Their aim of ennobling the gods by depicting them in human form was clever,' she thought, 'for the fact was that in so doing, they were glorifying themselves.'"

"She sounds more like a learned art teacher than a student."

She praised Phidias' huge marble statue of *Athena* in the Pantheon and *Zeus* in the temple of *Olympian Zeus* for 'their grandeur of conception-'as you know, the sculpture of Zeus is 43 feet high–as 'for the dignity and restraint they displayed. She considered that 'the repeated solemnity of their facial features was a significant change from the perpetual smile of the earlier era. However, she found that 'it expressed their view that the public display of human emotion was not only uncivilized, but also barbaric.'"

"My God, she must be a prodigy to be able to use such language! Were those the only examples she used?"

"No, it gets better. She chose the bronze statue of the *Charioteer of Delphi* 'to show the movement from stylized representation and idealism towards greater realism.' She pointed out that 'his facial expression displayed his self-control, modesty and restraint after a victory that would normally cause a moment of exhilaration.' In the architecture of the *Parthenon* and the temple of *Olympian Zeus*, she noted 'their imposition of order, moderation and harmony upon their work.' In both art forms, she felt that 'the artist sought simplicity, while disdaining decorative extravagance. Their deified human figures while beautiful, portraying types rather than individuals and suggesting that their artistic aim was universal rather than personal.'"

"My God, the language she uses and the breadth of her knowledge makes her sound like a professor delivering a lecture. Lee, are you sure this report was done by Serena Ahn, the preteen, without the help of background material?"

"She wrote it in my class, and in my presence. Of course, it's evident that she has a photographic memory, having reproduced what she had no doubt read somewhere. But the accumulation of her factual knowledge indicates the depth of her studies, her knowledge of and dedication to her subject and her evident love of art."

"It also indicates her intelligence! I can't wait to hear how she viewed the Hellenistic period," Yuk Lin stated.

"She chose the *Boy Jockey* to show 'the movement away from the idealization of perfect beauty towards a greater reality and naturalism.' She pointed to 'the expression of power, energy and tension in both horse and human caught in a moment of extreme exertion and exuberance.'"

"What were her critical remarks about the statues?"

"She said that 'the horse's head and neck are naturally drawn with dilated eyes, distended nostrils, swollen veins and ears pressed well back, depicting the sheer power of the animal under great strain. The facial features of the jockey too, are portrayed under great stress. Both horse and man express inner feelings of great effort and excitement. There is also the dramatic tension produced through exaggeration between the powerful body of the horse that dwarfs the puny figure of the boy. She considered that the *Boy Jockey* was a movement towards truth in art. "

"Her ability to write such a report while in class without reference material shows her incredible memory, her knowledge of the subject and her acute critical eye. She is more than ready to skip a grade. I shall have to be on my p's and q's with her in my class."

As a preteen, it struck Serena that there was a great disparity between the huge flourishing farm on which she lived with her parents, and the small unproductive farms far flung throughout the surrounding district. She knew that the crop production on those farms dropped alarmingly each growing season with disastrous results for the families. She decided to discuss the situation with her father.

"Dad, I notice that the neighboring farms are all small and unproductive in comparison with ours?"

"That's the truth. They've been growing the same crops, on the same fields, and using the same archaic methods for generations. They've robbed the soil of nutrients, exhausting it. The fact is that in past years, whenever their crops failed, they were forced to sell off parcels of land in order to survive. What you have to understand, my little inquisitive chipmunk is that their production like their farms, has shrunk. If they refuse to change, things will continue to get worse before they get better."

"But Dad, the truth is that many farming families are unable to adequately feed or clothe themselves. It worries me that they and their children have so little while we have so much. Have you noticed the very pale and piqued features, the big staring eyes and the string-bean bodies of their children? What you have to understand is that they've been wearing their clothes for so long that they've become threadbare. Their shoes are down at heel and few of them have socks. Can't we do anything about it, Dad?" Serena implored, her words spilling out over each other. Being anxious she kept rubbing her index finger with her thumb. Yet, she was sure that her dad could solve any problem in the world.

"Dearest daughter, if we put our heads together, I'm sure we can devise a workable plan. But the fact is that I've advised those farmers to change their methods till I'm blue in the face. The last thing they want is change. "What was good enough for our ancestors is good enough for us," is their mantra.

"Dad, can I think this matter over and discuss it further with you?"

"Certainly, my darling. And, would you like an appointment to see me in my study in a few days or so?" He added, in far too jovial a manner for his daughter's liking.

"Dad, please don't patronize me or treat what I've said as a joke." Her father recovered quickly.

"Serena, I would never make that mistake, especially after our last discussion."

"Today is Monday. How about next Monday, before you leave for work?"

"Next Monday it is!" Her father answered his face as serious as he could make it. Only his eyes were smiling.

Kim and Yong Sang were having a repetition of the same old argument.

"Darling, I keep telling you that girls often develop an early attraction to their fathers with a resulting resentment and even animosity towards their mothers. I believe that Leesa's behavior is no more than a juvenile hiccup, a fairly normal passing phase that she'll outgrow."

"I don't agree," Kim pointed out, "and I'm talking from experience."

"You're referring to that case file from your Psyche course?"

"Yes," Kim again lied through closed eyes.

"What happened in that case?"

"Things got worse. The daughter became cold and rebellious towards her father, always finding new ways to be vicious." Whenever Kim lied or complained she closed her eyes unconsciously.

"What harm could a small child inflict on an adult parent? She could hardly have murdered him," he joked.

"It's no laughing matter," his wife replied. "She cut holes in his socks and buttons from his shirts. When she grew older, helping with the cooking, laundry and ironing, she burnt his meals, ruined his shirts and stiffened his underwear with too much starch. Finally, she 'sweetened' his coffee with salt."

"What was her dad's response to such calculated wickedness?"

"He bought new shirts and underwear and made his own coffee. He was still convinced that his daughter's conduct was an aberration that would pass." Yong Sang noticed that her eyes were closed.

"He must have loved her very much to overlook such meanness and malevolence!"

"He did!"

"What was the mother's attitude?"

"She tried to convince her daughter that her father loved her in spite of her wicked ways. Then, she pointed out to her daughter that she had a darker side to her character that she'd have to control."

"You mean that she was evil?"

"Her mother didn't use that word, but she got her point across."

"Did it help?"

"No!" Kim didn't tell Yong Sang that she had substituted the case history for her own behavior.

Suddenly awake, Serena began trembling violently, her eyes clouded over, her face contorted with fear. She spread her hands before her face, palms forward, as though grappling with and fending off some unseen attacker. Her mouth opened wide in a scream, but no sound came from the corded muscles of her throat. She could again feel the vicious kicks striking her body, crippling her, and the stink of male musk rising in her nostrils was nauseating. She kept struggling against the nightmare images until exhausted. Her energy spent, she withdrew into herself, immobilized by the pain. Her shoulders and arms ached from the knees that had been pressed down upon them holding her prisoner, and a mass of scars and bruises had bloomed on her face and body. The pain from the bite marks on her breasts kept increasing as did the fire in her swollen genitals. And all the time, a face with parallel scars haunted her sleeping and waking hours. Even in sleep her thumb and index finger were in contact with each other and kept twitching too and fro.

Leesa's conduct grew worse. She refused to let Kim bathe, dress or undress her, demanding that her father usurp that maternal role. When thwarted by her mother's insistence that her wishes were inappropriate, she threw such violent tantrums that forced Yong Sang to take over her mother's role.

All through her youth and even into her early adolescence, she clung to her father as though he were her lifeline and every chance she got she continued to drive herself like a malicious wedge between her parents. The normal conduct that her father had forecast had spiraled downwards into gross abnormality. Leesa's resentment and jealousy had blossomed into full blown hatred that Kim read in the malignant stares her daughter darted at her. Yet, in each of those confrontations Leesa could never make eye contact for long with her mother. In spite of the anger that flared in her brain, Kim managed, with great effort, to smother the fiery blaze of her temper. Instead, she worried, fearing that Leesa's malevolence would one day break out into open warfare.

Monday morning finally came around for Serena's interview and it surprised her to find her father waiting for her in his study. He sat behind his enormous desk covered with papers, articles and tomes on farming while nibbling upon his fingers. One glass wall looked out upon a garden, and the others were lined with books dealing with every aspect of agriculture. Above them, framed pictures of his various university degrees and diplomas hung in a row. A number of framed pictures of herself, her mother and the family stood on his desk.

"Well, I haven't kept you waiting, have I?" He began, seeing that in her anxiety, Serena couldn't stop fidgeting. She was struggling to maintain her calm, evidently over-eager to get to the point. Like a tightly coiled spring, she could hardly suppress the impulsion to uncoil and spew forth her plans.

"No Sir," she replied. Oh oh, her father reflected. He knew the term 'Sir' instead of 'Dad,' forecast serious business. It was usually followed by a daring, well conceived plan. The last time she used the term, it had cost him dearly.

"I'm listening," he said.

"Dad, I have a proposition for you."

"Why don't you tell me what you have in mind?"

"At the moment, you have a number of fields that are not being used. They're lying fallow. I would like to lease one of them to start a poultry farm. Any vacant field having good drainage would be perfect."

"A poultry farm you said?" It's something I've been thinking about, he reflected. "What do you know about poultry farming?"

"I did an in-depth study on the subject for a project at school. I decided it wouldn't be very difficult to start one, especially since I can count on you and our farm manager, Mr. Sing, for guidance and support."

"You can always count on me, and it makes me happy that my daughter, at so early an age, is following in my footsteps in doing the work that my ancestors and I have chosen as a career. However," he added, "I'll have to treat your proposal as a serious financial transaction, then make it binding on both of us."

"I realize that Dad, but I'm hoping you won't drive too hard a bargain," she said with a winning smile. Her father pretended he was all business, smiling inwardly but ignoring her attempt to undermine his defenses.

"Do you have any financial assets in the nature of collateral to offer against the lease?" Her father asked, thinking he would catch Serena unprepared for such a question. But his daughter surprised him. She had spent considerable time thinking over exactly how her father would react. She had thus been able to forecast many of the questions he would ask and was well prepared.

"I didn't expect my dad to ask me for collateral," she said, still trying to throw him off balance and gain the upper hand, "but let me think," she said, pretending she wasn't ready for the question. She knew that she had him over a barrel.

"If I said that I have the financial backing of my father for collateral, do you think that would be enough?" She asked with another of her winning smiles.

"Is he a reliable fellow?"

"Totally! I can truly say that I've known him all my life and he's never let me down."

"Well then he must be quite a man., so I have to agree." He replied, momentarily stymied, and then quickly recovered. "But tell me how you intend to repay the loan?" In putting her on the defensive, he would learn if she was really prepared and to what extent.

"Repay the loan for the lease? But Dad, the land is lying fallow. That means it's vacant, not being used, so you lose nothing in leasing it to me." She stated breathlessly, with a nervous giggle, unconsciously aping her father's speech rhythm. It was one question she hadn't expected.

"Its topsoil has been lightly tilled and it is under heavy fertilization. Like money in a bank, it's gathering 'interest'–nutrients that next season will pay big dividends. So, I'll be losing a great deal."

"Well," Serena replied, again thinking quickly, "when the babies of my birds are mature, in less than four to five months time, that is, their eggs and meat will be in great demand. Once they are sold, I'll begin to repay your loans." Her dad was impressed with her ability to think on her feet.

"I'll speak to the nearby markets on your behalf."

"Dad, I wasn't thinking of those markets, I was thinking of *your* grocery outlets and farm markets. I've learnt in my research that there, eggs and poultry are always in short supply. I was counting heavily on your support. Dad, don't you see? With you backing my project, I'll be able to repay you far more quickly."

"Let's first consider the nearby markets," he replied, admiring her cleverness. "But if you are correct, and that plan fails, our outlets are always short of eggs and poultry. I'll buy your surplus eggs and birds whenever the other markets can't take them. That way, you'll have a guaranteed market. But, you haven't explained how you'll be paying for their feed," he replied, beginning to worry his fingertips with his teeth.

"That's the easy part, Dad. I've discussed the matter with many of the farmers' wives, those who grow oats, corn, barley, and wheat and others who grow millet, alfalfa, soybean and rye. These are the very grains on which my birds thrive. I've encouraged them to donate a portion of their grain and they've already filled fifty huge crocus bags. I've also drawn up a roster of those who will feed and water the birds. The families responsible have all agreed to my plan." This means that she'd already decided that I'd agree to all her suggestions, her father realized, smiling. There were still a few questions he needed to ask if only to show her that he wasn't a complete pushover.

"But Serena, don't many farmers have chickens, ducks and turkeys? Why should their wives be willing to donate their grain for your poultry? What do they get in return?"

"Sure, some farmers already have one or two birds that lay a few eggs. But, if they ate those birds, then they wouldn't have eggs. I've promised to exchange dozens of eggs for their grain once my birds start to lay, which I know will be immediately. Later, I've also promised to provide each donor with babies from chickens, ducks, turkeys and geese. They will then be able to start their own farms. The prospect of growing their own birds for eggs, meat and money appeals to them particularly."

"You get feed for your poultry; they get eggs in exchange. Later, while you keep getting grain for your poultry, they get meat, and in time, a 'starter' farm with four different kinds of birds. It sounds like a pretty good deal, all round," her father said, surprised at his daughter's shrewdness. "But, won't the farmers have to build larger coops for the starter farms?"

"Sure Dad. we've discussed that. They'll have lots of time before their babies arrive. But that's not all, Dad. I've made them promise to do for their neighbors what I'll be doing for them. You see, I've stressed that solidarity is my maxim. If we all work together, poultry farming will soon be spreading throughout the area and starvation will no longer be so widespread." John was surprised at Serena's humanitarian attitude as well as at her enterprise and good judgment, but asked: "Suppose the farmers refuse to share their good fortune!"

"I've warned them that I'll be coming around with Mr. Sing, our farm manager. We'll inspect the progress of their farms to make sure that they keep their promise. But Dad, I don't need to threaten them. They are delighted that they'll have a supply of eggs and meat for their families. That alone will make them keep their word. Besides, how could they turn down the possibility of a constant supply of protein?"

"You have a well conceived plan, but I'll have to give your proposition more thought before I commit myself to a final decision, okay?"

"Okay Dad, and thanks for listening sympathetically," she told him. While Serena's two fingers were clamped together, her dad was nibbling at his nails.

"We'll talk again in a few days time, and now I must leave for work," he said, lifting his daughter in his arms. "You're a precious gem that I'm very proud of." A warm glow suffused his daughter's cheeks after the loud smack she received.

"Yong Sang, don't you think that Leesa's hostility has gone far enough?" Kim asked her husband.

"There's no harm in her possessiveness darling. I'm sure it's not hostile. She's just a kid with strong notions of her ties to me. You shouldn't take it personally."

"Her animosity and dagger-like glares are not figments of my imagination. Apart from shoving me off the mat, she chooses the moment when we're talking or watching TV, to thrust herself between us, or to hop into your lap. Her eyes then light up, and her face becomes animated. When the hot blaze of my anger shows, she smiles, treating me as though we're competing and I am some sort of antagonist. Darkness clouds my brain, my anger intensifies and I want to slap her into next year. I have to clench my fists tightly and it's all I can do to calm myself and keep this hot temper of mine under control." Kim's eyes were closed when she added: "I keep worrying that she's cooking up some hostile plan of attack."

"She's been doing that since she was two. And you'd do well to keep your anger in check. It's unlike you to speak of Leesa as though she were some sort of predatory beast!"

"I suppose you're right. But she's not two anymore! She's thirteen, displaying the seductive wiles of an adult siren. Don't be surprised if she eventually makes me lose control of my temper."

"Darling, try to keep your cool and pay no attention to her juvenile antics! You must know that the way we feel about each other, no teenage daughter can come between us! Isn't that all that matters?"

"You may be right, but I still can't help worrying."

She had lost the power of speech and though she could see, she didn't recognize the woman who kept staring at her with an expression of unremitting sorrow. In sleep, nightmarish images flashed across her consciousness repeating scenes that had appeared in previous dreams. In some, she had fleeting glimpses of scarred features and half-naked men. In others, she was running from her Nazi pursuers. Images appeared and disappeared too quickly for her to interpret them. Like lights on a Christmas tree, they switched on and off; flashes of clarity followed by intervals of darkness. Their unexpected appearance only increased her terror and confusion. Whenever she awoke, the atmosphere of her room was tranquil, but her heart pounding like a trip hammer, filled her with dread. In confusion, she didn't know if the episodes in her head were real or imaginary.

Had they really happened to her or was she hallucinating? Oh God, she thought, had she lost her mind? What was happening to her made no sense. Worse, there was no one to help her, to tell her what had really happened or even who she was. In her confusion she kept rubbing her thumb against the finger next to it.

Chapter 3

Father Murphy would be blind if he didn't see the bigger picture. Hamyang was merely a microcosm of the worldwide catastrophe ravaging mankind. Like the winged predator she was, Evil stalked her prey using the whole earth as her hunting preserve. She coerced spouses into breaking their marriage vows and filing for divorce; goaded jealous or adulterous husbands and wives to fight and murder each other. After shooting their offspring, parents often turned the gun on themselves. Gun-toting students were breaking into schools and universities killing teachers, fellow students and then themselves. Civilian snipers embarked on killing sprees shooting innocent citizens at random. She compelled deranged mothers to drown their infants, abandon their newborn babies in dumpsters and she seduced young men and women into alcohol, drugs and prostitution. Those whom she drove to despair took their own lives. Perhaps, worst of all, were the suicide bombers whom she indoctrinated with her lies of paradise and the seduction of virgins. They not only detonated themselves, but also murdered a slew of innocent people in their vicinity.

As a creative artist, it followed naturally that Yong Sang adored beauty in all its forms and disguises. Not surprisingly, he worshiped women who embodied the beauty he adored. He was also a diligent woodworker, and John noted that he handled the woods on which he worked as adoring men treat their women. In choosing each particular piece of lumber, he closely studied the character of the wood, its shape, color and grain before making his selection.

Even before the wood won his approval, he had a habit of holding it gently, running his fingers up and down its length, lightly caressing its grain feeling for flaws. John thought that he behaved like a lover massaging the body of his beloved. Indeed, Yong Sang did relate to the different woods of his choice as though they were women, dividing them into categories based on their color and country of origin. There were the white woods of North America and Europe like pine, spruce, and fir that had endured the harsh winters of the Temperate zone. Since they offered themselves willingly to his tools and he had no difficulty in having his way with them, he considered them Caucasian. In his mind they represented the zany blonds of easy virtue.

The darker woods like ebony, teak and mahogany, he considered African. He regarded them as having won their spurs in their battle against the broiling heat of the Tropical sun. It had stripped them of their moisture so that they were dry, especially hard and resistant. He confided to John that they needed endless coaxing with the gentlest of touches, the tenderest of caresses for him to make any headway with them. Even then, with their sultry nature and fiery temper, it was not uncommon for them to resist his endearments and in rebellion, like the capricious broads they were, to ruin his tool.

"John," Leesa said to her husband, "have you noticed the change that has come over Serena since her accident?"

"Darling, as the doctor mentioned, the trauma of rape can be very destructive. The truth is that recovery has many phases and can take a long time for the healing process to take place."

"That's not only what I'm talking about. I know from experience that the feelings of shame, humiliation and guilt–the aftermath of such violence–are destructive, even crippling both physically and mentally. And they often take a long time to heal. But I was really thinking of what Serena was like before, don't you remember?"

"How could I forget? She had always been a bundle of energy, constantly on the move, running to fly her kite; racing on her bicycle around and around the yard; jumping onto the swing and propelling herself higher and higher, jumping off only after she'd had enough. You could always tell where she was by her trilling laughter, the happiness she always displayed."

"She was such a happy child, constantly involved in some new project or interest. Even when in her rocking-chair she couldn't sit still. She would rock herself violently from one side of the room to the other and back again. She would then begin tapping her feet or flicking her head back to throw her hair from her face. Her gold earrings would tinkle and glisten with each movement of her head, just as her bracelets would clash and jingle with each gesture of her hands. The repeated sounds and movements gave the impression that she was like a windmill in constant motion; an unstoppable force."

"It's that attitude to life that I had in mind. During the past week or so, she remains unmoving in her bed seeming painfully aware of what she has lost. Guilt and shame seems to have immobilized her, frozen her blood, and drained the vitality from her body. Before, she had always been a bundle of energy, ever on the move. Now, she seems like a corpse; as though someone has sucked the life force from her body."

"I supposed you've noticed: her two fingers are still twitching away."

Having tried to open Yong Sang's eyes to Leesa's malice, Kim realized that he was too blind to see. He refused to look behind her mask, to acknowledge her cruel streak, or to recognize her hypocrisy. But if the love for his daughter blinded him to her faults; if he were willing to remain blind, Kim was not. Despite the role of innocence played by the preteen, Kim could not fail to notice the malevolent glances her daughter shot at her. She remembered that even during her youth Leesa had begun to regard her father as her personal property and to detest her mother's encroachment on what she considered her personal preserves. She decided to show her mother the true extent of her hatred and hostility by devising a plan. She'd disguise the malice she felt by pretended love and affection. Then, when her mother least expected it, she would lower the boom. The beauty of her plan was that she thought her mother would not even know that she had been defiled.

During the following week, Kim noticed that Leesa had begun tidying up her room, rolling up her sleeping mat, tying a cord around it and upending it carefully in a closet. She had barely finished her meals before springing up from her cushion to clear the table and wash the dishes after breakfast and supper. When not at school on weekends, she also did the lunchtime load of dishes. At night, once a week, she did the laundry and really surprised her mother by ironing her own and her parent's clothes. At the end of the second week, Kim approached her daughter.

"Darling, thanks for doing so many of my chores. While it's very thoughtful of you and I'm really grateful for what you've been doing, it's taking away too much time from the study periods that you normally reserve for school work."

"Mom, I'm quite happy to do the chores. Don't worry, I'll find time to do my studies." With the sweetest of smiles, she continued. "I only want to help. It's my way of taking care of the mother I love." With that astonishing reply, she gave Kim a tight hug and a quick kiss on the cheek, before adding: "I also plan to bring you your morning tea with which you always start the day."

Her father told Serena that he had given a great deal of thought to her poultry farm proposal. While he admitted she had done some solid research and come up with a number of worthwhile ideas, the truth was that there were still a few questions he needed to ask. Abruptly he then inquired: "What birds do you propose to start with and how many?" She was ready for him, and replied immediately.

"I'll start with forty-five young adult Plymouth Rock hens and five roosters. I've chosen that breed for their meat. While they are also fair egg layers, certainly not as productive as Leghorns or Rhode Island Reds, they are far sturdier than both the others with more meat on their bones. Then, I'll need forty-five young adult turkey hens and five toms. I'll want the same breakdown in the number of ducks and drakes, preferably Muscovy, and the same number of geese."

"You seem to know something about the poultry you propose to raise. Do you have in mind any special breed of geese?" Her father enquired, trying not to show how impressed he was.

"I'll get the advice of the wholesalers and choose those birds that do best in our local conditions."

"When do you need the birds?"

"As soon as your manager, Mr. Sing and his farm hands can build me four separate enclosures on the field I've chosen, one for each of the breeds. For the ducks, I'll need one with a large built-in pond in one corner."

"I take it you know that the newborn offspring will need a separate coop within each enclosure that's warm and dry? They'll also need specially ground grain for the first few weeks?"

"Yes Dad, I've been thorough in my research, and I'll be there to explain to Mr. Sing what I have in mind: things like clusters of electric bulbs to keep the newborn chicks warm."

"Sing is very knowledgeable about all types of farming. He'll be able to offer you loads of advice, especially about the building of the coops and their laying boxes. But, your plan calls for a start with two hundred birds. That's quite a handful."

"I've told the feed donors what to expect and they have already begun collecting, mixing and bagging more grain in readiness. Since we spoke last, they have nearly fifty full bags of grain ready, each in the hundred pound range."

"Is that because you knew I'd agree?" He asked smiling. Serena thought it better to sidestep the question.

"Dad," she replied, "the fact is that they're almost as excited as I am."

"I've already alerted my veterinarian to inspect the birds you intend to buy. He will ensure that they have a clean bill of health. He has also agreed to check on them from time to time or whenever needed."

"Thanks Dad, I knew I could count on you." Serena's happiness had her flicking her thumb and forefinger to her own secret melody.

Kim was remonstrating with herself. She was hesitant about harboring suspicions about a daughter who had been showing such thoughtfulness and generosity. Yet, she couldn't forget those icy stares or the very abrupt change in attitude. She daren't let herself be taken in so easily while hating herself for vacillating; questioning herself over and over for thinking evil thoughts about her own daughter. Why did she keep harboring such un-motherly suspicions? Perhaps Leesa was really changing Kim thought. She then again berated herself for her unkind thoughts about a daughter who was showing such thoughtfulness, generosity and love towards her.

"So it's okay to bring you your tea first thing in the morning?" Leesa asked.

"That would be very sweet of you, darling," Kim replied while thinking: Oh God, had she misjudged her daughter all this time? Had she been wrong to read malice into all her looks, words and actions? Had her father been right in his assessment all along? From that moment on, Kim vowed to accept at face value her daughter's thoughtfulness and affection. Wasn't Leesa turning out to be the kind of daughter every mother yearned to have, and one for whom Kim had so fervently prayed? She began to feel ashamed of herself.

She was one of those babies born a 'plain Jane.' Yet, her mother knew that children changed as they grew. She hoped and prayed that her plain daughter would be so blessed. The ugly duckling did change. She grew uglier. During her youth and adolescence through school, her classmates picked on her every chance they got. She was constantly bullied, badgered and ridiculed, hence her life, like that of her mother, was one of intense misery. The torment that pursued her into her early adulthood stopped abruptly when she met and married a handsome farmer. For the first time she was the envy of the farming community of Hamyang where she lived with her husband.

Serena would stay in bed squirming, her legs crossed, knees pressed tightly together as she turned from side to side, fighting against the pressing need to go to the bathroom. She would restrain herself through fear of the pain that would accompany relieving herself. Urinating had become one of her worst ordeals. Just the thought of her burning flesh while her bladder emptied was enough to make her rein in the need to go until the very last second. The salted warmth of her urine would then set her raw and swollen flesh ablaze. With jaws clamped, flexed muscles, and closed fists, she'd have to control the flow of the fiery liquid, forcing it to leak out slowly. The salve she used to coat her insides was of little help.

"Determined to monitor Leesa's preparation of the tea she promised, her mother rose early. She wanted so badly to trust her daughter, but judging from past experience, she just couldn't. And so, from a concealed place, and still cursing herself for her suspicion, Kim watched as Leesa poured boiling water into the teapot to warm it. After throwing out the water, she carefully measured out three heaping teaspoons of tea leaves, put them into the pot and poured boiling water over them. Humming a popular tune, she covered the pot and waited for the tea to steep. When her mother saw that Leesa was going through the normal motions of tea preparation and failing to make any suspicious moves, her face reddened with shame as she cursed herself again for her un-motherly suspicion. She then began to withdraw from her hiding place.

During her pregnancy, Plain Jane's most cherished wish was to have a baby girl–a daughter who would be as beautiful as her father was handsome. Her mother couldn't wait to curl her long tresses, tie them with colored ribbons, dress her in frilly frocks and spoil her rotten. She yearned for the day when she would parade her beautiful child, dressed to the nines, in front of those neighbors who had made a living hell of her life, causing her such misery. She and her beautiful daughter would make them all envious, and finally, she would have the last laugh. Plain Jane did have a girl. She was the spitting image of her mother. The latter was so devastated by the ugliness of her child that she traded the frown she sometimes wore for a permanent scowl. Worse, she grew to detest the child she had been so eager to love. Though she tried to conceal the depth of her feelings, her words and conduct towards her daughter, Mona eventually told her the truth. The world confronting Plain Jane grew even more cruel forcing her to seek solace in religion. Her guilt and shame caused her devotion to become obsessive and she beseeched God to forgive her cruelty since it was the hardship she faced that had made her hate the daughter she should love.

On her return from school Serena ran in search of her mother. She was in the kitchen supervising the help. "Be sure to put enough red pepper paste in the prawns and scallops. You know they are some of our favorite dishes. Oh Serena! I can't believe you're back from school already? Come give your mother a big hug, dear. How did your day go?"

"Hello Mama. I made a new friend today."

"That's fine dear. What's her name?"

"Mona."

"How did you two meet?"

"I noticed that she was always by herself. At first I thought she was stuck up since she seemed to be ignoring everyone. But I was wrong. No one wanted to be her friend or talk to her."

"What made you think that?"

"Everyone kept calling her names and making her life miserable."

"You mean they bullied her. Oh, that's shameful."

"Yes they kept pushing her around. Knowing she wouldn't fight back they kept attacking her until she started to cry. I felt sorry for her. Some kids were calling her 'blubbo' and telling her that she was as fat as a whale. Mama, I don't like to see people cry."

"Neither do I dear. So what did you do?"

"I told them to leave her alone or else they'd have to deal with me."

"Did that stop them?"

"No!

"What did you do?"

"I shouted at each of them to stop teasing and to leave Mona alone. Then I hugged Mona and stopped her crying just as you do when I'm in tears." My God, thought Leesa, they're just kids and already showing their propensity towards evil.

Kim was already on her way to hug and kiss Leesa for her thoughtfulness, elated that her ugly suspicions had been wrong. Leesa was every bit the loving daughter Kim had longed to have. She promised herself to stop being so judgmental in future. She was about to call out to Leesa and show herself when her daughter's next move stopped her dead in her tracks. Leesa had placed the uncovered teapot on a low stool and stunned her mother by her next act. She stooped over the teapot, hiked up her skirt, and then shot into it a yellow stream of her venom. A cloud of darkness enveloped Kim's brain and a bright spark ignited her fury. Rushing into the kitchen, she grabbed her daughter by the neck and silently began to throttle her. Leesa freed herself momentarily and screamed so loudly that Yong Sang came running to the scene. In amazement, he broke the choke hold Kim had on their daughter's throat, permitting her to run away. Yong Sang scolded Kim for losing her self-control and for threatening their daughter's life. She listened to his tirade with closed eyes deeply ashamed of her conduct and unable to face her husband's anger.

"Calm down and collect yourself!" Yong Sang ordered in vexation. "Will you ever learn to control this aggressive streak of yours, or will someone have to die first? Tell me," he challenged, "if I weren't here, would you have killed your own daughter?" Kim's tear-filled eyes and bowed head expressed the shame she was feeling at her loss of control and at the violence of her action.

"I don't know what came over me. Until now, whenever she misbehaves, and despite my anger, I've been able to suppress the powerful urge to strike her senseless. But this time, a light flashed in my brain when I saw her urinating into my tea. Something inside me snapped and I lost control."

Yong Sang hadn't known the details that had prompted Kim's behavior but he was astonished at his daughter's evil.

"Mama, Serena has invited me to spend the weekend at their home. May I go?" Mona noted that her mother turned her eyes away from looking at her face, and knew the answer before it came.

"Aren't you afraid of catching some awful disease on that farm with their contaminated animals?"

"Mama, diseased animals would be quarantined and put down just as ours were. Besides, Serena's never ill." But I know you'll find another excuse to prevent me from enjoying myself, Mona thought, but didn't dare say.

"I just don't think it's a good idea. I worry when you're exposed and vulnerable." Mona knew it was a lie. Her mother had spoken to her so often about her dreams of vengeance against those who had humiliated her that she guessed the truth. Unconsciously, her mother was paying her daughter back for being ugly and thwarting her mother's plans for taking revenge on her earlier tormentors.

"Mama, Dad said I can go and that he'll give me a ride over. He knows I'll be as safe as Serena." Mona had long twigged to her mother's attitude towards her and often thwarted her plans by getting her father to rescue her. She knew that her mother wouldn't dare go against his wishes.

"What is this thing you have with that girl? It's always Serena, Serena, and Serena? I'm fed up with hearing her name."

"She's my friend," Mona replied, without adding that Serena's growing karate skills had been protecting her from the bullies at school who never stopped looking for an opportunity to torment her.

Chapter 4

After witnessing Leesa's conduct in the teapot incident, Kim's darkest fears arose bedeviling her mind. She considered that her daughter's act was not the prank of a naughty or willful child; it was a deliberate act of evil. She began to panic at the thought that the corrupt genes of her father might have leaked into her own and her daughter's gene pool. It made her think it was high time to tell Yong Sang the shameful truth that she had kept locked up in her mind–a secret that she had never dared divulge to anyone.

"Darling," she said, "I didn't tell you the truth about my father."

"He didn't die in the accident that you described in such detail?"

"No. He's still alive." Just thinking of her father raised her ire.

"Well dear, why haven't you introduced us? I'd like very much to meet him."

"No. You wouldn't. Yong Sang, why do you insist of being so blind and annoying?"

"Why do you get so angry whenever you discuss your father? And why wouldn't I like to meet him?"

"He's in jail."

"In jail? Was he a thief? Is that why you get so annoyed; why you didn't tell me the truth about him in the first place?"

"No Yong Sang, not a thief, a murderer. That's why I lied to you. I didn't want you to think that I, or any child we had, might be carrying his evil genes." Once the discussion centered on her father, she felt her fear and anger surfacing.

"Tell me about him?"

"He had a terrible temper that he was never able to keep in check. Although he loved us, he would get angry at the slightest miss step of my mother or me. Then, he would bellow at us as if we had committed murder." Yong Sang noted that her eyes were closed.

"Did he beat you?"

"No, I'm positive that he loved us in his own way. His ranting, which always included verbal abuse, would go on and on while we cowered before him. But he never resorted to blows."

"My poor darling. How you must have suffered!" There was genuine concern in his voice.

"We acted as though tiptoeing around egg shells when he was at home, and thanked God that he spent so much time at the office. During the trial, we learnt that dad had accused his business partner of cheating him, though he had no evidence. Wanting to keep an eye on his partner, he spent a great deal more time at the office. His suspicion caused the many heated arguments that arose between them. It became evident that they had grown to hate each other."

"So, what eventually happened?"

"Dad finally found proof that his partner was in fact fiddling the books. Their final quarrel had ended in a fight, and he broke his partner's neck. He was very strong–having been a physical instructor in the army. During the trial we learnt that the army had branded him 'excessively violent and aggressive.' Mother and I could have told the army that."

"Why didn't the army discharge him?"

"They said those were the qualities they needed to convert raw trainees into tough and hardened, war-ready fighting men."

"When does he get out?"

"He doesn't. He got life without parole for his brutality."

"So what triggered your need to unburden yourself about your secret now?"

"I'm afraid of what Leesa might do. I worry that she and I might have inherited my father's evil nature."

"You said he had an ungovernable temper that constantly led to anger and verbal abuse. But he never resorted to blows with you or your mother. Well, you do have a foul temper, but so far you've managed to control it most of the time. Leesa doesn't have a temper and she isn't violent."

"Perhaps, but she's mean, deceitful and holds a grudge. I'm afraid where those character traits may lead." Yong Sang was more worried about his wife's violent temper, but couldn't tell her so.

"Darling, our daughter is an innocent adolescent, maybe a bit quirky, but certainly not evil. Your fears are making you over react."

"And as usual, you refuse to see the obvious. You make me so mad Yong Sang, for never seeing what is so evident, never listening to what I say. Your problem is that you always think the best of people; even those close to you."

Were he to call attention to the evil afflicting his parish and those others throughout the world, Father Murphy knew that he would face serious obstacles. His early life as a chaplain at the Front during the Second Gulf War was well known to his congregation. There, he had witnessed the horrors of war: spending unbearably long hours helping the understaffed medics to administer needles, cauterize wounds, bandage and amputate limbs. Indeed, the flood of incoming wounded never seemed to stop. Those heavy duties and his cataloging the names of the endless rows of the dead, had finally taken its toll. The priest was driven to desperation at his helplessness when confronted with the stark reality of evil that kept increasing every day. When he could stand it no more, his mind had suddenly snapped. He experienced periods of hallucination accompanied by terrifying nightmares and was finally hospitalized with a nervous breakdown.

Under the present stress, similar to the experience he had gone through in Hamyang, the reality of his recurring nightmares and flashbacks convinced him that he was still in the field hospital. He kept inhaling the foul scent of blood, sweat and pus mixed with the odor of carbolic disinfectant stinging his nostrils. The constant moaning and screaming of the wounded and the dying kept echoing shrilly in his ears.

On that early spring morning, Kim followed the same routine as she had done so often in previous years. She rose at 4 A.M. to complete her household chores by five o'clock, needing the rest of her day and the long hours during the following weeks to work in her newly extended garden. She had already agonized over her loss of control, and apologized to her daughter. Yet, while doing her chores her thoughts returned to her assault. She kept asking herself again and again whether she would really have snuffed out her daughter's life if her husband had not intervened. The thought of her violent temper scared the life out of her. She finally put those thoughts aside to concentrate on finishing her chores.

Yong Sang and a number of the neighborhood farmers' wives, whom Kim had previously alerted, joined her at five o'clock to begin their task. She then explained for the benefit of newcomers:

"We'll start by pruning the rose bushes to keep the plants healthy and to promote new growth. Air and light will then more easily filter into the heart of each bush." After passing out pairs of gloves and secateurs to her volunteers, she told them: "Follow my lead in cutting out the dead, diseased and damaged brown wood until it becomes white. We'll then, rip out the suckers to prevent their regrowth and competition with the mother plant." She then set about to do the work and show everyone exactly what she had just explained.

Because of the gardening that would take up many of the following weeks, Kim had made arrangements to be replaced as the weekly organist for early Mass. At the end of their exhausting day, she again spoke to her co-workers. "You're all invited to my home to discuss plans for tomorrow's work." Yong Sang then chimed in. "Afterwards, everyone will be offered a steaming bowl of *bibimbap*, (rice mixed with vegetables and red pepper paste) and a glass or two of the strong cider pressed from the apples of our orchard." A cheer went up from the volunteers.

Both Serena's lips were split and stitches crawled across them like thin, filthy caterpillars. Her skin was still patchy with green and yellow bruises blooming everywhere. Her face and lower body looked as though she had failed to discourage a bull elephant in musk. Her swollen throat still hurt from being choked by her captors to stop her resisting, and swallowing was painful. She had lost the power of speech and still didn't recognize the people around her. She felt like a pain-crazed victim bound helplessly in a web of despair. Yet, being in a hospital bed and attended by nurses in starched uniforms, she knew instinctively that she was being looked after and for that she was grateful.

When the distraught parents consulted the doctor about their daughter's state of amnesia, he offered them an explanation in layman's terms that helped to clear up the mystery.

"The mind is a delicate instrument that sets a limit to the amount of stress or pain an individual can bear. Whenever the stress exceeds that limit, some kind of mental meltdown takes place. It can express itself in different forms, often occurring as an identity crisis through memory loss that is termed hysterical amnesia, or a fugue state."

"I suppose you're referring to her violation," her mother stated.

"Yes, you should remember that Serena must have suffered great pain with the additional stress of shame and humiliation as a result of that ordeal. She has chosen to hide from the incident, from herself and the world through forgetfulness. Ironically, she has mimicked a mild form of insanity as a means of safeguarding her sanity. But take heart, this fugue state, doesn't always last long. In fact, it is possible for her to recover at any time."

Serena heard the unknown woman, who sat in a chair watching over her constantly repeat the name, 'Serena.' The woman looked directly into her eyes calling the name and making it obvious that she was addressing her. Could that be her name? She pronounced it silently in her mind but it sounded alien, making no impression. The woman also talked about a colt named 'Will' that only made her think: what a silly choice of name. Neither name caused any stirring of memory. The woman's face registered grave disappointment. She then brought Serena a mirror and held it up to her face. "Serena," she asked, "do you recognize the face you see there?" Serena looked at the features appearing in the mirror–the pale face, the paler lips, the blank stare from the eyes, the drawn and piqued features, willing them to express some sign of familiarity. But the image of the gaunt face revealed nothing but the illness of the observer. There was nothing in the blank stare that told her anything she needed to know.

Once they completed the pruning of the rose bushes, Kim and Yong Sang assembled their helpers to begin the more arduous task of getting the soil ready for the new plants. Kim spoke while she worked, showing the newcomers the techniques of growing roses. "We have to make sure that the area selected for their planting is sufficiently far away from any nearby shrubs and trees that will compete with them for light, water and nutrients."

Yong Sang then broke in: "roses don't thrive in windy areas. As you can see, our house acts as a wind break from the prevailing wind."

"Where do you get your rose bushes, and how do you know which to select?" someone asked.

"From the local nursery," Kim replied. "I get the cultivars that perform best in this area."

"Are the plants very expensive?" One of Kim's helper's asked, hoping to get some free bushes to start her own garden.

"Recognizing the speaker's motive, Kim replied less gently than she intended: "Don't worry about the price, there are always lots of shoots and bushes that remain after we finish planting. There'll be enough to go around for those wanting them." Kim answered the next question before it was asked. "I select my bushes on the basis of color, fragrance, flower production and disease resistance. To do well," she continued, "rose bushes need soil with a rating between 6.5 and 8 pH. The soil also has to be especially well drained."

One of the volunteers asked what pH was and Kim explained that it was the term used to express the degree of alkalinity or acidity of the soil.

On one occasion, the unknown man speaking to Serena mentioned the word "sled" that brought back memories of winter and its cold that forced her to wear many thick, warm garments. The word also reminded her of being pulled behind a cantering horse. She remembered dodging the clods of snow that the hooves kept scooping up at her. But she recognized neither horse nor rider. On another occasion, the unknown woman kept talking about her paintings of the zoo animals that were her subjects. It recalled her struggle to capture the pain-crazed portraits of the animals on her canvases. For the first time, it seemed that with the woman's prodding of Serena's mind, snippets of her memory were creeping back. But whole segments were still missing.

"So," Yong Sang again spoke to his volunteers: "we'll first have to till the soil, and then raise the beds. Finally, we'll add peat moss to the surrounding area for better drainage. Grab a hoe, and follow my lead," he stated and then began to carry out the three processes showing how each was to be done. "Once we complete these phases, I'll show you how to use dehydrated cow manure and shredded bark to add organic matter to the soil. We'll then dig holes at least three feet apart to provide breathing room for each bush we plant." He then stated: "Look around you. I've chosen this particular area since the bushes will receive the six hours of morning sunshine they need to flourish."

"How long will you need us?" A newcomer asked Kim.

"Once the planting is done in two to three weeks time, I'll make up a roster for the volunteers we'll need to return each day to water the plants with my husband and me. We'll again be gathering at my home after each day's work for *jajangmyeon*, (noodles covered in a sweet black bean sauce) and cold cider." Another cheer went up from the helpers.

With her poultry farming experiment taking shape, Serena became a very busy body. She hurried home from school every day to join Mr. Sing and personally supervise the building of the coops for her poultry. As with the pig sty, they had chosen an area a good distance from the house where the prevailing wind and a thick barrier of trees would prevent the disgusting smell of poultry and their droppings from being wafted towards the house. After countless long discussions with Mr. Sing, she adopted his ideas to ensure that each enclosure was predator proof and allowed adequate room for expansion to house three times the number of birds she had originally planned for.

Mr. Sing was a mine of information with regard to the placement of nesting boxed for laying, the provision of food and water troughs, and the building of a small warm enclosure within each coop to house the first chicks. Her idea of using clusters of bulbs for warming the chicks was good, but not as efficient or energy saving as the electrical warmers manufactured expressly for that purpose. When the coops were finished, she accompanied Sing to buy her flocks and surprised both him and the owner/salesman by her tough negotiating stance. Playing hardball, she argued: "The huge number of birds I'm buying deserves a sizable discount from the usual price you charge. Otherwise," she left the sentence hanging, suggesting that she'd take her business elsewhere. Not surprisingly, the businessman agreed and gave her a 10% discount. She then asked a series of questions that surprised and puzzled both the businessman and Mr. Sing.

"Do you sell by the number of birds or by their weight?"

"Always by weight. We'll provide you with the exact weight of each of the four flocks."

"Perfect! Are you equipped to deliver the birds?"

"Yes, I usually deliver the birds myself."

"Please call me on the morning *before* delivery and give me the exact weight of each of the four flocks I'm purchasing." Her two fingers were doing their usual dance.

"Agreed!" The businessman replied.

On taking their leave afterwards, Sing inquired: "What was all that about 'exact weight' and 'calling the morning before' his delivery of the birds?"

"Well, Mr. Sing, I learned from my project on poultry farming that there are special wire cages used to transport poultry. But the birds are so overcrowded in each tiny cage that they can hardly move."

"It prevents them from fighting and wounding each other," Sing told her.

"I'm aware of that," she said. "The sharp top end of their beaks is also clipped to prevent wounding. Further, the birds have to be transported by truck in the dead of night or in the very early morning when the weather is at its coolest. The overcrowding, the heat and the fighting causes the birds to lose weight.

"That, I didn't know."

"If the owner gives me the exact weight on the morning before delivery, then, he will have already weighed the birds and placed them in their cages. That means they will be caged all that day and the following night before they can be delivered to our farm the next morning.

"Since the birds always lose weight when crowded together and transported under those conditions, I'd like you to get the hands to set up a few scales at the entrance to each enclosure. With their help in weighing each bird, we'll only pay for the exact weight of the birds in each flock."

"Do you have an estimate of the weight that each bird loses?"

"According to my research, it would be normal for each bird to lose at least one quarter of a pound as a result of crowding and the long journey from their farm to ours. So if my calculation is correct we won't have to pay for about ten pounds of meat in each flock. Bear in mind too that chicken is the cheapest meat."

"If your calculation is correct, and we multiply that by four, it will make a huge dent in the agreed price. I must congratulate you Miss. Your knowledge and clever calculation will cause us quite a saving."

"Thank you Mr. Sing," Serena replied, "delighted with the respect and admiration she heard in the farm manager's voice.

"Yong Sang, at last the brunt of our work is done. We've made the best selection of rose bushes, drained the soil properly, ensured that the plants will receive their need of morning sunshine each day and will be watered regularly. There isn't much more we can do, is there?"

"If the weather holds, the combined effort and long hours spent in their cultivation will produce a plentiful supply of fragrant and beautiful blooms. And once they begin blooming, each Wednesday, with Serena's help, you'll be able to make up your bouquets of long-stemmed white roses for the church."

"I was thinking that since we've doubled the area of the garden this year, we'll have a huge number of remaining long stemmed blooms to sell. Not only the remaining white, but the yellow, red and pink that we've planted for the first time."

"Do you realize that the colors, as well as the long stemmed variety, are all in great demand?"

"I've been thinking that in selling them bi-weekly we'll at least quadruple the sum we made each month last year for the remainder of the growing season."

"That's exactly what I was thinking. We'll be able to buy the best cultivars, organic fertilizer, and all our gardening needs for next season," Kim replied. And the remaining sum–which should be considerable this year–will buy food and clothes for those loyal families on whom we always depend for help. Without them, our garden would be neither as large, prolific nor as beautiful."

Evidently, Kim and Yong Sang took enormous pleasure in their gardening. After the hard work of planting was over and the long hours they spent in weeding, spraying against bugs once the blooms appeared, they thoroughly enjoyed just gazing at their beauty and inhaling their fragrance whenever they got the chance. However, apart from the pleasure they derived from the beauty produced with their hands and those of their neighbors, they also took pride in knowing that the operation went a long way to beautify the church and to feed and clothe the poor members of the district who so willingly volunteered their time, effort and energy to make their garden bloom and prosper.

Serena was again racing downhill pursued by the predators that she was in the habit of painting. No longer welcoming and 'alive with the sound of music,' the hills had turned dark and forbidding. Although she was exhausted panic drove her on. She rushed forward, plunging straight ahead into the darkness. Wolf and snake, eagle and hawk had all doubled their size and kept pursuing her as she rushed into the nearby forest. Hearing them right on her heels, she spurted forward. The carapace of terror that she wore began to restrict her movements more and more, slowly immobilizing her. In frenzy, she kept telling herself: "You can't stop, you can't stop. To stop is to die! Oh God, I need you beside me to rid me of these demons." Then abruptly she awoke.

Kim was troubled. Apart from the fiasco following the teapot incident, she had lied repeatedly to her husband about the conduct of the daughter in the case file. She had hidden the truth from him unsure of how he would react.

The daughter she was describing in the case file was herself and the behavior, her own youthful rebellion. She tried to banish her deep feelings of guilt not only because she had hurt her daughter, but because she had wanted to hurt her, had even enjoyed hurting her. Once she realized the wickedness to which she seemed addicted, Kim closed her eyes, followed her own mother's advice and knelt at her shrine to pray fervently for forgiveness. She kept wondering; was her mother right in her repeated warnings?

"Kim," she had stated, rumpling her daughter's dark curls, "prayer is only one part of the solution to overcome your evil nature."

"Mama, you've told me that over and over, so I keep trying to rein in my dark side by performing good deeds."

"That's right dear. Helping others is the surest means of atoning for wrongdoing. It may even help in being granted forgiveness."

"That's why I accepted Father Murphy's request and took the job of training the choir and holding choir practice one evening a week. Mama, I also agreed to become the organist for Matins on weekdays, and then I began planting the rose garden to decorate the church and to assist our distressed neighbors. I should think that's enough. Now I have little time for anything else," she said closing her eyes. But I'm not complaining. I feel much freer, much lighter since I've begun helping out."

"That's the right attitude, dear. Good deeds are a reward in themselves. They'll help you to turn over a new leaf; to become a better person. They also help to silence a guilty conscience. Otherwise, we stagger around bowed down by the weight of shame and guilt for the wrongs we've done. Like a disease that saps our lifeblood, they make us pay dearly for our wrongdoing and often prevent us from attaining the happiness we strive so hard to achieve."

"But Mama, there's something else troubling me. I believe that Leesa's cruel streak was inherited from me. Her behavior is too similar to be mere coincidence. Since I attacked her after the teapot incident, I've had to keep a tight rein on my self control. Now, I need to restrict my own wickedness, and at the same time try to restrict hers."

"Are you worried that at some point you'll both commit some unforgivable act?"

"Mama, that's exactly what keeps scaring me."

Kim was determined to show Leesa the error of her ways. But how do you begin to untangle the knots in a twisted mind? What hand could wield a scalpel skillfully enough to cut out only the diseased portions of the brain? How do you re-channel thoughts and actions that have ventured too far into the realm of evil? The thought reminded her of Macbeth's words that she wasn't sure she could recall exactly: "I am steeped in blood so far returning were as tedious as go o'er." Like Kim, he too seemed to be stating the fact that once you entered the arena of evil there was no turning back.

"Mama, I love Leesa in spite of her wicked ways. I only want her to love *both* her parents."

"It's what most parents want; a loving bond that unites all family members."

"Mama, you're so understanding!"

Kim began by explaining to Leesa that her malicious conduct had put an evil stain on her character. She explained that parents got married because of their love for each other. The constant attempt of a daughter to force herself between them was bad, but not as wicked as urinating in her mother's teapot. Kim then insisted that she and her husband loved Leesa as deeply as they loved each other. Her daughter had the grace to blush, expecting angry words of rebuke followed by a lecture. It surprised her that she was wrong on both counts. There were no angry words of rebuke; no lecture. However, Kim did make her promise to go to confession on the following day.

The unknown woman who sat beside Serena's hospital bed kept repeating the name, Serena, stating that was her name. Although Serena repeated the name again and again in her mind it sounded alien, evoking no mental response. The woman then mentioned a colt named Will. That too sounded hollow, and she again thought it was a silly name. On another occasion, the woman brought her a mirror and held it up to her face. "Serena," she asked, "do you recognize the person you see there?" She looked at what the mirror revealed, focusing on the sunken eyes with their blank, lackluster stare, the pale cheeks and the even paler lips. She stared hard at the drawn and piqued face, the dull hair, willing each feature to show some sign of familiarity; to express some signal of recognition. But the image of the gaunt face staring at her revealed nothing but the illness of the observer. It reflected not the slightest glimpse of the life history of the person she saw. The face remained blank and uncommunicative concealing all the secrets of an identity.

"Darling, I'm late for work and won't have time for breakfast." Yong Sang told his wife.

"Well, take this bowl of *jajangmyeon* with you that you can have while working." At this point, Leesa piped up. "Mama, it's Saturday, I'd like to go to the mall? If I catch the bus from the bus stop just around the corner, it stops right at the mall."

"Leesa, you're not old enough to go by yourself?"

"Mama, don't you have any confidence in me?" She spoke loudly enough for her father to hear, stealing glances at him from time to time. With closed eyes she pouted angrily, and wore a frown for her dad to see.

"Kim, I can give her a ride there on my way to work."

"But you're late. You haven't got time for breakfast and the mall is in the opposite direction from your workshop," Kim reminded him.

"I'll hurry. Get in the car, Leesa." On the way, her daughter paused just long enough to show her mother just who was in charge, shooting her another of her hostile glances. As they left, Kim was dumbfounded at the way her eight year old daughter could pull the wool over her father's eyes. She wondered how an intelligent adult could fail to see that he was being so brazenly manipulated. With a pout or a frown to show her displeasure, Leesa could get her father to run around in circles and behave like a trained monkey.

The same unknown woman sitting beside Serena kept badgering her trying to get her to recognize who she was. She mentioned that Serena rode into the mountain wilderness and talked about the cave that she and her father found there. In a flash, memories of Serena's life came flooding back. She remembered who she was, who her parents were, her colt, her zoo animals, her painting, her pigeons and finally her gang rape. So, she concluded, this event must have been the catastrophe that triggered her amnesia.

"Serena, what's the matter?" Mama shouted in alarm when she saw that Serena sat bolt upright in bed.

"Mama, I know who I am," she shouted back. I've recovered some of my memory. What you just said reminded me of riding into the mountains with dad and finding the cave." Mother and daughter hugged and kissed for a long time before Leesa rang her husband to tell him the great news.

Chapter 5

It became obvious to Father Murphy that his parish was a microcosm of the world that was under attack by the forces of evil. It left him in no doubt that the instigator of the attack was none other than Satan himself. Didn't the Almighty cast him from heaven into "outer darkness?" Wasn't it he who sought revenge against the Almighty for this humiliating debasement? Didn't he vow to destroy mankind by declaring war on the Creation? And in his obsession to destroy the human race, didn't he vow to seduce mankind into his evil web? Thus, the priest found it logical to conclude that Satan was synonymous with sin and evil in all its forms. Having spent a lifetime fighting the cause of the Just, he was convinced that the arch enemy had stepped up his campaign of evil. The priest also recognized with sorrow that being immortal, Satan had the upper hand against mere mortals. The priest knew too that man's sinfulness was an affront to God. The pastor also believed that He would not look kindly at man's collective disobedience. What words would he use to convince his congregation that evil *was* hammering at the door?

By the time Serena was twelve years old her poultry farm was flourishing, as were a number of those farms belonging to her neighbors. The speed with which the farms kept spreading was attributed to the number of eggs produced by Serena's birds.

"Dad," she had said, "the farm hands and I have collected more than a thousand eggs in the past two weeks, and I've already begun to supply the farmers with the dozen eggs promised each week. But Dad, I still have many more eggs remaining."

"Perhaps you should start selling them as planned!"

"Rather than selling all of them, I'd prefer to raise lots of chicks, ducklings, turkeys and geese and begin to distribute starter farms as promised. I also want to begin growing birds for market earlier than planned."

"How do you propose to go about that?"

"If I let the hens, ducks, turkeys and geese begin sitting, they'll stop laying and slow down egg production. I don't want that to happen."

"What do you want to happen?"

"I plan to get the eggs hatched without the long period of setting that stops egg production."

"Well, the only way to implement your plan is to use incubators."

"Dad, that's exactly what I was thinking, but ..." She left her answer hanging.

"I suppose you want me to provide you with a batch of incubators!" He stated, smiling indulgently at his daughter.

"Dad, doing so would be to *your* benefit." He knew that, but he still asked to hear her reply.

"How so?"

"It will speed up the number of eggs produced. Many more chicks will hatch in the incubators to become the basis of starter farms. Those birds not donated will be ready for market much sooner. The reality of it is that with the sale of surplus eggs and meat, the repayment to my benefactor will be speeded up considerably." She said, looking at him with raised eyebrows and grinning from ear to ear.

"Those are solid arguments, I'll have to agree, so I'll get Sing to help you choose the incubators."

"Dad thanks a million, and I can tell you one thing."

"What's that?" He asked fingertips in his mouth.

"The hens will continue laying and cackling proudly in thanks to you instead of boring themselves setting for weeks." Her father again smiled indulgently at the resourcefulness of his daughter and at her sense of humor.

As the abundance of eggs continued to increase and the array of new incubators began doing their work, four unexpected scenarios unfolded. First, Serena was able to distribute both her eggs and her chicks long before she had forecast. She could donate to twenty farmers instead of the twelve she had originally promised. Secondly, the remaining eggs were hatched and the chicks raised for market, again far more quickly and in larger numbers than forecast. Thirdly, a few months later, the new poultry farmers, following Serena's directives and supervision, began sharing their eggs and new-born chicks with others, and with time, the sharing had a domino effect. Just as Serena had planned, poultry farms kept spreading throughout the district. Finally, with the money from the sale of her own eggs and meat to the farm markets and to her father's outlets, Serena was able to begin repayment with a sizeable chunk for both the lease of the field and for the birds her father had bought her to start the business. As a reward for the success of her experiment, her father absorbed the full cost of the incubators. Much to Serena's delight, her profits began growing by leaps and bounds. Not only would she be able to repay her father's loans in a far shorter time than forecast, but she'd manage to salt away some of her profits into a bank account that would keep increasing to help her create other humanitarian projects.

"Dad, after selling many of my young fryers, I still have an excess of birds remaining that are market ready."

"Okay, I take it you already have a plan. What do you propose to do with them?"

"I'd like to buy a huge refrigerating unit to freeze the carcasses of the unsold birds. I don't want to flood the market as that will cause a drop in prices.
"

"I have to agree. That's the last thing you'll want to do."

"I've also been thinking of slaughtering some of the birds and starting a soup kitchen for those farmers still struggling to make ends meet."

"That will need quite a lot of organizing, if truth be told. Perhaps you should get the refrigerating unit first."

"I can use most of my growing profits to make a sizeable down payment for a part of its cost. Would you be willing to put up the rest of the money and add that figure to my debt?"

"I agree to help fund the refrigerating unit, but to start your soup kitchen, you'll need..." Serena cut him off.

"Thanks so much for your continued cooperation Dad. I know exactly what I'll need to buy: a few two burner stoves. I plan to set them up in one of your barns, with your permission of course. I'll also have to buy split peas for the soup base, flour for the dumplings, vegetables like squash, potatoes, rice, carrots, tomatoes and cabbage, plus some huge kitchen utensils and cheap plastic dishes like restaurants use for take out. Most of the vegetables and the seasonings: garlic, peppers, onions and tomatoes I'll get from the farmers' wives. Finally, I'll co-opt those same wives to butcher the birds and prepare huge caldrons of the soup and other meals for those in need."

"What you'll have to understand is that you'll then have the responsibility of distributing your soup and meals?"

"I'll designate a central point, perhaps a barn in the district where the farmers can gather to collect their meals. Don't you think it's the least they can do?"

"For free soup and meals they're sure to agree."

"Perhaps I can persuade some wealthy farmer to use one of his vehicles to truck the meals to the collecting point." She looked at her father smiling broadly with her eyebrows raised in pleading mode." John chuckled as he warned:

"Young lady, I firmly believe that you want to bankrupt me." But he was again smiling, pleased with the ingenuity, thoughtfulness and generosity of his daughter. He was already licking his fingertips.

Twice a week, Serena co-opted those wives who were not feed donors, to make gallons of soup with the backs, necks and wings of her birds adding the seasoning of onions, garlic, lemon grass, red pepper paste and those vegetables loved by Koreans. On week ends, she also organized a number of the neighborhood wives to use the legs, breasts and thighs to stew, fry or bake delicious meals with split peas and rice. Like the soup, the meals were parceled out in take out trays and sent in one of her father's vehicles to the designated barn where the meals could be housed in case of rain. Twice a week at 4 P.M. sharp, Serena was at the barn ready to distribute the meals to the crowd of farmers' wives or children gathered there. John was happy to lend the transport being especially proud of his daughter. She was turning out to be an astute entrepreneur, and he wasn't blind to her compassion for others, nor to the organizational skills and resourcefulness she displayed.

It was ironical that his love for his daughter blinded Yong Sang to the devious, vindictive and malignant nature that she possessed. And so it was that Leesa's natural beauty and elegance became barriers beyond which he could not see. Concealed behind her mask of hostility and guile, she appeared to him without fault or failure, clad in the protective cloak of beauty, purity and the innocence of adolescence.

Surprisingly, Leesa did keep her promise to her mother. Quite calmly the following morning, she confessed to the priest that her parents were both lazy and without ambition. "Unlike her," she stated, without meeting her confessor's eyes, "they were satisfied, almost elated with the status quo. If my mother were out of the way, I would then be able to take over the reins of the family and make changes that would be meaningful to all concerned."

"Whoa!" The priest almost shouted. "How do you propose to get your mother 'out of the way?"

"I haven't yet worked out the details, but that's of little importance."

"Oh, that's of the greatest importance!" The priest barked in reply.

"Father needs someone strong to chart a successful career for him."

"But he already has a successful career! He's a very talented woodworker."

"That's just the problem. You must try to see things as clearly as I do, Father. Dad could be a carver of exceptional brilliance, but at the moment, he's nothing more than a manual laborer. He needs to be pushed and my mother's not up to the task. However, if I were in charge, I'd make him use his ability to be far more creative. He would then earn much more and lift his family out of their obscure, squalid existence."

"So, you're really after a more prosperous lifestyle. Child," the priest then stated, "you have a gift for falsehood and great exaggeration! I know from personal experience that your family does not live in obscurity. They are well known and well liked in the district for all the good they do. I also know that you don't live in squalor, as you assert." The priest believed he had been listening to the fanciful tale of an adolescent, but he now knew that he was dealing with an astute adult mind as well as a liar and selfish manipulator.

"Child, what is this obsession you have with ill-speaking your mother?"

"Ousting my mother's influence is the only way to get my father's full attention?" Leesa replied casually. "I know you believe that I'm a selfish and wicked person, but having to live with a spineless woman lacking in ambition and intelligence is humiliating. She keeps dragging the family down because she's quite happy to remain a nonentity."

"A nonentity!" The priest erupted in alarm, "Your mother is one of the pillars of my church and the whole parish knows it. The time, effort and trouble she takes to beautify the altar with her fragrant and beautiful bouquets are a mark of her generosity of heart and her religious devotion. She also plays the organ every morning of the week and trains my choir. She's a college graduate, with a very astute head on her shoulders and singled out for some of the highest praise by her professors. To describe her as a 'spineless woman lacking in ambition and intelligence,' is not only a serious lack of judgment on your part, but an unmistakable mark of your wickedness. The deep hatred you evidently nourish for your mother has made you delusional for you to utter or even imagine such awful untruths," the priest scolded. Perhaps that's why you keep your eyes closed when you lie to me and cannot bear to make eye contact, he thought but didn't say.

"No Father! It's just that I can't stand her lack of foresight and her acceptance of things as they are." Pausing momentarily, she added: "She even made an effort to turn me into an obedient Christian. However, that's another story."

"My child, we have all the time in the world. I'd really like to hear that story."

She began kicking and kicking at the rapist struggling to straddle her. Suddenly, what felt like steel manacles on her ankles and the painful knees pressing down upon her shoulders immobilized her. A crowd had gathered. There were thousands of blank faces and staring eyes surrounding her but no sound came from her mouth. Instead, she could only see the scars on that awful face that became dyed into the fabric of her memory. As the terror and pain kept building with each thrust from the rapist, a shrill scream finally burst from her throat. She kept screaming and screaming for help with her mind in turmoil and with all those eyes boring into her. They made her feel as though the world had taken a front seat to scoff at her degradation. Since no one came to her rescue, she assumed that they were certain she deserved what she was getting. Eventually, someone took pity on her and stopped her body from thrashing wildly. It was then that her eyes opened and she found herself in the arms of her mother.

As the wife of a corporate executive, Leesa had a lot of time on her hands. Then, her freedom was greatly increased when she hired Tina, the teenage daughter of a farmer, to help with the housework and the preparation of the meals. With so much more spare time on her hands she kept recalling her past life and wondering how she could have been such a rebellious teenager. Worse, she kept asking herself how she could have been so spiteful towards her mother. Instead of giving herself up to the enjoyment of the freedom, affluence and higher status she had bought herself through her marriage, she spent a great deal of time brooding over the past, haunted by the conviction that she must have been born evil. She couldn't forget that even the gentle and compassionate priest, Father Murphy, had stated she was wicked.

Hamyang was a township spread over a large area of flat and rolling countryside with the majority of its inhabitants being peasant farmers. They rose early and retired late each evening after working long hours in their fields. Theirs was a harsh existence with little time left for entertainment. Unlike their urban fellow citizens, they possessed none of the technological marvels of the modern age that help to pass the time pleasantly. They had few phones, no televisions, computers or I-pads. Few could afford to go to the nearest cinema. But lack of money was not their only problem. A far greater problem was their lack of time. The men spent the early hours of their days and evenings slogging in the fields and their women often had to accompany them. Then, in a rural community where news is scarce, there is little to talk about besides farming: the work, the land, the crops and the weather. It is therefore not hard to understand why the main entertainment comes in the form of gossip about the indiscretions of neighbors. Indeed, the district buzzed with gossip like the drone of a power saw cutting through the hardest wood.

Tina, Leesa's household help, came in five days a week and was a prattler of renown. Through the thick and tangled grapevine of her neighbors and acquaintants, Tina had assimilated all the local gossip and knew the personal history of almost everyone. If put to the test, she could recite, non-stop, the detailed biography of every member of those families having the most lurid of histories. Since she had become the repository of the filthiest secrets in the district, everyone was in awe of the power she wielded, and kept their distance. Without close friends, she used the fear she inspired as a lever to pry out of her acquaintances the most deeply buried secrets of those living within the boundaries of her universe.

Tina was a survivor, one of those people who lay claim to that title by successfully overcoming the succession of life-threatening crises that life hurls in their path. As an adolescent, she worked tirelessly alongside her parents who slaved from dawn till dusk on their small unproductive farm. While she helped with the plowing, sowing, weeding and harvesting of the crops, she was as yet too young to make more than a token contribution. However, she took complete charge of the household chores that included the laundry, the cooking and the cleaning. It was a hard life for one so young, especially as she missed the love and affection that less busy parents were able to shower on an only child.

Kim realized that she had seriously underestimated her daughter's wickedness and didn't want to make the same mistake again. The make-over she had in mind for Leesa's character would have to be undertaken with the utmost care and with no hint of motive evident on her part. She knew that it would take deep thought and uncommon skill to accomplish the task. She'd have to give the matter serious consideration to come up with a workable idea.

Once the priest had encouraged Leesa to open the door to her past, she began to process the memories dominating her childhood that came flooding back into her mind. She thought of her mother, Kim, a deeply devout Catholic, who had set up a small shrine on the wall above her sleeping mat. She often wondered why her mother had never severely rebuked her for her wickedness. Instead, Kim had answered her daughter's questions explaining that she prayed as a means of asking God's forgiveness for her evil thoughts and deeds. Kim's words and actions had made Leesa focus on the many hours her mother spent embroidering the golden cross on the frontal drop cloth that turned the shrine she had erected on the wall into a miniature altar. When Kim knelt before it, at just about the level of her eyes, Leesa noticed that the tiny eternal lamp suspended from the ceiling, cast a warm glow illuminating the crucifix above the altar. The light from the red lampshade seemed to envelop in blood both the wooden cross and the divine figure nailed there. At its foot, on the altar itself, there were two figures. Both were kneeling with bowed head, weeping silently and prostrated in grief. One was the blue, shawl-covered statue of the Virgin mother. She was flanked by her white-cloaked companion.

Without realizing it, Father's Murphy's words, the scenes of her mother kneeling in prayer before the shrine and especially her mother's compassionate response to her daughter's wickedness, had had a profound and lasting effect on Leesa's character. Far more than words of rebuke or lectures would have done, they made her acutely conscious of the evil within her. She remembered that every foul trick she had played on her mother, the latter had responded with an act of love. Each time Leesa wedged herself between her parents, Kim, though very angry at the time, would later find some way to reply to her daughter with kindness and affection. After the teapot incident, when Leesa thought that she had deserved the severest of punishment for her deviltry, Kim had apologized before taking her shopping and letting her choose the dress she liked best. She couldn't understand her mother's behavior. It confused her. But like it or not, it had a profoundly subdued effect upon her wickedness.

Each day, the labor that their farm demanded of Tina's parents was exhausting. Each evening, the two adults looked and felt like worn and washed out dishrags. They were drained of energy and completely exhausted.

"Mom, your face is ghost-like and you look wasted," Tina said to her mother. "Where's dad?"

"He's still in the fields trying to finish the plowing. I tell you, he'll kill himself if he doesn't stop."

"But Mom, if he doesn't finish the plowing, we can't start the planting. And it's already getting late for that. I'll go out and help finish up."

"Child, just tell him to come in before he drops dead from fatigue."

"Okay, while you were doing the laundry, I made some *bibimbap* with the rice and vegetable from last night's leftovers. I'll go tell him it's ready."

"That should get him to listen and come in. He didn't have anything for lunch."

Eventually, as the work grew more and more exacting, at the end of each day, Tina's parents sought a reward to bolster their flagging spirits. They took to tippling on the pungent cider from their apple orchard. Once developed, the habit had a domino effect. As the days wore on, their increased tippling took a toll on their strength and energy, and the work on the farm grew harder. As they grew more and more dispirited at being barely able to make ends meet, they then sought further solace in their cider. It didn't take long before they got themselves besotted each night, and as their drinking increased, their hours of work on the farm decreased. Gradually, more and more areas became neglected and more and more work fell upon the shoulders of both parents and little Tina. Finally, unable to produce enough to feed themselves and pay their debts, the parents sold the farm, drifted off into oblivion, leaving Tina to fend for herself.

After the success of her poultry farming experiment, Serena spent long hours in her father's study searching to find another project that, if successful, would increase the crop production of the farmers and thus their standard of living. She couldn't rid herself of the guilt she felt at the profound difference between the lifestyles of her family and those of her neighbors. Both were farmers, but while their families were dirt poor, hers was extremely rich. It didn't matter to her that their wealth did not originated only from the farm, but was increased considerably by the corporate businesses owned and operated by her father and grandfather.

Tina had no problem whatever finding work on many of the neighboring farms. Since she was accustomed to do the household chores, and doing them well, her presence in their homes allowed the farmers' wives more freedom to help in the fields. Yet, she managed to keep her job in each household for a few weeks only, since she posed a constant danger to the farmers' wives. Tina, with her pretty face, alluring figure, her youth and beauty, was just blossoming into her late teenage years. She therefore made a striking contrast with their haggard faces, the shapeless figures, the muscular arms and legs of the toil-worn and middle-aged farmers' wives.

"What are you staring at?" The wife shouted harshly at her husband whose eyes had focused too long on Tina as she was bent over the wash tub. The husband's failure to reply and the scarlet blush on his face was enough evidence to proclaim his guilt. Unfortunately, it also sealed Tina's fate. Too great a temptation to husbands, the blossoming teenager was quickly dismissed by work-weary wives and forced to find work and lodgings elsewhere. Yet, as swiftly as she was fired, she was as quickly rehired in a district where the members of every household needed help to cope with its arduous workload. Moving from family to family, Tina couldn't help hearing all the ghastly family secrets revealed during the stormy quarrels and fights between husbands, wives and children. The sensational details stuck in her head, and she thought the knowledge would come in handy some day. It did, almost a year later, when after working in many of the farmers' homes, she was hired into the Ahn household.

In conducting her research, Serena recalled the way her father had described the decrease in productivity of the farming community. As she sat at her desk with her twin fingers already immersed in their dance, she recalled her father's words: "Their methods of farming are archaic," he had said. "They've planted the same crops, year in year out, for generations. The continued practice has finally led to the depletion of the nutrients from their soil, its exhaustion."

"Serena what have you been doing in your father's study every afternoon this last week, pouring over his manuals?" Leesa asked. "I've missed your company."

"Mama, I'm doing some research, trying to work out some problems and get some solutions."

"It must be some kind of farming since you are reading his tomes, why don't you just ask your father?"

"Mama, it's far more satisfying to research the problems myself. After I've done my research, then I'll question dad about any problems for which I've not found solutions."

"Okay, I'll be in the kitchen baking your favorite cake. Darling when you've finished, do come and keep me company. We'll have a slice together and talk about your future."

"Serena realized that while she was as yet no expert on farming, she was intelligent enough to draw a logical conclusion from her father's words. The solution to soil that had been robbed of its nutrients was quite simply, fertilization. Knowing little about the subject, she'd research the topic to learn as much as she could. At that point she'd be far better equipped to decide exactly how to accomplish the mission she had in mind.

She remembered her father saying that he had repeatedly told the farmers what was needed, but he had failed to change their minds or their methods.

"You have to understand that peasant farmers are a hard headed and stubborn bunch of characters," he had said. "The truth of the matter is that it's well nigh impossible to get them to change their ways. They were born in the same district, probably by the same midwife, christened in the same church, certainly by the same priest, brought up in the same religion, went to the same school, were married in the same church and buried in the same cemetery."

"'What was good enough for our ancestors is good enough for us,' they repeated to all suggestions about change. I firmly believe that change is the very last thing they are willing to accept or even consider," her father had said.

How can a mere thirteen year old schoolgirl succeed in doing what her father, a successful farmer, had failed to do? She asked herself. Finding no solution, she decided that she'd have to make another appointment with her father to consult a far wiser head than hers.

From the sleeping mat, Leesa used to watch her mother and listen to her humming a hymn, before Kim knelt in silent prayer before the altar on the shrine. There was a far-away look in her eyes and a smile on her lips. She behaved as if she were in possession of some mystical knowledge that brought a secret glow to her features and richness into her life. After each session Kim held with God, Leesa noted that her face always seemed flushed and glowing with an inner radiance. She had made a habit of relating to Leesa the story of the crucifixion, the injustice of the judgment, the cruelty of the Roman soldiers, and the suffering they had inflicted on their victim. This response to her daughter's malice was a part of Kim's plan to rehabilitate Leesa, and it seemed to be working.

Since her father was at work, Serena felt it would take too long to wait for his return. She decided to ask Mr. Sing how she might go about convincing the farmers to listen to her.

"Miss, you have to plan your strategy like an aggressive political campaign. Tomorrow we will begin by visiting each farm where you will take soil samples. After your generosity to them, they won't dare object. When they ask what you're doing, you'll tell them the truth, and that you'll inform them of the results once you have analyzed the samples. Second, you'll again tell them the truth a few days later: their soil has been severely depleted of nutrients and its fertility is close to exhaustion. Their harvests will be very, very disappointing. The bad news will spread through the district like wildfire."

"But Mr. Sing, they are already suffering. Such bad news will only distress them further."

"That's exactly what you'll have to do. Miss, you are fighting a war. Deep distress is what will put the fear of God into them. And that is when you shatter their peace of mind by forecasting that their harvest will be the worst ever. You'll further explain that many will face bankruptcy unless they change their ways immediately. They must not only *hear* the dire warning, they must *feel* its calamitous reverberation in their flesh and bones. It is terror, not logic that will force them to listen. Your warning will goad them into action and force them to change!"

"Mr. Sing, you would be a terrible man to have as an enemy, Serena said chuckling. I'm not sure I want to use such horrific Machiavellian tactics on those already distressed people? Such a terrifying forecast might lead to serious consequences," don't you think?

"That's the only way they'll listen to a teenage girl telling them the truth? Do you want to convince them to listen or not?"

"I do!"

"Then your next step is to convene a meeting in our barn for next Sunday after church, letting them know that you have a solution to their soil problems. I forecast that they will flock to hear what you have to say. Nothing else but stark terror will make them ready to eat out of your hand."

Chapter 6

The repetition of his nightmares, sometimes with the same content, convinced Father Murphy that they were divine warnings and therefore it was his duty to bring these warnings to the notice of his congregation. At first, he resisted the temptation for a long time. After all, he reasoned, wasn't his beliefs based solely on a series of bad dreams? Who would believe the hallucinations of an ailing priest? Yet, he argued, wasn't it his duty to protect his flock, warning them of the dangerous threat to their spiritual well-being? Shouldn't he point out that the worm of evil was actively boring into their hearts, forcing them to mock the virtues of a Christian life? Shouldn't he emphasize that it was goading them into temptation that they seemed powerless to resist? He then changed his argument. Wouldn't his presentation of dreams in the form of prophecy suggest that he had elevated himself to the level of a prophet? Wouldn't his parishioners regard such ranting as the height of arrogance? Armed with the knowledge of his nervous breakdown, wouldn't they regard his warning as delusional rambling? Yet, after all the self-searching, he finally decided to do his duty. Whatever the outcome, he argued, wasn't he their shepherd? And wasn't the mission of a shepherd to lead and to protect?

Serena could no longer stand her tremendous suffering and loneliness. She felt an aching need to unburden herself; to vent her feelings.

"Mama, I keep running and running, scrambling through the forest darkness. I feel as though I've been running forever. Working like bellows pumping my breath in and out, my lungs begin to burn. The rank smell of panic rises in my nostrils making me nauseous. Then, the retching begins. I feel as though there's a noose around my neck and the more I retch, the tighter it gets."

"Rina, don't take on so! You're making yourself worse," Leesa whispered frantically in response to her daughter.

"Mama, my nightmares resemble frames in a film sequence. The continuity is broken as though someone has deleted whole portions. I try to recall the missing parts, but they evade me. All sorts of terrifying images crowd my mind. That is when the terror escalates."

"Rina darling, you're frightening me!"

"Mama, I'm not the same person I was. I feel as though something is broken inside me."

"Father, until I witnessed my mother's devotion before her shrine, I never recognized the strength of her religious faith. Her loving response to my evil deeds and the depth of her devotion affected me in a way I could never have imagined. When I asked her what she was praying for, she replied that she was asking God's forgiveness for her sins. It occurred to me that if she, who led such a blameless life, should be asking forgiveness, shouldn't I be doing likewise for my evil thoughts and deeds? Her innocence and kindness forced me to realize more than ever: there was a very dark side to my nature that I was unable to control."

Serena was not at all sure that she should follow Sing's vicious advice. As a consequence, after she had completed her in-depth study of fertilization, she made an appointment to consult her father in his study. "Dad," she had said, "how do I begin to convince the farmers that fertilization is the solution to their serious decrease in crop production?"

"Daughter, the fact is that being farmers, they all know that proper fertilization would help considerably."

"Well, if they know, why don't they do what is necessary?"

"They haven't got the resources. Without the money to buy the organic fertilizer they need, they convince themselves that the limited amount of compost they make is sufficient to fertilize fields that have been exhausted from generations of under-fertilization. What they have to understand is that the little they succeed in doing is grossly inadequate."

"Dad, I have an idea. For the last two years the fowl dung from my poultry farm has been collecting in great mounds where the hands have shoveled it out of the way on the concrete apron behind the poultry enclosures."

"Yes, I know. The mounds have grown so large that they're causing a hazard. I've been thinking of ways to eliminate it."

"Dad, please don't do anything about that for the present. Do you think the farmers would listen if I were to speak to them about what proper fertilization can do for them? Of course, I'll expect you and Mr. Sing to be right there to back up my statements," she quickly added.

"Hold it right there!" He said. "This is *your* idea and *you* have to deal with it. *I* have a corporation to run and will probably not be available to help." He stopped talking, picked up the phone and immediately saw the disappointment that clouded Serena's face. She sat in stunned silence, unable to believe that *her* dad was unwilling to help her carry out the plan she had so painstakingly devised. Her thumb and forefinger were racing at full speed against each other and her face had taken on the look of the deepest dejection.

"Is that you, Sing?" Her father inquired as he clicked on the button of the speaker phone.

"Yes sir," the farm manager replied. "How can I be of help?"

"I'm sending Serena to you with a problem. I'd like you to advise her on the matter and give her the support she needs. I'm counting on you and the hands to help activate her plan."

"You can count on me to help her in any way I can, sir."

"Thank you, Sing. How are things going otherwise?"

"There are no problems that we can't solve, sir."

"I'm glad to hear that. Thank you in advance for your help."

At that point in the conversation, John was pleased to see the frown on Serena's face change into the broadest of smiles. Her eyes that were clouded over a moment ago were shining brightly.

"What a pretty picture you make when you smile." Her father said as he replaced the receiver and grabbed his hat.

"Dad thanks so much. But you won't escape so easily. I'll still need your advice and guidance, okay?"

"Okay my sweet. Now I must rush."

Serena's nightmares kept stalking her like predators pursuing their prey. The flora she painted joined together to launch furious assaults upon her. As she ran for her life branches struck her face and neck. Roots and bushes sprang up in her path trying to trip her. Fear had become a ball of ice in her belly, a roar of silence in her head. Both were fueled by the guttural whispering that came from her pursuers—a hoarse chattering of word-sounds that being unintelligible, served to increase her terror even more. She awoke with a scream finally aware of what was happening to her. In response, she could feel her anger building in violence ready to erupt and incinerate everyone and everything around her. But there was nothing upon which to focus her anger. Instead, an earlier fear mushroomed assaulting her. Something was radically wrong; something within her was broken. But she couldn't put her finger on what was it that made her feel so alien? As far as she knew none of her internal organs was malfunctioning. Yet, she could feel her heart beating too fiercely; her blood rushing too wildly; her anxiety and fear accelerating.

Although an inveterate gossip, thanks to her background, Tina was an efficient and indefatigable worker, and while she worked she talked. Leesa was hard put to stop her tongue from wagging as words tumbled from her mouth. She disgorged all the most salacious gossip she had amassed. She refused to let Leesa's apparent indifference stem the vitriolic tide flowing from her lips. Yet, since the two women spent so much time together, they had become close. So it was that Leesa learnt from Tina's incessant babbling, the husbands and wives who were cheating on each other, the wives who were being battered, the children who were being abused or molested, the adults and children who were ailing. Without realizing it, the knowledge provided Leesa with food for thought. She felt useless and seriously depressed at the idea that her preteen daughter had been helping the farmers while she stood by doing absolutely nothing. Each good deed that Serena did for the farmers was like a sword piercing into her mother's heart. However, the guilt and shame her daughter inflicted upon her were powerful motivators. Without even realizing it they tore at her conscience, ripped away at her complacency and humiliated her.

"Father it's not normal for me to feel drawn towards others or to concern myself with their welfare. Never before did I feel responsible for helping those in need. Indeed, I would have remained totally oblivious to the needs of the farming community were it not for my daughter's acts of kindness towards them."

"Perhaps you can follow her lead," the priest replied. "What do you propose to do?"

"I don't quite know, Father. Serena's thoughtfulness and generosity to the farmers has made me ashamed that I've remained blind to their misery for so long. But like a virulent disease, I find that compassion is contagious and I've begun to feel compelled to follow in my daughter's footsteps. Like her, I have to find something to do that will better the lives of the farmers and their families."

"Doing so would also make you feel better about yourself. So why don't you give it a try?"

"My guilt at doing nothing keeps troubling me, forcing me to ponder for long periods about what I can do to help. Finally, the obscene gossip I learnt from Tina gave me an outrageous idea, and I came to a decision."

"I hope you didn't do anything shameful, my child. Remember you can never be sure that gossip is factually based."

"I got into my limousine, drove to the twenty farms closest to my home that had benefitted from my daughter's poultry farm experiment, and issued an invitation. "I'd like to see your husband at 8 P.M. sharp this evening after he has returned from the field. Our farm manager, Mr. Sing will pass for him in my car."

"Your invitation sounds more like an arrogant command. That's hardly the way to get their cooperation."

"Anyway, each wife agreed with my suggestion that the hour I had chosen would give their spouses ample time to wash, have supper and clean up before being ready. I could see that the wives were curious at the visit to their humble homes of the wife of the wealthiest farmer/businessman in the district. I could almost hear their minds working, wondering what this woman, with her scandal-ridden past, wanted with their husbands."

Sing was an excited teenager driving from Hamyang to Seoul with both his parents.

"Dad thanks so much for getting tickets for us to see our national soccer team play some of the great world teams that are competing in the FIFA World Cup, and especially in our brand new stadium."

"As a past member of the national team, I was as anxious as you to get tickets to see some of those brilliant European and South American teams." His father replied.

"Do you think we have a chance to win?"

"Well, I think our team is playing very well. But to beat the best, your team has to be playing constantly against the best, and we haven't done enough of that. But I do think that we'll do well."

Soccer fever had gripped the nation, and while obtaining tickets was difficult this posed no problem for Sing Senior who had been a former member of the national soccer squad. He too had caught the national fever. Sing's step mother, his father's second wife, accompanied them. Her own son had drowned at almost the same age as Sing, her stepson, and she didn't appreciate sharing her husband with anyone, especially this teenaged boy. As the apple of his father's eye, she tended to be ignored whenever the son was present. To add fuel to the fire, throughout the long drive to the capital, father and son heatedly debated their team's chances of making the finals, totally oblivious of Mrs. Sing's presence.

The boy idolized his father for spending considerable time on evenings and weekends patiently teaching him the basics of soccer since he shared his son's goal of making the school's first soccer eleven.

"Run up slowly to the ball, place your left foot at about a foot from its left side and behind it at about the same distance. You then kick it with your instep, swinging your right foot in a scythe-like motion. The ball will rise in an arc over the other players." His dad did the drill showing his son how to practice the procedure using first right, then left foot. His son then took over until he got the hang of it. Over the next week, he would continue to practice the new skill each evening until he had it down pat.

"Your next drill is to run up slowly to the ball, place your left foot on the left side of the ball, then kick it with the instep of your right foot. Keep your weight directly over the ball as your instep makes contact with it. This will guarantee power and accuracy with the ball staying low, usually below the level of the goal's crossbar." His dad did the drill a couple of times, then let his son practice it until able to do it tolerably well with either foot. He didn't need his father's presence on those days that he continued practicing the drills after school.

"Over the following weeks, his father lobbed the ball to him and taught him trapping it under one of his feet or his chest as it came down to the pitch through the air. Once the ball was under control, he needed to use his peripheral vision to see where his team mates were so he could pass the ball accurately to one of them. Sing then learnt to head the ball in different directions, with his forehead and both front corners of his head. To get power, he'd learnt to use the whole upper half of his body above the waist instead of with the neck and head alone.

Finally, he had to learn ball control, the most difficult soccer skill. Planting six waist-high sticks into the ground in a straight line at about two feet apart,

Sing Junior would have to weave his way through them slowly, then later on the run, tapping the ball with the inside and outside of either foot without losing control of the ball. It took him many months to do it well. Later, he would repeat the exercise circling each stick using either foot alone. It took Sing more than a year to become competent in the soccer skills he was taught. Practicing at school, on evenings and on week ends, Sing finally made the school's soccer squad as its youngest member. Both his coach and his father congratulated him.

Unfortunately, father, step-mother and son never got to the stadium in Seoul. A huge semi-trailer interrupted their journey, crashing into them. Sing Senior was killed instantly, and the wife blamed her stepson for her husband's death. Her earlier dislike swiftly transformed itself into hatred.

"You know you killed your father," she began to accuse him viciously at home. If you hadn't pestered him to get tickets for that match, he would be alive today." She kept repeating her accusation, speaking harshly every chance she got.

"As a former national team member, Dad wanted to go as much as I.," Sing junior would reply.

"Go ahead. Excuse yourself for the guilt you should be feeling."

"Don't worry! I'm feeling enough guilt for both of us." But at night, he tossed and turned unable to sleep. His step mother deliberately left her door ajar so that he could hear the sound of her sobbing and the blame she kept heaping upon him.

"Oh John!" She wailed. "Why did you listen to that idiot son of yours? If you had let him go and stayed here with me, perhaps he would have died instead of you. Now, I'm here alone with no one to turn to and only your stupid son for company." Sometimes she would change her tune: "When you came into my life after the grief and isolation that followed my husband's death, you brought me such happiness. Now that your son got you killed, I'm alone again, with nobody to talk to but that moron." At other times, she'd say: "John, just looking at him maddens me. Forgive me for saying this because I know you loved him, but I've come to hate his very sight." Crippled by her own sadness, she was unaware that her stepson was even more overwhelmed by his father's death. But she never grew tired of twisting the knife.

"From now on, I'm not going to wash or iron your clothes or cook your food," she told him one day. "You'll just have to manage on your own." Then she dropped the bomb that condemned him to isolation. "You can continue to live in this house, but don't you ever speak to me again. I never want to hear another word from you."

Since he had another two years at school, Sing didn't know how he would get through them. Wasn't it enough that he had lost his beloved dad and best friend? Now he was forced to listen to the ravings of a mad woman who kept screaming at him every chance she got and making his life a hell on earth.

John had been a school and team mate of Sing Senior who had captained the school's soccer eleven. The two men had kept up their friendship into adulthood. During his visits to his friend's home, John heard a great deal about the son's soccer successes, and was particularly impressed by the boy's progress at school. Perhaps his interest was heightened because the son showed a special aptitude for agriculture and farming. John visited the home after the funeral to commiserate with the wife and son. He witnessed the way that step mother and son kept their distance from each other and never made eye contact, but he put their strange behavior down to the sorrow both were nursing.

The priest believed that Kim's plan for rehabilitating her daughter might be working and inquired:

"Did you ask your mother's forgiveness?" Instead of answering directly, Leesa replied:

"Mama's words and deeds encouraged me to begin changing. Seeing her devotion and listening to her stories made me acutely conscious of my corrupt nature, so I felt compelled to follow her example."

"Did you succeed in changing?"

"I think so. Her stories of the crucifixion and the cruelty of the Roman soldiers were so vivid that it was easy to visualize every lash of the whip, every drop of the spilt blood, every stab of the pain inflicted by the crown of thorns pressed down cruelly on the victim's head. Particularly moving were the words she used to describe the scorn of the onlookers for the prisoner: "the vulgar gaze of the rude and scoffing multitude." Those words brought tears to my eyes and shriveled my insides just visualizing the scene and realizing the humiliation he must have suffered.

"How had this changed you?"

"I became more compassionate, I think, having fixated on His suffering and humiliation. I tried to imagine the excruciating pain endured in the nailing of each hand, then both feet to the cross. I marveled at the mystery of his ability to withstand such merciless mental and physical torture."

"How did it change you?" The priest persisted.

"His suffering brought tears to my eyes, as I said, and made me more sympathetic to the feelings of others. But there was an even greater mystery that affected me. I found it incomprehensible that throughout the whole ordeal, the victim never once thought of himself. Instead, he kept praying for the forgiveness of his persecutors: "Father, forgive them for they know not what they do." Her next words galvanized the priest. "It came as a shock to realize that my mother was following his example in dealing with the hostility I had launched against her."

At school, Sing chose as his electives as many different types of farming subjects as he could handle. When, nearly two years later at the age of seventeen, he paid another visit to the Ahn farm, he surprised John with an admission and a request: "I'm really anxious to leave home Sir and I've done every subject offered by my college on farming. Would it be possible to get a job on your farm?"

"But the fact of the matter is that you'll be leaving your mother to live by herself. I don't think she'd agree," John replied.

"Oh she'll agree," Sing said quickly. "She's the reason I have to leave." It was then that John heard the sadness in the breaking voice, noticed that the boy's lips were trembling and saw the tears slipping down his cheek.

"Why don't you tell me about it?" He asked gently and found that the question opened Sing's floodgates. After he stopped sobbing, the young man answered.

"I can't cope with Mama's ill-treatment any longer," he said.

"Ill treatment?" John echoed. "Sing, you'd better explain." John was nibbling at his fingers.

"She blames me for urging dad to get tickets for us to see the World Cup match. She says that if it weren't for me dad would be alive today. Worse, she gives me hell for surviving the accident while her 'beloved husband' died. She wishes it had been me. These last two years she's refused to do my laundry or cook for me, and she's forbidden me to speak to her. Lately, she's been haranguing me to find a job. It's her way of urging me to leave the house for good." John couldn't believe the woman he thought he knew could be so cruel and guilty of such evil conduct.

"Sing, I know you loved your dad. He used to invite me to come and watch your soccer and basketball games, and was especially proud of your academic record. I also know that you did nothing to cause his death. So you have nothing to feel guilty about. Let me repeat that: you have nothing to feel guilty about."

"But Sir, despite ordering me never to speak to her, she hasn't stopped mouthing her cruel lies. The fact that my own mother hates the sight of me is bad enough. But her non-stop ranting and raving is driving me crazy."

"I don't want to come between you and your mother, Sing, but if you are determined to leave home, I'll certainly find work for you on the farm. However, if you accept my offer, I'll want you to begin taking evening classes immediately. The fact of the matter is that you'll have to learn as much as you can about the different aspects of farming and agriculture. On the weekends, I'll personally supervise your training on the farm. And no, don't thank me. You'll have to earn my respect by the initiative you show and the progress you make. Is that clear?"

"Yes Sir," Sing replied with jubilation in his voice.

So it was that John installed Sing in a tiny apartment above his garage. He gave him a modest allowance that permitted him to fend for himself in exchange for the various phases of work he kept learning to do on the farm. On the weekends, John personally supervised Sing's work as promised and for the next two years, the young man took evening classes, studying various agricultural subjects with a focus on farm management. Sing did everything he could to show his gratitude for what his mentor had done to better his life. No one on the farm was surprised that he was being groomed for the post of farm manager.

"But you haven't yet explained any change in your conduct, the priest repeated to Leesa."

"Father, you need to create so shameful a picture of yourself that it provides you with a powerful motive to change. My mother had acted towards me with the selflessness and compassion necessary to forgive her tormentor while being persecuted. I came to believe that it was only through the miracle of God's grace that such conduct was possible." She surprised the priest with this remark. Perhaps she has changed, he thought. "In comparison, how did you see yourself?"

"I was even more cruel than the Roman soldiers. Cruelty was part of their job description. It went hand-in-hand with their profession. My situation was totally different. I was being selfish, cruel and unkind to the mother who treated me with love and respect."

"How did your wickedness affect you?"

"Recognizing my own evil nature caused me such personal pain and suffering that it encouraged me to follow in my mother's footsteps."

At the mention of pain and suffering, the priest took the opportunity to point out that "everyone has some form of personal suffering to bear. I believe that the world's suffering binds us into a chain that links us together. It permits us to be accepted into that sacred body, the Communion of the Saints involving the living and the dead uniting us into a spiritual fellowship." As he deliberated in silence for a moment, his pale face grew even paler. "I believe," he continued, "that suffering permits us to share in the burden of Christ on the cross, thereby drawing us closer to Him." The priest then asked Leesa with gentle irony: "these feelings of remorse you talk so glibly about, were they sincere? Not too long ago you saw your mother as a despicable person."

"Yes Father, that's true. But I do believe I was sincere. The wrongs I had done to my mother made me feel remorse and inspired me with feelings of compassion. Isn't that why I'm here?"

"That's so easy to say! Why don't you give me an example of the change you talk about so eloquently?"

"My heart bled for the victim in my mother's shrine. I often took down the crucifix. My sorrow at Christ's suffering had me whispering words of comfort to him. I would then anoint the wounds on the hands and feet of the crucified Messiah. Finally, I would fix a tiny band-aid to the wound in his side."

The sincerity of her words surprised the priest since it echoed one of his most cherished beliefs: "The cruelty we inflict on others engenders such deep feelings of remorse and compassion in us that may well be the saving grace of our species. It thus offers us a chance at attaining forgiveness, and perhaps, redemption. Who knows?"

The oncoming darkness led Serena to bristle with fear at the thought of her accursed nightmares. Cowardice gripped her in its talons and she sought to erect all kinds of barriers to postpone sleep. She fought to keep her eyes open, forcing her eyelids apart, straining against blinking for long periods of time. The strain and the tears that resulted only tired her more with the shame of cowardice in her mind. Although her tears flowed silently, each breath of air, each sob was accompanied by a stab of pain. A sense of helplessness and self-pity washed over her. When suddenly she screamed for help, the sound tore into her throat like a knife severing her vocal chords. She then found herself imprisoned behind the bars of her cage. There, before her, was a semi-circle of the predatory wolves she had painted. Like Scarface and his pack, they kept barking out their aggression. She must have dozed off without realizing it. Only her mother's presence put an end to her terror.

"Over time, the mounds of fowl dung shoveled behind your enclosures have begun to pose a serious problem, Sing told Serena."

"Yes, dad said they had grown huge and unhealthy. His words gave me an idea. Mr. Sing, Would it be too much for you to ask the farm hands to convert the mounds of fowl dung into compost? With the help of time and weather we can transform them into humus." She quickly added, "There is only one condition. If they agree, I will not accept their assistance unless I am able to help."

"Miss, the majority of the hands are from the neighboring farming families. They already worship you for the help you have given them. They won't refuse your request but I'm sure they'll regard your working with them as taking advantage of a mere teenaged girl. Besides, the dung has begun to give off the powerful reek of ammonia, so they'll have to use masks. They'll also consider the shovel too heavy for a teenaged girl."

"Mr. Sing, you forget I've been doing my karate training for a long time now. I won't have any trouble using a shovel." During the following weeks, Mr. Sing, Serena and the hands were hard at work converting the fowl dung into compost that would in turn become rich manure. Eventually, with the additions made by the hands, Serena, the weather and through its own processing, it would transform itself into humus that was much richer in nutrients than raw manure. When the work was finished, they covered the mounds with large tarpaulins to prevent them becoming too dry from the sun's heat or too moisture-laden from rain. Serena then had another chat with the farm manager.

"Mr. Sing, I'd like to call a meeting of our twenty closest neighbors on Sunday to offer them my solutions. But, the reality of it is that dad, a successful farmer, failed to convince them. I'm still not convinced that they'll listen to a thirteen year old schoolgirl?"

"Most thirteen year old schoolgirls would fail to convince a bunch of stubborn adult farmers that their methods are archaic. But then, you are no ordinary schoolgirl. They've become successful poultry farmers, thanks to you, so they owe you, big time. Then, you've taken your soil samples and terrified them with a forecast of the truth. So don't you worry! I think they'll all come.

Time has a way of teaching stubborn people the error of their ways. Miss, you did say next Sunday, didn't you?"

"Yes, next Sunday, it is! The truth of the matter is that the week will give me time to prepare my words and my computer printouts of what I have to say and what I'd like them to do."

"I'll get the word out. Would you like me to be there?"

"I wouldn't dare do it without you. I think the very presence of both you and my father will show them, without words, that what I tell them is backed by solid agricultural knowledge and experience. They already look up to both of you for making our farm so successful.

Chapter 7

With pallid face and sorrow-filled eyes, a gaunt and skeletal Father Murphy shakily mounted the steps of the pulpit to address his congregation. His black cassock hung from his bony frame throwing into prominence his sallow complexion. When he began to speak, his reedy voice made it clear that he was not at all well.

"It grieves me to tell you," he began with a breaking voice, "about the harrowing dreams I've been having over the past months. Oh, I'm not complaining about the nightmares themselves or of their effect on my health. It is the content of these dreams that terrify me." He stopped to inhale deeply as though his lungs were starved of oxygen. "Night after night, I find myself stumbling about in a frigid no-man's-land engulfed in the stench and silence of the tomb. The landscape, shrouded in darkness, is scattered with the corpses of the dead and the dying." He again stopped to inhale deeply. "The stench of rotting flesh afflicts my nose, while the cries of the wounded and the dying afflict my ears. My worst fears are realized when the darkness is pierced by a shaft of moonlight revealing faces that I recognize. Some of them belong to you, my parishioners. Others are those of strangers that I've never seen before." He stopped again as a prolonged fit of coughing shook him. He then stumbled, grasping tightly to the pulpit to keep himself upright. He held on unsteadily for a moment of silence, faltered and slowly sunk to his knees in a faint. Two members of the congregation rushed to his aid, carried him down the steps of the pulpit and put him to sit and rest quietly in the vestry where he took a few sips of water. They then helped him to his home where he was found to have a high fever. They put him to bed and summoned his doctor.

"I'll remind them that, like the poultry farming *you* introduced, this too is *your* idea. So in future, when you have another new idea, they'll be willing to listen with due respect and patience to what you have to say, and to carry out any instructions you give them."

"Why do you think I'll have another idea, Mr. Sing?" Serena asked smiling.

"Oh Miss, seeing the way you operate, I don't doubt it for a moment."

"Anyway, I can't begin to thank you for your help, Mr. Sing. And I already have another idea," Serena told him smiling broadly. His reply came immediately.

"I'm not at all surprised."

Leesa was at a loss to understand how her mother could fail to detest a daughter who had planned to carry out such a cruel and despicable attack upon her. It made her recall the deceit she had practiced and all the acts of subterfuge she had undertaken. Her aim had been to fool her mother into thinking that she had changed into a loving and dutiful daughter. And then the dreaded questions arose in her mind, as they had done so often before: what had her mother ever done to make Leesa hate her with such passion? And didn't she deserve to be choked to death for the vulgar, spiteful and obscene teapot incident? Has she been in her mother's place, she wouldn't have stopped the choking. Didn't her mother's conduct show that she had always been willing to forgive her daughter for her vindictive and cruel acts? And as she considered her mother's behavior, she automatically began to judge her own past actions. Why did she detest a mother who had returned so many of her malicious acts with love and forgiveness? Where had the cruel streak come from that she displayed so often? And then the question that she most dreaded surfaced: Worst of all, she asked herself: was I born evil? It was the question that resonated in her mind, returning constantly to plague her; the question about whose answer she dreaded most to think.

Having seen the evil that was eating away at Leesa's heart, Kim felt more than ever compelled to come to her daughter's aid and help preserve her purity. She believed that revealing the feelings she had experienced during her acts of devotion before the shrine had perhaps helped Leesa to see her own wickedness and encouraged her to follow her mother's example.

"The scent of smoldering wax, the gleam of the eternal light, the immobility of the grieving women at the foot of the cross, and the silence of the pain-crazed victim," Kim told Leesa, "created the unique atmosphere that transported me to a spiritual plateau where communion with God seemed to follow naturally. Only then did I experience the sensation of spiritual peace that came over me. The experience strengthened my faith, making me even more steadfast." I know my daughter is intelligent. Let's hope my words and actions provide her with food for thought, she said to herself.

Serena saw herself ducking into that dark, foul-scented forest with the wind driving the rain like freezing bullets flaying her skin. The wet twigs of the trees she had painted as backdrops to her animal subjects whipped themselves against her face and body, clawing at her eyes. Roots sprang up in her path intent on tripping her. She skipped over them and kept running, terror spurring her forward. Her breathing came out in ragged spurts, her heaving chest burned as her eyes searched desperately for a safe haven. Startled, she saw the Nazi search party crouched behind the cover of some trees, waiting in ambush. Their presence, blocking her path, unhinged her. She tripped on the next protruding root and fell so violently that she awoke.

As Sing drove the farmers to the farm after collecting them in his employer's limousine, he learnt that Leesa had not enlightened them about why she needed them. She ushered them into her kitchen, seated them around her table. All were washed and dressed in clean clothes, sitting awkwardly, their faces gazing at her in expectation. They felt uncomfortable at finding themselves unexpectedly in the most luxurious and sparkling kitchen they had ever seen. Their eyes traveled from the recessed lighting down to the gleaming stove and refrigerator, the microwave oven, dishwasher, colored granite counters and beautiful crockery behind their glass-fronted cupboards. Staring down at the ceramic tiled floor, they waited anxiously to hear why they had been summoned to the wealthiest home in the district and driven there in Mrs. Ahn's personal limousine.

Despite what they knew of her checkered past, they were all kindly disposed towards her. Not only was she a very beautiful and wealthy woman–and most men feel drawn to women possessing beauty and wealth–but also each of them possessed a starter poultry farm that, thanks to her daughter, had been providing their families with eggs and meat for the last few months. Her daughter had accomplished what they had all been unable to do for their families–abate their hunger, and so ease their own suffering. And then during the past weeks, her daughter had also been providing them with delicious meals from various kinds of fowl. They all felt they were in her and her daughter's debt, and Leesa knew it.

"I would like to thank you all for coming and especially at such short notice," she began. "I'm sure you all know of the family tragedies that are taking place in our district." They nodded their heads indicating that they did, gossip being a major part of their entertainment.

"The victimization of women and children bothers me considerably, and so does cheating husbands and wives," she told them, before explaining what she had in mind. When finally she did and asked them to act on her behalf, they agreed. She then offered them drinks of her pungent cider and huge slices of rich chocolate cake before crowding them into her car.

Yong Sang had met Kim at college when like her, he was in his final year, studying for a degree in fine arts. He first heard her play the piano at a concert given by her department to raise funds that would help to defray the expenses of a sound proof room for their students. Afterwards, he went to compliment her on her performance. She asked if he too was a musician. He said no, and he explained that he had begun to specialize in sculpture but had decided, somewhat later, to switch to carving.

"What made you change your mind?" Kim asked.

"I went to the museum and saw some of the exquisite masks, pagoda panels and other artifacts that were carved and painted by Korean artists. Besides," he chuckled, "carving wood is so much easier and I think far more rewarding than clawing my way into marble and stone, though I still work with both." The two became friendly, the friendship blossomed. He asked her to accompany him on numerous outings; they fell in love and eventually got married. Apart from their other pursuits, husband and wife did their gardening for the beautification of the church and to bring some comfort to the neighbors living in their poverty-stricken district. Theirs was a strong and loving bond and both were delighted when a year after their marriage, their baby girl, Leesa, was born.

Yong Sang went to his workshop every morning where he designed, built and painted toys, birds, ships, planes and animals for his well-heeled clients. They came from all corners of the country to collect and pay for the items they had commissioned. All were delighted with his work and paid a handsome price for the models that were always built to scale. Once the couples' daughter was born, both parents began making plans for her schooling. Since education was the only doorway to a successful professional career, everyone sought to get his child into the best schools and colleges. There, space was at a premium and given only to the best and brightest students. Thus, education was not only very competitive, but also very expensive. The young couple immediately began a savings plan for their daughter's education.

The family lived in Hamyang's poor farming district where Young Sang, an able woodworker, made simple toys, trains, boats, planes and animals of all sorts that he painted as gifts, and distributed at Christmas to the poor children of the area. Both parents tried to get Leesa to help in the garden, but she showed no interest in helping. Yong Sang also tried to interest her in his work, but she shied away from him, his untidy workshop, and its sawdust-strewn interior. She hated to see him in his sawdust covered overalls that she viewed with distaste as the demeaning badge of a manual laborer. While there, she often turned her back and closed her eyes to prevent her looking at such a degrading spectacle.

While Sing was squeezing as many of the neighborhood farmers into the back of the truck to take them to the meeting at the Ahn farm, Serena, Leesa and Tina were at home busily slicing numerous hot rolls in two, lathering both sides with butter and making them into sandwiches with thick wedges of ham, slices of cheese, tomatoes, pickled cucumbers, lettuce leaves and a touch of mustard. The wives of two farmers were equally busy preparing gallons of hot coffee and laying out cream and sugar for the expected arrivals. Serena knew that once fed, the farmers would be more inclined to listen to reason, especially when they had nothing to lose.

On arrival, she greeted the farmers, assembled them in a warm barn and seated them around a couple of tables joined together. She then served them large mugs of coffee and sandwiches that disappeared in short order. When they were finished, she rose from the head of the table, got their attention by raising her voice loudly to address them.

"Thank you for coming and thank you again for the many gifts of fruit and vegetables you were kind enough to bring me after the success of our poultry farm project." She didn't think it would hurt to remind them that although she was a simple teenage girl, she had created a project that had put them all in her debt.

"Today, I have a new project for you that I, my father and Mr. Sing, our farm manager, consider would greatly increase production on your farms." The statement was greeted by a few smirks, restrained laughter, a bit of bickering followed by total silence.

"Let's hear about the new project Miss," someone finally shouted, breaking the silence.

"I'm sure you understand that plants are like people. Both need a constant supply of food. In order to thrive, they need water, sunshine and a balanced supply of nitrogen, phosphorous, potassium and sulphur to produce a vigorous root system and to establish a dense canopy that protects the soil's surface from weathering." She realized that they certainly all knew this, but felt it was important to tell them that she too knew what she was talking about. "As you also know, during every growing season your crops extract these nutrients from the soil of your farms. They must be replaced through various fertilizers that should be added to the soil annually..." A farmer cut her off.

"We are farmers, Miss. We all know that. Please tell us something we don't know," he said, speaking politely.

"Well, for decades your crops have been taking out from the soil more nutriment than you've been putting in. Let me repeat that: for countless generations your ancestors and you have been taking out more nutrients than you've been putting in. With the help of Mr. Sing, I have analyzed the soil samples taken on a number of your farms. The truth of the matter is that your soil has been severely depleted of nutrients. It has also been damaged by heavy tillage that mixes the fertile top soil with the less fertile subsoil. Therefore, each year you've been creating a top soil that is less fertile than previously.

"The reality of it is that over time," she continued, "in some instances the soil below the surface of your fields has become compacted, preventing water from being absorbed and stunting root growth. If truth be told, some of your fields are waterlogged from the heavy monsoon rains, and others dried out by sun. All these situations have severely depleted nutrients, and have killed helpful microbes, bugs, termites and earthworms that induce aeration and enrich the soil." She waited for a moment in the silence that her remarks evoked, before continuing.

"Over the years when bad weather destroyed your crops, many of you have had to sell off a portion of your acreage in order to survive. With shrunken farms most of you can't afford to allow your fields to lie fallow and revivify themselves. What especially surprises me is that only a few of you practice a constant cycle of crop rotation that proper farm management demands. I repeat, successful farming demands continuous crop rotation. These are the main factors that prevent you from having better crop yields." Mr. Sing had been listening intently and there were times when, but for Serena's musical voice, he thought that the expressions she used and the language she selected was very similar to that of her father. She didn't have long to wait for someone to answer her.

"Miss, my fellow farmers and I are disappointed that you blame us for a series of problems that you say we have caused. But isn't it true that many of the problems we face are the result of bad weather– too much sun, too much rain, severe drought and a number of blights that infect our crops? Wouldn't you agree that these are situations over which we have no control? Instead of the harsh criticism you have been dishing out, perhaps it is time for you to suggest some solutions." Serena was surprised by the wisdom of the speaker, and especially by the restraint with which he had made his points. She waited for the many 'yeahs' that followed what he said to die down.

"I'm sorry you think my criticism too harsh, and yes, I am aware that you are unable to control some of the problems that you face. But I want you to look at me. Yes, **look-at-me**," she repeated loudly, spacing her words, "and listen very carefully to what I say! In your mind, I am no more than a silly little child. Worse still, I'm a girl, a novice, whom you professionals believe has no real knowledge about the deep complexities of farming. But you are very, very wrong in thinking that. First of all, I have consulted both Mr. Sing and the most successful farmer in the area, my father on these matters. From them, I have got excellent advice and suggestions. Then, after making an in-depth study and research dealing specifically with the causes of your poor harvests, I have come up with some solutions of my very own. Finally, I want you to understand that being a little silly girl in your eyes, I have been forced to be blunt and severe in my criticism. Otherwise, not a single one of you professionals would take seriously what this **novice/girl/teenager** has to say." Once again silence followed her remarks. Then, the same speaker shouted.

"Okay Miss, you've made your point. Let's hear what you have to say."

"Mr. Sing, the hands on my father's farm and I have used a two-year accumulation of fowl dung. With much work we have converted it into humus. We have done so by adding water, kitchen scraps, spoiled fruit and vegetables, egg shells, coffee grounds, shredded plant material, twigs, tea leaves, fir needles, straw, grass clippings, ashes, old newspapers, horse and cow manure, soil and other types of material to form compost. Then, by regularly turning the mixture, we have aerated it so that aerobic bacteria, fungi, sub soil creatures like earthworms, termites and other living microbes have infused the material with heat, carbon dioxide and ammonium. The various elements in the mixture have created nitrates and nitrites and transformed what was once a mixture of raw dung and other ingredients into humus. I should point out to you that a single handful of humus contains more helpful microbes than the population of this whole planet. This most perfect compost when used to fertilize your fields will help it to retain moisture and create healthy soil that is resistant to erosion from wind and rain. The bottom line is that once fertilized with humus your fields will produce crops in such abundance that you will be shocked and delighted. In the mumbling of disbelief and uncertainty that followed she shouted: "I cannot hear you." Only at her urging did some ragged applause follow. She could see that they didn't completely believe her, but she pressed on.

"It is equally important for you to note that the compost you create annually, while showing good effort on your part, has never been sufficient to adequately repair the damage that has been done to your under-fertilized fields."

"Miss, we and our ancestors have been using our compost to fertilize our fields for generations. And since they hardly ever bothered themselves with crop rotation, and had very good harvests, why should we do anything different?"

"First, you no longer have good harvests. Low fertility, soil erosion by wind and rain coupled with under-fertilization prevents crops from getting the nutrition they need. Further, the compost you make is beneficial, but it is far too little to replace what has been lost over so many, many decades. And each season the damage gets worse." She noted that there was a lot of grumbling, but no laughter. She knew the farmers did not like to be reminded of their inadequacy, and certainly not by a teenage girl. Before things got out of hand, Serena again raised her voice to explain what she had in mind.

While at college abroad John couldn't help but be impressed by the striking figure, and encyclopedic knowledge of a British lecturer. He was a former don from St. Peter's Hall, Oxford who taught English Literature. Apart from being inspired by his insightful lectures, the student was equally impressed by the professor's stylish outfits. John's eyes sparkled with intelligence and he carried himself like a highly trained athlete. His muscles were toned from being accustomed to the hard work, discipline and routine needed to obtain his fifth degree Karate black belt. He loved to dress and since he had a slim tall figure that showed off his clothes to advantage, he looked like the model for an upper class, sophisticated clothing line. He was so taken by the stylish way the professor dressed that he determined to adopt his somewhat dashing and debonair look. On returning home after his studies abroad, he took to wearing well-cut dark blue double-breasted blazers with slender lapels. Four silver buttons stood out forming the corners of a square at the base of his lapels, and there were three more on the outer end of either sleeve. His shirts were starched white linen and he wore an open collar sporting silk baby-blue ascots. Onyx cuff links bearing his college crest adorned his French cuffs, and a rumpled white handkerchief was tucked carelessly into the wrist of his left sleeve. Sharply creased grey flannel trousers that allowed black socks to peep from highly polished black Florsheim loafers completed the outfit. On rainy days, he carried a tightly furled umbrella. John was savvy enough to realize that his dress clashed somewhat with his status as a provincial farmer, but he considered the foible a forgivable affectation. After all, wasn't he also a well-educated and well-traveled, very wealthy businessman?

"I do not want you to lose your farms through bankruptcy." She agreed with Mr. Sing that a little fear couldn't hurt. She then quickly added: "I am here to make you an offer," Serena told the farmers with the broadest of smiles, knowing that silence would follow immediately. "With the invaluable help of Mr. Sing and his farm hands, we have accumulated an abundant supply of humus from the dung of my birds. I am offering each of you four, I repeat, four full cartloads of humus free of charge." The earlier grumbling turned to loud cheers.

"However, in this first year you should use only half of what you collect, adding to it with your own compost. I repeat: you should use only half of your humus this year so that next year you will already have enough for your needs. This will give my poultry and me time to accumulate more dung to supply your future needs.

"Is that all we have to do, Miss?"

"No! I want to say a word about crop rotation.

Father Murphy, Leesa and the six burly farmers she had chosen, stopped at the homes of the wife batterers. She led them into each house where she confronted the abusive husband in front of his wife. Backed by the priest and her band of 'enforcers,' whose muscular bodies, clenched fists and scowling faces scared the life out of the abuser, Leesa warned: "My watchdogs and I are ordering you to stop the battering and ill-treatment of your wife immediately. Otherwise," she continued in the harshest voice she could manage, while spacing her words: "you-will-be-battered-into-mincemeat-yourself. Do-I-make-myself-clear?" She hissed her words loudly enough for the wife to hear. None of the visitors missed the fear that clouded the eyes of the cowering batterer, or the meek voice with which he promised haltingly to stop his abhorrent behavior. Naturally, each of the wives looked upon Leesa and her enforcers with grateful eyes.

"Father Murphy then told the husband: "I will be visiting your wife regularly to ensure that you continue to behave." He kept his promise over the following weeks and months.

Leesa's next stops were at the homes of the child molesters where she used the same strategy. "You should be ashamed of yourself for molesting your daughter," she told each of them. "If you persist in such corrupt and contemptible behavior, we shall see that you are publicly horsewhipped. Afterwards, you'll-be-banished-from-this-district. Do-you-hear-me?" Leesa didn't know if she could instigate a public horsewhipping or banish anyone, but to judge by the culprit's stammering reply, it seemed evident that he didn't doubt a single word she said and would co-operate. The molesters were even more terrified than the batterers. The priest promised them that he'd keep tabs on their conduct and again he kept his word.

The watchdogs next stopped at the farms of the husbands and later the wives who were being unfaithful. Leesa warned them that she and her crusaders were shocked by their adultery. If such promiscuity did not stop immediately, the miscreants would be publicly horsewhipped and banished from the district." The priest warned that he would visit each week to ensure that the infidelity had come to an abrupt halt."

On their way home, Leesa spoke to the priest and her six enforcers: "I want to thank you all for standing side by side with me to confront those awful characters. You all know that I couldn't have done it without your help. I'm very proud and particularly pleased with you all for agreeing to act as my watchdogs."

"Mrs. Ahn, you've made us proud of what we've done. None of us would have thought of doing what you did or of standing behind you without your encouragement and leadership," the priest replied on behalf of himself and the farmers. Later on, they all became even more proud of their accomplishment on hearing that the news of their actions had spread throughout the district and both Leesa and her watchdogs had become the community's heroes overnight. It made the watchdogs more eager than ever to continue the protection of their neighbors. Father Murphy went one step further. He had begun counseling the abusers and their families, and was able to assure Leesa that the abuse had indeed stopped.

Dang was John's best friend. He was stocky in build, but what appeared to be fat was solid muscle. In his late forties, he had a full head of hair. It was cut short and could best be described as salt and pepper. Though his broad face and aquiline nose reflected that of the Caucasian male, he had the full lips of Africa. His dark eyes brimmed with intelligence and were covered by horn-rimmed spectacles. He was a man of the earth, capable of using both his hands and his brains. Whenever John visited his friend, the latter couldn't refrain from poking fun at John's outfit. Through his thick lenses Dang stared goggle-eyed at his friend's attire. "Hey man! You look like a clothes horse for some big Brit designer."

In response, John struck the pose of a film star, pulled out the handkerchief from his sleeve and mopped his brow gently. He was not above playing the fool just to irk his friend.

"You know I'm not given to advertisement, Dang, John said, but I wouldn't be caught dead in one of your outmoded three-piece suits." The two friends hugged in greeting and joked with each other. Dang then put two shot glasses on the table and a bottle of Sojou, the preferred alcohol of locals. Following protocol, they poured shots for each other.

"So John, what brings you to my modest abode?"

"Modest abode? Ha! This luxurious mansion with its modern architecture, priceless paintings, and swimming pool is an advertisement for a debauched banker and his life style. If I didn't know better, I'd say it ran a close second to mine," John said, chuckling loudly. "But seriously, I need to discuss something personal with you." The tip of his little finger was in his mouth.

"I'm always available John. What do you have in mind?"

Of late, my conscience has been bothering me more than usual. It has me feeling very depressed, so I thought I'd express my thoughts and feelings to you and get your opinion."

"The last time we met, I was about to explain to you the mechanics of crop rotation," Serena told her audience. "Growing the same crop in the same field year after year, would cause a build up of insect pests and diseases that normally attack that particular crop. Doing so would also use up those nutrients in the soil on which that crop depends for healthy growth. The simplest rule of crop rotation is not to grow the same crop in the same field for two years running. Each grain crop must be followed in season two by one of the following legumes: beans, alfalfa, soybean or sorghum. However," she continued, "there are certain other guidelines that I'd like you to follow." There was an abrupt silence followed by slight grumbling. She waited for the question she expected.

"Miss, you must remember that we have our own ploughing and planting to do. Where will we find time to do what you ask?"

"I'm offering you suggestions only. You don't have to follow them, but I've already explained that it would be to your advantage to help one another. Remember, I stressed solidarity? Anyway, I've listed some instructions on a computer printout that I'll expect you to complete before you come to pick up your humus. Each of you can take a copy as you leave."

"We'd like to hear your 'guidelines' now, if you don't mind," someone said.

"Before adding half the humus, you should undertake *light* tillage of your fields to prevent further damage to the top soil and an even greater loss of fertility. That will keep moisture loss to a minimum, and prevent undue soil degradation by wind and rain erosion. You should also aerate the soil with light spiked rollers to break into the compacted sub soil that will allow roots to absorb moisture, grow and flourish. Aeration will also promote the growth of sub soil creatures, earthworms, fungi, aerobic bacteria and lots of other microbes."

"Miss, we don't have the means to do what you suggest."

"My dad has agreed to lend you a number of his light spiked rollers that you can begin to use immediately. Again I remind you of my plea for solidarity. Please offer your help to others and pass the rollers around as soon as you have finished using them. They will only be available for the next few weeks before the start of the planting season. To increase your crop yield and to help your soil regenerate itself, you'll also have to undertake crop rotation for the next growing season. When all these things are done, you can mix in your own compost and ashes and then put your humus to work. And yes, that is all, for the present."

"How will you be sure that we've followed your instructions," a clown asked, drawing from the assembly a gale of laughter.

"As soon as anyone lets me know that he has followed *all* my instructions, Mr. Sing and I will come to inspect his fields to see for ourselves that he has done what was necessary." With a free gift of humus on the horizon, there was no more grumbling.

"Miss, since crop rotation must be continued for several growing seasons, can you advise us about how best to do this?" One of the farmers asked.

"I'm glad you asked, although I've explained everything you need to do in the printouts. I'll start with an example. Corn requires lots of nitrogen and has specific insect pests and diseases like corn earworm, corn blight and other such diseases that attack it. By planting beans, alfalfa, sorghum or soybean in rotation, the legume replaces the nitrogen that has been lost. During the following growing season corn pests and diseases will have no plants on which to reproduce and replenish themselves, so they die off and decrease in number."

"Miss that example is very helpful for corn, but what about other grains like wheat, oats, barley, and so on?"

"I've set out for you a simple four year cycle: any grain planted in season 1, must be followed by a legume in season 2, a different grain in season 3 followed by a legume in season 4. Of course, if you planted a legume in a field last year, you'll be able to plant any grain crop in that field this year." Serena was pleased to see that twice as many farmers had come to hear her proposals. Evidently, the starter poultry farms had spread wider than she had thought.

"Oh, there is one more thing I need to mention," she said, having held back the good news deliberately. "World renowned scientists have succeeded to create seeds that are genetically engineered. These new seeds have been modified to increase nitrogen efficiency and to accelerate the process of photosynthesis. They also have greater resistance to insect pests and drought. I have managed to buy some of these seeds of corn, wheat, barley and oats." When she stopped speaking she knew that complete silence would follow before someone would ask: "Will you be donating those seeds as well, Miss?"

"Yes, but this first time only, and only to those farmers who follow **all** my suggestions. If all goes well, next year with the sale of your increased crops, extra eggs and meat, you'll be able to buy your own genetically engineered seeds. I hope you consider that fair?" A resounding 'yes' from the farmers brought a wide smile to Serena's face.

"I'd like to add one final word. With your starter farms, I would like to emphasize again that solidarity should be our watchword. So, if neighboring farmers were to help each other with the work to be done, the task would be much easier and completed far more quickly. She knew that her words would provide food for thought.

The farmers, being driven home by Serena and Mr. Sing, sat in brooding silence, aware that it would take a long time away from their normal work load to follow Serena's instructions. They also knew that doing so would greatly improve the fertility of their soil, and that the humus mixed with their own compost, ashes and extra soil would increase their crop production immeasurably. Regardless of the extra work involved, they could not let such a golden opportunity pass them by. If all went well weather wise and each farmer got the help of his neighbors, as Serena had suggested, the windfall of humus would go a long way to improve their harvests and their livelihood.

Leesa was studying in her room when the sounds of lovemaking came from her parents' adjoining bedroom. This was nothing new. As a preteen, she had often heard those sounds of passion before, since her parents were very noisy lovers, oblivious of the world outside. However, since she had become pubescent, she found that their love sounds had begun to affect her very differently. She heard each of her father's groans and her mother's gasps in response that sounded more like anguished cries of delight.

She felt a powerful surge of hatred aimed at her mother pour into her blood stream. Jealousy urged her to search for some act with which to accuse her mother. She immediately began to wonder if her actions before the shrine had been merely pretense. Her parents' lovemaking had wounded her so deeply, that she became convinced Kim's stories of Christ's victimization were a shabby attempt at role playing intended to cure her daughter of her wickedness. Leesa's deeply hurt feelings made her mother's motives clear. Her supposed goodness would, by comparison, make Leesa consider herself wicked. This would urge Leesa to cast off her evil ways to become a better person. Far more important, Leesa would no longer vie with her mother for her father's devotion. She convinced herself that her mother had played Leesa a cruel trick, prompted by the selfish motive of coming between daughter and father. Her mother had succeeded in manipulating Leesa in such an underhand way that her daughter felt betrayed.

While it was true that Kim was trying to get her daughter to follow her example, the devotion she showed before the shrine was sincere. Equally sincere were the words she had spoken and the compassion she had shown to the

Messiah and to her daughter. Yet, nothing could persuade Leesa that Kim hadn't betrayed her. She was determined to retaliate by devising a plan to show her mother once and for all the malice and vindictiveness of which Leesa was capable. She felt ashamed that she had fallen for the underhandedness and hypocrisy of her mother. How, she asked herself, had such a stupid person as her mother been so easily able to pull the wool over her eyes; she who considered herself such an astute and intelligent individual? Since she was unconsciously lying to herself, her eyes were closed.

However, what she had failed to consider was the profound effect that her mother's conduct, the shrine itself, and the stories that the crucifixion had instilled into her consciousness. She could not dismiss the fact that she possessed a darker side to her character. The guilt she felt for her evil thoughts and actions plagued her. She recalled the many times she had wedged herself between her parents, the hateful glares that she had darted at her mother and cringed at the memory of the teapot incident. Without realizing it, Leesa's struggle between good and evil had her standing halfway between the beckoning arms of God and Satan.

Serena looked forward eagerly to the arrival of the farmers for their share of humus. However, it took much longer than she expected for them to comply with her instructions. It was almost six weeks before the spiked rollers were returned and farmers began asking Serena to come with Mr. Sing to inspect their fields. Once that was done, a line of carts began arriving at her farm to collect their precious cargo and their genetically engineered seeds. She couldn't believe the number that came and kept coming. The news of her project had spread far wider than she had believed. It took far longer than forecast for the farmers and Serena to witness the results of this, her second experiment.

As harvest time grew nearer and nearer, the news grew from good to great. From all accounts, the crops were burgeoning on the farms and the forecast was that the harvest would be bountiful beyond their wildest dreams. Crops like corn, alfalfa, barley, beans, oats, sorghum, wheat, soybean, millet, rye, carrots, cabbage and tomatoes had almost tripled in production. Farmers and their wives began coming to the Ahn farm to congratulate Serena and bless her for her good advice. They began bringing Serena gifts of all sorts of fruit and vegetables. Then, without warning, just a couple of weeks before the harvest, a cold front had marched in, blotted out the glorious sunshine and froze everything in a bitterly cold snap. Farmers and their helpers raced into the fields to salvage what they could. The only thing certain was that those farmers who had followed Serena's directives would have far outstripped in production the crops of their two previous harvests. It was a crushing blow to both the farmers and to Serena to see, after all their hard work, the disastrous effect that the freak weather had had on their crops. But farmers are resilient. This catastrophe was made more acceptable by their knowledge that Serena's methods had worked exactly as she had forecast.

In preparation for the next season, they tilled their fields following Serena's methods with the remainder of their humus after again using her father's light spiked rollers. They also rotated their crops. With lasting good weather, they finally had a very successful harvest and again came in droves to thank and compliment Serena. The farmers couldn't understand how and why a mere teenager should take such an interest in the welfare of their families and their community. But their compliments scared Serena, making her reflect on the words of Father Murphy: "When God singles you out for praise and lifts you above your fellow citizens, beware! He's chosen a very tough row for you to hoe."

However, she was delighted to find that many farmers who had ignored her advice, came, hat in hand, to ask, with shameful demeanor, whether they too could share in the benefits of their neighbors. She was pleased to give them her humus, her seeds and her instructions, and again with her father's permission, to loan them the light spiked rollers. Even more gratifying was the fact that many told her they would listen attentively to any further ideas she might have for upgrading the production on their farms. She, in turn, promised to continue donating the humus as long as her four breeds of fowl kept up their production.

For Serena's successful experiments as for her generosity to them, the farmers' wives had been equally generous with their gifts to Serena. She had passed them on to the farm hands who had christened her 'the little dynamo.'

Left by herself after the farmers and their wives had departed Serena was delighted, even ecstatic. What an incredible feeling she thought, to have brought happiness and contentment to so many and to be worthy of their gratitude. She felt as though someone had taken a full bucket of joy and poured it into her heart. It was a feeling that she'd want to repeat and sustain for as long as possible, and as often.

Chapter 8

After regaining her ability to speak, Serena seemed to have improved. But some pieces of the puzzle were still missing. Her troubled mind was unable to piece together what remained or to grasp their full meaning. In her befuddled state, she remained an isolated stranger frozen with fear with no one to tell her what she most needed to know: why her pain-racked body felt so alien; why she felt that there was something seriously wrong within her; how she came to be imprisoned in the infernal limbo that she inhabited.

"The mind is a delicate instrument that sets a limit to the amount of stress or pain an individual can bear," the doctor had told Serena's parents. He then explained further: "Whenever that person has an experience during which the stress exceeds that limit, some kind of mental meltdown takes place. It can present itself in different forms, but often occurs in an identity crisis through memory loss that is termed hysterical amnesia, or a fugue state." The doctor had gone on to state: "Serena has been subjected to so harrowing an ordeal of pain and humiliation that she has chosen to hide from herself and the world through forgetfulness. Ironically, she is mimicking a mild form of insanity as a means of safeguarding her sanity. But take heart, this fugue state doesn't always last long." Her parents hoped that the doctor's forecast proved to be true. They then asked him:

"Doctor, can you say why she complains about feeling "awry" and "so different?"

"I think so. Serena's mind has blocked out the incident in order to permit her to retain her sanity. By hiding within her mind, she believes that she will be safe from harm. She has been showing many of the symptoms usually associated with a particular disorder. Apart from her forgetfulness she has a dazed appearance, together with disorientation and confusion. She is unable to figure out her true identity and has headaches, nightmares and heavy sweating. She feels differently perhaps because the rapists have trampled upon and stolen her youth, her vitality and worst of all, her innocence. She probably feels unclean; a sense of being tainted. After such violations some people feel the need to wash themselves constantly to remove the stain they feel is defiling them. A few also sense that they are no longer the same person. Some tend to think that they are broken inside; that they are no longer whole."

While her mother was away from home one day visiting a friend who was terminally ill, Leesa took the opportunity to confront her father with her plan for improving their place in society. She went to his workshop taking with her some of the candies that he loved, planning to use them as a bribe to manipulate him into seeing her point of view. Every little bit helps, she told herself. Her father was surprised to see her at that hour of the day since she usually went later each evening to tell him when supper was almost ready.

"Hey," he said, a broad smile showing his surprise and delight, "what's my little princess doing here?" She couldn't help noticing with distaste that he was sweating, his hair, overalls and forearms covered in sawdust. He looked every inch the manual laborer that she despised. She brushed that thought aside in order to begin.

"Dad," she said, "I wanted to talk to you about what you do."

"Really!" He replied. "Don't tell me you're impressed with my work and want me to teach you the trade," he said jovially."

"No no, it isn't that. I am impressed with your work. In fact I know that you're especially gifted and creative in the work you do..."

"But?..."

"But the small wages you make keep the family living like nonentities; humble folk with no chance of improving their status and moving upward in society." Her accusations astonished her father making him very angry and disappointed in the daughter he loved. His eyes turned hard and bored into her.

"What do you know about the wages I make? And yes, we are humble folk, so what Leesa? We make sure you want for nothing." His daughter could hear the surprise, anger and pain in his voice and could see his deepening frown, but she pressed on.

"Mom squanders the money she makes from the rose garden on the losers in the district. And you make beautiful toys that you give away freely to the same poverty-stricken street urchins."

"Your mother and I do what we can to help others in need, Leesa. She seems quite satisfied with what I earn, the work I do, and the way we live." Leesa could tell from the tight line of his jaw and the way he spaced his words that her dissatisfaction had deeply wounded him. The forced calmness of his tone showed how angry he was.

On another occasion, the woman who was constantly at Serena's bedside, talked about the zoo animals that she had painted over and over. Serena concentrated hard on what the woman said and found that her words made Serena begin to recall the hours she had spent trying to capture the pain and resignation reflected in the attitudes, postures and pacing of the zoo animals. So she was a painter and loved portraying animals on her canvases! Well, that was another new memory. Each small snippet of returning memory made her feel as though she had accomplished a huge breakthrough. The woman must have seen the glint of recognition in her eyes for she began to relate the journeys Serena took on horseback with her father into the mountain wilderness and the cave that they had found there. Suddenly, in a flash, the images came roaring back. Serena remembered who she was, and that the woman facing her was her mother. She remembered the farm, Will, her pigeons, riding into the mountains and visiting the cave. She sat bolt upright at the flurry of images that rushed into her mind and scared the life out of her mother and her.

"What's the matter? What's the matter?" Her mother asked anxiously, on seeing Serena spring bolt upright. When Serena told her mother that she had suddenly remembered who she was, they hugged each other tightly and both began sobbing. Her mother then rushed to phone her husband to tell him the good news.

"Dad, try to understand. I'm not criticizing you or your work," Leesa lied, turning away from her father and pretending to be petting the figure of a duck he had sculpted. "I'm just trying to make you fully conscious that you are falling short of your true potential."

"Are you sure it's me who's falling short, Leesa?" His words were spoken gently, but it was the sadness and challenge in his voice that disturbed her.

"Dad, as I said, you're an exceptionally gifted artist. At the moment, what you do is to fashion natural and man-made objects, like animals and ships in wood and various materials. You do that beautifully, but you could carve pieces that are far more creative in style, design and workmanship."

"So, you think that none of my work is original; that in short, I'm a copy cat?" Again aware of the wounds that her words had caused, she turned towards him but kept her eyes downcast and tried to soften the blow.

"Dad, I'm trying to make you see that a more creative style would increase the demand for your work and more than double your income. Now, do you see what I mean?" Though her eyes remained downcast, her voice was pleading for his understanding.

"It shocks and saddens me to realize that you are ashamed of the person I am, the work I do and the simplicity of our lives. If you weren't, you wouldn't make such harsh and false accusations."

"Dad, you're taking what I said the wrong way." Her father continued as though she hadn't spoken.

"While we do live simply, ours is certainly not a "hand to mouth" existence as you so colorfully describe it. Your mother and I make sure that *you* don't lack for anything."

"Dad, why won't you listen to what I'm trying to say?" Again he ignored her reply.

"Yes, we spend a lot of the money from the garden on the poor and the needy. But unlike *you*, who refuse to help even when we ask, *they* volunteer their help whenever we need it and without our having to beg." The sting of his accusation prodded her into attack mode.

"Dad, I hate doing manual labor like you, or soiling my hands like yours always seems to be. Just look in the mirror at the way you're covered in sawdust. It's lower class and undignified. "

"So now you're ashamed of me! You probably don't realize that everything you've said is about *you*, what you like and what you want! The world doesn't revolve around you or center upon your likes and dislikes. It breaks my heart to realize that you never think of anyone else but yourself?" He was frowning deeply and his lips were pulled back against his teeth as though he had the bitter taste of gall in his mouth.

"I'm here this minute thinking about *you*," she replied in annoyance.

"No, you're not! You're thinking about how your parents' work and earnings can promote you to a higher status; a life of luxury and sophistication. You're thinking about you, you, and you alone. And by the way, my work is not second-class. People from near and far come to commission my work. They respect my creative ability, and both your mother and I consider my fees more than adequate. Indeed, they're quite substantial!" She hadn't expected the stand her father was taking and his mention of her mother annoyed her intensely. It sparked her stubborn streak and her jealousy goaded her to anger.

"If they're so substantial, why do we live so "simply" as you quaintly put it. Why are we still nonentities in our community? Why does mama have to make my school clothes instead of buying them like everyone else? And why don't we go anywhere on holidays, or ever go away on vacation to different places like some of my friends?" She answered heatedly.

"Your mother and I decided to deprive ourselves of some of the things we'd like by putting aside one third of my income in the bank. That forces us to live simply, but we take care that all our needs, especially yours, are met. And you should never complain about your home-made clothes since your mother has created for you the latest and most stylish fashions that make you the envy of your friends. I can't imagine why or where she finds the time for such an ingrate..." His daughter cut him off. She made him so angry that the torrent of words rising in his mind became bottled up in his throat. He was left trying to convey his meaning with aggressive and dramatic gestures that, other than the fact that he was very angry, were impossible for her to interpret.

The terrifying images of Serena's present contrasted vividly with the joyous lifestyle of her past. She was a happy-go-lucky preteen living a serene and happy life on her parent's farm. She remembered saying so often: "Dad, it's snowing. Can we go sledding again today?"

"It's really cold outside darling, so you and your mom should dress warm. Make sure you put on two sweaters, a heavy coat, and don't forget your bonnet and mittens," her father would reply while her mother helped her into thick sweaters and thick, woolen mittens.

"Now, let me tie you both securely into your sled, one behind the other, then, I'll drag you behind my horse all over the pastures of the farm. You'll have to dodge the fountain of snow thrown up by the horse's hoofs," he'd say chuckling. They would have to wait a few minutes until he had saddled and mounted on Wizard. He'd then shout: "Ready?" And off they'd go.

"He'd start off slowly then build up speed, with her and her mother laughing and screaming their heads off all the way over the gentle hills and dales of the farm. She had to admit that she missed those winter mornings when the entire world was covered in a freezing white blanket that though cold, enfolded their family in its warmth. It was such an exhilarating time. When she was older, she returned the compliment, stuffing her father and mother into the same sled, tying them in, and dragging them behind her horse. As they tried to dodge the flying snow, their gales of laughter would echo over hill and dale all around the pastures of the farm. In late summer and autumn, her father, mother and Serena would cycle around the farm inspecting the animal enclosures, the fields and stop by the orchards to select the apples, pears and cherries that each of them favored. In the warmest summer weather, they would swim in the deepest pool in the river. This was a favorite pastime and even in winter they would sometimes take a quick dip in the freezing pool then sit warming themselves with chattering teeth before the fireplace. Her mother would listen to her shivering, red-cheeked husband and daughter as they related their adventures with much laughter over her hot chocolate drinks. At other times the three would just sit at home engrossed in the board games of yut, gangi or cribbage after which the loser would have to drink a full glass of water as punishment. They would often recall past outings or movies and chat together about the enjoyment they all had as a family."

"Father," Leesa said angrily, I don't care what plans you and mother have for a bigger house, a car or a luxurious vacation. Just answer me one question: why should your selfish desires come before a more sophisticated lifestyle for me?" She caught herself, then added: "for us."

"Our selfish desires?" He repeated, with a look of disbelief and deep hurt in his eyes. "I'll have you know that when you were born, your mother and I decided to put aside one-third of my wages for your university education. We've always known that you were an intelligent child." Leesa was caught flat-footed, but her selfish and headstrong nature compelled her to tough it out rather than backpedal and apologize.

"Why did you have to do something that I might not want? Did either of you ever consider that I might have plans than didn't include a college education? Did you ever think of consulting me? Dad, did you?" She challenged, with mounting rage and hurt in her voice.

Yong Sang was aghast at her intransigence and ingratitude. He thought of saying that it had been impossible to consult her since their decision was made when she was new-born. Instead of a rebuke, he merely asked what she intended to do after graduation.

"Did it ever occur to you that I might want to get married?" She barked belligerently.

"Then we'd use the money to give you the lavish wedding that you've always talked about and wished for." Even though he loved his daughter, he couldn't withhold his anger and sorrow at her less than gracious response to her parents' years of self-sacrifice. He couldn't help thinking that her soul was corroded with the leprosy of ego and its poison kept egging her on to create for herself one pitfall after another. He then questioned with gentle irony: "Do you think our saving for your welfare was worth the sacrifice?"

Finally, her father's gentle words coupled with his generosity had succeeded in shaming Leesa for her unfounded accusations, her selfishness and ingratitude. With her back to the wall, there was no retreat. Her parents' sacrifice on her behalf had finally made her see the selfish monster that she was. A crimson flush crept up her neck and reddened her cheeks. She bowed her head, lowering and then closing her eyes in shame.

"Oh Dad, I'm so sorry that I've hurt you. That wasn't what I intended."

"Well, you certainly chose the right words!"

"Dad, I do love you, but I'm so ashamed of living frugally and I hate, hate, hate being a nonentity!" She then added: "I wish I'd been a better daughter." She kissed him hastily on the cheek and in tears fled from the workshop.

After she left, Yong Sang couldn't help thinking of his thoroughly selfish daughter and the sharp arrows of ingratitude she had left embedded in his heart. He wondered: did those who were selfish ever think of themselves as cruel and wicked or were they so wrapped up in themselves, so twisted that they could always find justification for their evil? He could find no answer to his questions. A final question plagued his mind: did an ingrate recognize the depth of his ingratitude or how deeply it hurt those who had sacrificed for their welfare?

I remembered our visit to Mr. Dang, a banker, homing pigeon fancier, and one of dad's oldest friends.

"Dad, I didn't know that pigeons mated for life. While he showed me his birds, your friend also told me that if removed from their loft, when released, they would fly back to it even from another continent."

"That's quite interesting," dad replied distractedly, his thoughts obviously somewhere else. His lack of enthusiasm stung her and she asked: "Dad isn't it extraordinary that animals should display the virtues of loyalty and devotion that many people ignore?" This time he heard what she said since her question jolted him out of his reverie.

"Although still a teenager, Serena, you're quite perceptive. I'm really surprised to learn that such lofty principles as fidelity and devotion between partners should be important to someone your age. I suppose I should be delighted rather than surprised."

"Dad, since I do find those virtues impressive, I'd like you to buy me three pairs of youngsters. Mr. Dang says that's the best way to get started: before the youngsters have left their loft and get familiar with their surroundings."

"What you have to understand is that they'll need care and take up a lot of your time," he said, as she squeezed his hand thanking him silently for his generosity. During the following weeks, he was surprised and impressed at the interest she took in feeding her flock morning and evening until they had become accustomed to return to the new loft he had built. Only then, did she begin to train them; releasing them together at short distances at first, then at longer distances from home.

"After your birds circle and become tired, why do you chase them off when they try to land?"

"Dad, your friend explained that more exercise will develop their wing and breast muscles and build greater endurance."

"You're training them for racing already?"

"Yes, I'm following Mr. Dang's advice and the guidelines from the books you bought me. In a couple of weeks, I'll start releasing them further and further away from home. Later, the fastest birds will compete in the novice class races for prizes I hope to win. Do you know that your friend has some of the best racing stock in this country? He has imported thoroughbred pairs from England and France and keeps them in a special loft."

"I knew Dang was famous for winning many long distance races, but I didn't know about his imported stock. But why keep them in a special loft?"

"He's afraid that if they get loose they might fly back to their original countries."

Her dad kept up his interest in her pigeons and was almost as thrilled as she was when, some months later she won her first race for novices. He dragged her along with him to her mother so they could both share in her happiness.

Chapter 9

When John first met Leesa in high school as an adolescent, she was already a beauty. She had the charm and grace of youthful womanhood with her black silken tresses, her delicate bone structure of features and her litheness of body and limb. He saw such innocence and purity in her face, such elegance and poise in the way she carried herself that he thought of her as an extraordinary person. He fell in love with her immediately. He tried to focus on her evident allure, but had to confess that it was her eyes and lips that first commanded his attention. Her smile radiated such warmth and beauty it was like bright sunshine suddenly backlighting mountains at daybreak. Like him, there were others who were mesmerized by that smile. Then there was the attraction of her eyes. They were large, green and riveting while her rosebud lips invited thoughts that ignited the imagination. Her beauty created a number of rivals for him, some of whom were perhaps better looking. However, being from working-class backgrounds, they were in Leesa's mind, unworthy of the future she had projected for herself. Being the daughter of a humble woodworker, she saw John as the son of very affluent parents. She was tired of being someone of no consequence socially and believed that she could achieve her life's ambition by showing a special interest in him. After all, his father was a financial heavyweight. She knew that there were many affluent strings to his bow since he was a gentleman/farmer cum businessman, as well as the CEO of his corporation.

He had already told her he'd "soon be going to study at a university abroad."

"John, once you get your degree, will you stay abroad to find a job?" She asked, pretending naïveté yet knowing that he would return to Korea. He fell even harder for her by just hearing her speak his name and he was sure she knew it.

"Definitely not! I'll be coming back to take over the farm and our other businesses."

Those words were music to her ears. She therefore was able to calculate that though not the handsomest of her admirers, he was tall, and commanding in appearance, with a leonine head and broad shoulders on a lithe athletic body. Alight with intelligence, his eyes were cool, watchful and analytical as though trying to delve into the character and define the person to whom he was speaking. Unlike his competition, John had the distinct advantage of a very promising future. Marriage to him would lift her out of her nondescript background. She'd become the wife of one of the wealthiest businessmen in the community and have all the trappings of social status that came with such a marriage. Since she considered herself a very astute judge of character, she felt sure that she could use John's devotion to goad him into granting her every wish. She decided to wait on his return from abroad instead of wasting her time on good looks with bad prospects.

"Hurry back John!" she told him with a winsome smile.

"Mom, do you know why dad chose to follow the Catholic faith?"

"Darling, your curiosity never fails to amaze me. Why do you want to know?"

"I can't help wondering why he didn't follow the teachings of Buddhism, accept the philosophy of Confucius or gravitate towards the Shamanist beliefs like many others. I just can't help wondering why he chose Roman Catholicism?"

"Rina, why don't you ask him? As we both know it's the only way to find out. I believe he's in his study." Serena went in and was surprised to find him so engrossed in his reading that he didn't hear her enter.

"Dad, what are you reading?"

"Oh hello, Serena. Wordsworth, one of the Romantic poets I studied at college. Do you know his description of the leech gatherer?"

Before she could tell him that the portrait was one of her favorites, he handed her the closed book and began quoting from Wordsworth's poem: *Resolution and Independence*.

'I saw a man before me unawares
The oldest man he seemed who ever wore gray hairs.
Like a huge stone that sometimes seems to lie
Couched atop a bald hill or eminence,
Wonder to all who do the same espy
From where it had hither come and whence
As though it were a thing imbued with sense.
Like a sea beast crawled forth upon a shelf
Of rock or sand exposed there to sun itself,
So seemed this man. Not all alive nor dead,
Not all asleep. In his extreme old age,
His body was bent double, feet and head
Coming together in life's pilgrimage.
As if some dire constraint of pain or rage
Or sickness felt by him in times long past
A more than human weight upon his frame had cast.'

Before she could speak her father then added: "Sorry, I've substituted some of my own words whenever I wasn't quite sure of the originals. But what a fantastic portrait! The poet no doubt was aiming at extreme singularity. He sets the leach-gatherer apart by direct statement: 'the oldest man... that ever wore grey hairs.' He then presents him as a huge mysterious stone, an inanimate object that is rational. Next, the old man appears as a sea monster completely out of its element—from the bottom of the sea to the top of a land form: 'a bald hill.' Finally, the monster is again transformed into a human being. But this time he is 'bent double,' crushed by the weight of life's catastrophes. Serena, wouldn't you agree that it's a stunning portrait?"

"It is stunning, I agree. But Dad, you should remember that numerous critics used this poem and his other works to categorize Wordsworth as the poet of Nature, *par excellence*. His verse is filled with a hit parade of natural phenomena: night, wind, rain, sun, woods and morning among others. Not satisfied, he includes a number of nature's birds: the dove, the jay, the magpie and the sky-lark. Still dissatisfied, he adds a series of natural sound bytes: 'a roaring in the wind,' 'the rain' falling 'heavily in floods', 'the birds are singing in the distant woods,' 'the Jay' answers the chattering 'Magpie' and 'all the air is filled with pleasant noise of waters." Still emphasizing nature, he makes direct reference to the outdoors: 'all things that love the sun are out of doors.'

His obsession with the elements of nature makes his classification as a poet who leans heavily on the simplicity of the natural world to clothe his work in a pastoral setting is certainly justified. However, while the portrait is very cleverly created, the elements used to do so: the old man, the stone, the sea beast and a man bent double, are far too radically different and extreme to be regarded as **natural**. It is hard to believe that any such man ever existed or could ever exist. The portrait, far from being natural, is completely artificial."

Her father was surprised at the insightful analysis, but not wanting to disagree with his daughter's conclusion, he congratulated her instead on her intimate knowledge of the poem.

"Anyway Dad, I came to find out what made you choose the Catholic church we attend even though your parents are Buddhists."

"As a youngster, I naturally followed the faith of my parents. However, I believe that being sent to a Catholic school helped to change my way of thinking. Each day, we said prayers and sang beautiful hymns before school began. The refrain of a hymn and the tune I remembered stuck with me all through my travels abroad: 'Mother of God, star of the sea, pray for the wanderer and for me.'"

"I know that hymn," Serena told him.

"Anyway, my years first as a choirboy and later as an acolyte also helped. Serving my parish priest at High Mass before the altar and at the "Way of the Cross" services every Friday in lent, played a major role in my choice of religion and certainly in the formation of my character."

"Dad, I'm not sure I understand. Please explain what you mean."

"The priest was a formidable individual, combining tremendous charisma with solid intellectual mettle. His sermons based on the Scriptures, the Bible and the life of Christ, were both deeply meaningful and especially entertaining."

"Entertaining? That's not a word that one usually associates with the sermons of a prelate."

"Exactly! He had a habit of injecting high drama into the stories he told using his voice and his body language. The fact is that from the moment he began to speak, every member of his congregation was hooked. His brilliance as a preacher spread far and wide and people of every denomination crowded outside the church doors and windows whenever he preached. If truth be told, it was his incredible charisma that encouraged me to choose, and I began to examine seriously the teachings of Christianity."

"Are you saying that it was the player, rather than the game, that influenced your choice of religion?"

"In certain respects, it was. But at the same time, I noticed that Christian ethics fit in very neatly with the Confucian philosophy that pervades all Korean thought."

"You mean that we should love one another?"

"That was important, but you have to understand that as head of a family, fathers in the Confucian view are also responsible for the welfare and protection of their family members. I firmly believe that such a responsibility includes love. How can a father teach his family obedience and reverence towards their elders, as the Confucian ethic dictates, in the absence of love?"

"How were you able to overcome the dual attraction towards Confucius on the one hand and Christ on the other? In short, what made you embrace one and discard the other?"

"I didn't discard one for the other. I found that the basic principles of moral and ethical conduct that are at the heart of Confucianism are equally crucial to being a good Christian."

"So, your faith has a religious and a philosophical basis?"

"That sounds like a well thought out description."

"Thanks Dad. If truth be told, I now have a better understanding of the qualities that motivate you as a person." As she left his study, John couldn't help reflecting on the curiosity of his teenage daughter and the abstract ideas that circulated in her young but not so juvenile mind. What, he wondered, was the real purpose of her questions?

John had begun his career as a dedicated businessman with a difference. "Why don't you remain working late in your office like the majority of other executives?" His wife queried from her sewing when he had again returned home early one evening. He thought that she was fishing for a compliment and decided to tell her the truth.

"The truth of the matter is that I don't want to make a habit of carousing with my colleagues late into the night. When they leave work most of them go to be wined and dined under the care and attention of those females who serve their drinks and other needs. I've been there and done that and it leaves me cold. I'd much rather be at home where I'm loved and wanted. Even at work, I keep thinking of you both and missing you." From their first meeting, he admitted to himself that his wife evoked in him a desperate longing, an all powerful desire like that of a man dying of hunger might experience on gazing at a banquet from which he was excluded. Leesa couldn't help blushing at the admission. She couldn't bear to see the longing in his eyes. She turned back to her sewing, self-consciously.

"By the way," he said after a long silence, "there are some new films coming out that I hear are blockbusters. One is called *Silmido* and the other, *Taeguki*. The first deals with the action of special forces, the second with the Korean war that split our nation apart."

"I've read about them. They can't be new since, according to the newspapers, they've already been watched by more than ten million moviegoers. Anyway, you know Serena loves movies, so I'm sure she'll be glad to go with us."

"Talking about films," he said, "we should go to see *Shiri*, a film about a North Korean spy preparing a coup in Seoul, and there's *JSA*, (Joint Security Area) that outsold Western blockbusters like *The Matrix*, and *Star Wars*. That is, if they ever come to Hamyang. What do you think? "

"Well, we'll have to choose. There are a number of animated films coming as well and, as you know, they don't remain long in a small town like ours."

"You must be thinking of those reality-based Japanese films."

"Yes, they're totally different from the family-friendly Disney style films in which nobody dies and where everything depends heavily on make believe."

"Although the Japanese films are very popular here, I prefer the local blockbusters like 'Il Mare,' and 'My Wife is a Gangster.'"

"Those two dramas drew such large audiences here that Hollywood bought the rights of both movies to convert into American stories!"

"Really, I had no idea our films were so well thought of by foreign cinema moguls."

Since Serena was not available to see the blockbuster movies, John took his wife to see a number of the Japanese animated films. As in all agricultural societies, life in the household revolves around a closely knit family unit. Although Serena missed the first outing of her parents, she didn't miss the others.

"Kim, I didn't agree with your negative description of Leesa's conduct before, but I've noticed of late that there is something very wrong with her thinking."

"Don't let it bother you, dear. You're a man who sees only the good in people. But I'm glad that you finally agree with me. You've been unable to gage her behavior accurately because, by your own admission, you keep seeing her as a small child."

"That's true, but she's a teenager now. I only began to recognize the kind of person she is after she accosted me at the shop about my incompetence in the work I do. She suggested that I was a copycat, and insinuated that I was lacking in foresight, creativity and ambition. She also stated that I was always covered in sawdust and had the demeaning look of the lower classes."

"What! I can't think why she's so caught up with social status. Anyway, she deserves to be punished for such effrontery. But darling, you shouldn't pay attention to the ranting of a selfish and unbalanced teenager. God knows, she's my daughter and I love her, but her gross conduct and even grosser ideas give me the creeps."

"If you mean her selfishness, I'd have to agree. She knows how hard we work in the garden, and that we rely heavily on the help of neighbors. She also knows the pains you take over picking the roses, making the bouquets, and going to the church to decorate the altar each week. Then, there are the hours you spend collecting the long stemmed roses for the florists. Yet, never once has she offered to help. Even when I requested that she come and lend a hand, she didn't refuse. She just never turned up. She's totally wrapped up in herself; concerned solely with her own welfare. Nobody else seems to matter, or perhaps only in so far as they can get her what she wants."

"Tell me dear, what made you change your mind about her?"

"I noticed that she constantly twists facts to prop up her beliefs." Yong Sang replied.

"What are you talking about?"

"She believes that you purposely set out to shame and humiliate her by demonstrating that I love you more than her."

"How could she ever come to such a far-fetched conclusion? Her belief that I am her competition is so juvenile, and so destructive. How could she ever think I'd stoop so low?"

"She believes that your 'inferior mental ability' has prevented you from recognizing my true artistic creativity," he said with irony in his voice. "Otherwise you'd urge me to greater excellence and higher earnings."

"She's as ignorant about what you earn as about your artistic creativity."

"She also believes that your lack of ambition permits you to accept the 'status quo' of leading what she considers a 'hand-to-mouth' existence. Then, she detests the fact that our humble way of life forces her to remain a nonentity. She's also embarrassed by the fashionable clothes you make for her. I think she's afraid of what her friends might think of you if they knew you made her clothes."

"I know. She's ashamed to let her friends think that I'm nothing more than a lowly seamstress. In her book, working with my hands makes me a manual laborer, the lowest form of humanity. That's why she's never shown any enthusiasm for the designer dresses I make her. But darling, what's so wrong with the life we lead? Worse, how can she possibly think that I'm her competitor? Such weird ideas give further weight to my belief that she's delusional. Whatever did we do to spawn so unnatural a daughter? Evidently, she considers us the worst kind of parents."

"Do you think she'll ever change in her feelings of hatred towards you?"

"Oh! So you finally agree that she hates me?" Kim stated with surprise.

"Yes, after she accosted me in my workshop, I have to agree that she dislikes you intensely." The remark made Kim instantly recall the "teapot incident."

It took Father Murphy more than a week to overcome the virus that had knocked him off his feet. He had still not recovered his former healthy state, but was determined to finish what he had started and bring the message he had in mind to his congregation. Once more in the pulpit, he began.

"I am so sorry to have made a spectacle of myself during my last visit with you. It irks me considerably to have failed to bring you the message as I had intended. Let me inform you now that the repetition of my nightmares over a period of months has convinced me that their repeated similarity were meant to be divine warnings. As your shepherd, whose duty it is to protect and guide you, I bring this to your notice, urging you to take extra precaution against the temptation with which the evil one is using to seduce so many of us into wrongdoing. The growing volume of criminal behavior I keep hearing from the families of my parish is painful to my ears. It makes me aware that Satan has stepped up his campaign of violence in this and in the other parishes of the world. The most violent and sinful acts are taking place everywhere. With your safety in mind, I urge you to stand firm in your Christian convictions. I know that we mortals are completely helpless when subjected to the temptations of the immortal beast. However, do not forget to pray for God's protection for yourself and your family." After a long silence, he said, "I leave you with my blessing, and may God watch over us and keep us safe from the evil one."

Winter had swept in from the skies like a winged predator taking the citizens of Hamyang by surprise. One day they were basking in the warmth and playful fickleness of Indian summer and the next they were being crushed in her cold and cruel winter talons. Within the first week, the temperature had dipped so low that the cold had begun to freeze those farm animals outside the shelter of a barn. Two weeks later, the cold snap had tightened its grip on the land.

"Tina, why are you back here in this freezing weather after I'd given you a ride home? Did you forget something?"

"No Madam. I thought you'd want to know that the continuing cold spell has used up the farmers' supply of firewood."

"Is that what you braved the cold to tell me?"

"Yes Madam. They ran out of fuel some time ago, and many are confined to bed with all sorts of sickness, fevers and very bad colds." It took only a moment's thought for Leesa to see the problem as a heaven-sent opportunity for her to come to the aid of the farming community once again.

"We can't just sit around doing nothing," she said. "Come with me Tina, we'll invite the farmers to bring their carts and axes to cut the wood they need from the dead trees and blow downs around the farm."

"But Madam, their heavily loaded carts will bog down in the deep snowdrifts."

"You're right." Immediately, Leesa had an idea, and picked up the phone.

Father Murphy felt very uncomfortable seated in the overheated ante-room of the bishop's mansion, having been summoned there at short notice. The somber look on his pallid features reflected in the huge gilt-framed mirror clashed drastically with his colorful and luxurious surroundings. As he looked around him, he couldn't help but compare the oppressive warmth and opulence of the room in which he sat with the cold dilapidated hovel in which he lived. The comparison made him even more uncomfortable. Expensive paintings in gilded frames hung on the walls. The chair in which he sat was plush, deep and so comfortable that together with the warmth of the room made him want to fall asleep. There was a thick, beautifully woven carpet under his feet with gorgeous designs in white, red and purple, the colors of pomp and majesty. He sat propping his feet on the struts between the legs of his chair, fearful of soiling such a beautiful carpet. He felt a sense of defeat as he again contrasted the rich decor of this room with his own squalid living quarters. Indeed, he was both overwhelmed and intimidated by his surroundings. He kept wondering why the bishop had summoned him without disclosing the reason for doing so. He was hoping that the prelate had heard about the dedicated work he had done over these last years. Was His Lordship about to offer him a parish where he wouldn't have to work so hard just to keep body, mind and soul together? Was there a chance that he might be given a parish where he wasn't faced with starvation and have to wonder where his next meal was coming from? Oh God, he prayed silently: "Please let me get a new parish; one in which I don't have to scrape out such a meager existence as I do now." Immediately, he felt guilty for complaining. Wouldn't he be doing God's work wherever he was posted? He argued. After waiting a half hour, he was finally ushered into His Lordship's presence.

"Father Murphy," the bishop began. Thank you for coming at such short notice." In his confusion and humility, the priest mumbled something about always being at his lordship's service; ever ready to do his bidding.

"We've heard a great deal about your work but we've called you in to learn what we can about you from your own lips. We are deciding your future and want you to tell us anything you think we should know about you, that is, outside your church work."

The last four words struck him like a blow bewildering him. He had to think a long moment before replying: "My lord, nothing I do is outside my church work."

"Surely you must have other interests?"

"No, my lord Bishop. I visit the sick, sing the Mass, baptize the new born, confirm the children, marry the young couples and bury the dead. Attending to these chores and visiting the church school takes up my time. There is no time left for other interests."

"What is your connection with the school?"

"I interview new teachers and visit the school from time to time to consult with the Headmaster to ensure that it's being efficiently run."

"You make it sound as though your whole life is bound up with the church."

"It is, my lord! The parish is large, its inhabitants poor and their farms widely scattered. The church and the needs of my parishioners keep me very busy." He repeated: "I have no time for 'other interests.'"

"We're glad to hear of your dedication, Father, so let us be frank. We know that you've come from a poverty-stricken Irish family. We also know that you suffered tremendous deprivation in your youth, one of the reasons you joined the Church and emigrated to this country. Father, abject poverty is not unknown to you, neither is near starvation. We had a decision to make about placing you in a suitable parish, and because of the circumstances of your birth and background, we believe that Hamyang is the most suitable, indeed the ideal parish for you. It is certainly the poorest and most destitute parish in my

See. However, we believe that you, more than any of your brother priests, are very familiar with, and sympathetic to, the problems of its parishioners. We feel sure that you will be able to carry out your work there in the same way that you have been doing these past years. Is there anything you wish to say about our decision?"

"N-no, no my L-Lord bishop. I-I shall do my b-best to be w-worthy of your c-choice," he stammered. "Thank you Father, and God speed!" Realizing that he had been dismissed, he stood shakily and took his leave, deeply disappointed at the cruelty of fate and at the heavy burden His Lordship had thrust upon his shoulders.

Chapter 10

"Dang, I knew you were an ardent pigeon fancier but didn't know that you were beating the hell out of your competitors in pigeon racing and were renowned as well for the thoroughbred breeds you imported."

"Who has been maligning me?"

"Serena has been telling me about your fame as a winner and a breeder of the highest class."

"Thank her for the praise for me. But I think you had a more important subject to discuss."

"Yes, I do have a couple of delicate subjects that I'd like to discuss with you. But I know that not everybody is willing to listen to and offer their opinion about personal stuff." The two men were sitting in an alcove of Dang's beautiful living room and John's eyes moved slowly over the simple but tasteful decor of his surroundings. They lingered on the lovely drapes, the Persian carpet, the expensively upholstered furniture and the modern paintings on the wall. "So tell me," he continued after a moment, "if you'd rather not hear what I have to say."

"John, we've been friends since middle school here in Korea, then we again met at University in Canada. We've known each other so long that you should know by now that I'm always willing to listen to and to discuss any topic with you, personal or otherwise."

"Thank you Dang. I've been recalling some of the things I've done. If truth be told, it distresses me that despite my good intentions, I've often screwed up very badly."

"Recalling our past actions makes most right thinking individuals feel sad about some of the choices we've made. In doing that you are not alone. In fact you are in a huge majority."

"'Sad,' is too mild a term to describe the feelings I get whenever I think of what I've done."

"I hope it isn't your ego that's dictating those feelings. You're a good man, and I know you've always tried to act according to your principles and with the best of intentions. Perhaps you shouldn't let your ego betray you. We shouldn't forget that we're human, and like everyone else, subject to mistakes; sometimes serious ones."

"Dang, it's not a question of ego. I would be a jackass to think that I'm a special or superior being," John chuckled. "Quite the contrary. The fact of the matter is that I feel inferior when focusing on some of the idiotic things I've done. Having acted with good intentions shouldn't spare me from either the blame, or the guilt and shame that I feel for my shortcomings."

"We're talking in abstract terms; philosophizing. Why don't you tell me what's worrying you? Then, I may be able to better understand and tell you my take on your behavior, if that is what you want." He noted that John was attacking his fingernails with gusto.

"You're right. I'm so ashamed to think that I was playing squash when I should have been at the theater waiting for Serena after the movie. What you have to understand is that *my* absence made her decide to walk home. Can you imagine how guilty I feel? My irresponsibility led to my daughter's rape. Then, the long drawn out illness that followed and almost killed her is still wreaking havoc with her mental and physical well being."

And no doubt your own, Dang thought but didn't say. "John, there are quite a few other factors that led to Serena's calamity. It's true you were late, but not on purpose. Then, when you got there people were still strolling out of the theater. It wasn't your decision that made Serena decide to walk home. And you certainly didn't arrange for the gang of thugs to be in the field to greet her. Had Serena waited and remained where she was supposed to be, you'd have picked her up as arranged, and nothing calamitous would have happened."

"Are you saying that I shouldn't blame myself or feel guilty?"

"No! I'm saying that a number of random acts occurred. Yours was certainly one of them. You made a mistake, but you weren't absent on purpose. Of course you feel responsible as her father, but in view of the circumstances I've just stated, you should ease up on your feelings of guilt and shame."

"The reality of it is that I can't seem to shake those feelings or thinking that it's entirely my fault."

"Damn it, John! It's not *all* your fault. It's the fault of the men who raped her. You shouldn't lay such a heavy burden of guilt and shame upon yourself, especially since those burdens are self-made barriers to a positive way of life."

"The way you state the situation does make sense. But not a day goes by without the guilt and shame of my burden weighing heavily upon me. Even my wife finds it hard to absolve me from blame."

"Your own troubled conscience should tell you that you're a right thinking individual! I hope our discussion will lessen the weight of your burden."

"Hello, Sing here, Mrs. Ahn. How can I help?"

"Sing, the continuing cold has depleted many of the farmers' supply of firewood. Their families are suffering with all sorts of ailments. I thought that if we could fill one of our mobile containers with firewood, we could distribute the wood to the farms needing help."

"We certainly can do something to help."

"But I suppose it would be a miracle to find that we have the amount of wood needed. Do we?"

"We do have some large stacks of firewood, Mrs. Ahn. I've had the hands cut up the many deadfalls and blow downs all around the perimeter of the farm. An awful lot of them have fallen during the past month, what with the high winds and accumulation of snow."

"In this cold, they must all be covered heavily in a blanket of deep snow and ice."

"Fortunately not Mrs. Ahn. I've had them stacked in one of the barns."

"But why? Surely we don't need firewood."

"It comes in handy during a cold snap like this. And with the violent winds blowing trees down, a power outage can happen at any time. We'd then use it to heat the oil in the underground pipes that warm your home through the floor. At present we're using some to heat the barns that are already too cold for the animals."

"Do you have enough to get the hands to do what I ask?"

"I'll get to it right away and we'll take an extra tractor along to drag the containers out of any snowdrifts we encounter."

"Sing, it amazes me that you manage to solve any problem that Serena and I throw at you. You are truly a miracle worker!"

"Thank you, Mrs. Ahn. But it's you and your daughter who are the miracle workers for the good you do on behalf of the distressed farmers. I'll take along my mobile phone and let you know when our distribution is complete."

"Take Tina with you to show you the neediest households. Afterwards, you can give her a ride to her home. And thank you Mr. Miracle Worker."

"You're welcome, Mrs. Ahn."

"Your dad told me that when you were still a kid, he used to take you and your mother on walks to the furthest points of the farm where it merges with the foothills leading to the mountains in the *Jirisan National Park*. He still talks of the picnics that you all enjoyed there and later, your climb towards the *Banyabong* mountain peak. Do you all still indulge in what he described as 'real fun times with the family?' Sing asked Serena, his visitor.

"Yes, mama used to pack our favorite dishes and we really enjoyed those family outings together, but we don't go as often any more. On the way there, dad would tell us about the high pass above the picnic grounds from which he could see the elevated pastures and plateaux that lay below. It was only when I grew older and learned to ride a horse that he began to lead me up beyond those foothills and along the switchbacks into the heights. That was when the mountain wilderness began to impress me with its size and grandeur."

"I used to ride with him too, Sing replied. He loved following the narrow game trails along the base of the ridges and switchbacks that rose steeply to the towering peaks."

"Did you all ever get beyond the path where the mountain bulked? There's a high pass where you can dismount and look down into the valley below on the other side of the pass."

"We never took that route, but he talked about a place higher up from which he could see a wide open river valley bordered by mountain chains. He seemed enchanted by the heavily forested slopes and could actually name all the different trees we met."

"I've been there with him," Serena said. "Halfway up the mountain we would dismount to give our horses a rest before the steeper climb. She recalled her father's warning: "Serena, you must learn to observe the terrain and wildlife around you. Learn to recognize what you see because it can be either harmful or helpful. You never know, your very survival may depend on it one day."

"I've heard those very words from him," Sing added. "Being in the mountains fascinated your dad, but we never climbed to the high pass you mentioned," Sing told Serena.

"We did, and from that first moment, the vast panorama unfurling before us gripped me with its fascination. During the Ice Age, a massive glacier lay upon the mountains peaks and their valleys below, exerting enormous pressure. Moving only inches a year, the millions of tons of ice gouged, crushed and ground down the granite rock over which it moved. In so doing, it scraped out huge accumulated deposits of rich alluvial soil, or silt. Over the centuries, the melt water beneath the glacier formed a river distributing its silt over the broad flat plain on both its banks. On its passage down the main valley, the glazier had sliced away the lower areas of rock on both its flanks where tributaries drained into the main stream. A series of hanging valleys had formed and from them, silver waterfalls plunge down at right angles into the main valley."

"You describe the scene as though you were still staring at it."

"It had me mesmerized. I felt as though the massive and remote wilderness area was extending itself, making some kind of contact with me that I can't quite describe. In a way, the environment seemed to divine a need in me, a desire to reach out and have me become a part of it and it a part of me."

"Wow! You make it sound mysterious, even mystical."

"It was! You say that you never got to the pass, Mr. Sing. Then, you couldn't have been to the cave?"

"A cave? I didn't know there was one."

"Way beyond the pass, dad took me up to a huge cave that reached deep into the mountain. There was a small spring on one side of the entrance not far from a triangle of soot-blackened rocks that must have served as a cooking area."

"How did you all get there, Miss? I never saw any path beyond where your dad and I stopped."

"There was a steep narrow ledge on the flank of the mountain that wound its way upwards."

"Wow! I'd never imagined a cave higher up the mountain. That must have been quite an adventure!"

"It was indeed! There was a broad lip of rock in front of the cave that was almost completely sheltered by an overhang. The entrance was fairly narrow, no more than the size of a doorway that opened out into a roughly circular interior."

"If there is a cooking area, people must have lived there."

"Dad was convinced that it had been the home of many different families."

"What made him think that?"

"On the wall, there were primitive decorative drawings of stick-like animals and people, a sort of primitive mural. But the differences in the drawings of both the animals and the people suggest that different stages of man inhabited the cave. It was quite an adventure, let me tell you! But it wasn't the last." After a long moment concentrating on what she had seen she stated.

"Well Mr. Sing, thank you for the walk along memory lane. But I must be off now. I'll come and visit again when you're not too busy."

"Any time Miss. I'm never too busy for a chat."

The truth was that the discussion with Mr. Sing brought back to Serena the tremendous pleasure she derived from her sojourns into the wilderness. Since she was free, why not indulge herself? Better yet, why not ask her dad to join her. Since it was Sunday and he was well aware of her love for the mountains, he was happy to oblige. After all, he thought, he only had one daughter. Serena saddled her big roan gelding and then she and her father rode out of the paddock, her anxiety already on the rise. Her dad led them slowly allowing Serena to savor the pleasure she experienced as they headed for the mountain wilderness, one of her favorite places. When they reached the foothills, she watched as the landscape stretched out before them in a series of undulating plains, plateaux and tall snow-capped ridges. On the way up he challenged her.

"Serena, as an avid environmentalist, you should be able to recognize the flora and fauna of this wilderness area of Korea.'"

"Since you've repeatedly named the trees and animals we've met on our past outings" she replied, "I can name them in my sleep."

"Really! Why don't you name those trees you see bordering the upward path?"

"Gladly!" she began. "Dotting the hillside above us are a few *mountain ash* among a forest of *stone pine*. Another deciduous tree is the *levodia*, a few of which are on our left, their open branches spreading wide."

"Very good! How about those triangular shaped trees?"

"Those with their branches sprouting horizontally and displaying their grayish green needles are the *Korean fir*, and next to them is one of my favorites, the *Korean sweetheart tree* with its thick, glossy, emerald-green leaves and small yellow flowers. Its red, heart-shaped seeds stand out among the evergreens. She then began to point. "Over there I can see more *stone pine*, there,

Sitka spruce, and *fir* all over there. Near the clearing, there are a few *western red cedar*, *mountain ash*, *white birch*, and *alder*."

"Bravo! You do know your flora, how about the fauna?" He asked when they had again dismounted, tethered their horses and hidden in the underbrush. Pointing, she whispered: "There's a *white naped crane*, its head and neck pale grey and its legs red. Those ducks over there in the little pond with their yellow and green heads on a brown and grey body are *Baikal teal*."

"Name those two squirrel-like rodents fighting with each other among the rocks."

"Those are pica."

"Can you name that bird standing vertically on that dying tree trunk?"

"If you mean the one with a crimson crown, cheek patches and white belly drumming with his beak on the tree trunk, that's a *black woodpecker*. Normally, I'd expect to see the *spotted woodpecker*, the *hawk owl*, and the *black grouse*, but they're not around."

"What other animals should we expect to encounter? " Her father persisted.

"You can't be thinking of the *Korean tiger* or the *leopard*, because they are both extinct, but we sometimes glimpse the *Black Bear*, while deer, rabbits and squirrels as you know are quite common."

"I seem to have schooled you well," he stated smiling but pressed on.

"You've done extremely well, but I'd like you to name the bird that's most common in these foothills?"

"If you mean the one that stoops low while running through the undergrowth, that's the *ring necked pheasant*."

"You deserve credit as a good beginner," he said, chuckling at the stinginess of his praise for her remarkable progress.

"There's another problem I've wanted to discuss with you, Dang," John told his friend. It's the way I feel about how I treated my fiancée during our engagement."

"It appears that you've been brooding a lot lately, perhaps even obsessing on your past conduct."

"That's true I suppose, though the truth of the matter is that I didn't know it showed. As I said during our last discussion, I'm not at all happy with some of the choices I've made."

"Do you mean that with hindsight you'd make different choices?"

"I'm not sure. The reality of it is that I have a profound sense of dissatisfaction with myself."

"Well, if you're more specific, I may be able to throw some light on the subject."

"The truth is that I'm surprised that you're not tired hearing me lay my problems on you?"

"I'm here to listen and perhaps advise; just a friend giving you a chance to vent your innermost feelings. That has to be healthy, don't you think? Bottling up your feelings, as you know, can lead to frustration and dissatisfaction, even profound depression."

"Dang, during my courtship, I was faced with a critical test of my principles when my fiancée acted as though guilty of infidelity. Although I loved Leesa dearly, if truth be told, I was sorely tempted to abandon her for what I considered such outrageous conduct."

"What do you mean: 'acted as though she was guilty of infidelity'? Was she or was she not unfaithful?"

"The fact of the matter is that I thought she might be pregnant, and not by me. I wasn't sure."

"Thought she might be pregnant? Not sure? How could you possibly abandon her when you weren't positive that your accusation was accurate?"

"Exactly. Since I couldn't be sure, I didn't abandon her. I firmly believe that had I taken such a course, it would have raised the worst kind of scandal and the consequences would have been disastrous."

"I can see that. Among both your family and the locals, it would have caused a terrible scandal."

"The truth is that my intended bride and her whole family would have been condemned and ostracized. Even if she were pregnant, my love for Leesa would not have allowed me to put her and her family through such a scandalous ordeal."

"You must have realized as well that you and your family might not have escaped the outpouring of slander that such an incident would occasion, especially here in Hamyang."

"That's also true, Dang. But you have to understand, I took that into consideration."

"So what did you do?"

"I deliberated on the problem for weeks on end, finally seeking guidance in prayer and in the teaching of Confucius. Both encouraged me to emulate the qualities of acceptance, compassion and forgiveness that Christ had shown to the prostitute, Mary of Magdala and to others."

"Wondering about your fiancée's infidelity must have caused you incredible stress! I can only try to imagine what you went through."

"That's just it. I learnt that she wasn't unfaithful so my forgiveness was unnecessary. Some time later when she found that she was pregnant, she confessed to me that she had been raped. It made me agree to marry her immediately and to whisk her away afterwards. Doing so would protect all concerned from the wagging of slanderous tongues."

"In a small town like ours, slander can be both dangerous and humiliating. Facing it would take considerable courage and strong mindedness."

"I also had to protect the reputation of the unborn child. And as you suggest, there was the real possibility that I too would have been accused of impregnating my wife before marriage. I had to swallow the bile that rose in my throat as I considered the violation of my wife. I also had to keep up a constant fight with my conscience to be a loving husband and father."

"John, it is not a comforting thought that throughout human history, women have not been very successful in guarding against rape. However, I think you acted very honorably in the circumstances. Your conduct should give you no cause for dissatisfaction or guilt."

"Ah, but you see! I have to admit that it's the guilt of not having trusted my wife that distresses me. That, more than anything else, I find hard to forgive myself."

After John left, Dang reconsidered the doubts and fears expressed by his friend. The note of sadness and distress in John's voice showed that it troubled him deeply to realize that he had failed to be the loyal and honorable spouse he should have been. Berating himself for his shortcomings, Dang thought, testified to the innate goodness and solid character of the man.

Leesa had not forgotten that numerous people in the district were ailing as a result of the cold. She picked up the phone and dialed. After a few rings, she heard: "Hello, this is Doctor San's office."

"Hello, this is Leesa Ahn. Connect me with the doctor please?"

"One moment please, Mrs. Ahn, while I put the doctor on."

"Good day Mrs. Ahn," the doctor said after a moment. "What can I do for you?"

"Doctor, there are a number of sick people in the district that I'd like you to see."

"Certainly, Mrs. Ahn. How many are there?"

"I'm not quite sure, but would you be able to squeeze them in if I were to bring them to you today?"

"That will be fine." He paused before adding: "you know many of our farmers can't afford to visit me or to bring me their sick children. The few that can, give me fruit and vegetables in exchange for my services. Many can't even afford the medication I prescribe. Whenever possible, I give them the free samples I get from the drug companies."

"Oh, don't worry doctor. I'll take care of your services as well as any medication you prescribe." Pleased that Tina's gossip had again paved the way for her to do something meaningful, Leesa jumped in her car and with Tina to point out the homes of the sick, she was on her way to pick them up. Despite her thick coat, the cold had frozen her limbs and it took the deep heating of the automobile to slowly warm her body. Doing something helpful to others was, she thought, the best means of fighting against her guilt and inner shame. The act of kindness lifted her spirits considerably.

Each week day, Kim rose early to play the organ at the six o'clock Mass. On Monday mornings afterwards, she chose the hymns that were to be sung during the week until the following Sunday. She would then hold choir practice, drilling the boys, teenage girls, young men, mature women and men, in singing the hymns that would lead the congregation. She didn't consider it a difficult task since she had taken special care to choose each member of the choir herself to create the blend of voices she needed: sopranos, tenors, baritones and basses. She drilled them for weeks on end to ensure that the blend of joyous harmony in their voices echoed to every ear their praise of the Messiah.

It was Saturday morning and as usual, John was touring the farm with Sing, his newly appointed manager. It was the day he had chosen each week to see for himself how things were progressing. He regarded Sing as extended family, as he did with his other employees. As they wandered the paths alongside the fields of wheat, alfalfa, barley, soybean and corn, skirting the rice paddies and visiting the orchards and the barns, they also talked about other things of interest to them both.

"I like to take the family on one of the tour buses equipped with Karaoke stations so we can join in the singing," John confided. "That is," he added, "especially when we travel to the capital."

"My girlfriend and I, like most Koreans, also enjoy singing along to *No-raebang*, (Karaoke). But when we go to Seoul," Sing told his boss, "we usually take the Bullet Train."

"When there, have you noticed the many fast food outlets that have sprung up everywhere?"

"Sure, that's one of the reasons we go. Eating at Pizza Hut, having hamburgers at Mc Donald's or Burger King are some of the favorite choices of my girlfriend, Chin, and me. But another one of our favorites is *Pelicana Chicken*."

"We check out the coffee houses like *Dutor*, *Caravan*, or *Circle K* where we have breakfast, sample some of the Italian brews, and treat ourselves at the ice cream parlors and the other food chains that have been so swift in following Western models. It's plain to see that our choices reflect the strong foreign influence that is changing the eating habits of Koreans."

"Sir, have you been to any concerts in Seoul? Have you heard the popular music of groups like *Seo Tagi and Boys*?"

"No! My family and I prefer the movies. So unfortunately, we missed that group, though we did hear good things about their performances."

"Would you believe that they've incorporated the American genres of 'rap' and 'rock' into their repertoire?"

"I hadn't heard that. I wouldn't have thought that American pop music would blend suitably with ours."

"As far as I'm concerned, it doesn't! But Chin seemed to enjoy it. In fact, everything in Seoul enchanted her."

"I have to admit. There's a lot in the big city that's fascinating."

"Coming from a small town herself, she was surprised that so many of the pedestrians and bus passengers had mobile phones glued to their ears. I explained that almost 90% of Koreans own a mobile phone and that Korea boasts two of the world's largest cell phone companies, 'Samsung' and 'LG.'"

"Did you tell her that both provided innovative features, TV and Digital Multimedia Broadcasting, well before such programming appeared in the West?"

"Yes. I think that like her, Serena would be proud to learn that so great is their competition here that *Nokia*, the largest cell phone company in the world, can no longer compete here with our two giants."

"On our last shopping spree in Seoul, Serena was anxious to visit *Lotte World*, the world's largest amusement park. Have you ever been there?"

"Not yet. But we plan to visit later this year. We also plan to attend some of the games played by our professional baseball, basketball and soccer teams."

"On our last visit, we witnessed a series of exhibitions of Taekwondo, our national sport. We also went to the FIFA World Cup of soccer that Korea hosted," John told the young man."

"Did you ride the KTX Bullet train like us?"

"Yes, we traveled on the Bullet train," John replied, "and like so many others, were impressed by its beautifully streamlined appearance and especially its speed of 300 k/h. Serena was very proud of the technological progress of our country, when she learnt that the trains of few Western countries can compete with ours."

"How did you enjoy the World Cup, Sir? Did you catch the nation's soccer fever?"

"Oh, definitely! We were extremely excited to be there. The truth is that the impressive performance of the home team and the victories they notched up made us cheer until we were as hoarse as everyone else. What a fantastic performance they put on!"

Chapter 11

Yong Sang tried to bring about a closer relationship between Leesa and her mother. One evening, when his daughter came to the workshop, he decided to broach the subject.

"Leesa," he began, "I've noticed that you tend to be very cold and aloof towards your mother. Not only do you keep your distance but when you're close you never have a kind word for her. It troubles me to see the strained relationship that exists between the two people I love most."

"Why don't you speak to her instead of to me?" The vehemence in the voice surprised Yong Sang.

"Because despite your constant attempts to come between us, the numerous times that you answer her questions insolently, and the icy glares that you dart at her, I know that she still loves you."

"Well, I can't forgive her for the way she humiliates me by loudly proclaiming her ownership of you." Her answer again took her father by surprise. The anger was still there but the meaning escaped him.

"What do you mean?"

"I'm not a fool you know! Your screams of passion are deliberately uttered to let me know which one of us is your beloved and which one is not?" Yong Sang could not believe the grossly delusional views of his daughter. It made him realize that people are often led astray by interpreting reality through the filter of their personal feelings.

"Child, your mother and I could never be so cruel. Your mother is my wife and she does have the first claim to my love. But that doesn't mean she doesn't love you too. You have to believe that you are our most precious gift."

"That may be your opinion but don't expect me to share it. I believe that mama delights in hurting me through humiliation and that's why I've tried to come between you all these years."

"How is it possible for you to reach such a false conclusion?" He asked with a mixture of sorrow and incomprehension at her statement.

"False? Do you know what it feels like to be deprived of bonding with the person I love most? And by a stupid woman? Has either of you ever thought about *my* feelings?" Yong Sang thought that there was something really weird about the accusations he was hearing, and the evident delusion that fueled his daughter's spite, anger and hatred. Her unfounded and even weird conclusions, he thought, definitely pointed to a twisted and unbalanced mind.

"My darling misguided daughter, you and your mother are not in competition for my love. I love you both."

"You already said that she comes first." Leesa was frowning, her lips had formed into a pout and there was a tremor in her voice suggesting jealousy, anger and imminent tears.

"It's true she does come first. I fell in love with your mother, and she with me many years ago and we got married. We love each other dearly, but it's also true that both of us were extremely happy when you were born. Since that day, we've both lavished our love upon you."

"Well, you could have fooled me!" And she added silently: don't think she'll get away with it!

On John's return from his honeymoon abroad, he was supposed to learn the businesses that his ageing father expected him to take over and run. John's leave-taking was necessary to protect the reputation of his wife and child. But this was the time scheduled for his training. While his father managed in his absence without complaint, John determined to make up for his lapse and gently ease his father into retirement. But sidelining his father made him feel guilty. As usual when the stress of guilt weighed heavily upon him, he went to discuss his feelings with Dang.

"Dad has been suffering from the strain of overwork, he began. I feel guilty because I was not there to replace him when I had agreed to take over as CEO."

"Why weren't you there?"

"I needed to protect the reputation of my wife and child."

"So he's annoyed or perhaps disappointed with you?"

"No, he didn't complain. Since with age he isn't as sprightly as he used to be I'm sure he would have preferred to be at home where he could at least rest whenever business affairs got really hectic and took too great a toll."

"Well, he's at home now where he can rest and you're the new CEO, right? I'm sure he's proud of you."

"Right, but that doesn't prevent my conscience from acting up."

"So all's well that ends well. How is the work going?"

"I made a point of changing the way my father used Western models to run the corporation. I've been teaching my executives and employees new methods."

"You shouldn't fault your dad for having followed the Western models. They are evidently what he learnt while studying abroad. And they must have worked otherwise his business wouldn't have prospered."

"You're no doubt right, but the truth is that I wasn't at all happy with his Western thinking."

"I'm surprised that he expected Western ideology to work smoothly in an Eastern setting. Surely he must have known the two would clash sooner or later."

"That's exactly what disturbed me. He set up his office in the Western manner. He, the CEO, and each of his executives, closeted himself in his particular office because of the supposed need for privacy. The reality of it is that offices were compartmentalized and business was run from a rabbit warren of enclosures with each employee isolated from his colleagues and locked away in his 'prison.'"

"It seems to me that such an arrangement would prevent easy communication between employees?"

"Dad ignored that fact. In the West, friction between employees is natural since all are competing with each other for promotion. Here, close friendships are the norm and facilitate easy working relationships between employees."

"I think that close relationships would tend to boost efficiency, while barriers and open competition between employees would be counterproductive, each employee determined to protect his personal turf."

"That's my thinking exactly. As the new CEO, I changed all that by placing myself at the center of a large open area. I grouped my executives around me and our employees around them. Unlike the West, the arrangement encouraged much closer relationships between CEO and staff, making communication easier and work more efficient. Besides, instead of being hidden behind closed doors, each employee was exposed at all times to the eyes of both the CEO and his executives. It was far more efficient and made for greater productivity."

"Did your different organization create a barrier between you and your dad?"

"Fortunately not! Since I've taken over the reins, he hasn't objected to the changes I've made. I think he's impressed by the greater efficiency that is already evident."

"Were those the only changes you made?"

"No! It irked me that every event was scheduled to take place at a specified time; that punctuality and deadlines were rigidly enforced. Those idea were based on the Western assumption that time was the equivalent of money. Thus, in any business negotiation, there was the urgent need to get straight to the point–agreement on a price; signing a contract swiftly."

"You must admit, those principles can be effective and must have clinched quite a number of business deals for your dad."

"Dang, you're beginning to think like him. I see things differently. Business is not the speedy selling of a product; the quick agreement on a price; the swift signing of a contract. You have to understand that business is done with people. Therefore, to succeed in business, one must first establish a friendly working relationship with people."

"I remember listening to your strategy of starting each business meeting by drinking tea in a leisurely manner. It's a means of going slow fast. You use it to frustrate the Western approach, and according to you, it works."

Apart from the chores Serena the preteen undertook voluntarily on her farm–feeding the chickens, the pigs and milking the cows–she showed a special aptitude for art. She loved to first draw, then paint the animals she drew, always against their natural background. From very early, she made the link between them evident. The practice, repeated over and over through the years, gave her work a blunt reality. Her eye for form, composition and the subtleties of light and shade lifted her work to an artistic level beyond mere representation. Even in her earliest paintings, she was able to capture qualities with her brush that mere language was not always adequate to describe. Not surprisingly, art and especially painting, was her favorite subject.

When she was eight years old Serena had begun a serious feud with her mother. Mona's parents had invited her to journey with their daughter to the capital and spend a weekend visiting the zoo and the famous sights there. Serena was delighted at the prospect of such an unexpected adventure especially since it included being up close and personal with the exotic animals that she loved and about which she had read so much. With her eyes aglow and a dazzling smile she approached her mother for permission to accept the invitation, taking it for granted that her mother would agree. She couldn't believe she would be hard hearted enough to prevent her daughter from doing something that Serena had always longed for. When her mother refused Serena was so heartbroken she burst into tears.

"Mama, why can't I go?" She asked in the angriest voice her mother had heard.

"I've never told you this Serena because I didn't want to hurt your feelings but I don't trust Mona's parents or your little friend Mona. I know it's only a gut feeling but I don't think they are the kind of people you can depend on in a crisis. In an angry fit of tears, her daughter replied stubbornly:

"Mama what you said sounds like an excuse for keeping me always under your wing. You know that, if anything, Mona's parents are overprotective of their daughter. Why are you preventing me from going to see the capital and the big cats that you know I love? You never let me go anywhere unless it's under your supervision." Serena then stamped her little foot and glared defiantly at her mother. Leesa smiled at her daughter's tantrum of defiance and responded.

"Rina dearest, stop your tears. When it is convenient your father and I will take you to Seoul to visit the animals at the zoo and the other worthwhile sights."

"Mama, as long as I am under your wing you don't seem to mind me going anywhere," Serena replied with venom. Her index finger was moving frantically against her thumb.

"Serena, this discussion has gone far enough. It's not a matter for further debate. I'll ring Mona's parents and make an excuse." There was steel in her voice. Serena ran off angrily and deeply disappointed, crying her little heart out at the intransigence of parents and at her mother's overprotective nature. She ran unseeing to the barn where she always went to recover from the terrible disappointments that plague the lives of all kids. As always, she climbed and took a seat perched high in the window of a barn to watch the scenes that unfolded in the theater of the tall grass growing on the outskirts of the farm. Without realizing it, the view stopped her tears. Through her contact with the outdoors, her anger dissipated and her disappointment vanished like cobwebs in a high wind. Her interest in what was taking place made her aware that she had such an intense love of nature; so powerful an affinity with the environment that, like carbon dioxide on a fire, had doused the flame of her anger and calmed her distressed spirits. Henceforth, the affinity would become even more pronounced. As she viewed the action taking place in the tall grass she focused on the movement of raccoon and snake, fox and ferret that frequented the area and the airborne eagles and hawks that kept flying overhead scouting for prey. The truth is that as she learnt their secrets, she grew to admire them and the environment in which each lived. But while she began to absorb and love the natural beauty of their habitat, her eyes were drawn to the distant forested mountains and the mysterious and compelling attraction they held for her.

"Dang, we live in the East. Westerners come here to do business. They must learn from us. They love to base their negotiation on cold, hard facts believing that factual evidence is irrefutable. I differ radically from such a narrow belief. I agree that facts are important, but I'm not doing business with facts, I'm dealing with people. It is thus imperative to learn as much as possible about the people with whom I'm dealing."

"I have to agree with you there. You'd want to know their history, policies and guiding principles. You'd want to know if the people you are dealing with are trustworthy, if you'd be able to depend on them to keep their word. That's the way I do business at my bank."

"To me, personal information about my business partner is far more important than facts or figures."

"While we are on the subject of business relationships, I've often wondered how Westerners respond to our practice of "saving face?""

"As you know, saving face in our culture is of vital importance. It's a means of protecting one's image, and that of others. We feel that no one should be publicly or even privately humiliated or embarrassed. Therefore, our watchword is **harmony**. Overt disagreement is frowned upon. The reality of it is that I've created, for myself and my executives, a number of ways of saying no by simply refusing to say yes."

"Careful John, you're beginning to sound like a crafty con man."

"I try to be careful rather than crafty; otherwise I'd get screwed. By the way, I hope you don't mind me using you as a sounding board. I know that I can trust you to tell me the truth. If you disagree with any of my strategies, please say so."

"You wouldn't be discussing these matters with me if you weren't sure that I'd do just that. So far, your strategies seem both intelligent and sound. Of course, you'd change them if they failed to work."

"Now, you have to understand that it would be quite normal for a Western subordinate to make a recommendation to his superior. Doing so would be regarded as no more than a suggestion to be evaluated for its merits or otherwise."

"Here, such a recommendation from a subordinate would be a slap in the face of authority. It would suggest that the subordinate knew more than his superior. You can't run a business here with that attitude!" Dang replied.

"Exactly! I consider that it would constitute a serious breach of protocol. Our culture frowns on individuality taking precedence over respect for authority."

"I would expect that all your employees follow such a practice."

"I have ensured that they all do. Dang, another thing I've already mentioned: in Western culture, punctuality is regarded as essential, and deadlines are considered indispensable. Westerners behave as though they can predict the future; circumvent any unexpected event. Unlike us, they overlook the fact that random acts often occur. In our organization, I accord far less weight to punctuality and deadlines."

"It can be a more practical way of looking at things."

"Over here, relationships between employer and employee are far more personal than in the West. There, employees are always on the lookout for advancement and any such opportunity from a rival company is often accepted. Both employer and employee regard the exchange as normal. Here, we look after our employees as a father looks after his family members and the latter are expected to owe us, as their paternalistic employers, their full loyalty and support. When downsizing takes place in the West, companies stop payment to workers who are laid off whether or not they have found alternative employment. If we have to lay off employees, we continue to look after them until they find employment elsewhere. We treat our employees like family."

"Amen!"

"Darling, you've looked so worried and depressed this last week. What's the matter?" Kim asked her husband.

"Well, I didn't want to distress you, but I've had a talk with Leesa at the shop and from her statements it's evident that she hates you."

"So she's finally admitted it. What did she say?"

"She thinks that you and I go out of our way to humiliate her by deliberately throwing our love for each other in her face. Can you believe that?"

"She has some really weird ideas, but this one surpasses all others."

"She thinks we are purposely loud in our lovemaking to hurt and humiliate her. She stated that our motive is to show her that I love you more than her."

"I've always believed her thinking irrational. But from what you say it's delusional as well."

"I agree! I tried to explain to her that you're my wife, my first love, but that didn't mean we loved her any less."

"Her mind doesn't seem to be working normally, and there's a rage building inside her against me. It scares me that at some point it will explode. Darling, have you thought more about her need for therapy?"

"Yes, I have. But I've also considered the taint it can bring to both the individual and the family, especially here in Korea and in a small town like ours."

"I'm sure you recognize that our daughter's welfare outweighs any negative fallout that might sully our reputation," Kim stated.

"Of course, dear. But what if she refuses to go into therapy? Have you thought of that?"

"I don't suppose we can force her, but we have to try, don't we?" Kim questioned. "I think we should both sit her down and talk to her about doing just that. We have to make her understand that it is the surest way to make her well again." But in the back of her mind, Kim worried that her daughter's words and actions might be born of evil rather than delusion.

"Rina, it has been almost two years since you offered the farmers fertilizer."

"Yes Mama. And those who followed my instructions would have tripled their production but for the early winter frost that ruined their crops during the trial-year just before the harvest. However, as you know they did triple their production during the second growing season."

"Those that didn't follow your instructions must be cursing themselves, finally seeing the error of their ways."

"That's right. A number have already come begging for help. They've also admitted that next time they'll be inclined to listen more carefully to any suggestion I make, and act immediately upon my instructions."

"I'm sure you're right but their attitude is understandable. As your father states, the majority of these people hate change like the devil. I'm sure they also hate the thought of following the instructions of a teenage girl telling professionals what to do. But Rina, I have a proposition for you since we both seem to have a similar aim–helping the farmers to improve their lives."

"Mama, I know that you, your watchdogs and Father Murphy have cleaned up a lot of illicit acts in the district, so we have both been helping the farmers and their families. The fact of the matter is that the heroics of you and your watchdogs have spread far and wide. So while you upgrade their ethical conduct and keep them warm and healthy with firewood and medicine, I'll keep helping them to feed themselves and upgrade their standard of living."

"That's exactly what I want to talk to you about. I have a plan with which we can both help to raise their standard of living..." Serena cut her off.

"Mama, forgive my asking, but why is their welfare suddenly so important to you? You've never paid attention to their distress before."

"Thinking what I can do to help is not sudden. It's really a result of what you've done for them that made me see the error of my ways. I've been standing idly by for so long oblivious of their plight and doing nothing. You've made me ashamed of myself."

"Mama, you must know that was never my intention."

"I know that dear. But of late, with so much time on my hands, I've been thinking a lot about my past behavior. I'm ashamed to admit that before you came along I was far too preoccupied with myself; with my own desires and well being. Other people or their needs never seemed to matter to me."

"So helping others is a way to make up for your past; to make you feel better about yourself?"

"You've expressed my feelings exactly. Your compassion and generosity was catching. It made me see the error of my ways; made me want to help. So will you listen to my proposal?"

"Mama, I'd be honored to have you share your ideas with me."

"Dang, as you know, in the West, an applicant arriving for an interview is on trial." John was again discussing with his friend the changes he had made in the organization of his corporate businesses.

"Correct! He's expected to point out his reasons for applying, and why he thinks he's qualified for the job. He must sing his praises to convince his employer that he's the right man to fill the vacancy."

"Right! But an applicant who appears before me and my executives for an interview is already chosen for the post. We expect him to downplay his qualifications since, from his application, we are already well aware of his strengths. The fact is that we only need to see him and hear that he has no negative tendencies."

"Well, it seems that your attitude is both reasonable and sound. I know that many local corporations follow the same policy. I feel sure your changes will make for greater success in your corporation."

"Thanks for your reassurance. If truth be told, I've been wondering whether my changes have been too drastic."

"They are far more practical than drastic."

Long before reaching the eleventh grade, Serena had been an outstanding student in her art classes. Gifted in drawing and painting, she enjoyed learning as much as she could about the world's great painters. She studied the chief features of their work, spending a lot of her spare time studying the great art of the past. With her skill in painting improving each year, she was given a project to do on the Renaissance school of painting and sculpture. It was then that she became better acquainted with the great works produced by such renowned artists as Michelangelo, Leonardo da Vinci, Raphael, Titian and others. She was especially drawn to the period because of certain of its characteristics. The works were exceptionally large in dimension like da Vinci's *The Last Supper*–some thirty feet in width by fourteen feet in height. In the same way, Michelangelo's marble statue of *David* was more than 7 feet tall. The painted surface of the fresco, *The Last Judgement*, spanned the entire altar wall of the Sistine Chapel, a massive 2,000 square feet in size. She learnt that the size of a subject was important not merely for itself, but skillfully depicted, the canvas or sculpture could project its own dominance and grandeur, dwarfing the viewer into insignificance. Of course, greater size demanded greater skill in draftsmanship, since the smallest details of the subject would be larger and more exposed to the eye of the observer. Any shortcomings in draftsmanship would thus highlight the weakness of the artist. Few such weaknesses appear in the great masterpieces.

Serena was also impressed that these artists portrayed the world exactly as it existed before their eyes. Unlike their predecessors, they stressed the theme of individualism but did not ignore the symbolism that is a characteristic of the painting of the Middle Ages. They expanded the meaning and appeal of ordinary ideas by raising them to a universal level. Michelangelo's *pieta*, the marble Madonna with her crucified son in her arms, can be regarded as both an individual and an idealized woman. On the one hand she is a symbol of womanhood in general, facing the difficult problems encountered in her world. On the other, she is a mother suffering in anguish for her crucified son.

These artists also injected drama into their work. Serena couldn't help but recognize the excitement that is generated by the strain and tension in the marble figure of Michelangelo's *Rebellious Slave* straining to free himself both from his bonds as from the marble medium that imprisoned him. His fight for freedom is presented on the personal level as well as on the universal. It is obvious that it mimics all individuals struggling for their freedom. But while Michelangelo's *Rebellious Slave*, his *Dying Slave*, and da Vinci's *Adam and Eve* in *The Last Judgment* are all large-scale depictions, the skill displayed in their anatomical knowledge also showcased their incredible accuracy in draftsmanship.

Wanting her artistry to grow, Serena decided to follow the lead of these artists. Unable to study anatomy by dissecting corpses as Michelangelo had done, she began, like da Vinci, a regimen of drawing pencil sketches of the shapes, heads, body parts, beaks, tails and feathers of the animals and birds she planned to portray. Only when satisfied with every detail would she commit them to her canvas. To most people, such a routine would be an abomination of boredom. For her, the painstaking repetition would create realism and greatly improve her skill in draftsmanship.

"During the '88 Olympic Games that Korea hosted, dad took mama and me to Seoul via the Bullet train. Mona, that new stadium, built to hold over one hundred thousand fans, was really impressive. It made me proud to think that our architects had designed and built such a fantastic structure, one of the world's largest." As always, when Mona met her friend, she couldn't help cursing the fates for the beauty they had bequeathed to Serena and the ugliness they had reserved for her. She had to hide her jealousy but couldn't prevent a filthy swearword from silently slipping into her mind.

"You know I didn't go although I begged my parents to take me. So are you trying to make me jealous?" Serena stared a long moment at her friend before realizing that her question was serious.

"Mona, stop being so negative and so nasty! This is not about you! I'm explaining how much I enjoyed being in our nation's capital for the first time. Seeing some of the world's great athletes in action was quite a different experience from watching them perform on TV."

"You too would have a negative attitude if others were always trying to make you feel jealous!"

"I wouldn't have asked you here if that was my intention. We are friends, I keep telling you. Don't you know me yet?"

"Sorry, but to be honest, I don't understand your attitude. Have you never looked in a mirror and seen the huge differences between us? Christ Serena, you're a charismatic figure, poised and elegant, whom everyone regards as ultra beautiful. You exude charm like a fucking pot-bellied stove radiating heat. You draw people to you by the sheer force of your magnetism. Everyone wants to be *your* friend."

"Mona don't start that bitchy comparison between us all over again!" But Mona paid no attention. She found it impossible to suppress her jealousy.

"Serena, I'm overweight, a fucking ugly duckling with a horrid case of acne and an overbite. No one wants to be *my* friend. Now, do you understand my negative attitude?" She couldn't withhold the need to vomit out her urgent desire for praise. "So tell me, what the hell do you see in me to make us friends?"

"Mona, I won't dignify your questions with a reply. As I've said, I can never see you in the way you describe yourself. I'm your friend Mona, have been for years. She then added: "but you don't get it, do you?"

"What don't I get?" Mona hissed, frowning with suspicion.

"Anyone listening to your complaints would translate them as a plea for sympathy; for admiration; for compliments. I know the realization would make you cringe. It's the last thing you'd want." Mona's face turned red with humiliation, frozen by the truth. She acted like someone who saw a blow coming but stood her ground, knowing it was too late to react. Serena gave her friend a warm hug, advising: "Mona, you've got to lose that habit."

"It's hard to do that when you're the butt of everyone's jokes," she said, fighting to hold back her tears.

"Well, when you're with me, you should know better! Now, can I continue my Seoul adventure?"

"Go ahead," Mona replied wearily, wiping her eyes, mad with herself for once again verbalizing the pain originating in her ugliness that in turn spawned her lack of self confidence and her deep-seated envy and jealousy.

"While there, Dad and Mama insisted that I should see and learn at first hand some of the more important and popular points of interest in the city. We first visited Inchon, one of our two major seaports, and a modern world of container ships, and high-rise housing development. There was a long back up of ocean going liners crowding the harbor. The army of cranes that off-load them stretches for kilometers along the docks. I found the endless rows of containers sitting backwards from the wharfs and piled high atop each other in numerous rows far too numerous to count.

"It boggles the mind," Mona interrupted, her jealousy showing. It irked her to cede the floor to anyone who stole the spotlight. Unable to remain silent, she cut in sarcastically, "and the airport is just a little further away. The fact is that "the city rose to fame in 1950 when General Mac Arthur led UN forces in a daring raid landing behind enemy lines that brought the North Korean army temporarily to its knees."

Without scolding her friend for her bad manners, Serena cut her off: "The satellite town of Gyeonggi-do, together with our capital city, houses one third of the nation's population of almost 50 million. The three areas also form the hub of a major business and financial center with many international banks located there..."

"My parents never took me to visit Inchon International Airport, but I'm sure I know more about it than you, just from reading and watching TV." Mona then rattled off what she knew in a sing song manner to annoy Serena: "It's located on *Yeong Jong Island* and is responsible for almost all international flights and much of the local traffic. Along with Hong Kong and Singapore, the airport is one of the major transportation centers in South East Asia. Then, the Gangnwn district is one of the most affluent areas of the capital, and the upscale Apgujeong-dong area and the COEX- Mall boasts ultra modern boutiques that are famous the world over for its shopping."

"Mona, quit trying to upstage me. Can't you just relax and stop thinking I'm trying to make you jealous?" Mona ignored her friend and continued to spout her knowledge: "At those boutiques, one can see the latest designer fashions in clothes and accessories that have come straight from Paris, Tokyo, London, New York and Milan." Serena tried to ignore the jealousy that had prompted Mona's behavior as she looked at her friend with sympathy.

"Now may I continue Mona?" When her friend nodded her head dejectedly, Serena pressed on with her adventure.

"Before returning home, my parents thought we couldn't leave Seoul without a visit to the old Joseon Dynasty city. They regarded the visit as a part of my cultural heritage. They insisted that I had to see the renowned palaces, the architectural wonders of the government offices, and the many markets located there. The flower market with its blooms of every color and description was set up in sections. One was devoted to myriads of flowering potted plants. The mixture of delicate fragrances tended to waft you off to an imaginary fairy land. Another section was given to fruit and vegetables, their stalls laden with produce from all the fruit growing areas of the country. But it was the fish market that literally took my breath away with the pungent bouquet, not always pleasant, of its marine products. There were huge aerated aquariums brimming with live oysters, clams, crayfish, spiny sea urchins, shrimp, sea cucumbers, lobsters and crabs, most of them alive. The sharks, both great and small, were spread out on well washed concrete tables, or sometimes on the concrete floor. Close by were huge fish with their gleaming swords, giant blue fin tuna with their heads and tail fins lopped off, many more of the smaller yellow fin variety and loads of dolphin. Several mounds of king and Spanish mackerel were spread out over large areas and there were numerous piles of small fish that I had never seen before."

While observing the animals in the tall grass, Serena found that at times her mind would wander and gravitate towards those other animals she encountered and observed when riding in the mountains with her father. As she moved deeper into the trees she would feel more and more a part of her surroundings, certainly as much at home there as any creature of the wilderness. In her mind's eye she could actually see a woodpecker drumming away contentedly on the upright branch of a dead tree, its head a blur of motion. A Barn owl might suddenly hoot and appear on a low branch, head tilted sideways inquisitively, its huge eyes unblinking or a squirrel might scurry up a branch chattering his complaints to whoever chose to listen. There were times when the intensity of her concentration would permit her to inject herself so deeply into each scenario that she imagined smelling the acrid scent of sweat rising from her horse's flanks, hearing the creak of leather from her saddle or the metallic click of shod hooves striking against granite rock. On one occasion she even imagined hearing the agonized cry of some wild creature being crushed in the talons of a hawk or owl.

The couple had spent years trying to have a child but each time the wife got pregnant, she miscarried. After the third failure to carry to term, the doctors warned that a succession of miscarriages could seriously affect the wife's health and advised adoption. After considerable resistance to the idea, the couple finally adopted a five year old boy mainly on the basis of his good looks. His curly hair was blond . His face was appealing and his eyes were bright and sparkled like diamonds. The new parents couldn't understand how Frank, an angel at home, could turn into such a devil at preschool. His teachers complained that he seemed to be always in a black mood. He swore at his classmates and teachers alike and seemed to hold a special grudge against girls. He would tease them, take away their belongings–a box of crayons, a stuffed toy or coloring book–and the situation would always end in his picking a fight with the owner of the missing article. His parents had to keep changing his schools. Although they admonished him at home, his conduct at school didn't improve. As he grew older, his aggression intensified and as before, his victims were always female. Try as they did to force him to change his ways for the better, by grounding him, taking away his allowance and finally by flogging him, he remained faithful to his violent nature. After his expulsion from high school just prior to the long vacation, his parents decided to send him to work on a farm during the summer where they felt he would have no one on whom to vent his aggression. They failed to understand how he could be so affectionate towards his mother while displaying such violence towards all other females. They were left in no doubt that their beautiful child was horribly malicious.

"When he returns from the farm perhaps we should consider therapy," said his mother.

"I agree, but you should be prepared for the wagging tongues of the village community," his father replied.

"His cure is more important than village gossip."

Chapter 12

"During our visits to the different areas of the city, we couldn't fail to notice the industrialization and urbanization of the nation's capital that has greatly uplifted both the economic status and the lifestyles of so many of our fellow citizens. The truth is that our sightseeing wouldn't have been complete until we visited some of the most revered temples and pagodas, those 'tiered towers with multiple eaves,' and other palaces as well. It would be a part of my cultural heritage, my parents never tired of repeating."

"I hope that's all you've got to say about your precious visit?" Mona said with scarcely veiled jealousy and irritation."

"Nope, there's much more," Serena said, just to annoy her friend, but Mona refused to be upstaged.

"While you were so busy frolicking on your sightseeing tours in Seoul, I was glued to our TV set enjoying '*Autumn Fairy Tale*,' and '*All about Eve*.' Later I saw '*My Fair Lady*,' and 'Stairway to Heaven, all local TV mini-series that, as you know, have become very popular of late." Serena could actually hear the venom in her friend's voice.

"Tell me," Serena said in a moment of annoyance, don't you ever do anything enjoyable with *your* parents?"

"Isn't that obvious," Mona replied.

"Anyway, if you're quite finished interrupting me Mona," Serena stated with sarcasm dripping from her tongue, "I'd really like to continue what I was saying, but only if that's all right with you."

"Okay, okay," Mona replied, made to feel ashamed of her bad manners.

"The big city with its hustle and bustle was like the inside of a termite mound. Humanity crowded the sidewalks in chains of movement, people hurrying one way, others hurrying the other."

"I know you're going on and on just to bug me." Mona stated.

"Exactly!" Serena replied with a chuckle before continuing.

"Vehicles of all kinds crowded the streets–cars, stagecoaches, buses, motorcycles, gangs of bicycles raced together in a flurry of motion. There was the continuous roar of motors revving, drivers shouting, tires screeching, horns honking. The circling dust devils and the smoke belched from vehicles thickened the air. When inhaled, the foul-scented mixture forced every eye to stream and every mouth to cough. With people rushing madly to and fro, there was an impression of bedlam; everyone in a mad race to snatch whatever brass ring it was they coveted. Still sulking, Mona remained silent next to her babbling friend.

"At right angles to the sidewalks leading away from the streets, there were narrow walkways bordered on both sides by small shops. Knots of people crowded around shop-owners hawking their wares: clothes, cameras, luggage, jewelry, t-shirts, handbags, post cards and all sorts of knickknacks."

"Did you buy anything?" Mona asked in a small voice that echoed her defeat.

"If you mean outfits, no. But dad was pestered by a vendor holding a small suitcase with an array of watches carrying world renowned names: Seiko, Citizen, Rolex, Casio, Omega, Movado, and others. Dad thought he'd be smart by ignoring the vendor completely. As he stepped on board our bus, the vendor kept offering: "any two watches for fifty dollars." Dad made his first and final offer: "twenty dollars for both." To his utter amazement the offer was accepted immediately, and dad chose the two top makes.

Once seated, he began putting the Rolex on his wrist mentioning to the other passengers how he had bested the vendor with his negotiating strategy. Eyed by his audience, he then tried to tighten the watch onto his wrist. His audience gasped audibly, for to everyone's astonishment and chagrin, the band broke, the watch fell off dad's wrist to the floor accompanied by the sound of breaking glass. A loud gasp escaped from the onlookers and a look of total surprise and embarrassment appeared on dad's face. However, he was intent on showing everyone that he had an ace up his sleeve. He then fixed the Movado firmly on his wrist. When he held the tiny knob to set the correct time, the knob came off in his grip and the hands of the watch fell from their central pin. There were gales of laughter from the passengers until someone asked: "How much did you pay?"

"In a small voice of complete embarrassment dad replied: "Twenty bucks for two."

"I paid ten for three, but they won't make as good a conversation piece as yours." Dad kept blushing furiously with the laughter of his fellow travelers ringing in his ears. Even Mona couldn't help laughing at dad's predicament and Serena was able to continue.

"There were restaurants offering all sorts of goodies, like hot dogs, hamburgers and cold drinks to counteract the heat. Throngs of men, looking for bargains, sported colorful shirts worn outside their trousers. The women outshone them in their multicolored sun dresses. In the heart of this ultra modern scene, the temples and pagodas took me back in time, reminding me of a world in which saber tooth tigers and dinosaurs roamed the earth."

"Now, I hope you're finished?" Mona broke in with asperity in her voice.

"Yes. Now you can stay here and cool off or come help me with my chores. Your choice!" Serena stated, walking away from her friend.

Once again in the hospital chapel, Leesa recalled what so many of those around her failed to realize and take into consideration. Her courtship by John leading up to their engagement and marriage had been a terrifying trial. Few would understand, but she would never forget the guilt and shame she felt at having to wear a mask during all those years. No one would realize how hard it had been for her to fight her way through that painful and punishing ordeal. Yet, she remembered that the tall, gentle man whose proposal of marriage she had accepted couldn't have been more thoughtful, devoted or compassionate. As she looked at his grey-green eyes, his somber features that could so quickly break into a radiant smile, she wondered if he really believed the story she had told him a week after learning she was pregnant:

"John," she had said, "I stayed late at the school cafeteria one evening to have supper with some of my schoolmates. On my way home, I took a shortcut through a wooded area where I was confronted, overpowered and raped by a complete stranger. I haven't told this to anyone else, neither to my parents nor to the police. Please don't expose my secret. I couldn't stand the humiliation or the ostracism that would be sure to follow." Although he pretended to be thoroughly convinced, she wondered.

"I thought of something that will help to upgrade the farmers' standard of living."

"That's wonderful Mama! But why do you need me?" Serena asked.

"Because I haven't yet done the research to put it into practice. I'd like your help because that's become your field of expertise."

"I'll be happy to help in any way I can. So, tell me what you have in mind."

"Well Rina, while visiting quite a few farms with my watchdogs, I notice that many of their rice paddies are badly neglected, and in some cases, totally dried up. In some farms they are even non-existent."

"Mama, I am partly to blame for that. My instructions have created a new focus on poultry farming and later on fertilization. Many farmers have reacted favorably, but being short handed, they have had to exclude other chores. Their fields have increased production, but in last year's parched summer, their paddies shrunk, dried up, and were often badly neglected. As you saw, some were completely abandoned. So tell me Mama, what is this idea of yours?"

"The idea kept buzzing around in my head but I finally managed to capture it. I thought we could help them to rehabilitate their rice paddies and re-introduce carp farming on a wider scale."

"Wow! I see what you mean. Rice and fish would be important additions to both their produce and their diet. The truth is that even if their other crops failed, they'd always have enough to eat."

"Exactly! They'd have meals of fish and rice, in addition to their eggs and poultry."

"That's more than enough protein and carbohydrates for underfed people." Her mother said smiling. "So what do you think Rina?"

Mona carefully calculated the steps she would take to activate her plan. She was absolutely certain that men liked their women to be forward and feisty. They were impressed with women who showed their gumption. She was positive that doing the unusual, the unexpected, would turn them on. A real he-man wouldn't waste time on a wallflower. He'd want to fuck a firebrand. Thus, she'd use her 'womanly wiles' to seduce Frank, the new farmhand-hunk her parents had hired for the summer. His quarters were the cubicle built into a corner of the barn below. A successful campaign would allow her to turn the tables in her relationship with Serena. When Mona gave her a blow by blow recital of the incident, she would be the envious one for a change. For once, Mona would be the leader instead of the follower.

That night, she soaked herself in a bubble bath of scented oils while waiting for her parents to fall asleep. Next, she put on her push-up bra and the skimpy see-through panties that she had bought for the occasion. She sat before the mirror, layered on a thick coat of foundation to conceal what she could of her acne, covered her lips with 'crimson tiger,' the reddest lip gloss she could find, and used a blusher to color her cheeks. She brushed on eye shadow to create a look of mystery around her eyes, stuck on false eye lashes. To create a doe-eyed look, she traced a black line around, and made an upward arch just beyond the tail of each eye. She chose the tightest fitting dress in her wardrobe and cinched in her waist to magnify the thrust of her breasts and the flare of her hips. After smearing Chanel No.5 on her temples, wrists and the back of her knees, she donned her ballerina shoes. They would soften the sound of her passage down the stairs to the barn. It wouldn't do to wake her parents after all the thought and trouble she had put into her campaign. Finally, she looked in the mirror and liked what she saw. She was ready and couldn't wait for those muscular arms to wrap around her; to have that cruel mouth crushing against hers; to feel that tongue working its magic. Just thinking of the scene made her juices run and her blood sizzle.

John's loyalty and devotion were two of the qualities that had made Leesa come to respect and love him over their years together. She was also drawn to his tall athletic figure, his thick crop of black hair, his eyes and face that could be so kindly and loving. She had come to regard him as her rock since he had been the very essence of stability. As she knelt in the chapel, she asked herself for the thousandth time how could she ever have told him the truth? How could she even have begun to explain the enormity of her crime? Had she done so, it would have brought shame and dishonor on her, on her family, and especially on John, a loyal and innocent bystander. She just couldn't.

At that moment John touched her shoulder, brushed his fingers lovingly along her hair, cheek and chin. They then exchanged places. He kissed her hair and knelt to pray while she returned to their daughter's bedside. No prayer had escaped her lips.

"So Rina, do you think that my idea for the restoration of rice paddies and carp farming is a good one? Do you think the farmers will go for it?"

"It's a brilliant idea, Mama! It shouldn't be difficult to sell it to them in an attractive package, especially if we offer our help."

"If we begin the research at once, when we've accumulated all the information, we can discuss the best way to put the plan into action with your father. What do you think?"

"Sounds good to me, Mama!"

After their marriage, Leesa's feelings towards John had been anything but lukewarm, based especially on pure admiration for his loyalty, devotion and gentleness. Of course, it was helpful to recognize that he represented a huge step up the social ladder for her with an affluent future thrown in. Yet, so far, her improved social and financial status–so eagerly sought after–was in no way as enjoyable as she had imagined. Instead, the profound mental turmoil, born of her corrupt acts, had robbed her of that joy. And as she looked at the tall, athletic figure, the masculinity of the man she had come to admire and love, she cursed herself for having stooped to such an ugly betrayal.

It was his way of looking at, touching and caressing her face as though it were a precious gem that really got to her. That gesture, and his look of adoration, had made her heart go out to him. She had fallen in love with him for making her feel so special, and had admired him even more for the depth of his devotion. She could only hope he had accepted what she told him. However, she knew how implausible her hastily fabricated story of the incident must have sounded. Not only had he stood beside her, supporting her every inch of the way, but he had also made good his promise to marry her immediately as she had asked after learning that she was pregnant. What struck her most was that he never questioned a single detail of her story. She couldn't help but admire and love him for such unswerving devotion and loyalty.

There were times when Serena was with her parents, at other times when she was alone, involved in some task. A fit of trembling would seize her and her vibrating body would so terrify her that she would burst into tears at this new disaster threatening her sanity. She could never be sure when another panic attack would come without warning. Fear would make her nauseous, forcing her to vomit out her insides. After the terror and confusion brought on by the unexpected attacks, she had to deal with the humiliation of being regarded as a freak of nature.

Mona crept stealthily down the stairs to the cubicle; saw there was no light under the door, entered the darkened room and found her farmhand-hunk soundly asleep. She had fantasized often about the seduction scene, but never imagined that she would be faced with the bare back of a sleeping lover. She'd just have to be creative and improvise, she told herself. She removed her clothes in the darkness, then crawling onto his sleeping mat she snuggled up against his warm body. Ever so gently, she slid her hand inside his shorts. She planned to arouse him in this way, having convinced herself that all men were sexually aroused by a forward woman. She began her ministrations until she felt him stir awake. He turned towards her, rubbing the sleep from his eyes. She used the moment to plant an urgent kiss full on his mouth. Startled for a moment, he then motioned for her to turn the light on. When she returned to the bed, he forced her legs open and jammed himself into her. Without any foreplay, he began to rape her. He clamped his hand over her mouth so she couldn't scream or call for help. Then, with every thrust of his pelvis, he whispered the word: "Slut, Slut, Slut!" When about to climax he withdrew his penis from her and showered her with his ejaculation. He then shoved her away so violently that she fell over backwards, struck her head on the concrete floor so hard that it brought tears to her eyes. He then stared at her naked body splayed out in a heap on the floor and began to laugh at the ridiculous spectacle.

The world's race of ugly women like Mona would need to have tungsten smelted together with steel in their backbone. The resulting alloy would stiffen their spine and perhaps enable them to withstand the world's cruelty and ridicule without flinching.

Although John seemed to believe Leesa implicitly, she knew that he was puzzled by her many contradictions. They were both devout Catholics and she had accompanied him to Mass with her parents every Sunday. After the rape, she had suddenly stopped her churchgoing, giving no explanation for the abrupt change in habit. She could also tell, from his facial expression, body language and the sadness in his eyes, that some of the other changes she had made had deeply disturbed him. Previously, she had decided to adhere to the Korean traditions practiced before the wedding. She would ensure that her parents provided her with the gifts of ritual silk, *yedan*, that the bride gave to the groom's close family. She had also promised that the negotiation over the purchase price of the gift box, *hamgap*, would take place. She would then ensure that the box was carried to the bride's house by friends of the groom, on the night before the wedding, as tradition dictated.

She planned to have the traditional meal that was usually served at wedding receptions, dishes that Koreans had come to love. Few would be aware of the time and effort she had taken to prepare a full menu. There would be *bulgogi*, marinated barbecued beef strips, *galbi*, marinated short-ribs, *kimchi*, bowls of different kinds of fermented meat, or pickled cabbage with various spices and horse radish, and the variety of seafood that Koreans favored since the country is surrounded by sea on three sides. There would be clams, oysters, abalone, scallops, sea cucumber, squid, crab, octopus and large shrimp. She insisted on having huge quantities of *bap*, sticky rice, together with *gimbap*, rice, egg, spinach, crab, pickled radish and other ingredients rolled in seaweed and sliced. Her favorite was *mandu*, dumplings filled with carrots, cabbage, spinach, meat, garlic, chives, onions and clear noodles that could be either fried or steamed. *Doenjang*, a fermented soybean-paste soup with clams would end the meal. For dessert, there would be different varieties of melon, Korean pears and a variety of pastries.

In the end, she had done none of the things she had intended. Instead, her deeply troubled conscience had forced her to make a complete about face.

Mona scrambled to her feet, grabbed her discarded clothes, and ran from the cubicle. Hot tears of humiliation burnt her eyes, ruining her mascara. Her doe-eyed look had become a frightening Halloween mask. Having scampered up the stairs and into her bedroom once more, hot shame reddened her cheeks. She burst into a renewed fit of sobbing. Runnels of mucus dripped from her nose onto her chin that she wiped away with her forearm. She cursed the cruelty of fate for being so fat and ugly. She was angry and deeply humiliated that she had been fucked like a whore, sprayed with his cum and then rejected even by the lowly scum of a farmhand. Why, she kept asking herself, was she the target of everyone's hatred and ridicule while people like Serena had everything they wanted and were universally adored. Once again she had been taught the unpalatable truth: she and all those like her were doomed to a life of abuse, persecution and misery.

Chapter 13

For the next week, mother and daughter spent hours each day in John's study pouring over the texts and articles he had on the methods of Asiatic fish farming. Once they had completed the research and got their facts together, they believed that the idea, if accepted, would prove to be a godsend to the farmers. However, as always, there were difficult obstacles to overcome. They both knew from experience that nothing comes easily, but they had more than one ace in the hole. Both checked their research until they believed that they had compiled most of the required information.

"Mama," Serena suggested, echoing her mother's thoughts: "let's consult dad and Mr. Sing. I'm sure they'll have some worthwhile ideas to contribute." The suggestion was followed and their discussion with the two men brought them a great deal of new and valuable information.

"Not far from each paddy, there should be a pond, at least three square meters and one meter deep," Sing explained, before John chimed in: "Once the paddies and ponds are excavated, they will need a thick layer of compacted clay to waterproof the bottom and sides of the pond. The clay will keep the water from being absorbed."

"Won't fish be lost during the Monsoons when the paddies overflow?" Leesa asked.

"Both paddies and ponds should be located in an elevated area with a six to eight inch wall of clay around their rim. There should be a drainage pipe inserted six inches below the top of the pond to channel any overflow into a ditch leading to the nearby stream. A similar pipe at the bottom of each paddy will drain it when it's time to harvest the adult fish by netting. Those that are too small for eating can be replaced in the pond. They'll help to restock the paddy after the harvest when it is refilled and made ready for the next season."

"What will stop the fish from being lost through the drainage pipes?" Serena asked.

"The top drainage pipe will have fine mesh netting covering its inner entrance to prevent fish loss. The bottom pipe can be blocked on the inside by a cork that can be removed for a water change or for harvesting the fish," her father replied.

"Carp are prolific," Sing stated. "They spawn often on the floating weeds that need to be introduced into the paddies together with the adult fish. The weeds must be inspected daily and any egg-laden weeds gathered at once and transported to the ponds where the hatchlings will grow into fry. If the egg-laden weeds are left in the paddy both eggs and any hatchlings will be eaten by their parents."

"What about food?" Leesa inquired. "We know that carp are omnivorous, and will feed on snails, worms, mollusks, aquatic plants, seeds and insects. But there won't be any of that food in newly planted paddies."

"That's true. Initially, the food supply can be created and introduced with a few kitchen scraps, left over food, grass clippings, rice bran, livestock manure, chopped vegetables and mealworms that can be cultivated and placed in the paddies well before the introduction of the fish," John stated. "As it breaks down and decays, microscopic live organisms will develop–*infusoria*– that will serve as the first food for the tiny new born juveniles. Such a diet will increase their protein intake and speed fish growth."

"What are the main problems farmers will have to face?" Leesa asked.

"That's a good question Mrs. Ahn. Fish breathe oxygen from the water through their gills. Too much food would cause a high plankton bloom in the pond. This would use up the oxygen and force fish to come to the surface gasping for air. When that happens, oxygen can be increased by releasing half the fouled water, then replacing it with fresh water and cutting back on the food supply that created the plankton bloom."

"Dad, are there any other dangers we need to know about?"

"When introducing fish to the pond or paddy, the water being introduced with the new fish must be very close to the same temperature with that of the pond."

"How do we manage that?"

"The large plastic bags in which the fish are sold should be floated with the fish in the paddy for at least an hour before their release. During that time, every ten to fifteen minutes, a jug half filled with paddy water should be slowly poured into the bag with the new fish. This will help acclimatize the fish to the pond water and eventually make the water inside the bag almost the same temperature as that in the paddy."

"What about the danger of winged predators or aquatic animals preying on the fish?" Leesa asked.

"In commercial operations, huge nets are used to cover the paddies. But buying nets will be too expensive for the farmers. Their fish will soon get smart enough to hide among the rice plants and thick beds of weeds introduced for the egg laying and survival of the fish. That way, losses will be minimal," John replied.

"What other dangers are there?" Serena asked.

"There's the great danger of pesticides, Miss, that kill fish. But the clay wall around the rim of the paddies should keep out pesticides."

"Dad, now that we have the facts, how can you and Mr. Sing help us put the plan into action?"

"I suppose that I can lend you a couple of 'Cats,' mini bulldozers, to excavate the land for the new paddies or to deepen and enlarge the paddies and ponds that already exist on the neighboring farms."

"That's very generous of you, dearest," Leesa stated with one of her dazzling smiles.

"But Dad, some of the farmers have neither rice plants nor carp," Serena stated innocently.

"Don't we have more than enough, dear?" His wife asked, even more innocently.

"We have a plentiful supply of both, Sir." Sing hastened to add before John could respond.

"All right," John added smiling, seeing that his wife, daughter and manager, were silently conspiring to nudge him into coming up with the obvious solution.

"I see that you all want to make me a pauper. Go ahead, Sing! Give them all the help they need. But Serena, you can use some of your profits from the poultry farm to purchase more adult fish. I can't supply all the needs of the farmers. And don't you laugh or think you've escaped," he said with a broad grin aimed at his wife. "You too will have to contribute, and not from our joint account."

"Don't worry, dear. Serena and I have already decided to do that. And, let me add, we intend to be right there on each of the farms with Sing, supervising the hands as they carry out our instructions, and helping in any way we can."

"That's a good idea! The fact is that when the wives see you helping, I'm sure they'll all pitch in to speed up the process. After all, they alone will be reaping the reward." John added, before instructing his manager: "don't let this new 'adventure' hamper your supervision of our farm's needs!" By this time John was munching on his nails.

"Sir, you can depend on me to make sure that nothing on our farm is neglected."

"Good! One last caution! A large jug full of water must be taken from my paddies and poured into the water in each new paddy and pond, every day for about seven days, *before* the new fish are introduced. The water introduced will 'season' the pond and paddy water by spreading its own bacteria and preventing the new fish from dying of shock." He stated, before taking his leave. He was still gnawing at his nails.

It didn't take long for Serena to tell her grandparents of their plan to help the farmers. They approved and made a generous contribution to the sum put up by Leesa and Serena. These latter had assembled the neighborhood farmers, told them of their plan, and in less than a fortnight, Mrs. Ahn, Serena, Sing, his farm hands and the farmers' wives were busily excavating, enlarging and repairing ponds and paddies on many of the neighborhood farms. Each evening, on their return from the fields, the farmers made their own contribution by waterproofing the newly built ponds and paddies and making clay walls around their rim.

Meanwhile, Serena and her mother had bought large numbers of adult carp and introduced them into their own rice paddies. Within weeks, they were able to introduce the many egg-laden weeds into plastic bags half filled with water they transported to the farmers' ponds. Most important, there was the proviso "solidarity" clause: all those whoe benefit would donate eggs and fry to their neighbors. In a few short months, rice paddies and carp were being bred and spread throughout the district in the same way as the poultry farms. Within a year, there was a thriving rice crop and increased carp population in many of the newly flourishing rice paddies. By the following year, a steady supply of rice and fish would be added to the diet of the farming community, and thanks to the efforts of their benefactors, starvation and poverty would be slowly banished from the district.

It was then that Leesa came up with a novel plan. "Now that the production of rice and fish has grown considerably," she challenged her husband: "Why don't you buy the surplus rice and fish from the farmers for your grocery outlets? You'll be able to increase your stock of food and your benefactors will be happy to sell you their produce at a reduced price. At the same time, their sales would greatly benefit the farming community. If that were done both of you would profit."

"That's an excellent idea, Leesa. Our groceries can easily use the extra rice, once it's bagged. But the fish will have to be cleaned, frozen and packaged."

"I can organize that," his wife replied quickly. "I'll see that each farmer bags his rice, cleans and packages his fish in wax paper ready for freezing. I'll also designate a collection point where the produce can be brought together on the first Saturday of every month at the same time for pick up. John, will you lend a couple of trucks to collect and take the rice to your grocery outlets?"

"Okay. Once you have organized everything with the farmers, I'll let Sing take it from there."

"I'll take that as a yes," his wife replied, then added: "I'll arrange for the packaged fish to be brought to the freezing unit you gave Serena? Once frozen, the fish can be taken to the shops to be sold on a monthly date to be arranged. Right?"

"All right, dear. You realize that this phase of your plan will call for even more transport and labor?"

"Yes my darling. But I happen to know the owner of those trucks personally. I hear that he's a very generous man."

"Thanks, Leesa," John replied with a chuckle. "I'm really pleased that you and Serena are still taking the farming community under your wings."

A cloud of darkness enveloped Kim's mind as she recalled the insolence and ingratitude of her daughter towards her father at his workshop. The darkness sparked her anger and she sought Leesa out to deal ruthlessly with her: "How could you be so callous as to tell your father that he was nothing more than a manual laborer? Have you lost your twisted little mind?" The voice alone—apart from the insults—should have warned Leesa that her mother was furious. Not only was she shouting—and she seldom raised her voice in anger—but an angry blush had reddened her neck and face. Leesa remembered seeing her in such a rage only once before, during the teapot incident. Instead of disappearing as she should have done, the insult raised her hackles, goading her to anger and insolence.

"Well, isn't he?" Leesa spat at her mother. Kim overlooked the insolence and replied:

"And what got into your tiny addled brain to accuse him of being a copy cat? Didn't you realize how wounding such an accusation would be from the daughter he loves?"

"I didn't set out to hurt him, just to make him understand that he could do much better, for both himself and his family. All he needed was someone strong, with a less addled brain and foresight enough to guide him." Kim tried to overlook the insulting remarks to zero in on her daughter's self-centered nature. But the stinging insults merely increased her rage.

"Don't you mean for yourself, you selfish little bitch? After the sacrifice you learned that we've been making all these years was for your benefit, you didn't have the grace to show your gratitude, or to ask his forgiveness for your spiteful and vindictive accusations!" With the dark turmoil clouding her brain, Kim's voice had become a violent hiss, her eyes blazing with fury. Leesa should have taken note and disappeared. Instead she stood her ground and continued to spit out her insolence.

"What I said was true. You don't have to apologize for the truth!" Leesa again spat at her mother. But the darkness setting fire to Kim's brain had increased her fury and once again she lost control. She slapped her daughter so hard that it almost knocked the head from her body. Leesa was stunned, then her eyes became fierce and merciless in the stare with which she galvanized her mother. With her cheek stinging from the fierceness of the blow, Leesa drew her head back like a venomous snake about to strike, and then with uncontrolled fury, spat the venom on her tongue into her mother's face. Immediately recognizing the danger she was in from her mother's rage, she rushed from the room. Apart from her fear, she was too proud to give her mother the satisfaction of seeing her tears. But Kim's violent reaction, and the arguments she used to shame and belittle Leesa, had forced the daughter to realize that she had grossly underestimated the mother she had termed, 'soppy and weak-kneed.' Meanwhile, Kim felt ashamed at again losing control. She was conscious of once more having failed to control not only her own evil nature, but also the burgeoning evil of her daughter.

Kim regretted having struck Leesa even though she was still trembling with fury. This was the second time that her anger had made her lose control, and she couldn't tell what dark presence had inflamed her blood to such an extent. Surely she had overreacted in behaving with such violence. She began to feel ashamed and guilty not because she had hurt the daughter whom she loved, but because she had wanted to hurt her, had even enjoyed hurting her. Yet, hadn't that hot slap been the well-deserved punishment for the years of abuse she had suffered at Leesa's hands? But then, her behavior like a common fishwife had added to her guilt and shame. She realized that she now had to keep a tighter rein on her own wicked temper. In the past, it had made her rebel against the authority of her parents. At present, it made her feel self-satisfied with her violent outburst against her own daughter. Did that mean that she was the parent who had passed on the evil gene to her daughter? The fact that she couldn't tell increased her guilt and her shame.

When her anger had abated, she began to think that Father Murphy's words were true. "Evil is a powerful and ingenious hunter. A relentless predator, it follows the spoor of its prey by sound, scent and sight. The cool secluded sanctuary; the flagstones of the cathedral are no safer for the quarry than the tacky carpet of the whorehouse. Man is powerless against so skilled, determined and tenacious an adversary. She began to believe that once an individual surrenders to evil, it becomes rooted in his flesh. Lying dormant for a while, it perhaps feeds upon itself, growing stronger, she thought. But who really knows? She then began to wonder what malicious act her daughter might cook up in retaliation against her, and tried to fathom the source of evil that could so suddenly flare up in her own conduct. However, she was never able to pierce evil's impenetrable carapace. Perhaps evil concealed itself like the core of an onion, under many secret layers. She knew it was associated with darkness and cold, the first clouding the vision inciting wickedness; the second numbing the conscience against criminal action. Unwittingly, she had come to the same conclusion as Shakespeare's Lady Macbeth. Suffering from guilt at having goaded her husband to murder their king, she had tried vainly to fathom the same concept and surrendered in frustration with the anguished statement: "Hell is murky." Like Shakespeare's tragic heroine, Kim was sorely distressed at making no headway in unraveling the mystery.

Perhaps the most important change of plan had occurred with regard to the wedding itself. Leesa had insisted that Father Murphy should solemnize their marriage with organ and choir. She had finally decided to break Korean tradition by following the beautiful Western rituals that her priest had learned during his training abroad and had rhapsodized over. When asked, Father

Murphy had itemized the details for her. The wedding, she told John, would only be complete if it was held in church with organ and choir. She would have an exquisite bridal gown, a maid of honor, several bridesmaids and a ring-bearer. The huge reception she wanted would be held not in a home, not in a restaurant, but in one of the 'wedding-hall,' ballrooms that luxury hotels in Korea used specifically for that purpose. They would invite the families and friends of both spouses, and everyone would dance to a full orchestra. She had been adamant about having "a big wedding with all the trimmings."

"Leesa, I don't want a big wedding," John had told his fiancé with a frown. What you have in mind is traditional in the Western world. We live in the East and I, like many of your invitees, would be seriously disappointed to see you flout our own traditions. I'd much rather have a civil ceremony with only the immediate families present."

"Darling, a wedding is the most important day in a girl's life and I have every intention of enjoying mine to the full," she had replied, stressing each word. John didn't like what she said or the way she said it.

"To be honest, I dislike the elaborate style you have chosen, he said quietly. "It's far too showy. Besides, I don't care for the words you used or for the way they were spoken. They sounded too much like an ultimatum."

"I didn't mean to sound like that," Leesa stated with surprise at her husband's stern and unexpected reaction. "It's just my enthusiasm for having a church wedding." John thought for a moment before answering.

"Leesa, I'll do as you ask about bringing forward the wedding date but only if we have a small civil ceremony and reception with no one but the immediate families present." He spoke gently, without stating that he had no intention of backing down. He didn't say either that if she didn't accept his suggestion the wedding would be off. However, the look of determination on his face and the tone of his voice was enough to tell her that he meant business. Being pregnant, and having no alternative, she reluctantly agreed to have a civil ceremony without any of the invited guests. It didn't matter that the invitations had been sent or that a number of presents had already been received.

Since she had agreed to his decision, John didn't mind repeating again and again the humiliating apology he made to each previous invitee whose name had disappeared from their final list. He returned each of the gifts that had arrived with equal embarrassment and more humiliating apologies. Yet, he never spoke a single word of rebuke to her. She remembered the events as clearly as if they had taken place the previous day, especially John's reaction to the changes in her earlier decisions. He had been pleased that she had seen his determination and had agreed to his proposal. With a radiant smile, he looked as excited and jubilant as the soccer-team member who had scored the winning goal in a shootout. Yet, he never put into words whatever he must have thought; never once questioned her other changes of plan.

South Korea is a land whose high mountains often jut upwards to pierce their cloud cover. Their presence and the forested wilderness they support have inculcated in its people a close attachment to the environment. It may well account for their special love for mountainous country and more especially for the forests that grow on their slopes. Like their fellow citizens, John and his family loved the mountains and enjoyed hiking the trails and camping from time to time in the high wooded hills. On one occasion when they pitched their tent above the high pass, he set about pointing out to them how best as a farmer, he could utilize the area.

"In summer, when the fields below are parched and dry, there are pastures in these upper valleys and plateaus that are still lush and green. Look over there," he pointed. "Those waterfalls plunging from narrow hanging valleys have created deep basins from which their waters join the main stream and flow out onto a broad, open flood plain. It would be easy to dynamite one or even two of the upper rock faces on the valley slopes, then use the rock to build a huge dam across the two exits through which the rivers now flow." Neither Leesa nor Serena could ignore the enthusiasm that accompanied his words.

"Just imagine how the dam could be made to control the flow and used to irrigate the broad meadow below?" His wife and daughter listened without interrupting as he verbalized his thoughts. "The fact is that I could terrace the foothills on either side of the valleys for rice and fish farming, and then grow corn, alfalfa, wheat, soybean, barley, sorghum, millet and beans on the meadows below the paddies." Only then did his wife interrupt.

"John, I can almost see what you envisage. The crops you plant there would significantly add to the staples of grain and beans that you already grow on the farm. Likewise, there would be additional rice and fish to harvest for market." Serena's eyes suddenly grew large as she imagined the picture drawn by her parents. Caught up in their enthusiasm, she chimed in: "The whole area would be able to feed more than a multitude of five thousand. When the

pastures below become parched and dry, there would then be lush grass growing in the high meadows to supplement the food for our grazing animals. We
could even start a huge kitchen garden to supplement our vegetable sales to
your grocery outlets, Dad."

"True," said her father, "and the broad sweep of the river that overflows
with each Monsoon, would bring more layers of silt to its flood plain. The rich
soil would encourage the growth of grasses, interspersed with bushes, shrubs
and thick stands of riverine trees that, at present, border only the banks."

"I can see where you're heading," said his wife. "The wide variety of the
vegetation would attract an even greater abundance of wildlife. There would
be foxes, deer, coyotes, bear, small game and many species of ducks, geese and
some of the other game birds and waterfowl that already inhabit the region."

"Those are my thoughts exactly," John admitted jubilantly. And as the dam
filled and extended further and further backwards, a fairly large lake would be
formed to draw all sorts of wildlife and winged creatures to it. We could even
stock it with carp and trout. It would be quite an undertaking."

"And a windfall," his wife added.

"Sometimes dad talked wistfully about the earliest cave-dwellers who had lived
there, making the still wild area sound like a magical land that had beckoned
to people—probably our ancestors–who had given birth to unknown generations of the family from its earliest beginnings. I began to believe that the cave
had been in use by my ancestors from the very dawn of time.

"Dad," I asked, "what would it be like to live in such a place with only the
simplest of needs satisfied–the shelter of the cave, the availability of water, the
warmth of the fire and sustenance from the vegetation and wildlife of the
wilderness region below?"

"I can't truthfully say, Serena, never having experienced it. Yet, as we have
seen, people managed to live there for generations. I imagine that it provided
an adequate living, but the isolation of such a life must have been excruciating."
Then, remembering the stick drawings, he wondered aloud: "perhaps the creative outlet of art would have helped to alleviate the withering loneliness of
such an existence."

Chapter 14

"Just look at her face, John," Leesa whispered sadly as she watched her sleeping daughter."

"It seems as though her features reflect the suffering she's gone through during these last weeks.

"They do seem to mirror her pain." John agreed.

"Her pale, piqued features remind me of the pain-riddled animals in the zoo that had so fascinated her."

"Now that you mention it, I remember that she doted on them, painting them over and over, including the forest background sheltering them before their capture. She had used the subtleties of color, light and shade to portray the subdued panic and frustration of the caged beasts."

"It seems that she had not merely seen the suffering displayed in the bare patches of skin, their tattered coats, restless pacing, and feces-coated hind quarters. She must have actually felt their pain. The same anguish is reflected in her pale, worn-out features; her glazed, haunted eyes." Serena's loneliness was a dull ache that intensified her physical and mental suffering. It made her desperate to gain some relief; to find some means of escape from her private hell. Since there was none, her face contorted, her body shuddered and tears welled up in her eyes. When they flowed, they brought a soothing balm that was only a temporary respite.

Leesa resisted for as long as she could remember, struggling against a return to that dreaded past, since she felt there was no other choice. For Serena to recover, she believed implicitly that medicine by itself would never be enough. She felt absolutely certain that its treatment would have to be bolstered by the power of prayer. But how could she pray, she kept asking herself, when she had turned her back on God so many years ago? Then again, she quickly reminded herself that that had been the past. This was the present. Serena was her life, the breath in her body, the oxygen in her blood. Whenever Serena had an accident; a skinned knee, a cut finger or a fall, Leesa would actually cry, feeling her daughter's pain. She would apply band aids to Serena's scrapes and cuts, kissing them better with tears welling in her eyes. Few would believe that she treated the paintings her daughter brought home from school as though they were masterpieces from the Louvre. Serena was her sun, her moon and her stars. It was only through Serena's glowing presence that Leesa had been able to endure the years of guilt, shame and loneliness that, during her pregnancy and afterwards, had bludgeoned her mind and scorched her soul. She looked at the huge picture of her daughter on the bedroom wall, directing her words at the image. "It was through you that I had come to know the joys of motherhood, even though they were always tainted with bitterness; bitterness that kept intruding from the past. It was love for you that changed me from the rebellious person I had been. As a mother myself, I recognized through my feelings for you, the love my own mother and father had lavished upon me. How could I have returned their love with such monstrous conduct? From what corrupt sewer had my jealousy and hatred originate? Had I been born an evil child? Yet that was so long ago, I told myself, and thank God, hadn't I changed since then? Still, for the millionth time, I thought my crime so horrible that not even God could forgive me. At the same time, I truly believed that my daughter's rape was His way of punishing me; forcing me to my knees; breaking my stubborn pride. No one understood how hard I had fought against my foul obsession. Oh God, how I had fought!"

As John was about to leave his office, his secretary greeted him: "Sir, I was just about to give you the daily newspapers that you requested: the *Chosun* Ibo, the *Joongang* Ibo and the *Donga* Ibo."

"Thank you Lee. I can read the *Chosun* Ibo on line, so you needn't include it in future."

"All right, sir."

"But I'd like to have the *Korean Herald* and *PR Korea Times*, those English language newspapers that provide more news from around the world."

"I'll remember that sir. And would you like to have any of the main magazine publications like K *Scene* or *Korea Post*?"

"No thanks. I already have them delivered to my home."

"Please let me know if there is anything else you need."

"All right Lee, I will."

John drove the limousine that was taking Serena home from the hospital deep into the country. They passed the many unpainted one-story thatch-roofed farmhouses of stone and wood scattered widely throughout the neighborhood. Their outer walls were cracked, stained and scarred by countless generations of weathering through hundreds of parched summers and freezing winters. A few of the older and less sturdily built structures were crumbling, dilapidated and abandoned in a state of collapse.

Approaching the Ahn farm at last, the sleek automobile entered the long driveway leading up to the house and the unusually huge acreage of the farm. Groves of trees surrounded the central two-story home, almost hiding it from sight. Unlike the small, simple dwellings on the farms they had passed, this building was an evident transplant, architecturally designed and modeled after the solidly built upscale homes of the affluent West. The site was selected according to the Korean tradition of Feng Shui. It was built against a far-off hill with the house facing south to receive as much sunlight as possible. The site ensured that there was a balance between the *ying* and the *yang*, those positive and negative forces that oversee the welfare of those who dwell in the building.

As they approached the house, they had a full view of the garden that followed the traditional Taoist layout. Ironically, while there was an attempt to avoid all artificiality–great influence being placed on nature and mystery–the garden was man made, and therefore artificial. Its central feature was the lotus pond surrounded by flowerbeds with a tiny stream running beside a small pavilion. It was a scene fostering contemplation. Anyone nearby would enjoy listening to the flow of water murmuring over the pebbled bed while gazing at the stunning beauty of the flowers and mesmerized by thier lovely aroma.

The driveway led up to the huge white two storey mansion, whose entrance was through double doors inset with beautifully stained glass on either door. The building stood, steel foundations concealed under glazed white brickwork. The two white trailing wings receding from both arms of its central structure, created the impression of an immaculate virgin bride enveloped in her flowing bridal gown. Huge triple glazed windows graced the outside, while on the inside there was modern plumbing, a clay-tiled floor heated from below–a process known as *ondol*–and a state of the art kitchen.

In the dining room, glass-fronted cabinets displayed rare and beautiful sets of bone china dinner ware. On display too were delicately fluted Champaign glasses vying with solid Waterford goblets that overlooked a long table of burnished cherry with twelve matching chairs. In the living room, the light blue almond-shaped patterns in the dark blue carpet echoed the blue pools in the eyes of "The Artist's Wife," a portrait by Modigliani hanging on one wall. On another wall, the dark blue suit of her partner highlighted the shimmering white light of the dancer's dress in Renoir's "Dance at Bougival." But it was the tempestuous brooding vision of van Gogh's "Starry Night" that drew the eye. The heavy brush strokes of light and dark blue picked up the colors of the carpet while swirling crazily around the canvas often in collisions with themselves. There was also the vivid contrast between the dazzling light of the moon in the top right corner that was almost diametrically opposed to the maelstrom of darkness in the copse of cypresses near the bottom left corner. The canvas seemed to depict a chaotic universe afflicted by catastrophe. One couldn't help but consider that the portrayal also seemed to reflect the tortured spiritual interior of the painter who, like Father Murphy, was haunted by his vision of a world in the process of disintegration dominated by the forces of evil.

Wooden surfaces gleamed in furniture and floor, while carpets, cushions and curtains injected their rooms with the warmth of their coordinated colors. The many bed and bathrooms, sunken family room, library and study were all well furnished and suited to the needs, tastes and status of the corporate head of a very successful gentleman-farmer-businessman. A stone walkway separated the house from the paddock and barns.

On arrival at home, Serena was still too weak and frail to walk. Her father lifted her from the automobile, deposited her gently into a wheelchair and wheeled her to her suite in one wing of the house. He laid her in the four poster bed that held center stage in a bright room. Light filtered through the gossamer drapes over large windows. Apart from her bed, dressing table and stool, the room had few other furnishings. Her easel, canvases, paints and brushes were kept in an adjoining room. Its huge windows and skylight permitted a flood of light to brighten the studio. Thanks to one partially open window there was also a faint odor of horse and manure in the atmosphere. Serena considered it pleasant since it formed an invisible link with her beloved colt,

Will. Her parents tucked her into bed where she slept fitfully, anxiously watched over by each of them taking turns. When she first awoke some hours later, her father was kneeling beside the bed. He embraced her gently and whispered:

"Rina darling, your mother and I are so glad to have you back. Rest now and when you feel up to it, the doctor thinks you should resume the earlier pattern of your life, but only very gradually." Knowing that she was fragile and still hurting, he kept her feeling secure in his gentle embrace for a long moment.

"Rina!" Her mother mumbled, choking back her tears. Seeing that each of Serena's movements was painful, her mother bent over the bed and very tenderly enfolded Serena in her arms. "When you're better," she whispered, "I'd like to join you in feeding and caring for your pets. They all miss you, especially Will. But rest for as long as you need and when you feel strong enough, I know you'll want to get back to your painting." Serena nodded without speaking surrendering to the warmth of her mother's gentle hugs and caresses.

"Kim, do you realize that it's almost a year since this change for the better has come over Leesa?"

"I keep hoping that it will continue to last. But I'm not holding my breath."

"Why not? She hasn't given us a moment's worry."

"After our many attempts to get her into therapy, she was adamant in her refusal."

"So what are you saying? You expect an outburst at any time?"

"No. First, I'm happy for the change. But, I'm worried that her conduct might suddenly deteriorate and become a grave embarrassment. I know from past experience that just like her sudden change for the better, her moods cannot be trusted."

"Why can't you relax and enjoy the fact that she's improved considerably?"

"When evil takes root, I believe it handcuffs the individual. I also believe that after lying dormant, it will suddenly show itself. An eruption of some kind will take place. Oh God, I hope I'm wrong!"

"Kim, she has behaved so well that not a single word of criticism can be leveled against her. Darling, why can't you accept that?"

"I can't help feeling that some form of rebellion is on the horizon. So, forgive me if I can't relax just yet."

"Although you put on a brave face in front of Serena, I can see that you're deeply troubled by her condition," John said to his wife.

"Well, it's more than two weeks since she's been here convalescing and there's no real sign of improvement. Can't you see? The doctor has removed the sutures from her lips, but there's still some puffiness around them as around some of the other scabs on her body. A few still keep oozing pus showing signs of infection."

"Yes, but the heavily discolored bruising on her face, body, arms and thighs has all disappeared. Isn't that an indication of her healing too?"

"If she's healing, why is she still in bed listless, semi-comatose, and seeming to be lost in some other world? Then, she speaks little and eats less, while a low moan sometimes escapes her lips. The way she gingerly turns her body in slow motion, her eyes glazed with fear and sadness, indicates that her body is still painful. I believe that although not complaining she's still suffering severely."

"I didn't quite follow the doctor's reasoning. He thought that she had isolated herself from those around her, but there was something more that he couldn't quite grasp. He ended by stating that her problem was not wholly physical. It went deeper into the psyche."

"I wasn't quite sure what he was getting at either. He didn't fully explain what he really thought."

Father Murphy, who had come to visit the patient at her mother's request, agreed with the doctor's diagnosis. He believed that Serena's affliction went much deeper, but he awaited the medic's departure before expressing his view to her parents.

"Your daughter is afflicted with a spiritual disease," the priest stated. Some people who have been violated believe that their lost innocence is a defilement that has alienated them from God, the source of goodness and love. The separation leads them to believe that they're under the dominion of Satan. They presume that the evil one has shepherded them into a state of despair, inducing them to believe it impossible to recover their innocence; their purity. If she is one of those who loses hope, she may be seduced into thinking that self-destruction is her only alternative. We should never forget that Satan's diabolical aim is to destroy." The priest then squeezed Leesa's hand and left her with the advice: "Watch and pray for your daughter. I will do likewise."

Leesa couldn't help believing the priest's diagnosis when Serena's condition began to get worse. She lay on her side facing the wall, with knees pulled up, her body folded into the fetal position, her hands clasped as though in prayer.

She lay totally immobile for hours on end. She had bitten her nails down to the quick and her lips and fingertips were covered with blood. The condition signaled that her illness went well beyond a solely physical condition. Her guilt, shame and self-loathing had driven her to the dangerous habit of feeding on herself.

Leesa thought that perhaps Serena's nail biting was picked up from an unconscious habit of mimicking her father. But in her illness she had taken the harmless habit to an extreme.

Leesa found it impossible to make eye contact with her for Serena never looked at the person speaking to her. When her mother deliberately positioned herself to look directly into her daughter's eyes, she found them lackluster and glazed. She noted too that her zombie-like appearance and attitude suggested that her suffering, shame, guilt, and despair had drained the life force from her. The doctor's explanation that it was her means of shutting the world off from her and, more important, of shutting herself off from the world, made Leesa recognize that doctor and priest were not far apart in their diagnosis.

She confided to her husband: "It's clear from Serena's conduct that life had dealt her a stunning blow and she had chosen non-communication with, and isolation from others, as a defense against its cruelty." John agreed and replied: "Her lack of emotion, interest or motivation, and the fact that she had turned her back on the world, makes the diagnosis of priest and doctor more credible than ever. In her attempt to become invisible, she has indeed entered that "spiritual wasteland" to which both doctor and priest had alluded, though in different terms."

Serena remained confused, bewildered, despondent and depressed throughout the early stages of her recovery. She thought that there was only one person to blame for the rape and that was herself. Why, she kept asking herself, had she gone to the movie alone, dressed her self in one of her more stylish outfits and used her favorite perfume? Surely she was intelligent enough to know that seductive clothes and expensive perfume attracted attention. Both signaled sophistication, taste and money. Her decision to make herself alluring with a form fitting tank-top and mini-skirt had been a mistake. Then, being alone had increased her vulnerability. Finally, in choosing to traverse secluded woodland she had gone out of her way to invite the rapists.

It was evident that Serena had been so traumatized by the horror of her experience that she could no longer think rationally? Her reasoning was so skewered that she was unable to reach any valid conclusion. Her wild thoughts convinced her that the whole world would believe she got exactly what she deserved. Unwittingly, she created a block to both her mental and physical recovery by constantly flogging herself with the guilt and shame fostered by her disordered mind.

"Mr. Sing, you said that dad never spoke to you about either the cave or its inhabitants. I find that strange since he talked to me about them all the time?"

"Perhaps he only thought about them while he was up in the mountains with you, Miss."

"The enthusiasm he showed whenever he talked about them made me wonder more than ever before: who were those people, where had they come from and why had they decided to settle at that particular spot?"

"Their choice was certainly based on the presence of the cave. From your description, it seemed like the perfect spot, offering everything they needed. Being high up, they could see the approach of an enemy. The cave also protected them from the weather and was easy to keep warm in winter. The spring close by provided water and their home overlooked forests filled with an abundance of game and firewood for warmth and cooking. There was even a fireplace. What more could they want?"

"Something must have been lacking. Otherwise why would they have moved?

"Perhaps life was getting too hard," Sing suggested. "But before moving, they had lived there for generations according to the artifacts you found."

"Hunting in the same area over and over would have driven most of the game away, and generations of life there probably taught them that it was easier to supplement their hunting with food gathering."

"You're saying that time and the scarcity of game would have made them hunter gatherers, Miss?"

"Yes. The reality of it is that it would have made their lives less nomadic and eased their living conditions." After a moment's thinking, Serena added: "the fact is that gathering would in time have led to farming that would have ensured a more reliable food supply, and greater stability. So they must have moved because they could hardly farm on that rocklike terrain around the cave.

"I wonder how many generations it would have taken for them to begin cutting down the trees and clearing the land for farming?" Serena said, setting the farm manager thinking.

"They must have begun by using the clearings in the forest to start planting, because we both know the backbreaking work it takes to clear the forest."

"That's true, Miss. We both witnessed the difficulty your dad had in clearing a part of the forest to add to the acreage of the farm, and he had both men and machines."

The eyes of hundreds of spectators kept boring into her while she was being gang raped. In her panic, she couldn't understand why they kept their distance although witnessing her struggle and hearing her screams for help. She tortured herself with the belief that they all thought she deserved what she was getting. Although she screamed out her innocence as loudly as she could, all eyes remained glued to the scene but no one came to her aid. Inside and outside, her body was a mass of quivering jelly while she was being torn apart. The staring eyes of the strangers who watched and listened but refused to help were almost as terrifying as what was happening to her. Suddenly, she was in the arms of her mother and her terror evaporated.

"Mr. Sing, I remembered when dad and his workers started clearing the forest. It was backbreaking work. First, the trees had to be felled, their branches cut off, and the remaining logs carried to the edges of the clearing."

"One of the older hands told me about it. They had to burn the tree stumps before tearing the roots from the earth," Sing said. "Next, they had to dig out the rocks and boulders, and then collect and remove them. They could begin the plowing and planting only after leveling the earth."

"I used to sit high in the barn watching the men clearing the additional acreage. It had to be done with heavy machinery and even that demanded extra manpower."

"Miss, you wouldn't believe how arduous the work was even with machinery. It was the only time the older hand heard his colleagues complain even though your granddad hired numerous extras to help. And despite the many laborers, the work took ages to complete."

"Watching the men with chainsaws using their huge muscles felling the trees and lopping off the branches was really exciting Mr. Sing. The scene was a hive of activity. There were tractors dragging the felled logs to the edge of the clearing, backhoes ripping out the stumps and tractors carrying them away to be burnt. Mini bulldozers were digging out the rocks and boulders and filling huge trucks that kept up a continuous motion of coming and going to empty their loads and return for more."

"Even after they cleared the land, they had to bring in graders to level the badly scarred earth. Only then could they truck in huge loads of top soil. Finally, they needed more machinery for the plowing, the planting, the weeding, the spraying and much later, the harvesting. Those must have been hard times Miss. I learned that the backbreaking work needed to clear a forested area and get it ready for cultivation is just another form of slavery."

Chapter 15

Sing was right. The work it took to clear the land even with machinery and manpower made Serena believe that her ancestors had left the cave to begin their farming using the forest clearings. It would have taken the original couple generations to enlarge even a small section beyond the clearings. Perhaps, after generations of enlarging the acreage, they had gradually switched completely to farming. Certainly, it would have taken many years to change from hunter gatherers to contented farmers. The undertaking spoke of a people who had already faced considerable hardship, being well inured to the difficulties they had to confront. They possessed the toughness and determination necessary to survive in an unforgiving land of parched summers and bitterly cold winters. It is evident that the children would have learned from their parents and presumably, had very gradually changed their lives. She wondered how far back in the past those 'ancestors' had found the cave and how many generations it had taken for them to make those changes. Being cut off from the rest of the world, they would have led lives marked by severe hardships and loneliness. She couldn't begin to imagine the deprivations they must have suffered. Whatever problems they faced would have conditioned them to become survivors.

It was on that long ago day that Leesa overheard her parents' discussing her delusion and need for therapy. Later, on hearing their cries of passion, anger began pulsing within her. These were the thoughts that coursed through her mind: So they are both determined to humiliate me, pretending that I'm delusional and need therapy. I know that's just a ploy to get rid of me. They'll undertake any pretence to have me committed. I bet it was she who put the idea of my insanity into his head. She's such a manipulative bitch, and he's so gullible. But I've had enough of their secretive conniving; their conspiratorial aggression against me. It's time to retaliate. I've got to show them that they're not as smart as they think. Clearly, they don't know who they're up against. It's such a pity as I was trying so hard to show them that I could be a good daughter. But since they think that I'm insane and are determined to put me away, I'll open both their eyes and show them what madness really is, so help my God!

During the next few days after repeatedly hearing her parents' loud ritual of lovemaking, Leesa reverted to the spiteful and rebellious person she had been. Whenever she saw her parents together, she pried them apart, elbowing herself between them with a wicked grin. Kim could not ignore the glares of malevolence that Leesa shot at her. Her fears that her daughter's condition would worsen had become a reality. Evil had not only taken root. It had grown and intensified. She sensed that Leesa was hatching some vicious plot against her. If her daughter's behavior didn't improve, Kim and Yong Sang would have to take serious action.

On that night, like on so many others, Serena was afraid to close her eyes. She feared falling asleep, being terrified of trying to outrun the demons whose pursuit never let up. She lay in bed tossing and turning, forcing herself to stay awake, rousing herself again and again each time she began to doze off. Suddenly, she rose from bed and began running and running, her mouth dry, heart pounding, bosom heaving, lungs bursting for want of oxygen. When she became so exhausted that she began retching, she had to stop that mad race, or die. Yet, with her pursuers gaining on her, terror injected a jet of adrenaline into her bloodstream. She jumped up and began racing forward so fast that she thought she was flying. It was impossible to keep up that spirited dash, and fatigue eventually bowled her over. Her legs suddenly gave way and she fell crashing into the underbrush. There she lay panting, knowing that she was lost since the demons were hot on her trail. At their approach, she kept screaming and screaming and the noise forced her to open her terror filled eyes.

It took quite some time before her pain-riddled body recovered enough for her to be able to hobble around with her mother's help. Although it was quite an ordeal, she was at least able to move around, if only in limited distances. One day, she leaned on her mother as she helped Serena to the paddock. She wanted so badly to hug the colt at whose birth she had assisted. She had helped her dad separate the foal from his dying mother and had christened him, "Will." He had shown such courage and determination trying again and again to stand just minutes after his birth. With her last breaths, the mare kept licking away the amniotic fluid covering her foal's body before nudging him again and again to stand. Finally, he stood and moments later, his mother was gone. Serena didn't miss the instinctive generosity of her final act. Like all doting mothers, even her last breath was filled with concern for her offspring rather than for herself.

"Don't you remember, Rina? Each time Will fell he would climb unsteadily onto his wobbly legs, only to fall again with fore and hind legs splayed out from him. But until those same legs propped him up and he could stand, he never gave up trying."

"Mama, I won't give up trying either, if that's what you're trying to tell me." Since that first visit to Will, she had embarked on a new lifestyle. Instead of the painful walk to and from her bed with her mother's help, she decided to make Will's stall her bedroom, cuddling with him under his thick, warm horse-blanket. The following morning, Leesa was astonished to find her daughter sleeping peacefully with her arms around Will's neck. When she awoke, her mother said: "I can't understand the close relationship you share with the colt. There's an understanding, a companionship that goes well beyond the normal bond sometimes seen between humans and animals. The way you touch and interacted with each other; the way you know instinctively what the other's next move will be, indicates that more than a mere camaraderie exists between you two. You're sensitive to each other's needs like a couple whose finely tuned minds know what the other is thinking." Leesa soon became aware that Will had imprinted on Serena and had formed a tight bond with his new 'mother.'

While Leesa watched Serena and the colt asleep in his stall, she fell into a mood of reminiscence, recalling how, so long ago, she had made such an effort to cure herself of the wickedness she termed her 'disease.' No one would believe the amount of time and effort she had spent visiting different churches, confessing to different priests in the hope of finding a cure. All provided her with similar solutions based solely on prayer. Only Father Murphy was different. He was equally moved by her story but probed more deeply into the problem. When he told her to be more specific about the details, her explanation to him took a different turn. She finally confessed that her sinful thoughts and desires were driving her towards destroying her parents through fornication with her father. The priest was stunned by the casual way she had described her intention to break the powerful taboo of incest that Koreans, like most civilized societies, regard as unforgivable. However, despite his repeated questions, she refused to reveal her motive. When he asked her what had prevented her from sinning in deed, she replied: "I knew that if I had acted and my crime was discovered, it would have brought shame and disgrace upon me, and my whole family. We would have been exiled by everyone."

"Were you as worried about your family as about yourself?" The priest asked craftily.

"Both Father. But it was mainly the fear of abandonment that prevented me from acting upon my desire. I couldn't stand being scorned by everyone; of being condemned to eternal ostracism." She took a deep breath and hurried on. "The truth is that I finally managed to restrain myself knowing that it was wrong."

Finally, Serena had to admit that her peaceful sleep could be interrupted at any time by the most harrowing of dreams. The images were so familiar, so graphic that she swore they were indeed real and what she saw was actually happening to her. Four lurid scars on the face they disfigured materialized slowly out of the darkness to confront her. She again felt helpless. Scarface's teammates had her immobilized, restraining her with their powerful arms and knees. Scarface knocked her senseless to the earth and mercifully, oblivion blocked out whatever deviltry followed. Although this was one of her recurring nightmares, surprisingly, its repetition kept making it more and more familiar, so that eventually, it became less and less alarming. Unlike the trauma caused by its earliest manifestation, it provoked no more than a temporary panic attack. After its many reoccurrences, she no longer needed the calming influence of her mother.

However, other recurring nightmares proved to be far more daunting. She often found herself racing through the undergrowth of a dark forest where her demons had joined together to hunt her down. Wolf and snake, eagle and hawk had all tripled their size and kept pursuing her. She ran and ran her lungs ready to burst, sucking in great gulps of air. But no matter how fast she ran, the creatures stayed on her heels. When she fell, fear radiating through her, tears came to her eyes at the realization that in a moment she would be eaten alive. A scream of terror burst from her throat. That was when she awoke to find herself still in bed and a moment later, wrapped in the warm embrace of her mother.

When Father Murphy inquired how Leesa felt about the seriousness of her temptation, her answer disturbed him.

"Father, I feel that I'm a loathsome person and the realization leaves me no escape from my guilt and shame." Much to Leesa's surprise, the priest laid the blame elsewhere.

"There is an infernal disease on the wind that's sweeping across the earth," he said. "It's spreading its corruption throughout mankind. Alas!" He sighed, raising his head and staring into space as though he could actually see the corruption he was describing and using words she had heard before. "Evil never sleeps. It's sickening the world, blighting our spirituality, causing even the most devout among us to lose faith. Oh God," he continued, "darkness, darkness; death and darkness!" He paused before adding: "But your mention of grief and shame reminds me that they are the weapons we use to scar our souls and bodies for the wrongs we have done. The pain we inflict on ourselves gives rise to the remorse we feel for our wrongdoing and often forces us to behave ourselves which in turn permits us to retain our sanity. Otherwise, the shame of our wickedness would drive us insane." The priest then offered advice that his penitent had not heard before.

"Avoid the occasion of sin, my child."

When she said she didn't understand what he meant. He explained that she should avoid temptation by distancing herself from those who were inflaming her desires. Finally, he too gave her penance and absolved her of sin.

When Serena tried to resume her past activities, her mind and body refused to conform to her intentions. Blinding headaches assaulted her during her tasks and their throbbing pain caused dizziness. They made work impossible, forcing her to stop whatever she was doing. At times, a word, an action, even a smell would trigger the memory of her rape and she was catapulted back in time to relive the brutal invasion of her body. Once again she was defending herself against the violence of the rapists. The foul acts they forced her to commit returned to sicken her. She fell into a deeply depressed state of mingled shame, guilt, anger and self-loathing. During these panic-attacks, she indulged in further self-flagellation by questioning herself again and again. Shouldn't she have fought back instead of giving in to her aggressors? Couldn't she have done much more to fend them off? Shouldn't she have screamed much more and much louder? Wasn't she in some way responsible? And with these questions repeated over and over, she flogged herself into a paroxysm of fury, bludgeoning her mind with the question: Why did she feel guilty as though in some way she had cooperated with the rapists and deserved what she got? Why? Why?

In recalling the priest's words, Leesa kept asking herself: "How was it possible to distance herself from the persons who inflamed her thoughts and desires when she lived in the same house with both of them?" There was no answer. Yet, she managed to do the best she could. By going to school early, leaving home before her mother awoke, and before her father left for work, she would separate herself from both her parents during the day. But a problem arose. Each evening, it was usual for her, with father and mother, to take a walk around the farm. It was an occasion for family bonding and a means of making sure that all was well on the farm. She'd have to come up with some well-thought-out reason to excuse herself. She wasn't at all sure she would succeed.

It was another of those nights when Serena tossed and turned in bed terrified by the nightmare images that would tear at her mind once she fell asleep. Finally, when she found it impossible to continue struggling against sleep, she rose from her bed, hurriedly collected her paints and brushes and rushed towards the canvas already prepared on her easel. She was blazing with anger and bitterness at what she considered her victimization. Fighting against the demons of her fantasy, she slashed at the canvas letting her pent up fury pour out through her hand and fingers to gush wildly from her brush.

In firm strokes of black, red, white and yellow, the outline of a tawny animal began to take shape until the head, chest and forepaws of a giant tiger materialized, poised in mid-air, hurling itself out of the canvas. Its hackles raised, its claws extended, it spat forth its fury from its snarling jaws, pink tongue and malignant eyes. With its huge glistening fangs, it was ready to maul and mutilate every living thing in its vicinity.

The image echoed her retaliation against the demons pursuing her with an outpouring of her own venom. The result of her efforts gave her a temporary sense of power—a sense of revenge and release. She had learnt to use her brush as a wand to transform color into image and image into her personal reality. In doing so, she patted herself on the back for banishing her tormentors.

Unfortunately, the release was only a temporary fantasy, but it gave her the comforting feeling of having faced her tormentors head on.

Serena had always been attracted to the mountain wilderness, finding its ominous silences, its remoteness, and its solitude magical and captivating. The truth is that once in their midst, she became a different person. So clear is the air that whoever ventures into those heights becomes quickly familiar with the impression that he can almost reach out and touch the horizon or looking upwards from a mountaintop, caress the face of heaven. She was enraptured by inhaling its pine-scented breath, by the sight and sound of its gushing waterfalls, by the massive size of its granite rock face as by its incomparable grandeur. The emerald-clad valleys and their forested mountain chains stretching into blue oblivion awoke in her a spiritual sense of wonder. She felt closer to God, and therefore being blessed; being safe. Her being in the wilderness brought to her mind images of wild creatures, velvet tree-lined vistas and vast distances to cross. The mysterious sounds and silences nourished the soul encouraging thoughts of the past and of the future.

She remembered how in her early teens, she had been delighted to ride with her father into their mountain retreat as the tentacles of night stretched down along the mountain sides, absorbing the last fading light into their blackness. They would stop on their way to gaze at the heavily forested ridges that ribbed the valley below and the swift flowing streams, silvered by moonlight, cascading down from their hanging valleys. The rising moon would transform whole areas of the scattered stands of trees and rocky ridges into bulges of light and hollows of darkness that stood out like menacing ghostly figures.

On one occasion they had had to flee from a sudden summer storm. The driving rain, crashing thunder and lightening flashes had chased them scurrying to the cave for shelter. Under the overhang at its mouth, her father had made a huge bonfire using the bark, pine needles, dried twigs from blow downs and the coagulated sap from pine trees that they had stored in the cave for just such an emergency. He had then placed the marinated steaks he had brought on the flat fireside stone, evidently the cooking spot of their ancestors. The red flames leaping and clawing feebly at the darkness beyond the cave mouth kept them warm, snug and safe from the elements except when there was a shift in the wind. It would then blow the smoke into the cave filling it and almost overwhelming its inhabitants. Fortunately, the wind would soon shift back and the pine scented air would mingle once more with the odor of wood smoke and grilling steak. The scent and sound of juices bubbling on the hot stone and hissing as they dripped into the fire would create an unforgettable atmosphere. While they ate, her father would regale her with stories of his life in Canada. The repeated outings in such remote areas inspired her with a fascination for wild lonely places lost amid the pine-scented greenery of a mountain wilderness.

In recalling her childhood, Leesa remembered how her father, Yong Sang, had always adored her. He had made a habit of smothering her with love and kisses every chance he got. He called her his angel and she could never remember him but as an adoring parent. In consequence, she grew to consider him her idol. It was a natural reaction to his patience, understanding and devotion. By the time she had reached puberty, she had already begun to think of him as her special and personal possession. Yet, despite their close bond, no hint of sexuality had ever entered their relationship. It was only after she reached puberty that her parents' cries of passion had instilled in her a growing hostility towards them. Then, with each of their subsequent love trysts, the antagonism she felt towards them would return and its assault upon her senses would make her more and more furious. A bitterly cold hatred would fill her being. Eventually, the malice she felt goaded her into giving her hatred full rein. Yet, each time she tried to set in motion her plan for revenge, the repulsion she felt against her corrupt nature would take over and prevent her from carrying out her evil intention. If the priest's words were true that evil never sleeps, then she'd have to continue suppressing those vindictive impulses that kept urging her to be wicked. However, she knew that sometimes the impulse was so strong she wasn't at all sure that she would be able to suppress it.

Lately, she had begun responding to twin temptations, and from that time onward, and without warning, she would be sorely tested. A malicious hatred of her parents would captivate her and she'd feel an upsurge of wickedness propelling her to set her vile plan in motion. She would then recognize the feeling as a powerful attraction towards evil and Satan. Guilt and self-loathing would haunt her until she experienced an urgent need for grace that she sensed as an impulsion towards goodness and God. Yet, as horrified as she was by the malice that consumed her, she couldn't prevent herself from waiting impatiently for the sounds of passion coming from the adjoining room. The opposing temptations warred with each other and at times seemed to be evenly matched. Then, hatred of her parents would flare and drive her with the insane desire to destroy. Even when the other room was silent, her mind would riot with lascivious thoughts, her hands would begin roaming and groping of their own accord. As she became fully aroused, her body convulsed with passion. With the passage of time she no longer needed the trigger from the other room. Her sneaky hands would begin questing while she lay in bed and she would pretend that it was her father's hot fingers conducting the exploration. The fantasy would end with her squirming and bucking at the sweetness of his touch. After she imagined having done the deed, she couldn't wait to see the reaction on her mother's face.

Kim became deeply disturbed on reviewing certain patterns of Leesa's conduct. She remembered that as a small child, she had a habit of sitting in one spot and rocking backward and forward for long stretches. The behavior continued for weeks before tapering off, lessening in intensity and duration. At first, she suspected that her child was afflicted with autism, but the rocking finally disappeared and morphed into what could only be described as obsessive behavior. Like most children between the ages of three and five, all new games Leesa learnt, she kept repeating over and over. But while that was normal behavior for a certain period of time, unlike other kids who eventually grew bored, lost interest and abandoned the game for something new, Leesa's interest in the game persisted. When she began jumping on the sleeping mat, she would continue for hours until exhaustion compelled her to stop. On recovering however, she would start all over until again exhausted. She would continue the game for weeks on end. When her father taught her to catch a ball or pitch marbles, she would pester him not for hours or days, but for weeks. At such times, Kim could see that it was all he could do to keep his sanity. But, he never stopped smiling and never complained.

Leesa decided that it was solely up to her to rid herself of the pestilence that had so secretly invaded her mind and body, and was searing her soul. It forced her to confession where she could unburden herself. "Father, since it was impossible to share the knowledge of my unholy past with anyone other than you, I began following your advice."

"You were supposed to avoid the occasion of sin," her confessor reminded her with gentle insistence.

"Well, I distanced myself from both parents by rising earlier than usual, having a hurried breakfast and rushing off to school without seeing either of them."

"That must have been very difficult for you, my child."

"Instead of returning home after school each day, I closeted myself in the school library to continue studying for graduation. That way, I would miss being at home to share the evening meal with my parents.

"So you'd have supper at the school cafeteria?"

"No Father. I'd return home and eat a late supper by myself before slipping into my room. By following that routine, I cut down to a minimum my contact with both parents."

"But while it was possible to successfully avoid your parents in the short term. It must have been impossible to do that permanently."

"Very true, Father. But there were other complications as well. At the library, I found that distractions kept interrupting and I could never concentrate for any length of time on whatever material I was studying. Nevertheless, I prolonged the practice for more than a week despite the interruptions."

"What were the other distractions?" The priest asked to test her.

"After reading a single page over and over, I couldn't remember what I had read. Sometimes, a friend or a teacher would enter the library and surprised at seeing me there, would stop for a moment to chat. The lights would then go out a 6.00 P.M. sharp, when it was suppertime for the boarders. I would have to leave the library with nothing accomplished. I had wasted almost three hours."

Not long after Leesa had started kindergarten, Kim received a severe shock on the day her daughter's teacher, Mai, called her in for an interview.

"Kim, as your friend, I thought you should know that your daughter has been fibbing to both her friends and her teachers about the big beautiful house where she lives alone with her father."

"But Mai, surely you know that's only a bit of childish fantasy," Kim told her. "All children love to dream and embellish. Pretending is one of the ways kids deal with reality."

"She also told everyone that she's an only child..." Before the teacher could finish, Kim cut in: "But she is an only child. What she said is absolutely true," her mother replied, rushing to her daughter's defense.

"Yes, but what she finally said was not." The silence that followed forced Kim to ask Mai what it was her daughter had said.

"I have no mother. When I was born, she died."

Chapter 16

"Mama, there are times when I 'm delusional. I feel that I'm always un-safe and can be raped at any time, in any place, in the safety of my home, and even right in front of you. An unexpected sound, a footfall nearby, an odor is enough to set me off. It gets so bad that I can't trust my own thoughts. Unexpectedly, terror seizes me, gushing up from my insides like a geyser that erupts in a piercing scream. My body goes slack and I begin to tremble. When I can't stand it any longer, I scream and scream, shrieking out my distress, and that's when you appear to calm and comfort me."

"Oh darling, I'm so sorry that I can't do more."

Some incident would occur to distract Leesa whenever she tried to pray. Some-one would call in the middle of her prayer, the light would go out mysteriously in her bedroom or a closed door would open itself mysteriously then slam and break her concentration. Yet, her sincerity in wanting God to expunge the stigma of wickedness from her life forced her to return to the church. There, she intended to pour out to her priest as much as she could of the dreaded af-fliction that kept pursuing her.

"Where's Father Murphy, the priest who normally hears confession?" She asked Won, the sexton.

"He's gone to officiate at the Mass in a neighboring parish."

"Is there anyone who has replaced him?"

"No. It will be a week before he returns."

During that period, Leesa suffered the tortures of the damned. On hearing of the priest's return, she rushed to the church.

"Where's Father Murphy?" She asked the sexton. "I heard he had returned."

"He's here, but the hours of confession have been changed." Leesa had arrived too late to purge herself of her poison. She made sure to be first in line the following day. Yet, even before her entry into the confessional, she was frustrated and deeply distressed that so far, in spite of all her prayers, she had had no help from above.

"Mama, Oh God, Mama!" Serena almost shouted in her despair, "I need someone by my side to help me face the terror I'm going through." Leesa was taken by surprise at her daughter's sudden outburst.

"Mama, what's happening to me? I feel as though something inside me has died and its decomposition has corrupted me. Mama, am I going mad?" Serena raced on without waiting for an answer. "I feel as thought my whole inside is dirty. Is there anything I can do to recover what I've lost? People say that when tragedy strikes, you tend to lose your reason. Is that what's happening to me? All I see now is confusion and disorder, disorder and confusion." Her mother could see that Serena was scared at the chaos of her shattered life. She was trying desperately to impose order in a world gone mad.

"Talk to me darling, talk to me," Leesa encouraged, and Serena replied as though describing someone else's torture.

"You wait for a new calamity to smash into you," she whispered. "The waiting and the fear keeps building and building until you become traumatized. Your most private parts have been violated and you've become filled with self-loathing. Pain takes up residence within you from the kicks, cuffs, knife jabs and bruises. But that's not the worst, Mama. There's a fire smoldering in those private places that have been invaded, and every movement causes the fire to blaze, not only in your body, Mama, but in your brain."

Her mother stared at Serena with wide-eyed shock and sadness trying to silence her frenzied babbling. When she tried to hug and comfort her, Serena pushed her away roughly, held her at arms length and continued her anguished confession.

Kim remembered that as Leesa grew older, she began to show signs of a willful and compulsive nature. She insisted on breaking whatever rules her parents set. She refused to sit at the low table with them at mealtime and threw such violent tantrums that she got her way. She ate by herself. Kim couldn't forget the disgusting habit of permitting only her father to bathe, dress and undress her, nor could she overlook the vindictive habit of trying to drive her parents apart. Then, she felt impaled by those glaring looks of hatred. Try as she might, she could not erase from her mind the horror of the teapot incident.

"Bless me Father for I have sinned in thought though not in deed," Leesa began, so many years ago. At that point it was customary for the priest to intervene. But so pressing was her need to unburden herself that she blurted out her sin even before the priest could respond.

"I'm burning up with shame and guilt for my wickedness. All kinds of malicious thoughts fill my mind and are driving me insane. Help me to end these thoughts Father," she pleaded. "Tell me what I must do to stop this compelling temptation to sin." Yet, despite the pressure to cast off her burden, she still balked at telling the whole truth. Again, before the priest could intervene, she rushed on:

"Whenever I try to pray, something always happens to keep me from communion with God." She then added sadly, the shame making her whisper: "perhaps that's because I turned my back on Him when I thought He was not helping. I blamed Him for remaining silent despite every attempt I made to reach Him. Father, I kept cursing Him over and over."

"Child, you shouldn't stoop so low as to curse your Maker! Besides, you can't pray for forgiveness with hatred in your heart!" The priest responded sharply.

"Father, I became convinced for a while that He was the cause of my misery. You see, He kept ignoring me when I needed Him most." Father Murphy didn't interrupt, allowing his penitent to rid herself of the acid that was scorching her soul.

"With no help from above, I became even more crippled with guilt and shame thinking of the disgrace my act would bring upon my family and me. I grew wild with a passion to do violence to myself. But somehow, before I got seriously hurt, something always intervened to stop me."

"Your repeated statement that you got no help from above suggests that you believe God is punishing you for your sinful past. Is that correct?"

"Yes Father. That's why I've come to get your help." Her words stumbled over each other, and her voice was that of a distressed supplicant in mental and spiritual anguish. She was panting heavily, at the very end of her tether.

"My child, your despair and desperation has blinded you from seeing the contradiction between your thoughts and actions. The priest you have chosen to contact is the pipeline to the same God you earlier cursed, accused and abandoned."

"Oh God Mama, the pain never seems to stop!" Serena clung to her mother as she continued to verbalize her suffering.

"Where does it hurt most Serena?" Her mother asked, confused and distressed at her daughter's words.

"All over Mama. I've got rashes inside both my thighs, and there are places that itch so badly that I want to scratch, but those are the places I can't reach. Mama, I want to be whole and clean again. I want to be the old me."

"What do you want from me, Rina?" Leesa wailed, feeling totally inadequate to alleviate her daughter's pain.

"Mama, I feel stained inside and out. I've been showering constantly and washing myself but it hasn't helped."

"Why don't you lie down? Doesn't movement increase the pain?"

"Going to the bathroom is agonizing. I feel swollen. It's as though someone has opened an umbrella inside me. Mama, I'm no longer me."

In tears, her mother tried to stop the hot gush of her daughter's anguish, yearning to comfort her. But nothing she said or did could stop the outpouring of Serena's distress.

"Kim, you have a first class brain. You are capable of balanced judgment and can remain objective and unbiased even when assessing the conduct of the daughter you love!"

"I suppose you mean that I haven't been blind to her many mood swings, nor to the 180 degree changes she has made in certain of her choices and decisions. Yet, although considering the matter at length, I cannot account for any rational thought that might have prompted those changes."

"She seemed happy to accompany us to High Mass," Yong Sang added, "throughout her teenage years. After her engagement, she then went willingly with John. It was only in the final weeks before her marriage that she stopped without giving any explanation for her decision. And some of the changes began even before that."

"She was her high school's leading athlete. She had then abruptly stopped all athletics," Kim stated. She wanted a huge Western styled church wedding "with all the trimmings," then settled for a simple civil ceremony. Suddenly, she began going to confession as though there was a heavy burden of sin crippling her. I couldn't understand her behavior."

"Those sudden changes pointed to serious problems." Yong Sang added. Her conduct made you believe that there was a violent tug of war between good and evil taking place in her soul and you kept wondering whether your assumption was accurate. Don't you remember?"

"Most certainly! In assessing her behavior, I couldn't help concluding that she was unstable, irrational, and malicious. You didn't reach such absurd conclusions as she did unless you were flying on one wing only, or tiptoeing along the borderline of insanity. It struck me as possible that she might even have been bi-polar. Then, if the struggle against evil that was evident in her violent mood swings was accurate, it might have had the effect of tearing her mind apart."

Although so much time had passed, Leesa distinctly remembered Father Murphy's reply to her outburst in the confessional.

"My child," he had said, "every one of us is made in the image and likeness of God. And since He is the source of goodness and absolute love, it follows naturally that we all have within us the capacity for developing those virtues. When therefore He exhorts us to "love one another" or to "love our neighbor as ourselves," He simply means that we should exercise that divine spark of goodness and love that each of us already possesses. You should remember that and pray for forgiveness." Before the priest could continue, she replied: "Father, I have been asking His pardon and begging His forgiveness over and over for a very long time. Yet, never once has He answered my prayers. Don't you consider such behavior obnoxious and certainly unforgivable?"

"My child, I can't believe you are criticizing God. The only reason you are before me at this minute is because He has led you here. Be assured! He is watching over you. He knows that your innocence and devotion is genuine. Unfortunately, these are the very qualities that make you an attractive target for Satan. Make no mistake, the adversary is a powerful enemy, supreme in his use of lies and deception."

"Father, no one knows this better than the Almighty. So, why hasn't He come to my assistance?" The priest continued as though she hadn't spoken.

"The beast has been successful in distracting you from the true path, but only temporarily. He's trying to bring you under his dominion, drag you into the abyss. By heaping guilt and shame upon you for the evil that you contemplate, he will try to convince you that you are corrupt; that your life has no purpose. He'll rob you of all hope and deceive you into thinking that you are beyond God's love and forgiveness. That's false! False! Do you understand?" In raising his voice and repeating his words, the priest seemed to be trying to convince himself as well.

"Father, in spite of all you say, I am not convinced!"

"My child," the priest replied, "Satan is so cunning, his power so corrupt that he is able to falsify God's message." When he paused again, his eyes gazing into the distance, she broke into the silence.

"Father, I have malicious parents. They humiliate me with their loud love-making. They conspire against me stating that I'm delusional, insane and in need of therapy. Their insistence that I'm mad is driving me to hate them more and more. They think they're smart, concealing their plan, but I know they're anxious to put me away. Their conspiracy is urging me to strike out viciously at them." She wanted very badly to confess everything to the priest, but she still didn't think it wise to reveal her motive. In truth, the spiteful impulse driving her was born of jealousy of her mother and hatred of her father for abandoning her. "Father, she added, I nourished the wicked wish to destroy them both. Yet, the hatred urging me to destroy them made me realize that I possessed an evil streak; that there was no pardon for sinners like me."

The priest's answer was swift and angry: "No pardon? No pardon? Child, don't be so arrogant! You should guard against letting Satan inflate your ego! No one is so singular, so extraordinary as to be beyond the reach of God's love and mercy. Mary Magdalene was a prostitute and He forgave her for her sinful ways. And the penitent thief won forgiveness because of his shame and remorse."

Leesa had no answer to those claims.

Each time Leesa heard her parents making love in their adjacent room, anger flared within her and pangs of jealousy and sorrow pierced her heart. At the sound of another of Kim's moans of pleasure, the hatred towards her mother surfaced in her bosom. Although soon to be married, she felt as though she had been catapulted backward in time to become the wicked adolescent of her past. Rage against her mother exploded, surprising her. Leesa thought she had gained in maturity and outgrown that rebellious stage of her life. She believed that her wickedness had withered away. She then realized with surprise that it had not for she again felt the same venomous hatred that her mother had earlier inspired.

Since both her parents knew she was in the adjoining room studying, Leesa concluded that their yowls of pleasure were a deliberate performance put on for her benefit. It wasn't enough to emphasize the joy they experience in their intimacy; they needed to rub her nose in it. Theirs was a foul conspiracy to let her know that their love for her was a sham; a charade. She firmly believed that only parents who despised her could be so cruel. Angrily, she recalled their persistent attempts to force her into therapy, suggesting that she was seriously unbalanced or worse, insane. Any idiot could see through their intrigue as a ploy to get rid of her. She recalled her promise to show her parents the full extent of her malice. Struggling against her evil thoughts, she had broken that promise, again and again. Finally, she had done nothing. She tried to reason with herself, to impose strict control over her wickedness. She was determined to repress the rage she felt that was driving her towards committing a criminal act. She had been so sure that she had outgrown the rebellious nature of her earlier years. How could she have been so wrong? She fought against the powerful urge to destroy both her parents for thinking of her as a madwoman. Although she knew exactly how to accomplish that goal, she reined herself in, forcing herself to seize upon that wicked impulse and hold it in abeyance. She then asked herself? Wasn't that what she had done before? Weren't those the very thoughts that had made her fail to act? Didn't she have a will of her own or was she no more than a cowardly procrastinator?

Yet, the very stranglehold that she felt forced to exert over her impulses made her painfully aware that her thoughts were wicked. She determined to do everything in her power to resist her sinful desires; to remain pure. But would she be successful? That was the question. As the darkness seeped into her room and intensified, she began to shiver with the weird feeling that some evil force was creeping under her skin, insinuating itself into her very flesh and bones; imposing its stranglehold over her. She covered her ears with a pillow trying to drown out the sounds of passion coming from the adjoining room; to suppress her unholy urges.

In the darkness, her heartbeat quickened, her blood raced with mingled fury and desire. Suddenly, she felt as though she were no longer alone; as though a corrupt conspirator were at her side, within her. Yet, she was alone. Despite her efforts to eliminate her wicked thoughts, the vindictive need to punish her parents filled her with both excitement and dread. The malice in her heart pinpointed the strategy she had devised to destroy them both, once and for all. At that moment, the heat of sexual excitement filled her loins until her arousal became the very center of her being. Her body vibrated with malicious pleasure and she realized that she was no longer in charge. She had become a puppet and she felt as though some all-powerful puppeteer were pulling her strings.

Forbidden fantasies filled her mind as her father increased his impassioned urging and her mother's groans kept building in intensity. When the last animal yowl broke from Kim's lips, Leesa was amazed to find that her fingers had been secretly caressing her own body. She too had groaned, climaxed and soaked her underwear. On regaining her self control, she recoiled in horror at her incestuous thoughts and at the actions they had prompted. Shame, guilt and confusion assaulted her and reddened her face.

"If You don't want me to commit this atrocity," she shouted to the heavens, "then come to my rescue and rid me of this foul obsession!"

The sun disappeared, darkness fell, and the moon rose. It was one of those evenings that gave Serena a hankering to ride into the foothills leading up to their cave in the mountain wilderness. She saddled Will and cantered away. On that wild night, she was alone. The wind raced down the corridors and canyons in the valleys, whipping the tree tops and sending clouds scurrying across the moonlit sky. It was a time to think; to reflect on the possibilities of her future. Only a short distance away, the stands of trees merged into a blanket of darkness. All she could smell through the whirling darkness was the odor of a land still warm from the day's sunshine. All she could hear was the muted roar of the wind against the thunder of waterfalls plunging into deep ravines far in the distance.

The stories her father told at their mountain retreat had inspired in her a thirst for travel. Yet, travel she realized, meant a departure from her home, her country, away from so many of the things that she loved. Still, the impulse to travel was there, as was her curiosity to see the way others lived, to observe their habits and perhaps to learn and understand their values. That same urge goaded her to ask herself a series of questions. What was it that made her different from so many of her countrymen who were content to remain within their borders? What unknown germ of curiosity was there in her genes that made her akin to those footloose wanderers who yearned to cross oceans and continents, obsessed with seeing foreign lands; with leaving their footprints on distant shores?

The rage in Serena's bosom seemed to be endless as she continued to blurt out the venom that consumed her. "Mama, I'm not a person. I'm a caricature of who I was." Not knowing how to respond to such a statement her mother could only embrace and try to comfort her daughter.

"Hush darling! Don't take on so," was all she could think of saying.

"Mama, I feel as though the scent of corruption is on me! I'm sure others can smell it too."

"Rina, stop it! You're making yourself sick," she said in panic.

"I'm ashamed to have anyone near me Mama. Yet, being alone is worse. I can't stand it."

"What can I do? What do you need me to do?" Her mother asked helplessly.

"I don't know! Words of sympathy, perhaps. But then, I don't want anyone near me."

"Darling," Leesa began...but Serena cut her off.

"I'm a mass of confusion and contradiction. Mama, I must be going mad."

"Serena, don't you dare talk like that! You'll only make yourself worse."

"I can't help it, Mama. I feel like I'm dying here. What can I do to reclaim who I was?

"I don't know, Rina. I just don't know." Leesa wailed, tears staining her cheeks.

"The only solution is to rid myself of this repugnant life." The ultimatum spawned an idea in her mother's head: "Rina, you did nothing wrong! What happened was not your fault! You are just as pure as before!" The shocking cry for help induced Leesa to fold her daughter more tightly in her arms. While the two women wept together in their helplessness, Leesa recognized the truth of Father Murphy's words. Serena had been blinded by the glare of Satan's deception.

Chapter 17

The more Kim thought about Leesa's insanity, the more convinced she became that her assessment was accurate. She could see that a war between good and evil was taking place on the battlefield of Leesa's mind and the violence of the struggle was ripping her apart. Kim felt forced to give more serious thought to the matter since the welfare of her daughter's health and future was at stake. She consulted a psychiatrist to learn whether her assessment was accurate. While he tended to agree with her from the facts she related to him, he needed to see Leesa herself in order to have a far better grasp of the problem.

In considering the matter, Kim had to give serious thought to the way her countrymen viewed insanity. Like many of the world's rural backwaters, the unsophisticated farming community of Hamyang regarded insanity as a taboo. Their barbaric motto was borrowed from a misguided Roman credo: "Caesar's wife must be virtuous." Any personal miss-step or broken taboo was not limited solely to the evildoer. Its taint extended to every member of the family. The words 'psychiatrist' and 'therapy' spelled the word INSANITY loud and clear to the residents of Hamyang. It put the fear of God in them. The mere visit to a psychiatrist could not only ruin an individual and his future; it could also taint the reputation of his whole family. In short, the idea of going into therapy was so repugnant a taboo to the farming community that if given a choice they would rather contract leprosy.

After Kim confided her beliefs to Yong Sang, they thought that since Leesa had repeatedly refused to go into therapy, it would be best, for the present, to keep trying to change her mind. In the meantime, they would keep to themselves what they suspected about her condition. A short time later, when John proposed marriage to Leesa, they both breathed a long sigh of relief. They believed that her love relationship would help to stabilize her conduct and chase away the demons tearing her apart.

"Yong Sang, do you think it's possible for people like us to grapple with the notion of evil and come to any valid conclusion?"

"I suppose that in considering the nature of evil, and tackling it into its subterranean lair, we should begin at its source?"

"It sounds as though you've been giving the matter some serious consideration."

"Ever since you mentioned that Leesa was being torn apart by the struggle between Good and Evil, I've thought about it a lot."

"Well, the source is certainly Satan, the arch enemy of mankind. We should remember that he's also known as 'the beast,' the ultimate predator. With that in mind, perhaps we should examine the act of predation."

"I see," replied Yong Sang. You're evidently saying that there is something sinister, even malevolent in the act."

"Yes! While it always involves the unleashing of violence and cruelty, it is most often generated by the gratification of appetite." Kim thought a long moment before adding: "We shouldn't forget either that its ultimate aim involves bloodshed and destruction."

"It strikes me that as the supreme predator Satan follows the same pattern of predation as animals. They too are motivated by appetite. They too use violence and cruelty to destroy their victims with teeth and claw," Yong Sang replied.

"The difference is that unlike animals, the beast doesn't usually attack with teeth and claw. His teeth are deceit and his claws, temptation. He uses both to seduce and lure his victims into wrongdoing. However, like teeth and claw, wrongdoing also leads to perdition. In short, he traps individuals into destroying themselves so that the end result is the same as that of the animal predator."

"How in the world can puny mortals like us protect ourselves against that kind of an enemy that is, at the same time, immortal?"

Leesa was awakened out of the deepest sleep by loud muttering and movement coming from her daughter's bedroom. Getting out of bed and opening the door, she saw Serena in an angry fight, firing kicks, karate chops and head butts at an invisible assailant. The blows she threw were accompanied by the foulest language her mother had ever heard. Serena's wide open eyes convinced Leesa that her daughter was awake, but after she wrestled Serena back to bed, her daughter, without uttering a word, turned over abruptly and was fast asleep.

"We need to cling to our faith," Yong Sang answered the question his wife had posed. Our Creator has endowed us with the ethical armor-plate of a conscience that we must use to dictate our choice between good and evil."

"Darling, our armor plate is fraught with serious weaknesses. As creatures of passion and desire we are easily tempted into wrongdoing. Further, there are those who believe that evil is deeply embedded in the human heart and that Satan makes easy use of it to tempt and to lead us astray. If such is the case–and that seems very likely–what can an individual do to avoid temptation?"

"It's a losing battle, Kim. Can't you see? The odds are heavily stacked in Satan's favor. If we poor adults have serious problems avoiding temptation, how can we expect a teenager like Leesa, who is already flighty and delusional, to successfully resist such powerful urges?"

"Just as young prey animals need their elders to protect them by being always alert, so we, her elders, must do the same for Leesa."

"That my darling is easy to say, but almost impossible to do. How can we protect someone who despises us and refuses protection?"

"I agree it's a losing battle, but we just have to try. And since we're on the topic, I'd like to ask your opinion: "do you believe that evil can sometimes result in good, Yong Sang?"

"Yes," he answered, without a moment's hesitation or an explanation.

"Do you know that the French poet, Charles Baudelaire, composed a book of poems entitled *Les Fleurs du Mal*? Very roughly translated, the title means 'the flowers that blossom from evil.' Do you believe like him that there are instances where evil eventually results in good?"

"I suppose you are asking whether people who have committed evil acts can later rehabilitate themselves and lead worthy upstanding lives by benefitting others."

"Yes! But the conversions you mention are not limited to such people. Don't you find that the evil resulting from the planet's greatest catastrophes tend to unleash an outpouring of world-wide compassion? This virtue encourages those who are fortunate to do a great deal of good for the unfortunate victims of disaster. I also believe that we stagger around bowed down by the weight of shame and guilt that plagues us for the wrongs we've done. These 'secret weapons' are the whips we use to flog ourselves into leading more virtuous lives. They suppress our baser instincts, drain away our self-hatred, resurrect our self-respect and urge us to be better people. In short, good **can** result from evil. Without shame and guilt, we would surely become so deeply ensnared by evil that we would disappear into the vortex of sorrow that spirals down to despair.

"Are you saying that shame and guilt are the shields we unconsciously use against evil?" Yong Sang asked.

"I don't really know. What I do know is that without them urging us to become better individuals, the toll of suicides would be far higher."

"Mr. Sing, I noticed that there were many differences in the cave drawings of the stick animals and people. When I compared them with others that were more completely drawn, and saw arrowheads made of bone, stone and bronze, it seemed evident that different stages of man had left those records in the cave."

"Those artifacts no doubt speak the truth. But what did they tell you otherwise?"

"I began thinking about those long dead ancestors, wondering whether some of them had been there from the very dawn of time. Did they have dreams like mine? Did they believe, like me, that there was something out there somewhere, waiting to help them to complete their lives? Did they wonder like me, anxious and fearful about what the future might hold, about what they would become? Was their daily drudgery so onerous that in their struggle to survive they didn't have leisure time for dreaming? Were they content to lead their limited lives as hunters and cave dwellers or as farmers? Did some of them aspire to other pursuits? Did they have a yearning to better themselves like me and if so, what did they wish to become? Above all, did they ever realize their dreams and did it bring them the happiness they sought?"

"Miss, your thoughts, actions and especially your curiosity never ceases to amaze me!"

He was getting ready to leave the office when his phone rang: "Hello, John Ahn here."

"Hello John, this is Dang. Could you stop by my place on your way home? There's a problem that I'd like to discuss with you."

"Sure Dang. I'll be there in a little while." True to his word, John arrived a few minutes later.

"Ah, come in, come in." Dang looked at the outfit of his friend with a big smile and couldn't help ribbing him gently. "Your blazer, grey flannels, ascot and burnished loafers are as dazzling as ever," he said with a chuckle.

"Thanks. You must know that your compliments are what I live for," John replied with a sarcastic smirk. Now, what's the problem?"

"Wouldn't you like a drink first?"

"No thanks. Once we've discussed your problem, I've got to run. I'm taking the family out to supper. It's a surprise."

"Okay. As CEO of my family's private bank, I'm faced with a serous financial crisis."

"I suppose you mean the recent worldwide housing boom and bust."

"Exactly! It all began with the steep rise in house prices in the US over the last decade. It encouraged home owners to use the growing equity in their homes to refinance their mortgages at lower interest rates. This freed up huge amounts of cash through equity extraction. Then, after deregulation, several major financial institutions like Lehman Brothers, AIG, Freddie Mac, Merrill Lynch and Fanny Mae flooded the housing market by offering sub prime loans to borrowers who could just barely afford the homes they'd just bought."

"Right, and then with the unexpected rise in interest rates, millions of borrowers were unable to repay their loans. Thus, millions of foreclosures took place."

"To make matters worse," John stated, "unscrupulous US banks had boosted their own security by selling their loans to financial institutions around the world."

"The burst of the housing bubble in the US and the resulting blow to its economy, caused banking failures on a global scale," Dang continued. "Almost every bank had to sell some of its major assets to pay off its obligations."

"This led to a liquidity crisis which we in Korea are now experiencing. True?" John asked.

"Correct! Credit here further dried up as foreign investors withdrew capital to offset their own liquidity squeeze. Since however, our institutions were more scrupulous than our US counterparts, we ended up in somewhat better shape financially."

"But no doubt, you still have problems?"

"Exactly! That's why I want to discuss the steps I've decided to take to protect both my bank and my clients."

"Okay, go ahead."

"To offset the losses I and my family foresee, I propose to cut deeply into the profit margin that we now make until we can see how things develop in the future."

"And what about those small businesses that have payrolls to meet, and your mortgage holders who have monthly premiums to repay your bank? Are you going to foreclose on them following the American policy?"

"No! Thank God we have only a few businesses that are hurting badly. I've decided to carry those for the present until we see how things shape up. But it's the homeowners who have lost their jobs and can't afford to make their monthly payments that I'm really worried about."

"Well, what have you decided?"

"I'm willing to grant them a period of grace, say six months to a year, in which they pay only the interest?"

"That sounds like a worthwhile plan. It's exactly what I would have done. But, suppose the situation worsens?"

"Hopefully, that will be in the future. I'll have to decide on that eventuality if and when it happens."

"Good thinking! Regardless of what happens, a period of grace would be good strategy for the immediate present."

"I know that like the US banks, many of my Korean competitors won't be as generous. But when things improve, and they eventually will, those whom I've helped will develop stronger bonds with my bank, and their word of mouth advertizing will, I hope, bring new clients to join them."

"Dang, those are my thoughts exactly."

"John thanks for listening. It has helped to lessen my distress."

"You are very welcome! It's the least I could do. Now I must get going."

"Mrs. Ahn, in answering your question about the condition of your daughter, I can only tell you what I think, and what she should do to improve her health."

"I'd like to hear what you think, doctor."

"It is evident that the rapists have taken away the control of Serena's life. But eventually, she'll improve. When she feels better, I suggest she should attend a group session of rape counseling. It may be helpful for her to see how other victims react, certainly to hear their stories." A week later when Serena was feeling somewhat better, she followed the doctor's instructions and was introduced to a group session at which point its members were in the process of sympathizing with the rapists instead of their victims.

"They're misfits, incapable of controlling their urges. Can you imagine how badly they must have been abused in childhood," said one, her voice loaded with sympathy. "It's impossible not to feel sorry for them."

"Clinics should be set up for them," said another.

"Yes," agreed a third. "They need a hospital not a prison, but more than anything else, they need our sympathy, our prayers and all the help we can give them." And so, members of the group continued to pour out their sympathy and compassion for the world's congregation of sexual predators. Serena's reaction to the statements was not surprising.

"Mama, I'm so disgusted with what I heard that I feel both abused and betrayed by the outpouring of concern the group reserved for the rapists but refused their victims. I raged out of the room feeling more tainted than ever."

"Darling, I'm not at all surprised. I'd feel the same way."

When John saw the adverse effect that the group therapy session had on Serena, he began taking her for short walks that became longer each day. Within a week, their walks took them further and further away from home. The exercise and fresh air did wonders for Serena. After a week, her father no longer had to slow his pace of walking, and the long silences between them had become shorter and shorter. Most important, the exercise increased Serena's appetite and she soon regained her former taste for food. The piqued features and glazed eyes that had so distressed her parents were beginning to disappear.

"But what about your business, Dad?" Serena asked one day.

"I have many businesses but only one daughter. Your recovery is far more important to me," he had replied with a wry smile, adding: "I've told my executives to carry on in my absence, and explained that I'm taking care of my daughter. They understood." John thought it would be good therapy to take Serena into the mountains and to add to the elementary study of woodcraft that he had taught her previously. He had a plan in mind.

Together, they again rode into the *Jirisan National Park*, steering clear of the hiking routes leading to the many Buddhist temples. Instead they climbed towards the foothills of *Nogodan Mountain*. On the way, they followed game trails distinguishing between the tracks of raccoon and rabbit, deer and wild boar, ring-necked pheasant and black grouse that inhabited the thickly forested areas. Serena's enthusiastic response to their forest forays encouraged her father to prolong the adventures, but each time his destination was a different area of the vast mountain wilderness. Serena learnt the location of the deep pools below cascades in the river where the highly oxygenated white water attracted fish. She learnt to make snares to catch small game with the barest of essentials, "in the event," her dad said, "that you ever become lost in the forest." He showed her where edible plants grew, like wild onions and cabbage, non-poisonous mushrooms, certain juicy lilies, and roots like cattails that grew on the edge of lakes or marshes. All could be roasted, boiled or even mashed to make nutritious soup, stave off hunger and keep the body alive. He then took her to huge tangles of black, blue and red berry bushes where they ate their fill of the delicious fruit. Finally, he showed her how to make a safe fire, speeding up the process with hardened sap from pine and spruce trees. When, on one occasion, they remained in the mountains for a whole week. Only then did he think she was ready for his plan of action.

Father Murphy struggled with his secret shame while carrying on the work of God. He awoke every morning at 5 A.M. Following a routine, he fell on his knees, did his ablutions, ate two slices of buttered toast, dressed himself, and headed to the church to sing the Mass. Afterwards, he waited for his two vestrymen to hand the collection over to the sexton who put it into the steel safe, bolted the door and handed him the only key. He then returned home for a simple breakfast of porridge, toast and coffee that he fixed for himself while the key to the collection safe kept burning a hole in his pocket.

There were times when he couldn't keep the tormenting memories of his present and past to himself. Having no close friend in whom he could confide, he finally chose the sexton, Mr. Won since they spent so much time together. The sexton was a tall, thin man with a kindly face. His body was bent forward in a permanent stoop. His eyes, covered by spectacles seemed to be aimed at his feet and the swift movements of his head from side to side gave the impression that he was searching for something that he had lost. He was a pleasant, affable man devout in his duties to his parish priest and to his church.

One morning after Matins, Father Murphy felt so tormented that he needed to unburden himself. "Won," he said, "I wanted so badly to be what I was not, what I never have been, and perhaps what I never will be–someone with money in his pocket and a hot tasty meal warming his stomach."

"I don't understand," Won replied. "Was there something you wanted to buy with the money, Father, something you didn't have?"

"Yes and no. I don't really know how to explain this. There was nothing that I wanted to buy. The money in my pocket was there as a safeguard to stave off any crisis; especially the fear of starvation that, throughout my life, has pursued me like a rapacious beast."

"Since your family was so poor that your were faced with starvation, wasn't the Salvation Army, the Red Cross or local church groups there to offer free meals and soup kitchens?" Wasn't there some kind of state welfare being handed out to those in need?"

"There were such organizations helping the poor, but the sheer force of numbers of the starving was such that there was never enough to go round. I was the last of the many children born into a large Irish family of peasants. Like so many others, we suffered from the most numbing poverty. My parents kept fighting a constant battle to make ends meet, trying to prevent us all from starvation at a time when the nation itself was in the grip of terrible drought and famine."

"My family was poor too, but we always had enough to eat, even though it wasn't the food we would have chosen. There was always a huge pot of boiled potatoes and sometimes various kinds of pasta with which we could fill our stomachs. We had a few cows that gave us some milk, butter and cheese so we were never faced with the kind of poverty and starvation you describe."

"The deprivation has created in me a powerful urge to commit an act so sinful that it would be in violent conflict with my calling." He felt lighter just verbalizing his problem without details.

"Forgive me Father, but since you brought up the subject, did you ever give in to that craving?"

"Never! But the temptation keeps tantalizing me every moment of my life as a priest."

"Father, you are very highly regarded by your congregation. You never take time off for yourself. Every day after Matins, you hardly finish your meager breakfast before venturing out, regardless of the weather, to visit the sick and the bereaved scattered far and wide throughout this God-forsaken district.

"That," my dear Won, "is the work of every priest in every parish."

"But we, your parishioners, find it scandalous that the Catholic Church, with all its wealth, hasn't seen fit to build you proper living quarters or to be more generous with your stipend?"

"Won, I have no control over the Church, it's the other way around," he said jokingly. "As to my stipend, I just have to make do. I give thanks that there are generous families in the district like the Ahns and the Yongs. On weekends they send me hot meals. Both families also go a long way in finding all sorts of ways to benefit our parishioners. Besides, when all else fails, I can always scrounge something hot and tasty from Serena's soup kitchen."

"But Father, your cravings have piqued my curiosity. Did they arise from your envy of those families that were better off than yours?"

"Won, people here are poor, but their poverty can't compare with what we experienced back home. Here, everyone has a farm on which, besides his grain crops, he can grow vegetables. Some keep a few chickens, grow rice and a few even farm fish in their paddies. They can thus always find something to eat."

"That's not really true, Father. Their farms are mainly grain producing. They too are poor and perhaps no better off than you. Many were starving slowly until Serena's poultry, fertilization, rice and fish farming projects came along."

"We owned nothing, and at first, dad had a part time job as laborer that he lost once the drought hit. Then he, my mother, my brothers, sisters and I, like so many others, were sometimes forced to steal. Even then, there was never enough to feed the whole family. Many times I thought we would starve to death."

"During the Japanese colonization, we in Korea faced equally tough hardships. But I don't know of any families that were forced to steal."

"As a kid, my clothes were sewn from flour and crocus bags, passed down to me from my elders, I being the last child. I tired of hearing my parents quarreling over the little money they earned from odd jobs. The money evaporated long before our needs were met. I'm ashamed to admit that I and the half-starved members of my family actually bickered and fought over our food like a pride of vicious lions at a kill."

John approached Serena and questioned: "It's the end of summer, and you seem to be feeling much better. Are you up to spending a week in the mountains by yourself?"

"I think I am," she replied swiftly, taken aback by the unexpected challenge.

"Wait until you hear the rest of my challenge before you decide," her father cautioned.

"Go ahead Dad!" She said, forcing herself to sound far more confident than she felt, and wondering why her father would pressure her to undertake such a trial before she had fully recovered. Did his silences on their walks result from his guilt and shame for being absent when she needed him most?

"You can pick five items only to put into your backpack, besides the warm clothing you are permitted to wear. You leave with a single jumbo can of beans. If you succeed, you can name your reward." What if I don't, she thought, but didn't say.

"That sounds promising," she replied, forcing a smile. "When would you like me to start?"

"Now would be a good time, since you've already had a hearty breakfast." As an afterthought, he added: "if you decide to accept the challenge."

"Mama is out shopping. You know she'll be mad with you when she returns and finds out about your challenge."

"I'll cross that bridge when I come to it."

"Do I walk or go on horseback?"

"Your choice."

"I think I'll do both," she said, deciding that it would help to husband as much of her strength as she could before facing the ordeal ahead.

"Oh God," wailed Father Murphy after escorting Leesa from the confessional and bolting the church door behind her. Listening to the enormity of sin weighing on the hearts of his parishioners made him so sad that it was driving him to despair. That and the key in his pocket was creating the same kind of pressures that had so badly affected his nerves after the war. With his nerves raw and on edge, he always found it helpful to kneel in prayer alone in the silent church. Of late however, the stress building inside him kept forcing him towards that same troubled mental state that had hospitalized him after his tours of duty in the field hospital during the first Gulf War.

"Oh God," he moaned angrily, "if you won't help me to assist these persecuted people, why did you keep prodding me along this arid road?"

In that empty church, what he needed most was a brother priest to hear his confession. At that precise moment, he noticed a dimming of the lights as a sort of fog kept seeping into the church. He would then have sworn that someone shook his shoulder gently. He turned around and was astonished to see a priest, fully robed, standing in the aisle behind him. This must be an apparition, he first thought, being sure there was no one else in the church when he had shown Leesa out and locked himself in. He wondered if his depression was making him delusional, for the fog was getting worse. Was he imagining what he so badly needed or was this a new priest the bishop had decided to send him? Hadn't he searched the church and found that he was alone, he thought, beginning to feel the cold creeping into his bones? Had he not locked the doors to repel the cold? Then, how had that priest materialize from nowhere? The myriad questions going through his mind were making him more and more uneasy; more and more confused.

He was about to ask the priest to hear his confession, when he detected an unearthly smell surrounding him. The priest then pointed to the confessional, and began making his way there. The newcomer surprised Father Murphy by knowing what he needed without being told. Even more confused, he followed but couldn't stop wondering how the stranger, like the fog, the cold and the foul smell, had appeared out of nowhere. Still more mysterious, how did the visitor know the Father needed confession? Was his depression again playing games with his mind?

"John, what madness drove you to dare Serena to spend a week in the mountains by herself, and with only a can of beans for a meal? Have you lost your reason or did you want her to get lost and die of starvation?"

"Darling, this is late autumn. It's still quite warm so there's little to fear for someone who knows the mountain wilderness as well as Serena. I've spent a lot of time with her there, making sure she's very knowledgeable about her surroundings in the outdoors. I know that she's resourceful enough to take care of herself. However, I would not have issued such a challenge in winter, although I believe that she'd manage quite well even then."

"You'd better be right, John," his wife stated with menace in her voice. "Sometimes I really don't know what gets into that mind of yours."

In growing anxiety, John began attacking his fingernails

Chapter 18

"My father would hold a family meeting to explain his plan the priest told Won. 'We'll visit the market when it's packed with people. At such times, vendors busy with their customers will be less vigilant. You'll all form a line behind me with the youngest member last. I'll leave the family at one end of the most crowded vegetable stall and go to the other end. When I attract the vendor's attention, Annie will touch you on the shoulder,' he'd say to me. My father knew that the eyes of the vendors would be focused on the adults and adolescents rather than on a five year old kid. It was drilled into me that I should wait on my sister's signal before making my move.

"At the market, my dad would lift me onto his shoulder, take me into a deserted corner and whisper what he wanted me to do. 'Son, are you hungry?' He would ask. When I nodded, he would say: Your brothers and sisters are hungry too. I've told them to surround you on one corner of the stall. I will attract the vendor's attention at the other end. At that moment your sister, Annie, will touch you on the shoulder. Do you know what you have to do then?"

"Whip vegetables from the stall into her hands. I'd whisper in a trembling voice."

"Good boy! Now, I'll go to the other end of the stall, okay? When I nodded, he'd caution: "Wait until Annie touches you, before you make your move. If you do that we'll all have something to eat."

"My God," Won said to Father Murphy. "It's hard to believe that a father would encourage his son to steal, especially at your age. But did the plan work?" He asked, his voice alive with curiosity and impatience.

"It certainly did! On those occasions when we hadn't eaten for nearly two days, my dad resorted to a different plan."

"I keep telling you dear. It's wrong to keep Serena under your thumb. She doesn't need protection."

"So, Mr. Know-it-all, what does she need?"

"To build her self-confidence. It will help her to regain her strength and to recover completely. She needs every opportunity she can get to express herself."

"Doesn't she express herself in her painting, her karate, her pigeon racing, her poultry farming, her fertilization, rice and fish farming projects, her success in her studies, *dear*?" Her emphasis on the last word underscored the irony in her question.

"Can't you see? Each of those pursuits brings out a different facet of her personality. She needs room to develop, to grow even more, especially in the area of her self-confidence after her violation. That, more than anything else, is vital to her complete recovery."

"Is there some reason that makes you want to pressure her? Are you trying to compensate for your irresponsible act of playing squash when you should have been waiting for her?"

"That remark is unworthy of you Leesa," John stated, while hoping his wife didn't know how close her statement came to the truth. As he nibbled at his nails, he thought it necessary to strike back.

"What I'm trying to do is to give her the freedom that you're so keen to take away from her. Don't you see? Serena has no interest in the things like social position, sophisticated society or money that you consider so important. She's not cut out for the ordinary, like the grinding routine of office work in my organization. She's a go-getter, a leader, not a follower. She's one of those rare individuals obsessed with goodness, just plain goodness. With the recovery of her self-confidence she'll have a chance to try her wings even more. I can't help thinking that she'll make a life out of helping others." Oh God, he thought, I hope I'm right. He knew that he had never forgiven himself for his transgression that had had such tragic results for his daughter. As he continued to munch at his fingertips, he felt bound to ask himself whether his guilt over the misfortune he had caused was making him push Serena towards unnecessary risk or was her welfare his motive, as he believed. Perhaps, he decided that the truth hung in equal balance between his guilt and his desire for her welfare.

With heavy heart, Serena thought deeply before carefully choosing the five items. She then had a discussion with herself weighing the pros and cons of the situation. After all, she said, it's one thing to learn the elements of wood-craft with your father standing next to you, teaching you what he knows. It's quite another to undertake the exercise in the wilderness for a whole week by yourself. What kept worrying her most was the possibility of her nightmares recurring and having no one to turn to.

Should that happen, you'll just have to face the problem if and when it presents itself. Now, concentrate on the five things you'll need.

I'll take a large box of safety matches; dip their heads into melted wax so they'll remain dry even after getting wet. I'll choose a very thick, huge plastic sheet, the size of two large blankets, cut it in two and fold them both flat.

Don't forget a sharp machete to cut firewood and other things.

I daren't forget that, and a small sharp fish hook tied to a few yards of fish line.

What's your fifth item going to be?

Some yards of bailing wire rolled into a small flat circle to make it fit into my backpack.

Don't forget to take warm clothing.

I'll wear thick socks inside hiking boots, put on thick woolen trousers, a t-shirt and sweater with a zipper that I can open to remain cool in the warm autumn sunshine. I'll put my heavy hooded parka and thick woolen mittens into my backpack with the large can of beans and opener, before mounting Will.

So you're riding?

Yes, she thought. Her heart pounded anxiously to the hoof beats of her horse as she headed towards the foothills. Will's long, loping stride ate up the miles. On her way, she wondered what the next week of her life would bring. I'll use the time on horseback to focus on the best way to tackle the week's challenges. When we get deep into the foothills on the mountain, I'll turn Will loose to let him find his way home.

"Once my dad asked the vendor a question while pointing to produce that was furthest away from me, my siblings, screening me from in front and behind, would lean far over the stall staring in my father's direction.

"You're making an illegal act sound like an exciting adventure."

"As a five year old, you don't contradict your dad. When Annie touched my shoulder, my little hands flew. Tomatoes, carrots, cucumbers, cabbage, potatoes, corn on the cob, anything and everything small and edible disappeared into tiny hands. My siblings would swiftly conceal our next meal under their coats."

"And if you were caught? Was there a plan for that too?"

"Yes, my dad thought of everything. If I were caught, Mama would pretend to scold me while replacing the stolen item on the stall. She knew that few vendors would accuse a five year old kid of theft. In fact, most would probably let him keep the stolen item if it wasn't too expensive."

"Although your father's plan sounds foolproof, still, in your place, I would have been terrified of being caught. Just thinking about what you had to go through gives me the willies. But I suppose after doing it over and over so many times, you weren't even scared, right?"

"Not scared, Won. Petrified!"

"Father," Leesa told the priest, "I kept trying to put into practice your advice to concentrate on the words of my prayer as I said my penance. But despite my effort to concentrate, I found that my mind wandered constantly and I seldom finished the prayer I had begun."

"You just have to keep trying, my child," the priest stated.

"Whenever the desire to throttle my parents returned to taunt me, I realized that my prayers had remained unanswered, since the urge to be malicious was still firmly in place." Reaching back into the past, she recalled the desperate effort she had made to avoid the occasion of sin. She begged her parents to continue their customary evening walk around the farm without her, but her father wouldn't hear of it."

"Leesa make an effort!" He would say.

"Dad, I'm exhausted after a really hard day at school. Please let me stay at home and rest," I'd plead. But her father would call her forward to join them, stretching out his hand for her to hold.

"Come along dear, you can lean on me," he'd say, coaxing her forward with a broad smile and drawing her close against his side. She could feel the heat radiating from his body. Delicious warmth would steal over her and funnel its way down between her thighs. As the wintry darkness seeped into her soul, the feelings she dreaded began to take hold; hatred for her mother filling her breast, lust for her father suffusing her loins. Struggling against her wicked thoughts and feelings, she tried lagging behind, permitting her parents to walk ahead, hand in hand. But her father beckoned to her again, insisting that she accompany them. As he clutched her to his side, a flurry of improper thoughts crowded her brain as a cold sweat glazed her forehead.

"You see," he'd say. "Once we hold each other tightly, it's not so bad." She continued walking in the blissful confusion of shame and guilt, her head bowed and pressed tightly against his side; her face, deeply flushed, contorted with passion."

Serena's conscience kept contradicting her about what she should do as she made her way to the flat-topped hillock. It stood well above a large pool in the river below white water rapids.

What are you doing?

I'm choosing a place to sleep that's safe. This site is close to a large pool below a cataract. But it's above the reach of any flooding that might take place during the night. Hopefully, I'll be able to catch some fish later on in the highly oxygenated pool.

You're thinking of food after you just ate? You should be making a lean-to for shelter and sleep as dad did?

Be quiet. I've selected this 'V,' formed between the huge trunks of two deadfalls lying flat on the ground with a few covering branches above. When I remove the stones and sweep the pebbles from between them I'll have a place to sleep.

That's good thinking. Now collect a lot of tiny branches covered with leaves and make a thick carpet for your bed.

Why don't you shut up? Can't you see I'm doing just that?

So you're improvising? That's great! Now is the time that you should cut a fishing pole to try for your next meal.

If you don't mind, I'll first tie the four corners of one plastic sheet to the branches above my bed and spread it in a canopy over where I'll be sleeping. I'll tie it in such a way that it slopes slightly towards one of my feet.

I get it that the canopy is a shelter in case of rain and will also trap heat from your fire. But why the slope towards one of your feet?

That's where I'll catch rain water in my empty can after I've eaten the beans.

Excellent thinking! Now, collect the firewood you need and store it under the canopy at your head in case of rain. You can use the other half of the plastic as a blanket during the night, should the need arise.

Those are helpful thoughts, she had to admit. It's a pity you can't offer physical help, she thought as she set about collecting the fallen twigs and dry branches that littered the area.

Isn't verbal help enough? Maybe you should sweep the open end of the 'V' clean of any flammable stuff to prevent your fire from spreading during the night.

Good idea! But first I'll bring up some rocks from the river bed and arrange them into a tight semicircle enclosing the far edge of the fire site.

Why undertake all that heavy lifting?

With the fire blazing at some distance from my feet, the rocks close on its other side will reflect its warmth into my snug bower bed. Even in fall, the temperature can drop alarmingly once the sun sets.

I suppose you're right. The night can be very chilly.

After a while she made a large mound of the firewood she had collected and then began searching to select an adequate pole for fishing before putting the firewood under the shelter of the canopy.

When Father Murphy joined the priesthood many years ago, he regarded with pride and joy his entrance as a foot-soldier into the ranks of God's army. As a young chaplain during the first Gulf War, he was posted to a small field hospital a couple of miles from the Front. The fighting there had been furious during the first days of his arrival and the casualties had been returning in droves. He'd spent too many eighteen hour days and nights on his feet. He'd held limbs with wounds that needed to be cauterized or amputated. He'd commiserated with the wounded and ministered to the dying. He'd taken notes of their last requests and written letters to mothers, wives, and sweethearts. Not surprisingly, he was punch drunk with fatigue, unable to keep his eyes open almost asleep on his feet.

The heat together with the stench in that overcrowded space was overwhelming. When he couldn't stand it any longer, he began staggering towards the exit to catch his breath and recover his senses. At that moment, an orderly stopped what he was doing and stuck out his arm to bar the priest's way. With a push, the orderly exchanged places with the priest in front of a stretcher and whispered: "Take over Father. I have to go elsewhere and tend the living." His last words were: "He needs you more than me."

Only when everything was ready for the night to come did Serena think of food. And once again her conscience began its nagging.

I can't believe you're thinking of food. Dusk is more than two hours away and there are things to do yet.

I know that! I discovered a game trail with some rabbit droppings along which I intend to set some snares. But, I haven't eaten since breakfast, and after the long trek up the mountain, preparing my bed, cutting firewood and lugging those heavy rocks from the riverbed and arguing with myself, I'm famished.

Oh, poor baby! So, what are you going to do?

I'll bury the thick end of a sapling deep into the earth, securing it with stones dug into the ground around its base. I'll hook a branch around its flexible tip so that it bends down to the earth, above the rabbit trail. With my bailing wire, I'll hang a noose from its flexible tip across the narrowest defile in the trail. I've blocked either side of the defile with sticks pressed into the soil to form a tunnel. When Mr. Rabbit sticks his head into the noose and begins struggling, the noose in the bailing wire will tighten. Tomorrow, morning, I'll see if my trap is foolproof.

Let the noose hang about four inches above the ground so the head of Mr. Rabbit will enter the noose and spring the trap. And if you set another snare some distance away, you'll still have time to cut a fishing pole. If you hurry, you might even catch a fish for supper.

Can't you just simmer down! She hissed before continuing her work. At about one hundred yards further on, she set a second snare that was different. She took a heavy boulder that was flat and placed it over a broad flat rock embedded in the earth. She then lifted one end open like a yawning mouth and used a single ten inch stick to prop it up at its extreme outer edge. Next, she tied one end of fishing line to the top end of the prop, passed it around a low thick shrub growing ahead of the open 'mouth' and then back into the middle of the lower rock. The other end of the line she attached to a juicy wild carrot and placed a stone on the line just ahead of the bait to keep it tight. The slightest movement of the prop would dislodge the top boulder. It would fall and crush the intruder. Feeling satisfied with her improvised snare, she opened her large can of beans, started a fire and was about to congratulate herself for what she'd done. So far, she thought, things had gone rather well. But her thoughts of congratulations had come too quickly. There was a sudden change in the weather, and before she could warm her beans, the skies opened. With a roar, the rainstorm struck. Torrents of water kept drumming on her plastic roof, thoroughly drenching her firewood. Fortunately, she remained dry under her shelter, but without a fire, she had to eat half her can of beans cold. Being wrapped in her plastic blanket trapped some of her body heat, but the night was chilly and though fully dressed, she kept shivering. In her sleep, some unknown occurrence had triggered another relapse. Lurid dreams kept waking her so that all night long she tossed and turned between sleep and wakefulness on her bed of leaves. Tears burnt the back of her eyes making her feel miserable, lost and empty. When sleep finally came, it brought debasing images that stamped themselves anew into her consciousness. She awoke confused and terrified, screaming for her mother. Being alone, she twisted and turned trying vainly to sleep for the remainder of the night. A brilliant start to my week! She thought, on awakening to bright sunlight the following morning.

"Father, whenever I visit, I'm appalled at the poverty in which the diocese forces you to live." Won told his friend. "Don't you know that the last priest refused to accept this one bedroom hovel and appealed to the bishop for a transfer?"

"Yes, and he got it. Anyway, the bishop stated that I was admirably suited for this post, being the only priest intimate with poverty and starvation. What he said was grim, sad and deeply ironic, but true."

"Father, you're as poor as the poorest farmer in this God forsaken district. Your parishioners can't understand why you won't complain to the bishop about the dilapidated lodgings and the meager stipend."

"I can't complain. Since I believe that God has placed me here, I have to accept His will."

"Father, it pains me to see my parish priest struggling to prepare his own meals on a two-burner hotplate that doubles as his heating stove in winter. Worse, the meager amounts you cook are barely enough to keep body and soul together."

"Won, things aren't so bad. I get meals on week ends from thoughtful parishioners."

"Father, we your parishioners are amazed that you continue baptizing the children, visiting the sick, marrying the couples and finally burying the dead without complaint. You hardly have time to sleep."

"At my age, the body doesn't need more than a few hours sleep."

Serena awoke cold, tired, hungry and miserable. Since the day was sunny, warm and beautiful, she did her ablutions in the stream below. When finished, she collected dry bark and sap from the underside of felled trees, made a fire and heated the remainder of her beans for breakfast. She placed the damp firewood to dry near the new fire but out of reach of the flames. Then, she hurried to examine her snares. The first was empty, but the second had caught a rabbit. She reset the snares, cut a long flexible fishing pole the end of which she attached to her hook and line. Concealing herself behind a huge rock on the river bank, she then tied a wooden plug to the fishing line, two feet above the worm-baited hook. It would act as a bobber on the line that she lowered gently into the water. The bait hung just above the bottom of the pool. The trout were ravenous, the hook was sharp, and she soon had three trout gutted and cleaned, with their severed heads minus the gills in her bean can. She then split the fish open, each one held together like an open book, before seasoning them with wild onions. She threaded a long, thin stick broadside through the flesh of each one and grilled them slowly over the fire. They were tender, tasty and filling. She gutted, skinned and cleaned the rabbit, seasoned it and hung it high from an overhead branch out of the reach of critters. It would be her next meal in case her snares remained empty. That done, she added diced wild onions, mushrooms, wild cabbage and water to the fish heads in the bean can and made a rich tasty soup for supper. The next hour she spent cutting and collecting dry firewood for the night to come. When lit, it would help dry the rest of the damp firewood from the night before. After surviving her first day and night, the nervous apprehension she had felt at being alone in the wilderness was somewhat less daunting.

"My father, followed by the family, would patrol the market searching for an inattentive vendor. Won, you must understand that we were seldom able to steal enough to satisfy the appetites of the whole family. But on a successful day, it would mean fewer mouths to feed."

"How would you manage on a bad day?"

"We would visit those stalls on which the produce had remained too long. Often, they were almost bare since other families had cleared them before we got there. Thus, my father would end up using the little money he had to bargain for vegetables, fish or meat that others had rejected."

"You're telling me that you ate food that was already spoiled?"

"Long practice had made my parents skilled at cooking with strong seasonings, especially curry and black pepper to mask the smell of food that had seen better days."

Won listened to the priest with rapt attention, trying to imagine how he would have reacted in similar situations. After a pause, he asked: "You must have had a terrible childhood!"

"Not at all. We were a close family and passed the time playing board games. Then, both my parents told exciting stories about all sorts of interesting things to lessen our pangs of hunger. Besides, I had had nothing with which to compare my youth. What I'll never forget is the terror of being caught that overwhelmed me. The fear knotted up my insides, every long day and during the nights."

Chapter 19

"You couldn't have been successful every time!"

"Being a well trained monkey, I was caught only once. An iron grip immobilized my tiny hand with an apple in its grasp. Terror and nausea so overwhelmed me that I developed a chronic fit of vomiting, and became so ill that it brought an end to my career as a thief. My mother refused to let my father again put me through that ordeal."

"And what did the vendor do?"

"He gave me the apple."

"In the narrow stretcher before me, the bloody entrails were spilling out of a jagged hole in the   stomach of a young soldier. His bulging eyes looked on in panic as his blood-stained hands kept trying to stuff his bluish pink intestines back into his stomach. But with a wicked will of their own, they kept sliding from his hands onto the stretcher. The dying lad kept looking at me with the saddest eyes I had ever seen. Worst of all were the howls and screams of those having their arms or legs amputated. Their high-pitched shrieks had long since ceased to be human. The animal sounds and wide-eyed terror pleaded vainly with doctor and priest charged with severing their limbs. There were other wounded young men, traumatized and glassy eyed. They kept twisting in pain, silently playing at being heroic. When I could stand it no longer, I escaped to get a breath of fresh air."

"I waited a moment for my 'apparition' to intervene, but he remained as silent as a tomb. Did I really follow a priest to the confessional, or had my delusional state caused me to fantasize? Was I imagining what I so badly needed, or was I alone in the confessional talking to myself?

After that first night, the remainder of Serena's wilderness week fell into a routine of collecting firewood, setting snares, fishing and scouting through the forest for berries, wild onions, mushrooms and wild cabbage. She spent the early evening cooking her supper–fish, rabbit, pheasant or grouse–before going to bed at dusk and sleeping under her canopy. The heat reflected from the semicircle of rocks beyond the fire kept her warm and snug. The nightmares never returned and the weather held for the remainder of her stay. A number of times, she raided some bird nests to have a constant supply of eggs that she hard boiled in her bean can for breakfast. This feast would be followed by some of the berries she had stored in the hollow of a tree. On evenings, the smell of cooking often attracted a family of raccoons or a curious coyote. She threw them scraps so they reappeared each evening at dinner time promptly as though she had rung a bell. Her constant companion was a fidgety squirrel. Every time she threw him a few pine cones he kept chattering contentedly and so she always had company for dinner. She treasured his visits since they made inroads into the silence and loneliness of her vigils. She spent time gathering other tit-bits for him in appreciation.

Once she had taken care of her chores, she would journey into the forest and conceal herself in the underbrush to watch wild game as they went about their business. On one occasion, she saw a sow and her wild boar family rooting around for nuts, and another time, two does kept nibbling daintily at different bushes, oblivious of her presence. Suddenly, a magnificent buck with prominent antlers came striding regally out of the bush. He had sent his emissaries ahead to make sure it would be safe for him to venture into the open. The arrows shot from her makeshift bow often hit their mark, but instead of penetrating the hides of the animals she targeted, they bounced off harmlessly chasing away her quarry.

However, her bird's nests, snares, fishing pole, soup can, wild vegetables and berry patches provided her with more than enough to satisfy her needs. Despite the setbacks of being drenched by rain, frozen by cold, humiliated by escaping quarry and confronted by empty snares, she was alive and well. After her first two days and nights survival in the wilderness, she was no longer apprehensive about the days and nights that followed. Indeed, the rest of the week turned out to be a series of exciting adventures. Freed of her fears, it finally dawned on her why her father had issued the challenge. On her return, he greeted her effusively: "Darling, I'm so proud of you," he said, his voice choked with affection, admiration and what appeared to be relief. "Name your reward!" Realizing that his challenge had been aimed at boosting her flagging self-confidence, she hugged him tightly and whispered: "You've already given me that Dad. Thanks!"

"Father," he explained to his invisible visitor in the confessional: "the nightmares I kept having seemed so much like dire warnings that I felt an urge to preach my fears to my congregation. At first, I was reluctant to do so since those fears were based on the increased wickedness of my penitents and it wasn't Christian for me to judge them. Then, my warnings would suggest that I saw myself as a prophet. My listeners would believe I was treating my dreams as prophecy and would consider such conduct the height of arrogance. Consequently, I remained silent for a long time before preaching to them what I saw. I explained to my congregation that previously, these same symptoms had caused me to be hospitalized after the atrocities I had witnessed at the front. At that time I told them that I was diagnosed as being delusional, experiencing episodes that played out in my mind but had no basis in reality. Of course, that admission caused many members of my flock to disregard my 'prophecy.' The truth is that I felt it necessary to be honest."

"I fear for us," he told his congregation. "Repeated temptation has weakened our resolve to remain pure. Sin and iniquity, like virulent diseases, are roaring across the earth spreading their contagion. I see the destruction of whole cities struck by flood and fire, with hordes of the dead carpeting the landscape. I am no prophet. Still, I feel that I would be failing in my duty as your priest if I did not express my beliefs to you." He became so focused on telling his story that he had completely forgotten he was not alone. It was then that his strange visitor finally spoke."

Alone in the mountains, Serena had time to think about her future. She believed that somewhere out there, far greater challenges than were posed by simply living and working in a big city, lay in store for her. Yet, she still had no idea what those challenges might be. The truth was that the magical stories her father had told about that far off land, chock full of mountain wilderness and wildlife, had inspired her with an impulse to travel. She conceived images of a land where mysterious adventure always seemed to be beckoning; the kind she yearned to experience for herself. Yet, the images she cherished were so far out of reach that while she indulged her fantasies of wanderlust, there were stirrings of discontent and disappointment within her about the serene and pointless existence she had been leading. Not only was life passing her by, but the person responsible for letting that happen was her.

The capital city exerted little influence upon her, though she knew it certainly offered more of a challenge than her farm. Yet, she didn't think that particular challenge would be sufficient to fulfill someone of her temperament and tastes. Still, if she were asked what would bring her the fulfillment she sought, she would not have been able to say. She did know that she longed to travel, and this posed an eternal problem for her. To be anywhere else meant that she would have to desert her family and all the things about her home and country that she held so dear. She knew it would be impossible to cross continents and oceans without leaving home? There seemed no means of escape from the mental trap that she had set herself.

Leesa promised herself that she would beg off from walking around the farm with her parents on the following evening to 'avoid the occasion of sin.'

"Father, I didn't want a repetition of the previous shameful experience." When she explained to her father that she'd rather stay at home as she was feeling unwell, he began fussing over her, pressing his hand against her forehead, cheek, and neck to feel if her skin was hotter than usual.

"Did you have a fever?"

"No. But his closeness, the odor of his masculinity and his touch electrified me with a delicious shiver of warmth. Unseemly thoughts crowded my brain and set fire to my body."

"Under all that stress, did you misbehave?"

"No. But it was all I could do to restrain myself from grabbing his head and covering his mouth with hot passionate kisses. Instead, I fought against my base desires, willing my limbs to remain inert, immobile. But while I kept my eyes downcast and my body limp passion raged within me."

"Father Murphy," the voice from the confessional stated: "I trust there's a point to your endless digression!" The mellow voice paused: "You blame your fatigue, the claustrophobic atmosphere, the odor of the hospital, and even the symptoms of your past delusions. In fact, you blame everything but yourself.

In racing away to get relief, you abandoned your post, neglected your duty. Is that the reason you keep excusing your irresponsible conduct?" Ending in a chuckle, the mellow voice increased the sting of its rebuke. Even at this point, the priest still couldn't tell if the voice he heard was in his head, or coming through the grill of the confessional? He actually winced, as though struck with a whip, before stammering his reply.

"No! No! The sea of pain around me brought back a statement that a fellow seminarian had expressed a long time ago."

"And you're no doubt eager to let me hear those priceless words?"

"I didn't understand what he said at the time."

"Pray, do let me hear those words of wisdom."

"Suffering," he said, "should be regarded as a cardinal virtue."

"Is that really possible? Surely the Church has been teaching for centuries that suffering is a tool of the devil. So, how can one of Satan's most potent weapons be elevated to the level of a virtue?" There was a chuckle in the voice making Father Murphy unsure whether what he had said was rational or part of his delusion.

"I believe what he meant was that suffering elicits from the observer an outpouring of the deepest sympathy and compassion. Those virtues inspire in us the most amazing acts of generosity and self-sacrifice. In this context, suffering should be regarded as a virtue." He didn't think it necessary to make his case by using the outpouring of compassion and generosity that followed the devastation of Nine-Eleven, the Tsunami of South East Asia, or the flooding in New Orleans. So sometimes, good can come out of evil," he added with firmness in his voice.

This time, a sharply in-drawn breath accompanied the silence of the stranger priest. He reacted like someone who had known the answer all along and pretended that it had come as a surprise."

Although Leesa failed in everything she undertook to rid herself of her curse, she refused to give up the fight. Since library, prayer, confession and a galaxy of priests had all proved useless, she abandoned them and instead, focused her full attention on God Himself. She was seething with rage at her wasted efforts, as with humiliation from her many failures. She remembered how she began talking to God and how, without being able to stop herself the anger gushed from her heart.

"Perhaps you can tell me Father Murphy? Is there a point to this interminable irrelevance?"

"Yes! Oh yes there is! He replied quickly. "The scenes of the dead and dying brought the awful power and presence of Satan sharply into focus. It was the first time that I recognized the overwhelming power the beast wields. Only then was I also aware of the cunning he uses to engender hatred in men and nations, to spread the germs of warfare and bloodshed. At that time, I believed that human pain and misery were chiefly associated with warfare. But today, so many years later, I find that away from the battlefield and even in peacetime, there is in each parish just as much pain and misery in the human family and it comes from the same source."

"And what drove you to make such an amazing discovery?"

"Every day it is he who targets the world of the flesh he wishes to destroy. And every day his victims confess to me their lies and betrayals, their fornication and infidelity. They cry in despair about their broken marriages, the molestation of their sons and daughters, the myriad diseases, drugs and alcohol that devastate them and their families."

Over and over, Father Murphy's nightmares returned forecasting widespread calamity on the planet. He preached again and again about this nocturnal torment that was blighting his life, and because of their repetition, he believed that they were a divine warning. He repeated tirelessly that his words did not mean he considered himself a prophet. However, despite his sermons, he knew his warnings fell on deaf ears for the number of confessions had escalated alarmingly. He despaired over the success of the predatory beast that was silently stalking him and his flock.

Before she knew it, Serena's nose was thick with the scent of animal dung. Panting from her race to escape her pursuers, she couldn't help but inhale its pungent scent. The gorge rose in her throat forcing her to stop running as its bitter taste made her retch again and again. Although nothing emerged from her mouth, the nausea didn't go away and the urge to vomit continued. The terror of being caught remained, spurring her on. She again began running, her throat dry and burning, convinced that at any moment her demons would fall upon her and rip the flesh from her bones.

At their secret cave, her father often talked about his life in British Columbia, where he had gone to further his studies. He had become friendly with another student, James, one of the First Nation's people, who later invited him to experience the simple life of the reservation. There, he often spent part of the summer months learning about a culture that was so very different in its simplicity from his. The reservation was in the vicinity of Pink Mountain, a hamlet in the far north of the Province. With James as teacher, her father explored the interminable forests surrounding their reservation, learning to hunt and to fish. What he also found exciting were the stories that the old Chief told around a campfire about the deeds of his heroic ancestors: "In warring with other tribes they armed themselves with only spear, bow and arrow," he said. It was their strength and courage as warriors and their skill as trackers and as camouflage artists that allowed them to outmaneuver and overcome so many of their enemies. With such slight weapons, they were able to track and dispatch buffalo, elk, moose, caribou, black and grizzly bear, big horned sheep, deer and even cougar."

The Chief also related that "the tribe depended on a few of these braves to keep their larder supplied with game." He spoke of those individuals as though they belonged to a superior race. "They were tall, powerfully built braves," he boasted, "with deep chests, arm and thigh muscles hard and bulging. While tracking the animals they hunted and finally following their prey, they would run for days on end, starting at dawn and stopping only at dusk. They could maintain a steady mile-eating jog that they would repeat each morning and thought nothing of bringing back a three hundred pound buck or small elk slung across their shoulders. They were silent men, as strong, savage and cunning as the beasts they hunted." Her dad felt that the Chief was exaggerating somewhat when he stated that "the runners began their training as preteens and on reaching adolescence, continued practicing against horses, for distance of course, not for speed."

Another of his stories was about "the braves who fed the tribe with fish, armed with only a broad-bladed paddle. The fisherman would stand up to his ankles in the shallows of the river facing the bank a few feet away. The salmon, in these high reaches of the river, had to wriggle upstream with half their bodies out of the water. The 'fisherman' would place the paddle blade edgewise to the flow and flick fish from the stream onto the riverbank. His 'assistant' would slip the sharp end of his hook-shaped stick through the gills where it would join the rest of their catch. When the fisherman was tired, he would change places with his assistant." My dad had the distinct impression that the Chief was laying the groundwork for the braves of his tribe to recognize the strength, courage and cunning of their ancestors. He portrayed them as though they had already attained the status of heroes. But clearly, that was not enough to satisfy the Chief. He presented these individuals in a manner that surpassed mere heroism by attaching qualities to them that separated them from the common man. He used words and deeds to make sure that they mesmerized; even transcended. The language he used would encourage his braves to exalt them into legend. Perhaps the Chief was telling these stories as a moral builder, to unify the tribe and enhance its reputation. At any rate, such stories fired Serena with the desire to experience for herself the kind of adventures her father related. Unfortunately, she knew that her ambition was no more than a pipe-dream, since the setting of those stories was in a land she could only reach in her imagination.

"Yes, yes! I know," said the irritated voice from the other side of the confessional. "Satan is the ultimate archfiend, the cause of all man's wickedness. On the other hand, man is a saint, and totally blameless, right Father?" Father Murphy began shivering as he braced himself to withstand the foul smell that accompanied the cold. The gentle voice of the stranger was still smooth and beautiful despite the evident note of sarcasm and irritation. It made the priest think more carefully before replying. Could he be imagining all this? He asked himself. Wasn't this illusory manner of talking to himself one of the same symptoms that caused him to be hospitalized?

"No, no! Man is not blameless," he replied. "He possesses a God-given conscience together with the free will to act in favor of good or evil. So when he accepts and then acts on the infernal lie that anything good can be attained by wrongdoing, he incriminates himself."

"Oh, it's so good to know that you don't blame all the woes of mankind on Satan," the mellifluous voice replied, still laced with more than a hint of mockery. But Father Murphy was so deeply focused on the secret poison he was about to disgorge and the sense of shame it caused him that he was no longer paying attention to his confessor.

In spite of the cold, he was sweating and since his heartbeat had accelerated he had to take a series of deep breaths before continuing. He grew hesitant, ashamed of disclosing the foul thoughts and inner contamination that he had been battling these past years. "Satan was not content to limit his attacks to the laity," he continued in a hushed voice. "In the past few decades he has extended his circle of corruption to include the clergy. Not only has he corrupted many of my brothers inciting them to molest their charges," but, he blurted out shamefully: "of late, I too have become ensnared by his evil. A craving has possessed me to steal from the collection that lies in my safe, and from time to time I have the scent of my own corruption in my nostrils." The strange priest was quick to respond.

"And no doubt, Satan is again to blame for *your* evil, *your* corruption." There was repressed venom in the voice. "No vicious criticism should attach to you. No evil deed should stain your innocent soul!" The venomous stream of sarcasm and ridicule poured through the grill. "Isn't that right Father?"

"I'm not sure," he said, again taken aback by the pointed rebuke, the sharp irony in his tone. "I only know that the infernal urge has poisoned my blood, rages along my arteries and ends by tempting me into wrongdoing."

"Surely you have a 'God-given conscience? Surely you have the 'willpower to act in favor of good or evil? Why haven't you used those exceptional gifts and resisted?" The stranger challenged maliciously, using Father Murphy's own statements to wound him with the sharp blade of his irony.

"I have resisted but I know that I won't succeed much longer. Each day the urge grows stronger." His voice had dropped to a whisper, revealing his shame, and his guilt. He felt that the world had become a morass of sin, and now he too was a part of its corrupting influence. Of late, he was finding it almost impossible to look at himself in the mirror. Worse, he could no longer pray. These were both symptoms of his earlier depression.

"Oh Father," he pleaded, "Help me to resist; to remain pure. If I should fall by the wayside, what help will I afford my brothers in our war against Satan?"

There was a silence. Then, the musical voice from the grill chuckled: "Have no fear, my saintly friend. You won't have the chance to help your brothers. You'll be too busy fighting your own war." Another long silence followed.

Chapter 20

When Father Murphy rushed to the other side of the confessional, he was astonished to find it empty. In confusion, he pondered long and hard over the uncanny 'interview' he had just had. The musical voice and the words of the speaker were still ringing in his ears, but did they come from the confessional or from his own mind? Through innuendo and sarcasm then overt criticism and challenge, the invisible cleric has erased all guilt from the archfiend. Man alone, he had indicated, was responsible for his evil deeds.

His mind was knotted in turmoil and fear as he wondered about the incident. Had it all been a charade and was he alone responsible? Was there or was there not a strange intruder? Had he conceived the whole incident just as he had done when hospitalized for delusional behavior? He was beginning to believe that no one had been with him in the church. Yet, the last words spoken in that beautifully modulated voice filled him with an even greater alarm. Had he verbalized his own fears? Were the words a condemnation of his own moral conduct, or were they an unwitting forecast of his doom? The uncertainty only increased his confusion.

What he was certain about however, was that the rage to steal had come from outside himself since he had never felt such a temptation during his earlier years as a parish priest. He was being goaded into committing an act that would be in violent conflict with his vocation. He could never continue as a priest ministering to the spiritual needs of his parishioners once he had surrendered to his sinful urges. That, he knew, would be one of the most heinous crimes he could commit against the ethics of his calling.

As the temptation to steal grew stronger each night, he felt certain that it was only a matter of time before he surrendered. Yet, he made a superhuman effort to fight against his corruption; to find a way to expunge the desire; to stifle the infernal urge. God knew he had prayed and fasted. He had even taken the unnatural step of tasting the acid wine of self-flagellation, flogging his per-fidious flesh until it was blood-stained. But nothing he did deflected the urge to get his groping fingers on the key. He was being forced to make the hardest decision of his life. Each night, the descending darkness seemed to seep under his skin; to infiltrate his flesh. His body cringed with the oppressive sense of corruption. His mind became crowded with images of his defilement. He felt their tug, dragging him towards the abyss. The onset of night forced him into the habit of falling on his knees to pray for divine intercession on his behalf. But the prediction of the stranger clouded his brain and he could not pray. Would his God understand the forbidden solution to which his torment kept urging him? With his mind in turmoil and despair, he wondered. His heart pounding and his mind whirling in fear and distress, the priest then made the terrible and unholy decision.

Leesa was on her knees in church. Her chin was tilted upwards, her eyes raised to heaven as though she were in direct communication with her Maker before beginning her tirade.

"It was you who made me, and in your image," she hissed. "Since you are absolute Love and Goodness, that means I was born with the same potential. Yet, you never let me realize it. Why? It was you too who commanded that fornication, that most natural human urge, was forbidden. Worse still, within one's family, it became the mortal sin of incest. Why?"

She paused to find the next words, and when she again began to speak, her anger had evaporated and given way to sorrow and pleading. "You know how much I want to love and revere my parents, how important close family ties are or should be. You also know that the evil one is bent on destroying the bonds of love that unite us. If I give in to his temptation, that love will turn to hatred. You alone have the power to protect me from his darkness, from the threat to my life and the lives of my family." She paused again, wrapped in thought.

"You most surely know that no mortal can combat the cunning and power that the demon wields. In fact, you found his treachery so abhorrent that you banished him forever from your kingdom. Why then do you permit the monster to stain me, a mere mortal, with his curse; alienate me from my mother and push me towards dishonoring myself, my father and my family?" The sorrow dripped from her lips as she pleaded with her Maker to remove the accursed persecutor from her life. She then took a deep breath before continuing.

At that point, her voice took on the tone of a penitent and puzzled believer. "And when I turn to you in desperation and despair, how could you remain deaf and silent while the perverse one pursues and persecutes me? You know how hard I have tried to be one of your faithful; how hard I've been trying to remain righteous? Why have you let the monster lead me into temptation that each night becomes harder to resist? Why?" She wailed, overcome by tears and the wrenching need for forgiveness.

She began her prayer with a shrill hiss of annoyance and disapproval. The staccato beat of rising anger kept mounting and mounting until it reached the crescendo of excess. Her voice then changed to resemble the grieving moan of a cello, sobbing out its sorrow. Next, its tone reflected a deep, languorous sadness as she poured out her heart, expressing her religious devotion, her loyalty to family, her shame and her guilt. Finally, a new sound emerged pleading for forgiveness–the wail of a woman in despair. The anguished cry was wrenched from her soul and she couldn't tell whether or not it was heard.

Afterwards, her heartbeat quickened, forcing the blood to race through her body. She felt lightheaded, dizzy. Then, a feeling of weightlessness came over her and the burden she had carried for so long seemed to slip from her shoulders. Her spirits soared and she immediately fell on her knees and dissolved into tears. A refreshing balm of purity spread throughout her body and a smile crept slowly onto her lips. Yet, knowing the deception practiced by her evil mentor, she couldn't help wondering whether what she had experienced was God's truth or Satan's falsehood.

Leesa focused her thoughts on the happier times before Serena's violation, in a desperate attempt to obliterate her sadness at her daughter's inability to heal. Everything had been going so well and it was just a few more months before she would graduate with honors. Yet, she found it impossible to rid herself of the shameful past that kept tarnishing the joy and love in her heart. She knew that she didn't deserve such happiness and felt sure some punishment lay waiting in ambush. Since her conscience was overwrought with guilt and shame, she continued to obsess on thoughts of her sinful past and the price she was paying for her ungodly conduct.

She could never forget how the community had gossiped about her ill-concealed pregnancy and how humiliated she had felt as the target of their scandalous rumors; their ridicule. At that long ago time, her shame had forced her to keep to herself, brooding, brokenhearted and humiliated in her enforced isolation. The struggle that she had endured had seriously affected her mind and the tension of her tug-of-war between good and evil kept tearing her apart. Every day, the feeling that she was getting closer to a nervous breakdown terrified her. She was deathly afraid that in the grip of insanity she might blurt out her most closely guarded secret. She began to fear that after the hypocrisy she had practiced, and the lies she had told to conceal her atrocious act, she herself would reveal the truth and become her own Judas.

Terror poured through Serena's being and pulsed into her blood stream. Like some rogue tide powered by a malevolent moon, it surged through her veins and arteries. In her nightmare world with her demons in pursuit, she was alone, and being isolated, she knew she was vulnerable. A tremendous pressure crushed her body. She felt as though the jaws of a giant vice had gripped her chest and kept squeezing the last bubbles of air from her lungs. Her whole body was in pain, her mind in turmoil. She felt suddenly cut off from everyone and there was no peace for her. Someone had driven a hot knife into her brain and shredded away every vestige of hope. She clasped her hands and pleaded: "Oh God, I need You. Please, please help me!"

Although Leesa tried to focus her thoughts on the happier times she spent with Serena, her mind kept wandering and she found her thoughts again tending towards her own distress. One of her worst fears had been that Serena would leave home like so many others and go to the big city to find a job. How would she bear the sorrow that her daughter's absence would cause? She knew that life without Serena would be an empty, arid existence; one she couldn't bear even to think about much less to face. Serena had insisted that she wanted to leave home and support herself; to assert her independence. As if it were yesterday, Leesa remembered her daughter's response to her mother's attempts to change her mind.

"Mama, I know that dad would find an opening for me in his corporation."

"Well then, why won't you give it a try?" Leesa almost begged. "You know that working with him will earn you a big salary. You'll be able to live the luxurious life, mix with the right people, and be recognized as a member of the most elite society. Besides, doing so will allow you to live at home, and you know how much I want you to be nearby. Serena found it difficult to understand her mother's obsession with keeping her at home, under her wing, and imagining that she would want to mix with "the most elite society."

"Try to understand, Mama. I have to make my own way." Serena answered with youthful stubbornness. "Don't you see? However far I reach in father's employ, everyone will believe that I got there on his coat tails. That's the last thing I want." She had to be evasive in her answer, not wanting to tell her mother that earning a high wage, living a luxurious life or being part of an elitist group didn't interest her in the least. She couldn't understand her mother's belief that money and high social standing were so important. In her heart she felt that there were bigger fish to fry, but she couldn't say that either since she couldn't identify exactly what those 'fish' might be. Yet, when she asked herself what she really wanted to do, she thought it might be some sort of quest. Wasn't life a quest, a journey to realize the highest level of one's potential?

"Starting your career there would gain you vital experience in preparation for whatever you might want to do when you decide to move on. Why won't you at least try that possibility?"

"Mama, I promise I'll try that, but only if I can't find something that really appeals to me. Okay? Now will you please ring Mona's parents and invite Mona to spend the weekend with us?"

"Serena, you know how protective her parents are of their only child?"

"Yes Mama. They went through medical hell before they could have her, and since then they've been afraid she'll catch some horrible disease that medicine hasn't yet discovered."

"Don't be unfair, Serena. Can you blame them given the reasons that created their fear?"

"Not when I know their cattle got Mad Cow, their hogs got Swine Fever and both herds had to be destroyed. It almost drove them into bankruptcy besides sorely testing their rationality."

"Don't be so judgmental child! You'd have to agree that those are solid grounds for them never to raise animals on their farm and to be overprotective of Mona, especially after she nearly died at birth and their doctor's warning that she was 'born a delicate child.'"

"Mama, it's also reasonable for Mona to be fed up with her parents' attitude. She's told them till she's blue in the face that we raise all sorts of animals on our farm and that I'm not affected. But they still think she should be wrapped in cotton wool. They force feed her like a hog getting ready for market and then stuff her with all sorts of vitamins and medications to make her healthy. All they've succeeded in doing is making her fat and unhealthy. Have you seen her figure and face lately? "

"Yes, yes, I have! But Rina, I know Mona's been your best friend since kindergarten and I also know how lonely life on a farm must be for you both as teenagers. With her here you'll both be less lonely so I'll call and invite her. But, don't get your hopes up."

In our mountain hideaway, my dad talked about his love of salmon fishing, and often went to fish with James to the tiny village of Sooke on the South West coast of Vancouver Island. Having learnt the fishing techniques from James, his next step was to learn how to clean and cook the salmon, Indian style. After filleting the fish, and cutting the fillets into four inch sections, he learnt to marinade the sections for at least 8—12 hours in a 5 to1 mixture of Demerara brown sugar to salt. The mixture needs to remain neutral to the taste, neither too salt nor too sweet. The sections of fish have to be placed flesh down in the marinade that will turn into liquid goo. The sections should be broiled, skin side to the fire, on foil covering the grill of a medium heated oven or Bar-B-Q. They should be turned after about four to six minutes, depending on the thickness of the filets. The skin will separate easily from the flesh and the sections flipped over for another three to four minutes. The process is a marvel of simplicity and the taste of the fish, succulent and delicious.

My dad noted that Canada's northern wilderness was a land of forests that stretched on and on, endlessly. It was where James taught him the Indian style of still-hunting. He would have to stand immobile, take long moments between each few steps, while looking and listening intently before carefully lifting and lowering each foot so as not to make a sound. At each pause, he would again scrutinize everything in his vicinity. Moving forward had to be done so slowly and silently that an observer might think the hunter had turned to stone. Dad talked of seeing rabbits and squirrels, deer, elk and moose sneaking through the trees, skirting deadfalls or crossing shallow streams in the forest gloom. After the hunt, he learnt to field-dress the animals they shot.

Turning a buck onto its back, he would make a shallow incision in the skin of the stomach. Inside the puncture, he would hook the skin upwards with his index finger and run the knife's sharp edge upwards, sawing through skin sternum and neck as far as the chin. He would then return to the stomach, and cut the skin from there down between the hind legs on one side of the genitals. He would pry apart the chest and body cavity holding them open with two short sticks propped across the open torso to cool the insides of the animal. He would then core the anus from the outside of the body, with genitals attached, after severing the esophagus at the base of the chin. By carefully lifting the whole detached esophagus and entrails out of the animal, he would prevent the contents of bladder and bowels from spilling onto and fouling the meat. Once the lungs, pancreas and gall bladder were removed, he would cut out the liver, heart, and kidneys–delicacies for many hunters–leaving the carcass to be hung, skinned and cut into four quarters. The quarters would be immediately wrapped in cheesecloth to prevent blowflies from laying their eggs on the meat and fouling it with their larvae.

Serena begged her dad to teach her the basics of hunting and he stated that she should always begin by washing her hunting clothes in non-scented soap. "When in the field, you should hunt with the wind in your face, your movement following the pattern of a still hunt. Once the quarry is sighted, perhaps one of the deer families that include elk and moose–move forward only while the animal is feeding, head down. A swiftly twitching tail signals his intention to stop feeding and to raise his head abruptly. Freeze into a stoop at that signal, and remain motionless until he resumes feeding. Her father made her follow his instructions again and again while he played the role of the deer. She found it extremely funny each time her dad shook his behind.

Sometimes, he would halt abruptly to describe some scene in the forest, an animal crouched in a thicket, a bird perched on a branch, or the track of an animal that they had recently passed on the game trail they were following. He'd then ask her to fill in the details he had purposely omitted. Observation, he stated, was of vital importance. The repeated practice made her far more aware of her surroundings. She learnt stillness from him–willing every nerve and sinew in her body into immobility. She could become as motionless as a rock and as rigid. He also taught her to camouflage herself with small branches stuck into her clothing and hair, lying prone among clumps of undergrowth, or using the tangled roots of blow downs at her back to break up her outline and remain concealed. While still-hunting they saw an amazing variety of wildlife: squirrels, rabbits, raccoon, foxes, wild boar, grouse and ring-necked pheasant creeping secretly by. They even saw a few alert and easily spooked deer. It was so wild and exciting a time that it made her blood rush.

As her father recalled those glorious times of his youth, he wondered what had happened to his friend, James. Did he become a psychologist and marry his girlfriend, Gloria, after finishing Graduate School as they had planned? He fell into a mood of sadness at the realization that, as often happens, college buddies soon lose touch with each other after graduation. "Once they return home," he said, "their new lives take over and together with distance often create a barrier to continuing their former relationships."

After listening to dad's many stories of BC, Serena had a hankering to visit those places and experience for herself all that he talked so much about–the fantastic salmon runs, the whales of the West Coast, the National Parks "where animals came to see people," and the fascinating exhibits and artifacts of the Royal British Columbia Museum. Indeed, he talked about that museum as though its exhibits equaled in magnificence those of the Louvre or the Tate Gallery. He also mentioned Victoria's Buchart Gardens, but ended by saying that mere language was inadequate to describe the creativity that went into conceiving the great variety and beauty of their flowers.

As the days wore on after her joust with God, Leesa's attempts at prayer became more and more desperate as she struggled to overcome the hatred she felt for her mother and the malicious urge to have an incestuous relationship with her father. That, she knew, would destroy both her parents. But once she heard the noises from the other room, nothing could stop her heart from hammering, her blood from racing and her body from vibrating with desire. She became wild with arousal and the passion within her erased all thoughts and feelings about whom her diabolical act would injure. In her fight over the long years, she had become physically, mentally and emotionally exhausted. Finally, she accepted the fact that all her efforts to remain pure were useless. She permitted the dark and powerful persuasion of evil to overwhelm her. Ceasing to struggle, she surrendered.

"Serena thanks for inviting me," Mona said, after the two girls bowed to each other in greeting. Mona then asked to be shown to Serena's mother. Before entering the house they removed their shoes and placed them with their toes facing away from the house. Mona bowed to her hostess and using both hands, presented her with a small gift. All the while, she maintained eye contact with her hostess as was the polite custom. Mrs. Ahn bowed in return, smiled and welcomed Mona to her home. While she put the gift aside unopened, since tradition frowned upon opening a gift in front of the giver, Mona again followed the correct protocol of asking after the health of Mrs. Ahn and then of her husband.

Both girls were wearing the traditional everyday dress, the *hanbok* that consisted of *jeogon*; a pastel shaded long sleeved shirt, and the full voluminous ankle length skirt. Mona's was pink and Serena's blue. Dress was an important mark of social status and their clothing though colored was not bright. Both also wore a necklace, for jewelry like dress, set them apart from the lower classes who wore no jewelry and were often restricted to wearing un-dyed, colorless clothing. Both girls then changed into jeans and a t-shirt to do the chores as the Korean *hanbok* was somewhat restricting. While replacing their shoes, they took care to face the house since placing their backs to the building, in the same way as to a temple, would have been a breach of protocol.

"You are the only friend I can count on to get me out of a boring situation. My parents are visiting their friends and there's nobody my age I can talk to or do interesting things with," Mona stated. In appearance, she was the very antithesis of Serena: a rotund figure, with a moonlike face to match. Her eyes were small slits like her mouth and her nose was flat. She had an overbite and her cheeks were covered with a fiery case of acne. Whenever the two friends met, Mona was instantly struck with a pang of jealousy. Some people are blessed with looks, others with brains and still others with money, she thought. But for anyone to have all three like Serena? Good God, that's obscene! How is it possible to attract male attention when I'm standing next to a fucking goddess? She asked herself, while taking care not to let her jealousy show. To Mona, Serena wasn't just a stunning beauty because of her features. She was elegant and stately in her bearing. If that wasn't enough, the bitch radiated charm. Mona hated the way that her friend's presence drew all eyes away from her, and from everyone else.

"Hey, I'm glad you're here. You'll see how much Will has grown and you can help me with my chores." Serena told her with a radiant smile.

"Would you believe I'm looking forward to milking one of the cows?" Mona confessed.

"And drinking the milk while it's still warm and frothing, I remember," Serena chuckled.

"Afterwards, I'll drive you to the mall where I saw some designer fashions and we can shop until we drop for anything that takes your fancy. How's that?" Serena stated. As they passed the garage, Mona exclaimed:

"Serena, you didn't! A tomato-red Mustang Convertible! Don't tell me you have outfits to match?" Mona asked with a pang of envy.

"Why do you think we're going shopping?" Serena replied chuckling.

"A gift from your dad?"

"No, I gave myself an early graduation present. Since he was ordering a Mercedes SUV for himself, I decided to get the wheels I'd always wanted. Try it. Maybe you'll like it and get one for yourself."

"It would drive my mother crazy if I traded in my ancient VW for a new car. That, she'd warn, would be both extravagant and dangerous. She'd then say: it's extravagant because it will make you spend your savings uselessly since you already have a car. She'd say: It's dangerous because it will tempt you to speed. She'd finally predict: you'll have a terrible accident and kill yourself. You know how strict she is when it comes to my 'protection.'"

And so the conversation continued as the two friends deposited Mona's things in the guest suite before going to feed the animals.

Later, at the mall, the girls visited all the boutiques admiring the most recent fashions imported from abroad. They spent hours trying on different trendy dresses with belts, handbags and shoes to match but surprisingly bought little for themselves. They had a chicken burger and smoothie at *Pelicana Chicken*. After they returned from shopping they sat on the riverbank teasing each other about the hunks they'd undressed with their eyes in the mall's passing parade of young, good looking males. Once she was relaxed, Serena's fingers were dancing up a storm. Mona then confided that she had consulted a female shaman or *mudan* to help find a cure for her acne. Although the Shamanist belief had lost the powerful grip it previously held upon Koreans, it was still prevalent, and people from all walks of life consulted them to call upon the spirits to achieve the desires of their supplicants.

"The same was true about people consulting Fortune tellers for all sorts of things: babies names, success in final exams and other similar future events, yet ironically they rail against therapy and physiatrists." Serena stated.

"Mona, now that we've finished our chores, how about a game of *janggi*, (a Korean version of chess) or *baduk* (the Korean name for the English game known as *go*.)

"I'd much prefer to play *yut*, if you don't mind. (It's a far more popular family game enjoyed throughout Korea) By the way, I have a plan in mind that I want to discuss with you." Instead, Serena retrieved from the car, the few gifts they had got in the Mall for themselves and those they exchanged with each other.

"Serena, I'll embroider the white silk robe I got you with some of the colorful tiger lilies that grow on the edge of your farm."

"That's a great idea. I'll paint a flock of multi-colored pigeons on both thighs of the skinny jeans I got you Mona, with a herd of wild horses stampeding across your bottom. You'll have pigeons and horses all over the farm and your parents won't be able to complain," Serena joked before they began discussing plans about what they'd decide to do after graduation.

"My parents want me to go to university," Mona stated, "that's the one subject on which I agree with them."

"It's extremely difficult competing for the few places that exist for students educated outside the capital, as you know. It's tough to get into one of the prestigious SKY universities: *Seoul National*, *Korea* or *Yonsei*." But Mona, with your academic background, you'll have a very good chance of success."

"Well, I've been going to *hagwon*, (private academies that give extra tuition) while I was still in the womb. If I do get accepted, my parents will consider the exorbitant fees were well worth their sacrifice."

"I have no such ambition, even though I too have been attending *hagwon* all my life."

"So Serena, if no university, what do you have in mind?"

"I want to do something like my dad, helping people. I know it's definitely not the traditional university path."

"You haven't told your parents, I'll bet."

"That's true. But I've told mama countless times that I want to do something else with my life. She insists that if I don't go to university, then I should first work in my dad's corporation. It's her way of keeping me living at home. I don't know why my leaving home scares her so. She just refuses to understand that I want to support myself without any help from family. Dad won't mind, he'll back me in whatever I choose."

"Why can't parents realize that their children don't want to remain tied to them forever?" Mona stated. "Even before we reach the end of our teenage years, most of us are eager to leave home and parents behind, don't you think?"

"Definitely! As we approach adulthood, it's only natural for us to be eager for our first taste of freedom and independence. Parents should rush to help us achieve those goals." Serena replied.

"I can't imagine why such a basic need is so difficult for parents to grasp. I hate the farm, but my mom would murder me if I said so. She's so damn domineering and protective. Anyway, I'll be leaving too," Mona stated.

"She'll be devastated when you break the news."

"Oh God, I hate the way I'm so protected at home. Mama can be so dictatorial. But, you know what? There's a new really cute farmhand whom I've been meeting at night in the barn." She waited anxiously to see her friend's reaction.

"Mona, you must be mad!" Serena whispered, as though the world were listening. "How can you take such risks after the pledge we've made to keep our virginity intact?"

"Risks Rina? There's-nothing-in-the-world-like-fucking." She enunciated each word slowly to emphasize how she felt, pressing her thighs together to impress Serena. She babbled out her feelings, delighted to taunt Serena by having been the first to cash in her 'V card.' "I've never felt such passion," she lied. "God girl, you don't know what you're missing." Mona was reveling in the fact that her fabrication had allowed her to patronize her friend in one area at least.

"I'll find my excitement elsewhere, thank you Mona. I'm sure most people will find me old fashioned because I plan to remain celibate until married."

"I bet you'll do so just to demonstrate how extraordinary a person you are!" Mona spoke in a sing song manner to ridicule the stand Serena was taking and to imply that the notion of celibacy was silly and outmoded. Serena ignored Mona's attempt to ridicule her decision and whispered: "How can you risk the possibility of disease or pregnancy that could jeopardize your whole future?"

"Risk? Serena, you don't think about risk. Passion overpowers you and sweeps you away. You're no longer in charge. Futures don't matter, only the present counts." Then, with hardly a pause, she asked. "Do you think it'll be easy to find a job in Seoul?"

"We're both whizzes at computers and both on the honors list. Big business is looking for intelligence and skill. But I'm not sure business is what I want."

"Besides, if we fail, I hear the call girl racket's wide open there," Mona added.

"Stop trying to shock me, Mona!"

"Can't you tell I'm joking," Mona replied, but the lack of conviction in her voice left Serena surprised and wondering.

It had become a familiar ritual for Serena to lean on her mother and to proceed very slowly to visit Will. As she approached the stables she breathed in the scent of horse, hay and manure. It was a pleasant reminder of her friend. She whistled softly before showing herself when approaching his stall. In a flash, the colt whinnied, sticking out his head from his stall looking for his 'mother.'

"Will," she whispered, "Rina needs your courage and determination."

Will whickered, while nuzzling her cheek with his little velvet muzzle and tickling her neck until she giggled, pulling away but still holding him at arms length. She caressed him as he dug his muzzle into the pocket of her apron to find the apple she always brought him. Her mother looked on, marveling at the way her daughter bonded with and drew inspiration from animals. She could see that the special relationship between Serena and Will went well beyond the normal bond between human and animal. The way they followed each other's lead gave her goose bumps. Each seemed to know exactly what the other was about to do.

Chapter 21

"Mona, you think we'll be able to manage on our own?" Serena asked. "There'll always be your dad's businesses as a fall back position."

"True. But that will only be as a last resort. The idea of business doesn't inspire me at all."

"Anything's better than life on a prison-farm."

"How can you say such a thing?" Serena asked. "I love my life on the farm. But if you mean that communing with nature day in and day out eventually becomes a very lonely occupation, I know what you mean."

"Serena, hear me out. I've given a lot of thought to this and I'm convinced that since we are best friends, things would be much easier if we shared an apartment in Seoul. How's that for an idea?"

"Hey, that's a wonderful idea," Serena replied, although she didn't really want to go to Seoul. But not wanting to hurt her friend's feelings, she added: "It would make the idea of our leaving home much more palatable to our parents. And we'd certainly be able to manage with far fewer problems."

"Oh Serena, I'm so glad you agree. I was so worried you'd want to be on your own. Don't let me down now!"

"I said it's a wonderful idea, and I meant it," she lied. Her twin fingers started their twitching.

"Promise me you won't change your mind." Mona replied. "Friends should always be able to count on each other."

"Mona, there's no need to insist. I promise!"

Early one afternoon just before Leesa's wedding, Kim spoke to her daughter.

"My friend Vivienne is very low and has been asking to see me. I've got to go and visit her before she gets any worse. As she lives quite a distance away, it will take some time for me to get there and visit with her."

"What's she sick with?"

"She has Cancer of the lungs. Her doctors say it has spread into other organs and she hasn't long to live. Anyway, I'll be returning quite late so I'll leave you in charge of fixing your father's dinner and mixing the drink of hot chocolate that he takes before bedtime."

"Don't worry Mama. You can depend on me to prepare his meal and take care of him just as you would have done." Leesa replied, trying hard to conceal her excitement at the news of her mother's imminent departure.

Finally, Leesa was presented with the opportunity for which she had waited so long with both dread and delight. Her immediate reaction was to call on God to help her stand firm in her resistance. Until then, and despite the struggle within her, she had been able to restrain herself from the temptation to retaliate against her parents. But since she had decided to surrender to the evil urge within her, and she would be alone with her father, this would be the real test. With her mother absent, the way before her would be clear. Would she be able to resist taking full advantage of the opportunity or would her overworked mind and body betray her? Had she fought the urge towards evil all these years only to give in at the very last moment? She argued furiously with her conscience against such a betrayal. Since she was to be married in a short time, all she needed to do was to carry on the fight for a little while longer. Once married, she'd be able to leave on her honeymoon with her purity intact. Then, once and for all, she would leave behind her this infernal household where she was being constantly torn apart. She kept repeating that she had to stand firm. She just had to.

It was summer, yet night fell with a bone-chilling cold. The absolute darkness was complete, and its icy embrace filled her with a sick sense of recklessness. Like a relentless predator, the dark impulsion towards evil gripped her in its claws, ripping away her willpower; consuming her with its promise of gratification for the lust that was driving her. The hatred she felt towards her parents intensified. Her head buzzed and her mind raced with the thought of the prize so close at hand. Suddenly, desire bloomed within her, fanning her lust into a blaze that consumed every shred of her resistance. In a fit of trembling and confusion, she could hardly restrain herself from welcoming the night to instigate the malicious act she was about to commit. Yet, she crossed herself again and again to avert the atmosphere of evil that was palpable. At the same time, she thrilled with anticipation at unleashing the wickedness that needed all her willpower to suppress.

When Leesa made her way back to the church, she found a new priest in the confessional and on her enquiry as to the whereabouts of Father Murphy; she was astonished and saddened to learn that he was seriously ill. When she asked about the nature of his illness, the new priest refused to disclose any further information on the subject. But Leesa was not to be put off so easily. She stole around to the vestry and pressured the sexton, Won, into telling her what she needed to know. With great reluctance, Won revealed the mystery of Father Murphy's 'illness.' He had tried to destroy himself with an overdose of sleeping pills. What kind of suffering and desperation, Leesa wondered, could have driven the priest to so extreme an act?

Leesa prepared *tteokokki* for her father's supper in a fever of excitement. He loved rice cakes pan fried in red pepper sauce, and *bibimbap*, rice mixed with vegetables and red pepper paste served on a sizzling stone pot. Her excitement was so intense that more than once she almost dropped a dish from her trembling fingers. She had to squeeze her hands tightly together to calm herself as she sat and had supper with him. She became so lost in the fantasy of what was to come, that her father had to point out that she kept staring at him without touching her supper.

"Clearly you have other things on your mind," he said, smiling. "And you seemed to be enjoying whatever it was you were thinking of doing." She stammered a reply and a deep flush rose into her cheeks as with downcast eyes she picked at her food.

Later, as she mixed his mug of chocolate, wicked thoughts and feelings assailed her. She felt as though some malignant power had invaded her body and took charge of her mind. With Satan's own cunning, she took two sleeping pills prescribed for her mother's migraine, dissolving them in the hot milk she used for the chocolate drink. She then added a teaspoon of sugar to mask any aftertaste the pills might leave. In a fit of trembling and excitement, she looked on as her father sipped his drink leisurely while reading the newspaper. After a while, he kept yawning, and somewhat later, with eyelids as heavy as lead, he looked wasted with exhaustion. Retiring much earlier than usual, his eyes were closing even before he hit the sleeping mat.

After the way Father Murphy had ministered to the spiritual needs of her family and her own, Leesa felt duty bound to visit the ailing priest. She made her way to his modest cottage and was disturbed to find him alone, asleep on a threadbare cot in a darkened room. A single chair, a dresser with washbasin and jug, a small mirror, were the only furnishings other than the cot with its sheet and thin blanket covering him. She had brought him a dish of *Sam-gyetang*, a small chicken stuffed with rice and boiled in a ginseng broth, and decided to sit and wait until he awoke to see if he was hungry. She also needed to talk to him.

The priest lay on his side facing the chair on which she sat. His face was drained of color and his features radiated the same innocence as the face of the child he had been in the yellowing photograph on the wall. In it, he was an acolyte carrying a cross high above his head, proudly leading a procession. What trouble, she wondered, could have made this holy man take such a desperate step? In all her visits to Mass and to confession, she had never thought of him as a person with a life of his own; never considered it could have been so troubled that he would decide to end it tragically. In fact, she had never thought of him as having a normal life at all, realizing that the majority of people seldom see beyond the robes of a priest. She was lost in the reverie of her own thoughts when he opened his eyes.

When Serena's parents consulted the doctor about the worsening condition of their daughter, he told them that rape recovery was sometimes a long and very difficult journey. Unlike the wounded body that healed relatively quickly, the damaged psyche often lingered in a kind of limbo. Progress was often slow and relapses frequent. A great deal depended on the victim's mind and the strength of the support system. Indulging in pastimes too was of considerable help. Occupying the mind with an interest was vital since it freed the individual from preoccupation with the self. "Give it time," he advised. "When she's up to it, let her slip back into the pursuits of her former life as gradually as possible. That," he felt sure, "would be of great help to her recovery." He left them then with a pronouncement that was anything but reassuring.

"Your daughter is paying so high a price of suffering for the terrifying ordeal she experienced that she may well emerge a very different individual."

Leesa waited for her father to fall asleep, and then with evil's own cunning, she scented herself with her mother's perfume, undressed and crept noiselessly onto his sleeping mat. The heat of desire raged within her as a cold sweat broke out on her forehead. Icy fingers of darkness gripped her heart and the obsession to victimize her parents cut off all feelings of regret or self-reproach at the barbarous crime she was about to commit. She cuddled close against her father as she had done so often in her fantasies. Then, her face ugly in its contortion with lust she very gently began her sexual ministrations.

After intimacy with her father, she stole back to her sleeping mat, her lust spent; the promise to destroy her parents kept. Although she had finally struck the blow to achieve her goal, yet she felt neither the elation nor the triumph she had imagined. Guilt, shame and remorse had already begun to torment her, for with the return of reason came the full recognition of the heinous crime she had committed. She kept repeating to herself: "Oh God, what have I done!" She twisted and turned on her sleeping mat, contemplating with horror and loathing the havoc she had brought on herself and on those who were closest to her. So deep was her sense of shame that she felt the compelling need to itemize her crimes. Even before she took her marriage vows, she had broken them by betraying the trust of her intended husband. She had fornicated with a married man, had wronged her mother by sleeping with her husband, and her father by tempting him into infidelity. She had also sinned against heaven by breaking at least two commandments. She had "committed adultery," and "coveted" another woman's husband.

"So you've come to hear my confession and absolve me?" Father Murphy asked his visitor with a soft voice and a gentle smile.

"Sorry Father, I have no cure for the soul. Only some hot soup for the body." Leesa smiled back.

"We have to stop meeting like this, my child." The priest said, trying to lighten the moment. But his visitor stalled his attempt at levity, surprising him by coming straight to the point.

"Father," she questioned, "what could make you do this to yourself? If you lose faith in the system, what model is there for the rest of us poor mortals to follow?"

He thought of replying: Oh, you know, I just got tired of life, hiding behind meaningless words. But even to him, those words were empty and lacked conviction. He also realized with shame that he would be practicing deceit, one of the devil's tools. His shame urged him to tell the truth. "I've been yearning to steal from the collection box with the key to the safe in my pocket urging me on," he said. Unconsciously, his head was bowed in shame.

Nothing could have surprised Leesa more. She would never have imagined that the priest was driven by the same obsession that had goaded her to commit a sinful act. Thoroughly confused, she didn't know what to say when the priest continued: "before I could act, I was racked by guilt and shame. My corrupt thoughts tormented me, making me conscious of my wickedness. While swallowed up in darkness, I felt an urgent need for God's grace. Night after night, a craving would seize me to use the key in my pocket. So powerful was the temptation to steal that it almost overpowered my will. I would then struggle in an effort to exert my willpower knowing that my yearning for the key was sinful. Yet, no matter how hard I tried, the urge was too strong to resist. Although I fell on my knees, I was unable to pray." His visitor immediately realized that the priest had described the same pattern of temptation that had haunted her. He too had been caught in the universal struggle between good and evil. Like her, he had lost the battle.

"What will they do to you?" She heard herself whisper.

"I'm not sure. I'll probably be defrocked and dismissed from the Church. The bishop is determined to stamp out evil in his See." Immediately, an idea came into Leesa's mind. She remained silent for a long moment, battling with the idea, pondering deeply, wondering if she could succeed in so ambitious an undertaking. She then changed the subject, convinced that what she had in mind would be far too difficult, almost impossible. Instead she asked:

"Father, I notice that although you're sick, you're here alone. Don't you have anyone taking care of you?"

"My child, when you disgrace yourself, you'll find that people shun you. You become a pariah that everyone avoids. Worse, you become sure that you're contaminated and you begin to detest yourself. From that point on, everything is darkness and desolation." His features became suffused with profound sadness. He then said: "You must have spent a long time watching me sleep. I'm sure the members of your family need you. You should go home and take care of them."

"I'm here with my family," she replied simply. After a pause she added. "Father, I'm giving you notice that I'll be coming in every day to look after you and do the cooking, washing and cleaning until you're fully recovered. And don't you argue or get out of bed. You look so poorly, I'm sure that you haven't eaten properly in days. You don't even have the strength to stand. I'll bring you lots of food to strengthen you up, and to see that you take better care of yourself in the future. For starters, I hope you like chicken soup."

"Future?" He said. "I don't have one."

"We'll see about that," she said and made up her mind to try to give him one.

Leesa spent the next eight weeks feeding and nursing the priest back to health. When the priest was back on his feet, she wrote to the bishop requesting an audience with him.

Leesa knew that her worst crime was having committed the mortal sin of incest. Despite the excuses she made to herself about the hatred she felt towards her parents, she knew that there was no justification for her act. There were other problems she had to face. If she became pregnant, how would she tell John that he wasn't the father of her child? And when she did, how would he react? As self-recrimination swept over her, she felt more defiled than ever by the galling stain of evil. And so her downward spiral began with shame, followed by guilt and a loss of self-esteem that progressed into a deep sense of self-loathing that ended in a mood of the blackest depression. Haunted by the lurid memories of her guilt-ridden past, she felt that she was falling apart; a lightening blasted tree too feeble, too infirm to hold itself together.

Her belief that she was living in a state of damnation convinced her that her crime had severed her from God. The burden of her corruption had already begun to make her hate herself, and was driving her to despair. She had entered that spiritual wasteland from which the Church is excluded. In a word, she had become the handmaiden of Satan.

What happened was inevitable. The knowledge that she had become pregnant persuaded her to follow in the footsteps of her evil mentor, the supreme master of lies. It was the only path that lay open to her. She staged her "rape," fabricated a story to tell her husband to be, stopped going to Mass, changed her wedding plans, then lied to everyone about the reasons. Finally, she justified her hypocrisy by telling herself that since God had turned His back on her, she had merely retaliated in kind. From that moment she found it difficult make eye contact with anyone.

Once the rage to destroy her parents had been satisfied, the terrifying consequences of her act began to trickle into her consciousness and to overwhelm her. Oh God, how could she have exposed herself and her family to the vicious rumors that are sure to circulate when her diabolical secret comes to light? And once it does, the family will be ostracized by society. They'll probably have to run away to some place where no one knows them, with their heads hanging in shame. Oh God, how could she have placed herself and her family in such jeopardy?

Leesa worked herself into a passion that she could neither repress nor control. She thought of the disdain she would meet in the eyes of her parents and the heavy toll they'd all have to pay for her ungodly act. Each time she thought of the consequences, she became sick to her stomach, and had to rush to the toilet. Once there, she couldn't stop vomiting; the sense of her corruption knotting up her insides. From that moment on, that dreaded 'albatross' hung from her neck and nothing she did could dislodge it or obliterate the mental and spiritual anguish resulting from its crushing weight.

Yong Sang's corruption of his daughter weighed heavily on his conscience. Both he and her mother, Kim, had taken such pride and pleasure in the grace and beauty with which Leesa had blossomed after the rebellious period of her earlier years. They considered that their lives had been blessed by the inexplicable change for the better that had suddenly come over her.

"How could so radical a change for the better have come over such a rebellious child?" Yong Sang had asked Kim in amazement.

"She wasn't only rebellious," Kim reminded him. "During those early years her behavior had been so monstrous that I was convinced she was going insane." It was a miracle, they both agreed, that their daughter had so abruptly changed for the better, then remained totally unaffected at a time when rampaging hormones drove adolescents to such violent extremes. Lately, there had been no periods of dark brooding, no prolonged silences, no grunted replies and no aggressive behavior to exasperate them or to sorely try their patience. That had all been in the past. Leesa seemed suddenly reformed and became free of former weird and reprehensible conduct.

Indeed, their daughter had become a beautifully behaved young lady, obedient and responsible at home, hard working and successful at school. She had also become a superb athlete leading her volleyball team to many victories and bringing credit to her school for the gold medals she won in the one hundred and two-hundred meter races against competitors from other schools. Wonder of wonders for a teenager, she seemed to enjoy going to Mass every Sunday with her parents and her fiancé. How, her father tortured himself over and over, could he have contaminated so upright and so elegant a daughter? Each time he considered the sinful act he had committed, an avalanche of darkness crashed down upon him to shatter the tranquility of his mind. Like his daughter, he was forced into the hypocrisy of pretended innocence and, in despair at being helpless to right the wrong he has done, he too began to loathe and despise himself.

After Leesa looked on helplessly at one of her daughter's violent panic attacks, she felt that she could no longer remain silent about her own revolting secret that she had kept concealed, a festering wound in her bosom, these long years. She hugged Serena tightly, cuddling her for the comfort that she needed as much as her daughter, before divulging her loathsome secret.

When Serena's tears and sobbing subsided, her mother shocked her with an astonishing revelation: "Rina dear, I too was brutally raped as a young woman. I suffered many of the symptoms that you're going through."

"You were raped?" Serena replied with her eyebrows raised in amazement.

"Yes. It was your father's love, sympathy and support that started me on the road to recovery." Even in the depths of her despair, Serena was stunned and listened in chilled silence to her mother's confession: "I was too ashamed to seek therapeutic help which would have meant exposing my horrifying experience to the world. I confided in your father only after learning I was pregnant and made him promise never to reveal my secret to anyone."

"But you needed help," Serena said puzzled.

"Your father passed on to me the advice he has spent long hours researching at the university where he lectured on agriculture."

"You mean father is a specialist on rape recovery?"

"Well, he certainly was in my case. You see, he discussed my case in detail with a psychologist friend and helped me to follow the advice he had gleaned from both his research and the doctor."

"Mama, was the advice helpful?" Serena's face showed that she could hardly believe what her mother had said.

"Rina, his advice forced me along a tough, bleak and lonely road, but it turned out to be the beginning of my healing process."

"Why are you telling me this now, Mama?"

"So you'll understand that I know what you're going through; so you'll let me help."

"Mama, I'll do anything to stop this misery."

"First you have to make sense of the terrible confusion in your head."

"How do I begin Mama?" The mingled hope and sadness in her voice indicated the immature and confused young woman that she was; the suffering she believed would never go away.

"Start by writing down the whole incident. Describe where and when it happened, the number of assailants involved what each one said and did, and how it affected you."

"Mama!" Serena's voice rose in shock. "Do you know what you're asking?" Serena's eyebrows were raised, her eyes wide open. Distress and hopelessness was etched on her face and in her voice. But her mother was relentless.

"Record every detail and then paint a series of pictures depicting each facet of the assault."

Chapter 22

Leesa needed to learn something about the bishop she decided to confront. One of his colleagues explained to her that he had come "from old money. Had he gone into the family business, he would have been filthy rich. No one knew why he had forsaken a life of wealth to embrace the poverty of the Church." Another very close college buddy of his told her: "He's an extraordinary man. One early morning I went to visit him at his manse. I knocked on his bedroom door thinking he was still asleep. Since the door was ajar, I went in thinking that he hadn't heard me. He had already left for church, but what I saw amazed me. There was a huge four poster bed, with embroidered lace-covered pillow slips and matching counterpane. It was still made up so it hadn't been slept in. There was a thin pallet on the floor beside it and its sheet and duvet was in disarray where the bishop had evidently slept. His position in the Church had acquired for him the luxurious manse in which he lived, a chauffeured Rolls Royce and all the trappings that come with his post. But he created quite a spectacle of himself through one of his habits that indicated clearly the type of man he is. People are amazed to see him, clad in his purple robes, his girdle swinging in one hand as he strides along, about twenty meters ahead of his chauffeur-driven 'Rolls.' That's how he visits the sick and the churches of his See. He's a simple man who disdains show, refusing to live luxuriously or to drive in style." What Leesa learnt about the bishop made her far less apprehensive about the audience with him that she had requested.

"Thank you for seeing me at such short notice," Leesa said to the prelate. She found him a striking figure in his white clerical collar, purple robe cinched in with matching girdle. His big head, square jaw on a bull neck and huge muscular frame was suited more to a powerful athlete than to a man of the cloth. A large photograph on the wall above his head showed him brandishing a tennis racket. Behind him she could see the green and purple colors of the Wimbledon Stadium. In real life his eyes were kind and although they seemed to bore right into her, yet they were both warm and compassionate. They made his visitor feel somewhat more comfortable about the mission on which she had come.

"Thank you for coming Mrs. Ahn. I fear that as a devout and prominent member of our diocese, you've come to complain about the disgrace to the Church caused by the scandalous act of Father Murphy." She found his voice, like his eyes, was kind and gentle even when referring to the "scandalous act."

"No, my lord bishop. I'm here to state some of the facts you should know about the man condemned by no one else but the Church."

"I'm anxious to hear what you have to say about a priest who has so badly damaged the reputation of Mother Church." Again, the tone of his voice held no malice even though he spoke of the Church's "badly damaged reputation."

"First, I should paint him against the backdrop of an earlier incident, my lord. His predecessor begged you for a transfer since he couldn't cope with the personal deprivation he had to face even before seeking the welfare of his flock."

"Yes. He did complain to me that he found it impossible to live what he referred to as "the intolerable hand-to-mouth existence forced upon him by his meager stipend and the hovel that passes for a presbytery." I was sympathetic to his complaints and remember giving him a transfer to a less demanding parish."

"Well, my lord. We his parishioners didn't consider his departure a mere 'transfer,' as you term it. We saw his departure as a cowardly act, an irresponsible desertion of his duty. Furthermore, he was thinking only of himself and his running away was done to the detriment of his flock that was in dire need of his spiritual leadership."

"I believe you said that you were here to speak on behalf of Father Murphy," the prelate reminded his visitor with gentle irony. However, she had made him aware of something about which he was ignorant. The parishioners had looked upon his "transfer" with deep animosity and distress.

"Well, Father Murphy too was hoping for a transfer, and for the same reasons. But unlike his predecessor, although you invited him to do so, he did not express that hope nor did he complain. His dedication over the years is well known throughout the parish. Apart from doing all that is expected of him as a cleric, he often rolls up his sleeves, hikes up his cassock and pitches in to help the farmers till their fields, feed their animals and repair their broken fences. He can even be seen shoveling manure whenever the need arises."

"Tell me more about this er, this amazing priest," the bishop replied not without a hint of sarcasm. The question made Leesa think it necessary to describe the priest as he appeared in the pulpit.

"My lord, his deeply lined features and exhausted appearance make him the living replica of the corpses he buries. Yet, his kindly smile lights up his face so amazingly that he puts everyone in his presence at ease. No member of his congregation doubts that this humble priest is truly a man of God, as devoted to his calling as to his flock."

"Apart from his appearance, is there something more you can tell me about this, er, er...'man of God?'"

"He collaborated with me and my 'watchdogs' to stop the parish's husbands and wives from cheating on their spouses. With him, we then visited and counseled the wife-battering husbands and child-molesting fathers and mothers of our district to stop their abuse."

"Yes, I heard about that admirable undertaking of yours. You deserve a great deal of credit for the success of the venture. You and your watchdogs are to be congratulated. Would that we could have them in every parish!"

"Thank you, my lord bishop. But Father Murphy played an important role as one of us. It was he who followed up our visits giving counsel to both the evildoers and their victims. By his repeated follow up visits to their homes he also made sure that the abuse was halted permanently. If that were not enough, he preached sermons to raise awareness about the plight of those unfortunate children of the area who can't attend school."

"We built them an elementary school," the bishop immediately replied with a deep frown. "Why can't they attend?"

"My lord, during the day when school is in progress, some of those children have to remain at home to help their parents on those farms where they are shorthanded. The Father arranged to get volunteer teachers, school supplies and the loan of a barn to use as a school. With his volunteers three evenings a week, he teaches the children reading and writing, feeling a pressing need to overcome illiteracy and offer these young people the chance of a better future."

"Is this man as exceptional a priest as you make him out to be?"

"My lord, I wouldn't be here if I wasn't convinced of it. I should add that he does all this on a pittance for a stipend without enough to eat and with a hovel for a presbytery. His parishioners and I think it's far too much to ask of any single human being? We are surprised that none of his superiors have noticed. Had they done so, I'm sure they would have corrected the situation and come to his rescue long ago."

"I get the impression that you have a somewhat different agenda to the one you stated. Why are you really here, Mrs. Ahn?" The bishop asked with a benign smile.

"To remind you, my lord, that the Church preaches forgiveness as one of its central principles, and to beseech you to show Father Murphy the compassion both his parishioners and I are convinced he deserves."

"Did this exceptional priest ask you to come here and speak on his behalf?"

"Oh no my lord! He is too humble and self effacing a man to ask such a favor. He would blush scarlet to hear what I said about him, or even to know I was here on his behalf."

"While you and your parishioners evidently think that the saintly Father is a monument of dedication and fidelity to his calling, as to his flock, you should understand that those qualities don't stand up very well in the face of scandal. I have to take into consideration that he has dealt the Church a fearsome body blow. It's the kind of sin that not even God can forgive."

"My lord," his visitor replied swiftly, "doesn't the Church preach that there is no sin that's beyond the forgiveness of God? Didn't he forgive Mary Magdalene for her immorality and the penitent thief for his crimes?"

"Touché," was the bishop's reply. He then questioned: "Mrs. Ahn, I'm curious. What would you and your parishioners have me do?" There was no hint of sarcasm in the bishop's voice this time.

"My lord, we would like you to follow the ethics of your Christian calling and pardon Father Murphy for his transgression. I know he is filled with remorse for what he tried to do. But, his congregation is convinced that his act was a desperate attempt to avoid the evil one's temptation of theft from the collection. Had he submitted to the temptation he would not have been able to continue as a priest."

"Is there anything else you and your congregation would like to add?" The prelate asked. Again his voice was devoid of sarcasm. This time his eyes were twinkling brightly and he was smiling. He seemed to know already the plea that would come from his visitor's lips.

"Yes, my lord bishop. We would beseech you to raise his stipend and find him proper lodgings, ever mindful of the fact that he is the right kind of shepherd the Church needs to lead his flock."

"Well, my dear lady. With supporters like you in his congregation, Father Murphy is indeed blessed. I shall give your appeal all the consideration it deserves. And thank you again for coming." Leesa thought she had said enough. She again thanked His Lordship, rose from her seat and bade him goodbye.

In the same way as with his daughter, Yong Sang's conscience was destroying his peace of mind. In a single act, he had set in motion shock waves that would destroy his marriage, ruin his reputation and have serious repercussions on the welfare of his daughter. His thoughts turned morbid as he considered that his conduct had destroyed forever the bonds uniting his family. He saw himself as some kind of degenerate sexual predator whose darker side he had kept closeted all these years. Finally, the beast had escaped its cage and mauled all those closest to him. Indeed, he became so haunted with recrimination at having corrupted his daughter that it affected his work as a skilled carver. The problem began with a slight trembling of his hands that grew with time and the cruelty of his self-chastisement. As he continued to flog himself, the trembling got worse and the quality of his work deteriorated. With time, his commissions became fewer and fewer.

The night Leesa returned home after visiting her ailing friend, she undressed, lay down next to her husband on their sleeping mat and scraped her nails gently along his spine. She felt his muscles ripple in response, indicating that he was awake. She then began the gentlest scratching of his back, her tacit invitation to intimacy. While it was Yong Sang who often initiated their sexual bonding, it was not unusual for her to attract his attention when she felt the need. She listened carefully to the sound of his breathing while again moving her nails lightly across his back. Normally, as she continued to scratch, his breathing would change from a regular rhythmic pattern to grow deeper and deeper until a soft moan would escape his lips to signal his arousal. He would then turn to her and they would begin the mutual kissing, caressing and fondling that would eventually end in intimacy.

However, on that fatal night, since Yong Sang had just finished betraying his wife in the sexual embrace of his daughter, his mind was still reeling with the guilt and shame of his act. Another sexual encounter, especially with the woman he had just betrayed, was the furthest thing from his mind. Unmoving, with back rigid and muscles tense, he never felt the urge that usually thrilled through his body and heated his blood. Indeed, intimacy with his wife had suddenly become abhorrent to him. Kim was stung and deeply puzzled by his rejection. He had never failed before to respond to her invitation with alacrity. Since she knew that he was awake, the rejection was a severe blow to her self-esteem. She remained between sleep and wakefulness all night long puzzling over his resistance and arousing her suspicion.

"Mama," Serena replied, her voice edged with anger, "you want to make me relive that terrible past instead of blocking out those memories that I've been trying so hard to lock away? They are the ones that return again and again each night, punishing me with the nightmares they spawn."

"I know what you're going through, believe me."

"You're not satisfied that I already feel dirty and ruined for life, Mama?" The anguish in her daughter's voice was palpable, but her mother pretended to take no notice.

"Write and then rewrite your version of each experience. Paint them in a series of pictures. Finally, under each picture, describe what is taking place."

"Mama, isn't there any other way? What good could possibly come out of reliving my violation? How can that possibly help?"

"You'll be confronting your demons for the first time. You need to do that, Rina. Trust me."

"Recreating those scenes of my degradation is going to hurt more than help, Mama." Serena's tearful voice rose in anxiety and disbelief at the renewed torture she was being ordered to undertake.

"By confronting your true feelings, you'll begin to see the incident from a different point of view. Just do it, Rina." Steel had replaced the earlier note of sympathy in her mother's voice.

After the first few attempts to follow the advice, Serena rushed to Leesa begging her permission to stop the suffering. "Mama, writing the facts of my rape is revolting. Recalling the scenes bring a whirlwind of humiliation. They paralyze me. My body becomes the center of an emotional storm. My mind recoils from the memory, and my breath comes in spasms. In my mind, terror, guilt, shame and anger war with each other. Reliving the incidents by day encourages their return at night and the nightmares that occur terrify me with their realism."

As John approached adulthood, an acolyte attending Sunday Mass, he searched the congregation for Leesa, the girl who had won his heart. He was drawn to his beloved, by the youthful glow of her face, the green piercing eyes with their long lashes. He had been smitten by those pink rosebud lips and the mass of raven black hair that helped to set off her singularity. She radiated so powerful an aura of purity and innocence that she captivated his heart all over again each time he saw her.

He then waited with mounting excitement for that part of the Mass when he had to ring the gong three times. It alerted the congregation that the mystery of transubstantiation was taking place at the altar. Each time he struck the gong, the hair on his arms and neck instantly stood erect at the thought of the miracle that he was highlighting.

John often lit the candles before the start of the Mass, and he sometimes replaced the oil in the eternal lamp. Standing on tiptoe, stretching with arms uplifted to steady the lamp hanging above the sanctuary, he looked to the congregation like a saint in his ascent to heaven. The image displeased Leesa, jarring as it did with the lascivious fantasies she had woven about John. So saintly a person could hardly plant the fiery kisses on her lips and the passionate caresses of her body for which the hot blooded teenager secretly burned.

On John's return from university training in Canada, he continued helping his father run the farm, but noted with dissatisfaction the way his other corporate businesses were run. His dad, who had trained in the US and Canada, had followed very closely the Western way. True the corporation was making a profit, but John knew that Korean thinking was so far different from that of the West that he decided to introduce changes that would improve the efficiency of his employees and the profit margin of the family's businesses.

However, he decided to wait until after the retirement of his father before making the changes he envisaged. In the meantime, he set aside two afternoons a week to visit the workshop of Yong Sang. There, he watched the master craftsman at work, gazing in admiration at the miniature ships, planes, ducks, toys and other items, many built to scale, that he had already painted. Many were works commissioned privately. The rest went to Korea's upscale department stores where their simple beauty fed the taste of affluent customers. The exquisite lines of each carving showed the loving care and skill that spilled from his fingers demonstrating that he was as much an artist as a master craftsman.

"Rina," Leesa counseled, "confronting your demons is one of the toughest things you have to do. It will cause you untold suffering. But, believe me, it is necessary."

"Oh Mama, you make it sound so much easier than it is. You have no idea of the misery and suffering you are forcing me to face."

"It takes misery and suffering to confront your demons."

"Each time I recall the memory of a vicious act, it takes enormous effort to keep it in focus as it triggers all the other brutalities I had to endure."

"You have to keep trying Serena, until you clear away the confusion and misery."

"But each time I try, the cruelty forces me to stop. I have to dismiss the memory almost immediately."

"Rina, it takes courage to face down your fears while suppressing your guilt and shame. You'll also need determination and willpower to stifle your anger and confusion."

"Then why subject myself to such pain when there's no guarantee that it will help?"

"Because finally, you'll be able to observe and record the images in detail, just as you did in the series of paintings you made of Will's 'trial.'

"Mama, what does Will's trial have to do with the suffering I have to endure?" Her voice rose in a wail of annoyance and despair.

"Remember, he kept falling each time he tried to stand. But each time he fell, he picked himself up, gaining strength with every attempt. Eventually, he was free of his handicap. Rina, he could not only stand, he could run."

"Mama, I hope you don't really expect me to run. Will you be satisfied if I manage to limp?"

"Your father and I are here whenever you need support and reassurance. But whatever you do, don't stop trying. And don't stop praying either." Great advice, she thought with irony, from the likes of me.

"Okay Mama," Serena replied in the most dejected voice her mother had heard. And so she began confiding to her mother the sordid incidents of her rape, the threats of the rapists, and the demeaning acts they made her perform.

Leesa listened in alarm, disbelief and sorrow, trying desperately to maintain her poker face. But she found that impossible. As she listened, her lips trembled, her eyes filled with tears, and the anger mounted in her breast at the pain and suffering the rapists inflicted on the daughter she loved to distraction.

John felt excited when the great man began teaching him the use of saw, plane, chisel and square. While he became passionate about woodworking, he had a far more important reason for his visits to the workshop. Each evening, Leesa came to tell her father when supper was nearly ready. While waiting for him to put away his tools, John devoured his beloved with his looks, intent on showing her with his eyes the depth of feeling he had for her in his heart. His beloved soon got the message and the two began conversations showing their interest and affection for each other.

Yong Sang noted the attraction of the young man towards his daughter, and as he approved, began inviting John to share supper with the family. As the woodworker got closer to his apprentice, he took to addressing him as JC, (John's second name was Claude) which made John infinitely proud. He considered it more than a coincidence to be called by the same initials as Jesus Christ and to be unwittingly involved, if only passively, in doing the same work as the sacred carpenter. More important, the realization helped to strengthen his earlier resolve to practice the virtues of his namesake whenever possible.

One evening at supper, the topic of religion came up when Kim, began talking about the Crucifixion. She expressed her astonishment "at Christ's extraordinary conduct during His torture." It disturbed her, she told her listeners. She couldn't "fathom why He kept praying for the forgiveness of his oppressors while being scourged, even while he kept falling under the weight of the cross on his marathon march to Golgotha." It was "unthinkable," she said, "that anyone could take time to forgive his persecutors while falling under the weight of the cross or enduring the pain of being nailed to a cross."

The idea had never occurred to John before and it struck him so forcibly that, like Kim, he found it inconceivable that anyone could respond to such cruelty and injustice with compassion for the evildoers. At home and at work during the next days and weeks, John fixated on the virtue of compassion that allowed his Maker to forgive the sins of others. These thoughts led him to consider Christ's forgiveness of the remorseful 'penitent thief' and of the prostitute, Mary Magdalene. He then remembered His compassionate words for the cruelty of the soldiers crucifying him: "Father, forgive them for they know not what they do." In amazement, he kept asking himself: where did a suffering individual find room in his heart for the virtues of compassion and forgiveness.

Though the idea amazed and plagued him, he could find no answers, but the conduct has so captured his imagination that those two Christian virtues became the chief models of conduct that he considered worthy of emulation.

Chapter 23

"Come in Father," Leesa stated. "You look not only very well but also very happy. What brings you here?"

"Oh thank you, thank you so much for what you did." The priest stated enthusiastically, staring at Leesa, and reaching out to hug her, his eyes filled with tears.

"You have me at a disadvantage, Father. What did I do?" Leesa replied with the inscrutable poker face born from a lifetime of practice.

"I got a letter from the bishop explaining in detail the strong case you made to him on my behalf. Instead of being sacked and defrocked, I am to remain the priest of this parish," he said, wiping his eyes that lit up with a radiance approaching religious ecstasy. His features then glowed with such boyish enthusiasm and charm that he seemed to grow younger before her eyes.

"Oh, I'm so happy for you, Father. No one could be more deserving of a second chance," she said, hugging the priest enthusiastically. "Is there any other good news?" She asked archly. He looked at her for a moment wondering whether she had had the temerity to press the bishop beyond asking for his reinstatement.

"My hovel is to be renovated and transformed into a real presbytery with all the furnishings necessary," he said, peering closely at Leesa trying to gauge if his suspicion was accurate.

"Oh, the bishop is as compassionate as his looks and bearing imply, but is there anything more?" Leesa insisted.

"Yes, my stipend has been doubled and made retroactive for the last three months." Her two questions and her insistence made the priest realize that she did have the courage to importune the prelate into providing him with a new lifestyle. He felt bound to thank her again and to ask:

"What stories did you tell the bishop to make him so generous and forgiving?"

"Stories?" She asked, with surprise. "I merely told him what all your parishioners know about you. But, I'm sure he must have conducted his own investigation and found out for himself that what I told him was true."

"Well, thank you again so much. You've actually given me a new life!" Leesa blushed deeply at his words. The crimson of her features also displayed the surge of pure joy that good deeds engender.

Serena explained to her mother that the pain and the bleeding she suffered was less than the humiliation of being alone and so shamefully exposed—the one half-naked female facing five males—each waiting to take his turn. With broken voice, amid tears and sobs, she described the stink of sweat and musk that pierced her nose and the perverted eyes that punctured her body. She repeated the foul language with which they abused her, and the humiliation of being ridden. By that time, she hardly felt the knife jabs and the kicks they administered before abandoning her. She couldn't help fixating on the shame, humiliation and guilt that garroted her, cutting off her breath. By the end of each 'purge' that she repeated for days on end, Serena became sick to her stomach and emotionally exhausted. Her mother then gave her hot, herbal tea, heavily laced with rum and condensed milk, that sent her blessedly off to sleep.

The recurring nightmare of her flight and pursuit then invaded and poisoned her sleep. Her mother kept vigil, caretaker over her daughter's troubled restlessness. Her heart lurched at every sudden twitch of Serena's face and body, and every moan caused a wrench in her gut. She watched, bowed over with sadness, yet incapable of easing either her daughter's torment or her own.

"My little baby girl, what have they done to you?" She whispered again and again, her eyes burning as the tears flowed; grief and sorrow crumpling up her features. She rocked back and forth on the bed, nursing her own sadness at her daughter's pain and revealing the depth of her own suffering. She recognized that her only recourse was to approach her Creator for help. She knew that He alone could accomplish this mammoth task and so she knelt at Serena's bedside. Once again, she prayed, pleading that He would hear her prayer and intercede on her behalf. But, she also knew that when He came, it would be in His own time. Although they "grind exceeding small," she knew that "the mills of God grind slowly..."

Serena became really excited when her mated pigeons began the ritual of nest building followed by cock chasing hen to the nest that forecast the laying of their two eggs. Once they were setting, both parents shared in the demanding task of incubation, and later feeding their blind, helpless hatchlings. Each parent seized the beak of its delicate chick dressed in its yellow fuzz, then, their beaks locked together; the adult bowed its head vigorously again and again to regurgitate a milky fluid that fed its hatchling until its crop bulged. Two weeks later, their fuzz exchanged for the tiniest of feathers, and three times their size, the chicks would get a milk-like mixture of finely-ground grain to speed their growth.

Serena remained riveted to each rite of passage, as the adult birds passed from mating, to nest building, to laying then incubating and finally to feeding their young. She and the youngster's parents then waited impatiently to witness the solo flight of their fully fledged offspring. Through each of these stages, the conduct of the pair was a study in patience, devotion, co-dependence, fidelity and single-mindedness. Once again the pigeons' relationship with each other and with their offspring set an example that inspired in her the deepest admiration for their unique qualities.

She couldn't help but regard the devotion and dedication each pigeon showed towards its mate and its youngsters as a parallel to the love and devotion her parents lavished on each other and on her. Indeed, the conduct of her parents, and especially the solid rock of her father's religious faith, was the major influence that had created her self-assurance, courage and determination to carve out for herself the future she wanted.

Although John had dedicated himself to follow a unique example, he was well aware of the perils that he had set himself. He had no illusions of trying to follow the highroad to sanctity or even the less lofty road to the monastery. The life of austerity to which both saint and monk condemned themselves was far too extreme for his liking. He knew that he was not of the caliber to follow either of those lonely and perilous paths.

Unlike saint and monk, he could never take the vow of silence. That would mean cutting himself off from verbal communication with the world. He couldn't imagine becoming a deaf mute and living in total isolation. Such a life would not be merely painful, it would be utterly inhuman. It was therefore out of the question. He knew too that unlike saint or monk, he could never take the vow of poverty. To jettison everything he owned would be a severe trial for him and an even more austere one for his wife, Leesa and his daughter, Serena. For him, the toughest of the three vows was that of chastity which would mean becoming a virtual eunuch, and perhaps indulging in self-flagellation to purify his profane body. His love of worldly pleasure made it impossible for him to indulge in such grisly self-sacrifice. He considered that life without the pleasures of the senses was no life at all.

Yet, his admission to being an ordinary man did not free him from serious responsibility. It certainly didn't preclude his following the ethics of Confucius while living a righteous Christian life. Neither did it rule out the determination, as far as was possible for him, to practice the virtues of compassion and forgiveness that were at the Christocentric heart of the Church's teaching.

Serena began the resumption of her old life, gradually putting behind her the horror of her gang rape. This was due in large part to the support of her parents, the comforting sense of belonging to her farm and especially to the habit of painting that she very frequently indulged. The latter was of special therapeutic value. While absorbed in the act of creation, she was able to discard her worldly worries and distress as though they had never occurred. The long hours she spent practicing her art helped to free her from obsessing on her corruption as on her isolation in the enchanted circle of her private hell. Although she didn't realize it, the major catalyst that had accelerated her healing process was her painting. She had also followed her parents' advice and kept praying for the strength to endure.

The farm had become a school that provided her with a special kind of instruction since her father had followed the practice of his ancestors. Any animal that died or was stillborn–calves, pigs, chickens, turkeys, geese, ducks, pigeons and even eggs that were spoiled–was carted off to a distant corner of the acreage. There it was left for nature to take its course. Serena would climb to a perch in the loft of the tallest barn to watch through binoculars as foxes, raccoons, coyotes, opossums, and various birds of prey and carrion descended on the carcasses.

Each group of animals would gorge themselves. To her amazement, she once saw a family of wolves ripping and tearing mouthfuls of offal from the insides of a dead calf. The sight amazed her since no one was aware that there were wolves in the area. The spectacle gave her the idea that death was nature's clever strategy of providing food and sustenance for the preservation of many of her species.

From her overhead perch, once again she became a spectator in the theater of the tall grass of those pastures on the edge of the farm. She would watch avidly as a feral cat stalked a rodent; as rutting animals enacted their mating dance; as an opossum, laden heavily with its young, scurried from the path of a marauding snake. When she saw a rabbit concealing itself in some bushes while munching away at its lunch, she knew that it would be effort wasted if the hawk circling above had its way.

After observing their habits of hunting for food, mating and then expending so much time and energy in the protection and upbringing of their young, she concluded that the animals resemble us humans much more than we like to think, and we resemble them far more than we cared to admit. It was easy to understand how the farm, in her eyes, had become a complete ecosystem. Like many modern Koreans, she thought of life and death as a continuum of the same circle. Living in such close harmony with the land and its animals, it was natural for her to see herself as an extension of the environment.

So many years ago, the knowledge of her pregnancy had come as a shock, thrusting her headlong into a vortex of confusion and misery. With her mind a muddle, Leesa tried to imagine the best way to solve the problem of her possible discovery. She first noticed a slow but steady increase in her weight. She began checking daily in the mirror trying to gauge whether her parents would notice her developing body. To prevent this, she began wearing very loose fitting clothing. However, she found that hiding her fits of morning sickness from her mother became more and more difficult. Her vomiting would leave her so exhausted that her mother, Kim became suspicious that something was wrong.

"Child, you look like a ghost. Why are you so pale and breathing so heavily?"

"Mama, I'm feeling so out of sorts, I must be coming down with the 'flu."
Kim believed her at first, but on a later occasion she questioned:

"I heard you bringing up your breakfast and retching in the toilet. What's the matter dear? You know you can talk to me about anything that might be troubling you."

"Mama, I'm sure it's something I ate that didn't agree with me. But I'm feeling better now that I've got rid of whatever it was." The reply didn't quell her mother's suspicion but she decided not to pry any further. Whatever the problem was would become evident sooner or later, she said to herself. Leesa knew that she would soon be married and the maternal inquisition would end. Unfortunately, she also knew that her husband's questions would then begin. But she had a plan to take care of that. She'd have to scrap her plans for a big wedding, agree to a civil ceremony and most important, bring forward the wedding date. She'd have to get married almost immediately and conceal her growing pregnancy beneath a tight corset and layers of clothing. But no matter how well she hid her condition there would still be serious problems to face.

A civil ceremony, with only family present, would mean that she'd have to return all the gifts already received with apologies to all those invitees who would no longer be in attendance. She knew that John would take care of the return of gifts and the apologies, but she also knew that such a radical change in wedding plans would give rise to the foulest rumors and speculation that would threaten to expose her ungodly act, not only to the world, but to John. The scandal and derision it would cause would not be limited to her alone. Its devastating effects would engulf her whole family, including her father, whom she knew was innocent.

She then thought that if she got married immediately, John could whisk her off to one of Korea's smaller cities for their honeymoon. They'd take a prolonged trip and return only after the baby's birth. She believed it would be the best way to keep a lid on things. While she also knew that it wouldn't prevent vicious rumor and rampant speculation, she felt sure that those problems would be easier to face than complete exposure. And thanks to his love for her, she felt sure that John would be willing to carry out her plan. After all, his consideration for the welfare of their child's reputation would encourage him to agree.

Leesa began by detesting the 'thing' growing inside her, as though it, and not she, had been the cause of her catastrophe. With the passage of time, she began to feel differently about the "growth," later the "unborn child," that had gradually become the "innocent infant," inside her. She began going for long walks in a nearby wood, both hands cupped upon her growing stomach while she heard herself singing lullabies to what had finally become her 'beautiful baby.' She never imagined that she could muster an ounce more of the love she felt for her unborn child. But after her birth, when the newborn began suckling at her breast: "My God! What an experience that had been!"

Soon after John became engaged to Leesa, but before she had learnt she was pregnant and confided her 'rape' to him, John spoke to Yong Sang about the changes he'd noticed in his fiancée's conduct. Her father was quick to point out that he too had noticed those changes: "She's done so well in her academic studies and is the school's best athlete, but she does seem to be going through some sort of crisis."

"I didn't know you'd noticed," John replied. "With graduation approaching, she's resigned from all sports. Instead, she goes to the school library to concentrate wholly on her studies."

"Have any of the other athletes done that? I mean resigned from all sports?" Yong Sang asked.

"No sir. I'm sure you know she's also been spending a lot of time at the church in confession." What John couldn't tell her father was that she'd stopped the kissing and fondling that they'd both enjoyed so much, that she'd even stopped holding his hand, and as though ashamed, she could not look him in the eye. Equally disturbing was the fact that she suddenly stopped going to Mass, abruptly changed all her carefully made wedding plans. Finally, she had asked him to marry her immediately and to spend their honeymoon in one of Korea's obscure islands where they'd be unknown.

At that point, he suspected that the problem of his bride-to-be resulted from some kind of infidelity. Yet, her life was so circumscribed. The only friends she had were classmates whom she met solely during school hours. There were no parties, nightclubs or clandestine meetings outside the home. Still, he couldn't get the idea of pregnancy out of his mind. For days on end he was plagued by that thought, wondering how such a thing could possibly have happened.

One evening while dining in a restaurant with his fiancée, John noticed an odd looking woman staring fixedly at them with a peculiar concentration. She stood out among the Korean diners, she being Caucasian and in Western dress. He tried to ignore the woman's rudeness and was surprised to see her call the waitress, hand her a quickly scribbled note, then point to John. At that moment, Leesa rose, excused herself to powder her nose leaving John alone when the waitress handed him the note. He pocketed it without reading its contents and when he again looked for the woman, she was gone. He and Leesa enjoyed their meal and he had completely forgotten the incident until later when he felt the note in his pocket. "You need to see me," was all it said, and it was written in English. John found the incident mysterious. It made him wonder how the strange, dark-haired woman knew he spoke English and why she thought he needed to see her.

The following evening as he was exiting the elevator after work, John recalled the incident and that the woman's face had struck him as being quite masculine with a somber cast to her features. When she stood to hand the waitress her note, she was wearing a long black cloak of peculiar cut that made her look like a priest. He was still lost in thought wondering if he'd ever see the woman again when the elevator stopped at the foyer. Astonished, he no longer needed to wonder, for there she stood, again cloaked in black, evidently waiting for him. He noted that her bright intelligent eyes, shining from a face of sallow complexion, contrasted sharply with her coal black hair and cloak. Approaching her, he tried to fathom the mystery of how she knew where he worked, and the late hour at which he left, often after all his employees. Before he could address her, she turned away, walked slowly through a glass door into the adjoining café where she took a seat. He followed as he was meant to do and she accepted his offer of coffee. While waiting to be served, he asked: "Who are you?"

"Mary Cuchulain from Ireland." She needn't have stated her country of origin since it was evident in her broad Irish brogue.

"Why were you staring at me in the restaurant?"

"At you and at your fiancée. People's anxiety and sadness draws my attention."

"Anxiety, sadness?" John asked, speaking casually. "Why do you think there is anxiety and sadness between us?"

"Haven't you been worrying about whether or not your fiancée might be pregnant?" Although John was taken aback by her knowledge, he prolonged his casual role-playing.

"Are you trying to tell me that you're a prophet; that you can forecast future events?" He asked with raised eyebrows and an ironic smile of disbelief.

"I didn't expect you to believe me since I'm a stranger," she answered, "but you should think about this: I am of Celtic origin and way back in antiquity, the Druids conquered us and later adopted our beliefs. After you check on who they were and what they did, we'll meet again." With those prophetic words, she left John wondering at the mysterious woman, and her knowledge about him and his fiancée.

Since school and church were the only two venues Leesa visited outside her home, John convinced himself that it wasn't possible for her to be pregnant. Yet, he forced himself to seriously consider the crucial question: if that were the case, would he forsake his sullied bride-to-be and cancel the wedding? He kept deliberating on the question for days and nights on end, unable to think clearly, or to sleep. And during all those troubling days and nights, his thoughts kept returning to the mysterious Mary Cuchulain and to the plight of Mary Magdalene. Try as he might, he couldn't seem to get the images of the two Marys out of his mind. Then, thinking about the Magdala woman forced him to recall his earlier resolve to cultivate the two virtues that were at the heart of Christian doctrine.

Chapter 24

Intrigued by the mysterious Caucasian stranger, John gave a great deal of thought to the questions that arose in his mind about her uncanny knowledge. How did she know that Leesa was his fiancée, and that he spoke English? Even stranger, how did she know that his mind had been in turmoil over the possibility of Leesa's pregnancy? He had never mentioned it to anyone. Again, how did she know where he worked or what time he left? He then wondered what was the significance of her being of Celtic origin, and of her Druid ancestry, both of which she had stressed. Well, he thought, there was only one way to find out. His first stop on the way home was at the public library.

It didn't take him long to learn that the word Druid was a combination of 'dru' and 'vid,' 'to know' or 'see.' Thus the Druid was the gifted one, who knew and presumably saw into the future. They belonged to 'a mysterious religious sect' predating Christianity, and wore long priestly robes at their ceremonies. At that point, he realized that the mysterious woman had made him learn for himself that if all she said was true, he had to believe she had the gift of knowing. She also said that she was Gaelic and that her name was Cuchulain, so he continued to search the Internet for that name in Gaelic antiquity. The closest he came was to a legendary Gaelic warrior, Cuchulainn, a heroic superhuman figure, given to extraordinary exploits. Alone, he and his sword slew an army of hundreds. After the battle, his body radiated such heat that it 'melted snow for thirty feet around.' Later, when he bathed in the sea to cool himself, 'the water boiled.' John was amazed at the knowledge

Mary had urged him to inquire about her background. He had quite a few questions for her. But would he see her again?

While John kept telling himself that the idea of Leesa's infidelity was too far-fetched to consider, yet his thoughts kept returning to that accursed Magdalene woman and his vow to emulate the Carpenter's virtues of compassion and forgiveness that had cleansed her of sin. Suddenly, he caught sight of Mary Cuchulain in the adjacent café. She was seated as before, no doubt again waiting for him. He confronted her.

"How did you know I wanted to see you, and how am I to know what you say is true?" He asked.

Mary remained silent for a long moment, and then finally stated: "People with serious stress problems exude a peculiar aura that I can feel and sometimes see. Their stress creates a powerful attraction that allows me to feel their pain; to get an idea of their problem. Experience does the rest. Once I looked at you, I could tell that you were under great stress. Then, when I saw your lady, with the bulge of her bosom, the bloom in her face, but without a ring on her finger, I had a good idea of the problem troubling you both."

"What makes you think I've been under stress, worrying about whether or not my fiancée is pregnant?"

"It shows," she replied simply. "Isn't that the problem that's been bugging you?" Her wide staring eyes and raised eyebrows goaded him to admit his feelings.

"I have been considering that possibility, but neither you nor I know the truth. Although I am impressed by the facts you've stated and with the uncanny knowledge you seem to have of both present and future, I don't...I still can't believe you. So, now that you've made me aware that you have the gift of prophecy, is there anything else you think I should know?" His arrogant smile of skepticism made it clear he didn't believe a word she said. Stung by the fact that he had accused her of falsehood, she decided to clear up the mystery.

"Your fiancée *is* pregnant." She said simply, rising from her seat, her face white and twisted with anger at his unspoken accusation. Then she added. "She will bear a son who will need one of mine to care for him. But I won't say more than their will be bloodshed, broken bones and blindness."

"Wait!" He almost shouted when she left the café before he could stop her. Her departure left him with a dilemma. Should he take the word of a complete stranger and accuse his fiancée? Or should he be patient and wait for her to confide in him of her own volition? The decision he had to make kept torturing him day and night until he asked himself and answered what he considered the only pertinent questions. Was he still in love with Leesa? Would he still marry her if she were pregnant? His answer to both questions was a resounding 'yes.' It was somewhat later that Leesa fabricated the story of her rape, her pregnancy, and the way she decided to overcome the problem with his help. Since she had confided in him of her own volition, he agreed to her plea to spirit her away directly after the wedding. It would solve a number of problems, the most important of which was the reputation of their child. Yet, not surprisingly, he couldn't stop thinking of Mary Cuchulain.

After Kim failed to arouse her husband with her back-scratching technique, she snuggled up and pressed her naked body against his. While whispering "I need you," she slipped her hand between his legs and began to gently massage his member, but much to her chagrin, there was no result. Despite more eager coaxing, the organ remained limp and lifeless. While she began to wonder what had happened, she couldn't help glaring angrily at her indifferent husband and feeling bitterly humiliated at his rejection. The white light in her brain flared igniting her anger. She lost control and slashed savagely at her husband's back with her long fingernails. She felt satisfied that she left deep gashes on his back. She then leapt from the sleeping mat in a huff, went to her own mat and saw blood on her fingertips. It serves him right, she thought, glad that she had really hurt him. She then tossed and turned in a rage of dissatisfaction and suspicion before actually dozing off. From that time onward, each time she signaled her invitation to intimacy, Yong Sang's back grew rigid, his muscles tensed and he kept his distance.

His wife's persistence drove him crazy with increased guilt and shame at his inability to give her the love, warmth and comfort she sought. What irked him equally was the irony of his conduct. He had begun by doing what he shouldn't have done, and ended by refusing to do what he should. He saw with deep sorrow that the evil he had initiated had driven a wedge between his wife and himself, destroying the bonds of love that had cemented the family together. But neither guilt nor sorrow could undo the wrong he had committed, and there seemed to be nothing he could do to heal the wounds he had inflicted on his family and on himself.

Over the ensuing years, after their daughter's marriage, both parents visited their daughter and son-in-law, John. And whenever their preteen granddaughter, Serena, prattled to them about the life-long fidelity and devotion to each other of her mated pigeons, each spouse fell silent becoming sick-at-heart at the ever growing distance between them.

Serena's painting went hand in hand with her life on the farm. She drew her models from nature, yet she focused her attention on the wild animals seen on the farm, at the zoo or from enlarged photographs she took or bought. Unconsciously, while painting her subjects, she would try to imagine what each of them was thinking. From long observation, she knew their habits and often could accurately forecast their next move. Because of her knowledge and insight into their conduct, she began thinking of them as her kin. Soon, she was silently communicating with them. She would sharply criticize the wolf gorging on carrion for his bad manners then excuse his behavior by concluding that otherwise he would starve to death. The episode would set her wondering how she would react in a similar situation. It made her realize that there would be no alternative if she wanted to stay alive. To the eagle in flight above his realm hunting prey far below, she wondered whether his majestic soaring would encourage a tendency towards arrogance and egotism.

In this way, she would converse with, question, comment on, criticize or sympathize with the conduct and the attitudes she had conferred upon the animals she painted. Her love of nature and her painting of its subjects created and developed for her a rich and rewarding life of the mind. While this was a world of pure fantasy, the unrestricted use of her imagination in the practice of her art provided her with a vital outlet. It served as a buffer against the painful reality with which she was surrounded. Painting channeled her thoughts away from the dangers of introspection and acted as a restorative to a healthy life. It helped her to endure, and while being of immense therapeutic value, served to enrich her existence.

The morning after Kim's rejection was overcast. Clouds of a sinister darkness had gathered and the sky was ominous. The gloom that penetrated her household had affected her mood. She was already angry after carefully searching her husband's sleeping mat and finding a few pubic hairs that didn't seem to have come from her body or his. When there was no corroborating evidence on her daughter's sleeping mat, she was so perplexed that she didn't know what to think. Yet, the very idea that the mortal sin of incest might have occurred in her own home, drove her frantic, especially between the two people whom she most worshiped.

Some would say that John was a punctilious man, since he was meticulous in his habits. He rose at 5 A.M. each morning, did his calisthenics for exactly thirty minutes, followed by his bath and ablutions for exactly twenty. He then supervised his daughter's regimen of exercises, dressed in one of his Oxford don outfits, breakfasted on a cup of coffee and two slices of buttered toast and was driving on his way to work by 7:30 A.M. exactly. Rather than take vacations, he spend that time visiting any department store or manufacturing branch of his corporation that was failing to meet its quota. He thought of himself as a quiet man, seldom speaking unless he had something worthwhile to say.

Acting as a trouble shooter, he interviewed managers and employees scrutinizing their work ethic as well as the financial system that was in place. He often found that an unhealthy balance sheet could often be traced to poor managerial skills, the thoughtless distancing between employee and customer or even to shoddy window displays that failed to advertise the promotion of weekly loss leaders. By the time he left the branch, the problems were usually diagnosed and solved, and the branch on its way to meeting its quota.

He had given a lot of his time to his family, conversing with them over board games like *yut* and *go* that are so popular in Korea. He had taught them *cribbage*, another popular board game played with cards that he had learnt during his years in Canada. As a family, they looked at the televised computer game contests and at the films on TV that they hadn't seen at the cinema. One day, he took his teenage daughter aside and asked if she had made plans for the future. "You'll be graduating in a few months. Have you thought of anything you'd like to do?"

"Dad I'm not sure what I'd like to do," she told him.

"You know there's always an opening for you in our organization. You only have to say when and where."

"Is that the echo of Mama's voice I'm hearing somewhere in the background, Dad?"

"Yes, she wants me to encourage you to begin working with us. You'll get some experience of what you'll encounter in the business world. But darling, the decision is entirely yours. You know that I'd never pressure you into doing anything against your will."

"Thank you Dad. I want you to know how much I appreciate your offer. But working in the world of business is low on my priority list. The little I do know doesn't appeal to me and I don't feel I have anything to contribute to that world. I want to do something that really counts."

"It makes me really proud to hear the daughter I love say that the work I do in business doesn't really count," he replied, his tone turning from sympathetic to deeply ironic.

Kim's mind was in turmoil as her depression grew and darkened her already black mood. Finding no solution to her problem, her anger increased. She was ignorant of what to do next and in a state of mental and physical confusion. She rushed to the church to ponder over the ghastly possibilities as she fixated upon the lecherous images that seared her mind. Her haunted thoughts coated all those images in the deepest pessimism, giving rise to unanswerable questions. Was it her daughter who had whored herself with her father, or had her own husband initiated the wicked seduction of his own daughter? More and more lewd and disgusting images flooded her brain. Frantic that she couldn't tell whether or not her worst fears had been realized, she decided to observe the conduct of husband and daughter during the next few days. She would then surely know the truth.

"Dad, I apologize. I didn't mean that the work you do is unimportant. The fact is that business never has, nor ever will, hold any interest for me."

"Really Serena? Tell me, what do you know about the world of business?"

"Very little, Dad. I know you employ a lot of people, and that I suppose is helpful. But the bottom line in business is making a huge profit. Isn't that why we can live a life of affluence, while your workers, whose hard work provides that affluence, lead a life of deprivation? I hope you're not going to tell me that my assumptions are wrong." Her father laughed at her naïveté, setting aside his exasperation, before explaining.

"My darling child, your assumptions are so very wrong. Your words suggest that we're still living in the Dark Ages. Your description couldn't be further from the truth. Serena, your grandfather and I employ hundreds of people. That means there are hundreds of families that owe their livelihood, their very existence, to our organization. Like other corporations, we go a long way to help those we employ. With a deduction from the wage of each worker, we pay the medical and dental expenses of the whole family. We provide additional employment for spouses of our employees who need it. We use our influence to get the children of our employees into good schools and universities and when needed, pay half the cost of their extra tuition. It's an incredibly competitive world out there! A good education is the only way to a successful professional career, and education is extremely expensive. We help. We've also bought hotels in resort areas where our employees and their families can spend their vacation at greatly reduced rates."

It took numerous attempts at stifling her feelings before Serena was capable of writing down the incidents of her assault. She persevered, although failing again and again, until finally she managed to finish the first draft. She entitled it: "Serena's Gang rape." She noticed, as she recorded the events and the emotions provoked by each of the acts, that the repeated process of reliving each episode from beginning to end was cathartic. Gradually, she began to feel differently once she got past the revolting feelings experienced during the assaults. When she analyzed these strange new feelings, she realized that what her mother had told her was true. She had radically altered her point of view with the familiarity that grew from confronting her demons again and again.

When Yong Sang rose early, Kim scrutinized his actions from partly closed eyes. He brought her a glass of orange juice, prepared his breakfast and a bowl of *bibimbap*, rice mixed with vegetables and red pepper paste, for lunch. After kissing her warmly, he went off to his workshop behaving as he always did, without any suggestion in his conduct or appearance that could be construed as guilt.

Leesa rose about an hour after her father left. "Mama, why is the house so gloomy and cold? I'll turn on the lights," she added, kissing her mother warmly. She ate a portion of her breakfast then busied herself, listing what was done and what needed doing for the wedding. She then asked whether Kim and her father would survive a civil ceremony rather than an elaborate church wedding.

"We'll agree with whatever decision you make." Leesa then left for school to study for her approaching final exams. Otherwise, she kept her distance from both parents exactly as she had done ever since her engagement.

"Dad, you're right. I had no idea that corporations went so far, or were so generous to employees and their families."

"Many large corporations run their organizations along those lines, though few mid-sized corporations go as far as we do."

"So you've been treating your workers like family."

"They are family. As their paternal employers, your grandfather and I have taken steps to set up our own department stores. Since our businesses manufacture the products we sell in those stores, we are able to provide good quality household products like furniture, large and small appliances, and clothing for our workers at lower prices than our competitors. Then, we have supermarkets where we provide the most basic food for our families. We offer them rice, milk, lentils, pork, seafood and vegetables, your eggs, chickens, ducks, turkeys and geese. More recently, we have included fish from the farming community. We have been able to undersell out competitors since we farm and manufacture many of the items ourselves. Since we can buy in bulk at reduced prices we pass on to our employees for only a marginal profit those items that we neither farm nor manufacture. The major share of our profit comes from the customers who don't work for us. And thanks to our prices that are lower than those of the competitors we have a very large customer base. Finally, there are other improvements that we are about to implement."

"Dad, I don't understand. If the prices of your items are fixed, how do you differentiate between the prices paid by employees and non-employees?"

"Our employees have company credit cards that guarantee them special prices."

Chapter 25

"Mama," Serena blurted out, "you were right. Once I became the observer rather than the victim, I was able to see my rape in a completely different perspective. It was a random act." In tears, she related how she had eventually arrived at the conclusion through reasoning.

"And how did that make you feel?" Her mother asked intent on urging Serena to continue the therapy.

"Since it was a random act, I had done nothing to provoke it as I could do nothing to stop it."

"Did you feel better, worse, what?" Her mother persisted.

"I began to feel a sense of lightness, of release, but it didn't happen right away. It was gradual." Her mother could hear the amazement in her voice.

"All the horrible things I had thought before; things causing my black moods of depression were totally false."

"Be more specific Rina," said her mother, determined to prolong her daughter's self-revelation. "What was false?"

"I felt that I hadn't struggled enough, screamed loudly enough. Mama, I even felt that I had attracted and encouraged the rapists by the way I dressed."

"How could you possibly think that?"

"I wore fashionable clothes, expensive perfume, and of course being alone, I was vulnerable. Once these false beliefs took hold, I felt that I deserved what I got. Oh Mama, I was so wrong!" As she hugged and comforted Serena, her mother whispered: "I'm so glad you're managing to shake off those false beliefs darling, so very glad."

"Dad, you've really astounded me with your information. But how does the cost of living of your workers compare with that of others? And what are these grand plans that you and granddad have?"

"Our benefits allow our employees to live at about three quarters of the cost of others. Therefore, they lead lives that are far more comfortable than many other workers in the country; better even than the workers in some bigger corporations. Equally important, they have easy access to the things they need. We are also arranging through our organization for them to get help with the mortgages on their homes. Further, every worker will be encouraged to buy shares in the corporation through deductions from his wages. Most important, those workers who have a proven record of efficiency and loyalty to the company will be offered a special credit card. At the year's end, these card carriers will receive a 10 % rebate on the full amount they have spent at our shops. Once these innovations are set in motion, no other corporation, big or small, will have gone as far in creating a better life for their employees."

"It sounds as though what you spend on your employees must plunge your organization into total bankruptcy," Serena said with a laugh.

"No. We do make a profit, but that is not the bottom line. You see, while our workers do provide us with affluent lives, we make sure that a hefty part of our profit is used to allow them to lead decent and comfortable lives themselves. But in offering them these benefits, we expect them to show their appreciation with excellent service and loyalty. So now that I've given you a peep into our world of business, I hope you think that what we do is worthwhile. Now, my dearest, what do *you* want to do with your life? I hope it begins with further study at a university."

"Dad, as you know from my past, I've always felt that the most satisfying job lies in helping the less fortunate in some way. Now that I know what you and granddad are doing, I want very much to follow your example. But exactly how, I've not decided. I see life as a kind of quest, the pursuit of which can bring out the best in an individual. Please don't laugh at my puerile thinking, but I don't believe it involves going to university. I also hope my view doesn't disappoint you too much."

"Darling, I never laugh at your thinking, and believe me it's anything but puerile. How could I possibly laugh after seeing all you've done for the farmers of our district? Without realizing it, you've also shown tremendous promise as a business woman. But I'm not at all pleased with your decision to avoid a university education."

"Dad, let me think about it please."

"Most students with an academic record like yours would jump at the chance to go to one of the SKY universities, especially with all the years of *hagwon* you've done. But, it's early yet, and I hope you'll change your mind. However, I think that when the time comes, you'll be mature enough to choose the career that appeals to you most. You know that you're our most precious and beloved daughter. When you decide on a career, please let me know. I'd like very much to help."

"Mama, I'll trust you always." After a pause, she added: "And you know what? Being the observer made me reason that since I wasn't responsible for the attack; I don't need to feel guilt or shame, or to blame myself as I've been doing."

"So you're finally rid yourself of those destructive emotions?"

"Only to a point." She replied puzzled. "You see, the rape should be losing its hold over me, and I keep telling myself that I shouldn't need to feel any guilt or shame. But even though the feelings are much less intense, they're still there." The puzzlement and profound grief in her daughter's voice wrung her mother's heart.

"Rina dear, what you'll learn is that reason alone is not strong enough to erase deep feelings immediately. This is especially true of feelings that you have repeatedly drummed into your consciousness."

"Are you saying that these feelings will always remain to plague me and that they'll never go away?"

"Rina dear, some remnants of guilt and shame will continue to distress you. They too will gradually lessen in intensity, but they'll never disappear completely. They're part of your history. Repeated reasoning will help you to accept the changes you're going through, the strengths and maturity you're building."

"In short, I'll recover fully?" There was such hope in her voice that her mother's heart melted with love.

"Yes darling. You've moved out of the darkness towards the light. You're becoming a new person. Be patient dear, it's a long, and difficult process, but oh so rewarding."

There were times at night when Serena would awake to the sound of the heavy rain drumming down on her skylight. Sleep would elude her and she would set up her easel and canvas and decide to paint. She sometimes found that while painting, her mind would wander and in the twinkling of an eye she would be riding into the mountains with her father. In her mind's eye she would actually smell the fat sizzling on the grill, see the flare of flame and hear the hiss of droplets falling into the fire. These scents, sounds and images would come unbidden to haunt her. As she struggled to return her focus to her painting it would suddenly occur to her that apart from the environment, her thoughts had been occupied with the presence of her father only. Her conscience would then attack her for not having given a single thought to her mother who had given Serena life, and unswerving devotion. With selfless dedication, she had brought her daughter back to the land of the living during her long and dangerous illness and recovery. Serena felt like the world's worst ingrate. At that moment, she thought that ingratitude had to rank as one of the gravest sins. Yet, it wasn't long before her focus would automatically shift back to the forested mountains where she would identify herself once more with its wild creatures.

Kim grew more and more angry at a husband who continually rejected her advances. Since her daughter had left home after her marriage, the once loving home they shared and treasured, had become a dreary prison. In it, two strangers were sentenced to live out their isolated lives. In Yong Sang's state of self-imposed impotence, he had discarded his wife like an old shoe that no longer fitted. Not only did this state of affairs increase his torment, but it also struck him then that he had destroyed any possibility of salvaging the broken fragments of his marriage.

John couldn't help noticing the strain that existed between his in-laws on their visits to his home. He noted their unnatural silences, the distance they kept from each other and the fact that they never made eye contact. On one occasion, he mentioned his observations to Yong Sang and on receiving a non-committal response, decided to hold his tongue rather than pry any further. He knew that every marriage had its own problems. While he let the matter rest, he wondered why, unlike Serena's pigeons, human beings seemed incapable of maintaining an untroubled relationship. Why, he asked himself, was the bond of fidelity so delicate and tenuous that the slightest tension could destroy it? And why did the resulting discord so often begin in betrayal of one kind or another?

Although John could see that his wife was troubled, he was never quite sure of the cause of her distress. His wife however, did not need a reminder.

"With each passing day her unforgivable act had scandalized her more and more. The lies she had told her husband, and those she felt compelled to use to cover her tracks, sickened her. She sometimes became nauseous with bouts of vomiting and got such violent migraines that she needed strong pain-killing drugs and sleeping pills to help overcome the problems. Perhaps what troubled her most was the feeling of exclusion; the steel wall of alienation erected between her and everyone else in her world. Her secret shame and guilt festered within her and she could find no way to escape her feelings of depravity and contamination. Yet, without help, she had no alternative but to weather the physical and spiritual storm as best she could.

Chapter 26

The days dragged on into weeks and Kim could never pinpoint the slightest evidence that would tell her whether or not the dreadful event had taken place. As ever, she found that her mind, like her house, was always clouded in gloom. She began to wonder if it was her anger and disappointment at rejection that had induced her to imagine the worst. While she couldn't see any change in the conduct of either husband or daughter, the mental anguish of not knowing yet thinking about the calamity every waking moment, had seriously affected her state of mind. The outrageous act, the terrible suspicion and accusations it spawned, caused a dramatic change in her conduct.

She felt that she had to get out of that darkened house and began to distance herself more and more from both its evil occupants. She spent more and more time outdoors away from home, especially when the two were indoors. Her long walks and visits to the church became more frequent and lasted longer. And all the while she brooded over the betrayal of her two Judas' as she came to think of her husband and daughter. At the same time, neither of the two culprits dared to question her about her long and frequent absences from home. There was also no comment on the looks of accusation in her eyes, the awkwardness of her body language or her long silences in their presence.

Serena was elated at the progress she was making in exorcizing her ghosts and decided to return to school to complete the few months before graduation. Mona's absence bothered her. She had never come to visit. Impulsively, she phoned to tell Mona the decision she had made. Her mother answered the phone, evidently surprised to hear Serena's voice and that she wanted to speak to Mona. She told her that Mona was out and would return her call later. When the whole weekend passed without her friend calling, Serena began to suspect that something was wrong.

While she was definitely on the way to recovery, she was by no means fully recovered. She was still being plagued by nightmares. The same predatory beasts that she painted by day had so etched themselves into her consciousness that they returned to haunt her by night. In sleep, they shattered her newfound peace of mind, launching attack after attack upon her. She always seemed to be terror struck racing through one of the forest-backdrops that she had painted for her subjects. As she ran, the wet branches of the trees slashed at her face and body, clawed at her eyes. She could feel the blood running down her face, arms and legs, while she continued running for her life. As she searched desperately for a safe haven, her ragged breathing came in spurts and her chest burned from a lack of oxygen.

She didn't let the nightmares change her mind and forced herself back to school on the following Monday. She found to her dismay that her classmates avoided her. They all averted their eyes and her sense of isolation intensified when no teacher mentioned her absence or welcomed her back. Everyone treated her as though she had a terminal illness and kept his or her distance as though the disease were contagious. Rape had made her a pariah, with everyone refusing to look in her direction. At school, she had suddenly become invisible.

Sometimes, Kim sat on a park bench in the nearby square with her hands laced together covering her head. It seemed as though she was trying to prevent her brains from exploding. She kept asking herself: what could she do, where could she go, how could she escape the dreadful isolation that her family was forcing her to endure? And inevitably, she began to wonder what mortal sin had she committed to bring such calamity into her life. She lost interest in her household chores that she had done so willingly for the husband and daughter she loved. She lost her appetite for food and drink and was unable to sleep at night. Like thick black smoke curling and uncurling, pessimistic thoughts swirled crazily in her head. Nightmare images of incest poisoned her sleeping and waking hours. Images of her husband and daughter locked in sexual embrace bedeviled her mind. And what was driving her to distraction was the mental picture of her daughter's face contorted in delight.

She began to hate the world she lived in, and detested even more her own loathsome life. In order to shut out the ever growing gloom, she had developed the habit of keeping the lights in her home turned on day and night. But that failed to dispel either the gloom or her rage. She lost weight and all interest in maintaining her appearance. In a few short weeks, she became a gaunt creature with bowed back and lackluster eyes. And while these changes for the worse took place, the anger within her kept building and building until it became transformed into full blown hatred that, bottled up, threatened to explode and shatter her insides. Mentally and physically exhausted, she could no longer withhold either the bitterness of her anguish or the potency of her rage.

Serena looked at her former classmates, their faces pinched with a mixture of suspicion, guilt and shame. Their eyes slid away from her direct stare, unwilling to make contact. They seemed to be thinking of themselves faced with the same situation. Since she had been friendly to all, they seemed ashamed of their act of collective cowardice and betrayal. During the lunch break, she summoned up her courage and approached her very embarrassed friend.

"Mona, why are you and everyone else avoiding me?"

"Serena, Mama says I can't be friends with you anymore. You know," she continued, "mixing with a person who's badly tainted, you run the risk of becoming taint..." her voice trailed off. Then she added: "The other students seem to have got the same message from their parents."

"You surprise me Mona. I never expected you of all people to be a Judas." Her voice trembled with the ache and humiliation she felt at her best friend's disloyalty. It made her loneliness more acute, more heartbreaking. This was the time she most needed the support and loyalty of a friend. The bitterness she felt building inside her, rose in her throat like vomit, and the frustration of being helpless to fight against her estranged friend forced her to sob out her gall.

"Oh Mona," Serena whispered through hot tears, "how could you? Weren't you the one who lectured to me that friends should always be able to count on each other?" The hurt in her voice and the tears in her eyes should have created a deep knife-wound in Mona's heart. But if she felt the bite of the blade entering her flesh, the shock did nothing to change her attitude. She seemed to revel at the thought of at last being the one in charge; the dominant one. Perhaps, it was the envy and jealousy she felt when confronted by Serena's beauty and charisma that had made Mona so relentless an enemy. Her animosity must have developed into full blown hatred that obliterated all considerations of friendship and compassion. Serena knew that Mona hadn't been able to stop herself from spreading the most scandalous rumors about her and her family. Mona's face was radiant, glorying in the fact that she was no longer the underdog. She was cherishing the situation that had finally made her the dominant one in their relationship. She couldn't suppress the taunt that she had in store for Serena: "So the star had finally fallen," Mona stated with glee in her voice. But thinking quickly, Serena refused to give Mona the upper hand and replied: "I'm surprised at your ignorance Mona. Stars pitch. They never fall."

Mona took the hit but was not easily shaken. She wanted to grind Serena into the dust. She could hardly contain a perverse smile as she began paving the way for the execution she had painstakingly planned." Mama doesn't believe your trumped up story."

"What does your snake of a mother accuse me of?"

"My snake of a mother knows you are lying." Mona replied angrily, riled at Serena's slanderous description of her mother.

"What story Mona? What story am I lying about? She thinks I deceived the doctors at the hospital's Rape Crisis Center pretending I was raped. I then lay in bed at home play-acting at being sick?"

"No! She says she's seen you out and about wearing the skimpiest of tank tops and the shortest of mini skirts. She considers it disgusting that you flaunt your body so shamelessly as though advertizing it for sale. She can't believe your family permits it."

"Mona, you've been everywhere with me and you know that's a lot of lies. So tell me, while snake number one was tearing my reputation to shreds, did snake number two just listen and accept what was said or did she defend her 'best friend?'" Mona hadn't expected the question or the vicious irony with which it was shot at her. Caught off guard, she reacted automatically. With shock on her face and a crimson blush that betrayed her guilt, she remained in tongue-tied silence for too long a moment before stammering unconvincingly: "I-I tried, but y-you know Mama. When she gets an idea into her head she doesn't listen to what anyone else has to say."

"So you listened to that snake slander your 'best friend' and never said a word in her defense! Well Mona, you vipers can slither back into the subterranean sewer where you both belong—deep underground and out of sight."

One very windy day while her birds were circling, Serena held her breath on seeing a hawk soar upwards from a tree top. Its immense wingspan and powerful muscles made it quickly airborne. She grew apprehensive as it pumped its wings against the blustering wind striving for height. She felt positive it would climb to the level of her circling birds to hunt them. But the hawk appeared to be oblivious of her pigeons. It kept powerfully mounting the air, increasing its height until it became a tiny speck high above and behind the pigeons. They continued to circle, fighting the wind, ignorant of their airborne menace.

The raptor zeroed in on the flock with its acute vision. It lusted at a fore-taste of the living flesh that would quell the sting of its hunger. It kept pumping itself upwards towards the sun, oblivious of all but the terror and destruction it would visit on its prey. It flexed its powerful talons, eager to rip into the body of any laggard it intimidated and separated from the flock.

The penny only dropped after Serena suddenly recognized the age-old technique of the aerial assassin. It had gained height to use the shelter of the sun's brilliance as a backdrop. Camouflaging itself, it remained invisible to its intended prey. Patiently, it waited until one of the younger birds began falter-ing in its struggle to keep up with the others. The moment it fell behind, the hawk pumped its wings vigorously and dove headlong at the stray. When the predator had built up enough speed, it locked its wings into a swept-back po-sition and bored down like a bullet towards its quarry.

Serena was as startled as her birds when they suddenly became aware of their dangerous adversary. The tight formation of the flock erupted, as though a bomb had exploded in their midst. The panicked birds veered crazily in all directions. Some tried to gain height–a dangerous tactic born of terror. Others dove in a frenzy to exit the air as quickly as possible. The fierce wind kept pummeling the pigeons, forcing them to drift sideways, frustrating and ham-pering their escape. The more mature birds dashed towards the shelter of the neighboring trees, while others zoomed under the eaves of houses for protec-tion. All but a few had careened towards the earth, their own wings folded back for speed.

But the speed of the pigeons was no match for that of the raptor. It had already locked upon its prey. Despite the bird's mad zigzagging attempt at evasion, the hawk expertly shadowed its every move. Serena's heart leapt to her throat in anxiety over the safety of the youngster, for with the swift ap-proach of its nemesis, the bird's fate seemed to be sealed. When the raptor was within a few meters of its prey, the pigeon tried a last desperate tactic. It suddenly braked against the air stalling on its wings and dodging sideways to evade its pursuer.

"Stop calling my family names, Serena. The members of your family are no angels according to the things I've heard my parents discussing."

"I thought your assault was aimed solely at me. What does my family have to do with any of this?"

"Leave it alone Serena. You don't want to know. Your parents are angels, right?" Mona said goading her friend onward so she could plunge the knife more deeply into her heart. Unknowingly, Serena was cooperating with her.

"Why don't you spill what other lies you and your parents have on your forked tongues? Isn't that what you've been dying to do all along?"

"So you really want to know? Okay, I'll help you with the truth. Your mother is a scarlet woman! There! You're satisfied now?" Although the statement shocked Serena, she pretended it was a lie and couldn't affect her. She replied breezily, giving Mona the opportunity she had been waiting for.

"Is that the best you can do, Mona?"

"It's not a lie," she said. "I checked." Serena gave up her act of pretense and shouted:

"How the hell could you do that?" Rejoicing at the opportunity to do the damage she had painstakingly orchestrated, Mona drove the knife deeper in, and then twisted the blade.

"Your mother brought forward her wedding date by more than four months. So, let me help you with the math: she betrayed her intended husband, then disappeared with him for ages, before returning with a baby. In short, your mother's a slut, just like you, and your father is probably not your biological father. Leaving those terrible words ringing in Serena's ears, Mona turned to leave, elated at having seen the whites of her enemy's eyes. But Serena hadn't surrendered yet. Mona's slander of her parents goaded her to spew out her own venom.

"Go tell viper number one which one of us sluts was sneaking out at midnight and fucking the life out of your new farmhand all last summer. She'll be delighted to learn that her daughter is following in her footsteps."

Once more alone, Serena's distress encouraged that sickness of soul leading to a mood of the blackest pessimism. Her whole mind became focused on blame. She couldn't remove from her thoughts her best friend's filthy attack on her family. It made her green eyes turn steely with anger, and then they quickly flooded with tears of humiliation. Human beings, she thought, were like the weather; fickle and unreliable. Neither can be trusted. When your corn is ripening and you're counting on the harvest to make a killing, an early frost comes along and destroys it all. It's the same with people. Those, whom you count upon to be loyal, deceive you with their lies and hypocrisy. Their betrayal obliterates all thoughts of compassion or forgiveness.

Chapter 27

The hawk intercepted every one of the pigeon's moves. Swiveling sideways, it extended its talons. In a split second, it struck and torpedoed the straggler with its razor sharp talons. On impact, it ripped into the flesh, crushed the bone and knocked the pigeon senseless. Serena's heart pounded and, as a burst of feathers mushroomed into the air, an involuntary moan of sorrow rose from her throat.

The collision hurled the pigeon clean out of its flight path. Its red stained feathers tumbled into the violent wind, standing out against the white cloud-patterned sky. The driving force of the predator killed the quarry instantly, slashing deep into its terrified heart. As the pigeon's feathers pin-wheeled through the air, a triumphant scream broke from the hawk. It then turned steeply, swooping down upon the falling bird and, snatching the prey in mid-air, flew off with its next meal. The whole violent episode had played out against a serene, dispassionate sky on the one hand and an impassioned observer on the other.

Serena's grief was short lived at the loss of one of her prized youngsters. At first, she was overwhelmed and outraged at the cruelty of the raptor, but couldn't help admiring its lightening speed, its cunning, and its aerial acrobatics. Its sheer physical prowess left her speechless. It was as accurate in its aim as a guided missile zeroing in on its target, and equally deadly. Like the ultimate predator it mimicked, it seemed the incarnation of evil.

She wondered whether she could ever be as steadfast and direct in her purpose. The stunning areal display so deeply affected her that after her violation, the hawk kept appearing in one of her recurring nightmares. She would see the pigeon zigzagging crazily through the air in a desperate attempt to elude its pursuing nemesis. The life and death contest of flight and pursuit went on and on until the pigeon became an image of herself in panicked flight. Her own demons were hot on her trail, and although she had eluded them so far, she felt, with growing terror and exhaustion, that in their relentless pursuit, they would eventually overtake and destroy her.

As dusk approached, storm clouds, heavy with their moisture, accumulated over the little township of Hamyang. In the descending darkness, the clouds burst, and from the heavens they spewed out their contents. In the howling wind, the rain drummed upon the roofs of houses; lashing the sides of buildings; overflowing the eaves; flooding the fields. The deluge broke branches, fell trees and turned the unpaved roads into raging torrents. In minutes, everything was soaked so that much later when the storm abated, the town remained crouched and shivering like a wet cat.

After the deluge, Serena walked gingerly over the splashy earth, skirting the huge puddles and jumping over runnels on her way to the riverbank. She needed the peace and seclusion of one of her favorite spots to suppress her anger and confusion; to silence the growing noise in her head and to calm her fears. Yet, she found it impossible to stop her mind and body reeling from the verbal stab wounds that Mona had delivered with such accuracy. She stood aghast, gazing in amazement at the change that had come over her favored spot on the riverbank. After the storm, the lazily flowing creek had become a raging flood no longer emptying into a crystal-clear pool. Instead, it had burst its banks transforming the pool into a chaotic mud-charged torrent.

Although appearing calm and composed on the outside, Serena resembled her pool on the inside. She struggled to control the raging flood of images swirling crazily, choking the canals of her brain. But try as she might, her doubts and fears kept bombarding her mind and she couldn't repress the horde of questions about her mother and father that, without answers, kept driving her to distraction.

"Mama, no one at school talks to me. No one whom I counted as friends even looks in my direction, not even Mona." Serena blurted out, sadness dripping from her words, yet looking at her mother with new eyes, wondering at Mona's accusations. What her mother wanted to reply was: Don't let their attitude bother you dear. Things will change. They'll eventually realize their mistake. However, she knew that such words would be meaningless to Serena in her present grief. Cold reason is grossly inappropriate at such times. The only worthwhile remedy is silence and sympathy expressed in a tight, warm hug from a fellow human being. In silence, Leesa embraced her daughter. But Serena, still wrestling with her isolation and unable to withhold her anger and frustration posed the question: "Mama, do you know what it feels like to be all alone?"

That I can lecture about, thought Leesa. Instead she advised: "Try not to think about it, Rina. It will only distress you more."

"Even the teachers didn't welcome me back and they too refused to make eye contact with me. Everyone was so cruel. The few who did speak to me never made eye contact. They all looked at a space beside me."

"They didn't make eye contact because they were ashamed of their betrayal." Leesa spoke from personal experience.

"Rina darling, this is the time you need to be strong. Those who turn away from you don't know the meaning of loyalty. They aren't worthy of your friendship. Besides, you don't have to go back to school."

"Mama I have to go back if I'm to graduate. I won't let the disloyalty of those I counted on as friends prevent me from graduating. Besides, I can't give up. I'm not a quitter."

"Rina dearest, you don't need the aggravation or the pain. You've had enough to last you a lifetime. You need to stay away from people with such shabby principles." And in her mind, she thought with deep regret that the criticism was aimed more accurately at herself.

"No Mama. I have to go back to finish. And I also need to face up to betrayal, to bear its burden and, in spite of the heartache, to stand up and to endure."

"Oh Rina, sometimes you seem bent on suffering needlessly, on destroying your peace of mind," her mother replied in exasperation.

Serena's last jibe had hurt Mona so deeply that she took special care to paint Serena, her mother, father and family as black as possible. "Not only is her mother an immoral monster, who betrayed her husband-to-be by becoming pregnant for someone else during her engagement," she told anyone who would listen, "but the daughter, Serena is the worst cock-teaser imaginable. She enjoys exposing herself in the skimpiest of clothes to invite male attention. She finally went too far and got what she deserved: she was gang raped."

By the time Mona and her family had finished spreading their rumors, the reputation of Serena and the Ahn family was in tatters. In fact, the rumor-mill was so successful that shortly afterwards, as Ahn and his employees were leaving their office building one evening, a number of paparazzi suddenly descended upon them. They poked their cameras in Ahn's face, snapping his picture to authenticate the vile rumors they intended to print. They shot the foulest of questions at their victim hoping for an angry response or insult that would lend further credibility to their story. They knew too that any scandal centered on hot illicit sex would greatly increase the circulation of their newspapers and magazines.

"Was your wife pregnant for you or for someone else while you were engaged?"

"Your child was born only six months after your marriage. Were you the father?"

"Is your child a product of incest?"

"Now that you know that your wife is a scarlet woman, will you divorce her?"

John was white with rage at being vilified to his face and before the eyes and ears of his employees. Although humiliated and incensed by the insistence of reporters that he had married a scarlet woman, and that his daughter was not fathered by him, he faced the inquisition with silence and stoicism. His height and bearing gave him a commanding presence that was increased by the sheer force of his personality as by the esteem with which his peers accorded him. With the reporters thick on his heels like marauding dogs, he behaved as though their poisoned fangs failed to penetrate the armor-plate of his self confidence. His employees were secretly proud of his reaction. He remained ramrod straight, ignoring his attackers as though they were no more than a tiresome swarm of insects beneath his contempt.

Kim's active imagination replayed the scenes she dreaded so vividly in her mind that she might have been actually standing at the door of her bedroom observing the spectacle. She saw her husband's trouser legs tangled around the outfit her daughter had discarded on the floor. The white blood-stained sheet was thrown aside and she could almost inhale the rank scent of sex filling the room. She shook her head vigorously trying to erase the image of the two sweat-covered bodies on the mat locked in passionate combat. But she was helpless to dispel the images flooding her brain.

Her daughter's eyes were tightly shut; her legs wide open. The muscles and tendons in her neck and limbs were stretched taut and her bared teeth indicated she was in the throes of passion. Her husband was the jockey violently goading his mount towards the post. The lurid images so nauseated her that she rushed to the toilet to vomit up her insides. When her retching stopped, she blanched in humiliation, trying desperately to focus her mind on less disturbing thoughts. But for a long time she found that impossible.

Immediately, the shame that her images inspired, forced her to repeat the questions that tormented her most. Was her daughter the evil temptress, whoring herself with her father, or was her husband the corrupt initiator violating his teenage daughter? With these questions bludgeoning her mind, she became so angry that she could no longer withhold her anguish or her rage.

Serena tried to impose some kind of organization on her frenzied thoughts and the questions flowing naturally from them that bedeviled her mind. Could the loving and devoted mother she knew be really a scarlet woman? Could she have betrayed her husband-to-be even before their marriage? Was Serena really illegitimate? And if so, who was her real father? Each question repeated over and over was like a sledgehammer pounding down on her skull and she could find no way to stop each resounding blow.

At school Serena was devastated by the betrayal of her friends, classmates and teachers, but she doggedly stood her ground, refusing to surrender to their cruelty. She was determined to graduate despite her isolation and approached her teachers to get tuition for the lessons she had missed. They agreed, but remained coldly aloof. However, her persistence in turning up for evening classes over the following weeks made them admire her determination. Yet, the fact that they willingly provided the extra tuition she needed did nothing to lessen the feelings of alienation and humiliation that had become the central pillar of her life.

During the nights of her daughter's illness, Leesa could never tell when the screams from the adjacent bedroom would wake her, sending her racing to Serena's bedside. Whenever they did, more often than not, Serena would appear traumatized, her face transfixed, staring with unseeing eyes. Serena's exhalations would erupt out of her in short panicked bursts, her bosom heaving. Her lips would be drawn back over her teeth, her snarling mouth open like a cornered beast facing an apex predator. Sweat would drench her body, standing out on her forehead and temples. Leesa would call softly to her trying to break into her alien world. "Rina? Rina? I'm here with you darling. There's nothing to be afraid of. It's only a bad dream." Sometimes, as Leesa tried to embrace her, still traumatized, she would fight her mother off violently as though she were the enemy. At other times, she would sit up abruptly, with deeply furrowed brow eyes wide open, fists clenched, ready to defend herself against whatever demons were pursuing her. A moment later, she would fall back on the bed, mumbling incoherently, still sound asleep.

That night, Kim had reached the end of her tether. Like a match, darkness had ignited the spark in her brain. A white light had flashed, goading her into a demented rage. She grabbed Leesa from behind by the shoulders, spun her around violently and threw her to the mat. Like a wrestler, she pinned her there, throttling her with a choke hold. Kim's facial muscles were tense with rage as she gazed into her daughter's terrified eyes. She then spat out her accusation:

"What madness drove you to sleep with your father?" The surprise attack had stunned Leesa for she lay spread-eagled, her head aching at its contact with the floor through the thin mat.

She stared into her mother's pain-crazed features, seeing each new wrinkle up close, the dried white saliva on her lips, the fury and hint of madness clouding her eyes. Immediately, Leesa recognized there the dawning of insanity. She dared not tell the truth. Doing so, she was convinced, would not only put her in jeopardy, but would probably lead to her mother's permanent madness.

Then, scared by the terrifying consequences she envisaged if the truth were known, she rushed ahead impetuously, forced to save herself and her family from being hounded and ostracized. She had no alternative but to tell one more gargantuan lie.

"Mama," she replied, gathering as much shock and puzzlement into her voice and demeanor as she could muster, "you must be mad! What are you talking about?"

Kim gazed fixedly into Leesa's eyes, remembering that although she had often been wicked, Kim had always been secretly proud of Leesa for blurting out the truth. Even in difficult confrontations, when a lie could get her off the hook, she could always be counted upon for telling the brutal truth. The shock, puzzlement and hurt expression on her face brought a tidal wave of relief sweeping over Kim. Impulsively, she hugged her daughter tightly, kissing her again and again, all the while apologizing for her loss of control, her outrageous accusation.

A rush of sadness, guilt and shame stabbed into Leesa's heart, but she took care to continue acting the role of the innocently accused. Fortunately, she needed to keep up the pretense for a short time only. With her marriage a short time away, she'd soon be whisked off by her husband on their honeymoon.

The outcome of the confrontation brought such tremendous relief to Kim that she suddenly seemed like a new person. Brilliant sunshine had elbowed away the darkness corrupting her mind, heart and soul. The sunlight brought the beginning of a smile to her lips, and with time, she even surprised herself by humming a tune. Since her daughter was innocent, it followed naturally that her husband couldn't be guilty. There would be no need to confront him now. She emitted a deep sigh of relief, thinking that she could finally return to the peace and contentment of their earlier lifestyle. Immediately, she fell on her knees to beg God's forgiveness for her evil thoughts and accusations. The lights in her home were still on in broad daylight, but they had not succeeded to dispel the ever-thickening gloom.

Serena refused to let her profound discouragement and unhappiness show. She worked doubly hard, using revenge as her motive to rise to the challenge of outperforming her classmates in the by-weekly tests, a part of the school's educational program. Her humiliation at placing last in the first test, made her study even harder. In the second test, she still didn't do well enough to return to the honors list, but while the success gave her some solace, it did nothing to alleviate the isolation she was being forced to endure.

It was not easy for her to focus on her studies while dealing with the pain of enforced isolation. Despite the teachers' change in attitude, rather than follow their lead, her classmates continued to ostracize her. The experience was both cruel and humiliating. Yet, balanced against this cruelty, was the enduring love and support of her parents, the joy of her existence on the farm and the therapeutic value of her painting. This last allowed her to escape into her fantasy world that like an old and loyal friend had never deserted her. When finally her hard work placed her back on the honors list, it gave a boost to her deeply wounded self-esteem.

Serena lay in bed feeling a tremendous sense of relief at being at last free of the images from her tortured past. She thanked God that the terrifying nightmares had gradually disappeared and she could look forward to a glorious future of nightmare-free nights spreading endlessly and painlessly before her. She had come a long way from those nights of pure terror, and before closing her eyes, she began detailing her itinerary for the day ahead. She'd rise early, drive with the best of her young racing birds at least one hundred miles from home. This time, she'd release each one separately, instead of in a flock, at ten minute intervals. It would be a stringent test for each bird to find its way home by itself. She knew that one or two might be lost, but the one hundred mile flight would be important to test their strength, courage and endurance. It would also test their ability to avoid predators.

On her way home, she planned to visit a few malls to do some much-needed shopping. She'd lost a few pounds and some of her skirts and tops were 'hanging' on her. She'd check out the latest designer labels that had caught her eye in one or two of the malls. Once satisfied that she had settled on her plans for the following day, thoughts of contentment put a smile on her face as she closed her eyes.

Suddenly, her arms and chest were locked in a vice. She began struggling desperately to break free, but could neither move nor scream. Something alive and powerful had wrapped its coils around her torso. It had to be a giant serpent because with each exhalation of her breath the coils grew tighter and the pressure they exerted made it more and more difficult to breathe. She fought against her panic, struggling to disengage herself from the powerful muscles immobilizing her. Sweat beaded her forehead, plastering the hair to her skull. In the darkness, she grappled with the monster's head, hoping to prevent it from sinking its fangs into her flesh. She was almost out of breath. A momentary shift in its coils gave her the chance she wanted. It permitted her to take a ragged breath and she screamed and screamed at the top of her lungs. Suddenly, her mother was at her side as she switched on the light. With caresses and comforting words, she embraced Serena's trembling body before untangling the twisted sheets wound tightly around her. Once her terror subsided, she fell into a troubled sleep.

After her graduation, she resumed her old life. On the downside, although two years had passed, the peace she had fought so hard to reclaim could still be shattered unexpectedly by a nightmare. She would spring awake sweating, breathless and terrified. Fortunately, these episodes kept growing further and further apart. On the upside, the farm was flourishing, Will had developed into a strong and healthy colt and the special relationship between them continued. Her pigeons had multiplied and were performing well in club races from distant points all around the country. She had resumed her karate classes at the dojo, her calisthenics at home, mucking, milking, feeding the farm animals, and occupying herself with her painting. She seemed to be fully recovered to all outward appearances. The resumption of her regimen of physical exercises together with riding and hiking in the mountains had firmed up her muscles making her fit. There was a sparkle in her eye and a definite spring in her step. She was just about ready to leave home and start a new life of her own. Then, something happened that changed her life forever.

Part 2

Chapter 28

For the first leg of his trip from Vancouver to Seoul, Stephen took the non-stop flight on Singapore Airlines on the advice of his Uncle Tom, Professor Emeritus, who lectured on International Relations at Kings College, London in the UK. He was on leave in Victoria, but would soon be on his way to attend learned conferences in Europe. Uncle Tom was big, bald, and blue-eyed. Though as tall as his brother, Stephen's father, there unfortunately, the resemblance stopped. Uncle Tom was a brain, his brother, an idiot. The former had hanging jowls that were badly in need of a shave. When he talked, they shook, and since he was talkative, they shook often. It was he who had suggested that Stephen might think of spending his vacation in South Korea and that he could do worse than look up his old college friend, John Ahn. The latter had done exceptionally well in farming and business, as the CEO of a middle sized and very successful corporation.

Stephen was Canadian, a systems analyst trained in Intelligence Technology and a supposed wizard with computers. He had traveled the English-speaking world gathering as many state of the art computer courses as he could muster under his belt. When his uncle advised him to vacation in Korea, at the home of his wealthy friend, and CEO of his own corporation, Stephen was elated. He immediately agreed, seeing the suggestion as a possibility of deriving some sort of profit from living in the home of the well-heeled business-man-buddy of his uncle. He knew his uncle was a workaholic and would be too busy, between lecturing to students and attending learned conferences, to go to Korea. He also knew that his uncle's company would spoil his trip, so he didn't want his company. Yet, he pretended differently by asking, but knowing the answer before it came: "Why don't you join me on the trip to Korea? Your friend would be delighted to see you."

"I'd love to do that, but my busy schedule won't allow me to take so long a trip. Anyway, I do have some gifts I bought for John and his wife, Leesa. I'm sure you can find room in your suitcase to take them for me. I know they'll be both surprised and pleased with the gifts."

"I hope you're not sending them a fridge or a stove. I travel light, using only a single suitcase."

"I'm just sending the carving of a mask by Hunt who's a friend. There are also some hand-woven sweaters for his wife. But you sound as though you're planning a speedy getaway." His uncle said, chuckling. I hope you won't do anything to let me or the family down." Uncle Tom stared him straight in the eye.

"Perhaps I should warn you that although the Ahns are very wealthy, they have chosen to live a simple life on a farm buried deep in the countryside. I hope that won't spoil your plans. I know that you regard yourself as an urbane man of the world," his uncle said, chuckling again.

"Why does everyone always warn me about the past?" Stephen replied, sounding like a petulant child.

"Perhaps it's because your past is somewhat checkered. You should have learned by now that ladies shouldn't have to pay for your company, or that emptying their pocketbooks for your pleasure is a no-no." As an afterthought, he added: "The Ahns have a teen-aged daughter, so do try to behave yourself."

"Well, any woman who wants to present me to mama as a potential husband will have to pay for the privilege. And as for teenaged kids, in my book they're sub-human, so you needn't worry on that score."

"Stephen, the people you're going to meet are not as laid back as we Westerners are. You'll need to be on your best behavior in your dealings with them. They're far more formal, some might even say straight-laced, in their attitude to life. Perhaps a word of advice would be helpful."

"I'm listening, since I'm sure that any information about these people would be useful." So used to lecturing to his students, Uncle Tom began:

"To better understand the Korean mind, one must be aware of the powerful influence of Confucius, a Chinese scholar and statesman whose philosophy permeates the whole society. His teachings imposed a rigid code of moral and ethical conduct in a hierarchal chain that governs all existing relationships between members of a group. His main idea was to preserve harmony." Stephen was already bored and asked: "I'm not sure I understand what you're getting at, or why what you're saying is even necessary."

"It's necessary to understand the people you're going to meet, especially your host and hostess. The information I'm giving you will lessen the number of times you put your foot in your mouth. To Koreans, protocol is vitally important and an overview of their conduct will save you a great deal of embarrassment. Preserving harmony is also a means of saving face. For that to happen, individuality is suppressed in favor of adherence to an iron-clad principle of reciprocal responsibility to each other, based on the hierarchy of rank. If you still don't understand what I'm trying to explain, the bottom line is as follows: All members are subservient to the group leader in the same way that subjects in a state owe their full allegiance to their ruler. So in the family, in business or in a team, members owe their allegiance to the father, the CEO or the captain. I hope you understand, because when you get there you'll be constantly on trial. To cut down on the mistakes you are bound to make, try to be ultra observant and follow exactly what you see others do."

"You talk as though you're sure they'll have me."

"John and I are good friends. He won't refuse my request."

Once Stephen got the word that the Ahns would be glad to have him, he began to plan his first extended vacation since beginning work at the Ministry of Health in British Columbia, Canada's most western province. As team leader, he had helped to design the software that issued 'Care Cards' to all British Columbians in their upgraded 'medical care' system.

Stephen, at six foot four, possessed a powerfully muscled body built along the lines of the statues of classical Greek sculpture. To reinforce this image of the Grecian powerful figure and good looks, he exercised with weights, dyed his black hair golden, styled it into ringlets and fixed an errant curl dangling over his forehead. It was an invitation to feminine fingers to pat it back into place. His huge frame, exuding a sense of enduring solidity, inspired confidence, while the innocence that radiated from his features, especially his eyes, reinforced the impression of complete honesty. He seemed to be so trustworthy that if he told you he had been on a flying saucer, you'd believe him. Those eyes, his proudest asset, were even more striking than his body. They were big, and of the deepest blue. He used them as a secret weapon, since they increased the impression of his trustworthiness, his total sincerity. With Stephen's good looks and his eyes that radiated charm, women flocked to him like flies to carrion, and like carrion, he was rotten to the core.

Women found him fascinating because his face, eyes, and tall muscular body at once captured their imagination. Then, his golden curls in magnificent disarray invited the caress of feminine fingers. When women looked up at him and listened to his voice, their hearts would melt. They saw his eyes as holding unfathomable mysteries. For some, they seemed able to bore straight into their hearts to ferret out and unearth their most closely guarded secrets. For others, they seemed like deep blue pools in which they were invited to swim. Inevitably, they soon found themselves out of their depths, drowning.

Stephen was aware of the devastating effect of his appearance on the fairer sex and he used it to become the quintessential con artist. He practiced assiduously before a mirror to hone his role-playing skills to perfection. In the blink of an eye he could adapt in his voice, features and mannerisms to whatever attitude would best allow him to win the prize he happened to be seeking. He pretended to be the most affable of companions and would go to any lengths to be convincing. But he always used his charm and good looks to profit at someone else's expense. He had a number of weapons in his arsenal apart from his appearance, and when cornered, found that one of the most successful was a deeply pained expression followed by absolute silence. In a number of scrapes, it had got him off the hook.

During his college years, Stephen saw every woman he met as a challenge to his powers of seduction. He was a regular Don Juan, and his many conquests had earned him his nickname, 'the leopard,' since the quarry he hunted was always the naive, the unwary and the weak. He gloried in each conquest since it put another feather in his cap and gave a boost to his self-esteem.

Before leaving Canada, Stephen determined to become acquainted with as many of the ideas and beliefs of the people with whom he planned to spend his vacation. He knew that knowledge was power. If, as he intended, to profit financially or otherwise from the trip, he needed to learn as much as possible about the geographical and historical background of Korea, its weather conditions, its economy and above all, the views and values of its people. But since the research required to get this information would be too time consuming a process, he devised a method that would save him the trouble.

He drew up a document on his computer promoting himself as a movie producer. He then explained that he was in the process of making a documentary advertizing South Korea as the newest Asian vacation paradise, with the capital, Seoul, as its center piece. He advertised an essay contest in English, offering a prize of US $1000.00 for the winner. The subject was: "The influence of the geography and history of Korea on the culture, conduct and values of its people." There was a deadline date and a Post Office Box address to which the essays should be sent.

Stephen rang the Secretary of the Victoria Intercultural Association to activate his plan. He explained who he was and that he would be sending a number of printouts for her more advanced ESL Korean students inviting them to participate in an essay competition. He informed the secretary that the information on the printouts would be self-explanatory and added that he would mark the essays himself and award the prize of US $1000.00 in person to the winner. The Secretary agreed to distribute the printouts.

Of course, once the essays were received, Stephen would be long gone and no prize money would be awarded.

You could have got the information you needed from any public library or the internet, his conscience told him.

Yes, but either alternative would entail an unnecessary expenditure of time and effort.

Aren't you ashamed of relying on deceit to get what you want? Haven't you learned yet that hoodwinking others and reaping their rewards for yourself is a no-no?

If you didn't know, outsmarting others gives a decided lift to my ego. Information is power and I intend to use what the essays teach me to become familiar with the geography and history of Korea and more especially with the views, values and attitudes of its people. They will also provide me with the way that Koreans think and how they perceive other nationalities.

So what do you hope to gain from this exercise of deceit?

I hope the information will allow me to derive some sort of financial benefit from my vacation that I see as an enterprise for gain. After all, I'll be living in the home of the CEO of a wealthy corporation. That alone is a distinct advantage of which I hope to make use.

Stephen found his seat, stowed his small single suitcase in the overhead bin, sat, fastened his seatbelt and watched the air hostess as she helped the other passengers find their appointed seats and stow their gear. She was Oriental and Stephen was immediately taken with her, he being one of those men particularly attracted to the beauty of Eastern women. The air hostess had exquisite ivory skin, almond shaped eyes, high cheekbones and black hair pulled back severely against her head and coiled into a neat bun at its back. Her turquoise, tight fitting uniform accentuated the lift of her breasts and her short, tight skirt revealed a prominent posterior. When she walked, the sway and swish of her behind was as enchanting as it was obscenely sexual. Any observer would agree that she was stunning, and Stephen thought that he could overcome the boredom of the long flight to Korea by flirting with her. You never know, he thought, I'm not yet a member of the Mile High Club.

Go ahead his conscience told him, everyone should have a goal!

He waited until she had alerted the passengers about the safety features of the aircraft and let her finish her spiel before pressing the button to summon her. She arrived, bent over, giving him a prolonged look at her cleavage. She pressed her face so close to him that he caught the scent of her perfume.

"How can I be of service, Sir?" She whispered the words with a saucy grin and a twinkle in her green eyes. Her unexpected conduct made Stephen realize immediately that she wasn't just being friendly and efficient. She was definitely flirting; coming on to him.

"Can you please bring me a pillow and blanket? I really need to sleep." He whispered back with a naughty smile and a sparkle in his eye.

"Going to bed so early?" She again purred, and this time she stooped in the aisle displaying an ivory slice of thigh for his benefit. It was with deep satisfaction and her heart a flutter that she saw his eyes riveted to the spectacle.

"I'm ready for bed, how about you?" He whispered, throwing the ball right back into her court.

"You know," she said, "My job is to take special care of my passengers." Then she added: "even after they go to bed." On that note she rose and left to do his bidding.

"Back in a sec," she said, and true to her word, she returned quickly with a pillow and blanket. Stephen took the opportunity to say: "Thank you. You're a lady of impeccable taste."

With a somewhat puzzled look and raised eyebrows she questioned: "Impeccable taste?"

"You're wearing "Joy," by Jean Patou. It's one of France's most highly renowned perfumes. In my estimation it qualifies you as a woman of taste."

"Well, thank you," she purred, her smile as wide as that of the Cheshire cat that had just polished off a bowl of cream. "Is there anything else I can do for you; anything at all?" She added archly.

"Perhaps you'd like to join me when we get off the aircraft?" He queried.

"Well, we do our best to serve, Stephen."

"How do you know my name?" he asked, mystified. "You must be a seer."

"Yes, and I foresee that you and I will soon be much better acquainted," she replied, again smiling playfully. She then confessed that she had consulted the passenger list to get his name. When he inquired why, she told him calmly:

"It isn't every day that we get a hunk on board without the encumbrance of wife or girlfriend." Stephen considered himself very adept at the flirtation game she was playing. Since she had thrown the ball back into his court, he though he'd better pick it up before she left.

"The color of your uniform accentuates the green of your eyes," he whispered softly, "and that mouth of yours was specially crafted for kissing." He used the twisted smile and arrogant curl of lip that he had practiced so hard to perfect, and his tone was that of a priest conferring a benediction.

Although she was used to such compliments, they had never come from someone with the physical attributes of Stephen. She sashayed up the aisle blushing and smiling shamelessly, very pleased with herself. She swished her hips from side to side a little more than usual deliberately titillating the imagination of every male in sight.

The blanket she brought came with a note. My name is Shellie. If you haven't yet made a hotel reservation, you're welcome to crash in my pad at the Somerset Palace. We can meet at the taxi stand in front of the airport and share a cab to the hotel. He nodded, smiled in assent before whispering:

"You are full of surprises, and I was making such devious plans to snare you into my web."

"Really!" She replied. "Since I find webs mysterious, I'll have to give those plans some serious thought." She walked away seductively, all male eyes following her hungrily.

As the plane approached Korea during its descent, a heavy cloud bank of what appeared like stained cotton wool engulfed the aircraft. The limited view persisted, forcing a definite change in the mood of the passengers. Their earlier gaiety and lively conversation had disappeared. The sense of their imprisonment made them serious, apprehensive and silent.

From the angry patchwork of blemished white, the aircraft penetrated an even darker zone of smog. Suddenly, it emerged into bright sunlight. The sharp contrast had an immediate effect on the mood of the passengers. There was a collective gasp of relief and the earlier stony silence gave way to the hum of animated chatter. Everyone leaned towards the windows, peering outside at the magical transformation of the scenery.

"As the plane banked, Stephen had a birds-eye view of the country below. He saw the Korean peninsula as a giant thumb thrust out from China into the Sea of Japan in a north-north-west to south-south-easterly direction. The Taebaek Mountain mass running north to south along its east coast rose steeply out of the ocean. In the southwest the Sobaek Mountains ran northeast to southwest. In the north and east the mountains rose steeply then sloped westward towards lower hills. These then merged gradually into a broad coastal plain in the south and west bordering the Yellow Sea. As the aircraft got lower and lower, Stephen could see hundreds of islands, stretching along the southern coast and grouped thickly around the south-western tip. The plane then passed over a green, heavily cultivated agricultural area with a series of cities strewn in an almost unbroken line along the western plains. They looked like a beautiful string of pearls lit from the inside.

Stephen found the ultramodern airport impressive and picked up a brochure on the way to enter customs and immigration. If what he read was accurate, South Korea was much further advanced than the stagnant backwater that he had considered it. Inchon International Airport was "the largest and perhaps busiest in Asia," and rated as "the best airport in the world." True, he had found its ultra modern appearance striking, but he considered what he was reading the kind of hype that most countries boast about themselves, their products and their culture. Still disbelieving, he read on. "Its baggage handling system was computerized and state-of-the-art, as were its security facilities, created in response to terrorist threats," the brochure stated. The population, descendants of Mongol tribes, gradually became a homogeneous people developing their own language, customs and culture. The people tend to be somewhat aloof with strangers since throughout their history they were subjected to constant attack and foreign domination. However, they could be warm and friendly especially after they got to know the visitor."

"We'll see about that! Stephen mused, as he kept reading.

"The climate is similar to that of Canada's west coast, with four seasons. Spring starts in late March with a light drizzle occurring until May. The summer stretches from June to August but the Monsoons, beginning in late June, cause that season to differ significantly from Canada's summer. Since their heaviest downpours occur in July, "Koreans have built large drainage canals to remove the overwhelming excess of water from the downpours. At this time of the year people on the street cannot do without their umbrellas. Towards the end of September autumn begins and continues its reign into November. As in Canada, the weather is cool and dry and the trees are dressed in their most flamboyant fall colors. Like Canada too, the autumn landscape is eye catching. Winters tend to last from December to mid March and as in Canada, one has to contend with rain, snow and weather that is bitterly cold."

Before he knew it, Stephen was at the head of his line, and thanks to the numerous and efficient passport and immigration inspectors, his documents were swiftly, and politely processed.

Chapter 29

While waiting for Shellie, Stephen's brochure informed him that South Korea is one of the "Four Asian Tigers" with the "third largest economy in Asia," and "the 11ᵗʰ largest in the world."

It's also one of "the most highly developed scientific and technologically advanced countries," with the "world's largest shipbuilding industry, and is the world's third biggest manufacturer of steel." Korea is also "the global leader" in the production of semiconductors. Huge corporate conglomerates, *chaebol* dominate and oversee the economy with Seoul as the headquarters of such corporate giants as Samsung, Hyundai, Daewoo, the LG Group and Kia." The capital city of Seoul makes the greatest contribution to the country's economic success. Its renowned SKY universities are located there. Indeed, Korea's education standard is rated as being "among the world's highest;" far higher than both the US and Canada who lag far behind. The literate in Korea is almost 96%, no doubt because of its 12 year education system that starts at age 6 and continues until 18. After Stephen read the brochure touting Korea's successes, he was forced to admit that the qualifications of the country to being world class were extremely impressive. Yet, he still found the information hard to swallow. After all, he thought, doesn't every nation tout its wares with a huge dollop of exaggeration?

He met Shellie as arranged and they shared a cab to the hotel. On the way, the doubt he first harbored about Korea as a first world nation was being swiftly whittled away. He was flabbergasted at seeing the ultramodern metropolis of concrete, glass, steel and marble that confronted him. He couldn't believe that the country he had earlier considered to be third world, was instead striking and modern. The taxi drive was a definite eye opener. Seoul, the country's capital, was a modern city encircled by an ancient one. He had to admit that its modern 'sky- scrapers' stood in marked contrast to its ancient palaces, temples, shrines and pagodas that dated some 1500 years. They were every bit as spectacular as stated in the brochure. He blanched at the thought of Canada's few hundred years of history in comparison and began to consider the centuries of wisdom and culture that Korea must have accumulated over that span of time. It dwarfed that of his own country. The high-rise buildings rivaled, and often surpassed in beauty, those in many of the world renowned capitals he had visited. Having expected none of what he was seeing, Stephen began to have a completely new concept of South Korea.

Shellie's view of the city was somewhat different. She saw its architecture as stunning, but struggling fiercely against itself. In her mind the smooth ultramodern structures of glittering glass, marble and steel sought to dominate and outshine the palaces, temples, shrines and pagodas. She pointed out some interesting facts about the temples and palaces.

"Their architects had a preference for using Korean granite rock for their solidly-based foundations supporting a massive wooden beam super-structure. Wooden pegs rather than nails held the wooden structure together so it could be moved. The main beams holding up the roof were painted in spectacular color schemes of stark reds, blues, greens and gold. There were tiny figures of animals along their roof-ridges that were supposed to prevent fires and ward off evil spirits. Paintings on the beams depicted highly imaginative scenes. There were masks ridiculing the observer; rabbits dancing in the moonlight; water-craft freeing souls from the clutches of Satan." Without pausing to draw breath Shellie pressed on: "Music and dance are important parts of Shaman ceremonies and paintings of musicians and dancers appear on the ceilings and main beams of Buddhist temples. The figures on the roof-beams represent the spirits that dwell in the beams. Should these spirits become disgruntled by being ignored, they would withdraw their support permitting the roof and building to collapse. The performance of Shaman ceremonies (kuts) was needed to placate the unhappy spirits." Shellie did pause but only for a second. She then continued like a teacher in front of a class.

"Longevity is an important aspect of Korean culture so that life itself must be nurtured towards extending its limits for as long as possible. So great is the goal of longevity that Koreans have created a number of symbols that work towards the impossible aim of immortality. To prolong life the individual needs protection that is attained through a series of symbols that include good luck, repelling both evil spirits and danger. On the one hand, there is protection by tiger, dragon and others creatures. On the other, there is good luck induced by turtle and phoenix among others." Shellie then returned to her impression of the city and stated:

"Seoul gives me the impression of modern man struggling against the completely different mind-set held by the city's ancient architects. The violence of their country's division makes me imagine that the moderns were in combat with the backward architectural thinking of an era reminiscent of the saber-tooth tiger and the dinosaur."

What astonished Stephen and reinforced his conviction of the city's modernity, were the video screens hanging on the side of high-rise buildings. No such state-of-the-art screens appear in Canada, the US or Europe as far as he knew. They made him sit up and take notice. Not only were they gigantic, at least 30 feet tall by 60 feet wide, but they showed full-motion videos. Since Shellie soon realized the unexpected impression that the city had so far impressed upon Stephen, she told the cab driver to give them a short tour of the city that she appeared to know intimately. A moment later, Stephen began to feel a bit of home sickness as he caught sight of the famous golden arches of a Mc Donald's and a few Burger King and Pizza Hut establishments. Shellie told him that Koreans were proud of *Lotteria*, their own fast food mega-chain, while *Pelicana Chicken* was Korea's fast food chain specializing in chicken and French fries. She also mentioned that there were local chains like Circle K, *Family Mart* and *7-Eleven* where you could have Western styled breakfast with coffee. She also pointed out that *Caravan, Dutor, Jardin* and *Mr. Coffee* were very popular coffee houses. As they passed by the World Trade Center, Shellie pointed out the huge, very modern building complex surrounding the COEX Convention and Exhibition Center. She promised that they would visit it later on one of their tours. By then, Stephen had had a much improved view of Korea that had begun to make him a believer.

"As a computer analyst, you are no doubt intrigued to see the huge letters "PC" on a number of buildings," his tour guide stated. "They are Internet Cafes that are very cheap to use. They cost only about US $1.00 per hour, and remain open 24/7." Everything Stephen saw made him realize that Korea was every bit the forward-looking country about which he had read and was now seeing at first hand. Until that moment, he had not believed the hype. Shellie interrupted his thoughts.

"Buddhism is deeply rooted in Korea's past and forms its largest religious sect. Although it plays a significant role in its culture, its arts are restricted to its temples and museums rather than to its homes. However, as observers, we can witness its influence in paintings, sculpture, ceramics and architecture. Surprisingly, we will see that different sects appear together in Buddhist paintings so that Shamanistic beliefs exist side by side with Confucian ethics. When Buddhist artists abandoned their earlier practices of representing Buddha in terms of sacred symbols, they began to portray him as a human being, but with a difference. Since he was an extraordinary being they incorporated his many attributes into his sacred figure. A large head might represent wisdom. A hand-held fly whisk would suggest his swatting away of problems while a lotus blossom would indicate the continuous generation of a species and its ability to grow into a beautiful flower from the corrupting depths of its soil. In an attempt to stop the continuous gush of information from Shellie's mouth, which Stephen had begun to consider superfluous, he thought of a question that might stem the flow. Clearly, he wasn't yet aware of her habit of persistence.

"You weren't always an air hostess, were you?" He asked, since Shellie seemed to know so much about the country.

"No," she replied. "I taught history and geography at high school in Vancouver. But I've been traveling to Korea for years in this job, and I've spent considerable time visiting places of interest, reading about Korea and steeping myself in the customs and culture of the country." Stephen had to admit that she was a mine of information and never seemed to tire of dropping him a nugget of her knowledge. Since he was far more taken with Shellie's erotica, he began to find her nugget dropping intrusive and somewhat irritating.

Without any inquiry from him she mentioned: "When you visit Hamyang that's located in Korea's southern rural area, you'll see numerous stone remains scattered all over the hilly countryside. They mark the sites of temples, pagodas and shrines that were once busy places of worship.

"In times past," Shellie continued a moment later, "the state adhered to Neo-Confucian thought believing that its tenets would create an ideal society ruled by a wise monarch. The ideals were so impractical that they could never be realized. For example, the family was deemed to be the most desirable social unit and considered four generations living under the same roof as the norm. They thought too that filial piety was the highest virtue. The death of a parent obliged the eldest son to live in a hut at his parent's graveside and spend the next three years eating nothing but thin, vegetable-based broth. This period of mourning demanded total celibacy.

"Following these teachings, a new hierarchy of relationships evolved. Obedience was mandated "from subject to ruler; child to parent; wife to husband; younger brother to older brother." Girls were victimized from birth while boys were revered. Women's education was restricted to serving men in silence and giving birth to male children. Men had the prerogative of divorce "by word of mouth for reasons including his wife's talkativeness, sterility, and disrespect to parents-in-law." The Confucian dress-code for women dictated that they wore clothes that hid their breasts and bodies, perhaps motivated with the aim of making them as "unattractive as possible." Shellie then looked sternly at Stephen with raised eyebrows and a serious expression of irritation on her face. She was behaving as though he were to blame. Since he was male, he couldn't care less about the condition of Korean women. In fact, judging from present company, he thought it was a fine idea to punish them for talking too much. After a long pause, during which Stephen luxuriated in the silence, Shellie returned to teaching mode.

"Koreans are very superstitious and you'll find that 4 is an unlucky number here." Why the hell should he care, he thought, but didn't say. She continued to stare at him.

"No why?" He finally asked almost rudely at again being interrupted from admiring the contour of her long shapely legs.

"It sounds like *sa*, the Korean word for death. As you will see, neither hotels nor hospitals have a fourth floor." She quickly dropped another nugget.

"Every man in Korea serves a two-year stretch in the military?" Why did she think that was important for him to know? He thought she was just rambling with information that was totally disconnected. Without drawing a breath, she again continued:

"The natural resources of Korea are coal, graphite, lead, tungsten, and molybdenum. Then, because of its mountainous nature, the country has a huge potential for hydro electric power." This time, he shook his head negatively, tempted, in his growing irritation, to tape her mouth shut and prevent any further interruptions to his erotic musings. Her eyebrows were raised once more and she stared at him with widely opened eyes. He swore that she was about to whack him with her teacher's ruler. He stood his ground and stared back at her while remaining silent. For his insolence he got a stern earful:

"You don't seem to know very much about the country you're visiting," she scolded, before adding with wrinkled forehead: "Didn't you do any research before coming? Didn't you think it would be interesting to learn as much as you could about Korea?" There was a mixture of irritation and amazement in her voice.

He remembered that information was power and whatever he learnt would help if he wanted to profit from his vacation/venture. So he admitted that he hadn't done much research and would have to postpone for a while his intention of getting Shellie into bed. She refused to let him off the hook so easily, promising to drag him–'kicking and screaming if necessary'–on a tour of the city to improve his education. Shellie was displaying a different side of her nature: intelligence, curiosity and persistence that, until then, he had overlooked.

"We're staying at the Somerset Palace Seoul," Shellie told the taxi driver and in a short while, he pulled up before the building. "It's centrally located and is within walking distance of Seoul's most popular tourist destinations," she said while getting out. Stephen jumped out of the cab, busying himself with removing their luggage from the trunk. He was trying to avoid having to split the taxi fare. He quickly handed over the luggage to the bellhop and excused himself to Shellie, supposedly to phone and inform his hosts of his arrival. He headed for the nearest rack of phones, pretending to call his hosts by dialing a series of random numbers, then shot up to the room in time to tip the bell hop for bringing up their luggage. After all, he had let Shellie pay the taxi fare, settle up for their room at the front desk and he was going to have her all to himself. So the two bucks he tipped the bell hop were no more than a niggardly investment.

"He then complained of a raging hunger that he explained made him decide to go out for dinner. Since he didn't invite Shellie to accompany him, he expected her to suggest that he remain at the hotel and let room service take care of them both. Women are so easy to manipulate, he thought, convinced that Shellie wasn't going to let so worthy looking a bed mate slip through her fingers.

"Stephen, I don't want to start our relationship with a quarrel, but I'd hate you to take me for a fool, Shellie stated. You busied yourself with our suitcases when I was about to pay our cab fare, then you were again absent at the front desk when I was about to give reception my credit card..." She let the statement hang in the air.

"Are you saying that I'm guilty of not paying my fair share?" He replied, frowning deeply and pulling out his wallet.

"Don't you trust me?" He asked, frowning and looking insulted. But in truth he was taken aback by Shellie's astuteness and admired her stance. Trying to appear hurt, he kept wearing his frown and used a prolonged silence to get him off the hook. Shellie paid not the slightest attention.

"Let's just go down to the front desk and explain that we're sharing for the few days we're staying. And while you're at it you can also give me your half of the taxi fare." He was again surprised that Shellie had caught on to his con game. But he had other aces up his sleeve and did as Shellie dictated with a deeply pained expression on his face and a silent tongue.

"Let me surprise you with dinner, using the hotel's room service," Shellie offered.

"That's very kind of you, but the least I can do in response to so generous an offer is to surprise you with the choice of our meal. And don't worry your pretty little head. It's my treat, not yours." When dinner arrived, she opened her eyes wide in surprise at the expensive steak and lobster dinner that he had ordered, and at the ice-filled bucket with a magnum of "Moet & Chandon" that came with it.

"Not to worry," he told her, "I've already taken care of the bill in return for your generous invitation to share your pad. It was her turn to thank him for his generosity.

They were both so tired from their long flight and brief city tour that after eating, and chatting over the champagne, their exhaustion from jet lag drove them to sleep in their own beds. However, Shellie couldn't miss the opportunity to promise that she'd take him on various tours of the city which she jokingly said would cure him of his 'ignorance.' Since we only have a few days, she added, we'll have to cut short our guided tour.

The next morning, Shellie woke him bright and early, making it a point to acquaint him with some of the cultural aspects of Korea. While he had other far more interesting plans in mind for his hostess, she prolonged her role as teacher and, while they had breakfast, regaled him with stuff that he thought he had read or heard before.

"The invention of a phonetic script–*hangul*–for the Korean language, led to a vast increase in literacy. Today, Korea ranks about second among the world's nations. Their literacy rate is 96%, far higher than either Canada or the US," she stated.

"Its standard of education is among the four highest in the world while Canada and the US rank far, far lower, not even among the first sixteen." He had already heard or read those words as well but couldn't remember where. Were they from the student essays or from the brochure? He couldn't be sure but he remembered clearly that he had refused to believe them. Affecting a tone of disbelief, he made the mistake of asking her where she got such trumped-up statistics. The insult got him another earful, encouraging her to harangue him with an overview of Korea's education system. He couldn't help grinding his teeth as he listened. Shellie was too busy pontificating to notice.

"Kids attend kindergarten from ages 3 to 5. They go on to elementary school at 6 and climb through six grades. Their progress is by age rather than by performance. When they are 12 they enter Middle School where they complete three grades by age 15. Math, English, Korean, and Science are their core subjects but they also study history, ethics, art, computer science and home economics." Stephen tried to stem the flow of her babbling without actually stating that he found the information boring. He thought the look on his face would be enough to do that. But, he was wrong. Shellie could be rather insensitive at times. Although he didn't want to insult her, he also didn't want her to prolong the boring lecture.

"You didn't believe me," she accused, looking at his face and seeming seriously hurt. Still, she decided to fill him in about her 'trumped up statistics' and rattled on:

"They study six subjects every day and they are given an extra lesson of the teacher's choice. When the school day ends at 3 pm, many students choose to go to after-school academics-*hag-won*- or they take private tuition. What makes their education system superior to ours," she stated, is that *hag-won* continues until midnight."

"What!" He exclaimed, pretending that he was listening. Unfortunately, Shellie interpreted his exclamation as one of surprised disbelief. He had succeeded only to prolong the lecture. "Exactly! She replied. "This is almost impossible for foreigners to comprehend especially when they are told that being accepted into the best High Schools, all located in Seoul, is difficult. Adding to the problem is that acceptance in any of them is almost indispensible to gaining entrance into a reputable university."

"Isn't that interesting," he said, feigning interest. But he should have kept his mouth shut for his remark had only succeeded to egg her on.

"There are competitive entrance examinations that students must pass at age 17 in order to attend a High School that specializes in Fine Arts, Foreign Languages and Science. Students go through three grades in these schools before graduating at the age of 19. Since competition is so fierce, education is both highly prized and extremely expensive." He breathed an inaudible sigh of relief when Shellie remained silent for all of one whole minute. He didn't know how she managed it, but perhaps it coincided with their completion of breakfast. Suddenly, she broke the silence.

"I hope you know that Korean currency is the won. There are about 600W to the Canadian dollar, and banks give you a more favorable exchange for Travelers' checks." Stephen thought that two could play at the same game and questioned:

"Did you know that Korea has moved from its traditional manufacture of cheap goods for export to up-market high technology and service industries?" Before she could answer, he continued: "And did you know that all sectors of government are involved in the economy while huge conglomerates, "*chaebol*" dominate it?" The response was not what he expected.

"Bravo! Stephen. I see you've done a little homework!"

That night, and on the following day, after prolonged and exhaustive frolicking together, Shellie tugged him out of bed urging him to accompany her on a subway tour of the city. She explained that, like all public transport, the subway was cheap, easy to use, very punctual and quick. Before he could catch his breath as he wondered where she got such energy after so little sleep, she rambled on. The stations were only two to three minutes apart. Since he had thoroughly enjoyed his bedtime frolicking, he would have preferred to linger in bed all day with Shellie, so it was with great reluctance and almost silent groans that he allowed himself to be dragged along with her. Where the hell had she got all that energy, he again wondered as he stood gazing up at the Gyeongbokgung Palace. But he had to admit that the building was striking especially the stonewall facade with its three huge arched entrances.

"This "Palace of Shining Blessings" is perhaps the best example of the royal palaces of the Joseon dynasty and a gem of Korean traditional architecture," Shellie pontificated. Of course, Stephen had quite a different gem in mind. But something was troubling him. A number of Shellie's descriptions resonated in his mind. There was a familiarity about them that kept puzzling him.

"Notice the two tiered roofs with their corners ending in upturned wings," Shellie pointed out eagerly. "Often, notches are used instead of nails in ancient building construction so the upper structure can be moved." He nodded his head vigorously in silence, amazed at the building's beauty yet being sure he had heard those words before. He took in the large flagstone area approaching the stone wall on either side of the entrance. Six round pillars with green walls between them soar upwards. Resting on it is the lower roof whose pillars seem to pierce the beam in support of the higher roof. The two roofs curve gently upwards at their ends like the upswing of the tips of birds' wings in flight. A white ridge outlines the top of both roofs and their black tiles together with the red pillars, green walls, and gold-flashed beams make a fine display of color giving the building a distinctive and majestic appearance.

After visiting a number of other places in the same compound, he stated sarcastically:

"Now that we have seen the whole of Korea, isn't it time to return to bed?" Shellie only smiled, took his hand and dragged him along the crowded walk-way. It was a mistake. As soon as she held his hand, people began to move out of their way. They got a series of disdainful looks, and then a belligerent pedestrian elbowed Stephen hard in the ribs as he passed. The blow was deliberate. Shellie immediately let go of his hand as though bitten by a snake.

"Oh my God, I forgot," she said, with her hand over her mouth. "I look Korean and you are a foreigner. It's a no-no for Korean women to be intimate with foreign men. Any such intimacy in public is frowned upon and can cause trouble. It's even worse at night, since many Korean men have a drinking problem as can be seen by their habit of puking in the gutter or on the sidewalk. A few get really hostile when they see Korean women too close to foreign men. So the 'accidental' elbow that jolted you was definitely not accidental. Please remember that!" Stephen made no reply, but if he remembered correctly, it was Shellie who had grabbed his hand.

"You'll love what we're about to see." Before he knew it, they were in Myeongdong, one of Seoul's trendiest tourist shopping districts.

"Although it's beautiful by day," Shellie mentioned, "by night it's a land of neon lights, electronic billboards and brightly lit department stores. You'll see the mid-to-high priced retail shops selling clothes, shoes, handbags, accessories and cosmetics." Everywhere he looked there were people crowding the trendy shops, restaurants, cafes, and coffee shops. From these, he could smell the blend of their products filling the air. Buildings towering above the sidewalks added to the traffic jam in the street and the crowds swarming the sidewalks. There were stalls along some of the walkways selling food, clothes and an assortment of touristy items. The smell of the cooked food was mouth watering, and there were little groups standing around each stall eating or waiting to be served. Shellie informed him the most popular dish was '*gimbap*,' "small rice and seaweed rolls served with pan-fried spicy squid and diced radish *kimchi*.

A little later, they stopped at a restaurant as Stephen said he felt "famished" and needed something stiff to fortify his "sagging spirits." While they waited to be served, he could smell the leather goods from across the street that blended with the perfume of flowers from next door. The aroma of spices being used as seasonings merged with the cooking from the restaurant's kitchen. When the waiter arrived Shellie suggested Stephen should try a shot of 'soju,' Korea's most popular alcoholic drink. It was a clear rice vodka not unlike wine, but very potent. It was sure to lift his spirits. The waiter deposited two shot glasses on the table and a plastic covered cardboard box. Stephen poured a 'shot' for Shellie and following Korean protocol, she returned the compliment. It was quite potent and bucked him up somewhat. Shellie then had a '*bokbunjaju*,'a raspberry wine that thankfully kept her silent while she sipped it slowly and waited for the meal they ordered: '*samgyatang*,' a small chicken stuffed with rice and boiled in a ginseng broth which they shared. She also ordered '*Bibimbap*,' which she described as one of Korea's most popular dishes. It consisted of a bowl of rice mixed with vegetables and red pepper paste served in a sizzling stone pot. Once again the scent of pungent spices filled his nose and made his eyes water. The pepper burned his lips, tongue, throat and stomach. For a very long moment he couldn't speak while his nose and eyes watered and his tongue kept burning as though it were on fire. He grabbed a quick drink from Shellie's wine, used a number of tissues to wipe his lips and the tip of his tongue before the burning gradually subsided and he could feel normal again. He didn't dare try to finish his meal. Afterwards he got a sharp jolt of energy and couldn't tell whether it came from the food, the drink, the pepper paste, or a combination of the three.

"We'll have enough to take back to the hotel for our next meal," she said, "unless you can finish it all."

"No thank you. That was the closest I've ever come to fire-eating in my life. You can have it all." Not long after leaving the restaurant, Stephen had a compelling need to go, and thought it might be difficult in the city. However, Shellie advised him that there were toilets everywhere, in restaurants, bus and railway stations, department stores, parks and museums. But, she suggested that he arm himself with toilet tissue as it wasn't always available in the toilets. He did so and ventured into the nearest public washroom which was clean, but of the squat-style variety. He imagined that tourists and especially older women would find balancing in a squatting position over a hole with nothing to hold on to, rather challenging. Shellie was right, there was no toilet tissue.

On the way home, Shellie decided he needed a history lesson which she began to expound without even a 'by your leave.'

"After the Japanese occupation of Korea and their defeat at the end of WW11 by the Allied Forces, Korea was divided between north and south at the 38th parallel. The Soviet Union administered the north and the US the south. Unable to agree on Joint Trusteeship, the Korean War ensued and split the countries into North and South Korea after a truce was declared. The corrupt government of Syngman Rhee brought slow recovery before a military dictatorship took over and under the efficient, if tyrannical government of the Park administration, South Korea experienced an economic miracle though fluctuating between democratic and autocratic rule. The present regime, the Sixth Republic, is democratic and has developed substantially in education, economy and culture. You've already heard about its education, so let me brief you on its culture. This last you'll find especially interesting." He disagreed silently, but did not object since he didn't want to queer the pitch of his gushing guide. It could cost him dearly later on.

"Boy, you must have been a really dedicated teacher!" He lied, preferring small talk to a lecture. "Why did you leave teaching?" He asked, trying to forestall the avalanche of useless information that he knew was about to drown him.

"I wanted to personally experience those countries that I had only known from books. Besides, my superior considered me 'overenthusiastic and demanding too much from my students." She said I was 'overzealous, long winded' and suggested that I 'find another occupation.' I took her advice." He agreed silently with her superior, but added:

"You certainly know your subjects intimately and do an excellent job. Then, you express yourself intelligently. That and your enthusiasm, makes what you say educational and interesting," he again lied realizing that a little compliment couldn't hurt.

"Thank you," she replied, looking at his poker face with suspicion, before continuing to display two of the greatest weaknesses of teachers: over-enthusiasm and long-windedness.

"When WW11 ended there was a split in culture between North and South Korea. The musicians of the South created more popular music with new groups that became K-pop stars. A few musicians followed American pop models and produced their own version of hip-hop. Inevitably, Korean youth used the new music to invent new dance crazes. However, the older folk retained their preference for *Trot*, the traditional popular music. I've found the recorded music of stars like Tae Jin Ah and Song Dae, quite innovative." Shellie stated in her non-stop flow of useless information that Stephen found annoying, but stoically withstood the onslaught, buoyed by the thought of again frolicking with her in bed on their return home.

"Later, even though he was visibly wilting, she dragged him to the COEX Mall, located in the Gangnam-gu district. She confided with scarcely veiled pride as though she were Korean:

"It's the largest shopping mall in Asia and it might surprise you to learn that it is underground." He saw numerous shops displaying expensive clothing, pottery, jewelry, ornaments and paintings about which Shellie talked animatedly. Fortunately he didn't have to listen until she began asking questions. They also visited a mammoth multi-cinema complex and food court. They followed with interest the filming and broad cast of the popular computer tournaments. Afterwards, he suddenly perked up at the aquarium that attracted him with its numerous varieties of fish. He was especially taken with the many species of sharks. There were lemon, nurse, blue and tiger sharks, the black-fin reef shark and the open ocean white tipped shark. To his disappointment, the Great White was missing but he realized that its predatory nature would pose a danger to the other fish. The fascinating display jerked him out of his lethargy momentarily and he stated:

"We have many zoos in Canada but, I believe, there is only one really worthwhile aquarium in Vancouver."

She agreed having visited it many times.

While at the Mall, he tried to follow his uncle's advice being ultra observant of the surrounding crowds. On expressing surprise at two men holding hands as they walked, he learnt that their bond was no more than one of friendship. Many girls and women also held hands while walking for the same reason. When the two men stopped in the middle of their walkway continuing their discussion, he noticed that a number of pedestrians passed between them. His 'guide' stated that it was impolite to make someone pass behind your back. How strange, he thought. It's just the opposite in the West.

Before parting, the two men shook hands, using both their hands, one in the palm, the other holding the wrist. He made no further comment. Like the many others shoppers, he gaped at the exquisite merchandise that had to be worth millions. Some of the shops seemed to breathe a fragrance somewhat similar to perfume. Shellie thought it was used to encourage the shopper to spend. He did not follow her philosophy. But as he kept observing the frantic buying of the shoppers it seemed that what Shellie said might be true. As they passed through the crowded throngs of people Shellie commented on the stares that targeted them.

"Wherever foreigners go, people will stare, even in cosmopolitan Seoul. I find it rude!"

"I like it," Stephen replied. "I'm used to being stared at on account of my looks and size." She ignored his evident conceit and continued her trend of thought.

"In the small township of Hamyang, people will not only stare, they'll also approach you to start a conversation." He later found that what Shellie said about Korean women was also true. They did cover their mouths when laughing, and both sexes often stood so close together that, in the West, would be regarded as an invasion of one's space. They were then made to feel nostalgic having a cappuccino at the only Starbucks in the whole of Korea. The pungent smell and the familiar taste of latte' wafted him back to 'his own' Starbucks in Victoria. It's tucked into an area of the Safeway grocery store located at the corners of Mackenzie Avenue and Shelbourne Street. There he often sipped a latte' while reading the 'Times Colonist.'

He finally got up the nerve to tell Shellie that he'd had enough education and pleaded with her to return to the hotel. She replied fiercely:

"You keep saying that knowledge is power and that you want to learn as much as you can about Korea and its people. Yet, when I show you around their palaces, temples, shrines, pagodas and shopping centers; when I explain important facts about Korea, you're not as interested to learn as you state. You should realize that what you see is only a bird's eye view of the place and its people. You'll need to recognize that while this is an important aspect of your learning. It's only a small part. You'll never get to really understand and know the Korean people until you are immersed in a family and begin to interact with its members."

"What you say is only partially true. I may seem disinterested but I am looking and listening very carefully," he lied unconvincingly. Shellie surprised him with her reply:

"I know that you want me in the bedroom, but from time to time I need you in the class room. It permits me to tell you what I think you need to know and gives me a chance to use the knowledge I've gained through experience and observation over the years. There'll be enough time for frolicking tonight. After all, we can't spend all our time in bed." Of course, he disagreed totally and pouted to show his disappointment, but she paid no attention. Soon, they were en route to the Changdeokgung Palace. Once there, she again spouted a stream of what he considered unsolicited and useless information.

"King Taejon began building it as a royal residence. Behind the palace grounds she pointed out the beautiful landscaping of the Huwon Gardens that were added later. He frowned. Shellie was again using words that he found familiar but just out of reach of his memory. It really bugged him that he couldn't remember where he had seen or heard them before.

"Don't frown" she stated, with a smile. "It's a UNESCO World heritage site and I think one of the finest examples of Korean garden design." He had to agree, the landscaping was definitely eye-catching, but he daren't say so. It would only increase his guide's tendency to prolong his torture. They then visited Gyeongbok Palace and the continuous flow of useless information recommenced.

"King Taejon built it to serve as the main seat of power for Korean kings from the Chosen Dynasty to the present. As you can see," she droned on in her uniquely boring manner, "like the earlier palace we saw, its architecture is equally striking." He looked at the gently-sloping roof-top covering the building like a half-open book, its cover uppermost, and its four corners curving upward in traditional Korean style. Perhaps it was striking to those interested in architecture, but since it resembled so many others he had seen, to him it was nothing new. Anyway, how many tourists are interested in architecture, he mumbled to himself. He certainly wasn't.

"The visits to such ancient structures," Shellie stated, "made her recognize the radical changes that the industrialization of South Korea had brought about." The enthusiasm with which she made this remark, and the way she suddenly stared at him, made him feel obliged to pretend that the statement was of special interest to him. He had no alternative feeling obliged to ask a question since she had raised her eyebrows expectantly and continued to stare at him. Evidently, she was prodding him to show some interest by at least asking questions. He was tempted to state candidly that he wasn't the least bit interested, but he behaved himself because of the special prize he had in mind. Instead, he inquired with pained lethargy injected into his voice:

"What were the changes brought about by industrialization?" He asked. His question was all Shellie needed to prattle on with her lesson in her uniquely verbose style.

"It made job seekers rush to all the major urban centers, and the effects were far-reaching." He cursed himself for not merely permitting, but actually encouraging Shellie to spout her knowledge. But he didn't dare hurt her feelings. It could cost him dearly later on.

Chapter 30

"What were the serious effects of urbanization?" He asked with a complete lack of enthusiasm in his voice. Of course, his indifference was completely lost on Shellie. She began, as eager as ever, with an in-depth explanation. As usual, she reverted to her long-winded teacher mode.

"Industrialization created a huge new job market that induced a rush of population from the provinces and rural areas to answer the call of the new vacancies in urban centers. This generated a giant upsurge in the earning capacity of the new employees. It also spawned an increased demand for additional housing complexes and both these facts caused a major change in the lifestyle of the new workers." Since Stephen was not listening carefully to what Shellie said, he found her explanation somewhat puzzling.

"You're confusing me with the changes you describe," he stated, realizing too late that he had spoken without thinking, urging her to prolong her lecture. She jumped at the chance.

"The change in the economic situation of the new employees had a major effect on their lifestyle. It was traditional for the family to be the central pillar of Korean life. Its members formed themselves into a sort of clan, *tonjok*, in which as many as four or even five generations lived together in a main building. The eldest family member made decisions that affected everyone." Shellie then looked at him, eyebrows raised, expectantly.

"Did men and women live together?" He asked the first question that came into his mind.

"No. Men and women lived separately on either side of the building and men were forbidden to enter the domicile of the women." When she added: "and this you'll find really interesting," he was forced to feign attention once more.

"The *tonjok* formed a miniature government with an appointed member to run the household. However, in their movement to the urban areas and the boost to their earning capacity, the traditional family became transformed."

"Transformed how?" He asked dejectedly, knowing that the answer would bring a flood of information in which he'd again drown.

"The multi-generational families were no longer compelled to live under one roof. They became instead, a 'nuclear family' with a father, mother and their children living together." He was sorry to have given her an opening, because the voluminous flow continued unabated. However, he couldn't help being astonished by her remarks. He believed that the multi-generational family she described would be considered not merely absurd but totally unacceptable to a Westerner. What she went on to say about traditional marriage was equally astounding.

"Unlike in the West, Marriage there was arranged not as a union between two single individuals but rather an alliance between two families. Among the moneyed class a family member was chosen to conduct research into the background of candidates. Once a worthy partner was found, the two were expected to marry after a brief period of dating. People do things differently today. There is intermarriage between individuals from different social classes." Stephen made no comment, and for a moment there was blessed silence. He couldn't believe his luck. His refusal to reply had stopped the one-sided flow of information. However, his luck didn't last. On their way home, Shellie dropped another unexpected gem.

"Koreans are justly proud of their ancestry. They revere their elders and their dead, erecting shrines for those who have died. However, when a parent dies, the eldest son goes into mourning by wearing a hat of reeds, and covers his face with a fan. He then detaches himself from everyone including family members." To Stephen the conduct sounded not merely strange, but weird.

On the subway home, at last, he found that no seats were available since it was rush hour. He was standing holding bags of his purchases in both hands. He felt a tug on one bag and looked down to see that a seated old lady had relieved him of his bag. She held it securely in her lap. Not understanding, he looked at Shellie with raised eyebrows for an explanation. She whispered: "the lady is helping you." He bowed to the old lady in thanks, but her eyes were closed, so she didn't respond. Later, expecting her to hand the bag back as he was disembarking, he found that the old lady had fallen asleep. When he tried to tug the bag gently away, she held on to it even more tightly. Not surprisingly, the tug-of-war that took place created a bus full of laughing passengers. Finally, her neighbor gently pried the bag loose and handed it back to him amid a chorus of laughter. Although no word was spoken, he bowed in thanks at the stranger's polite and thoughtful gesture. He needn't have bothered. The old lady was still asleep.

On another day, Shellie dragged him off to Insa-dong. "This," she began, "is the center of a thriving cultural and financial area of Seoul. It is also the location of the Joyesa Temple and one of the most active Buddhist places of worship. Here, in May on the Buddha's Birthday," she continued, "the temple presents a display that showcases the country's culture." Once she mentioned 'culture,' he knew he was trapped. There would be an elongated explanation to follow. But he shouldn't complain. She had been especially generous in their frolicking on the previous night.

"Visitors are invited to attend The Lotus Lantern festival and to celebrate the birth of Buddha. It is a very colorful parade that displays many thousands of multicolored paper lanterns and beautiful hanbok costumes.

"I would imagine that the riot of color is extraordinary!" he said, in lame response to Shellie's irate stare. "Are there other festivals?" He then felt constrained to ask.

"There is the festival of Seollal that celebrates the traditional Korean New Year. It allows visitors to experience the very best of Korea's cuisine. There you can get a taste of *galbi*, barbecue ribs, a very popular Korean dish. Also very tasty is *bulgogi*, marinated beef. Perhaps you shouldn't try *Hongeohoe*, since it is sliced fermented skate. I find that its high ammonia content makes it unpalatable. The smell is somewhat disgusting and often causes puking. Another dish you should ignore is *san naki*. It is octopus whose tentacles are sliced. Although they are served pan fried, they have a habit of wriggling on your plate and persist in doing so in your mouth when you try to chew them."

Shellie gave him no peace until they visited the National Museum of Korea.

"It is," she informed him, "especially worth seeing since it is the sixth largest exhibit of its kind in the world. According to Korea's guide books "it is the flagship museum of Korean history and art, offering a variety of exhibits and educational programs." He concluded that it, like the rest of their sight seeing tour, gave her the opportunity she so evidently needed, to further extend her lesson plan. She continued:

"As you can see, the wings that we visited provide a glimpse into both the past and the future. Showcased there is Korea's most priceless collection of historical artifacts and religious art work.

On the ground floor level there were exhibits from the Three Kingdoms period. Shellie pointed out the work of their incredibly gifted artists and artisans. Their gold, silver and bronze cast in ornate shapes highlighted a fifth–century crown and belt set worn by a Silla king. They skipped the next floor and headed straight to the upper floor that displayed numerous metal sculptures and a wide assortment of beautiful pots that were evidently centuries old.

"The main purpose of our visit is to see the Gyeongcheonsa Pagoda which is in the glass case before us." Shellie then amazed him with a detailed description.

"As you can see," she began, "it is ten storeys tall, and being made from marble, differs considerably from most of the others that are traditionally made from granite or wood." Before she could continue Stephen cut into her narration much to her amazement: "It is considered one of the finest examples of Joseon dynasty pagoda art. The first three storeys follow the shape of the base and the next seven storeys are shaped in the form of squares. Dragons, lions, lotus flowers, phoenixes, Buddhas and the Four Heavenly Kings are carved on each panel of the pagoda. While made of stone, it is carved to look like wood and imitates a wooden pagoda design. Each tier had a hip-and-gabled roof, eaves and carvings that resemble tiles. It's truly an impressive work of art! Don't you think?"

She applauded his effort.

As they left, he remarked that "certain people whom he saw sitting at a table or standing in a group seemed to be programmed robots. They showed both respect and deference to each other as though they followed some invisible unwritten law or principle of hierarchy."

"Oh yes," Shellie replied, quick on the uptake: "Koreans tend to follow a strictly adhered to code of conduct between husband and wife, father and son, old and young, even between friends." She then paused for a moment before adding as an afterthought: "Yes, just as they do between ruler and subject. You see, it was the protocol of social ethics taught by Confucius that they were following when showing deference to others." Stephen thought this gave him the opportunity to catch her out. He asked:

"But why then did we notice so much jostling and queue jumping at that crowded bus stop? You'd have to admit that there are some people who obviously don't follow those rules?"

"People in a queue or a crowd are strangers who are ignorant of each other's background," Shellie pointed out. "Thus, there is no basis on which to classify each other in terms of their relationships. However, when introduced, strangers will immediately change their conduct. Higher status is gained through prestigious job, wealth, age, and especially by those who attended a better school or university. Such people are given greater respect." While Stephen was irritated at not having caught her out, he noticed wives being subservient to their husbands, helping them on with their coats, and walking a few steps behind, before hurrying forward to open doors for them. Pointing out these facts, he stated sarcastically:

"This must be a female oriented society. Don't you think?"

"Unlike in the US and Canada, women rights have made little progress here. Korea is definitely a male oriented society. However, women do dominate to some extent in the home." Shellie said in response to his observation. "There, she has the responsibility of raising the children and providing the family with a comfortable home. They also take charge of the household finances. When a husband gets paid, it is customary to give his entire salary to his wife. She is the one who gives him an allowance. So, it can be said that in some respects women do dominate in the home."

On more than one occasion, Stephen noticed that in answering a question, people tipped their heads backwards and audibly drew in their breath. Shellie explained that it was the Korean way of saying no. She then inveigled him into trudging up the "Old Pilgrim's Way" to visit a shrine in the "Diamond Mountains."

"If you don't mind," she stated, "we have to climb upwards along very rough and steep terrain to visit an old monks' burial ground." But she continued with a complimentary bribe: "You're a big, athletic, muscular man so it won't bother you." He refused to respond to the evident massaging of his ego since after all the walking he was quite tired and angry. But Shellie goaded him into climbing higher, leading him into an even more remote area.

"To arrive at the Mychissko Shrine, the path is so steep that those pilgrims who are too weak to walk, have to be lifted upward on stretchers to see the Shrine. Its age predates the Roman occupation of Britain." On arrival, Shellie and Stephen saw the colossal carving of a Buddha that stands out of the living rock.

"It's the place where pilgrims come to pray in order to propitiate the vengeful spirits of the dead," she said. Despite his fatigue, he agreed that the magnificence of the carving was well worth the effort. For once he couldn't fault his guide for urging him onward and upward. But he promised himself that this was the end of the road. He was eager to do some urging of his own.

Against both his will and his better judgment Shellie kept her promise. She dragged him kicking and screaming to the Namdeamun Market, an outdoor affair where almost everything is sold 24/7. Stephen couldn't believe that all the things he saw could be bought in one single location. There were fabrics, food, house wares, toys, flowers, clothing, shoes, socks, jewelry, accessories, stationery and appliances. In both the wide walkways and the narrow alleys there were crowds of shoppers. Above the shops on either side was a daunting array of colorful signs—large and small—naming the shops and advertising their wares. Present too was a large number of street-vendor stalls some selling 'street food,' while others sold anything a person could care to name. The aroma of cooking exotic dishes hung over everything awakening the appetite and lending a special atmosphere to the market. "Wasn't this visit worth the effort?" She asked. He smiled at her but refrained from stating that he had a different effort in mind.

On their way home as they passed a little kiosk where guide books were being sold, Stephen caught sight of one hanging by a string from a shelf. Its name, *Korea*, was on the cover printed in large white letters that stood out against a black background. On the cover was a man standing with his back to the camera. Stephen recognized the book immediately as he had bought and read it after receiving so many quotations from it in his student essays. It was written by Robert Story and published by Lonely Planet Publishers. He then knew why so much of the information that Shellie kept quoting sounded familiar to him. Hanging next to it was another guide book: *Korea's Cultural Roots* written by Jon Covell and published by Hollym International Corporation. He again knew of the work from student quotations and recognized some of those used by Shellie. His tour guide was a fraud. She pretended to dish out information about Korea as though it came from her own study and observation. Instead, most of her comments about the history, politics, architecture, education, economics, festivals, cuisine, temples, pagodas and other places of interest came from the two guide books and no doubt from the Internet. In fairness to Shellie though, he had to admit that her descriptions were very seldom quoted verbatim. She also possessed a first-class memory. However, on thinking over the situation, Stephen decided not to unmask her. It would serve no purpose except to cause an argument. Far more important, it might eliminate the possibility of any further frolicking.

The rest of their stay passed in a flash. "Where are we going?" He asked Shellie.

"We are heading to Yeonido dock to take a romantic cruise on the Hangang River that bisects Seoul from east to west." They boarded the double decked boat and were soon gazing interestedly at a gorgeous display of ancient glazed pottery before taking their seats, side by side. On leaving the dock they could feel a refreshing breeze that brought different scents from either the bank or from the surrounding islands where they originated. There was a musical performance and though they didn't know any of the songs they agreed that they were all lovely. Throughout the performance they held hands concealed under his coat. During the concert except for the lapping of the waves against the hull and the peculiar odor of the river, Stephen was able to enjoy the silence of the night and his tour guide. They also saw a series of striking panoramic views of the colorful lighted bridges with their curved blue arches above them. Specially highlighted too were the N Seoul Tower, Jeoldusan Park, the 63 City Building and Jamsil Sport Complex. Later, on returning to their hotel room, they frolicked in bed, slept late, ate voraciously, then frolicked some more.

Stephen arose early on the morning of Shellie's departure, and was fully dressed and packed before waking her. He excused himself for not being able to accompany her to the airport as promised, since he had "to catch the only early bus" to his destination. He thought Shellie knew he was lying, as there were buses leaving every hour. She must have thought it futile to confront him with the lie. Being practical, she no doubt realized that there was nothing to gain since she would never see him again.

Perhaps she thought that a confrontation would spoil the wonderful time they'd had. He believed she consoled herself with the thought that she couldn't have found a better lover. This view occurred to him since he gave her an evaluation of her sexual performance, being aware that some women would kill to have such a critique. He had a standard assessment with which he complimented each of his conquests and thought Shellie was delighted with what he said, for she had committed it to memory and before he left, repeated it to him verbatim: "In the throes of passion, you behaved like a wildcat, writhing in frenzied delight. The passionate things you do and say make your partner's experience unforgettable. When I entered you, the way your inner muscles tightened around my member made my senses sing. You must have enjoyed yourself too, since everyone within a mile would have heard your screams of agonized rapture."

When Shellie went to check out of the hotel, she was stunned at the news from the front desk. "Before leaving, your companion charged all your meals and drinks to your room," the receptionist told her. The employee averted her gaze when she saw Shellie's startled reaction and the tears that sprang from her eyes. Although Shellie had enjoyed every moment of Stephen's company, and would never forget their lovemaking, she couldn't withhold tears of annoyance and deep regret that so gorgeous a creature on the outside could, on the inside, be such a thoroughly rotten bastard.

The *Korea* guidebook pointed out that before the founding of the three kingdoms (1122 BC) there were few historical events worthy of note. The first to emerge in the peninsula was the Goguryeo kingdom in the north. Later, the Paekche kingdom arose in the southwest. The last to emerge was the Silla kingdom. It conquered the other two and unified the whole country. During this period, the Confucian code of ethics was introduced. Confucius, a Chinese philosopher/teacher believed that leaders should be highly educated and that government should be in the hands of the most capable people rather than in the control of the nobility. Each individual in society had a role to play and if each person carried out the role allotted to him, there would be justice for all in the society.

The Korean peninsula is sandwiched between three of the world's powerful giants, Russia, China and Japan, who, from the earliest years, pursued a policy of aggression: they all wanted to extend their borders while harassing Korea to open its markets. Today, with the recent break up of the Soviet Union and the Chinese introspective policy of navel gazing, harassment from these nations has become less of a threat. Instead, China is far more willing to support the economy of North Korea.

Japan too, imposed its own brand of torture. From very early times, its pirates ravaged Korea's costal villages. By the end of the sixteenth century they had begun to invade and terrorize the whole Korean peninsula. In the early 20th century, Korea remained hard at work trying to avoid foreign influences.

Russia, China and Japan were grappling with each other to occupy Mongolia and Korea. After Japan defeated the other two, it forced Korea to accept the "Protectorate Treaty" which gave Japan control over the functions of Korea's administrative and foreign relations. Japan's military was able to suppress the many uprisings from Korean students and labor movements until finally it controlled all aspects of Korean life.

The student essays also repeated the following: In a war between Chinese backed North Korea and United Nation backed South Korea, the Communist troops of Kim Il-Sung invaded the South, seized Seoul and the nation became divided at the 38th parallel. Japan's brutal invasion and colonization from 1910 to 1945 ended with that country's conquest by the Allied forces in WW11. At the defeat of Japan, the Allied Forces drew an arbitrary line across the peninsula and made each half a protectorate of the superpowers. The American forces moved into Seoul and the Russians occupied the North. Disagreements between the USSR and the United States on unification caused the permanent establishment of the two separate regimes. In 1948 the Republic of Korea was born with Rhee Sygman as president. A month later Kim Il-Sung became head of the Democratic Republic of Korea.

The Internet states that during their colonial rule, the Japanese oppressed the Korean people. Any attempt at independent thought or action was brutally suppressed. The scenes of torture depicted in Korea's Independent Hall offer the observer a graphic view of the depths of Japanese depravity. The Colonizers increased the psychological torture by making the Japanese language mandatory in schools and eliminating Korean history from the curriculum. Finally, they forced Koreans to take Japanese names, follow Japanese rituals, and conscripted hundreds of thousands of young men and women into the Japanese workforce to boost the Japanese economy.

Certainly, the most morally destructive blow to Korean pride was the rounding up and transportation of thousands of young women to the front to serve as prostitutes and sex slaves for the Japanese armed forces. Such ruthless acts of oppression no doubt help to perpetuate Korean bitterness towards the Japanese.

As though these disasters were not enough, North Korea began a series of assaults against its southern neighbor. Then, since 1953 both sides were heavily engaged in espionage and terrorist activities. North Korea has continued its policy of aggression, trying to conquer and occupy the South. Their agents planted a bomb in Burma killing a whole South Korean delegation.

Then, in attempting to sabotage the 1988 Summer Olympics in Seoul, North Korean terrorists planted a bomb in a South Korean airliner that killed all on board. Even today, North Korea pursues its threat to the South and its neighbors with panic creating tactics like the firing of missiles over the Sea of Japan. Worse still is its constant boast of nuclear weapon-production that threatens the safety of its neighbors, and indeed of the whole planet.

Against such a background, Stephen found that the animosity the South harbors for the government of the North was hardly surprising. He also learnt that other Occidental nations had been a pain in South Korea's butt. Over the years they had used every vicious arm-twisting tactic they could devise to persuade South Korea to change its economic policy of seclusion and open its markets. They and the West are still trying to do so. As a result of its past history, it is not surprising that Koreans feel one or more of their neighbors can, at any time, bare their aggressive fangs and threaten their security. This recognition has not created for Koreans a comfortable relationship towards foreigners.

The essays assured Stephen that the pressures of harassment, war, conquest, colonization and subjugation had seriously influenced the character of the Korean people. They had become suspicious and intolerant of all other nationalities. Thanks to the greed and aggression of their neighbors, the people of South Korea had become xenophobic, and there are those visitors who claim they could actually feel their scarcely veiled hostility. However, the essays also told Stephen that Koreans could be warm, friendly and hospitable, if rather formal because of their protocol-ridden culture. The consensus was that by Western standards, they were somewhat reserved in their ways, but tended to become good and loyal friends once they got to know you.

Stephen was to learn later the important role that their Confucian philosophy, together with their Christian teaching, their Buddhist and Shaman roots, played in conditioning their character. He would have to determine for himself the extent to which each, or all of these strands, helped to influence the conduct of the Korean individuals he met. He felt sure that the information recorded in the essays would help him to understand the strengths and weaknesses of the people among whom he was about to take his first and only extended vacation.

After leaving Shellie at the hotel, Stephen took a taxi to the Tong Seoul Bus Terminal where he boarded a bus traveling the Gyeongbu Expressway that passed through the city of Daejeon, and headed further south along the Jungbu Expressway to reach his destination, Hamyang. This small country township was 100 kilometers north-east of Kwangju, the ancient provincial capital of Chollanam-do.

Stephen sat at the back of the bus watching the mix of Caucasian tourists and Orientals as they entered. He was soon joined by a striking couple. The man was a tall powerfully built, black African with scarified face markings. His partner was a peach complexioned doll-like Japanese young woman. Both wore sunglasses. The couple was striking because of their sharply contrasting features. What also compelled attraction was that they kept holding hands even on the bus. Their entwined fingers seemed to give them a dual solidity. After hearing their stories, Stephen realized that they felt the need to protect themselves from an enemy world that had invaded their privacy too often to gape and to mock.

They made a bee-line for Stephen with timid, engaging smiles and both removed their sunglasses at the same time before entering into conversation with him. They both seemed friendly as the man made introductions. "I am Joe, and this is my wife, Sally. We heard you speak English in the immigration line and guessed that you were American."

"No no, I'm Stephen, a Canadian. Forgive me for asking, but it seemed odd to me that you both removed your sunglasses at the same time before speaking? Was it just coincidence?"

"No, it's impolite in Korea to wear sunglasses while in conversation," Sally replied. "Perhaps it has something to do with concealing the eyes and the supposed sincerity or otherwise that might be seen there."

"You're both fluent in English, are you on vacation like me?"

"No. We're both ESL teachers working at different high schools in Jeonju."

"What do you think of the architecture you saw in Seoul?" Sally asked him a few minutes later after being seated, and they were both gazing at the city slipping by.

"I find it a paradox that the old and the new should confront each other in such hilarious discord. The ancient and modern architects must have had vastly different objectives. The first, supremely confident in the knowledge of the person he knew he was seems to have chosen simplicity to satisfy the national taste. The second, a dislocated personality produced by the division of his state, had become schizoid, seeking fulfillment in the accolade of others.

"That's a rather harsh criticism," Joe said, yet I agree with the division you state. "To me, Seoul is a modern bustling metropolis of powerful contrasts. Its ancient shrines, pagodas and temples sit cheek by jowl with modern office blocks and giant manufacturing complexes. It is symbolic of innovative planning and architectural creativity." Stephen thought that foreign dollars had fueled the building of almost every school, hospital, university and monument in Africa. Many, he had read, were in a state of disrepair bordering on collapse. The drought of African architects, he thought, encouraged Joe to see Seoul's architecture as "the forward march of an artistic people obsessed with progress."

Sally differed from them both. She had come from the ghastly urban sprawl of downtown Tokyo. "There, skyscrapers dwarfed and dislocated the landscape, with millions of people jammed together in hotel rooms, streets and sidewalks, cars, trains and buses. They live, in a kind of frenzied yet sophisticated chaos. "For me," she said, "Seoul brings to mind the neurosis of high-density population, congested living, continuous motion, and noise, whereas the mountains in the background, wreathed in clouds, suggest tranquility, harmony and repose. In comparison, Seoul is a travesty of muddled thinking, a sin against the environment and the national soul." Sally's overtly harsh criticism was clearly the result of being a died-in-the-wool environmentalist.

What was written about Seoul's architecture offered a more balanced assessment. The building of high-rises was an innovative attempt to provide big corporations with easily accessible living accommodation for the huge labor force that needed to live close to their workplace. True, it was a giant step forward in urban planning and organization, but Stephen believed that these people who had stunned the world with their beautiful shrines and temples, pagodas, highways and bridges, had put a lasting stain on their reputation for simple beauty.

The trees bordering the Expressway were festooned with storks, huge ungainly shaped birds with small heads, large elongated beaks and pink, oversized goiters. They blossomed from the tree branches, standing on one or two matchstick legs, like ugly, forbidding fruit. Their nests, large mounds of untidy twigs, vied with the architecture for the prize of having defamed the landscape. As if to compensate for this hideous display, vast swatches of "dazzling royal azalea, forsythia and fragrant gardenia" sprung from the soil on hills, roadsides and untilled fields stunning the visitor with their loveliness.

The traditional style of the old buildings they passed in villages provided a great contrast with Seoul. "Their inhabitants have resisted transfer into the present preferring a closer relationship with their Neanderthal forbears." Stephen's listeners failed to find any humor in his tasteless remark.

Chapter 31

Stephen received a shock when he asked Joe and Sally where they made their home. They looked at each other and the earlier smiles disappeared. "We have none," Joe replied sadly. Clearly they had a story to tell and Sally soon began.

"I was one of Joe's students at the Yonsei University where he taught courses in ESL and Business English."

"She was my star student with a gift for languages and a wide area of interests."

"After classes, I began meeting Joe who challenged and inspired me by discussing all sorts of topics. I found him charming, knowledgeable, civilized, and above all, gentle–so very different from the sense of power and savagery that his huge figure and scarified features first evoked."

"It was no mystery that I fell in love with my very curious and beautiful student. Even more incredible, she fell in love with me."

"He proposed, I accepted and we decided to wait until after my graduation to get married. When I broke the news to my parents, my father, whom I had always respected for his liberal views, stunned me with his response."

"If I married a black African, it would bring shame, embarrassment, and disaster upon the whole family. We would be shunned and alienated from our world. He gave me an ultimatum: "call off the marriage and stop seeing Joe at once, or you'll be outcast from the family.""

"Sally, strong-willed like her father, carried out our marriage plan and afterwards wanted the family to meet the man she loved and to whom she was married. She knew that the timing of introducing me to the family was crucial and chose the time when they were all together at the evening meal."

"When I introduced Joe, they behaved as though a fire-breathing dragon had suddenly charged into their midst. My father turned his back on us and following him, the family–my mother, brother and sister—literally ran from the room. As we were about to leave the house, my mother reappeared carrying a basket in which my belongings were neatly packed. She kept her back towards Joe and me, placed the basket next to the door and fled."

"Since that day, no member of the family had spoken a word to either of us, Joe said sadly." The couple left Japan immediately, and brooding over the offensive behavior of certain human beings, started their sad and lonely pilgrimage teaching in those Asiatic countries that would hire them. It was only because of his impeccable qualifications, coupled with the Asian obsession to learn English, that Joe was hired and tolerated by Asian colleges. Stephen suggested that they should go to Canada where "countless thousands" of Asian students are studying courses in ESL."

There's always a need for qualified teachers, and you'll find that Canada is multinational and that the government vigorously promotes a policy of equality and multiculturalism."

Joe's story was somewhat similar to that of his wife and he hastened to tell it. "At the age of twelve as a houseboy in Zimbabwe, I would often sit under the verandah and listen to the discussions of my white bwana and his farmer friends. Carousing late into the African night, they often discussed "the local situation." African war veterans and civilians were fencing off sections and taking over ownership of farms belonging to white farmers with the encouragement of the Mugabe government. The policy was supposed to correct the injustice that had occurred almost a century earlier. Large tracts of land had been given to some 700-800 white foreigners. These latter were the employees of the white pioneer/founder, Cecil Rhodes, in a country with just under a million black Africans. I listened to the blistering comments falling on my ears like molten metal from above. The speaker reserved "a special contempt for the black shiftless creatures" whom he employed. A heated argument ensued in which all present seemed to be in vehement disagreement with the drunken speaker, but the calumny was enough for me. I left the farm that very night and over the next years worked and studied to get an education and become a well-qualified teacher." Stephen lowered his eyes in pretended grief, but indifferent to the racism and the resulting scourge of solitude that is not limited to an individual, a community or to a country, but is worldwide in its scope.

Sally pointed out the smaller cities on the bus route, describing each as "a miniature Seoul, displaying the same urban sprawl, the same concentration of industry, and on its outskirts, the same ugly high-rise housing" that she found impersonal and dehumanizing. "The same vehicle traffic clogged the streets while the pedestrian traffic clogged the pavements. There were similar unending stretches of lots crammed with new cars; the same urban pollution of noise, dust and exhaust fumes."

The bus stopped for a bathroom break and Stephen complained that he felt somewhat lightheaded at not having had breakfast in his rush to catch the bus. Before he could finish his spiel, Joe and Sally invited him to join them for breakfast as he had anticipated. While they both had a single cup of coffee, he surprised them by having a large bowl of cereal followed by a huge four-egg omelet, a slew of pancakes and numerous cups of coffee before returning to the bus.

After a moment's silence, Sally asked: "Weren't Asians supposed to be the world's most accomplished copycats?"

"True," Stephen agreed, "but they often followed their cheap imitation with innovation, when a new vastly improved product would be born to dominate the world market at a lower price. It had happened with cars, cameras, motorcycles, bicycles and an untold number of electronic gadgetry. The fact that they could ship their products to distant Western markets, undersell the homegrown competition and still make a profit was adequate proof of their economic creativity and even more of their marketing strategy. They all agreed that Korean cities pulsated with the same frenetic energy that reflected the innovative ideas and the thoroughness of their planning and economic know-how.

On the outskirts of Daejeon, Sally pointed out the popular 'hanyak' shops displaying in their windows glass containers of snakes next to stacks of deer antlers, and piles of dried insects. Joe explained that many Asians including Koreans "firmly believed that animals possess medicinal qualities in their meat, skin, bones and blood. They made soups with the meat from dog, snake, eel, octopus and the powder of deer antlers. They ate fried beetles, spiders and bugs of all kinds. In some countries, rats and live monkey's brains were regarded as delicacies," he added. "Koreans also used parts of these creatures as aphrodisiacs to boost their libido."

"We should be saying our goodbyes," Joe told Stephen. "We'll be getting off at the bus station in Daejeon, a couple of minutes away. We'll be changing buses there heading for Jeonju where we live. Here's our phone number. Perhaps you'll call and come to spend with us any week end that you are free." The repetition of the invitation and the enthusiasm with which it was delivered seemed to echo the aching loneliness of their lives.

In spite of himself, Stephen was moved. "Thank you both," he replied. "You can rest assured that I'll call and come at the first opportunity." At the same time, he couldn't help congratulating himself for having spun his web of charm successfully enough to ensure that the couple would be ripe for the pickings whenever he had the time and inclination to visit them.

After another hour, the bus drove into an area that Stephen at once recognized as a new realm. The landscape was one of terraced foothills and open plains. The whole country seemed to be tilted westward towards the Yellow Sea. A carpet of lush green pastures, broken by areas of black, untilled fields seemed to stretch towards infinity. The sight and powerful odor of manure that permeated the atmosphere at once testified that it was "a land of farmers, the agricultural heartland and rice bowl of Korea," as Joe had stated earlier. Stephen saw women planting rice in shin-deep paddies on the terraced hillsides. The plants sprouted above the surface of the water in lines so straight that they seemed to have been drawn with a ruler. Joe had told Stephen that it was "a seriously disadvantaged area, economically depressed since it was totally lacking in heavy industry." Sally disagreed of course. Before leaving the bus she insisted that "the region had the distinct advantage of the cleanest air and the best-preserved natural environment in all Korea."

Stephen disembarked further along at the tiny township of Hamyang, where he took a taxi to the Ahn residence. On arrival, he noted that the Ahn property differed considerably from the widely scattered farmhouses he had passed. While they were all thatched roofed, single story dwellings, their unpainted stone walls pockmarked by generations of time and weather, the Ahn residence was an imposing structure of two stories. It was built and designed along the lines of upscale Western architecture. Mr. and Mrs. Ahn greeted him on their front steps with a bow. Stephen responded in kind, noting that the bow was from the neck not from the waist like the Japanese. Both wore the Korean traditional dress that had become familiar to Stephen during his stay in Seoul.

They welcomed Stephen warmly, before removing their shoes to re-enter the house. Stephen remembered his uncle's advice to carefully observe and follow the conduct of his hosts. He removed his shoes, and like them, pointed the toes away from the building. He was again surprised to note that although Korean women were accorded equal status with men, some wives continued to regard men as superior. Mrs. Ahn scurried forward to hold the door open for her husband to enter their hallway. Stephen then quickly held the door open for his hostess to enter before him, having learnt from the essays that he was the lowest in rank and thus the least important.

On entry, the pungent aromatic blend of spices prickled his nostrils. He had only once smelled so overpowering an aroma in the outdoor market in Seoul and concluded that the scent, like that of the market, could only have come from blending all the world's most potent spices. He couldn't even guess at the piquant odors that filled his nostrils making his nose and eyes run although he was far from the origin of the scent that no doubt came from the kitchen. He noticed that the Ahns used non-verbal communication, sometimes with their hands, eyes or even facial gestures. Unfortunately, he was not yet sure of their meaning. There were two portraits of men he assumed were the long dead Ahn ancestors, hanging on either wall of the large hall through which he was passing. Their eyes peered down at him conveying, he thought, a sense of pride at the successes they had achieved on the farm and the rich legacy they had passed on to their descendants. Their stern faces suggested that life was a very serious business in which there was little room for hilarity. No portrait of a female ancestor graced the wall.

His hosts conducted him first to his upstairs room to freshen up, but he had learnt that custom didn't allow them to show him over their home as Westerners sometimes do. Yet, what Stephen did see gave him the idea that a building could absorb the character and emotions of its inhabitants. Their presence seemed to be lodged in the paint, the furnishings and the masonry. It manifested itself so strongly that he thought it would pervade even the damp of the bathroom and the soot of the kitchen. However, since the home was a model of Western luxury and elegance, no hint of either damp or soot was present. He had the impression that the home exuded the atmosphere of the warmth, love and simple contentment of the generations that had lived in its interior space. It made him feel humble to accept the hospitality the Ahns were extending to him, a charlatan and an interloper. It seldom happened that such unbidden thoughts came to Stephen's mind, and whenever his better nature surfaced, and they rarely did, he objected strenuously to such reprehensible thoughts, and banished them forthwith from his mind.

"How's your uncle?" Mr. Ahn asked, and Stephen remembered the essays explaining that a safe subject of conversation with strangers was asking after the health of a close relation.

"Very well thank you, Mr. Ahn, (Stephen had learnt that he should use the full title in addressing strangers) but busy as ever lecturing at his college in London and attending learned conferences in Europe somewhere. Afterwards, he'll be returning to his college in London to continue teaching."

"Tom was brilliant at everything he did. If he had gone into business, he'd have made a huge success of it. But he always loved teaching."

Stephen remembered from his research on the Internet that Koreans ask rather intimate questions trying to find some link in their relationship with a new acquaintance. They use age, family, school, university, hometown or even a hobby to do so. It is a means of finding some common ground with which to start a conversation. More often it helps to determine which of the two is of higher status and therefore demands greater respect. An important talking point fosters social bonding. With these thoughts in mind, Stephen offered the topic of Haida art.

"Uncle Tom mentioned that you were fond of Haida carvings. Do you have any of their work?"

"No," his host said smiling. "Students in a foreign country are always short of money, and the better carvings of the aboriginal people of the West Coast are quite expensive. So, I never could afford to buy anything I liked. If I ever get the chance to return to BC, I'll get myself some of their works." Stephen was impressed with the fluency of his host whom he thought spoke with only the barest hint of an accent, if a little more slowly. He wondered if it mimicked the speed of normal Korean speech rhythms, or if its slowness was a result of speaking a second language.

"Well, when Uncle Tom mentioned your interest, I thought you might like something done by Hunt himself, so I got you an example of his work. Then I saw some hand-woven Haida sweaters with raven and whale designs emblazoned on the front in black, red and white, their favorite colors. I couldn't resist getting a few of them for you and Mrs. Ahn."

"What! Ahn exploded. That was very generous of you Stephen. But we really can't accept gifts from you. It wasn't at all necessary for you to do that." Stephen knew from the essays and the Internet that Korean protocol demanded that his gifts would be immediately refused and that he'd have to insist more than once before they would be accepted, and with practiced reluctance. He kept insisting until they were finally accepted.

"Oh, it was the very least I could do," Stephen said smugly, handing over the gifts that, if memory served him right, "had to be done with both hands." He expected the Ahns to open the gifts in front of him, unaware that Korean custom frowned upon doing so. He was therefore surprised and disappointed that his hostess took the unopened gifts and spirited them away somewhere inside. It wasn't until much later that both his host and hostess showed that they were as overwhelmed by the gifts as by Stephen's generosity.

"Thank you so much for the mask, Stephen, it's an exceptional piece, exquisitely carved and painted."

"The mask is by Hunt himself; a worthy example of Haida art," Stephen stated.

"Carved by Hunt himself, you say. However did you manage that? He has museums, airports and universities clamoring for his work." Stephen was tempted to say, you don't want to know. Instead, he remained silent and smug, seeing that Ahn was delighted with his gift. He held up the mask examining it closely and exclaimed: "This is one of his priceless pieces; something I've always wanted. I can't thank you enough, Stephen." The donor smiled and replied: "I'm so glad you like what I chose."

"The sweaters too are beautiful," said Mrs. Ahn. They'll surely in Korea stand out." She quickly added: "We have too lovely sweaters, but no intricately hand-woven ones with so original animal designs." Stephen noted that his hostess also spoke English fluently though she sometimes changed the word order. She too spoke at a much slower pace and her accent was more marked than that of her husband. Both the Ahns thanked Stephen again for his thoughtfulness and generosity, and even more for his extravagance. Stephen congratulated himself for having begun to spin his web with evident success. No one could say he hadn't started off his campaign with a bang.

There was a quiet beauty in the rooms of the Ahns home–pastel shaded walls, tiled floors in muted colors that Stephen later learned were heated from below, a process called 'ondol.' There was the gleam of bright glass windows framed in dark polished wood. The lower half of the dining room walls was paneled in burnished cherry, the upper half enclosed in etched glass that climbed to the vaulted ceiling. The staircase, with its highly polished banisters, ascended in a gentle curve to an upstairs gallery.

Stephen's suite, (it couldn't be termed a room) was for him, the 'piece de resistance.' The huge bed, stretched out before him like a football field. It faced a towering unlit fireplace where a vase with bare pine branches were fixed in a floral arrangement. The room was warm and its pine-scented breath mingled with the perfume from a bouquet of roses sprouting from an exquisite Waterford vase on one of the two bedside tables. Blue flecks on the green bedside rug were repeated together with green ones in the blue drapes, while the recessed lighting gave an additional dimension of space to the area. The bedroom was equipped with its own dressing room, an ensuite with washbasin, toilet, bidet, bath and shower. Stephen was duly impressed. The affluence that the suite exuded gave Stephen food for thought, and while undressing for bed that night, he began to consider the stratagems he might use to advance his campaign for profit. He kept rubbing his hands together.

On the following morning, he came downstairs and saw Serena framed in the doorway. Her back was to him and she was wearing the hanbok, an outfit consisting of a white, long sleeved *chogori*, the Korean short jacket, with the *chima*, a white voluminous high-waisted floor-length skirt. In stature, she was petite, her head was raised, held with the poise and elegance one associated with royalty. Her black silken hair was pulled back severely against her skull then gathered and wrapped into a bold knot that sat on top of her head. It suggested the presence of a crown and made her seem taller. Her back was facing him; she was looking at the distant mountains and the sun set fire to her hair. Its rays, shining on the white fabric of her outfit, made her seem to shimmer with light. It also silhouetted her shapely figure through her clothing, so that even from behind she exuded a rare sexual quality. When she turned towards him at the sound of his footsteps, her face jarred him into a standstill of confusion, holding him spellbound. There was a draining away of his blood, and a hand seemed to clutch his heart in a grip of iron. He could hardly breathe. It was as though the oxygen in his lungs had evaporated. He noticed too that her almond-shaped eyes were tilted, outer ends upwards, emphasizing the high Asian cheekbones and the faultless porcelain skin. Her lips formed a cupid's bow and her jaw line was set at a stubborn angle of determination. The hair on his neck stood on end and he lost the power of speech temporarily. Never before had he been confronted by so striking a face. He could only think of one word to describe it: "spectacular." He saw too that her allure went well beyond mere sexuality. She possessed the solemn beauty of a child-woman that made her appear innocent, mysterious and unreachable. He remembered his uncle mentioning that the daughter was a teenager and his reply had been: "you needn't worry. In my book teenagers are sub-human."

The fiery glow of her hair gave him the impression of looking at a finely-carved exotic ornament that had suddenly come to life. Her perfectly white teeth lit up her face and her blatant sexuality inflamed his blood sending furtive messages to his loins. Looking into the sparkling lagoon of her eyes, he felt irretrievably lost. They were the deep green of emerald gemstones flecked with gold. She exuded a regal air and moved with the feline grace of a jungle cat. The impression of her purity leapt out at him, making him feel that in her presence, a charlatan like him defiled the very air she breathed. She was so natural, seeming unaware that she carried herself in a way that turned heads. Her proud breasts thrust themselves forward against the thin fabric of her *chig-ori* and her narrow waist flared towards her hips. The image of that figure stalking like a predator along a catwalk suggested that she would make a highly paid super model or a very busy call girl. Stephen had to forcefully bring himself under control as fanciful intimacies stole into his mind. He shoved a hand in his pockets to hide the bulge in his trousers, but wasn't sure he was quick enough. He then greeted her.

"Hello Serena, I'm Stephen, here on vacation." He thought he saw a flash of fear ripple across her features and then it quickly disappeared. Her face was deeply flushed with embarrassment or was it anger. He couldn't be sure. The expression she first wore was stiff and unsmiling, but when he added: "I'm your houseguest," stressing the last word to impress upon her the obligation she had as his hostess, her features shifted smoothly into an embarrassed smile. She bowed to him in greeting ignoring his outstretched hand, and Stephen caught a look of alarm that flashed from her eyes before she made it disappear.

Serena repressed her annoyance, trying to bring herself under control after refusing to accept his handshake. She considered him an uncouth lout, since in the first few minutes of his greeting he has already twice broken Korean protocol. Women never shook hands with men, not even with male friends. Worse, they never allowed their given name to be used without their express permission. Despite Serena's effort to remain calm, Stephen couldn't help noticing her discomfiture or was it annoyance, he couldn't be sure. Her eyes looked through him, he thought, as though searching for something of worth, and apparently finding nothing, they moved on. Once she was again in control of her emotions, her eyes emitted such warmth and energy that their impact struck him forcibly.

"I am Stephen, your guest." He emphasized the last word to make her again aware of her responsibility, and thrust out his hand. She again ignored it while she bowed saying: "Hello Stephen, welcome Korea. Ahn family trying make happy you vacation." Her English was halting and he noted that her word order was misplaced like that of her mother. But the smile she wore made his heart ache. It was not merely her beauty that her seeming sadness enhanced. She projected an air of such complete innocence that he was at a loss for words. It swept him away and took more than a moment for him to recover his senses.

"I'm relieved that you speak English," he said haltingly, "so that I'll be able to talk with you." He was smiling sheepishly, trying hard to calm his rioting thoughts, to make himself affable.

"Talk slow, Serena understand. Father teaching me the English. When he busy, Serena go Frankie."

"Frankie?"

"Frank Sinatra? 'The lady is a tramp.' 'I've got you under my skin.' 'Fly me to the moon.' 'I get a kick out of you.'

"Yes," he said smiling, and thought I certainly get a kick out of you too. "You learnt English from listening to Sinatra's CD's? That's tough to believe."

"Why? Singer's words, music affecting brain 'like the bubbles in a glass of champagne.' Coffee?" She offered, throwing him off balance. He thought it was the name of a song he hadn't heard. She smiled handing him the bowl. Despite her apparent friendliness, he could see in her frozen features that she was fuming inside for her eyes signaled a subdued irritation. Since she had twice ignored his handshake, he realized that it must be against protocol to shake hands with a female or stranger. She evidently considered him insolent; he realized then began quickly to apologize:

"Forgive me if I have offended you by offering to shake your hand. As a stranger, I don't yet know your customs, but I'd like you to teach me, especially when I make a mistake." She bowed without speaking, ready to forgive him and responded politely.

"Perhaps," she replied, "Serena too quick judging." Stephen wondered if she was just trying to keep her distance since it took some time before she could bring her emotions under control. But, he noted that her eyes were on his hand in his pocket.

"Serena," he began, "I'd like you to give me a tour of the farm," but she was shaking her head negatively even before he finished his request. To save face, he added: "that is if you have the time."

"Today feeding animals, sorry. Other day perhaps?" Her voice was almost pleading. Stephen knew she was trying to avoid him and didn't press her.

"Okay, another day then." He saw the relief settle into her features. Left to himself, Stephen couldn't believe what he could only describe as the magnetic force of her presence, a kind of spell that had drawn him towards her, almost physically. It was the sort of raw magnetism that he had never before experienced with any woman, surprising him with its intensity. While he was with her, he noted, she made him forget about his profit motive. Since she refused to show him over the farm, he decided to explore the acreage by himself and familiarize himself with his surroundings. It was a means of nursing the unexpected insult of Serena's refusal to grant his simple request. He wondered why she seemed so determined to keep her distance, and why she appeared so vulnerable. Was she afraid of him? It couldn't possibly be that she disliked him at first sight? That, he refused to believe. There was a hint of sadness in her face that made him remember a line of Keats' *Hyperion*: "sorrow had made sorrow more beautiful than beauty's self." He wasn't sure he got the words right but the idea stuck in his mind.

Chapter 32

From where he stood in the tall barn, he had a bird's eye view of rural Hamyang. Open country stretched in every direction, flat in some areas, gently undulating in others, but all sloping gradually from the far distant eastern mountain chains towards the western coast bordering the Yellow Sea. He saw that the farm was huge, and after leaving the barn he poked around taking his time. While his eyes focused on the different crops and his ears balked at an unaccustomed sound of snorting, he quickly nosed out the hog enclosure marveling at the size of the huge hairless pink-skinned beasts. He had only known pork as sliced chops or roasts packaged in a refrigerated grocery showcase. Holding his breath at the stench, he was amazed at seeing some of the many sows in their enclosures. A few were surrounded by as many as ten to twelve piglets. Since there was only a single boar, he thought it must consider itself lucky to have so many ladies at his disposal.

He tramped alongside fields lying fallow and around others growing grain, when the sharp scent of ammonia, mixed with the stench of fowl dung, assaulted his nose. He came upon four huge poultry enclosures standing in a separate field, hidden behind a barricade of trees. He noted that like the hog enclosures, they too were located behind a thick stand of trees where the prevailing wind blew away from the house. The barricade, no doubt, was to deflect the foul odor in the event of a shift in the wind. Edging away from the revolting scent, he thought, there had to be at least a thousand fowls of all sorts in those enclosures.

He skirted the terraced rice paddies, stopping for a moment to stir his finger in the water between the thick beds of floating weeds. Suddenly, what seemed like hundreds of full-grown and smaller carp crowded the surface sucking air where his finger had been. They probably thought it was feeding time. He wandered through orchards of apples, peaches and pears savored the odor of ripening fruit on the trees and nauseated by the rotting fruit on the ground. He checked out the huge barns and found that some were packed with bags of grain, others with huge stacks of firewood and still others with the scent of well-oiled farm machinery hanging in the enclosed atmosphere.

He passed a field in which a few cows were all lying down chewing their cud in the shade of tall trees. The scent of the warm earth and cow patties merged with the odor of fresh green grass. In another pasture enclosed with a fence, a couple of horses were grazing. A colt was running free and kicking up a fuss. The pungent odor of farm animals and manure mixed with the warm-scented earth kept prickling his nose making him aware that everywhere he went he was surrounded by raw nature and thus totally divorced from the urban world in which he normally lived back home. He climbed into the loft of another barn and gazing through a window, caught sight of a silvery flow in the distance. Following it closely with his eyes, he saw that it was a stream snaking through its riverine bushes on the outer edge of the farm. He made his way there realizing how unusual it was for him to be so completely enveloped by nature.

Serena sat at one of her favorite spots contemplating the awkward and embarrassing situation that had been thrust upon her. Here she was, still unsure of herself, still not fully recovered in body, mind and soul after her attack by male assailants. And what had her parents done? They had actually brought a strange man under her roof, sharing her household, invading her own very personal space. Especially annoying, they hadn't even consulted her. She was furious at their thoughtlessness, worried that it might be too soon to test whether or not she could accept or even share her secluded life with strange male company, especially one so ignorant of Korean customs. Imagine the gall of calling her by her given name without her permission. Not even some of her friends were on a first name basis with her. He then made matters worse by offering to shake her hand! He must be thick headed not to have realized it was bad form to do so a second time after her first refusal.

Still, he was a stranger to their customs and he had apologized very politely, she reasoned. Yet, there was another side to the coin. She knew that on their first meeting, Stephen had seen her flash of anger at his unexpected appearance. He was an innocent bystander, unaware of what had happened to her. Whatever she felt, the fact remained that he was a guest in her home, as he had insisted. That made her his hostess and thrust a strict code of conduct upon her shoulders. At the very least, she had to be polite and friendly. Her behavior, so far, was neither. It was a serious shortcoming on her part. She knew he had already seen her reaction of discomfort and alarm at his presence, and she had refused his request to show him over the farm, with the lamest of excuses. She was forced to admit that she had behaved abominably and would have to find some way to make amends for her lapse in good manners. But could she bear to be alone with him? It felt so awkward trying to repress her fears in strange male company. How could she act naturally when she wanted so badly to flee?

Stephen could hear the subdued flow of gurgling water long before he came upon an open area on the riverbank. He then entered a secluded spot ringed by a majestic grove of towering trees. Some of their branches overlapped to form a bower. The shaded area beneath them was cool and redolent of the scent of pine, fir, green ferns and mosses scattered about the area. To his surprise, Serena was sitting a few yards ahead and to his left, leaning her head and shoulder against a knobby weather-beaten tree trunk. She seemed to be gazing at either the pool or the stream slipping by and was obviously not busy doing anything.

In the dappled light that fell through the branches on what was visible of her profile, she appeared to be a merger between mortal and wood nymph. When she bent forward, her hair hung freely, a veil of black silk fanning out over her arms, shoulders and back, echoing the polished sheen of the dark water flowing by. When struck by the sun, the silken veil was burnished with reddish tints. He again thought she exuded an ethereal quality with a rare blend of sensuality. To say that she was captivating would be an understatement, for each time he set eyes upon her, her beauty struck him even more forcefully. It was the second time he had come upon her unawares, and this time he didn't want to startle her. Suddenly, she balled her hands tightly into fists and bent forward as though ready for a fight. She kept talking to herself and her aggressive pose suggested that she was arguing or quarreling with someone, or perhaps with herself. In fact, she was struggling with her feelings. In Stephen's company she felt fearful, restless and uncomfortable. She needed to keep some distance between herself and him. She felt nervous as though she couldn't trust him or herself. To Stephen she still seemed furious.

He gave her time to let her anger drain away and then, remaining where he was, called: "Hi Serena." On hearing his voice and realizing his closeness, she almost jumped, feeling trapped. Yet, knowing that she couldn't escape with another lame excuse, she summoned up her courage, and turned to face him with a fixed smile. She waved her hand in a gesture suggesting he come forward, pointing to another tree where he could sit at a discreet distance from her.

Stephen took the hint, and sat where she had pointed, exclaiming: "What a beautiful place! How fortunate you are to have such a glorious spot surrounded by lofty trees all to yourself! And it's shady, cool and directly facing a deep pool in the stream." He was stretching out the description, making small talk and trying his best to put her at ease. He was anxious to get her talking, asking any question that might cause her to answer. He was mesmerized by her rose-bud lips no doubt inherited from her mother. They were full and perfectly formed and their movement delighted his eye and quickened his pulse.

"You like?" She asked, evidently pleased with the description. "It Serena favorite spot! Ancestors digging, enlarging stream-basin." He realized that she was comfortable once the topic didn't center upon her. To make her less uneasy, he thought it best to talk about the obvious. "I'm quite unused to being so deep in the countryside and have never been on a farm before. Perhaps you can tell me about the farm, the crops you grow and the animals you raise?"

"Father growing vegetables, small acreage—tomatoes, cabbage, carrots, potatoes, peas, beans, various lettuce types. He devoting big acreage growing grain: wheat, rye, barley, corn, millet, soybean, alfalfa. He growing rice also, with carp in paddies, fruit in orchard. He raising also many hogs, but cows, horses few only. Serena making huge enclosures, raising chickens, ducks, turkeys, geese." Stephen noticed the pride she took in relating her own contribution and decided to keep her talking about it. It couldn't hurt to get friendly with the daughter since it might help to get him into the good graces of her tycoon father.

"What made you decide to start a poultry farm?" He asked.

"When younger, Serena seeing neighborhood farms failing. Farmers unable buying food clothes for children. Serena getting dad, Mr. Sing, farm manager, help starting poultry farm for helping neighbors."

"I don't understand. How did you help neighbors by starting your own poultry farm?"

"Poultry thriving on grain neighbors grow. So Serena asking they feed birds during first weeks, months. In return later, Serena giving eggs. Still later, giving dozen farmers twelve babies from chickens, turkeys, ducks, geese. They starting own farms." He found her quite talkative once she got started. It was hard to believe that she had conceived such a daring and humanitarian idea while so young. The thought immediately gave him another crisis of conscience, reminding him of his own selfish lifestyle. He had never ever thought of the hardships of others. Speedily, he banished the somewhat humiliating comparison.

"Was your project successful?"

"Yes. Each neighbor farm Serena starting, farmer giving others same amount chicks from four different fowl. During two years, through whole district poultry spreading. Now, farmers having eggs, meat. They enough for family meals and sales."

"The farmers must think very highly of you as their benefactor, he thought before asking the obvious question: "How did you, a teenager, persuade professional farmers to take your advice? That must have posed a difficult problem."

"Serena preteen then, not yet teenager," she corrected. "She negotiating. Farms providing grain feeding Serena birds. Later, in exchange, Serena giving farmers eggs, chicks. With starter farm, each farmer raising chicks, ducklings, turkeys, geese; getting own eggs, meat. So farmers getting something for almost nothing."

"I see! You must have been quite persuasive."

"Father and Mr. Sing telling farmers Serena idea very sound. More important, they not lose anything. Farmers can't eat grain. But they getting eggs and meat tasting real good." Stephen couldn't help smiling at her clever description. To keep the conversation going smoothly, he talked about his impressions of the capital.

"I was very impressed with the ultra modern Inchon International Airport, and the spectacular architecture of the high-rise building complexes I saw in Seoul."

"Koreans proud. Best airport in world. Employees there polite, efficient?" She asked.

"Yes, I got through customs and immigration very quickly. I was surprised at their politeness and efficiency."

"What else surprising you in city?" He wasn't sure if there was a hint of sarcasm in the question, but he let it pass.

"I was amazed at seeing the huge video screens on outside walls of buildings. I don't remember seeing such advanced technology in any of the foreign capitals that I've visited."

"Koreans not backward. Many ways advanced." He used the pride she took in her country and her countrymen to keep the conversation going.

"I also visited the temples, palaces, pagodas and shrines in Seoul. I found the simplicity of their architecture very striking."

"Thank you," she said blushing. "Stephen compliments making Serena head spinning," she stated with a giggle of embarrassment. As he had predicted, the compliments seemed to be having a calming influence upon her and if he was any judge of character it was evident that she no longer felt as alarmed by his presence as before.

However, becoming somewhat less familiar did not mean becoming comfortable. While talking to him, answering his questions and listening to his voice, it took some time before she felt courageous enough to make eye contact while they spoke. But, even those contacts were no more than fleeting glimpses. She still couldn't look directly into his eyes. She only stole glances at his face while his eyes were focused elsewhere. When, with the passage of time she finally did look him in the eye, she was startled then transfixed by the handsome golden head of massed curls tumbling in disarray; the lightly tanned skin and the apparent innocence of wide-set eyes that were the deepest blue. A lock fell over his forehead and it surprised her to think of smoothing it back into place while Stephen talked to her about being a city man.

"I'm only completely at ease in a city where I'm surrounded by tall solid buildings, asphalt roads and hard, concrete sidewalks."

"Stephen disliking life in country?" She asked pointedly.

"I don't know anything about country life and I've only been here a single day." Chuckling, he continued: "I love residential areas with scads of houses, and perhaps you'll find this hard to believe, but I've never before been buried so deep in the heart of nature, as I now am."

"Stephen disliking heart of nature?" She persisted. "Yet, it having you say special charm?" She asked, smiling. He could see that she was wondering whether he had lied to her in his earlier lavish praise of her surroundings.

"I said that your spot has a special charm, all its own." Of course, it's one thing to recognize a beautiful spot and quite another to live there permanently." He noted her cleverness in trying to catch him, thinking that he had never met someone who was so straightforward and honest in expressing her thoughts and feelings; certainly no one with so sharp a mind. Indeed, he had to admit that her honesty was disarming. However, he was sure that the praise he heaped on her capital city and her natural surroundings had warmed her heart. Such praise, he felt certain, had to make her feel less uncomfortable to be with him.

Serena was attracted to Stephen's good looks and found his interest in her flattering. Once she got used to his voice and his presence, she also noticed that he was young, handsome, friendly and warm. More important, she no longer felt threatened by his male presence. After all, she reasoned, he hadn't come all this way across the world with the sole purpose of violating the unknown daughter of his host. The very idea had her shying away from the images her reasoning evoked.

Serena wondered why Stephen sought her out and accompanied her everywhere while she did her chores. She refused to believe that such a handsome man would be interested in her romantically, so she asked him. At first, he hesitated to tell her the truth preferring to sidestep the question with a lie. But after a moment's thought he blurted out what he felt. "I really enjoy your company and hope you don't find my presence an intrusion." His words made her blush and brought out a huge smile that, with her dazzling white teeth, lit up her face as if by magic. On seeing her smile Stephen thought he was on a roll so he continued.

"I'm very lucky that my uncle and your father were old college friends," he said to her, after they had spent so much time together during the first two weeks of his vacation and they had discussed numerous subjects of mutual interest. She frowned at his statement shaking her head to show she didn't understand what he meant.

"What old college friends having to do with you and luck?" She asked.

"I couldn't have met you otherwise and fallen head over heels in love." He spoke slowly, placed both his hands over his heart. "Just being near you and spending so much time in your company, has made these last weeks the happiest time of my life." His serious facial expression and the flush of his features mirrored his sincerity. Serena blushed in confusion, at once flattered and unbalanced by Stephen's unexpected avowal. Deep emotion was not something Koreans expected from virtual strangers. She blushed crimson and kept struggling to make sense of her confusion.

Stephen too was confused and surprised by the words he had uttered. He had no idea where they had come from. He'd better watch himself if he didn't want to spoil any chance he might have of profiting in some way from what he considered his vacation-enterprise. But he wasn't about to take his words back.

"Two weeks only Stephen here. He not know Serena," she replied, still flustered but recovering somewhat.

"Oh, I've accompanied you every day for the past weeks and watched you at work, Serena. You're so efficient at everything you do, and even more important, always seem to be happy at whatever you're doing. And with your raven-black hair, high alabaster cheekbones, your almond shaped eyes and your perfectly feminine figure, you're a knockout." He turned sideways to hide the bulge in his pants. Serena again flushed in deep embarrassment showing the naive child-woman that she still was. She hid her face in her hands and began to sob silently. No one had ever spoken such words to her.

"Oh God, Serena, I'm sorry. Please forgive me," Stephen spluttered. "I didn't mean to alarm you. It's just that I haven't been able to think of anything else but you since my arrival. I know I'm an idiot."

His words, uttered with such sincerity, made her stop crying and when she raised her eyes, his look of dejection and embarrassment made her feel warm and sympathetic towards him. His sincere apology, the tone of his distress helped to calm her, allowing her to bring her emotions under control and the compliments surely didn't hurt. With a mischievous look in her eyes, and a smile, she replied haltingly: "Stephen only idiot Serena know. Perhaps she getting to like him." Pausing she added: "In year or two, maybe?"

He smiled, remained silent as she continued: "Stephen seeming good person. Serena no experience, not understanding feelings. Stephen words confusing; scaring her." Then she dictated: "We go house."

It took many attempts in the days that followed before Serena was finally able to show her mother the paintings she had made of the rape. As Leesa looked in stunned amazement at the graphic details of the paintings, Serena, speaking swiftly between halting breaths, related the methods she had devised for her revenge.

"I'd tie each rapist to a post, pry open his mouth, seize his tongue with pliers and tug on it. Deaf to his garbled screaming, I would saw off his tongue with a dull jagged blade, but slowly. That Mama, was for the things he said."

"Gripping each penis with the same pliers, I would then stretch it, before slicing it off, slowly. I'd ignore the babble from his tongue-less mouth, the blood flowing from his torn body. That Mama, was for the things he did." Her mother was too horrified to interrupt.

"Afterwards, I would build a slow fire around each one of the bleeding, roaring beasts. While roasting them alive, I would be deaf to their unintelligible screams as I watched their blood bubble and boil on the red-hot stones around them."

Leesa stood aghast, as much from the graphic details of her daughter's words as from the heaving bosom that accompanied the over-enthusiastic rush with which Serena delivered them. She recognized that Serena was overwrought, panting heavily, almost hyperventilating in a state of near delirium. She seemed to be rejoicing at the vicious methods she had devised. Worse, she kept looking expectantly at her mother for approval.

The words had gushed from her mouth as she confessed: "Mama, in practicing this fantasy, I managed to release some of the pent-up anger and bitterness that the rape had generated. Each time I performed the exercise," Serena rattled on, "I experienced a greater sense of calm." Since her mother noted she was anything but calm, she thought it necessary to remark: "Serena, you seem seriously disturbed. You're still panting heavily as though you had just run up Mount Everest."

Chapter 33

It was clear that Serena was in an unnaturally troubled state. The images of her violators were unnerving and confusing her. They kept spinning around in her brain like a ceiling fan out of control. Further, she was overwhelmed by the powerful emotions released by repeatedly reliving the rape and the methods she had devised for her vendetta. Only after relating the ghastly details and seeing the look of consternation on her mother's face, did she finally become aware of the way she was shamefully overreacting. Suddenly, she burst into tears, overcome by agitation and exhaustion.

"Mama," she blubbered, "I've become as cruel and as immoral as the rapists."

"No, no Serena," her mother corrected. "You must never think that. There's a vast difference, don't you see? The rapists committed a series of criminal acts on a *living* victim. You only fantasized about what you'd *like* to do. There were no live victims. *You* didn't hurt anyone."

"Mama, you're not saying that just to make me feel better?"

"No, no Serena! You merely found a way to release your anger, resentment and bitterness without hurting anyone. It's one of the methods victims use to purge themselves of those feelings. Darling, believe me, it's healthy."

"But Mama, I still feel angry, guilty and ashamed."

"Yes, but the feelings are milder than previously, aren't they?

"Yes, I suppose so. But they're still there." She concluded sullenly.

"Be patient and continue repeating the exercise. You'll feel much better as time goes by. In the meantime try to use your reason to rid yourself of your anger and guilt. Once you accomplish that, your shame too will evaporate gradually."

With the passage of time, Serena found that her mother's advice was accurate. By repeating the exercise and using her reason, she succeeded in gradually whittling away the anxiety, the white-hot anger and the hatred blazing within her. She was also able to rid herself of some of the shame and humiliation they caused. It took time for her to eliminate the poison. Yet, while her bitterness slowly evaporated, the desire for revenge remained.

On sunlit days in late autumn before her assault, she enjoyed wandering the lanes between the apple trees in an atmosphere rich with the aroma of the ripening fruit on the trees and the rotting fruit on the ground. She would wonder about the generations before her whose feet had trodden the same paths, and whose hands had harvested the ripened fruit from the same trees. What were their dreams? Were they ever realized? She wondered, tramping through the muddy edges of the rice paddies or elbowing her way through the tall stalks of corn, heavy with their bounty. At such moments, she saw her Creator's presence in the guise of nature surrounding her. To her, the farm kept repeating the miracle of the five barley loaves. A single grain multiplied itself miraculously into feeding millions. Absorbed in such reverie, her spirits would soar in contentment at the infinite beauty of nature and its rich spirituality. In doing so, she felt sure that her spirit would be mingling with those of her revered ancestors.

Once more at home, she confided to her mother the conversations she'd been having with Stephen over the past weeks. "Mama, he seems such a sympathetic and gentle man. He's such pleasant company."

"Then, you're attracted to him?" Instead of answering the question, she countered:

"He's big and powerful and is quite impressed with the architecture of Korea, its temples and pagodas, and the Inchon Airport in particular."

"Well, are you or are you not attracted to him?" Her mother persisted, forcing a smile.

"I do think he's good looking," She stated, refusing to be drawn.

"Your refusal to answer my question indicates that you are attracted to him. If I'm right, you should give the relationship time to see what his intentions are."

"But Mama, his attraction to me as a woman and his emotional outbursts of love, excite and scare me to death at the same time."

"Love?" She queried, taken by surprise. "What do you feel when you're with him?"

"Confused and excited that someone like Stephen could find me attractive. How can I tell him I'm a ruined woman," she said with abject horror in her voice.

"What! Her mother exclaimed in astonishment. "Serena, I too have been brutally raped, but I'm sure you don't think of me as a ruined woman," her mother replied. "You really must tell Stephen about your assault before the relationship goes any further."

With womanly curiosity, Serena decided to test Stephen's interest in her. She rose early, did her chores and then hid herself high in one of the barns to see if he would search the farm looking for her. It wasn't long before she saw him roaming the fields, going to all the places they had visited together. Totally satisfied with the experiment, she kept up the practice for another day. She knew that Stephen would realize that she was deliberately staying away from him but he couldn't understand why. He possibly thought that she was trying to drive him crazy. That was the only way he could explain her behavior. On the one hand, she smiled at him with mouth and eyes that he must have interpreted as a combination of invitation and challenge. Yet, when he spent hours searching for her, she was nowhere to be found. She would then suddenly reappear out of thin air long after he had given up the search.

On each meeting with Serena, Stephen had to force himself to act naturally. She so inflamed his senses each time they met that he wanted to clasp her in his arms and cover her mouth with the hottest of kisses. He wondered how far she would let him go if he ever got the chance. He couldn't believe that this mature looking and sexually alluring person was still a teenager. He just had to get his hands on her body.

Sometimes, while they walked together on the multi-scented paths of the farm, she would purposely lean her body so close to him that he could breathe in her fragrant-scented hair; catch the scent of her mint-fresh breath. When she spoke, she pressed herself against him as she pointed at something she wanted him to see. She began to enjoy tempting him. Her closeness and femininity, she could tell, set his blood on fire, for his hand would be plunged deep into his pocket.

Indeed, whenever Serena was close to him, Stephen liked to imagine that she had surrendered to him completely. Only with his hands imprisoned in his pockets was he able to repress his overpowering urge to surrender to his caveman instincts and drag her to his cave. In his mind he rubbed his hands together with a smile behaving like someone ogling an object he was determined to possess.

"Mama, I'm feeling so much better and it's all thanks to you."

"I think it's partly due to the new arrival," her mother replied smiling. "I'm so glad you're feeling better. But Rina, your problems aren't solved."

"What do you mean?" She replied with a deep frown.

"It's true that painting and writing about your assault has eliminated some of the symptoms of your abuse. But surely there are others that must be equally troubling?"

"What do you mean?" Serena repeated, pretending she didn't understand. But her mother persisted.

"I know from experience that it's impossible to relive the rape scene without feeling the most acute sense of bitterness and anger. Yet, you've never mentioned either of those symptoms." When Serena remained in silent confusion at the truth, her mother continued.

"Rina, rape is the violation of your most precious and private parts. To such a personal invasion of your body, bitterness, rage and the desire for revenge are the most natural reactions." Again Serena remained stubbornly silent, her head down, her face suddenly contorted in pain and rage. She stubbornly maintained her silence, but as she listened to her mother's scolding, her anger kept growing until finally she blurted out:

"Mama! How can you be so ignorant of the way I feel? Haven't I done everything you asked?" Her cupped hands flew to cover her mouth, as shocked as her mother at the insolent outburst. She immediately began to apologize. Apart from the breach of etiquette, she knew that by her impertinence she had committed the equally grave sin of disrespect to an elder. What made it much worse, the elder was her parent. She knew that these were cardinal sins, for in the Confucian hierarchy of relationships, filial reverence, from youth to age and especially from child to parent, was instilled into all members of society. However, with great restraint and compassion, her mother understood the impassioned reaction and chose to overlook the grave transgression.

"There you are!" She said. "You've never dared speak to me like that before, Rina. I know you're not really mad at me. It's that anger of yours smoldering just below the surface."

"Oh God Mama, I'm so sorry. Please forgive me. I really don't know what came over me."

"That rage of yours needs to be controlled before it again explodes. And it'll flare up, believe me. It'll overwhelm you when you least expect it." Serena's look of shame and defeat was all too evident.

"What do I have to do now?" She groaned dejectedly.

"You need to recall your rapists, write or better still, paint a vivid picture of each of the situations you were forced to endure and bring those paintings to me."

"But Mama..."

"Just do it, Serena! Steel had replaced the sympathy in her mother's voice and its sternness instantly stopped her daughter's appeal.

Stephen exulted in the chase. Being at base a predator, he was adept at following the spoor of his quarry and tracking it to its lair. But once he had brought down and captured the quarry, his enthusiasm waned before deserting him entirely. Yet, he found that this habit of his did not extend to his relationship with Serena. She possessed qualities he had not met before; qualities he had yet to experience, explore and savor. The simplicity, honesty and innocence she exuded had a profound and unexpected effect on him. It forced him to look inside himself and to recognize the empty and worthless shell of his own character. Confronted by her honesty and purity of spirit, he felt ashamed of his selfish and deceitful nature; his tendency to con others; his habit of being always on the lookout for profit. He had to admit that he had never met a woman who had exerted so powerful an influence over him.

There was a swing in the Ahn's backyard that Serena's dad had erected for her when she was much younger. As a teenager, she seldom used it anymore. However, on very rare occasions she would sit on it to work out a problem or even do a bit of daydreaming. She was doing just that when Stephen snuck up behind her and grasped at the opportunity of putting his hands on her body. He gave her a push that startled her at the unexpectedness of those male hands touching her for the first time. She had been daydreaming about Stephen before he began pushing her. She was wearing a tank top and noted that with every push Stephen's fingers were inching closer and closer to the uncovered outer edges of her breasts. She soon began to feel the tingling of her flesh where he touched her. The stirring in her breasts became more intense until her nipples stood firmly erect and a surge of hot lust funneled deep into her womb. She blushed scarlet and couldn't help wondering what her feelings would be like if he ever made love to her. Suddenly, he stopped the swing, came around to face her, clasped her cheeks in both his hands and brushed his lips against hers. The gentle kiss was quite casual but her earlier feelings of arousal had her warring with the rising passion within her and the aching need to respond. She opened her lips. He immediately thrust his tongue into the opening, probed into every corner of her mouth and began to caress her tongue expertly. Her excitement grew when she heard a soft groan and was surprised to learn that it had come from her own throat. Both his hands then began caressing her breasts through the fabric of her tank top. She had to fight hard to suppress the urge to surrender to the delicious sensations coursing through her body. Eventually, she pushed him away, panting hard, her exhalations like the bellows of a blacksmith. Without a single word she then returned to the safety of the house. Stephen followed.

As the days wore on, Serena's life seemed to be divided into four distinct strands: her existence on the farm, her painting, her courtship by Stephen, and in the torture of her private hell, the concentration necessary to recall the features of her rapists and to do what her mother had ordered. She found this last an ordeal as harrowing as the rape itself, for in her mind the two were inseparably linked. In recalling the faces of her assailants and remembering what each had done, she found herself again surrendering to her assailants and reliving the rape. Each time she tried, her anger and humiliation kept erupting. Their intrusion stopped her dead in her tracks. Yet, by repeatedly imagining the diabolical onslaught she planned to unleash upon her violators, she finally began to confront each one boldly and to exact her revenge.

Stephen continued to accompany Serena everywhere on the farm, showing an interest in everything she did. The alarming and uneasy attitude that he had detected on their first meetings was no longer evident or had evaporated whenever they were together. At the same time, Serena couldn't fail to notice that Stephen showed more interest in his tour guide than in the tour. And she was not above being flattered by the attention. Of particular importance to her was the fact that she was becoming more and more accustomed to his male presence. The realization brought a special excitement to being in his company. She couldn't wait to experience another romantic episode with him.

"Come," she told him, with a twinkle in her eyes after finishing her chores and leading him to a closed barn. His heart leapt as he flattered himself into thinking that he was about to get lucky. Instead, she led him inside and pointed proudly to the large fleet of farm vehicles–tractors, bulldozers, backhoes, forklifts, other farm machinery used to plough, fertilize, thresh, and harvest crops. While showing the machines, she pointed out the two mechanics "repairing broke machinery." Stephen couldn't help noticing that the air reeked of hot oil and exhaust fumes. He realized that the mechanics had probably been repairing engines that had been working. He hardly glanced at the machines or the mechanics, preferring instead to focus on the mysterious slant of his tour guide's eyes, the seductive curves of her body and of course the full pink lips that he thought were especially created for kissing.

When she led him to her favorite spot, she no longer took care to keep her distance. Closer to her, he caught a scent of the floral freshness of her hair. The fragrance of roses from her cologne merged with the pine scented air. He took note of the seductive way she glided instead of walked, and the clean scent of glowing skin and fragrant soap that just masked her adolescent sweat. The mixture together with her femininity unmanned him again arousing him sexually, shoving sinfully delightful images into his mind. His hand disappeared into his pocket.

Serena sat next to him under tall pines and huge old oaks, their branches overhanging a deep pool on the outskirts of the farm. Strange odors of sodden mud on either bank of the stream saturated the air. They mixed with those from the thick green foliage of the plants and trees surrounding them and forced Stephen's awareness of being deep in a natural and unfamiliar setting. In discussion with Serena she surprised him by communicating quite adequately on fairly abstract topics that he had deliberately chosen to trip her up. He was trying his best to get her at a disadvantage, expecting that she would be unable to express herself; to make herself understood. He wanted to have her at a disadvantage, hoping she would surrender to his superior knowledge of the meaning of words; the expression of an idea. He began by asking about her "ancestral background." Purposely choosing such an abstract topic, he was attempting to force her to defer to him, anxious to assert his dominance.

"This tree family," she told him. "Ancestors planting it." As she wrapped her arms around the trunk then clasped her hands tightly to indicate their close bond, he focused on the tiny hands with their exquisite fingers. While pronouncing the word 'ancestors,' she thrust her thumb over her shoulder many times repeating: "far past, far past." While talking, she would sometimes flick out her pink tongue to lick her lips frowning as she wondered whether he understood. Sometimes she would blink several times or her eyes would flash before moving rapidly from side to side as she expressed some thought or feeling. Stephen followed every movement with delight.

"In life, ancestor muscles, flesh, sweat working soil. In death, ancestor flesh, bones, blood nourishing soil. Many, many generations making flourish farm," she told him, using hand gestures to express herself, to help him understand. Stephen scarcely heard, taken as he was with the liveliness and energy pulsating from her movements. He nodded to show he understood even before she continued.

"For dreaming, capturing peace, Serena coming this spot." She placed one hand on her heart, and patted the earth with the other. She then pointed her index finger to her temple. Closing her eyes and swaying her body to some unheard melody, she used her calm facial expression to indicate her sense of peace and contentment. He gazed at her mouth and fantasized about planting long, hot kisses there.

"Wind sound, stream noise, fish splash, bird call... nature talking, Serena listening. Here nature, Serena, one." She looked at Stephen anxiously to see if he understood, all the while congratulating herself that she was succeeding in being polite and friendly towards her guest. She was definitely making up for her earlier unmannerly conduct. And to be truthful, she was enjoying herself immensely. In the fantasy world that he had created around his hostess, Stephen had forgotten his attempt at one-upmanship.

"It's a lovely place," he agreed. "Just the right setting to show off a beautiful lady." He smiled and remained silent to see the effect of his words. Serena blushed and said:

"Stephen good person. Serena confused. You words scaring her." A moment later, she again dictated: "We go house." On the narrow foot path leading upwards like a stairway to the house, Serena walked ahead of Stephen. His eyes remained glued to her as she ducked under a branch. When her hair fell forward, she swung her head in a semi-circular motion tossing her hair behind her. Then, with head held high and straight back, she glided upwards with such elegance that he imagined an Asian princess ascending the steps to her throne. He was entranced.

Stephen was ultra conservative in his taste for food. His Canadian parents had inherited one of the unique virtues of their British forbears–total incompetence in the kitchen. They had a natural flair for whipping up such mouth-watering fare as lumpy porridge, soggy vegetables and greasy, overcooked meat. Like evil magicians, they performed their black magic between stove and table, transforming the best cuts of meat into the rarest cardboard. On special occasions, they crowned the banquet with a dollop of rice pudding for dessert. Incredibly, the family enjoyed these feasts, clearly proving the truth of the maxim, 'there is no accounting for taste.'

Koreans, unlike the Imperial British, are proud of their competence in the kitchen, and the Ahns displayed all their culinary skill for Stephen's benefit. Some of their most popular meat dishes appeared repeatedly at mealtime. There was also an array of dishes of vegetables, noodles, and succulent herbs that it was their country's custom to serve in a series of small dishes at the same time. Once on the table, the dishes emitted a profusion of powerful smells with the scents of their myriad seasonings uppermost. Since Stephen was accustomed to unseasoned food that was neutral in smell and bland in taste, the powerful scents of highly seasoned dishes confused, clouded his senses and unnerved him. Indeed, no one had to notify him about the approach of mealtime. The atmosphere, in and even outside the house, reeked with a mixture of pungent spices. That was warning enough.

A dish of *kimchi*, pickled cabbage with many different spices done with beef, pork, fish or some other meat he didn't recognize was always camouflaged in many of its different forms. He sometimes thought that mother and cook had created a conspiracy to embarrass him. There was also *gukbap*, marinated raw beef and various vegetables on rice served with very hot sauce. Just the scent of the pepper made his eyes water. He learnt that *bibim-bap* consisted of vegetables on a bed of rice with egg, beef and red pepper paste, while *chueotang* was a soup made from fish. He regarded such fare as innocent-looking but well-concealed traps to catch him off guard. However, the description of Korea's cuisine in the students' essays came to his rescue. Some stated that their food was often seasoned with onions, ginger, garlic, hot chili peppers and horse radish. Others used adjectives like "fiery " to describe the taste while still others mentioned that visitors uttered sighs and even shed tears after tasting the pungent spices. Stephen would never forget his introduction to the first peppered spoonful of something he had tried at the Ahns' table.

It was so hot that he leapt from his sitting position, his mouth on fire. While still in the air, he realized that apart from his scorched mouth, the meat he was about to chew on was probably eel, octopus, skate, snake or dog. His stomach lurched at the thought. When once more in contact with the floor, he bounded up the stairs to upchuck in the privacy of his suite. To their credit, the Ahns pretended not to notice his antics. On his return, he apologized haltingly to his hostess claiming a queasy stomach, and took care to praise her dishes. He assured her that they would delight those of the adventurous palate. Alas! He exclaimed. He did not belong to that courageous clan. He preferred to stick to the neutral dishes of noodles, vegetables, salads and eggs which thankfully, were always in abundance. He praised their variety and taste explaining that he found them thoroughly enjoyable.

His uncomfortable seat on the floor, at their low table, with only a thin cushion beneath him, made him tend to slouch. In comparison he noticed that all the members of the family sat with their backs straight, displaying proper posture. He immediately tried to follow suit. However, the uncomfortable position of sitting cross-legged on the floor made his legs fall asleep. He had to scramble up on more than one occasion hopping around to eliminate the numbness in his legs and to get the blood in them flowing again. Once more, his host and hostesses pretended to ignore his comic antics. They acted as though it was expected.

After they had become more familiar with each other, Serena no longer felt it necessary to keep Stephen at a distance. She noticed that he would look longingly at her and on one occasion drew close to her and began to caress her hairline. He then ran his fingers along her cheeks and jaw. It sent the blood rushing to her cheeks and to her surprise she felt that she would have liked to do the same to him but of course, she didn't dare. Protocol stood in her way. Even so, it made her blush prettily and turn away from him. She then made a bee-line for the safety of the house much to Stephen's chagrin.

Stephen couldn't ignore the fact that red meat was often absent from the menu, while chicken, pork and seafood were the preferred meat dishes and were often present in different forms. He had learnt from the essays that Koreans considered that eaters of red meat gave off an offensive smell, while he, like other Westerners, found the scent of spice eaters somewhat disturbing. Thank God, the subject never surfaced in the Ahn household. However, he was struck by the mosaic of color in the presentation of their dishes, for the rice, rich soups, and other side dishes, *branchan*, added their riot of color to the table. It became evident that their cooking did not merely aim at creating exquisite taste. While it pleased the eye with its color, it also had enjoyment and good health as its goals. After the meal, the Ahns passed around toothpicks and Stephen followed their example by covering his mouth when using them. At table, there was little talk. The Ahns ate with such relish that it discouraged conversation. He also learned more of their meal-time protocol: each person had a rice and soup bowl to himself, but all other dishes were shared. Finally, no one was to start eating before the oldest person; he of the highest rank, their father. He was always served first and every one left the table after him. As the lowest ranked guest, Stephen left the table last.

While Serena sat daydreaming at one of her favorite spots beside the pool, Stephen crept up behind her and embraced her gently. Serena, taken by surprise, hardly had time to react when she felt an array of kisses that began at her temple, continued over her eyelids, the tip of her nose and along her cheek. She had been kissed like this only once before by Stephen. Previously, the rough, playful and inexperienced teenage kisses she had received were closer to peccadilloes that had little emotional effect. Stephen's kisses by comparison made her feel delightful tingles spiraling through her breasts to arouse her nipples. Her knees turned to water and she had to press her thighs together to withstand the flurry of erotic shockwaves that scurried from the base of her abdomen to the apex of her thighs. Stephen's numerous kisses had left her with swollen lips, butterflies in her stomach, a too-swiftly pounding heart and trembling knees.

During the meal Stephen managed to learn even more about Korean protocol. Everyone followed Mr. Ahn according to the strict Korean code of respect for status and veneration that followed the hierarchy of honor. Mrs. Ahn sat after her husband and was followed by her daughter. The guest, as the lowest ranked person, sat last. Each time Stephen sat at the table of his Korean hosts, he couldn't help assessing their manners and conduct. Although warm, generous and hospitable towards him, the whole process at mealtime seemed like 'déjà vu;' an exact repetition of the practice at the previous meal. The fact that the guest was always last struck him as awkward since in the West, the guest is served first as the most highly honored. It is one of the marks of respect and politeness that Western culture demands. In the Ahn household, everyone repeated the same ritual at mealtime. The dishes were the only difference at the table. Korean protocol-ridden culture stood out in their repetitive conduct. Since Stephen learned that their culture frowned upon individuality, their behavior seemed to be a deliberate attempt to repress their natural impulses. He therefore had the strange impression that everyone was pre-programmed, even choreographed by some unseen robot director.

When Serena learned that Stephen enjoyed swimming, she invited him to try out their heated pool. She hoped he would accept since it would give her the chance to see his muscular body almost in its entirety. "Ahn family swimming a lot when younger Serena. Since dad CEO, family swimming only few times. Seeking to embarrass Serena, Stephen asked: "Did you ever go skinny dipping?" The question was so unexpected that Serena's face turned crimson and as she covered her face with her hands, she didn't answer him. In the silence that followed, she was unable to suppress the images of both she and Stephen in the nude—her tiny figure nestled against his hard muscular body. Immediately, she felt erotic sensations spiraling throughout her body and ending between her legs. Ironically, instead of annoying her, Stephen's insolent question and the images it evoked made her begin to feel a strong kinship with this rascally fellow who aroused thoughts and feelings within her that she had never experienced before. With him next to her she began to feel more like a woman than a teenager.

Because of the hot spices used liberally in Korean cuisine, the very mention of mealtime in the Ahn home tended to freeze Stephen's blood, and on more than one occasion it did. Having actually sprinted from a family meal, he had to be resourceful enough to devise a plan that contained if not eliminated his mealtime distress. Since hamburgers were a family favorite, he promised to introduce them to "home-cooked-burgers" with him doing the honors as chef.

He took two pounds of regular ground beef, dry onion soup-mix and kneaded them together with the help of two whisked eggs and about three tablespoons of teriyaki sauce. Knowing the family's taste for pungent seasoning, he cut numerous wafer-thin shavings of garlic and ginger, let them liquefy and burn as he cooked them in a skillet with hot virgin olive oil. After molding the seasoned ground meat into patties, he grilled them in the hot oil. He then made a mixture using red pepper paste with half a tablespoon of Worcester and Oyster sauces. While the patties were cooking, he lathered both sides of the warmed hamburger buns with mayonnaise.

Inside each bun, he put toppings of sautéed onions, sliced mushrooms, a doubled lettuce leaf and a large tomato slice smeared with half a teaspoon of mustard. Since the family found his burgers delicious, they welcomed his offer to repeat the performance as often as he wished. It then occurred to him that he could alternate the presentation with his own special recipe for hot dogs. He surprised them by steaming the buns before adding jumbo-sized wieners and all the hot spices together with onions, mustard, relish, a half tea spoon of red pepper paste, mayonnaise and tomato ketchup. The family loved his hot dogs almost as much as his hamburgers.

Lying in bed at night, it struck him that the essays he had collected in Victoria were extremely helpful. They had saved him from making a fool of himself a number of times. Equally important, he found them quite accurate. The people he met on walks with Serena in the small town of Hamyang were always friendly, and more than one had singled him out to start a conversation or to try out their English. And as Shellie and the essays had predicted, people stared at him as though hypnotized by his huge, powerful build. However, there was something in their furtive gaze that labeled him alien. Both men and women stared, but while the eyes of the men were always grave and serious, those of the women never made eye contact. Walking with Serena among these porcelain-skinned people, all smaller in stature than himself, he couldn't help thinking of himself as superior. It was not that his greater size and good looks were guarantees of greater worth. On the contrary, it was his instinctive sense that he had come from a country with a higher standard of living and a culture that he considered superior. It never for a moment occurred to him that he might be wrong.

At mealtime once again, he carefully observed the actions of the family, never again leaving his chopsticks atop or lying parallel across his bowl at the end of the meal as he had done earlier. This, he learnt, brought bad luck to the family. Instead, following his hosts, he placed them on the rest that was provided for that purpose. When passing a dish, he followed the merry-go-round of protocol and did so with his right hand, and when necessary, supported it with his left. He also politely filled his neighbor's small dish with soy sauce as had been done for him. When offered extra helpings, he did not accept on the first or even on the second offer. He waited patiently until his host insisted more than once before finally accepting the offer.

Chapter 34

Later, he learnt that it was okay to eat everything in the bowl of soup or rice, but never to finish any of the other shared dishes. It gave the impression that his host was neglectful in not providing him with enough, and would be a grave embarrassment.

He found that the Korean preoccupation with courtesy paid to hierarchy was obsessive and it irritated him to note that Koreans often turned abruptly from the middle of their conversation with someone of lesser rank to speak to someone of higher status. His un-tuned ear was just beginning to catch the patronizing tone a superior would use to a subordinate and the deference the latter would use in his reply. It made him recognize that the Korean disease of superior versus inferior was worse than the equally inhuman game of racism that was played in other countries. While at university abroad, he noticed that there was always an attempt to be subtle about the same subject; to sweep what might be considered indelicate under the rug. A non-white university applicant was never referred to as black. Instead he was introduced as an 'overseas' student. Perhaps it was done to spare the applicant any embarrassment. However, in Korea the stigma was even worse. Each citizen had to verbally admit his superiority or inferiority each time he opened his mouth.

Serena's presence filled Stephen with a kind of joy that was new to him. When she absented herself, he thought of her as the beautiful but wicked witch who had first turned his head, then cut out his heart. He convinced himself that she had set out to make him fall in love with her, and then rejected his advances by disappearing from sight.

After her miraculous reappearance, they would sometimes walk together. Her woman smell, the scent of her freshly washed hair or even the perfume she wore would set fire to his blood. On occasion, her hand would brush against his accidently, or her body would be so close that his other hand would automatically slip into his pocket. Whenever this happened, he imagined what he would like to do with her body in an attitude of complete surrender. He had to hold himself under strict control so as not to give in to his overpowering desire to blurt out his true feelings and make violent love to her.

When she was away from him, he had developed the habit of picturing the different images of Serena that he could conjure up. There was the angelic country bumpkin in long braids, bright yellow Mac and matching muddy galoshes feeding her hogs in the rain. This picture was balanced against the affluent sophisticate, beret at a rakish angle, at the wheel of her red Mustang. He would then imagine the staid high-school student, immaculate in white blouse, tie, blazer, plaid skirt, white knee-high socks and glistening shoes. This image contrasted markedly with the stunning sex-siren in revealing tank top, micro-miniskirt, stiletto heels and angled peaked cap. There was then the reserved teenage adolescent in her budding womanhood as well as the struggling artist with paint-stained smock and colorful palette, frowning in concentration before a canvas. Finally, he found it hard to dismiss the obsessed environmentalist babbling away about the call of the mountain wilderness, and its precious wildlife. What surprised him was that in each of the images, he found her equally appealing.

"I hear your dad challenged you to spend a whole week in the mountains taking only a few items and a large can of beans with you. How did you manage to survive the cold, the dark and the isolation?"

"Serena loving mountain wilderness. She not having problems there."

"You're a hell of a person, Serena," he said, his voice heavy with admiration at her courage and resourcefulness. Most people would not have dared to accept such a challenge. Just the thought of being alone in the wilderness and enveloped in total darkness each night would have been enough to scare the living daylights out of them."

"Serena knowing mountains like back of hand. Wild animals minding own business. Not harmful if she leaving alone and at distance keeping them."

Stephen thought that Serena was arresting in her loveliness. Her grace and beauty often struck him so forcibly that it left him tongue tied. Although he had had his share of women, he had never kept the company of anyone with such staggering beauty. This last was partly because grace and elegance came so naturally to her. Then, she was so unaware of the effect she had on others that her presence was especially disturbing. While he was with her, there were times when he could no longer find the words that had slid so effortlessly off his tongue with other women. He found that although the words he needed filled his mind, they were often blocked by some constriction in his throat. At such times, when Serena questioned him at his failure to reply to her, he had to lie, saying that his thoughts had wandered. The truth was that she made him feel so much less than the man he had always thought himself to be. How could a mere schoolgirl turn him inside out and make him feel like a lily-livered girl? It was little wonder that she had made him jettison his 'hidden agenda' without the least regret.

The feminine scent trail that Serena left so aroused him that his senses reeled. He breathed in the faint aroma of her cologne and the clean delicate fragrance of her skin lotion. He found the mixture, together with the whiff of her femininity, erotic in the extreme. He believed, though he couldn't be sure, that the whole 'show' was a deliberate attempt to torture him. He then thought it impossible that so naive an adolescent could have such womanly wiles as to be playing the desirable temptress. On such occasions, before he could control himself, his manhood was again aloft.

Lately, he found that she was far more at ease with him. It could only be because they had sat together so often on the riverbank, or walked together so often around the farm exchanging ideas and discussing various topics. He knew too that the kisses they had exchanged had helped to make her feel more comfortable in his presence. That was before she began playing the game of hide and seek that seemed to be her way of torturing him. After she pulled her second disappearing act, he decided to follow her lead. He'd disappear too by going to spend the weekend with Joe and Sally whom he'd met on the bus. He knew that staying on the farm with an absent Serena would only exasperate him further. She had cast her spell over him and since he had completely lost his grip, he reasoned that there would be little point in staying on the farm. It was Friday morning, he'd take his leave of Mr. Ahn and not return until the following Monday. Nothing like distance to make the heart grow fonder, he thought. But whose heart was he thinking of? He wasn't at all sure."

"When from her hiding place in the barn, Serena didn't see Stephen for the whole weekend she was shocked to realize that he had gone off on his own without a word to her. She cursed him in her mind for complimenting her, expressing his love, telling her she was the most beautiful girl he had ever seen and even saying that he hadn't been able to think of anything else but her. She paced up and down in anger and frustration on the riverbank, arms tightly folded, head bent, convinced that he had not meant a single word he'd said.

"So, if I'm the most beautiful girl you've ever seen," she argued aloud, "how come you just disappeared without a trace? It can only mean one thing. Your words are false, no more than hot air. That means you're dishonest, deceitful, underhand, disloyal and untrustworthy. No one should ever believe a single word you say." Of course, Serena had conveniently forgotten that it was she who had started the disappearing act. "One thing became clear to her. Her deep feelings indicated that Stephen's presence meant more to her than she was willing to admit.

The truth was that Stephen had begun to capture her heart. In fact, his absence had thrown her into such confusion that she sulked and pouted all the time he was away. Angrily, she decided to show him who was in charge. On his return, she again kept away from him, and from various hiding places, she watched smugly as he tramped the farm in his vain forays to find her. At mealtime, she excused herself before he could finish his meal and disappeared before he got the chance to speak to her.

During the days after Serena's disappearance, her face kept materializing in his mind's eye, haunting him. As he leaned against a tree trunk on the riverbank, lost in thought, he saw her face everywhere: it was reflected in the surface of the pool, in the strange and clever formation of clouds, even in the green foliage of the trees. Deep in the reverie of his missing beloved, he wondered at his irrational reaction to everything she said and did. He found that the stream, crashing over its rock strewn bed, echoed the way she dislocated language and destroyed grammar. Sometimes, he imagined catching the scent of her fragrance. It would set him looking around, searching to see if she were truly nearby. At night, as he wrestled with his conscience, wondering what he had done to make her desert him her face would reappear to torment him. Overwhelmed by the absence of his beloved, he waited on tenterhooks, every moment fraught with fear and apprehension. And eventually, when in exhaustion he closed his eyes, the last images confronting him were those tantalizing features."

He kept wondering what he had done or said to make her disappear. In his desperation over her absence, he composed letters to her in his imagination, but the words he used far outdistanced the reality of their relationship. He kept hoping illogically that she might hear his words through the vacuum of silence between them. "My darling, I am cold and miserable, because you're not with me. I want to feast my eyes on your face, savor your fragrance of roses, feel my heart quicken at the way you spray your words, and dismember language. I long to inhale your perfumed presence, hear the music of your voice, listen to your laughter and feel your touch. I have become a recluse to everyone here because of the profound distress that has come over me. Fortunately, no one can guess its cause. Oh my darling, if you only knew how I curse myself for having driven you away. I have so much more in my heart to say to you, but until you come back to me, those words must be left unsaid."

The nights without sleep caused dark circles around his bloodshot eyes and when Serena finally reappeared, he rejoiced at seeing her looking so radiant. It was then that he recognized, with an ache in his gut, that Serena was what he wanted. She was everything he wanted. Her stunning beauty and her sexuality made him understand, as he had never understood before, why he had abandoned his hidden agenda. He felt the compelling need for her to be a permanent part of his life. In the past, he had scorned the thought of needing any member of 'the weaker female of the species' for anything other than the pleasures of the bed. At that moment, he knew for certain that he would be completely lost without having this beguiling child-woman as a permanent part of his life.

Stephen couldn't help seeing the irony of his situation. In the past, love was a concept that was not only unknown to him, but also completely alien. He had even scoffed at the notion of love at first sight. Had anyone suggested that such a phenomenon existed, he would have made him have his head examined. Thus, he found it almost impossible to come to terms with what had happened to him. To make matters worse, he had fallen for a teenager, a species that he had never before considered human. Yet, when it happened, he was struck by lightening. The mere sight of Serena affected him so deeply that his senses quickened, his pulses raced. In her presence, the world took on a rosy glow. As he began whispering her name over and over, her image would appear before him and he would hear the music in her voice, the curiosity in the simplest of her questions, the gaiety of her laughter. Indeed, she laughed so heartily that her head shook and her black silky hair flew in all directions covering her face and shoulders. Her green eyes, as green and clear as the open Atlantic, glistened and made her look so beautiful that Stephen's heart melted with love. There was an unconscious ease, a carefree manner in the way she glided through life that stirred in him a desire to be carefree too. He couldn't have said why, but it made him want to shed his wicked ways and become a better person; one of whom he could be proud.

In the past, he had reacted with scorn at witnessing the way love-sick men acted, fawning over their beloved and appearing pathetic, even delusional, whenever their goddess' attention happened to be riveted elsewhere. He now saw that he was one of those deluded idiots making the most asinine spectacle of himself. The most brilliant and witty remarks crowded his brain when his idol was absent. In her presence, he became a tongue-tied sot.

It irked him to think that Serena was deliberately keeping away from him and he wondered what he had done to annoy her. He had fallen in love with her and realized that because of her, his hidden agenda had completely vanished from his mind. The confusion, doubt and heartbreak that came over him when he began to believe that she detested him, made him realize how much she meant to him; how deeply he was smitten. He tortured himself, going over everything he had said to her in an effort to discover the wrong he had done. Finding nothing he had said that could be misconstrued as embarrassing to her in any way, he finally gave up trying.

"He was reduced to begging and pinned a note to the door of Will's stall. He knew she would see it since she fed the colt every day, though maddeningly she had changed Will's feeding times to forestall his thrusting himself upon her. She never materialized although he waited for her on several occasions. Eventually, he wrote a note explaining his deep concern."

Dear Serena,

I don't know what I've done to hurt or annoy you to such an extent that you block my every attempt at being with you. Whatever it is, I apologize. What you don't know is that during the past few days I've spent hours searching vainly for you all over the farm. I've already told you that I've never met any one who has affected me in the same way as you have. My time is getting short, so I'd very much like to be with you so we can at least talk.

Stephen.

Serena relented after reading his note. So, she thought, when he's not in control, he resorts to pleading. And what if his pleading doesn't work, she wondered? She permitted him to 'ambush' her while she was feeding the animals. She began by being somewhat standoffish and cool, at first feigning indifference. She couldn't help using her womanly wiles for a bit longer since they had proved to be so effective. Finally, she made an effort to be friendly by insinuating herself closer and closer into his presence before actually invading his space with silent signals and body language.

Sometimes she held his hand unexpectedly or leaned on him as they walked. In a surprising move, she looked deeply into his eyes as they talked, then brushed back the lock of hair from his forehead. Her conduct seemed to confuse and baffle Stephen almost as much as her disappearing acts. He was at a complete loss to understand this beguiling witch of a woman.

He told her that he had never met anyone like her before and didn't know how to interpret her behavior. With his mind clouded by emotion, he failed to see that she was trying to manipulate him, urging him into making a commitment. She thought, he could either fish or cut bait. At first, he seemed confused and didn't know what to do. Finally, on the next occasion that she came close to him, he drew her gently into his arms and kissed her on the lips. Since he took her by surprise, he kissed her again before she could recover, slipping his tongue past her lips. Desire rose within her in such a powerful surge that she couldn't believe the mere touch of a tongue could so jar her senses and rattle her bones. Its intensity consumed her entirely. The experience reminded her of Mona's statement: "when passion overwhelms you, you don't think of the future. Only the present counts." In her confusion, she barely heard Stephen's proposal:

"I've fallen in love with you, Serena. Will you marry me darling?" Stephen heard himself say. "I want to love and protect you for the rest of your life." He was almost as surprised as Serena to hear his avowal of love and his proposal. Then, he stammered: "I have only a short time left before I must get back to Canada and I'd like to take you with me."

She was so astonished and confused at getting her wish that she couldn't immediately decide what to answer. Instead, she too stammered a reply. "Serena needing t-time to t-think. Ev-everything too q-quick happening. Serena answering later Stephen."

She again disappeared to think seriously about Stephen's proposal while he patrolled the farm looking vainly for her. Finally, he waited for her at Will's stall knowing that she would show up there eventually. When she did, he explained haltingly:

"I've already cleaned out his stall and fed him just as I saw you do, Serena. Will you please let me talk to you?" He spoke sitting on a stool, keeping his distance. In her sternest voice, she admonished him, her eyes sparkling with mischief: "Stephen not supposed feeding Will. That Serena job."

"I'm sorry," Stephen replied, dejected at the sternness of her voice. "I did it so I could get a chance to talk to you without interruption. Why do you keep avoiding me? I've been honest and sincere with you and it hurts me to realize that I scare you away. Will you please talk to me, tell me if I've done anything wrong." Once again the apologetic, imploring tone of his voice made her stop her game playing. But he answered her earlier question: when pleading failed, he resorted to more pleading.

"Stephen," she said, "it my problem, not you."

"How do you mean?" He asked, failing to understand

"Serena say you next time." Now that she had got what she wanted, she wasn't so sure she wanted it any more. Could she really leave Korea and all it meant to her? Yet, she had to consider that a fresh start was what she needed most. Further, his offer included travel abroad and to the very country that her father had talked about so animatedly that it made her heart ache with desire to go there.

"Yet, whenever she considered the vile rumors that were circulating about her and her family, her cheeks flushed an angry red and the light in her eyes blazed with a green fire. She pressed her lips together so that her mouth became a thin line and she ground her teeth in her clenched jaw. The rumor mill Mona and her family had created about Serena took care that the notorious circumstances of her mother's engagement, marriage and too-soon pregnancy renewed in everyone's mind the faded memories of the past. Slanderous tongues had resumed their wagging and the burden of shame and humiliation descended once more upon the shoulders of her family and on her. Again, she was made to feel like an imprisoned predator, prowling the confined space of her cage, pawing and rattling its invisible bars and enraged enough to claw and tear to ribbons her detractors. She began to curse that kindergarten day she had rescued the girl being bullied because she was over-weight and plain looking. Since then, Mona had followed her everywhere and she had extended her hand in friendship. She began to think that a new country would be the only way out of her dilemma. With marriage to the handsomest of men thrown in, could she really refuse?

Chapter 35

"Stephen, say me about Canada life." It was the following day and they were under the trees by the river where she had let him 'find' her. Although she was sitting still, each time she spoke, he noted that her head would tilt at various angles as her hands gestured swiftly this way and that to clarify her meaning. Whenever she swung her body around to make a point, the golden loops hanging on delicate chains from her ears would swing crazily. Their dizzying movement and their sparkle added to her fascination. She seemed a bundle of energy to Stephen, a life force in constant motion that had helped to captivate him.

"If you marry me I'll take you to Canada with me. I'd rather show it to you than talk about it. Victoria has so many interesting things to do and beautiful things to see, in fact so does the whole province. No one can fail to fall in love with it. There's so much I want to show you myself. You'll never believe the attractions my city and province has to offer. Can you believe that the natural beauty and wildlife is so extraordinary that writers describe the province as "super-natural?" I can promise that you'll agree with their description."

"Then say me about it. You words telling Serena she a lot missing."

"Darling there'll be plenty of time and opportunity to show you the things that I know you'll enjoy after our marriage, but they will have to wait. Instead, I want to know more about your country. It's such an enigma to me." She noted his insistence on getting his way, but his mention of their marriage made her heart quicken. He could gage its acceleration by the movement of the fabric covering her bosom. It breathed with her and each forward motion of her breasts struck him with a jolt of desire. He imagined getting his hands on them and running riot over their nipples with his fingers and tongue. If only she'd accept his proposal. He then found himself wondering if possession of her body was what mattered most to him, and had to admit he was always in a state of arousal in her presence. He swiftly tried to banish such disturbing thoughts from his mind.

Yet, on deliberation, he managed to convince himself that lust couldn't be the main reason that attracted him, stirring his senses and constantly forcing his hand into his pocket. He thoroughly enjoyed being with her even though they had never been intimate. He couldn't accurately define it but her beauty apart, her simplicity, honesty and purity of spirit, were virtues that made it exciting to be with her. This surprised him, for if he were honest, he'd have to admit that virtue, simplicity and honesty had never attracted him before.

Whenever he was alone, he always felt depressed and distraught by Serena's absence. He no longer chided himself for having abandoned his hidden agenda. What he wanted most was for her to accept his marriage proposal so he could have her all to himself. She had breathed clean, fresh air into his life, making all those selfish, deceptive and shoddy thoughts of gain disappear. Could the upright and honest person she was make a new man of him? He wondered.

Serena saw his reaction and was delighted at the power she could wield with what she imagined was only her 'breathing.'

"Stephen wanting to know more about Korea?" She asked. Delighted to talk about her country, she began eagerly: "Korean flag not only symbolic, okay? It philosophical too. Representing purity is white background, while Taegu– circle with S at center, lying horizontally– standing for balance, harmony. Representing heaven is red top half S, the Yang, representing day and male gender. Bottom blue half, the Yin, standing for earth, night and female gender. In perfect harmony twin forces, yet seeming in opposition." As Stephen looked at a picture of the flag, he was stunned that she managed to describe its symbolism so accurately.

"I suppose all flags represent certain aspects of their country, but none that I know of is so pointedly steeped in symbolism," he replied lamely.

"Traditionally, Koreans using floor for sleep because below floor, pumped through pipes is hot water. Everybody warm sleeping. Today in Korea, more

Western beds, but people going back to floor in winter, getting more warmth, more comfort."

"I can see the logic in that," Stephen agreed. But he added:

"I want to ask you some questions about your government. Is that okay?" She realized from the way he asked the question that he knew he was treading on dangerous ground. But she agreed:

"Okay."

"South Korea calls itself a democratic country like Canada and the US. But is it?"

"Compared to totalitarian governments of Rhee Singman and later Park Jung-Il, South Korea *trying* become democratic. After all, Prime Minister by people elected. But, Korea not truly democratic many citizens thinking."

"Would you please explain that?"

"Too many anti-government protests; too much rioting university students, citizens, labor groups. Government treating civil uprisings like terrorists. Administration harsh measures using, including batons, bullets. Government forces killing many students, members labor groups. Constant civil unrest annoying citizens. They not understanding why government treating as enemies civilian protesters. That not democratic. Government conduct making very confused, discontented citizens."

"Do you consider those shortcomings the major failures of your government?"

"No. Students protesting also government widespread corruption. They demanding North South unification Korean biggest problem perhaps. Families between two countries split. Both sides citizens wanting unification."

"But the North has been trying again and again to bring about unification through conquest. And the students have been trying to unify through rioting and violent protest. Both attitudes seem to be short-sighted and wrong."

"Yes, Serena understanding. She thinking successful unification needing patience, negotiation, not violence from North or South. This especially true when economically, socially two countries so divided deeply. Both needing much compromise. Both imposing with force unity. Not possible imposing on people democracy!"

"So from the way you speak you seem discontented, dissatisfied with your government."

"Dissatisfied yes. Serena and many women having serious issues against government. They permitting women bad treatment. Korea woman worst sin: failing produce son for husband. It worse in past when mother naming daughter for expressing family shame: *soun* (disappointment), sosop (pity), yucan (regret). Confucius bad cultural message in citizens entrenched deep: for him woman useless property; good for babies, cooking, housework only. Women asking: Why not like sons daughters treated? Why people offering to parents sympathy? Why having daughters so wrong?"

"But that's not the case today, is it?"

"Not always. Some parents like Ahns very liberal. Love daughters very much." She looked at Stephen with a mysterious smile and eyes alight with what seemed impossible to interpret. Perhaps, he thought, it might be parental adoration.

There were times when Serena would look at Stephen with so innocent and deceptive a smile that he could only guess at its true meaning. Perhaps, he thought, she was trying to drive him insane with her beguiling ways. Whenever he met her outdoors, he became acutely aware of every detail of her person—the way she glided instead of walked; the way her long thick ponytail swished from side to side like a metronome whenever she hurried; the shiny white pearls that drew attention to her ears; the golden glint of the locket that brought his eyes to the cleft between her breasts. In her presence, he often felt breathless, tongue-tied, no longer in control of his emotions, and far from being the big masculine Don Juan that had mesmerized so many of his earlier female companions. Perhaps the truth was that they had never really mattered to him.

Thinking about Serena's dissatisfaction with her government, Stephen paused for a moment before asking:

"So you no longer love your country." How could he ask her such a question that could so easily lead to an argument, create disharmony and loss of face? She wondered at his thick headedness, but answered anyway with scarcely veiled irritation.

"No, no, no Stephen! That never true! Korea very dear Serena. But, she not blind; stupid. Confucian ethics guiding citizens excellent manner. But they conformity creating; individuality stifling; making for authority blind obedience; discontented citizens."

"Tell me more about your people. I find them an enigma. It seems that their Confucian training keeps them always in agreement." After her detailed explanation about Korean protocol and its obsession with harmony, he persisted in asking questions that were bound to cause disagreement, disharmony. Still, because of his lack of understanding and in spite of her Confucian training, she felt obliged to break protocol and disagree. To her, the truth was sometimes more important than protocol.

"That not true Stephen. Korean constant civil unrest showing everyone *not* agreeing. But Stephen need understanding Confucian behavior code. It **demanding** citizens avoid always conflict. So citizens not expressing true feelings. Family, friends discussing problems taboo. Discussion leading to conflict eventually causing quarrel, ending in disharmony, humiliation; taboo in Korea."

"I'm not sure I understand," Stephen replied.

"Korean obsession avoiding always disagreement, confrontation. On everyone tremendous pressure for creating **harmony**; **saving face**." Serena's eyes were flashing signals of irritation in her failure to convey her meaning. Was it her inability to express clearly what she meant, or was it Stephen's inability to understand? She wasn't sure.

Meanwhile Stephen seemed oblivious of any problem. He persisted in his inquiry.

"In my discussions with Korean students in Canada, I was told that Koreans tend to be xenophobic. Is it true that they hate all foreigners?" Serena shook her head in disbelief at his thick headedness, his intransigence but hid her annoyance. It seemed impossible for him to understand what *harmony* meant to Koreans. He couldn't see that it was both embarrassing and humiliating for her to disagree with a guest on the one hand while admitting his criticism was fairly accurate. His questions kept putting his hostess in a very difficult position. She had to tell the truth yet be loyal and uphold the good name of her countrymen. To do less would be a betrayal. Gritting her teeth she answered.

"Not true at all. Of culture, heritage, traditions Koreans proud. They happy sharing views with others. But, sometimes standing in way problems of past. History explaining constant struggle maintaining borders, independence, against giant USSR, Chinese, Japanese. All wanting piece of Korea. Eventual war outbreak, then Japanese occupation. Superpowers scarring badly Korea. Treachery, deceit, hatred, envy, they teaching. Koreans begin thinking constantly conspiracy. So some Koreans hating, envying Japanese. Others thinking Chinese "dirty yellow bastards." So racism deep rooted Korea true. But, not true all foreigners Koreans hating. They courteous, respectful, generous, friendly when getting to know foreigners. Very fine people, Koreans."

While walking the paths of the farm together, Stephen's hand accidently brushed against Serena's. Before she knew what was happening, he held her hand turned her towards him and began kissing her on her lips. With each kiss, his tongue exerted gentle pressure on her closed lips. When he embraced her tightly, her soft breast became pressed against his chest. Immediately, she began to feel erotic tremors coursing through her body heightening the sensation of her arousal. Her lips parted, permitting Stephen's tongue to enter her mouth. Her hands then clasped his body in an even tighter embrace. The reaction was exactly what he sought. His tongue took to swirling expertly around her tongue and mouth probing into every nook and cranny. Her breathing quickened, her blood raced and her mind went blank as Stephen set her body on fire. Passion flared within her and at once she remembered Mona's prophetic words: "when passion sweeps you away it blots out every precautionary thought. The present is all that counts; gratification of desire all that matters. So, although aching with desire to continue she refused to surrender to passion and perhaps compromise her future. With an effort of will, she swiftly pulled herself together and in silence stepped away from Stephen. She continued their walk and changed the subject: "Stephen wanting know more about Korea? She asked.

"I'm learning a great deal more about Koreans from you than from all the information I've been fed by others. It gets me much deeper into the mindset of your people. I feel that I'm really getting to know them." Serena thought it was high time to correct her guest.

"Stephen, excuse what Serena saying *please*. She stressed the last word. Impossible any foreigner understanding Korean thinking without long, long years training very complex Confucian ethical code. Example: foreigner not understanding ancestor worship; not understanding deep respect, reverence for elders or parental authority; never shaking lady hand; never using first name between friends, acquaintances without permission; never touching Korean on head, shoulder; never expressing deep emotions or exhibit intimacy in public; never disagreement with other; never conversation about lesbians, homosexuals; never asking questions creating disagreement, disharmony. Foreigner **never** understanding paramount importance of rank, status in Korean life; never understanding why rape rarely reported; why it reaching court rarely; why deep shame on victim whole family; why victim accused of ruining life of someone's precious son. Throughout long years every individual in Confucian ethics deeply entrenched. Without deep indoctrination, all foreigners failing understand very complex Korean protocol. So no! Stephen *not* learning great deal about Koreans. He just scratching surface."

"Thank you for the correction," he replied with scarcely concealed sarcasm. Then, failing to understand what Serena had just explained, he asked:

"May I continue to ask you questions?" Her training forced her to agree. But while Stephen was congratulating himself at finally penetrating the inner sanctum of Korean thought, his question made Serena realize that her words, which she thought had carried meaningful messages, had slipped by Stephen's mind without registering any sign of their passage. It became evident to her that Stephen's mind was like a dead tree stump; immune to life-giving sunlight.

"Carry on," she answered but her eyes were smoldering with irritation. Insensitive as ever, Stephen continued the inquisition.

"When in Seoul and even here in Hamyang, I noticed that there are very few women around. At the same time, there are always a far greater number of men. It made me wonder at the serious imbalance in the population. "

"Today families wanting children only two. Two boys or one girl, one boy. This acceptable, but two girls not."

"But why?"

"First, males only passing on family name; women not. Also, Koreans worshipping ancestors, but only males performing ancestor ceremony Koreans practicing still. Then, daughters for marriage needing dowry. So draining family finances, therefore daughters bad."

"With a shortage of women, what do marriageable men do?"

"From other Asian countries, importing brides." His essays had informed him of the practice and its attendant problems. So he asked:

"How come only fair-skinned brides are acceptable to most Korean bachelors?"

"Never bachelors making choice. Families only making arrangements marital. So families exposing sons to fair-skinned brides only."

"Are you saying that Koreans are racist?"

"Disqualifying dark-skinned brides families deeply racist." He noted her honesty about the shortcomings of Koreans with amazement.

"I understand that Korean men don't treat their wives as equals." There he goes again, she thought, failing to understand the meaning of harmony in social relationships. But her own conscience quickly intervened: *Didn't you state clearly that foreigners could never understand Korean protocol. Well, Stephen is a foreigner, isn't he?* Serena had to agree and replied grudgingly.

"Much male oriented Korean society. Much slow closing gap men-women." Stephen thought about her reply before deciding to change the subject.

"I understand your education system is one of the best in the world. Is that true?"

"Yes, but formidable task entering university. Seoul having best high schools in nation. Seoul High school students filling most available places at university creating for provincial students serious problem. Many having brains, spending years studying 'hangol,' preparing entrance exams. But Sky universities few students from provinces accepting." Stephen again decided to change the subject.

"Can you describe what life is like in the farming areas?" This was the kind of question that Serena answered with alacrity since it gave her the opportunity to praise her country and countrymen.

"Life on farm simple. Koreans ambitious, having more jobs than one; working hard. Everyone much interest at progress."

"Yes, I-I, er no-noticed," he suddenly began to stammer, caught off-guard and fighting to control his straying erotic thoughts thanks to the allure of his hostess. "I've seen how hard they work, and don't need supervision to be always busy."

"Much work on farm: tilling soil, spreading fertilizer, planting, spraying crops, weeding every day. Then if bug infestation or other blight not happen; if weather hold; successful harvest making everyone happy; making hard work easy. Mechanics all time repairing machinery, farmhands all time clearing irrigation ditches. All work, no supervisor." She spoke in rapid bursts so that the thin cotton fabric covering her breasts jerked forward and backward in a manner that caused Stephen to stammer, his thoughts to stray. When her earrings caught the sunlight and dazzled as they danced, he found it both disturbing and delightful, convinced that no man possessed the kind of emotional armor to guard against such a host of unsettling images.

"I suppose the workers are to be praised for their work ethic," he mumbled in a voice thickened with desire. Although his words were complimentary, Serena noted that his tone was somewhat patronizing. Perhaps, she thought, it was because he was talking about people who were hired for brawn rather than brain. She couldn't be sure, but she put it down to a bit of egotism. Perhaps he thought that such people were his inferiors.

"At end war, dad saying much farm workers go towns, working restaurant, construction, manufacture, travel, hotel, transport, communication," she reeled off the words in rapid gunfire fashion.

"I know," he replied. "Korea exports automobiles, mobile phones, televisions, computers, appliances, shoes and textiles to the whole world." Serena was already smiling and nodding her head in agreement even before he finished. Her sparkling eyes and dancing earrings kept Stephen enchanted.

"Not backward, Koreans," she said. "Not backward at all!" Stephen understood that she was praising both her country and her countrymen for the progress made since WW2. He was annoyed with himself for falling so thoroughly under her spell that he kept losing his objectivity and sometimes had difficulty thinking at all. Her voice, her every movement, her very presence mesmerized him to such an extent that his manhood was being constantly tested, too often on high alert.

"Two medicine systems Korea, Western and "hanyak." From ginseng, red or white traditional medicinal brew coming. From animal antlers in powder, horn of rhinoceros, droppings of cockroach, dead bees, bile from snake and bear all making important treatment."

"How effective are they as cures?"

"Toothache to ageing, they curing all illness." While she talked enthusiastically, he was captivated by the movement of the fabric covering her bosom. When she caught his eyes, he blustered.

"Yes, yes," he said hastily, forcing himself to regain control of his emotions and to think logically, "but you're telling me what Koreans do. I'm more interested in what they think." Why does he disagree and insist on correcting her, she wondered.

"Say me what Stephen wanting to know. Serena trying answer."

"I believe that Confucian, Buddhist, Shaman and Christian beliefs all play a part in shaping Korean thought and conduct."

"That true," she replied, realizing he seemed to know more about Korea than he pretended.

"Tell me," said Stephen, "how is it possible to blend such radically different views into a single philosophy?" Serena noted that his questions arose only after he had divulged a number of little known facts. It struck her as a means of asking a question to show off a broader knowledge of the subject about which he was asking. Was he trying to test her or to showcase his knowledge? She thought as well that his intonation and body language suggested a hint of condescension, even smiling skepticism. Why was he trying to win an argument when all he had asked for was her opinion? Was his ego so fragile that he needed to be always right, always in charge? She tried to overlook the shortcoming. After all, he was entitled to his opinion, she told herself. Then, it struck her that his earlier questions concerning her ancestry, her government, Korean thought and now about religion and philosophy were all abstract topics. Was he deliberately choosing difficult subjects to spotlight her inadequacy of language or her inability to think in abstract terms? Was his questions chosen to assert his dominance; establish his superiority? She couldn't be sure.

"Stephen, Buddha, Confucius, knowing life of humans having much pain, much suffering, through mainly selfish desire. Buddha making *individual* develop selflessness, compassion to others, wisdom. That way *individual* finding enlightenment–Nirvana. Confucius making *ruler* develop similar virtues. His wisdom, enlightenment obliging him rule in just, virtuous manner. So, both selfishness, suffering eliminating."

"Whoa!" Stephen exclaimed loudly, only half understanding. I'll go slowly and you'll tell me if I've translated your explanation accurately. Okay?"

"Okay."

"First, Buddhist and Confucian teaching grew out of the realization that human life is fraught with suffering arising from selfish desires. I got that. Then, both seek to eliminate selfish desires that give rise to this problem. Right?"

"Right!"

"Next, you state that Buddha worked through the individual encouraging him to develop the virtues of selflessness, compassion and wisdom that would bring him enlightenment or Nirvana, thereby putting an end to suffering. Is that correct?"

"That correct! Now go on."

"Instead of working through the individual, Confucius worked through the ruler, encouraging him to develop these same virtues together through justice. His own enlightenment would oblige him to rule his subjects with justice and wisdom thus eradicating the problem of human suffering."

"Bravo! Serena applauded, clapping her hands and leaving Stephen amazed that she could think with such clarity on the abstract subjects that he had deliberately chosen to trip her. He wasn't at all pleased, but had to admit. Even though her grammar was limited, this teenager had a far better mind than his in dealing with abstract subjects. He couldn't believe that he was being constantly outmaneuvered by a teenaged girl. For the first time it got him hot under the collar instead of below the belt.

While Stephen was silently feeling defeated, Serena pointed out: "Koreans blending into one old, new ideas. Example: Western fashion together in street with old Korean dress. Husband, wife equal, but some wife behind husband walking."

"Yes, yes Serena," he said impatiently and irritably:

"I understand that here the traditional and the modern exist side by side. But how can you blend the two philosophies we just discussed with Christianity?" He asked. Unhappy with the outcome of the last discussion, he was determined to defeat his companion in an argument, to display his greater knowledge and intelligence and especially his greater command of language. By dominating her in the argument, he would reestablish his sense of superiority as well as his self-esteem.

"Stephen," she replied with irony. "Both teachings discarding selfishness. Both encouraging virtues wisdom, compassion. So, both teaching for others sympathy, affection. Same as Christian 'love one another,' no? More important. People *today* helping others. Not awaiting future heaven *after* death." The last statement, contradicting everything Stephen believed from his Christian upbringing, increased his annoyance.

"But that amounts to blasphemy, the very reverse of Christian teaching," Stephen exploded. Serena couldn't help noting his anger and that he spoke as though Christianity was the only true religion. Worse, he behaved as though it belonged only to him and his kind. Was there any limit to his arrogance? She wondered. The truth was that he pretended to be scandalized by her answer, but his explosion really arose from the recognition that she had again beaten him at his own game. His disbelief made Serena wonder why his head was like a rock; impervious to reason.

"Your farm is quite an operation, Mr. Ahn. You are to be congratulated." Stephen spoke as though conferring an honor. His host smiled at his arrogance.

"Well, thank you Stephen, but the truth of the matter is that success began with my dad." Ahn's reluctance to continue made Stephen state: "The neighboring farms are quite small while yours is huge in comparison. Does size guarantee success?"

"No! Intelligent farm management does."

"By the end of WW1, the Japanese colonial government neglected agriculture in favor of urban industrialization. What did you do to keep the farm solvent?"

"What you have to understand is that my father recognized a new strategy was needed." Ahn thought that Stephen's questions seemed intended to impress with his knowledge.

"What new strategy did he devise?"

"Dad used the loans granted by the Park administration to enlarge his holdings considerably. He bought more of the nearby farms that were going bankrupt."

"But if small farms were failing, why would a big one succeed?"

"Well, the reality of it is that small farms no doubt flourished in the past. But the farmers' archaic methods of farming gradually exhausted the soil. And since the work was all manual, few farmers without help could cope adequately with the additional labor required to run their farms successfully. Bad times–drought, weather, soil erosion, plant infestation and the like–caused crop failure and forced some farmers to sell parts of their acreage to survive. The fact of the matter is that over time farms gradually dwindled in size until the small farmer barely managed a subsistence livelihood. Eventually, the whole district became a poverty-stricken area."

"But," Stephen persisted, "if the soil was nutrient poor and farming methods archaic, greater size would guarantee greater failure. Why hasn't your farm failed?"

"Dad imitated the Canadian methods using crop rotation, restoring nutrients that had been leached from the soil. He planted soybean and alfalfa that put nutrients into the soil and alternated them with crops like corn, wheat and barley that used those very nutrients to grow strong and healthy."

"Was that enough to guarantee success?" Stephen asked sitting, Ahn thought, like a monarch, his left ankle propped upon the knee of his right thigh. Ahn's repeated glance at his exposed shoe sole reminded Stephen from his essays that it was insulting to display the dirty soles of one's shoes or feet. He quickly put both feet on the floor, hoping that his host would overlook his breach of etiquette.

"No. He also switched from manual to mechanized labor and began using organic instead of chemical fertilizers that had robbed the soil of its nutrients, killing many of the microbes, bugs, termites and earthworms that help cultivation to thrive. Finally, he also allowed fields to revive by letting them lie fallow for a season."

"And these new policies accounted for your success?"

"Partly, I also taught farmers the new methods." When the phone on his desk rang, Stephen excused himself and left the room.

"Stephen, why aren't you inside instead of outside my husband's study?"

"He had a phone call and I excused myself allowing him some privacy. I thought we could continue the discussion later."

"Then perhaps we can talk." She couldn't wait to find out his plans.

"Certainly Mrs. Ahn. By the way, your English is excellent. I've always thought you must have been one of those language whiz kids people hear about."

"I was pretty good at high school English, then I've been getting a refresher course ever since my marriage, although I still had to take private lessons to keep up." Since she didn't know how much time she would have with Stephen, she felt pressured to get the information she needed quickly.

"Tell me Stephen, you seem very interested in Serena, but with only a short time left..." She left the sentence unfinished, hanging in the air. Stephen grasped her meaning immediately.

"Mrs. Ahn, I'm in love with your daughter. I've never met anyone like her. I've asked her to marry me, so we can go back to Canada together. I needed to get her reply before I could ask for the consent of her parents."

"I see," she replied, a wintry chill settling around her heart. "What about her feelings for you?"

"I'm not sure. Although she seems willing, she's so young, so attached to the family, to Korea and its culture, that although she's attracted to me, she's still debating her final decision." Leesa's heart beat with trepidation as she tried to reassure herself by asking:

"And has she already decided? Is she prepared to leave everything behind to start a new life in a foreign country?" It embarrassed her to be so pointed in her questions, but not knowing the answers was worse. She dreaded what they might be. She didn't know what she'd do if Serena decided to leave. She'd definitely have to think about that and then consider her options.

"I've often wondered if she's seriously considered what it would mean to move into an urban world that's so very different from the natural tranquility of her home," Stephen told his hostess.

"You believe it might be too much of a shock for her, that she might not fit in?" There was a moment's pause before Stephen could answer. He then heard Mr. Ahn calling to him.

"I'm glad I've had a chance to talk to you Mrs. Ahn, and was able to let you know my feelings for Serena," Stephen said before reentering the study.

"Sorry about the interruption, Stephen. I was telling you that I taught the new practices to other farmers."

"Why would you share your successful policy with your competitors?"

"They weren't competitors. By combining our efforts, we got the big cities to increase their dependence on us and made us more successful."

"Did you then invest in new machinery?"

"No. We bought more farms, deciding to expand and diversify. At that time, the economy was shaky. Many businesses were reeling, needing greater cash flow. We thought the economy would recover, and bought into good businesses with cash flow problems. They were unable to keep their heads above water without an infusion of cash. Some manufactured furniture, others household appliances. We also bought a few department stores. Rather than go bankrupt, all agreed to sell us 51% of their stock."

"How did you make the businesses you bought become successful?"

"We placed their best workers in key positions and gave them incentives to turn the businesses around. Most of the risks we took paid off. The economy soon recovered as did the businesses. We bought out the remaining shares of those companies that seemed viable."

"So you ignored the farm?"

"Not at all! We invested heavily in organic fertilizers, formed an agricultural cooperative with farmers and increased production. The urban areas became dependent on our produce, but there was still a problem. The loss of farm labor to urban areas was eroding our productivity. We applied to government for guaranteed farm subsidy with additional price support."

"How did government respond?"

"Very favorably! They guaranteed farm income, positioned industries in rural areas and farms just outside some cities. This policy also provided employment for those wishing to remain on the farms."

"So thanks to your foresight, things turned out well. But tell me, don't your scorching summers, monsoon rains, your bitterly cold winters and typhoons, affect your crops adversely?" His host was now certain that Stephen was again using inquiry to showcase his knowledge. He realized then that Stephen, while asking intelligent questions was something of a manipulator.

"What you have to understand is that we have huge reservoirs with powerful pumps that play a dual role. During the monsoon season, they help to drain excess flooding. In the event of drought, they irrigate the fields."

"So," Stephen asked, "when the Asian economic crisis ruined many businesses and Korea had to apply to the IMF for loans, weren't you hurt financially?" He's again showcasing his knowledge to indicate how well informed he is, Ahn decided.

"No! Our heavy investments in Canada's banks paid off. They allowed us to buy companies that, without our infusion of capital, would have gone bankrupt."

"Do you lay off your less zealous workers as they do in the West?"

"No! Taking advantage of others is not the Korean way. We find them alternative jobs where their lack of enthusiasm doesn't affect us negatively."

"I'm not sure I understand," Stephen said, wondering whether Ahn had seen through his insincerity and with his subtle use of language was gently hinting at it without being insulting.

"Well, if you have no more questions, I do have a heavy schedule..." Ahn didn't say: and I would like you to leave. But Stephen understood that he was being dismissed and began to look at Ahn with new eyes. He was far more astute than Stephen had believed, and far more than the benevolent husband and father that Stephen had seen up until this interview.

"What you've done sounds very impressive..." Before he could prolong the discussion, Ahn stood and said: "Give your uncle my regards. He knows he's welcome here anytime." Stephen understood that he was being dismissed and thought it prudent to show that he got the message.

"I will sir," he replied, "and thank you for everything, and especially the warmth of your hospitality."

"You're very welcome, Stephen," his host stated as Stephen left the study.

"Your philosophies are no more than a haphazard patchwork of ideas." Stephen lied, as he continued his argument with Serena. She was feeding the hogs and considered his tone patronizing, with more than a hint of annoyance in his manner. There was that arrogant curl of lip she had noted before. My God, she thought, did he always have to be right? Did he think that his opinion was the only one possible? Is his head so hard that reason cannot enter it?

"More mosaic, not patchwork," she stated, knowing it would annoy him. "Buddhist Monks building Joyesa and Gilsangsa Temples all over Seoul mountains. They teaching disciples help poor, old, sick. Stephen," she emphasized, "helping others same as loving, no? Koreans taking highest philosophy ideas, blending together; they making progress!"

"Serena, listening to such radically different views makes me think of a constantly changing chameleon rather than a mosaic," he replied with a superior smile and arrogant curl of lip. Although she realized that he was the one constantly changing his arguments, she asked:

"Explain please. What means cam-mee-lee-on?"

"A lizard that keeps changing its colors." Serena thought for a moment before answering. She was tired of his pontification.

"Stephen, when change making progress, that good. So, constantly changing, Korean searching, gaining perfection, no?" Stephen saw he was getting nowhere and being prone to seeing only his point of view, shied away from opinions that had never occurred to him. Worse, since he detested the reality of being bested by a mere schoolgirl, he again shifted his ground and changed the topic. Being angry at another defeat, he tried once more to get even and to humiliate her.

"When I was in Seoul, I noticed that some of the younger Korean women seemed obsessed with looking European. They had used surgery for nose and eye jobs and then injected their lips to make them fuller and sexier in appearance. Their hair was dyed gold and their bodies tanned. They were evidently prouder of beauty standards that were European rather than Korean. In fact, they were embarrassed to be Korean. I thought 'loyalty was the tallest virtue in Korea?'" Stephen felt confident that he would win this argument by humiliating Serena. In doing so he was hoping to re-assert his superiority.

"Stephen, some younger Korea women in Seoul following Hollywood not European styles. Every society Stephen having fringe minorities. They craving attention; wanting stand out. When such minorities having no attractive qualities they aping others for gaining attention. Unfortunately, fringe minorities also lacking intelligence. They choosing from Hollywood false models for imitation." The clarity of her thought made Stephen again realize that he was no match for her in intelligence. Fuming with rage he again switched his argument.

"What is this thing you have for animals?" He asked in a voice of cold and angry condescension. "I don't understand why all your paintings deal only with animals." Before answering, Serena wondered if all he saw in her work were the animals. Didn't he see anything else on her canvases?

"Stephen, animals living at nature heart, in forests, valleys, mountains. They wildness, freedom, representing environment richest elements."

"But your animals are all sick!" He pronounced triumphantly, as though he had finally caught her out in a lie. Again, she noted the tone of disapproval that had crept into his voice, the angry and patronizing way in which he spoke.

"Not true! Only zoo animals. They sick at prison, separation from wilderness home. Freedom lost creating deep longing; basis of sickness."

"So," he insisted, again switching his argument, "explain to me what your paintings say." Again, there was the same curl of lip, the same challenging smile of disdain as though he was defying her to reply intelligently. She wondered why he seemed so resistant to any idea that differed from his viewpoint. Or was it his arrogance that made him always imagine he was right?

"They saying things observer should be seeing himself." She replied with irony, before adding to herself: if he has insight, imagination and intelligence. "Painting backs showing nature creating animals by harmonious evolving. One stage further in process every animal. For model, painter using nature. Clever, no?" Stephen was totally baffled by Serena's explanation: the background of her paintings revealed her animals as being in harmony with Mother Nature whose goal was perfection through the process of evolution. Every stage, she was trying to make him understand, was a step forward in the process. She couldn't blame him for not understanding her inability to explain coherently. She made an effort to explain further.

"Stephen, two important points for grasping evolution theory. One: parents passing genes to young that, over many generations, changing, mutating. Eventually, young growing different from parents. Two: young, and offspring of young, adapting to environment, also changing, growing different. But over long years, environment also changing, so present animal species much difference from long ago ancestors. Using adaptation evidence, Darwin introducing Evolution Theory later."

Stephen was again dumbfounded by the clarity of her thought, but tried not to show how baffled he had been before her explanation. Though acquainted with the evolutionary argument, he understood it only as a process working towards 'the survival of the fittest," through attrition, the eventual death of the old, the wounded and the weak. He hadn't understood it as one creating change through the gene pool, as well as through adaptation to the changing environment, or of having perfection as its goal. As usual, he was unwilling to accept a viewpoint that he had never considered or understood.

He shifted his ground once again. This time the repeated loss of his argument had made him angry enough to become insulting.

"I don't understand your decision to remain on the farm after graduation. Weren't you interested to go to the big city and to find a job like so many others?" Stephen was ashamed of losing arguments to a girl, and worse, to a teenager. His anger prodded him to ask questions that trespassed on insult. His bad manners made it difficult for Serena to keep her cool.

"Not everybody deserting farm, Stephen," she said simply, but he noted that the eyes she turned on him were flashing danger signals. When she assumed a certain pose, it suddenly struck him that Koreans had invented a secret body language that began with the eyes. Her eyelids had suddenly narrowed, the irises slid to the left corners of her eyes, their smoldering stare directed downwards. Her arms, fists folded, rested akimbo on either hip. Her torso was bent forward slightly as she turned her head placing him sideways and behind her. The fiery stare she then unleashed on Stephen squashed him like an odious and malicious bug. In the plainest language possible and without a single word, she told him that he was an insufferable son-of-a-bitch. Only after she considered that he had got the full message, did she deign to answer.

"Stephen, people staying on farm, loving simple life." This obvious truth that had eluded him increased his annoyance and his questions became even more insolent and insulting.

"Weren't you ambitious to get ahead? Didn't you want your independence? Surely this life of working on a farm and keeping pets doesn't fit you for anything besides being a farm girl!"

She couldn't fail to note that he spat out the last two words, nor that his questions were couched in a manner that amounted to accusations. He was downright insulting, having had the audacity of taking her to task, questioning her motives. She bit down on her anger and smiled as though the questions were quite acceptable. Instead of taking offense, she pointed out facts that would correct his view if he applied reason to them. Why did he have to be so stubborn, always wanting to have the upper hand? Only a person lacking in self-confidence behaved in that manner. Sometimes she thought his neck was no more than a prop supporting an irrational head.

"That answer easy," she replied. "Loyalty for family, parents, ancestors, tallest virtue in Korea. Also, Serena loving simple farm life, enjoying close animal contact. She belong at land where ancestors working, sweating during generations. Also, at favorite places by river, cave on mountain, Serena listening, talking at nature. She contented, happy farm girl." She spat out the last two words.

"It sounds as though you've decided never to leave the farm." His voice and body language had suddenly changed, showing his discouragement and dejection at the belief that she would never abandon the things and family she loved in order to marry him and leave Korea. His words and attitude made her realize he thought that she had already decided against marriage to him. She didn't want to let that happen.

"Stephen," she quickly stated, "you company pleasing, attracting Serena. But love, marriage talk exciting, frightening her. She confused, not understand self. Need time for thinking, making feelings sensible."

"Serena, I only have a couple more weeks," he said slowly approaching her. Surprising her and himself, he held her by the shoulders, drew her close and kissed her. The first kiss was gentle. She closed her eyes to savor the sensation. The next kiss was more urgent, more demanding. Before she had time to react, he kissed her again, this time the tip of his tongue probed. past her parted lips. Her mouth became the source of an electric current of arousal that coursed through her body. When his tongue began caressing hers, she became so overwhelmed by the thrill of enjoyment that she felt herself losing control as shockwaves of passion pulsed through her, making her blood rush, her head spin. As she gloried in the excitement thrilling through her, she noted with surprise and delight that his advances and his masculinity were no longer threatening. She opened her mouth thrusting her tongue between his lips and giving herself up to the glorious sensation of arousal. When she later considered the situation, she realized that her parents had been right in bringing Stephen into the family without consulting her. Had they done so, she would have disagreed vociferously.

Since she hadn't resisted, Stephen kissed her again. He embraced her so gently, as though the slightest pressure would shatter her delicate body into a million pieces. After the kiss, she held her breath. With eyes closed and trembling lips, she stood immobilized like a wild creature ready to bolt. When she parted her lips and he skillfully stroked and caressed her tongue, her breath quickened, her heart hammered in her bosom as desire coursed through her, threatening to sweep away her defenses. With singing heart, she stood erect on tiptoe surrendering to the heat raging within her. She did not know that kissing could teach her things about her body that she hadn't known. Blushing to the roots of her hair, she felt wafted away on a cloud of pure bliss and was amazed that passion and need had so quickly and completely suffused her body. She concluded that the mixture of confusion and excitement she was feeling had to be love.

The feel of his beloved pressed tightly against him sent Stephen's blood pulsing through his body, and the heady scent of her femininity together with his arousal drove him wild. His innate nature surfaced and surprising himself, he poured out his innermost feelings.

"Darling Serena, I really do love you. Please say you'll marry me. I'll spend the rest of my life loving and protecting you." Serena remained silent, her cheeks burning. Then, giving in to the wildness within her, she again tiptoed and kissed Stephen passionately. Suddenly, she remembered Mona's statement that "passion sweeps away your defenses" and decided it would not happen to her. She refused to be swept away by her arousal or the press of Stephen's male organ against her. Yet, nodding her head in assent to his plea, she surrendered once more to the excitement of his kisses. It surprised her that the plan she had so hastily devised had actually worked, and made her proud at the recognition of her devious nature.

In bed that night, Stephen recalled the arguments he had had with Serena and his attempts at controlling her with his views. He remembered how embarrassed she had made him feel by winning every argument he had deliberately started trying to embarrass her into silence. Not only had she evaded all the traps he has set for her in his game of one-upmanship, but she had made him feel dumb in the process. Thinking of it made him feel like a moron. More than anything else he hated to be ridiculed; to be a laughing stock. It reminded him of the humiliation at his father's hands. Making it infinitely worse was the fact that this slip of a girl showing up his ignorance and putting him to shame was no more than a naive teenager.

His attempt to control and dominate her had failed miserably, and each confrontation had caused him a further loss of self-esteem. Clearly, he had to admit that when it came to intelligence and knowledge, she outdistanced him by miles. It was then that he remembered his marriage proposal. Would he be able to live with a wife whose mind was sharper than his? As a husband, how long would he remain in the driver's seat if he failed to dominate and control his opinionated wife? These were questions his conscience told him he would do well to consider before taking a wife who could easily wrest from him the position of dominance and authority in his home. Like his father, he could not conceive of being dominated by a 'female of the species.' But, since he really loved Serena, he would not dare go back on his word.

In bed on the night after she had received her first kisses, Serena tried to recall accurately the way in which the experience had affected her. Stephen's first unexpected kiss had evoked little more than surprise. However, in the kisses that followed, the sweetness of Stephen's tongue had exploded her senses. Such powerful sensations had invaded her, making her body tense, with stirrings in her breasts making her nipples stand erect. Blood charged through her veins, swifter, fiercer, hotter than ever before. She could scarcely breathe or stand the dazzling sensations. Her head spun, her body trembled, her knees weakened. She had no idea that she had waited all her life to experience those moments. Oh God, she thought, Stephen had brought her the one thing she desired most–love. She couldn't wait to be again with this man who had turned her life upside down. She imagined hurling herself at him, clinging like a leech and kissing him until she fainted. If she failed to create a repetition of those tumultuous sensations, she'd just die.

That same night, alone in bed, Stephen had the strange awakening of a new self. He began to feel the stirrings of a desire to jettison his checkered past that had brought with its successes a fair share of humiliation, guilt and shame. He felt a novel ambition to attain those qualities that had attracted him to Serena–her simplicity, her sincerity and above all, her honesty. He knew that his arrogance, his egotism would be serious barriers to achieving his ambition, but he determined to chip away at those obstacles. If only he could curb his baser instincts, he'd be the kind of character of whom he could be proud.

Chapter 36

In bed, during Stephen's week end at Joe and Sally's home, sleep eluded him. All he could think of was the green-eyed Korean beauty with the black, silken hair falling around her shoulders almost to her sinewy waist. He even thought he kept hearing the beating of her heart and the music in her voice. He tortured himself picturing the lurch of her bosom beneath her blouse reacting to each of her movements and the magic in the metronomic swish of her pony tail from side to side as she jogged. But it was the delicate pink of her unpainted lips and the magic of her trilling laughter that drove him to distraction.

When Stephen returned from Joe and Sally, he boasted to Serena about the lavish hospitality he had enjoyed during his week end away. He was so jubilant that Serena thought he was celebrating some sort of a victory. She wondered too if he were enjoying as much the lavish hospitality she and her family were extending to him during the time he had been here. Being unaware of his hidden agenda, she didn't understand why he was so pleased with himself.

"Serena, you've been spending a lot of time with Stephen and he seems to be just as taken with you."

"That's true Mama. I like him a lot, but he puzzles me too. Sometimes I get the feeling that he dislikes Koreans and Korea," she said. "He also seems to have a mean streak."

"Yes, I've noticed that he sometimes looks on Korean customs and conduct with a jaundiced eye. Maybe he feels out of his element with people who are so different from him. But that certainly doesn't apply to you."

"That may be true, but I don't like what I've been feeling."

"Moonstruck?" She asked, trying to draw Serena out.

"No, it isn't that. Each time he gets close to me I feel excited, but I also feel guilty and ashamed. It's so maddening. I thought all that was past and over. Why hasn't it gone away?"

"It never goes away for good, dear. It's part of your history. You have to accept that, control how you feel about it, and then move on with your life."

"I suppose you have a recipe for that kind of control?" Serena said, with a blend of asperity and discouragement in her voice.

"Not a recipe, just what I think might help. Remember, I had those same feelings. I learnt that writing down and drawing episodes of the events would help. They did, but they weren't enough. That was when I told my darkest secret to my intended husband. His devotion, sympathy and support were of tremendous help, and made all the difference."

"I have no intended husband at the moment."

"Hasn't Stephen asked you to marry him?"

"Yes he has and I've said yes, giving him hope. But I haven't definitely made up my mind. I'm not at all sure what I should do."

"Well, lately you've been going out of your way to confuse and fascinate him. Surely you're not beginning to lose interest now? Don't you love him?" Although Serena was surprised that her mother had accurately interpreted her behavior, she pretended not to notice.

"Sometimes I think so, but I still have problems to solve. He wants to take me back to Canada, away from everything here. I thought that was what I wanted; to travel, to see new places; meet new people; start a new life. But now I'm not so sure. I worry that I'll regret leaving behind everything that I hold dear."

"Isn't that what you've been leading him on to do? Leesa thought but didn't say. "Darling, you mustn't let your love for us, for your home and the farm stand in the way of your own happiness. Working on the farm and keeping pets holds no future for a young woman with your potential."

"I know Mama, I know!"

"Isn't a fresh start what you need most; a new life and a man who loves you dearly?"

"That's what I keep telling myself. Stephen is offering me all that I need, but I'm still not sure."

Although her mother seemed to be urging Serena to leave, she was really hoping to learn whether or not she had already made up her mind. Outwardly, she spoke with conviction, but inwardly her heart was breaking. With great effort, she managed to conceal the pain she had already begun to feel just thinking of her daughter's absence. Leesa knew with certainty that if Serena left, her own day to day existence would be shattered. She was sure that she could do something to change Serena's mind if she decided to leave. But, should she interfere in her daughter's life? That was the question. She would have to deliberate far more seriously on the matter.

"I'm so confused, Mama. There's so much here that I love, that I'll miss terribly. Yet, I feel drawn to Stephen, ever though he can be so contradictory. Being with him is exciting and annoying at the same time. Is that what love is?"

"It can be. But Rina, you don't have much time. Stephen will be leaving soon. If you really love him, and decide to marry him, there's something you must do at once. You know, your problems are not over."

"No, I don't! She said abruptly. "Especially since you and father keep telling me that I've made such great progress, that I'm so much better." There was acid in her voice.

"It's true. You have made progress, but there's a way to go yet."

"What would you have me do?" Serena asked with mounting annoyance.

"Writing and painting the details of your assault has helped, but telling your story to your intended husband is mandatory and can also be therapeutic." Leesa thought this was her ace-in-the-hole. It might just tip the scales in her favor. She was sure that if Stephen learnt the brutal facts of Serena's rape, he would change his mind about his proposal of marriage. Few men would accept 'damaged goods' for a wife.

"Why do I need to involve Stephen? I'm the one who was abused. It has nothing to do with him."

"Wrong! It has everything to do with him. You'll need to see his reaction to you when you tell him what happened."

"I don't want to tell him what happened." Serena replied stubbornly.

"Unless you do, you'll never know what he really thinks or feels about you. Besides, once you begin to harbor secrets, you'll find yourself forever trying to prevent their leakage. Rina, keeping secrets is living a lie. You'll be hiding what you believe is an ugly part of yourself, a part that you don't want others to see."

"Doesn't everyone have secrets they keep hidden from others; intimate parts of themselves they don't want others to see?" Her mother ignored the truth in her daughter's question.

"After a while you'll become terrified that knowing your 'ugliness' will change their opinion of you for the worse."

"If he never knows, he can't think ill of me."

"What about how you think of yourself Rina? Surely that's even more important. Can you imagine how tough it is to fool everyone around you, every day of your life? Do you want to live the life of a hypocrite?"

"Mama, you know how I abhor hypocrisy," Serena replied angrily. "It's just another form of lies and betrayal."

"Exactly! Living a lie is a deliberate practice of deceit; a corruption of your moral principles. It will fester within you causing guilt and shame and end by corroding your soul." Leesa knew intimately the experience she had described.

"Aren't you exaggerating, Mama?"

"No! That's the price you'll have to pay for being secretive about your abuse. You've made such good progress, you mustn't fall back now."

"Mama, you really want me to humiliate myself?"

"Serena, the corruption, like acid, will eat away at your insides, and the torture will weigh so heavily upon you that it will impair your judgment and cause you to be delusional."

"Whoa Mama! You're going too fast. How did you get from my keeping secrets to making me delusional?" Her mother though shocked at the insolence, overlooked the outburst in favor of answering the question. The matter at hand was too important to be sidetracked with protocol.

"Very simply. Your being secretive stems from your fear of exposure. Once your secret is revealed you become afraid others will dislike you. That fear will make you apprehensive. Like gays and lesbians, you'll worry constantly that your secret will be discovered. You'll be always on guard, always uneasy, never totally free. Soon you'll become suspicious of the simplest statements and motives of others. You'll turn harmless remarks into barbed missiles aimed at you. You'll be locking yourself in a prison built by the criminal behavior of others. Now, is that what you want?"

"Oh Mama, you're so persuasive, so wise, even though your wisdom makes me cringe in terror. But you're right. That's not what I want."

"Well, once you understand that telling Stephen what happened will help lighten your own burden you'll realize that it's the best path to follow." And she thought: it will surely destroy any possibility of your marriage to him.

Chapter 37

"Mama, do you know how hard it is to do what you ask? God knows, you're making me undergo a sense of my own degradation."

"That's exactly what you have to do. Bow to your fate. Accept!" And she thought: is this Leesa of all people giving such advice?

"Mama your words sound like some cruel joke. I'll loathe myself even more. It will make me sick!"

"Why sick? Because he's a man?"

"Yes!" she burst out. "Just like the rapists, with the same unconscious aim."

"My God, Serena! Don't you see how wrong you are? You're becoming suspicious and cynical already. That's your paranoia responding. From what you've said, Stephen is a man who loves you, and wants to spend his whole life loving and protecting you. He'll never hurt you."

"How do you know that? You're just using arguments to prop up your viewpoint? Stephen is a man. Aren't all men essentially rapists?"

"Oh God, Serena. How can you be so cynical, so callous? You don't really believe that of Stephen, do you?"

"No Mama, I suppose not. But after my experience, it's always there, lurking in the back of my mind, nudging me with the possibility."

"You should be able to tell Stephen anything and everything. He'll never judge you only love you all the more because he feels the pain you're suffering."

"Mama," Serena smiled, "you've just described Papa. Not everyone is as understanding or as loving as he."

"I know dear," she smiled, but persisted. "So you will talk to Stephen?"

"Yes Mama," she groaned. "I'll talk to him."

"That means you've already decided to marry him," she said, chuckling with pretended delight, trying desperately to conceal the deep distress she felt at the thought of losing her daughter.

Serena hugged her mother, giggling. She was so swept away by her own emotions that she remained completely oblivious of the pain that, like a rapier, pierced her mother's heart and was reflected on her face.

"On the bus, I notice that houses in the closest city to this township are modern, Western styled apartment complexes, while many in the rural areas are single, one-story dwellings." Stephen and Serena were once more on the river bank discussing Korea. Despite her annoyance with him for his earlier attempts at dominating her in argument, and controlling her views, she couldn't stay angry for long once they were together.

"Yes, houses traditional. They making with brick, concrete; having tile roof."

"Yours is a very modern two-story home, vastly different."

"Yes. Father renovate, following Canada models." Serena held his hand guiding him to a nearby field, changing the subject. "Here grow soybean, sweet potato, cabbage, onion," she told him, making a sweeping gesture to cover the fields she was describing. Having found that Stephen's maleness no longer made her uncomfortable, she longed for the excitement that his earlier kisses had aroused. She was hoping that her closeness would lead to a repetition of that romantic episode.

"Such large scale cultivation must be for urban markets, right?"

"Right," she snapped, irritated at his failure to give her the response she needed. "There," she pointed to the hill slopes, "rice paddy terraces, with fish inside water. Over there," she pointed to her left, "more soybean and further, barley, beans, wheat, corn. Still further at orchard, growing apple, pear, peaches. Urban market for all." Her words, like barrages of gunfire, expressed her impatience, disappointment and annoyance at Stephen's reluctance to approach her with romance on his mind, heart and tongue. She drew him closer, again holding his hand and taking him strolling lazily along the outer reaches of the farm. He could feel her warmth and inhaled her perfume that almost masked her youthful sweat. He became instantly aroused when she held his hand telling him she "could gaze at land capturing beauty, fragrance, wildness, stamping images on her brain." Then, leaning backward against him and rubbing her head against his chest, she explained further: "capturing on canvas, they staying Serena forever."

The temptation was too much for Stephen. He placed his hands on her shoulders and pulled her against him even tighter. He kissed her temple and trailed a succession of kisses along her cheek moving towards her lips. Turning her around, he heard her swift intake of breath, followed by the quickening of her breathing. Her eyes were closed and he kissed them both before returning to her mouth where his steaming kisses left no doubt of his desires or intentions. On the outside, she appeared calm, except for the crimson flush on her cheeks. On the inside, she was all a-flutter, feeling a fullness in her breasts, her nipples tiptoeing to attention with a tightening of her pelvic muscles. An ache began in her loins and, as though a wand had been waved, she was once again in a state of enchantment. When with closed eyes she whispered: "Stephen, Serena never having such feelings before. Maybe this is love?"

Suddenly, while Serena and Stephen were enjoying their intimacy, a deluge, signaling the imminent arrival of the monsoon, had come earlier than expected. Shafts of forked lightening and deafening roars of thunder accompanied the heavy downfall drenching the couple to the skin. Rather than slog across the muddy fields in their soaked clothes to take the long way towards home, Serena opted to take shelter in a nearby cabin. It was built for the farm hands to use in just such an emergency. As her mind wrestled with the plan, she fantasized about the opportunity for seduction that it would offer to Stephen. She then wondered whether she had the will to resist his advances. She had to shout above the roar of the storm to make herself heard: "We going nearby cabin for drying clothes and warming bodies." Immediately, the thought of disrobing before the fire sparked ideas of erotic intimacies in her mind. Stephen too, also thought of a ready-made seduction scene. Once they rushed into the cabin, he found that it was stocked with all the basic needs. The fireplace was already laid with logs and Stephen only had to light the kindling to get the fire started. Meanwhile, Serena turned her back on Stephen and began to undress. She removed all her clothes except her underwear then wrapped herself in a towel. Stephen quickly followed suit but since there was no towel for him he remained in his boxers.

Serena wanted to feel the muscles of Stephen's huge masculine body and run her fingers through the curling blond hair on his chest and head. She then wondered what it would feel like to touch what was causing the bulge in his boxers. Of course, she dared not. But immediately, her juices began to flow, her heart began to pound and the blood rushed to color her cheeks. Stephen couldn't miss the change that had come over her and understanding its cause, he drew closer to the fire and to her. "You know Serena," he began, "if I hold you next to me we'll both get warmer far more quickly." Since that was exactly what she wanted, she hastened to reply: "Serena agreeing but only if Stephen behaving."

"Of course, I won't do anything without your permission." She sat on the floor in front of the fire and edged closer. Stephen took the opportunity to circle her waist with his arm and drew her even closer. The reality of Serena's almost naked body clasped against his side had his mind racing with indecent possibilities and when her inquiring hand fell onto his lap, his erection almost burst through the fabric of his boxers. Since she had leaned her head back against his shoulder, her closeness and the lingering scent of her cologne drove him wild. As an automatic response he began showering gentle kisses that started at her temple and cheek descending very slowly towards her mouth. Serena's senses sang at the feel of the bulge in her hand and at the array of kisses scattered over her face and lips. She became almost as hot as the fire. Stephen's hands crept up from her waist until his fingers played with the soft edges of her breasts to find that there was no bra to hamper his progress. He lifted her onto his lap so that he could more easily reach her mouth. She opened her lips at the gentle pressure of his tongue seeking to enter her mouth but it was his maleness pressing upwards in the space between her upper thighs that set a series of explosive sensations ripping through her body. It made her wonder what it would feel like to throw caution to the winds, remove her towel and surrender to Stephen. But not being completely healed she couldn't do that. So, again recalling Mona's warning about passion being the universal enemy that encourages you to give yourself up to the ecstasy of the moment, she exerted her willpower. She felt the deepest disappointment at stopping the unbearable pleasure she was experiencing. Besides, she and Mona had made a solemn promise to each other to keep their virginity intact until they were married. With no intention of going back on her word, she broke away from Stephen and put an end to the seduction.

Stephen surprised her by also stopping at once. "Serena," he said. You've avoided answering my question these last few days and I don't know why. Have you decided not to marry me?"

"No Stephen, not that." She remained a long moment wrapped in thought. It was as though she was trying to come to some decision. He burst out:

"If there's a problem darling, maybe I can solve it for you. As I've said before, I love you, want to marry you and take care of you for the rest of your life. Please say yes and come with me to Canada. He cupped her face in his hands, pressed his lips to hers and kissed her deeply and longingly. It was exactly what she wanted. With relief, she wondered: What the hell was he waiting for: The sun to come down and the moon to shine? Then, she caught herself.

"Wait!" She said suddenly. Catching her breath, she willed herself to stop what she found so exciting and since the downpour had stopped she dressed herself quickly and rushed away. Stephen cursed himself, wondering what had happened, what he had done to break the spell. He could do nothing but let his passions cool as he followed her to the house. She returned holding what appeared to be colored pictures in her hand. He became curious but she didn't let him see them.

"You wanting Serena answer marriage question? Right? First, she thinking marriage partners must know each other." She then launched into her explanation. "Two years ago, Serena walking home from movie. In field five men grab, overpowering, raping her, leaving her for dead. Now, you turn answer," she challenged. "Why Stephen marrying ruined woman?"

Stephen stood transfixed. Nothing had prepared him for so dramatic and damning a disclosure. In tears, Serena handed him the graphic pictures of her rape. She then explained amid sobs: "all males scaring Serena so much after rape that she recovering still two whole years later. Sometimes," she sobbed, "Serena still feeling uncomfortable with men, even friends she knowing well. Perhaps Stephen recalling Serena reluctance on earlier meetings." She concluded that spending time in Stephen's company had helped considerably, but she still hadn't fully recovered. She burst into a renewed fit of sobbing, telling him that there were times when she felt uncomfortable even with him. "Such feelings Serena not able control."

Stephen stood speechless for a long moment, hypnotized by the brutality of the pictures that provided so brilliant a contrast between the advance of the five burly male aggressors and the retreat of their diminutive female victim. While looking, he listened to the bitterness and pain pouring from Serena's mouth. He could see she was reining herself in, straining to keep control over her emotions but continued sobbing silently while waiting for Stephen's response to her challenge. Finally, he exploded.

"On my God Serena!" He took her gently into his arms so that his warmth and sympathy started Serena on a new bout of tears. Then between sobs, she repeated in a tone of puzzled dejection: "Why Stephen wanting for wife ruined woman?"

Stephen couldn't believe what she was asking. The shocking question immediately aroused his compassion for the deeply wounded child-woman. How was it possible, he wondered, that someone radiating such innocence, beauty and raw sexuality could regard herself as ruined? He responded with words of sympathy.

"Darling, bad things happen to good people, and such unfortunate events are not uncommon in this evil world. You just happened to be in the wrong place at the wrong time." The hackneyed explanation, he knew, offered little solace, so he kept hugging her tightly until her sobbing stopped. "Go back to the house and wait for me," he told her. "I have some serious thinking to do." After she obeyed and left, he sat down to think.

His mind was in turmoil. All he could see were the graphic images of Serena's rape. His eyes, having left their focus on the assailants, were riveted on the expressions stamped on Serena's faces. In the first picture, she resembled one of the caged zoo animals of her paintings. The stark terror in the bulging eyes, the rigid facial muscles and the silent scream echoing from the gaping mouth conveyed the agony of the victim. Reflected too in the other pictures, was her helplessness, her resignation to the ghastly fate that was only moments away. Half naked and backing away from that terrifying semi-circle of assailants, she projected an attitude of complete resignation to the approach of evil.

With an effort, he tried to stop focusing on the event. He needed a special clarity of mind to carefully consider his own thoughts and feelings towards Serena with the knowledge that had just been thrust upon him. But the raw power of the paintings had paralyzed his brain. He shook his head, forcing himself to concentrate. It took a long time and great effort to clear his mind and make the horrific images disappear. Eventually, he succeeded.

He knew Serena was blameless and thus her 'punishment' unjust. He also knew she had been honest enough to tell him about her rape and even to show him the ghastly pictures. In his mind, she was the same beautiful young woman with whom he had fallen in love. Further, he hadn't forgotten that he had twice proposed marriage to her, and twice promised her his undying love and protection.

For a moment, he couldn't believe that these were his own thoughts, the thoughts of Stephen, the liar, con man and hypocrite; the seducer and cruel betrayer of women. Yes, he had to admit, it was the same selfish Stephen who had never done anything without harboring a motive for gain. Yet, he had never believed that he had betrayed the women he had dumped. In fact, he convinced himself that he had always given as much or even more than he had got. After all, he considered himself a superior lover, and his arrogance made him certain that the women he had loved and left were always satisfied that they had got the better end of the bargain. He consoled himself with the rhetorical question: how often had they met someone with his special gifts?

Yet, something strange, weird and wonderful had happened to him since his meeting with Serena. He had never had such a powerful attraction to any woman before. Sure, he had enjoyed making love to the others, but he had always been in charge. During those relationships, there had always been a separation, a detachment on his part, from start to finish. His intimacy with those women had been a physical thing, nothing more. He had never let himself become emotionally involved. His taking from them had never bothered him, knowing that he could leave them without so much as a backward glance. In fact, that distance he kept from his women was very important to him. He prided himself on never having made a verbal commitment to a single one of them. The words 'I love you' had never entered his mind; never crossed his lips. That, he convinced himself, left him with a clear conscience.

Before meeting Serena, he saw and used women as sexual objects; objects that would bring him to orgasm. Sex with them was the equivalent of a desired ejaculation. For him, intimacy with a woman was merely a tenuous and temporary sexual bond, far more enjoyable than the manual equivalent. Everything else was an empty, meaningless embrace. Since he felt nothing more, he was free to walk away from them without a thought. Women stirred his body responding to his sexual need. Their warmth never reached his heart. But Serena was a very different proposition. She had changed him. Although he hadn't slept with her, he realized that she possessed qualities he had not met before. Since he believed that she had the power to make him change, she was someone precious and mysterious.

For the hundredth time he asked himself if these feelings he had for Serena, this new way of thinking and acting, had anything to do with love? And then he began to consider those deeply intimate feelings of devotion that women had whispered to him so often. Could he have caught the disease? If so, it must be strong medicine indeed, for it seemed to be making a new man of him. He had already begun to think, feel and act differently. He was already turning himself inside out; already making a conscious effort to separate himself from his past. Why else had his hidden agenda, his earlier craving for profit, evaporated so suddenly and so completely?

These new feelings that had surfaced had provoked such a surprise that he needed to deliberate carefully on the decision he had to make. He had proposed marriage and only afterwards found out that his bride-to-be had been cruelly gang raped. He now had to decide whether or not to honor his proposal. He gave only a passing thought to the fact that in marriage to Serena he would not be taking a virgin bride to his bed. That was a secondary matter to him since, as a husband, he was not virgin material himself. How could he demand it of his wife? Then too, it was common knowledge that most modern brides eagerly cashed in their 'V' cards, impatient, even eager to jettison their virginity long before marriage. Besides, his loss of virginity had been deliberate, his own doing. Hers was not.

The only question left to consider was whether he loved Serena any less with his new knowledge. He also had to keep in mind that more than once, he had promised to love and protect her. How could he turn his back on so delicate and lovable a creature–a tiny, fragile bird with a broken wing? How could he betray this precious young woman? He just couldn't. He rose and went inside to search for Serena. And as he went, the decision he had made gave a powerful jolt to his self-esteem. He felt refreshed, renewed, revitalized. He considered himself a new person, a changed man, ready to show the world that a vicious leopard could change its spots in the same way that a venomous serpent could change its skin.

The simple fact was that Serena's confession and conduct had bowled him over. It forced him to look within himself and consider his own grossly deceptive and reprehensible nature. He found it almost impossible to believe that anyone could be as forthright as Serena had been. He didn't have to ask her about her past, she had offered the explanation willingly, from her heart. She had even backed up her words with the most horrific pictures. Evidently, she just thought it was the right thing to do. Could he ever act in so simple, truthful and straightforward a manner? He wondered.

An idea came to him so foreign to his nature that it shook him to the core. Since Serena had been honest enough to express the details of so personal and private a degradation of herself, such purity goaded him to follow her example.

He could never forget her challenge: "You wanting me answer marriage proposal? I thinking marriage partners must know about each other. So, I say you about me. Two years ago, Serena walking home from movie. In field five men overpowering, raping her, leaving her for dead."

That kind of honesty from that kind of woman, he thought, had the power to make him turn over a new leaf, start his new relationship with a clean slate. Rising to Serena's challenge he decided to confess the dark and shameful past of his father's dominance and its negative influence on his character. As he deliberated on the painful memories of his past, he began to view the incidents as the same kind of violation that Serena had experienced.

Leesa had a momentous decision to make. Either she could do nothing, in which case Serena would leave Korea and marry Stephen, or she could create an obstacle to the marriage that would prevent Serena from ruining her life. Leesa used these arguments to justify the action she might decide to take. No one would understand the heartache she would experience in losing her daughter, and perhaps never seeing her again. The stark realization evoked a series of images. She saw Serena as the baby girl she had carried within her for nine months. Thus, she would always consider her a vital part of herself. No one would believe the terror and confusion she experienced when she first learnt she was pregnant. She had nowhere to turn, no one to help or to advise her. That was the worst experience of isolation she had ever endured.

She then recalled the shame of dragging her bloated body around, stared at by a silent and hostile world. Later, there was the series of appalling events; the humiliations of having to face the filthy rumors swirling around her husband and herself. She remembered the nausea, the vomiting and having to crawl to the toilet on hands and knees, being too dizzy to stand. There were the weeks of growing ravenous for food yet the fear of vomiting forcing her to starve herself. Finally, there were the kicks and blows from the baby and the joy she felt since each one testified to the life she bore within her, the life on which she couldn't wait to lavish her love. Looking back, she wondered how she had been able to withstand the icy prison which she had inhabited during those long months of fear, shame, dread and humiliation.

She recalled the terror of childbirth itself, the way her body would spasm each time the pain roared through her, each contraction ripping her apart. It was so bad she convinced herself that she was dying. Even worse was the deep humiliation of her experience in the birthing room. She had to spread her legs, stretching them widely open–like the curtains in front of a movie screen—before the start of a movie–exposing the most intimate view of herself for the entire world to see. She'd had to close her eyes and mind to the silent eyes boring into her most private parts. But perhaps worst of all, was the horrifying indignity of emptying her bowels to the staring eyes of her sanitized audience at the very moment of childbirth.

She then recalled the baby that had gladdened her heart and providing her with the armor to face the abuse of a cruel and judgmental world. Then, to her amazement, she found that the appalling series of events had made her baby more precious than she had thought possible. She recalled suckling her first born. Oh God! Did every mother feel the same indescribable moment of rapture; the same outpouring of love, pride, and joy she had experienced at that miraculous moment?

Memory then took her to Serena as a two year old toddler, running around their dining room in her new red shoes, stamping again and again to exaggerate the sound of her heels on the wooden floor. She just couldn't contain her energy as she raced around in her red party dress, her hair gathered in a pony tail pointing skyward and spilling like a fountain from the tiny red bow holding it together. She was so exuberant, so full of life, that Leesa was almost envious of the outbursts of hilarity that nothing could contain. Serena was the daughter that every mother dreamt of having. When Leesa held her warm tiny hand as Serena skipped along at her side, Leesa knew that she had been granted a grace, a gift and a reward.

Indeed, she convinced herself that her beautiful child was a signal of God's forgiveness. She believed the suffering, humiliation and shame she had experienced during the months leading up to her pregnancy had softened His heart; made Him more compassionate and forgiving. The pride and joy she took in the belief that her daughter had brought her forgiveness was such that no words could express her feelings. The love bubbling up inside her was so overpowering that it left her gasping for breath. And when Serena asked a question, looking at her mother as though gazing at her own personal oracle, Leesa felt as though she held in her hand the secrets of the universe, the keys to the kingdom. It was then, as a teenager that the incredible change had come over her. She was almost blinding in her beauty and elegance. In fact, the only words that came close were: gorgeous, ravishing and spectacular.

Chapter 38

Leesa remembered how her heart had almost burst with pride when Serena won the first prize for painting in the school's art contest and again the first time she topped the honors list. In her mind's eye, Leesa marveled at the picture of Serena sitting for hours, wrestling with her homework or her painting, struggling against exhaustion until satisfied. Only then would she exude a radiant glow of fulfillment on completing the task she considered worthy of her.

Leesa silently thanked God for giving her so beautiful, talented and intelligent a daughter. Then, her eyes filled with tears at the thought of the rag doll they had brought home from hospital and her long, hard fight for her recovery. She had looked on, battling down her fear, praying for her daughter's life and sanity. And finally today, Serena was blooming again, even more beautiful. Oh God, Leesa didn't deserve such happiness. She couldn't abide losing this golden gift. No, she wouldn't lose her. But then, she tried to be fair, giving a long hard look at her daughter's situation, and trying, as far as it was possible for her, to view it as an unbiased observer. But of course, she could never admit that where Serena was concerned, it was impossible for her to be unbiased.

Why don't you force yourself to see the reality of the situation without bias, her conscience demanded.

"Okay, my daughter is very young, inexperienced and in love with Stephen and he with her. How's that?" Leesa asked.

Well, that's a beginning. Of course she's young and inexperienced, but she's never been flighty. You know very well that she's level headed enough to deal adequately with any problem that arises.

"I know my daughter. Can you imaging what would happen if I failed to intervene?"

Yes! She would agree to marry Stephen and try as hard as possible to be a good wife.

"Serena has had no experience of an emotional relationship with a man. She knows nothing about what love really is. And when she finds out her mistake in a foreign country, it will then be too late. You don't seem to understand. She'll have no one to turn to for advice and help."

You know very well that Serena can cope with whatever problems life poses for her. Besides, in a new country, she'll have the golden opportunity of a new beginning with a husband she loves. Your objections are based solely on a selfish desire to keep her with you. You worry about what your life would be like without her.

"Of course I worry. But as her mother, I worry more about how **her** whole life could be destroyed by the mistake of a too-early marriage, and to a man she hardly knows. You'll have to admit that these are solid grounds for my opposition to the marriage."

They would be good reasons, if those were really your main concerns. But you know in your heart that your true motive is selfish; you want to keep Serena near you. You don't want to lose her.

"Of course I don't want to lose her. She's my firstborn, my only child. The hell and heartbreak that I've gone through over her, has made that only child especially precious. I love her with my whole heart for the unremitting joy that she has brought me. You think I could stand idly by and let her ruin her life without opening my mouth?"

Try telling the truth, Leesa. What is the real problem?

"I did not know that just the fear of losing a beloved child could so sorely sicken the heart and grieve the soul. I can already feel the cold claws of separation and loneliness raking across my heart. If I let Serena leave Korea, there would be a gaping hole in my life, my soul. How could I let Stephen cut out my heart? No real mother could let that happen without lifting a finger to stop it. Am I or am I not a real mother? That is the only question I need to answer.

"Serena, I can only imagine how humiliated you must have felt explaining this outrage to me and showing me those awful pictures." She caught the notes of deep concern, sympathy and sadness in his voice. The sincerity, he hoped, lessened her mental anguish, bringing her some little comfort. "Believe me what happened to you doesn't change anything. I love you now, more than ever, and want to protect you for the rest of your life. Darling, please say you'll marry me."

The love and sympathy evident in Stephen's voice evoked similar sensations within Serena's heart. She was attracted to him and wanted to say yes, but once again the thought of leaving behind everyone and everything she loved, deeply distressed her. Yet, the relief and the joy of having successfully accomplished her mission swept over her. Once again the choice was hers to make, but first she needed to be fair to Stephen.

"Stephen, Serena not answering now. Needing untangling feelings, sorting out confusion. Not understand why Stephen wanting damage person, not deserving love, to marry."

"Serena!" he almost shouted. "You have to stop thinking of yourself that way. To me, you're beautiful, innocent and completely unspoiled. You're just a woman-child who has been unjustly molested, and victimized." She kept looking at him with love in her eyes as he continued. "What you need most is love and protection. If you marry me, I can assure you that you'll have both and a new beginning. Then, when we get to Canada, I'll show you all the things and places I find so fascinating. When you see what I plan to show you, you'll be exchanging your old world for the new. I'm sure you'll come to love your new world as much as I do. Equally important, my darling, you'll have a new life of happiness in Canada, a fresh start. You have no idea how much I'm looking forward to that."

As she listened to Stephen's compassion, his tender and loving words, her thoughts diverged in different directions. She became positive that Stephen couldn't be the same man whose unsavory image had emerged from his attempts to dominate her with his arguments. She felt suddenly happy since the realization lifted a curtain that had darkened her earlier thoughts of what marriage to him and the future might hold.

On the other hand, she noted with alarm that he was offering her a door to the future that hinged on her leaving home. Now that she had prodded Stephen into proposing, she again had to ask herself the dreaded question that she had been avoiding. Could she be happy leaving behind everyone and everything she so dearly loved? For the moment, she again shied away from answering the question. But, the short time that remained of Stephen's vacation kept pressuring her.

Serena's honesty, her sincerity had such a profound influence on Stephen that he deliberated for days and nights on the best way to answer her challenge. What could he do to make her feel that he was deserving of her love? He took her to the riverbank to expose to her his earliest experiences and the way they had affected him.

"Serena, I want to be as frank and as forthright with you, as you have been with me. I want you to understand how the influence of my parents during my earliest youth and adolescence has molded my life and character as an adult. I consider that its effect is, in a way, similar to your violation. The main difference is that you came through your ordeal as an honest and upright person. I strayed in the opposite direction.

"My father fit almost perfectly into the British stereotype of the stoic with the stiff upper lip. He even had the short legged, solidly built, squat body and ugly face of the British bulldog. A Sandhurst man before retirement, he was stubborn. Like mule and milepost, he refused to change his mind. Instead, he followed in the tradition of his fellow officers by cultivating a relentless and decisive stubbornness that they alone translated as the virtue of perseverance."

Serena listened in silence to Stephen's story. "I remember most of all the raging quarrels that took place between my parents," he said, and recreated the scene for her.

"John, I don't agree with your belief that experience is the best teacher. Certainly not always. That may be true when Stephen grows older, but he's only a three year old. Don't leave matches for him to play with. He'll only get burnt." My mother would try to intervene whenever she disagreed with the methods my father used in my upbringing.

"That's the whole point, woman, he'd reply angrily. Getting burnt will teach him never to play with matches."

"The stern military discipline that applies to soldiers is unsuitable for a toddler, John. Stop being so narrow minded and dictatorial in your views. It's stupid to use such strict methods on your son unless you enjoy hurting him."

"Woman, leave me to my narrow minded, stupid and dictatorial views on training my son. As the authority figure in this household, I'll continue to use my own methods, thank you."

"Can't you see that there are other less cruel ways to attain the same ends? Must you march forward, ramrod straight in military fashion, believing that your way is the only way? Are you incapable of bending; of showing at least some affection and taking into consideration the tender age of your son?

"My father paid no attention to my mother's logic and common sense. He left the matches where I was sure to find them. My curiosity soon got the better of me and it didn't take long before I began playing with them. My clothes caught fire and I raced around screaming. If my mother hadn't been nearby to smother the flames with a blanket, I would have been burnt to death. My mother, enraged by my brush with death, plowed into my father: "You idiot!" She screamed. "You almost killed your son. Why do you have to be so stubborn and stupid? Must you be the rock against which all reason shatters?"

"You mother having strong, cruel words for husband! Serena thinking her vitriol making father even more angry."

"True, but my father didn't change his view or his behavior. Later on, he found that the steep staircase held a particular fascination for me, and created another minor catastrophe."

"John, why did you remove the barrier from the top of the staircase? Do you want Stephen to break his neck?" My mother accused my father angrily. Meanwhile, the magnetic temptation of the stairs worked their magic on me and I rushed to follow my dad as he descended and then stood half way down the stairs. I tumbled down, head over heels, striking my head again and again, and would surely have broken my neck if he hadn't caught me. Screaming from the painful blows to my head and the terror generated by my fall, I held out my arms to my father seeking sympathy and comfort. Instead, I received two hard slaps on my behind. The unexpected shock made me pee my pants as I listened to my father's words that I didn't understand, echoing in my head:

"The world is a tough place where crybabies like you won't get far." He put me to kneel in a corner for my transgression and called my mother to see what her mollycoddling did to her 'hero.' "He pees his pants every chance he gets, crying out for sympathy instead of taking his lumps like a man," my father told her. His ears were deaf to my mother's angry reply that I was "just a toddler and such harsh discipline would hurt more than it helped." Meanwhile, I continued to weep shamefully in my corner, deeply humiliated at words and punishment I didn't understand."

"From that day, I always cringed inside at my father's laughter. It made me feel small and ridiculous. Worse, I began to hate people ridiculing me. It would make me become that little boy again, ashamed and humiliated at peeing his pants. The experience made me want to be always in control, always in the dominant position. And as his laughter rang in my ears, I ran from his ridicule, rushing through the door, slamming it behind me.

"Good Christ, John! When are you going to learn that Stephen is just a kid? He's too young for your dumb theories. You act as though you're still in the army ordering your subordinates. I wish you'd stop being such a jackass. So saying, she swept me up from the corner into her arms in a challenging manner."

"Damn it wife! We've had this quarrel before. By countermanding my orders, you're getting Stephen used to sympathy whenever he finds himself in a tough spot. Besides, you're letting his conduct come between us, and making a mockery of our marriage. It's *your* conduct that's turning our home into a madhouse where we keep flinging hateful remarks at each other."

"Well," she responded. "I'm sick of your commands and your refusal to bend your military principles. You're not being steadfast as you like to pontificate. You're just being stubborn and stupid. Worse, you're hurting our little boy." And so with my father's stubbornness and my mother's insulting words cutting my father down, the fighting escalated, making me sadly aware of the severe stress I was putting on my parent's marriage, and the equally severe strain they were putting on me."

"Very hurtful, you mother's words, making angry, stubborn father. But father very cruel, showing no affection at Stephen," Serena stated, at once thinking of her own gentle, loving and protective father. In comparison, she considered Stephen's father a monster.

"My God, such cruelty having crippling effect at Stephen's life," she said sympathetically.

Stephen continued his confession, his eyes watering as he thought of what happened next.

"Whenever I tearfully approached my father in an appeal for sympathy after some juvenile misfortune, I always met a stern face followed by a sterner lecture on stoicism."

"Real men didn't cry, snivel, whine or complain over every piddling accident. Emotional outbursts, pleas for sympathy and kissing to make it better, are reserved for 'the weaker female of the species.' Real men are supposed to be tough. In whatever trouble they find themselves, they learn to take their lumps, to grin and bear it. Developing toughness and learning to display true grit will help you to avoid the need for your mother's sympathy and affection." The incidents of the matches and the stairs burnt themselves into my consciousness together with the lectures that would take me years to understand.

"Wife, if it were possible for Stephen to join the army as a toddler, I'd have him conscripted," my father once said. "The rigid military discipline and training, the regimen of hard work and physical fitness would toughen up his tender muscles and replace his rubber spine with a steel rod. In that man's army, you wouldn't be there with your sympathy and affection to spoil him. Stephen would learn, at first hand, that the world has no place for bellyaching crybabies." Listening to Stephen's words brought tears to Serena's eyes, and in a gesture of sympathy and compassion, she took his hand in hers.

"John, you never fail to criticize Stephen for the least shortcoming. You believe that constantly cracking the whip will make a man of your son. Further, whenever he approaches you with any request: a raise in allowance; a bicycle or even to go out with his friends to a movie on the weekend, you always find an excuse to refuse. Worse, you've never let him address you as Dad, it's always Sir, as though he were in the army. I'm really fed up with the cruel way you keep treating your own son."

On another occasion, my mother had heard my father refuse my plea for a bicycle to go picnicking with my buddies. On the following day, when my father saw me ride off on a new bicycle with my friends, he confronted my mother angrily.

"Woman, I don't like the way you undermine my authority by catering to Stephen's every wish."

"I don't like the way you refuse every appeal he makes to you, the father he worships. You suspend his weekly allowance for the smallest of infractions, cut down his TV privileges, use the flimsiest excuse to ground him and refuse to buy him a bicycle to join his friends. How can you be so cruel to a son who loves you?"

"When I want your input in the way I bring up my son, I'll let you know. Your giving in to his every whim will only spoil the child; get him to expect mollycoddling and getting things the easy way in life. He must learn to do without."

"You've been a brilliant teacher in that respect since you deny him everything he should expect from a loving and affectionate father."

"I prefer to win respect from him before I can think of offering love and affection."

"Well husband, respect has to be earned. Refusing whatever he asks for, and never attending any of his games–basketball, football or squash–is not the way to do so. Besides, you don't even know that your son is a credit to his school?"

Much later, as an adult, I remember my mother's words to him. "You keep abusing your son, calling him names like a 'spineless simpleton.' You kept needling him about being unable 'to face authority or the difficulties he encounters.' You then tell him sarcastically that he'll 'need to resort to dishonesty to survive.' What kind of a father tells his son to be dishonest?"

"My father turned his back and left the room without replying." This was the hostile atmosphere in which I lived. Not surprisingly, I began to think of my father as a cold inhuman machine totally devoid of emotion; the empty husk of a man who reigned in a stifling atmosphere charged with angry violence and the guarantee of criticism. Such a person, I was sure, could never give me the love, affection, and respect I craved. I grew to fear and hate him intensely. Serena kissed him chastely on the lips to let him know that she understood.

Although Serena had not yet decided to accept Stephen's proposal, she was both excited and anxious to learn as much as she could about the people and the culture of British Columbia where she would probably spend the rest of her life, if she married Stephen. She spent hours at the nearest library learning that BC was "the province located on the west coast of Canada." But she also learnt from her reading the true meaning of culture: "the lifestyle that distinguishes one community from another through its traditions and values, its special skills, knowledge, and beliefs. These were the attributes of the legacy passed from one generation to the next; from the past to the present." If she accepted Stephen's proposal, would their two cultures clash violently or would she be able to make them merge together seamlessly? It was therefore important for her to become familiar with the culture of Canada. She placed a large map of British Columbia before her so that she could check the location of everything about which she read.

Vancouver, she learned from a travel guide borrowed from the library, "stood between the Fraser River, the Coastal Mountains and the Strait of Georgia." What really excited her was the list of recreational activities and interests that the city offered, promising the numerous amenities of any modern day metropolis. Certain parts of the coast, while a part of the mainland, could only be reached by boat or aircraft. Living on her farm very far from the sea, she found it delightful to learn that in BC one had access "to the sprawling acreage of green pastures, rugged coastline and long stretches of sandy beaches."

On consulting the Internet, she learnt that Vancouver Island,' where Stephen lived, was "an off shore island similar to Holland in size and situated about 55 kilometers west of the mainland. Victoria, the capital city of the province was nicknamed the Garden City and situated on the island's southern end". Serena was excited to learn that the island was considered 'a jewel,' because of its "breathtakingly beautiful scenery." In the province, after hockey, fishing was certainly the most popular sport, but there was ample provision for visitors who would rather scuba dive, ski, sail, snorkel, bird watch, go horse riding, roller-blading, canoeing, white-water rafting, snowboarding or mountain climbing. She couldn't believe that any one place could offer such a diversity of activities. She saw too that some trips were specially organized that combined fishing with numerous other activities.

Although seduced by what she had read about the myriad exciting adventures that BC offered, she still thought that she would have to be mad to accept Stephen's proposal. It would mean leaving her home, her parents, and the farm she loved. She'd be trading her country and language for a series of unknowns. A million questions leapt into her mind. How long would it take her to wrestle with the language before she became competent? Wouldn't her inadequate speech and different accent immediately brand her an outsider; a second class citizen? Could she ever become a sophisticated urbanite like Stephen or would she always remain the country bumpkin, the farm girl, hankering after her humble roots? Would the people she met be friendly? Would she be able to fit in, or would she always remain a foreigner? Most important of all, did she really know Stephen after so short a time together? And could she really trust an unknown person with the rest of her life?

What if her marriage turned out to be a mistake? Would there be anyone to confide in; anyone she could turn to for advice, comfort and support? Confusion and uncertainty swamped her mind at the decision she had to make. But then, didn't she have to stick to the decision she'd already made? Hadn't she already told her mother that she had agreed to Stephen's proposal? Wouldn't it be too humiliating to change her mind? Oh God, she thought. What should she do? There seemed to be so many obstacles in her way. Yes, she'd have to be mad to marry Stephen. Despite these thoughts, she hurried back to the library determined to learn more about the place with which, like her father before her, she had already begun to fall in love.

She learnt from the Internet that "the Aboriginal culture of the First Nations people has made a significant contribution to BC's life and culture." It was a legacy passed down through the oral tradition of story telling, dancing, traditional ceremonies, drumming and art. These people lived in many of the coastal areas and islands where there was an abundance of food from the nearby forests and the sea. The first offered wildlife, fruit and vegetables. The second offered marine creatures. Their situation between forest and ocean, both of which provided a plentiful supply of food, permitted them to settle permanently. Once they had stored their food in the fall, they regarded winter as their time for ceremonial practices, story telling and artistic creation. Oh God, Serena thought on reading the paragraph, these words were chosen with the specific aim of seducing her.

"Rina, leave the dishes to me. Go talk to Stephen and decide on your future."

"Mama, how do you know that I haven't already decided?"

"Oh, I had a chat with Stephen." Her mother tried to sound as casual as possible, although she knew perfectly well what her daughter's reaction would be.

"About what?" The question was as blunt as her mother had expected.

"Well, I wanted to know how he felt about you and what his plans were," she told her daughter.

"What did he tell you?"

"He's in love with you and, as you know, wants to marry you."

"But...?" Serena asked.

Leesa couldn't stop herself from what she considered as a fight for her daughter's happiness.

"He thinks that perhaps you're too young and scatterbrained, and that you don't know what you really want." The words were like an unexpected whiplash against Serena's skin. Her hackles rose instantly, just as her mother had intended.

"Mama, did Stephen use those very words?" It took all her willpower to repress the anger boiling inside her, for Serena couldn't believe that Stephen had spoken those damning words about his intended bride.

"He said you're so fixated on the people and things here that you can't think straight. Perhaps," he thought, "you're too juvenile." This ought to make her mad enough to put a huge dent in her plans, Leesa said to herself.

Serena learnt from her reading that the potlatch was the most revered ceremony of the First Nations people. Their drumming, dancing, their carving of totem poles, traditions and beliefs all tell of the past. Their legends point to a 'Transformer Age' in which 'shape shifting' took place; where people and animals exchanged places. They believed that their Creator came to earth, disguised in the form of Coyote, Bear or Raven. In short, he was a trickster who came in disguise to see for himself whether or not the Aboriginal people had practiced the traditions they had been taught. Serena considered that these people were fortunate to have inherited so rich and wonderful a legacy. Myth, legend, reality and art were so skillfully blended together that they produced in their ceremonies an extremely colorful tapestry of events. What she read made her lean dangerously close towards accepting Stephen's proposal.

"Was that all Stephen said, Mama?" Serena had to put a choke hold on her rage to speak calmly. Yet, the tremor in her voice betrayed her. She thought: who was this jellyfish of a man to complain that she was too young and flighty to make an intelligent decision?"

"No dear." Then, to force an even more violent reaction from her daughter, she added:

"Leave it alone Rina, or you'll just get yourself more worked up."

"Serena hissed at her mother through clenched teeth:

"Mama, tell me what else he said?" Leesa breathed deeply, then told the final lies that would accomplish the break up she hoped for.

"He didn't think a farm girl would fit into his urban world. He would have to think over the matter before making a final decision." She knew the spin she put on Stephen's words would make Serena explode. I've done my best to prevent her from ruining her life with a bad marriage in a foreign country, Leesa said to herself. Please God, she thought, let her stay!

Serena kept pacing up and down the riverbank fuming with rage at the way in which Stephen had characterized her to her mother. She couldn't believe this was the same gentle, considerate man who'd admitted that he was besotted with her. How could he blow so hot and cold? How could he be such a traitor? One minute he was planting hot kisses on her lips and proposing marriage, and the next he was running to complain to her mother about her flakiness, and the confusion of her juvenile mind. The very thought of his going behind her back made her spitting mad. How could he insult and humiliate her to her own mother? And now, how could she have anything to do with so treacherous a Judas?

Chapter 39

She could just see her mother agreeing with everything that…that foreigner told her, then, speedily communicating the news to her father. What a humiliation! She knew that the only treatment the slimy foreigner deserved was to be totally ignored, left to his own devices. But how could she succeed in doing so, she asked herself. If she remained on the farm, he would pursue her as he always had, and then beg her forgiveness. She would not allow that to happen. She would simply go somewhere else; get clean out of his sight until he left Korea. He only had a short time left anyway. If she disappeared at once, she would never have to see him again.

"Hello?"
    "Hello Grandma Kim?"
    "Is that my little darling, Serena?"
    "Yes Grandma. Can I come over?"
    "Sure, baby girl. But your voice sounds strained. Is everything all right?"
    "I'll explain when I get there."
    "When are you coming?"
    "I'll just put my stuff in the car and come right over."
    "Looking forward to see you darling."

"Serena come in, come in," Grandma Kim said eagerly. "I knew something was wrong as soon as I heard that strangled voice I'd heard so many times before." The tears were streaming down Serena's face, she was so mad; so deeply humiliated.

"Come baby girl. Tell Grandma Kim what's wrong."

"Grandma," she began, but stopped abruptly at what she saw. The drained features, the slouched and shrunken figure of the woman before her was a poor semblance of the grandmother she knew. "Are you feeling well? You look like a ghost," Serena stated with the blunt honesty of youth.

"I haven't been sleeping too well, and seem to have lost my appetite these last few weeks," she lied. "But I'll be okay." The truth was that she too had heard the rumors of both present and past raked up by Serena's imminent departure from Korea with an unknown single man. The rumor mill had been reactivated and had brought back to Kim's mind all the horrifying images of incest that had weighed so heavily upon her and almost ruined her earlier life. Serena found it so comforting to be hugged by a loved one just when she needed it most. She poured out her problem.

"It's Stephen, Grandma," she blurted out in distress. "After he'd just told me how much he loved me and proposed marriage, he went skulking behind my back and complained to Mama that as a 'farm girl, I was too scatterbrained, juvenile and muddleheaded' to make up my mind."

"Are you sure dear? That doesn't sound like a young man in love who's serious enough to propose," Kim replied.

"Those were his exact words and they came from Mama herself." Then, as an afterthought, she added: "Why would Mama lie?"

"Aha," said Kim, "so this is your Mama's version? You haven't spoken to Stephen then?"

"Why should I, after the humiliating things he said, Gran. He betrayed me."

"Yes dear. Now as I remember, you'd like some hot chocolate, a hot bath, and grandma will come up and tuck you in," she said with an encouraging smile.

"Gran, I'm not ten years old anymore," she said smiling, "but, I'll settle for all three."

Serena saw her grandmother as a loving, generous and intelligent woman always there for her whenever life's hiccups intruded during her youth and early adolescence. She was exemplary in her religious faith, striving to maintain a loving bond with her husband and making a serious commitment to her church. Grandma Kim had mentioned to her jokingly about the rebellious attitude of her daughter during her teenage years, but only in the vaguest of terms. She had never provided Serena with a single detail. Of course, Serena could never see the loving mother she knew in the role of rebel.

Her grandma was a gardener of renown. For a number of years she had grown a selection of long stemmed white roses, solely for the decoration of the altar. Lately, she had extended her garden considerably and cultivated other colorful roses with the market in mind. After buying what she needed for the next season the remainder of the profit from their sales would go to feed and clothe the many volunteer gardeners and their families. Twice a week, Serena helped grandma make a series of bouquets of baby's breath, ferns and the green leaves of white lilies and long stemmed white roses. She and Grandma Kim then went to the church and replaced the previous week's fading bouquets on the altar with fresh ones. Because of Grandma's efforts, the church was always redolent of the perfume of roses. Indeed, the scent of roses in the church brought to the mind of many parishioners the image of Grandma Kim; gardener/choir master/organist/mother/wife/and relentless care giver to the farming community.

As an accomplished seamstress, and from just looking at the window displays in department stores, she created for her daughter, Leesa, some of the latest designer outfits. She had a definite flair for dressmaking so that no one could tell that her daughter's clothes were home made. Of course, while Serena knew that her mother's friends had often complimented her on her 'designer fashions,' she also knew that her mother had never confided to anyone that her designer/dressmaker had been her mother. Serena concluded that instead of being proud of her mother's skill, Leesa was ashamed to admit to her friends that her 'designer fashions' were really home made. Instead of seeing her mother as a very clever and talented couturier, Leesa was afraid that they would view her as a humble dressmaker.

She thought of the times when, from the pulpit, Father Murphy would compliment Gran for the time and effort she spent in growing and providing the church with her beautiful roses. He would mention her brilliant college career, during which she had majored in music, the reason he had co-opted her first as organist, then later as choir master. Whenever the priest commended her for the time and effort she spent in her church work, she would bow her head and her cheeks would flush with a pink glow, embarrassed at being singled out for praise. She preferred to remain anonymous, and left out of the limelight to attend Sunday Mass with her husband and daughter.

Serena said to her grandmother while she was being tucked in:

"Grandma, your life seems so simple, so serene and pure. You spend so much of your time helping others and taking care of the church. People like you are so lucky! You've showered your love on your husband and daughter who, I'm sure, never gave you cause for a moment's worry, right? Father Murphy has every right to praise you to the skies for all the good you do. If others were like you, the world would be a far better place."

"Right!" Her Gran answered after a moment, but was unable to accept the lie without revealing the sudden change that came over her features. When Serena saw her chin pucker, her facial muscles crumple, her eyes brim and the tears slide down her cheeks, she sat up abruptly in astonishment and alarm.

"Oh Gran, I'm so sorry. Did I ask an awkward question? I didn't mean to pry." She then continued to pry anyway.

"It had to be grandpa who gave you cause to worry, because I can't see Mama creating problems for anyone, especially for you, her mother." The simple statement caused her grandma's eyes to fill and silent tears to turn into loud sobs. And as Serena had unwittingly broached the subject that had caused so much pain, she listened to her grandma confessing the deep hurt that had lain dormant in her heart all those years. She didn't want to, nor could she discuss the subject in its completeness with her granddaughter, but she felt the necessity to clear her innocent husband of blame.

"It wasn't your Grandpa, Yong Sang, who had caused me so much worry and distress during our marriage Serena. It was your mother's rebellious nature and open hostility." But Kim knew when to stop and went no further in confessing the origin of those salacious rumors that had caused her so much shame and humiliation. On realizing the awkward situation she had caused, Serena finally held her tongue.

"Hello, John Ahn here."

"Hello John, this is Kim. Your daughter is here. She's mad and in deep distress."

"Why is she mad and in distress at your home?"

"She's staying away from Stephen."

"What did he do to her?"

"He ill spoke her to her mother."

"What did he say?"

"That she's a farm girl who's too juvenile, scatterbrained and confused to make up her mind about marrying him. She's too attached to all the people

434 · Clive N. Ramkeesoon

and things that she loves in Korea to leave; too scared at the thought of starting over in a new country."

John considered Stephen quite intelligent from the incisive questions he asked. He also thought him somewhat insincere, since he used little known information to appear knowledgeable. He wondered whether he was the right person for Serena. Yet, he knew that if he interfered, and tried to stop Serena from marrying Stephen, he would only succeed in driving her closer to him.

"Kim," he said, "let me call you back." But Kim stopped him before he hung up.

"John, your wife is my daughter," Kim began. "You know the way she idolizes Serena. Do you think she could be trying to prevent the marriage?"

"Why would you say that, Kim?"

"I found it strange that Serena heard the whole story from her mother, not from Stephen."

"I know what you're saying. But I don't think Leesa would go so far. I don't think she would create an obstacle to her daughter's happiness." John stated.

"Anyway, why don't you have a talk with Stephen yourself and get to the bottom of this?"

"All right, Kim. Thanks for letting me know Serena's safe and with you."

After putting down the receiver, John again tried to assess the character of the young man with whom he had recently spoken. He thought that Stephen was somewhat conceited since he asked questions in a way that was meant to display his knowledge. His tendency to offer compliments to make himself agreeable suggested that he was insincere. Yet, he did sum up situations quickly, and was by no means a fool. He seemed to be in love with Serena and it sounded unlikely that such a person would express his love for a woman, propose marriage to her, and then go behind her back to ill speak her to her mother. Such conduct, he felt sure, would be out of character for Stephen.

John took his wife into his study, sat her down, before speaking: "Thanks for lying to our daughter," he said in one of the coldest voices his wife had heard.

"Lying to our daughter? You must be mad to think that! I love her and want to keep her here with us." Her brows were knitted together in a frown.

"Love, ha! You lied to her, almost wrecked her future happiness. Is that what you call love? Love is never underhand, never deceitful." He was so mad that he had leaned over her and almost spat the words in her face. Deeply stung by his words and aggression, Leesa snapped back in sudden anger.

"What the hell do you know about the love of a mother for her child? What do you know about the pain and suffering of pregnancy that binds you to a child, Mr. Know-it-all? Have you ever carted around another person inside you for almost a year? Were you ever blown up like a blimp, riddled with back pain and so constipated that you thought you'd explode like a bomb? Were you ever so nauseated that you couldn't think clearly? Tell me, did the child inside you ever make you starve yourself because to eat was to erupt with vomit?"

"You're getting off the point," he remonstrated in icy tones. "You were supposed to be lecturing to me on the subject of love. You know that men never experience pregnancy symptoms. So why even mention them?" He asked, his voice softer, less sure of himself. His wife ignored his words as he began gnawing at his nails.

"Because when during childbirth you learn that the baby is in the wrong position—upside down—and that baby begins to rip your body apart, the doctors then advise that the only way to bring you relief, is to slice you open. When your suffering is so intense that you fear the life of your child is in danger, you learn that child is so precious that you never want to lose her. That, together with your nurturing her through all the years from birth to maturity, creates so powerful a bond that it is impossible to make anyone understand who hasn't had the experience." When she saw the look of sympathy in John's eyes, she stopped shouting, calmed down and finished with the remark:

"Nobody has the right to take that child away from you, nobody!" She found that her tirade had exhausted her and panting with the effort it took, she whispered:

"So John, what do you know about love?" Leesa asked less belligerently.

John realized that the difficulty of his wife's pregnancy and his own unexpected attack on her had little to do with their quarrel. She was seeing Serena's departure as another installment of divine punishment. Then, the vision of loneliness, of a future without Serena, had driven her over the edge. She was retaliating to his accusation as a means of venting her frustration and anger. He saw clearly that her love for Serena had developed into an obsession, an addiction, exposing all its unsavory symptoms. Rather than let her anger drive a deeper wedge between them, he decided to leave the scene. Before leaving however, he said gently: "Leesa, I know how much you love Serena, but you've gone too far. You've driven her away from home with your lies." Leesa was so dumbfounded to learn Serena had left home that she no longer tried to defend herself.

"Oh God," she moaned. "What have I done? John, where has she gone?"

"I won't say, until you admit that you lied. You have to apologize to her for doing so."

"If I admit that I lied, it would mean I was selfish enough to destroy her happiness." She could no longer look her husband in the eye.

"Leesa, the truth is that you almost destroyed her love for Stephen, her chance at marriage and a new life? And the fact is that's just the beginning," he added sternly.

"What else have I done?" She whispered in consternation.

"You've broken a commandment, bearing 'false witness' that was harmful to others. You even went further," he said with still more gravity.

"John, you're exaggerating to punish me. What could be worse than breaking a commandment?"

"You've tried to decide the destiny of others; to arrange their lives to suit your desires. You've been playing God, Leesa! You're guilty of pride, the first of the Seven Deadly Sins." His voice though still grave, was gentle and sad.

"Damn it John, don't you dare criticize me so brutally!" Leesa shouted her tormented reply at her husband as though she could repudiate his accusations by the sheer vehemence of her words. Yet, she kept looking everywhere but at her husband's face.

"You know I only acted out of love for Serena. I want her to stay here. She's brought us such happiness that I don't want to lose her. Is that so wrong?"

"What you said made her leave home?" The realization stung her so deeply that she burst into tears anew. When her sobbing stopped for a moment, she stated:

"John, I didn't think I was breaking a commandment or playing God, and you know I never meant to drive Serena away." She spoke with her back towards her husband and her sad response ended in a series of sobs before she added: "besides, she'll never accept my apology. She'll think I betrayed her and probably never speak to me again."

"That's a risk you'll have to take. Otherwise, I'll tell her myself. You need to show remorse and ask her forgiveness. If you don't, she'll never have anything to do with you."

"All right, I'll do what you ask. Where is she?"

"I'll take you to her. I want to be sure you tell her everything." His fingers were again in his mouth.

Chapter 40

As John was getting ready to drive his wife over to Kim, he tried to recall Father Murphy's words to his wife when she had asked him if good deeds might permit an evildoer to deserve forgiveness, redemption. John couldn't remember the exact words but he did recall the gist of the response. The priest began by saying that after his cruel act the aggressor would have to experience a sense of guilt and shame leading to deep feelings of remorse. As in the case of Mary Magdalene and the penitent thief, remorse would inspire the persecutor to undergo a radical change in his attitude making room in his heart for feelings of charity and compassion. But, he branched off, forgiveness must begin with yourself. If you can't forgive yourself, how do you expect anyone else to forgive you?"

"But what about forgiving the evildoer," my wife asked. Instead of replying, the priest seemed to turn a mental page for he began talking about grace, divine grace. And as the idea of grace crept into my mind so did the words of the hymn: "Amazing grace how sweet the sound that saved a wretch like me// I once was lost and now I'm found was blind but now I see//. Those words made me realize for the first time that grace is amazing because it is all about saving sinners. In other words, it is about forgiveness of others; redemption.

Indeed, in this context, Grace is a mysterious process since it would permit the persecutor to assimilate the true spirit of Christ. Only then would he be permitted to love those whose actions made them unlovable.

The priest then answered Leesa's earlier question directly. "Saving grace can neither be earned nor deserved." Evidently, the priest believed that charity and forgiveness could only be attained from above. Thus, grace was divine. Like the priest, John believed that guilt and shame were the weapons the evildoer used against himself to engender feelings of remorse. He also understood that Leesa was deeply sorry for the wrong she had done, and believed that her feelings of remorse were sincere. He hoped Serena could be persuaded through her charity and compassion to forgive her mother. However, he knew Serena's attitude towards betrayal and realized the hurt might perhaps be too deep and fresh in her mind for her to overlook the wrongdoing. As he was about to leave home, the phone rang.

"Hello, John Ahn here."

"Hello Mr. Ahn, may I speak to Serena please."

"Mona? Ahn stated, stunned that the rumor monster dared to call his home. Serena is at her grandmother." His anger at the gall of Mona calling to ask for Serena made him add. "And even if she were here, I'm sure she wouldn't want to speak to you."

"I didn't think you'd recognize my voice, Mr. Ahn."

"Well I did, and can't help wondering why *you*, of all people, would dare to call the Ahn home after all the nasty rumors that you and your family have spread about us? Why would you imagine that Serena would even want to speak to the friend she refers to as "the deceitful viper?" He didn't try to mask his anger. Mona's response came back equally fast and angry.

"Don't you dare judge me, Mr. Ahn. You know nothing of the circumstances that prompted my action." Listening to the hiss in her voice, Ahn was reminded of a serpent; cold, slithering and poisonous. The angry response kicked his annoyance up a notch. He remembered how deeply hurt, angry and humiliated Serena had been at Mona's betrayal; how she had brooded for days on end, suffering at the treachery, the deceit of someone she had trusted.

"On the contrary, young lady, I know you're a Judas. You turned your back on Serena when she was shunned by everyone else and depended on you, her best friend, for support. There's nothing more to know about *your* circumstances?" He shouted into the phone.

"I'll let Serena be the judge of that! And thank you Mr. Ahn," she spat. He then heard the loud click as the line went dead and he began wondering what on earth would prompt Mona to call Serena.

"Phone call for you, Serena," her grandmother called out as she passed Serena the phone.

"Hello, this is Serena." There was a long silence form the other end and an audible intake of breath before any answer came.

"Serena, please don't hang up." A rush of anger constricted Serena's throat as she recognized Mona's voice. Then, calming down with great restraint, she replied in the sternest of voices:

"Give me one good reason why I shouldn't hang up!"

"Serena, can I come see you. I can't say what I need to on the phone." Mona's pleading tone mollified Serena somewhat, but she couldn't help asking:

"Why do you want to talk to me now? When everyone ostracized me at school and I turned to my best friend for support, you treated me like a leper and fled the scene. Mona why is my leprosy so suddenly cured?"

"You're making this very hard for me Serena."

"Hard? Hard for you? Serena shouted. "After the way you betrayed me. What the hell did you expect? That I'd be smiling sweetly with arms extended in welcome? I'm surprised you have the gall to call me."

"Perhaps when you hear what I have to say you'll understand." Mona said. In the smallest of voices she added: "Please let me come and talk to you. At least listen to what I have to say." The pleading tone and the catch in Mona's throat put a choke hold on Serena's anger. She relented, fought to get her emotions under control, and calmed down.

"Okay," she said. "I'm at my grandmother. Meet me there."

"Can I come right over please? I'm speaking from my car." Again the plea in her voice and words made Serena pause to wonder what had caused Mona to make so abrupt an about face.

Mona's phone call sent Serena's mind reeling back to their last quarrel and the vicious things Mona had said about her and her parents. She remembered how Mona's cruelty had destroyed Serena's peace of mind sending her racing to her favorite spot. Her mind had been in turmoil piecing together the outrageous falsehoods she had heard. She had never thrown herself at any man, and she was certainly not a slut as Mona had stated. Perhaps her statements about her parents were also false. But she seemed so positive, even stating that she had checked. Yet, the semblance of Mona's certainty gave Serena pause. Could the mother whom she knew as so loving and devoted be a scarlet woman? Could the loving and devoted wife she knew, have betrayed her husband-to-be before her marriage? Her knowledge of Leesa as mother and wife made Mona's slander incredible. It was equally incredible that her father was not her real father.

And then, she remembered grandma's saying it had been Leesa, not Yong Sang, who had caused her such heartache. Then, into her mind crept the sneaky idea: could the slander be true?

She was forced to play hardball, asking herself the toughest of questions. Did she want to know if the mother she loved so deeply, who loved her without reservation, and who had labored so hard to help in her recovery, was a scarlet woman? And the gentle man who has loved and respected her all her life, did she want to know if he was her father? Yes, she answered. For, if he wasn't, wouldn't she want to know who was? And wouldn't that answer the question about her mother?

As she deliberated on the issues, it became clear that learning the truth would be difficult. As a beloved daughter, she could hardly confront her parents with Mona's slander. Whether true or false, such a confrontation would be a grave betrayal. It would be as embarrassing to her parents as to her. Another question arose in her mind. Would it serve any purpose to discover the truth that could destroy the two people she loved most?

Further, knowledge of the truth had the potential of affecting her adversely. After her recent illness, would her mind be able to withstand the upheaval the truth might reveal? Could it affect her sanity? She then asked herself: Did the past really matter? Since she'd be leaving Korea to start a new life abroad, could it affect her adversely? Yet, despite all the logic, she would still want to know. Instead of confronting her parents, she'd have to find the truth by other means. After much deliberation, it seemed that the person sure to know the facts would be Grandma Kim. Besides, the truth could not possibly affect her. So, with the impulsiveness of youth, she went to her grandma.

At the sight of her grandmother, Serena had a worse shock than her previous one. How could she have missed how ill Grandma looked?

"Grandma, you don't look at all well. You've lost more weight, and those circles under your eyes are much darker. Haven't you been sleeping well? Haven't you regained your appetite? What you really need is rest and relaxation. Let me tuck *you* into bed for a change. And don't worry I'll get what I came for another time." Kim looked like an empty husk, eaten away from the inside. Her skin, pulled tightly over her bones, made her skeletal in appearance. How could Serena have missed the radical change affecting her grandmother? Had she been so wrapped up in her own problems? Was she so selfish that she'd become immune to the problems of others; even the members of her own family?

"Serena, tell me what you came for." Grandma's stern voice made her unload her burden. She came to the point immediately."

"Did Mama advance the date of her wedding?"

Oh my God, she's heard the worst, her grandmother realized, and she's come to me for confirmation. Well, I have to protect her and her parents. She won't learn anything from me. She paused for a long moment before answering.

"Yes, she did, and she had good reason to do so!" In the silence Kim took to collect her thoughts before continuing to lie, Serena shot out her next question.

"Was Mama pregnant before her wedding?"

"Of course not! Wherever did you get such an idea, Serena? It's certainly not true."

"Are you sure Grandma? How could you know?"

"I'm positive!" She lied. "She had her period on her wedding day." That should put an end to her speculation, she thought.

"You have to understand Serena," her grandma continued, "your father is a very private man and his businesses were going through hard times. Your mother wanted a huge, very expensive wedding but your father explained that a huge wedding would have bankrupted him. Knowing our financial circumstances, your father offered to pay for the wedding expenses. We agreed, but also helped financially. That was the reason they brought forward the wedding date, and had a small civil ceremony instead of the big expensive wedding your mother had planned. There were no invited guests and all the gifts were returned." Serena stared at her grandmother in silence. The frown Serena wore seemed to disturb her grandmother forcing a further confession from her.

"Little one, we live in a very small community where gossip abounds. Tongues run riot when the incidents surrounding a marriage flout local tradition without any rational explanation. All sorts of speculations surface. No one would expect your father to make his reasons public." She breathed a deep sigh before adding: "In the same way, Serena, a schoolgirl like you, rushing from your parents' home, leaving Korea with an unmarried stranger, supposedly to get married and live in a foreign country, started the rumor mill going full blast all over again. It also raked up all the nasty speculation circulating about your parents in the past. We who know the truth won't be bothered by such gross falsehood, but that doesn't stop the scandalous rumors or the speculation." There, she thought, that should put Serena's mind at rest. Under the pressure of what she was hearing Serena's fingers were twirling in a rhythmical jig.

The raking up of those old rumors had led Kim to reassess the past confrontation she'd had with her own daughter. It now seemed clear to her that Leesa had lied to protect herself and her father, just as she had just done to protect her granddaughter. Those were the thoughts that would come back to haunt her. Those were the thoughts that would cause a further loss of appetite and destroy her sleep. Those were the thoughts that would spawn even more lurid and turbulent nightmares.

"Oh my God, Mona! What happened to you? You look like death warmed over," Serena blurted out. In truth, Mona's deathly pale color, serious weight loss, and gaunt features threw Serena completely off guard. The concern and compassion in Serena's voice shook Mona's resolve. On her way over she had steeled herself, determined not to go to pieces and humiliate herself by breaking down before Serena. But the flood of sympathy in Serena's voice broke the dam. Mona burst into tears and Serena could do nothing but hold out her arms. Mona rushed into them and the two former friends hugged each other tightly.

With her arms around Mona, Serena could feel she was all skin and bone. Her corpse-like color and almost skeletal body showed that she was evidently facing some catastrophe and going through deep suffering. While Mona blubbered in her arms, Serena wondered for the second time what kind of calamity could have so transformed Mona's appearance. Had her parents both died in some terrible accident? Had their investments or their crops failed, or had their house burnt to the ground? But no such news had come to the Ahns. She waited while a very agitated Mona got control of herself and was ready to talk.

"Sorry about the blubbering, Serena," she said with an apologetic and nervous giggle. "And thanks for letting me come to talk with you after the way I let you down. It wasn't my fault really. You see, I've always tried to obey my mother. She warned me that any further relationship with you would bring scandal to me and to my family." Serena was exasperated at so flimsy an excuse. She was tempted to ask Mona whether or not she had a mind of her own, then thought better of it.

"Believe me, Serena. At the time, I didn't realize what a shitty excuse that was until I found myself in your shoes."

"You were raped?" The question burst from Serena's lips.

"No. This is not about rape, she replied too quickly."

"What then?" Serena demanded with a quizzical stare.

"You remember the clandestine meetings with the farmhand hunk I told you I was seeing?"

"You fell in love with him and he left you?"

"Yes, I fell for him. But no, he didn't leave me."

"What then?" Serena asked, exasperated that she had to tug the information out of Mona.

"My parents caught us and kicked him out."

"Oh my God!" That would have been so-ooo embarrassing, Serena thought, then asked: "So what are you planning to do?"

"I don't know yet. That's why I'm here. My parents won't have anything to do with me; haven't talked to me in a week. They want me to leave home."

"They're kicking you out?"

"Yes. I have another week to pack up and leave."

"But why? An affair that nobody knows about is no big deal." Serena stated.

"Well, it is with me. They're afraid of the scandal."

"But Mona, no one else knows, so there won't be a scandal."

"Oh yes, there will be!

"Why?"

"I'm pregnant."

"You're what? Mona! Don't tell me you didn't take precautions?"

"Yes, I did. But not every time. Sometimes we got carried away." Mona continued to lie, too ashamed to let Serena know about her brutal rape and rejection by their farmhand.

"Carried away?" Serena whispered. "You must be mad, Mona."

"You'll find that when passion overtakes you, it sweeps you away," she paused and then added, "nothing else seems to matter; nothing."

"What about the farmhand? Doesn't he love you and want to marry you?"

"Serena, he's been kicked out, driven away by my irate parents. They even threatened to take him to court. Besides, he doesn't even know I'm pregnant."

"So contact him and let him know. For Christ sake, he's the father."

"Serena, I don't want to marry a farmhand. I don't want to have anything to do with a farm for the rest of my life. Can you understand that?"

"Yes. So what have you decided? Why come to see me?"

"To remind you of the promise you made." She stopped the reply about to come from a stunned Serena and begged her former friend to listen and let her finish before answering.

"All right. I'm listening," Serena said.

"You made a solemn promise that we'd both go to Seoul and share an apartment. I'm here to beg you to keep that promise. Serena, it's the only chance I have to get out of this horrible situation. I'm sure you can understand. I've lost my appetite. I can't eat or sleep. My parents despise me and refuse to speak to me. Oh God, Serena, I'm so alone." Mona was again blubbering. "Please don't forsake me when I need you most," she begged. There was a battle going on between hope and despair in Mona's eyes. At the same time, a slow burning was taking place at the back of her throat as she fought against the tears that again threatened.

"Do you know how painful it is to be totally alone? To live all by yourself, with no one you know to talk to, or share opinions with? You'd have no one to whom you can bitch about the inequalities of life?" Serena cut her off. Mona's words brought back all the hell and heartbreak she had suffered during the weeks after her friend's betrayal.

"What about having your best friend betray you? What about having 'friends' who ostracize you? What about the isolation of living alone; ignored by everyone as though you didn't exist; making you feel invisible? The punishment of Serena's isolation made her oblivious to Mona's suffering. She spat out:

"You of all people deserve to learn the true meaning of isolation, how it gets under your skin, seeps into your flesh and bone, shrivels you up inside and out. Since you believe that no one cares about you, you soon learn that you don't matter. You feel useless and deserve to be ignored. Suddenly, your life has no purpose. Your one wish then is to destroy yourself." Despite Serena's harsh words, one glance at Mona's anguished appearance brought back the compassion she felt at the plight of her old friend. Not knowing what to say or how she could help, she took the bull by the horns.

"Mona, if it's money you need, I can help you out. And if things get tough, you don't have to repay me."

"I'm not here for your money, Serena. My parents will give me whatever I need, as long as I leave home and go so far away that no scandal touches them. I can't for the life of me understand why they are so deathly afraid of scandal. After all, it's just words often spoken only in secret."

Chapter 41

"So what you need is a friend, someone with whom you can talk. Otherwise, you'll be alone, cut off from everyone. You'll go to bed at night and dream of seeing strangers wherever you turn. Mona, it'll get really scary. Instead of blending in, you'll be standing out. Your difference will draw all eyes stabbing into you like daggers. You'll feel exposed and vulnerable like a bug under a microscope; an inferior species. Your confidence and self-esteem will desert you, and you'll wish you could evaporate into thin air. That being impossible, you'll just want to shrivel up and die." It suddenly dawned on Serena that Mona was well aware of the isolation being described, for with each of Serena's awful forecasts, Mona flinched as thought taking a hit. Her features had then become even more gaunt and corpse-like. The realization made Serena stop her cruel prediction, before adding:

"Mona. I'm sorry to see you hurting, but there's little I can do to help. My situation has changed completely since I made that promise. In spite of the way you treated me, I would stand by what I said. I would go with you to Seoul..." Mona cut her off.

"I hear a 'but' in your statement."

"But I can't." Serena said sorrowfully.

"Why can't you?" Mona challenged, anger making her shout. "What you mean is you won't. So after all, you're just big talk and promises. When it comes to the crunch you're just like me."

"Just like you, Mona?" Serena answered almost choking with anger. "I was raped. That means violated and forced against my will. You, Mona entered willingly into a sordid sexual relationship. So don't you dare compare our situations. There's no similarity between us whatever. None!"

"You're deliberately misunderstanding me, Mona shot back. When I said you're just like me, I meant that you too are a betrayer, a treacherous Judas. At least I was obeying my parents' warning. What's your excuse, Judas?" Mona challenged angrily.

"I'm getting married. That's my excuse. My situation has changed. I'm going to Canada to get married." As she thought of her decision and the happiness it promised, her anger drained away.

"If you don't believe me, I'll introduce you to Stephen, my fiancé."

"So that's the male stranger everyone's talking so much about," she mused. "No thanks." Mona's eyes bore a look of total defeat. With head bowed and shoulders slumped, she turned and began walking away in slow hesitant steps, so that Serena could sense the dread inspired by the uncertainty of her future. She caught the terror displayed in Mona's awkward body language at the trial of loneliness she was steeling herself to confront. Serena became filled with compassion. "Mona," she called out with an audible catch in her voice. Mona stopped walking away, but she didn't turn around.

"We shouldn't part like strangers with this barrier between us. We're both going away and we'll probably never see each other again. Can't we remain friends?" Serena's voice was pleading. The words of sympathy were exactly what Mona needed to hear. She turned around and the two friends, all differences forgotten, rushed into each others arms.

All thoughts of Mona vanished from Serena's mind when she saw her parents get out of their car with her mother in tears leaning against her father.

"Papa, Mama, what's wrong?"

"Oh God Serena, I'm so sorry. I've come to apologize to you and beg your forgiveness. I'm so sorry," she said falling to her knees.

"Mama," Serena started, trying to lift her mother from the floor. "Why are you apologizing to me? What have you done?"

"Oh God Serena, I lied to you. I twisted Stephen's words. True, he was anxious to learn your decision, but he never called you scatterbrained or said you were immature or a juvenile farm girl." There was a long silence and Serena's face grew grave, hard and angry before she could reply.

"You lied to me, Mama?" Serena asked with disbelief, her voice stern, cold and hard. She then repeated: "You lied to *me*?"

"Yes Serena, but I never meant to hurt you, or destroy your chance at happiness. Please believe that, please," she begged, but her eyes couldn't meet those of her daughter.

Serena again remained silent for a long moment, her face ugly with shock. Before she could speak, her mother begged her to listen.

"Rina, I'm so sorry. I didn't want you to ruin your life with a bad marriage. But most of all, I just couldn't face the prospect of losing you. My life would never be the same..." She was not finished before Serena broke in.

"And what about my life, Mama? Have you any idea of the pain you've caused me? Mama, you have a cruel streak. First you betrayed my father and now you've betrayed me."

"Betrayed your father? What the hell are you talking about?"

"Don't try to deny it, Mama! Mona told me the conversation she overheard between her parents about you."

"Serena, I don't know what you're talking about," she said, but her voice had lost all conviction. Her eyes were again downcast.

"You suddenly brought forward your wedding date by almost four months."

"I had personal reasons Serena. Ask your father. He'll tell you the truth."

"Stop lying Mama! I didn't believe my saintly mother could stoop to lies, betrayal and infidelity. Do you know what everyone's been speculating about since my birth?"

"What Serena?" Her mother asked, but her voice held a tone of defeat.

"That I'm illegitimate. That my father is not my father." Her mother decided she had to tough it out and said with renewed conviction:

"Serena I hope you're not stupid enough to believe the lies that Mona and her parents are spreading." She hadn't been prepared for her daughter's reply.

"So instead, I should be smart enough to believe your lies? Can you imagine what you've done to me, mother?" At that point, Leesa gave up all pretense of arguing with her daughter and broke down.

"Serena, I'm so sorry, Leesa sobbed. You know how I love and want to protect you from harm." She blubbered. "Can't you forgive me?" She pleaded.

"Mama, you made me curse and desert Stephen. But it wasn't he who betrayed me. It was you." The accusation set her mother back on her knees, groveling.

"I didn't mean to hurt or make you unhappy, Serena, you must believe that."

"You made me hate the man I love. You almost wrecked my marriage plans; my chance at a new beginning. You never considered my happiness for a moment. Your only thought was for yourself."

"Oh Serena, I've always tried to protect you. I never meant to hurt you. I love you..." But before she could continue, Serena cut in. "Love Mama? You don't know the meaning of that word. Love is a free gift of oneself. Your love doesn't give. It's a taking, a total grasping, a possession."

"Serena my love for you is pure. I'd die for you."

"What you call love is venomous. It poisons your mind so that you do evil things to those you say that you love. You contaminate, Mama! You kill!"

"Oh Serena," her mother wailed, "I never thought I'd hear such soul-shattering words from you." Kim, standing nearby, looked sadly at her groveling daughter, and knowing the love she felt for Serena, helped Leesa to her feet. She hugged her daughter, trying to comfort her, hugging her and patting her back as she had done so many times before.

"Mama," Serena said with icy sternness, "I'll say no more to you.' She then turned her back. "Papa, I'll go home now. Later, Stephen and I will tell you our plans." As she left the room, her father was comforting his wife, trying to stop her whimpering and her tears.

"Serena, I'm ashamed of the way you behaved towards your mother. I can understand your surprise and anger at her betrayal, but you didn't need to show such hostility and disrespect. You behaved like a fishwife. Don't you understand? She loves you and was trying to protect you."

I'm sorry Dad, but I was so angry that I lost control. I promise it won't happen again."

"I trust you'll keep your promise Serena because you behaved abominably. That aside, I never believed you would accept a marriage proposal from Stephen."

"Dad, you mean I'm breaking the taboo of Korean tradition leaving here with a man, and without the blessing of marriage. Together with my rape, I'll have committed the worst crimes in the eyes of our community, right?"

"The violation was not your fault. But you are flying in the face of tradition. The fallout of your actions upon us, your family, is *not* what concerns us most. We are far more worried about *your* welfare. Listen to the questions that plague us: do you really know Stephen after so short a time together? Have you thought through the risk of spending the rest of your life with a person you hardly know, in a country where you'll be a foreigner, unable to cope adequately with the language? Are you fully aware of the ramifications that result from your act? You have never before had an emotional relationship with a man. Do you, still a teenager, really know your heart? After your serious illness can you take on the full responsibility of a wife? These questions seriously disturb your mother and me. Of course, while we would both like you to stay, we would not stand in the way of your happiness. I hope you believe that, Serena."

"Dad, I don't know Stephen as well as I should, but he has been compassionate and understanding about my gang rape, even after I showed him the ghastly paintings. As for the language, I don't think that will pose a problem. I'm a quick study. But in spite of what you say, you and,—and your wife, are more distressed by the shame that will fall upon you because of my actions." Her father couldn't help hearing the hostility in her daughter's reference to her mother and responded angrily.

"Serena, don't make me ashamed of you for the evil thoughts you harbor against your mother. Have you forgotten the promise you just made to stop being hostile towards her? Have you forgotten whose love, devotion and advice pulled you from death's door? You must know that you owe her your life, a debt that is impossible to repay! You must know that she lied trying to protect you from making a horrible mistake. Besides, how could you forgive Mona for her betrayal and refuse to grant your mother the same consideration?" Serena didn't know that he had seen her embracing Mona. But with youthful stubbornness, she replied:

"Dad, leave that aside. Tell me if my leaving as an unmarried Korean teenager with Stephen, a Caucasian, is what really disturbs you."

"I can't leave that aside. I don't know what has come over you? You've never been so disobedient or disrespectful to your parents before. How can you so casually ignore your unconscionable behavior? You're not acting like the daughter I knew." He paused to take a breath. "Now, as to your marriage plan, I can honestly say that I'm very displeased that, unmarried, you plan to leave your country with a man who, by your own admission, you hardly know. But I am also aware of what he is offering you—love, marriage and a fresh start—with the exciting adventure of life in a new country. However, I repeat: do you really know Stephen? Can you trust a virtual stranger with the rest of your life? Have you thought that in the event of problems between you, problems that are bound to occur, you'll have no one to turn to for support or advice? These are the questions that plague your mother and me. The slander, we can deal with and ignore, just as we've done in the past." At this point, he admitted to Serena something that he should have told her many times but had said only once before. "After all, you are the most precious person in our lives, and your welfare is what we consider most. As you must know by now, *we* both love you dearly, more than anything else in the world."

"Dad, I love and admire you very much, as I always have, but I'm not sure how I feel about mother yet. Will you give me your blessing and wish me good luck? And don't worry too much. You know I can take care of myself. Above all, don't let slander worry you unduly. You can always depend on me to do the right thing." Since she seemed completely unaware of the irony of her words her father thought it was time to fire off a couple of salvos of his own:

"Doesn't it trouble you that your irresponsible decision to leave Korea with an unmarried man is causing so much malicious gossip? Don't you care the slightest bit it's your family that has to bear the burden of the slander you are causing?

"Well Leesa, they'll be leaving once they've finished their packing."

"How long," she asked.

"A day or so."

"Won't she accept my apology? Won't she forgive me? Won't they even come and say goodbye, John?"

"I don't think so. But you should understand that accepting an apology and forgiving the wrongdoer is not the same thing."

"What do you mean? If she accepts my apology doesn't it means that she's forgiven me."

"Not at all. If she accepted your apology, it simply means she agrees that you are sorry for what you did. Forgiveness is another thing entirely. She still bears the rancor at the pain you've inflicted. Remember you made her curse Stephen and desert him. Anyway, we had a long talk."

"What did she say?"

"Stephen assured me they'll get married as soon as possible."

"Not Stephen, Serena!" His wife said harshly with expectation stamped on her sorrowful face.

"She said I was not to worry," John replied. Leesa caught the singular "I."

"She didn't mention me at all?" Her tone was almost begging. There was disbelief in her voice.

"Well, she told me her plans. When she didn't mention you, I told her again that she should forgive you; repeated that she should do so before she left." When John then remained silent, Leesa demanded angrily:

"What did she reply? How can she leave without at least saying goodbye?" To spare his wife's feelings, John told her to let the matter rest. He knew it would be better if she didn't know her daughter's reaction.

"John," she almost spat through clenched teeth, "Tell me, damn it!"

"As you know, she considers betrayal an unforgivable sin…" His words hung in the air.

"But John, I don't understand. First, how could she disobey you, her father? Then, how could she so blatantly disrespect me and my wishes again and again? Besides, I lied because I love her and didn't want marriage and life abroad to destroy her. I wanted her to stay here, to be a part of my life, our lives. Now, I'll never see her again, she moaned bitterly. She won't even invite me to the wedding. Oh John, I'll miss her so," she continued, her heart breaking between sobs.

"Shh darling, I'll take care of you."

"John," she wailed, "Serena came out of my body; she's a vital part of me."

"Shh darling, I can only try to imagine how you feel."

"She is the spitting image of me, with my mop of black hair from the moment she was born. Our eyes are exactly the same shape and color, and she walks with a fluid motion, just like me." Leesa continued to mourn the loss of her daughter through parallels of their similarity.

"Shh dear, I know."

"When happy, she even skips and struts like I used to do. But when angry, she's silent and remote; her face as hard as stone. Have you noticed that she tilts her head when listening, and smiles just like me? Oh John, her leaving without a word to me hurts so deeply." Leesa was already fighting against the separation. Her voice, a harsh whisper, was burdened with bottomless sorrow.

"Shh darling. Don't take on so."

"John, she's cut out my heart." And in an afterthought she added: "Did you tell her that anything she needs she can have? Did you give her a blank check?"

"Yes dear, but she refused it." She said her husband will take care of her needs."

"Oh John, she's turned her back on us. And it's my entire fault." Feeling guilty, Leesa couldn't face her husband.

Before going to Korea, Stephen had always styled himself as a confirmed urbanite, a man who felt at home in any city. He was comfortable in a setting where the streets were bordered by scads of buildings, where the sidewalk felt hard under his feet, where he saw gas stations, department stores, groceries and shopping malls vying with each other for prominent street corners. He was used to the wail of police, ambulance, and fire engine sirens stopping traffic as they wailed their warning from a distance. Above all, he was accustomed to seeing people—pedestrians crowding sidewalks, men and women rushing to their personal destinations, people milling about in malls or alighting from buses and trains. He felt comfortable amid the loud hum of vehicles of every description—cars, trucks, motorbikes and buses—clogging the streets and making them impassable at rush hour.

Serena's conscience kept troubling her and she was in deep distress. She thanked God that her mother was unaware of the resumption of her friendship with Mona and bitterly regretted having rejected both her parents' plea for forgiveness. She couldn't believe she had disobeyed her father and shown such disrespect to her mother. She couldn't believe that she had forgiven the betrayal of her friend, but had refused her mother the same consideration. As her father had reminded her, her mother had been her constant support; had made Serena the central pillar of her life. During her illness she had often vacated her husband's bed to lie at Serena's side. She was always ready to comfort and protect her during her troubled sleep. And whenever Serena's nightmares struck, terrifying her with their reality, it was again her mother who was always there to hug, comfort her and soothe her jangled nerves. Her mother had never reeled off the hackneyed suggestions: 'that these things happen,' or 'that everything would be all right,' or 'just give it time.' Instead, she had held Serena close, letting her vent her anger, agreeing with her every word as her daughter railed against the hardships of life and the calamity that had singled her out for punishment. Her mother had always been there to comfort her in her hour of need. *She* had never abandoned her daughter.

Stephen had no knowledge of the outdoors, having grown up with the hum of city life pulsing through his veins. Yet, his vacation in Korea had brought about a radical change in his thinking. In that tiny town Stephen found himself isolated from city life for an extended period and living on a farm sandwiched between animals and cultivated fields. At first, he felt buried in the heart of nature. But place and time had conspired to bridge the divide between him and the environment. Helping Serena feed the animals milk the cows or mucking out Will's stall had made his nose familiar with the odor of the pigsty, the paddock and the barn. Listening to her preoccupation with wildlife habitat and her constant discourse about the tight bond between man and nature had made him feel more familiar with the outdoors and more comfortable in his new setting. He had walked with her through the orchards and sampled the fruit. He had skirted the acres of grain and vegetables. He had fed the carp in the paddies or just sat with her on the bank watching and listening to the river gurgling along over a deep pool or gushing over its shallow bed. Finally, she had exposed him to the wild animals in her paintings and upgraded his understanding of the changes that take place in the environment. Above all, he had learnt the basic principles underlying the process of evolution. He had to admit that she had helped to open his eyes and mind to a very different world.

Although pretending otherwise, Serena was ashamed of the way she had behaved. She hadn't yet disclosed to her father that she had wanted to make peace with her mother but every time she tried, something changed her mind at the last minute, stopping her cold. She couldn't put her finger on what was happening to her but she just hadn't been able to do what she wanted. Although she kept asking herself how dare she disobey a parent? How dare she disrespect her mother's wishes? How dare she criticize her conduct when she was equally guilty of similar shortcomings? Hadn't she forgiven Mona? Hadn't she disobeyed both her parents by flouting Korean protocol, the central pillar of her training? Wouldn't her actions cause a tidal wave of scandal to engulf her parents while she would be abroad, safe from the vitriol of wagging tongues? Thus, wasn't she equally guilty of hypocrisy? How dare she don the mask of the innocently accused?

"John, the daughter I love hates me. The same child I would give my life for. Can you believe that? Serena really hates me! And after the lifetime I've spent showering my love upon her. Isn't that ironical? When her husband remained silent, she asked:

"John, tell me. Is it a crime to love someone too much?"

Leesa's reaction to Serena's imminent departure, her breaking of Korean protocol and her refusal to obey him or her mother were like arrows piercing John's heart. He could find no way to stanch the flow of blood. His eyes filled as he watched his wife's suffering. Apart from trying to comfort her, there was nothing more he could do to eradicate her pain other than to offer his sympathy, closeness and comfort. The thought that Serena was the cause of her mother's suffering, struck him like a stab in the back from a loved one.

Stephen believed the sudden change in his thinking had come on a day when he was sitting on the river bank listening to Serena describe the natural scene. It was on an early morning just before sunrise that she made him see the setting through her eyes.

"Look Stephen" she pointed in excitement: "mist creeping gently over valley, slowly glowing golden in sunlight" was the statement that got his attention. He found her next exclamations equally arresting: "Sunlit mist covering landscape like glowing counterpane setting whole sections ablaze." At that precise moment the sun began to creep over the mountainside. Listening to Serena's near poetic language made him focus more intensely upon what she was describing. He gazed and gazed until the scene she had described suddenly materialized before his eyes. A sense of serenity washed over him. It made him aware of the power nature wields over the human spirit, inspiring him with the quiet joy of its magnificence; its simple grandeur. It was Serena who had opened his eyes and mind to nature's magic and its mystery.

Yet, the turn of events that had catapulted him from his dishonest urban existence into the simplicity, the honesty of life on a Korean farm, brought with them an inability to fully understand the changes that his character had undergone. How could his deceit and dishonesty, so natural to him, have so silently slipped away? How did his earlier obsession with a profit motive disappear as though it had never existed? How could his new burgeoning love for the natural environment almost equal his love for an urban world? Perhaps most important, after his success with so many sophisticated women, how could he have become captivated by and even besotted with a naive farm girl?

"My mother was a very beautiful woman, unlike my father," Stephen stated continuing his confession to Serena. "She had long golden hair set in ringlets about her face and her figure resembled superb Greek sculpture. She was especially proud of my appearance, seeing my strong resemblance to her as a special tribute. Since she loved both my father and me, she went to great lengths to wrap my father in a warm blanket of excuses, mostly lies, in an attempt to deflect the cruelty of his criticism.

'Your father really loves you,' she would say, 'but his war wounds make him irritable and he drinks a bit too much to stifle the pain. Stephen, you should realize that liquor and pain do not mix very well. They account for your father's undue harshness.' She was a loving mother, and tried her best to make amends by lavishing on me, all her warmth, tenderness and love."

Chapter 42

"Stephen fortunate having a so loving mother," Serena told him, her guilt growing as she thought of how she was repaying hers for all the love that had been lavished upon her. Stephen hurried on, hoping to help the burden he was still carrying slip from his shoulders.

"The family was financially comfortable, and over the years I found that each time I approached my father for a favor–a toy, later, a bicycle, still later, an increase in my allowance, and finally a car–my father's refusal would goad my mother to grant my request. Yet, I didn't see her conduct as proof of her love and generosity. Ironically, heeding my father's lessons, I interpreted my mother's conduct as what I should expect from 'the weaker female of the species.' I despised her for it and quickly learnt to use her love as a weapon to pry from her everything material I ever wanted."

"Oh Stephen, that so wrong! You mother goodness deserving you respect, sympathy, love. Serena's words made her realize that she was preaching as much to herself as to Stephen while he hung his head, and continued.

"Of course, my father saw his wife's behavior as countermanding his authority and bitter quarrels ensued. I realized that I was responsible for causing the rift between my parents that kept growing wider and wider. The heavy burden of guilt I carried helped to twist my already unstable mind. I believed that my mother taught me a lesson in the way that women behave and I promised myself that I would never become emotionally involved with any woman. Instead, I continued to play the dominant role in my relationship with women, which was always that of manipulator. Serena's features immediately took on the cold disapproval of a stone statue. Stephen hastened to correct his mistake.

"My darling, what I'm trying to explain is that the cruelty of my father and the love of my mother, warred with each other in my brain and I believe, negatively affected my mind. Their conduct tended to alienate me from them, making me fall back on what I considered my personal assets. I believed that my powerful physique, my charm and classical good looks gave me all the attributes I needed to take advantage of other lesser mortals, especially 'the weaker female of the species.' The success I achieved with women following this belief soon qualified me as the ultimate con man. It wasn't long before I became the quintessential predator." Serena couldn't believe that the man she had fallen in love with could have been such a cruel, calculating and reprehensible human being. She told him so.

"Darling, I agree. That's exactly what I've been trying to explain. I became a shameful and selfish person, always on the lookout for profit, always on the take. My motive in coming here was also an attempt to gain some sort of profit from my uncle's friend, the very well-heeled business tycoon and corporate executive, your father. But after meeting you, all that changed. Your sincerity, honesty and overall goodness has made me see the error of my ways. Darling, I will do my best to be worthy of you and of your love. From now on, I'll always try to do what is right rather than what will further my interests, or bring me profit. Do you understand what I'm saying?"

"Oh Stephen, hearing that promise making Serena happy. And she not person so angelic as Stephen believing. At best, she trying make him proud."

"So John, it has finally come to this." Leesa's trembling voice carried to her husband the anguish that had been lacerating her mind and heart ever since her daughter had refused to have anything to do with her. As with the death of a loved one that is expected imminently, the final event comes with no less a shock of bewilderment and grief. In her state of paranoia, Leesa saw the rift between herself and her daughter as retribution for the grave crimes of her past. In the darkness of her turmoil, she kept twisting and turning like a wild animal skewered on a divine spear, vainly seeking escape from its imprisonment, its torment. Her mental confusion set her wondering what she could do, where she could go, how she could endure this new agony that was draining her very lifeblood.

John watched his beloved writhing at his bedside, powerless to bring her comfort or to ease her pain. With each new wave of suffering that she imagined was thrust upon her by divine decree, Leesa had become more and more obsessed with her guilt. She knelt at John's bedside, her head tilted upwards in unconscious preparation for the confession she was about to make both to God and to her husband. She would plead for forgiveness from the husband she had wronged and the God she had abandoned, hoping that both would be more compassionate than her daughter.

Her tiny hands wrung each other on the bed. Under the skin between her wrist and fingers, the veins stood out like a blue spider's web. Suddenly, she began to tremble and her head swiveled from side to side, like a trapped animal seeking respite from the pain inflicted by the jaws that held it prisoner. Her face was drained of blood and it crumbled into an ugly grimace of tears as a series of sobs broke from her lips. Her hands clasped each other and the words that followed scorched her tongue with the bitter taste of gall.

"John," she whispered, "I have wronged you so deeply all these years of our marriage with a lie." Her husband's face was drawn into a bloodless mask as he listened without looking at his wife. He had waited for years to hear this confession.

"My darling, what Serena said was true. I lied to you about my rape." She paused to take a deep breath and the air rushed in and out of her lungs with relief as though she had jut cast off a weight too heavy for her to bear. But there was an even greater weight that she rushed to discharge. All the while, John never moved a muscle, never interrupted.

"One night when mother was away and father asleep, I crept naked onto his sleeping mat and had intercourse with him. *He* was not at fault. It was *I* who had drugged him and initiated the coupling." She waited for the explosion of disgust and anger that she felt sure would erupt from her husband. Only after his long silence, did she continue. She did not say that she had overheard her parents stating that she was insane and planning to put her into therapy. She didn't explain that she thought they were conspiring to commit her to a sanatorium and that her act was retaliation to their cruelty. In short, she didn't try to deflect condemnation from herself or her act. She simply stated what happened. But in her own twisted mind she regarded her act as a complete family suicide.

"By the time mother was back from her visit I had already returned to my own mat. I never found out if father knew what had happened. I suppose he must have known, but he never once gave any indication of it. Later, when I found that I was pregnant, I cried 'rape' to you, to prevent bringing shame and disgrace on myself, on the family and on you. Oh John, I knew it was wrong but after the act I couldn't let the taboo of incest ruin all our lives. That's why I had to get married immediately after finding I was pregnant." Again she paused, expecting an outburst from her husband. Once again he said nothing.

"Oh John, I beg your forgiveness. Can you ever forgive me?" Although she emitted a loud keening that rose from the depths of her soul, she directed her eyes everywhere but at her husband's face. Her hands then covered her face in shame and her head, in constant motion, swung from side to side as though shamefully trying to deny the truth she had spoken. Slime leaked through her fingers, and a long drool wormed its way down onto the sheet.

"So, Serena is not my child," John stated suddenly, pain and regret breaking his voice. Yet, he was as deeply moved by his wife's distress as by the appalling facts she had stated.

"No. But I've admired and loved you for the way you've always lavished your love and affection on her as thought she were your own."

"She *is* my own," he roared. "I'm the only father she knows, he insisted, as though the angry outburst would transform wish into fact. A long moment passed before he spoke again.

"But Leesa, your news is not a surprise. When you made all those changes in our wedding plans, I had my suspicions. Then, on his deathbed your father confessed the truth of what had happened."

"What!" his wife whispered in disbelief. "You both knew, yet neither of you issued one word of rebuke? Why John? Why? Oh God," she continued: "It would have been so much better if you had spoken then. This horror would be behind us."

"Well Leesa, true love includes compassion and forgiveness. They allow a spouse to overlook the grievous faults of the beloved." She thought he was rebuking her earlier ranting about the nature of love, but changed her mind when he enveloped her in his arms. Oh my God, she realized, he was following the model he had chosen for his conduct.

"Oh John, I never really knew the depth of your love, but you should know how much I've loved you all the years of our marriage; how much I love you this very minute for your enduring devotion, your compassion, and especially for your forgiveness."

It hurt John deeply to watch his wife suffer. Tears burned his eyes and throat as he listened to the sobs wracking her body; the violence of grief ripping through her. He held her closely in his arms, lifted her gently, and crying shamelessly himself, took her to his bed. There, he comforted her in the only way he knew how.

But, while Leesa's sadness overwhelmed her, John was grappling with an equally overwhelming heartache.

"Father, I need to get this burden off my shoulders."

"That's what confession is for, my son."

"On his deathbed, Yong Sang sent for me. He confessed he had impregnated his teen-aged daughter, Leesa, who is now my wife. What he said, confirmed what I had suspected: my wife was pregnant for someone else before our marriage. I never would have guessed her own father was the animal in question."

"That must have come as quite a shock," the priest said, deep sympathy in his voice as he tried to comfort his penitent.

"It meant that my daughter, Serena, was not my child but his. His confession made me feel as though I had fallen into a cesspool and its foul contents were clinging to my body. I wanted to choke him to death, but controlled myself as I quickly rose to leave. But he grabbed my hand and pleaded:

"JC, forgive a dying man. I need you to listen."

"Listening to the confession of the dying is a duty, my son. No one should neglect it, even in such a morally contemptible situation."

"Damn you! I said to him, not wanting to hear more of his depravity. But he ignored my words and replied."

"When you commit a criminal act, disaster strikes and your whole interior becomes a void filled with darkness. No light JC, no light at all! Only silence; silence and darkness. Its weight is crushing me." The truth is that I had no idea what he was trying to say. His voice was weak, his face ashen, his eyes glazed.

"Don't you remember, I visited you two weeks ago and you complemented me on how well I looked?"

"I remember your visit. But what the hell are you getting at?" I spoke harshly wanting to distance myself from this monster.

"Well, don't you find it strange that I'm on my deathbed just two weeks later?"

"Old people get ill unexpectedly. That's what ageing does." I hissed.

"That's not the case with me. I need you to know, John. There's no one else I dare tell."

"I turned to go, but he grabbed my hand again and begged me to listen."

"I trust that you did, despite your anger," said the priest. "It's your duty to ease suffering regardless of the sins of the individual."

"I listened to his confession, Father."

"The fact that I impregnated my own daughter has haunted me every day of my life. I can never make up for the irreparable wrong I've done," Yong Sang stated.

"His voice was thin, dry and as arid as a withered leaf ready to fall from the tree."

"His wrongdoing had very serious implications, not only for his daughter," the priest interjected. "It was disastrous for you and for your whole family as well".

"But JC," Yong Sang continued, "Everyone knows how much I love my wife. I've never been unfaithful to her before or after that terrible night. My incestuous relationship, coupled with my infidelity to the only woman I've ever worshipped, burns like a fire in my entrails." Suddenly, he whispered: "JC, I need forgiveness!"

"He needed a priest to hear his confession," Father Murphy stated.

"The truth of the matter is that his words, and the intensity with which they were spoken, got my attention. My curiosity got the better of me. Well, what did you do?" I questioned.

"I confessed my sin to every priest I could find. They all said the archfiend had a compelling urge to tempt, corrupt and destroy families, especially those of devout Christians. Finally, they gave me absolution."

"So how come you're dying?"

"That's another story," he replied. "When nothing I did eased my tortured mind, I began to hate myself and even thought of suicide. But I was too much of a coward. Worse, it would have been unfair to Kim."

"There was a moment of silence while I waited. Why the hell don't you come to the point? I finally shouted, but he paid no attention to my outburst."

"I decided there was only one way to get relief. I would have to confess to my wife and get her to grant me forgiveness."

"That was very courageous on his part," don't you agree?" The priest asked.

"Father, I had no sympathy for so immoral a creature. So did you confess?" I asked him.

"Yes, I explained to Kim the anguish that was destroying me; told her how I had confessed to numerous priests, but nothing I did eased my tormented conscience. I then told her how much I loved her and begged for her forgiveness."

"There was another long silence while he took short shallow breaths. For Christ's sake, how did she respond?" I finally barked.

"She surprised me with her compassion and tenderness. Can you imagine the tremendous relief I felt JC? I prostrated myself before her. The next few days were pure ecstasy. I made love to her as though I were a young and vigorous man. I thought she seemed happy, but her moods seemed to be shot through with moments of deep sadness. At least, so it *seemed* to me."

"Seemed? I questioned. "Why have you emphasized the word seemed?"

"You see, on the very day of my confession, she had begun to poison me."

"What?" The priest exploded, exactly as I had reacted. His statement was the last thing we both expected.

"But I thought Kim had forgiven you." I stated.

"That's what I thought too. And I told her those last few days that we loved each other had been some of the happiest of my life." She gave me a look of the deepest hatred before explaining:

"What I had done," she said, "was to commit a sin that she found it impossible to forgive." Since she paused, I asked: "Why?"

"Her answer came as a complete surprise. She said I had had years to learn and become intimate with every inch of her body. She was certain that I must have known instantly that it wasn't her body I was fondling that night. For having given in to my lust, for not having pulled away," she said, "I deserved to die."

"Everyone deserves a chance at forgiveness," the priest said, before adding: "especially if they feel remorse that is sincere."

"God knows that I was not in a forgiving mood but I didn't contradict the priest."

"So once you knew you were poisoned, why the hell didn't you call a doctor? I almost shouted at Yong Sang."

"I agree," said the priest. He should have called a doctor right away!"

"Well you see JC, she was right. Once I was aroused and began fondling the body next to me, I knew immediately it wasn't my wife. I knew, but in the heightened state of arousal I couldn't stop myself."

"So now that you've transferred your burden to me, what will you have me do?" I asked angrily.

"Pray for me JC," he said. "You've listened to my confession. That's enough to help me die in peace."

"I hope you called the doctor," were the last words of the priest.

John stood immobile, feeling paralyzed. The filthy secret Yong Sang had just disgorged was so explosive that once revealed it would surely destroy the sanity of his wife and the happiness of his daughter. His wife was already heartbroken at Serena's imminent departure from Korea. The absence would profoundly disturb her mind and shrivel her soul. To inform her of the violence that she had set in motion would do irreparable harm. Her paranoia would make her assume that she was still being stalked by divinity. He felt certain that she would never recover from so final a blow.

And his daughter too needed to be protected from such terrible news. Good God, he said to himself, what was he to do? No solution came to his mind.

Kim had left her husband at death's door, refusing to believe the explanation he had given her of what she considered his betrayal. The spin he put on the incident played over and over in her tortured mind like the detested recording of a filthy song that refused to stop repeating itself. He was in a drugged sleep, dreaming of a sexual encounter with his wife and felt her fondling him. By the time she placed her hand on his member, he was already fully aroused, his body pulsing with desire. He was still in a drugged semi-comatose sleep when his fingers found her hot and wet. He entered her and they rocked together in a passionate embrace until they both exploded in climax. It was later, when Leesa came to his mat and began scratching his back, that he became fully awake. Only then did the truth dawn on him. What he had experienced was no dream. He had been intimate with a woman who turned out to be someone other than his wife. In a welter of shame and confusion, he then realized it had been his daughter.

As John entered the cold, darkened house of his father-in-law, the noisome scent of corruption and decay struck him like a whiplash. It was overwhelming. He felt as though he had walked into a wall. Although it was less than a week since John's last visit, the atmosphere of the house had undergone a radical change. The darkness and the malignant atmosphere should have warned him what to expect. Instead, the sight that confronted him made him stagger. His heartbeat quickened, his stomach lurched violently, and he almost lost his lunch. Tears filled his eyes as he saw the twisted face of Yong Sang, the emaciated body bent sideways. His knees were drawn upwards, and his hands were still clasped in a parody of prayer. His body had shrunk and his face was contorted in the rictus of death.

John began to feel so dejected, so overwhelmed with sorrow that he found it difficult to accept the fact that someone so close to him had been struck down and murdered in so cruel a manner. It was then that he recalled the gentle hands of the master craftsman guiding the clumsy ones of his pupil. He remembered the pride he had taken in learning each new skill he was taught. He thought of the pride he took in Yong Sang's naming him JC, and his generous invitations to share the warmth of his family at supper time. He thought of the loving way the craftsman inhaled the scent and caressed the grain of the woods he selected and Kim's story of the crucifixion that had so influenced his thinking. He then recalled the shameful secret that Yong Sang's festering conscience had forced him to disgorge. When he recalled the effort Yong Sang had made to gain atonement and forgiveness, a wave of pity washed over him. He felt deeply saddened at the way passion succeeded in goading humans beings into criminal conduct, and at the guilt, shame and humiliation it made them suffer.

John could not believe that Kim, who had loved her husband so deeply, who had been so devoted to the church and to helping others could have turned out to be a cruel murderess. He wondered how she could have denied Yong Sang the charity that had played so central a part in her stories of the Crucifixion. How could she have contradicted the principles she had so eloquently expressed in her tragic story of the Roman victimization of Christ? No answer came to mind.

Serena was tired of letting others make her decisions for her. It was high time to take the reins of her destiny into her own hands, to decide her own future. She went to Stephen and accepted his proposal of marriage. She suddenly felt elated; carried away by thumbing her nose at the whole world. Once Stephen had got Serena to agree to his marriage proposal, his next step would be to seek her father's approval. He hastened to do so and once again met with Mr. Ahn in his study. He got right to the point.

"Sir, I have c-come to ask your c-consent for your daughter's hand in marriage," Stephen began, stumbling over his words. The news was not totally unexpected.

"Let me be frank with you Stephen," Ahn replied. I would not have chosen you as the husband of my daughter. I suppose few parents are happy with the spouses their children choose and often with good reason. The fact is there are certain serious problems that concern me about this marriage. You have known each other for a few weeks only. That is not enough time for you to really know Serena or for her to know you. That's not enough time for her to risk her whole future life and happiness on marriage to a virtual stranger. Serena has had no experience whatever in affairs of the heart, and she has just recovered from a long and debilitating illness. I consider therefore that she is far too young and inexperienced to know her heart; too fragile to undertake the heavy responsibility and the full duties of a wife. Then, you'll be taking her to a foreign country where she'll have no one to turn to in the event of the numerous problems that both marriage and life creates. Since she doesn't speak the language fluently, she'll be branded a second-class citizen. It's evident that she'll encounter great difficulty coping with the many problems that are bound to arise.

However, despite all that I have stated, I know that Serena is intelligent. She has a level head on her shoulders, and you no doubt have convinced her that you're an upstanding and responsible young man. Most important, you both seem to love each other. Since her mother and I won't be present to seek our daughter's welfare, we look to you both to keep your wedding vows. With that in mind, I would consent to your request on one condition only. You must be married before leaving Korea.

"Thank you for your approval, Sir. I should hasten to add that I do love your daughter and will do my damndest to make her happy. On that score, you should have no doubt whatever. But Mr.Ahn is marriage at all possible given the short time we have before leaving?"

"I have already arranged everything with Father Murphy. So I trust you are in agreement?"

"Most certainly, Sir. It never occurred to me that there would be time enough, what with the need for the publication of the banns that usually takes three weeks."

"Serena I've already spoken to Stephen and expressed my views. Before I say what I have to, I want you to think of me as I believe you always have: a very loving, proud and protective father. Only then will you understand that I cannot permit my teenage daughter to leave home and to venture abroad in the company of a man who is a virtual stranger. Even though your plan is to get married, the move you are making is ill-advised."

"Tell me Dad, what disturbs you? Is it that I'm too young and inexperienced or that Stephen is a stranger?"

"Both! Let me show you your behavior through Korean eyes. I consider that we are the most conservative people on the planet. The fact of the matter is that strict ethical and philosophical codes of conduct guide our thoughts, customs, behavior; our very lifestyle. Respect, filial obedience and reverence to parents–the most basic elements of the protocol by which we live–have been deeply ingrained in you throughout your upbringing. Your intention to flout tradition in so blatant a manner would be a surrender to temptation. It would be putting passion before propriety; self-gratification before moral obligation. The truth is that you'd be acting like a common slut. Doing what you plan would be one of the most disgraceful and undignified acts that a young lady of your background and training could undertake."

At first, the knowledge of her husband's incest was like the scorching flame from an acetylene torch searing Kim's brain. It numbed all thought, leaving her a creature faced with turmoil, confusion and calamity. The shame and humiliation that filled her gave way to loathing and finally to anger. How, she wondered, could her husband let his passion so consume him that it obliterated all sense of moral and ethical conduct? Only the worst kind of depravity could have driven Yong Sang to commit so heinous a crime. Was the man she married, and thought she had known so well, no better than an animal?

Unconsciously, she had dismissed her daughter's role in the affair. She believed that Leesa was too young and innocent to have acted in the way she was portrayed by her husband. There was no way that the incident could have played out in the way he had described. Kim had no doubt whatever that he had put his own careful spin on his explanation. Her daughter had been led, and her husband was the leader. She was convinced that he alone was the guilty beast.

The next questions that plagued her were the most frightening. What did she propose to do about the situation? She had given Yong Sang her love, her loyalty, her very life. After his confession, she couldn't pretend that nothing had happened, could she? She couldn't continue living with and loving so degenerate a monster, could she? Oh God, she wailed, what could she do? She needed to come up with some plan, to devise some strategy, perhaps even to take desperate measures. But, how far was she prepared to go? She was convinced that Yong Sang had to know that the woman he was caressing was not the wife he had known for over eighteen years. To her way of thinking, that was the bottom line. The final question that crossed her mind was: what do you do with slime?

"Dad, I'm going to a country where no one will know anything about my background."

"And what about your knowledge of your own behavior?" How will you erase the knowledge that you broke every ethical code of conduct you were taught? Think, Serena, think! First, you have disobeyed your father's express wish that you reunite with your mother. Then you have disrespected your mother's wishes. Thus, everything you've done should make you thoroughly despise yourself in your own eyes. Both your parents and family would be devastated by such conduct. Even if the slanderous tongues remained silent, we'd hang our heads in shame."

"Dad, you've spelled out only the negative aspects of my plan, 'through Korean eyes.' Why can't you see the positive side?" She ignored his mention of her disobedience and disrespect.

"Daughter, I've stated the negative aspects where only Korean protocol is concerned. Equally disturbing to your parents are the obvious problems arising from your intentions."

"You're referring to my youth and inexperience; the fact that Stephen is a stranger. Dad, I consider that our plan is simplicity itself. The truth of the matter is that Stephen and I love each other and we are returning to his home to get married. Why should that disturb you or anyone?"

"Daughter dear, if truth be told, you're using blinders to make the ugly truth disappear."

"What ugly truth, Dad? What ugly truth?" She stated with the heated impetuosity of youth.

"You have to realize that Stephen is the first and only emotional bond you've had with a man. As a naïve infant in affairs of the heart, you haven't begun to understand the true meaning of love or the exceptionally onerous responsibility of marriage. Then, after your recent illness, I'm not at all sure that you are capable of bearing the full burden of a wife's responsibilities without suffering severe physical and mental consequences."

"Dad I admit that I am young and inexperienced. But I also know that Stephen has been sympathetic, tender and loving even after I showed him those horrible paintings. The truth of the matter is that he was generous enough to see me as pure and innocent, despite the gang rape. Dad, you have to understand that we are in love, and want to commit to each other. Isn't that what matters most?"

It was only after she had learned of her husband's death that Kim fully realized what she had done. She brooded over her ungodly act and berated herself for committing it. Her conscience barraged her with the cruel act of revenge that she had undertaken to get even with her husband. Then, the realization made her ask herself: is she the same devout person who had prayed morning and night before her bedroom shrine? Could she be the same person who had taught her daughter the virtues of compassion and justice? Could she have forgotten the lesson learned from the cruelty of Christ's victimization? She was well aware that compassion was the virtue that, with God's grace, bred forgiveness. Yet, how could she have failed to show the least bit of compassion towards her husband? How could she have remained deaf to his repeated pleas for forgiveness? Those virtues that she had held so dear, where had they vanished? How could she have undergone so radical a change? How had she become so cruel and cunning in the act of murder? Who had schooled her in the science of hatred and turned her heart to stone? Her conscience plagued her with these questions though she knew there was only one answer. She had surrendered unwittingly to the diabolical mentor urging her to murder the man she loved.

Chapter 43

"Yes and no Serena. Yes, your love for each other is a very important factor. No, because Stephen is a virtual stranger. Can you really trust a stranger with the rest of your life?"

"Yes Dad, I feel that I can. The truth of the matter is that I'm drawn to his warmth, to his charm and especially to his sincerity. He confided to me the most intimate problems of his past. Then, his reaction to my violation tells me a lot about the person he is. You have to understand that he didn't renege on his marriage proposal as everyone would have expected. After all, few husbands would take to his bed a wife who is not virgin."

"Serena, you'll be in a foreign country where your poor language skills will brand you a second class citizen. Then, should an emergency arise, you won't have anyone to advise or support you. Those are the major facts that worry your mother and me."

"Dad, you know I'm fairly level headed. I know I'll be able to cope with any problems that arise. Besides, you can trust me to do the right thing."

"Can I? When you insist on doing what is so wrong?"

"Dad, I have to follow my heart. Can't you understand that?"

"Yes Serena. I knew you would resist my every argument, just as you've disobeyed me with regard to making up with your mother, just as you have disrespected her wishes. So, to save you from yourself and safeguard your reputation, I have to insist that you get married before you leave. With that in mind, and with Father Murphy's help, I've made the arrangements for your wedding. Otherwise, you won't be permitted to leave Korea or get my blessing as a father."

"Oh Dad, of course we'll get married. But, I didn't think we'd have the time. Afterwards, I hope we'll get your blessing and your wishes for our happiness."

There is one final thing I want from you. You must forgive your mother." His daughter remained in tight-lipped silence.

"Serena, I understand that your mother has tried again and again to make her peace with you, but each time she asks your forgiveness showing her sincerity and telling you how sorry she is, you turn your back on her and leave the room."

"Dad, there is something I wish to tell you. I have tried more than once to forgive Mama for what she has done. I've made several efforts to go to her, but each time I've been unable to do so. It isn't that I've had a change of heart. It's as though something or someone keeps stopping me. At such times I feel as though I am no longer in charge, as though some outer force has shaken my will. Dad it's as though I'm being manipulated." Can you understand what I'm saying?

"No Serena. I don't understand what you're saying, her father replied angrily. Are you so cruel that you enjoy seeing your mother's suffering? She's the person who went through hell to bear you in childbirth; the same person who nursed you back to health when you were floundering at death's door." The sternness of her father's rebuke rattled around in her brain. After all, wasn't her stubborn disobedience of a parent flouting Korean protocol? Wasn't her ingratitude as grave a sin as betrayal? The awareness of her shortcomings laid a severe guilt trip upon her that was especially onerous to bear. But she had to get something off her chest before again trying to explain what was happening to her; why she seemed to be refusing to relent; why she was disobeying her parents.

"Dad, you must agree that infidelity and betrayal are horrible sins not easy to forgive. They are in a league of their own."

"And what about disobeying your own father and disrespecting your mother? What league are they in? You forgave Mona, and it was hatred and jealousy that motivated her conduct. Your mother was motivated by love. She doesn't want her beloved daughter to destroy her life with a too-hasty marriage. She doesn't want to lose her beloved daughter at all. Can't you see the difference between the two situations? Can't you feel compassion for the woman who loves you unconditionally?"

"Dad, you're very persuasive and I know what you've said about Mama is true. I would never have recovered without her caring and advice. And I do know the enduring love that she has for me. In fact, I've thought of little else since my verbal attack on her. I have also realized for some time now that my behavior was not merely harsh but hostile in the extreme. I know too that I've caused Mama enormous suffering by refusing to see or speak to her despite the many times she has apologized and begged my forgiveness." Before she could say another word her father interrupted:

"If what you say is true, why haven't you relented and made your peace with her?"

"Dad, please let me finish."

"Okay, go ahead."

"I'm especially sorry for excluding Mama from the wedding ceremony. More than anything else, I know that mothers live for the day on which their daughters get married. They look forward to dress them in their bridal gown; to be present at the ceremony; to see and hear them take their vows before God; to congratulate the bride and groom and to join in the jubilation that follows."

"If you are aware of all you say, I can't understand why you have refused to bridge the gap in your relationship."

"Please Dad, I haven't finished what I'm trying to say." Her father bowed in agreement and she continued.

"To a mother who has loved me unconditionally, I have responded with utter selfishness and a total lack of consideration. I have committed the grave sins of ingratitude on the one hand and disobedience to parents on the other." She paused to breathe deeply and perhaps to grant herself a moment of relief after her burdensome confession. "Dad," she said finally, "I've been trying to do what I should, but each time I summon up the courage to act, something gets in the way. It's as though I've lost my willpower. I feel as though someone is manipulating me; pulling my strings. I've been trying Dad. I've been really trying. That's what I've been attempting to tell you all along. It's as though you don't hear what I've been saying or you clearly haven't understood. Anyway, I'll obey your wishes and keep trying to make my peace with Mama."

Leesa's household had been a very unhappy place during the days leading up to the wedding. Stephen spent a couple of days badgering Canadian immigration authorities trying to get landed immigration status for Serena to enter Canada as his wife. Serena kept busy shopping for her bridal gown and last minute things for her wedding while her mother waited on tenterhooks to be invited to the ceremony. She never thought that Serena would be married under such circumstances nor that she, the mother of the bride, would not be welcome at the wedding. She lay in bed, sick at heart over the recognition that she would not be allowed to dress her daughter in her wedding gown, watch her walk up the aisle on her father's arm. Worse, she would not be there to see her stand before God and hear her make her matrimonial vows. Aren't those the sacred moments that all mothers live for? Aren't they the dreams that all mothers have? How could Serena rob her of that joy?

An unholy darkness had penetrated Kim's being, freezing her blood while she listened to Yong Sang confess the ravishing of his daughter. The anger it had ignited burst into flame, inciting her to focus on revenge. She, who had been filled with the virtues of compassion and forgiveness, had become transformed into a vengeful fiend of destruction.

She used the deceit of her diabolical mentor, by pretending to forgive her husband. His relief was so sincere that it almost deflected her from her purpose. But an angry darkness had flooded her being, stifling all feelings of compassion. Yet, Yong Sang was so tumultuous, so vigorous in his love sessions with her, so sincere in his remorse, that she was sorely tempted to forgive him. But her infernal mentor refused to free her from fulfilling his demands. Each time she vacillated, he fanned the flames of her hatred and humiliation so that they consumed all feelings of compassion, all thoughts of forgiveness.

"Ironically, it was Yong Sang himself who provided her with the means of his death. As he begged for forgiveness, he hoped that his crime had not 'poisoned' her love for him. The verb that he used had dictated the way he would die. When he took to his bed from the earliest mild doses of poison Kim had administered, he believed that his illness was no more than a bad case of some new virus that would soon run its course.

"What immigration people telling you?" Serena asked anxiously on Stephen's return.

"To enter Canada, you'll need a tourist visa from Immigration Canada. Once that expires, you'll have to leave Canada. That's why they insist on your buying a return ticket."

"What is alternative?" Serena asked, swiftly becoming numb with disappointment.

"You have to apply for landed immigration status, but can only apply from outside Canada."

"How long Serena staying outside?"

"At least seven months, but it could take longer."

"Suppose Serena leaving with you on tourist visa?"

"Once it expires, you'll have to leave Canada and apply from Korea or any country outside Canada. You'll then have to go through the same period of waiting."

"Leaving Korea once very hard, Stephen. Leaving twice unthinkable for Serena." Her voice was sad. The hopes, dreams and excitement of married life in a new country had been shattered in an instant.

"What do you mean?"

"Dad, Father Murphy arranged marriage almost immediately. After marriage, going Canada impossible, so Serena deciding stay Korea. She applying landed immigration status at once. Then, she upgrading the English here."

"I'll lose my mind waiting seven long months for the lady I love."

"Maybe good thing, immediate separation."

"How could separation be a good thing?"

"After violation, Serena enjoying kissing, cuddling Stephen, but she not able go whole way. Separation providing her time full recovery. While Serena getting immigration status, Stephen getting real wife."

"That seems like a fair exchange he thought smiling, but accused:

"You seem relieved that you're not traveling with me?"

"No, no! Serena wanting travel with husband; seeing 'super-natural' country. But she already explaining repugnant feeling around males. She needing time overcome bad feeling. Stephen helping her recover but Serena not ready for all wife responsibilities. She not wanting frustrate, disappoint husband. Understand?"

"You do have a way of speaking your mind, don't you? But I have no choice, do I?"

"None darling! Now, Serena filling out application forms at once."

Chapter 44

"Darling Kim, I'm not feeling at all well. Will you keep my company while I lie down? I'll feel so much better with you at my side. You've been such a wonderful wife. You'll never believe how grateful I am for your compassion, understanding and forgiveness."

"Yong Sang, there are a million things I have to do, but as soon as I'm finished, I'll come and sit with you. Is there something more I can bring you, some more soup perhaps?"

"I'd prefer a bowl of rice noodles. The last soup you brought had a bitter after taste."

"Okay my dearest. Perhaps I used too much red pepper paste." I'll have to be more careful in giving him smaller doses of the poison, she told herself. An hour later, she returned to his room.

"Darling, I've brought you the rice noodles in broth. I hope it's not too hot. Taste it and tell me if it's all right."

"I'm so grateful for your love and forgiveness. I don't deserve you. Any other woman would have murdered me for my unforgivable transgression." Good God, Kim thought, he's so annoying with his repetition of my supposed forgiveness. Anyway, now that he's had quite a few doses, it won't be long before he begins to feel worse. Only then would she inform him that his is a very different kind of virus.

"Will you stay with me while I have this snack? Your being close reminds me of the forgiving wife that you are. You'll never understand what your compassion means to me."

Over the next days, Yong Sang wearied and annoyed Kim with his repeated expressions of gratitude. But it was his insistence on her supposed forgiveness that finally goaded her to anger. Then, little by little, the darkness accumulating in her brain ignited her fury. Finally losing control, she spewed the bile from her throat. It erupted from her lips like shrapnel from a bomb.

"Forgive you, for violating your daughter? Forgive you, for disgracing me with your betrayal? You must be mad! No sane person could forgive such barbarism." Yong Sang shrank back in awe at the unexpected onslaught.

"You animal!" she screamed. "You've had a lifetime to learn every inch of my body, so you knew it wasn't me you were fondling. You knew, you sick bastard, yet you didn't stop, didn't pull away. Like some masochistic cannibal, you relished feeding off your own flesh. For that, you deserve to die." Then she shrieked: "And that's why I've poisoned you." An eerie silence followed as Yong Sang stared at her in stunned amazement. She broke the silence with an exultant roar: "I've been poisoning you in every meal from the moment you confessed." The cruelty of her words made his heart begin to slam against his ribs. He remained silent with shock, then, aware that he was dying he began to feel as though darkness were filling the whole of his interior. After a pause, she spat:

"Now, go call the doctor!" It was then that Yong Sang summoned his son-in-law.

After the death of Yong Sang, John found himself in a terrible bind. He couldn't tell his wife that her incestuous act had not only destroyed the marriage of her parents, but had driven her mother to murder her father. The shock Leesa had received at her rift with Serena had almost unhinged her mind. Since she saw it as another divinely inspired wallop, her paranoia had thrust her into an advanced stage of depression bordering on despair. John believed that she could not withstand another shock of such magnitude. But how, he wondered, would he be able to shield her from the news of her father's death? That would prove almost impossible, but if he could manage it, he felt sure that time would help to cushion the shock.

He also considered that he would have to withhold the news from Serena, seeing that she had enough problems of her own. The truth is that he didn't dare tell her that her mother had committed incest and that she, Serena, was illegitimate. He didn't dare tell her that her grandmother, Kim, was a murderess who had poisoned her husband. Nor did he dare tell her that Mona's story was true; her mother had been unfaithful as his fiancée. Worst still, how would he tell her she was not his daughter? Any words he used to do so would choke him to death. The truth is that he could never be so callous as to destroy her one chance at happiness, or her excitement at the prospect of starting a new life abroad. What a wedding present that would be!

It was his fate to be the guardian of this obscenity that he could never divulge. He was like a ship filled to the brim with sewage and no port where he could discharge his odious cargo. The filthy details, with all their salacious images, were driving him to distraction. He would have to find some spiritual cesspool where he could disgorge the scandalous perversion. Yet, he knew that such an evil secret could only be deposited in a church. There, he could lay it gently on the shoulders of Christ. But, before he did that, he had to visit his mother-in-law and confront her with her villainy.

When Serena entered the driveway to her home after the long absence, she was surprised to find that many of the most cherished memories of her life on the farm came rushing back to overwhelm her. Immediately, the very questions that had plagued her for so long struck her again with the force of a speeding locomotive. How could she have deliberately torn herself away from this place where so many of the pleasure-filled moments of her life had occurred? How could she have disrespected then abandoned so callously the mother who had orchestrated the majority of those events? Finally, how could she have refused again and again to obey her father when her entire upbringing had been steeped in the rigid code of ethics that stressed, above all else, filial obedience and respect to parents?

After administering poison to her husband and leaving him to die, Kim moved back to her parents' home, locking herself into her old bedroom. There, she lay in bed pondering over the cruelty of her act against the husband whom she had loved so dearly; a husband with whom she had spent eighteen long and happy years. She recalled the excitement of their first meeting when he had come to congratulate her after her piano recital. He had been so young and handsome then, as he told her how the feeling she put into her playing had affected him. He felt that she had been playing for him alone, he said sheepishly, and they both laughed. He then talked to her about his change from sculpture to carving. From the enthusiasm with which he spoke, he communicated to her the dedication he felt for his craft. But, the tremor in his voice conveyed his shyness in talking to a girl he evidently admired.

She fell for the kind and gentle nature of the handsome and promising artist whose love of life and laughter had so impressed her. She remembered the happiness they shared during the early years of their marriage. He surprised her with tickets for their first ride on the Bullet train that took them to Seoul where they stayed in a luxurious hotel. It was an especially exciting time, loving each other by day, visiting the sights of Seoul, enjoying the diverse culinary art of the city's fine restaurants each evening and loving each other again each night. She could never forget how the over enthusiasm of their sexual appetites had left her with swollen lips and the burning sensation at the apex of her thighs. They saw interesting plays and some of the new film releases. They often went to museums where he showed her the exquisite wood carvings and masks that had made him change from the sculpture of stone to the carving of wood.

He took her to various areas of the city to gaze in awe at the serene beauty of the pagodas and palaces, the temples and shrines of a bygone era. They made plans for the birth of their first child, and he surprised her with the gift of a piano. Back at home each evening, during those exquisite early years, he would sit and listen to her play his favorite music: Rachmaninoff, Chopin, Beethoven and Liszt. She recalled the help he gave every year in their garden, and the pride she took in his devotion to her and to their daughter. Then, it was he who had suggested that they bank one third of his earnings for their daughter's education. She knew that at heart, the husband she had married was a good and decent man, deserving of her love in so many ways.

It was only after she kept repeating the story he told her over and over until it numbed her brain, that she began to believe what he said was true. After all, had she put herself in his place and the incident occurred as he had described it, she would probably have acted as he had done. Yet, the proof that her husband and daughter had committed the taboo of incest so appalled her that she became sick to her stomach. At that point, the only thoughts that crowded her benumbed and sickened brain were those incestuous images associated with wickedness, sexuality and corruption. Those were the images whipped up by her cruel mentor that ignited her fury and rendered her incapable of logical thought or action. Illogically, she argued: even if what her husband said was true, she found it impossible to absolve him of blame. Yet, despite the enmity she felt towards him, as she tried to put the incident and its aftermath into proper perspective, she knew in her heart that there was no justification for murder. In her deep hurt and anger; driven by an overwhelming desire for revenge, she had followed the lead of her mentor and convinced herself that poisoning her husband would be a fitting outcome to his betrayal. Hadn't he destroyed their love, their marriage, their family, their reputation and their lives with a single ungodly act? Thus, in her tormented mind, she accepted the infernal advice: no punishment was too severe for such a monster.

In considering their reunion, Serena still couldn't face her mother without thinking of the terrible wrongs she had done. Instead, she phoned and brought her mother up to date about all that had transpired in Serena's absence. She then informed her mother that she would be leaving Korea in a few days and was off to Grandma Kim to say her goodbyes. She then promised to return before her departure. But she still did not invite her to the wedding ceremony.

When Kim heard the news of Yong Sang's death, only then did she realize, with mounting alarm, that she had committed murder. Even before the case came to court, the scandal and shame she'd have to face would be enormous. The stories circulating about her could no longer be dismissed as mere gossip or speculation. They would have the stamp of truth, the sanction of the law. Once the toxicology report surfaced, she would be arrested, tried for premeditated murder and imprisoned. She would no doubt have to face a life sentence or perhaps end her days on death row. Her mind reeled at the guilt, shame and humiliation that her act would visit upon her and on her unsuspecting family. In considering the enormity of her crime and the shattered future awaiting her, she began to feel abnormality creeping over her. Under the crushing weight of misery over the man she had killed and the future she envisaged, she soon lost her appetite and was unable to sleep. She had finally come to the realization that she was evil, and that it was she who was the carrier of the evil gene in her family. In a very short time, she reverted to the gaunt and wizened scarecrow she had been when the rumors of her daughter's tainted marriage had first struck so long ago.

Day and night, the terror that kept creeping into her thoughts added to the shame and guilt that was bludgeoning her mind, sickening her soul. In despair, she fell on her knees before her shrine, but each time she tried to ask for forgiveness, her throat choked on the words and no prayer passed her lips. How dare she ask for forgiveness? Hadn't she refused to forgive her husband? And so, wherever she looked, the sad and shocked face of Yong Sang would appear, alarming her further. She tried to dismiss the images from her mind, forcing her thoughts to seek more pleasant paths. She rushed to the church. The stained glass windows above the altar drew her eyes to the figure of the grief-stricken mother contemplating her dying son. But Kim could find no comfort in the invitation on the stained glass: "Come unto me ye that are heavy laden and I will refresh you." There was no trace of the forgiveness she sought. Instead, every image she conjured up metamorphosed into the accusing face of her husband. Thoughts of her imminent arrest, the ensuing trial, her future execution and its disastrous effect on the family kept bludgeoning her mind until the torment became too much to bear. She locked herself in her bedroom thinking it was too late for Father Murphy to hear her confession. Instead, she sought vainly to cast off the burden that kept growing heavier by the hour. Eventually, as the deepest despair gnawed away at her sanity, she entered a downward spiral of darkness and confusion that led inexorably to the arid portals of insanity.

The wedding ceremony was anything but the happy occasion that any of the individuals present would have envisaged. Serena had refused to invite her mother even though they had been reunited by phone. Her father felt annoyed with her and deeply hurt that his daughter had disobeyed him and that his wife was absent. Once the couple had taken their vows, bride and groom would be separated. Stephen would be heading to the airport and Canada, while Serena would be heading home to her farm. Amid tears and kisses, the newly married couple began saying their goodbyes vowing that they would miss each other and would write as often as possible.

"I don't know how I'll be able to survive without you," Stephen confided to his bride, warming her heart.

"Darling, you here," she struck her heart. "Always Serena thinking reunion at husband."

She couldn't help feeling like the discarded spouse in a ruined marriage: abandoned, empty and useless. Then, after the couple had said their goodbyes John approached his son-in-law.

"This is for you, Stephen," John said, handing him a manila envelope that Stephen opened while the plane was speeding from the airport and Korea. At the same moment, his newly-wed bride and her father in sullen silence were speeding from the airport towards their home.

"Oh my God!" Stephen exclaimed silently on opening the envelope and seeing two hefty checks attached to a letter. He began reading avidly.

Dear Stephen,

Welcome to the Ahn family. However, as a concerned father, I have to exercise caution on my daughter's behalf since, in my mind, she is married to a virtual stranger who spent only a short time with us. What you have to understand is that the following involves some hard business decisions I've had to make. Should any split or falling out take place between you two, I have taken the precaution of putting the ownership of the new three bedroom house, our wedding gift to you both, in Serena's name. That way, she'll always have a roof over her head.

I was able to purchase the newly built home through the bank of my friend, Dang. It is fully furnished, mortgage free and located in an area of fairly luxurious residential homes in Gordon Head. The latter is a district of Victoria on the Saanich Peninsula of Vancouver Island. The house consists of three bedrooms, living room, kitchen, two full bathrooms, and a laundry area upstairs. There is a two bedroom, ground level, basement suite with a separate entrance. It is fully furnished, with its own living room, kitchen and laundry area and completely self-contained. It can be rented out to students or faculty since it is close to the University of Victoria. The rent should take care of all your utilities, the annual municipal taxes, phone, TV, cable and the internet, while leaving you a fairly large cushion to help with living expenses.

One check, made out to you, Stephen, is for the purchase of a new car. The second check, made out to Serena, is to be deposited at any Toronto Dominion bank of your choice. It will furnish her with whatever she might need and a new car. The remainder will act as a cushion for any and all eventualities that might occur. I trust that you will take good care of Serena and I wish you both a long and happy life together.

John Ahn.

Stephen found it ironical that he had received a huge financial benefit from his Korean vacation without having to use lies and deceit to attain it. On arrival at his new home in Victoria, he immediately wrote an email to his father-in-law thanking him for his generous gifts and assuring him that he would take the greatest care of Serena and try to make her happy. He then wrote to his wife.

My very own darling Serena,

Leaving you behind while flying back to Canada was the hardest thing I've ever had to do. My heart ached as the distance between us increased, and I have been miserable ever since leaving you. My home here is definitely not where my heart is. I've lost my appetite, cannot concentrate on my work, and am unable to sleep without your face constantly popping up in my thoughts. I want to resign my job, rush back to Korea and reclaim the happiness I had with you in my arms. I miss sitting with you on the riverbank and listening to the rattle of your words clashing with those of your charm bracelets. I miss your animated gestures and seeing the glint and flutter of your ear rings that accompany every shake of your head. I miss witnessing the flurry of your two fingers whenever you became angry or excited. Most of all, I miss you and the tender moments we shared together.

My darling, without you I'm a useless hulk, but racing back to where my heart is in Korea would not solve our problems. So I wait impatiently for the hours, days, weeks and months to creep by until we are together again. God keep you safe my love,

Stephen.

As Stephen re-read the letter, he noticed that once again he had communicated his innermost feelings to Serena. It struck him forcibly because he had never before expressed such intimate emotions to anyone. He pondered long and hard to discover the motive underlying what he considered his epiphany. At first, he thought it was his love for Serena that had exposed the nakedness of his emotions. But gradually, he came to realize that while the love he felt for her was important, he thought it had not played the major role in triggering the change that had come over him. On further analysis, he reasoned that his sincerity had been stimulated by the character of the woman he had married. It was hard to believe that at the age of eleven she had singlehandedly undertaken the poultry farming project solely for the benefit of others? She had followed that up with her fertilization project, and later had joined her mother to undertake the rice paddy and fish farming experiment with the same motive. Then, she didn't have to tell him about her gang-rape or to show him the odious paintings of the event. And she didn't have to describe herself as a ruined woman, unfit for marriage. In his mind, Serena was the very essence of sincerity, generosity and just pure goodness. His love for her was important, as was her love for him. But he'd had the love of many women before and it had never affected him emotionally. He believed that it was his exposure to the kind of person Serena was. In short, it was the character of his wife that had triggered the change in him. He was trying hard to follow her lead. Not long after this debate with himself he received an email from her.

Chapter 45

Darling,

Stephen email making Serena happy, but she preferring him here. Marrying husband followed with immediate separation was cruel disappointment. Serena worrying you so far away and she for reunion waiting so long. Serena suggesting Stephen begin flogging severely immigration officials for so long separating married spouses. Anyway, Serena needing address and phone number ESL teachers Joe and Sally Stephen meeting on bus. Serena wanting upgrade the English, grammar and fluency. If Joe and Sally willing teach Serena, she saying Stephen outcome next email. Meanwhile, Serena sending husband all love. God blessing, keeping Stephen safe.

Serena.

On the way to her grandmother, Serena kept thinking of the decision she had made about forgiving her mother. The truth was that her father's arguments were very sound. Since she had forgiven Mona, she was glad she had finally done the same for her mother. The recognition of her disobedience and disrespect had forced her to lean in that direction anyway. Yet, she felt sorry that she had not done so before the wedding and invited her mother to attend the ceremony. She had had to make a superhuman effort to overcome the "invisible" opposition she had met again and again in trying to do her duty. She couldn't understand it herself so how was it possible to make her father understand the stubborn resistance she had tried to explain. Anyway, she thought, there would be time enough to discover what had repeatedly prevented her from doing her duty after she told her grandmother of the most recent developments. On entry to her grandmother's home, the gloomy atmosphere that engulfed the house broke into her reverie. She was taken aback immediately and began to wonder what was amiss when she saw Kim's mother, her great Grandma, Yuk Lin, bent over the kitchen table sobbing softly.

"What's the matter great Gran? Why so sad?" She asked, hugging her anxiously, with deep concern in her voice.

"It's your grandma Kim. She's locked herself in her room for the past couple of weeks refusing to come out, or even to eat. She keeps muttering to herself, and shouting."

"What made her lock herself away, and why is she shouting?"

"I'm not sure. She was completely silent for the first few days. When I knocked and offered her something to eat, she wouldn't answer. A week ago, she began muttering words that were incomprehensible and some time later she began speaking in an abnormal voice then alternated between muttering and shouting. Sometimes she sounds as though she's confessing to Father Murphy, or begging forgiveness from her husband. But she's alone. There's no one with her."

"Why does she need confession and forgiveness? What has she done?"

"I don't know, but her weird behavior makes me worry about her sanity." Her great Gran, Yuk Lin, didn't want to shock Serena with what she knew. Instead, she advised:

"Go fetch your father. Maybe he'll be able to help."

"I can phone dad at the office from here, explaining that there's an emergency. But I won't go anywhere until I find out what's going on." At that moment, Kim began speaking and the two women kept silent so they could hear her tear-filled voice beseeching the priest. Immediately, Serena positioned herself outside her door to listen, with her great Gran not far behind.

"Oh, oh, oh, oh, will God ever forgive me, Father? It was Yong Sang who started it all." The voice was hoarse, definitely masculine, not that of the Kim they both knew. There followed a deep bass mumbling that neither of the listeners could understand. After a long silence, the muttering resumed growing louder. Then Kim began to shout. This time, she seemed to be remonstrating with her husband. The voice, again male, was harsh and angry carrying with it an underlying note of deep sorrow. "How could you do such a thing, Yong Sang? How could you? And look at what you made me do! How will I ever be granted forgiveness?"

"What did he do?" Serena asked her great Gran, but before any reply came, Kim shouted.

"Leesa lied to me, Father. She's equally to blame!" More mumbling followed.

"What did Mama lie about?"

"I don't know what Kim is talking about," her great Gran lied as the mumbling ceased.

"Can you understand what she said?" Serena questioned.

"No! Her voice is too deep and she keeps slurring her words then muttering. Besides, you know I'm hard of hearing."

"I'm so sorry, so sorry and so ashamed, Father. I couldn't believe Yong Sang's story. What happened will destroy the reputation of the whole family. They'll never live down the scandal."

"What story is she talking about, and what scandal?" Serena asked. Fear had crept into her voice as the deep muttering began again. No answer came from her great Gran. Kim then spoke in a normal voice and her words were clear.

"No sane person would believe you, Yong Sang. Everyone will agree you're the guilty one. And yet I am the one who needs forgiveness. Father, tell me. Will I ever be granted forgiveness?"

"What is my grandfather guilty of?" Serena almost spat at her great Gran, furious at Yuk Lin's refusal to answer her questions and at her own ignorance of what was going on.

"Oh, oh, oh, oh," Kim shouted, before again beginning to mutter. Between silences, the bass muttering resumed and continued. Then, after a long period, Kim proclaimed quite clearly: "that's why I did what I did."

"Oh God, please tell me great Gran," she pleaded. "What did Grandma Kim do?"

"I don't know, I've told you." She stonewalled, before adding: "Don't you see? She's muttering to herself, then confessing to Father Murphy and finally shouting at her husband. She doesn't know what she's doing. Since she's alone, it seems that she's lost her mind." There was a long silence before the loud muttering resumed and came through the locked door. The only word that both women heard clearly was 'murder.'

"Murder?" Serena whispered with fear and incredulity in her voice. "Who committed murder? For God's sake, great Gran, tell me what is happening!" She again pleaded. Her tone was a mixture of anger and distress.

"I can't hear or understand what she says," her great Gran lied as Kim continued to shout.

"I'm so sorry, so very sorry for what I did, but I just couldn't believe your story." Since Serena couldn't make very much sense of what she had heard and was wondering if grandma Kim had indeed lost her mind, she decided to wait until she could hear more before piecing together what all the muttering and shouting was about. Suddenly, Grandma Kim screamed:

"Incest? Incest? And in my own home, between the two people I love most!" A sound of deep and sorrowful moaning followed, before Kim again confronted her husband:

"Damn you! How could you have corrupted your own daughter?"

"Oh God, oh God," Serena wailed, turning towards her great Gran, begging her with a gesture of raised arms and eyebrows, palms upward to falsify what they had both heard. "Tell me that isn't really true? How could they have stooped so low?" Serena whispered. After a moment, Grandma Kim continued in a normal voice.

"Don't you see, I couldn't help it? I had to poison you." There was a long silence before she added in the innocent voice of a child:

"But, murder is always wrong, isn't it!" Then she began crying and laughing hysterically in a voice that was distinctly male. "Tell me Father, who will grant me forgiveness, who?"

On hearing those words, with bowed head, Serena decided to take matters into her own hands. She pounded loudly on the door, calling for Grandma Kim to open it. A long silence followed, and although she kept pounding on the door and calling, her grandmother refused either to answer or to open the door. The words Serena had heard were impossible to accept. It was like trying to swallow a bucket of water in a single gulp. Her mind choked on the colossal mass of depravity she had just heard. She rushed from the house, jumped into her car to find a place where she could be alone to contemplate the terrifying words and the implications of the confession she had just heard.

Hours after leaving Yong Sang's home, John felt constrained to find Kim, tell her of Yong Sang's death and confront her with his knowledge of her wickedness. He knew she had left her husband and gone to her mother's home. On his arrival, the dismal atmosphere of the house and its cold, struck him forcibly. Yuk Lin then told him that Kim had got some bad news, then had locked herself in her bedroom for a couple of weeks, talking to herself, screaming, and refusing to come out of her room or even to eat. She explained that Serena had come by and that they had both heard Kim's confusing confession.

"She kept talking to herself, to Father Murphy and to Yong Sang. What is also puzzling is that she kept speaking in different voices. She talked in a bass masculine voice like a man, then like herself and sometimes like a small child. But since she was alone, I believe that the torment plaguing her had unhinged her mind. Serena and I pounded on the door begging her to open it but she refused. Since then, there has been an eerie silence for the past few hours. I'm afraid that the seriousness of her problems has jarred her mental state. She might do injury to herself."

"What was the bad news?" John asked.

"She never told me." Yuk Lin replied.

"Perhaps she heard of her husband's death," he suggested. They then pounded on Kim's door and called to her a number of times. When there was no answer, John struck the door with his shoulder and flung it open. Immediately, the sickening scent of human feces mingled with the coppery scent of blood assaulted their nostrils and turned their stomachs.

A revolting sight met their eyes, as a shriek of despair rose from Yuk Lin's lips. She stood a moment in silence, shocked at the sight of her mangled daughter. A moaning escaped her lips, her legs gave way and she crumpled to her knees. The horrifying sight made John experience a sharp and painful sorrow. It was as though a steel shaft had been driven into his heart. Kim was on her knees in a sea of blood. Her body, before the shrine, was leaning backwards, propped up against the headboard and bedside. Her position made it obvious that she was dead, for her head hung backwards and her eyes, still open, stared upwards at the crucifix in an imploring manner. Her hands had fallen from an upright position and still clasped, rested against her bosom. She was evidently at prayer when death overtook her, but before praying, she had not only opened one wrist, but in her rage, she had also slashed at her neck, directly across the jugular vein. Though cut, it was not completely severed, but her blood had drained down one side of her body and pooled on the floor.

How she had managed to clasp her hands together after such cruel blood letting struck him as odd. Like her husband, she must have been obsessing on what she had done, perhaps with expiation in mind.

In the bathroom, Yuk Lin was slumped on the floor retching violently. When she stopped, John helped her with wet towels to clean herself. When he returned to the bedroom, the sight of Kim struck down like a broken doll wallowing in her own blood, made him sick at heart. He felt that no one should face death in such terror, and loneliness. As he looked at the tortured face, the blood encrusted wrists and her imploring gaze heavenward, he thought of how much she must have suffered before she so fiercely attacked herself. Her wrist was not only slit, it was butchered in what must have been a paroxysm of anger and hatred. He could only guess at the way her twisted mind had deteriorated, and wondered from what abyss of evil that hatred of herself had sprung.

Like a cop, Kim had written, God was never there when you needed Him. It was the last thought that she had scribbled on a pad before she had brutally attacked herself. John couldn't help thinking about the moving stories she had told of the Crucifixion and Christ's forgiveness of his persecutors while being tortured. She had been the person responsible for strengthening his faith; for making him a better Christian. The horrifying spectacle reminded him of the priest's words to Yong Sang: "The archfiend destroys families, especially those who are devout." He became convinced that such a frenzied assault upon oneself was a symptom of Satan's dominance, his evil.

Tears filled his eyes and grief rose up to overwhelm him with sorrow and regret at the death of another loved one. He thought of Kim's dedication to the church, the time and effort she expended to train the choir, play the organ, cultivate her garden and beautify the altar with her roses. He thought too of her generosity, giving the profits of her garden to the needy of her farming district and he remembered how her story of the crucifixion had become the trigger that led to his forgiveness of his wife. He turned his eyes away from Kim's mutilated body, mute testimony to a life worn down by inexpressible suffering. Indeed, the deplorable sight caused him an outpouring of compassion. Devout Christian that he was, he couldn't help wondering how He could permit the evil one to turn loving spouses so savagely against each other? Then, prolonging his blasphemy, he wondered what good was the crucifixion if it failed to bring hope to the distressed, the disillusioned and the dispossessed? He could find no answer. Instead of the peace and serenity that should have ended their lives of devotion to each other and to the Church, both Kim and Yong Sang had died scandalously from criminal conduct. Once again, evil had triumphed.

It seemed that hatred and humiliation must have twisted Kim's mind, inducing her to murder her husband. Perhaps only the cold rage of insanity could have allowed her to watch Yong Sang suffer while dying from her poison. She had then used the same cruel detachment of insanity to destroy herself. Wielding the knife, she was at once assassin and victim. He could only guess at the infernal rage that had goaded her to commit so vile and unspeakable a crime. Such horror, he thought, only played a part in Greek and Shakespearean tragedy. There, the heroes usually died from the clash between some character flaw and circumstance. Here, as in the loving bond between Romeo and Juliet, evil had been at the root of striking both spouses down. He could only wonder at the unearthly power that could transform the love that both felt for each other into such abject hatred.

Now he had to find Serena and try to console her.

Chapter 46

]n the chilling predawn hush, Serena saddled Will and rode up to the high pass, gazing at the vast and magnificent landscape stretching into the distance. Its seclusion and silence soon engulfed her. At first, the beauty of the scene did nothing to counteract the sorrow and disgust tormenting her heart and the turmoil and confusion immobilizing her brain. The shocking words from the mouth of her grandmother had smashed into her brain like bullets, shattering her reason. Since the revelation was too huge and solid a mass to digest quickly, she needed the seclusion, meditation and time to dwell on the revolting disclosure before she could work out the ramifications it held for her and her family.

So, Mona had told the truth. Her mother was not only a scarlet woman. She had also committed the revolting crime of incest. Good Christ, how does a daughter deal with so shocking a discovery? And since the man whom she thought was her father was not her real father, how should she relate to an incestuous one? Besides, did my supposed father not know of his wife's conduct? And if he knew, why did he accept it? Then again if he knew the truth and accepted it, shouldn't she do likewise? Finally, how should she relate to him? Oh God, oh God, this catastrophe was too confusing and complicated a mess. But what could she do about it?

Needing time to think, to give her fevered mind a rest, she turned her thoughts towards prayer and meditation. Her meditation over, she then opened her eyes to the panorama spreading out before her and focused on the green wildness of the mountain chain and its incredible vastness. Immediately, the grandeur of the scene struck her with its majesty. Faced with its immensity as with the limitless vault of the sky, she suddenly saw herself as less than a grain of sand enveloped in the vastness of the universe. Ever so gradually, the consuming disgust, the sick sense of despair weighing her down and overpowering her spirit, began to dwindle, to evaporate and slip from her shoulders. Perhaps it was her prayers or perhaps it was the breathtaking grandeur of the scene that had granted her a grace. Its very majesty had seeped into her being, calming her spirit; tranquilizing her soul. She couldn't help but glory in the therapeutic experience.

Of course, the sensation was only temporary, for those two unspeakable words, 'incest' and 'murder' that had exploded from the lips of her grandmother, rocketed her back to reality. She couldn't help asking herself: How could her grandfather commit so heinous a crime against his own daughter? Worse, supposing that her mother had been the seductress, would Serena still want to welcome her back into her life? And since her grandfather was her biological father, how could she consider living at peace with such severely depraved creatures?

When Serena took time to deliberate on the incestuous act that had driven Grandma Kim into so jealous a rage that she murdered her husband with poison, she felt sick to her stomach. She realized that it was the initial reprehensible act of her mother that had set in motion the whole web of evil. Now that she knew the true character of her mother, would she be able to love such a creature? Would she be willing to welcome her mother back into her life? Could she? Now that her mother needed the love and support of her family, wouldn't Serena's renunciation of her be another betrayal? Her mind was so tortured, confused and in such turmoil, that she could no longer think logically.

It suddenly dawned on her that once the autopsy took place, and the poison found, Grandma Kim would be arrested, tried as a murderess and sentenced to death. But long before the case came to court, the scandal would rock the family to its very foundations. Oh God, oh God, this mountain of corruption had her wondering if the evil genes polluting her incestuous mother and father lay dormant in some secret part of her being. Was it possible that she could be exempt? She then set about researching her past to see whether the term evil could be attributed to any of her actions. Since she could only think of her refusal to forgive her mother, she concluded that perhaps she might be exempt from the curse, but only so far. What did her future hold? Finally, she began to think of the influence that the ungodly acts of her real parents would have on the rest of the family and on her? Those were the questions that kept tormenting her; questions that she'd have to put to the only father she knew.

Once again captivated by the majesty of the scene, all concerns about herself again gradually evaporated. It was as thought the mountain wilderness had expunged her ego. She felt cleansed, reborn, like the wilderness washed by rain. The calamity that had dominated her life a moment before had ceased to exist momentarily. Nature had granted her the grace of centering herself, feeling whole again. She rode up to the cave, and kneeling under the overhang at the entrance, prayed that God might grant forgiveness to her family and to her. Next, she prayed that she, and the man she loved, would find happiness together.

Dear Stephen,

Since you departing Korea, Serena learning much bad news about family. Serena ashamed saying you how mother committed incest with father, Yong Sang, both grandfather and Serena real father. Knowledge of own disgraceful act forcing Yong Sang confession to wife, Grandma Kim. In jealous rage, she pretending forgiveness but begin poison him slow. Yong Sang death making her murderess. When autopsy revealing poison in Yong Sang's body, Grandma Kim facing arrest, trial, conviction, sentencing to prison, perhaps death. Great scandal descending on whole Ahn family from mother initial act.

Serena not wanting innocent husband, Stephen link with degenerate Ahn family. Already she consulting lawyers, agreeing with advice. Before marriage, Stephen ignorant Ahn family corruption. Thus, no problem removing himself at unsavory situation. Lawyers also pointing out husband wife separation immediately after wedding, thus marriage unconsummated. So Stephen obtaining annulment easy.

Serena so sorry, so ashamed describing disgraceful family problem. She asking forgiveness from husband. She understanding Stephen feelings. He not knowing if Serena carry evil gene of parents. Stephen not wanting possible monster in offspring. Serena needing know when Stephen wanting begin annulment process.

Serena.

After John had learnt that Serena had heard her grandma's confession, he tried desperately to reach her. He rushed to his home, but she wasn't there. He tried to reach her by phone, but got no answer. Finally, he tried his office, worried about the devastating effect Kim's confession would have on her. He was in deep distress until alerted that Serena was on her way to his office. On arrival, she was ushered in by one of his secretaries who immediately withdrew. Serena appeared white faced and exhausted. In silence, John opened his arms and Serena burst into tears as she rushed into his embrace. She clung to him sobbing helplessly. He hugged her in return until her crying stopped. "Dad," she pleaded, "Tell me everything you know about mama." Before he could speak, she added: "truthfully, without defending her in any way."

Chapter 47

"Dearest daughter, according to Yong Sang, her husband who knew her best, the truth of the matter is that your mother was born a very dissatisfied person, and grew to become a deeply disturbed personality. The close and clinging bond she initiated with her father, from the time she was little, was an attempt to shut out her mother, whom she regarded as a rival. The fact is that she became hostile towards Kim, wedging herself between husband and wife at every opportunity. As early as kindergarten she began lying: 'her mother died when she was born.' She was always rebellious towards Kim, refusing to let her dress, undress or bathe her, then threw the worst kind of tantrums to get her way. Such conduct forced Yong Sang to usurp his wife's role as mother. Kim managed to ignore her unacceptable behavior throughout her youth and early teens, but lost her temper when, from a concealed spot, she surprised Leesa urinating into her teapot."

"What! Oh my God! Mama did that to her own mother? She had to be a real monster! Serena stated with a deep frown, her face contorted in an expression of intense distaste.

"So, what did Grandma Kim do?"

"Kim grabbed and choked her within an inch of her life. Fortunately, Yong Sang heard the screams and the ruckus, appearing just in time to save Leesa's life. But instead of blaming his daughter, he sternly censured his wife whose ungovernable temper had almost killed their only child."

"Perhaps it would have been better if Yong Sang hadn't arrived in time." Serena whispered, without even realizing that she had spoken.

"But then, you wouldn't have been born, and that would have been a greater tragedy," her father stated. "On hearing the lovemaking between her parents, Leesa became angry, taking her father to task with the mistaken belief that he and her mother were deliberately conspiring to humiliate her. She complained that they were shamefully parading the fact that his wife, Kim, and not his daughter, Leesa, was first in his affections."

"So, she was not only wicked, she was also delusional!"

"Just before our marriage she kept having severe mood swings. She was the school's best athlete then gave up athletics without explanation. She attended church regularly then suddenly stopped going, again without explanation. She demanded a huge Western style church wedding with bridal gown, bridesmaids, full choir, orchestra and dancing. After inviting a long list of friends and family, she then sent back the invitations and gifts settling for a civil ceremony with family alone present. As a result of her unseemly conduct and twisted reasoning, her parents concluded, like you, that she was irrational, delusional and seriously unbalanced. However, it was Kim's belief that there was a terrible struggle between good and evil taking place within her daughter that was tearing her apart. Yong Sang agreed and both considered that she needed therapy. They told her that from her many false conclusions, she seemed delusional and needed help. They then begged her to see a psychologist."

"Did she agree with them? Did she see a psyche?"

"Instead of interpreting their concern as a means of helping her, she saw it as an attempt to get her certified so they could put her away. Their humiliating inference that she was insane drove her wild. Her deep resentment caused her anger to flare and in a paroxysm of fury, she decided to destroy them both by an incestuous act. They believed that it was spite; a desire to destroy through revenge rather than lust that motivated her."

"Oh my God! I didn't know it was she who initiated the seduction."

"It was. While Kim was away tending a sick friend, Leesa drugged her father with sleeping pills, then, when he was unconscious in sleep, she went naked to his mat."

"Oh my God! Dad, I can't believe that you knew all this and still married her."

"No Serena. I didn't know any of it. I believed the lie that Leesa told me. She said that she had been raped and pleaded with me to keep her secret. It was only recently that I learned what really happened from Yong Sang. He begged me to listen to his confession while he lay dying and told me the truth. Then, after your mother lied to you about Stephen and you cut her off, she confessed that she had lied to me. Only then did she confirm Yong Sang's story."

"Dad, I can't understand how you could live with, let alone love, such, such, a hideous monster."

"Serena, my darling, there's another whole side to the story about your mother that you need to hear."

"I'm listening dad, but I hope you're not excusing Mama for the horrible crimes she committed?"

My very own darling Serena,

How could you possibly think that I would permit the immoral conduct of others to stain you with their evil, my innocent wife? It is absurd to blame the innocent family members for the gross indecency of the family's black sheep. I want you to know that as far as I'm concerned, the scandal of the family that you described has nothing whatever to do with you. I know from personal experience that you haven't got one iota of evil within you. Therefore, I want you to forget the advice of your lawyers, and put that silly notion of an easily attained annulment out of your head. I have no intention of extricating myself from our marriage and of losing the innocent and beautiful bride that I married. Serena, you should know by now that I love you very much. So, you had better get on with your study of English. I do agree with you that living with Joe and Sally will allow you to make rapid progress in speaking the language correctly and increasing your fluency. It will also allow you the choice of being away from contact with your mother.

I have no doubt that rumor of the scandal will run rampant from the chattering jaws of your neighbors. I wish I could be there to protect you from some of the awful things they will say. But since doing so will solve nothing, I've put the idea out of my mind.

I need to tell you that your father sent us a gorgeous wedding gift of a luxurious three bedroom home that is mortgage free. It is located in a nice neighborhood and comes complete with a two bedroom apartment downstairs that is fully furnished and self-contained. He suggests that we rent it out and use the proceeds to pay our utilities, taxes and help with living expenses. He was extremely generous in giving me a check to buy myself a new car and anything else that we might need. I have also opened an account in your name into which I have deposited the second check that he made out to you for a new car and anything else you might want or need. I have already emailed your dad thanking him for his thoughtfulness and generosity. You should do the same. Now I must go to work, my darling and send you my love.

Stephen.

"No, Serena. I offer no excuses for your mother's conduct. However, there are facts that you should know. Your mother, from her earliest youth, has had an ongoing struggle between good and evil that kept tearing her apart. She knew that two opposing characters existed within her, a good and an evil person. She had to keep up a constant and desperate battle to stifle and expunge her evil nature. She spent years, Serena, years visiting different churches, confessing to numerous priests, begging for help to break the evil spell that threatened to paralyze her conscience and dominate her life. In short, though she was always drawn towards evil, she kept trying to be good.

"Dad, where did you get this information?" She kept rubbing her two fingers together with the rising tension of her voice. Her father noticed but continued as if she hadn't spoken.

"She prayed fervently, even confronted God, cursing Him aloud for permitting Satan to pursue and persecute her, knowing that mortal humans stand no chance against an enemy that was immortal. She fought long and hard, resisting again and again the urge to be wicked, repeatedly postponing the earlier decision she had made to destroy her parents. Eventually, getting no help from priests or God, and in physical, mental and emotional exhaustion, she surrendered." There was a long silence between them before he stated:

"Serena, I would like you to answer a few questions truthfully. Will you?"

"Certainly Dad, if I can."

"Tell me; in the eighteen years that you've known her, has Leesa been an exemplary mother to you?"

"Yes Dad, she has been everything that a mother could be." After a pause she added: "I can never forget all she did to help me recover from my violation. I owe her my life!" While stating these facts she had the grace to blush.

"From your knowledge over the same period, has she been an exemplary wife to me?

"Yes Dad. I can't deny that. She has watched over you like a guardian angel."

"Didn't she confess to you that she was ashamed of her badly checkered past, and that she wanted to turn over a new leaf by helping the farmers?"

"Yes. She also admitted her shame of being so selfish that she had completely ignored the needs of others."

"Did she say that your example of helping the farmers made her guilty and ashamed?"

"Yes. She did say those were the reasons motivating her to rack her brains and come up with the rice paddy and fish farming project. But I hadn't recognized her decision as the outcome of an ongoing struggle against her wickedness." As Serena began to feel less antagonistic towards her mother the motion of her fingers were no longer going at full speed.

"Well, I can tell you. That was definitely a major part of her motivation. Then, she was also following your example of generosity to the farming community by creating her 'watchdogs, wasn't she?"

"Yes, that's true. She made a vital contribution to the farming community and actually admitted later that she was trying to atone for her sins of the past."

"So you *were* aware of the continuous battle she was fighting against her evil nature?"

"I suppose so but that didn't really register since I couldn't believe that the mother I knew then could be guilty of any serious wrongdoing."

"And did she later take it upon herself to organize the distribution of firewood to the farmers during that terrible winter?"

"Yes. When Tina made her aware of their needs, Mama got Mr. Sing to distribute firewood to the distressed farmers."

"Did she, in certain emergency situations, round up the sick and the suffering of the district, drive them herself to the doctor, and pay for both the doctor's fees and their medication out of her own pocket?"

"Yes, she did. Throughout that terrible winter each time she heard from Tina about any illness in the farming community."

"Was it her idea to get me to buy the farmers surplus rice and fish?"

"Yes Dad. She knew that the extra money they made would go a long way to better their lifestyle."

"Wasn't it she who organized the collection of rice from the farmers for it to be shipped and sold to my grocery outlets?"

"Yes, and I remember it was mama who arranged for the fish to be cleaned, packaged and frozen so it could be collected and sold. She also managed to organize a fish collection point and its transport to your groceries. Her idea proved to be a great financial benefit to the farmers."

"Are you aware that while you were at school she visited Father Murphy after his attempted suicide, and did his cooking, cleaning and washing? And, did you know that she cared for and fed him every day for almost two months nursing him back to health?"

"No. She never mentioned it. Dad, where did you get this information?" At this point the speed of her fingers was moving far more slowly.

"Did you know that when your mother learnt that Father Murphy was about to be defrocked and dismissed from the priesthood, she took it upon herself to visit the bishop without the knowledge of the priest? She then defended Father Murphy so fiercely that the bishop reinstated him as our parish priest."

"No! She never mentioned it, and no one knows she interceded on his behalf."

"Did you know that she also succeeded in getting the bishop to convert the hovel in which the priest lives into a respectable presbytery?"

"No! No one knows anything about that. But are you trying to tell me that Mama is a saint?"

"I haven't finished. There's a bit more about your mother that you need to know."

"I'm still listening, Dad."

"Your mother got the bishop to double Father Murphy's stipend that was made retroactive for three months?"

"Dad, where did you get all these incredible stories?"

"Yes, they are incredible and I got them from Father Murphy himself. The fact is my darling daughter, that throughout her life, your mother has been involved in a lifelong fight against her evil demons that kept tearing her apart.

Therefore, before condemning her for her evil, as you already have, you need to balance your judgment by considering her good deeds as well."

"Okay Dad, but when I focus on the evil things she did, I begin to tremble with rage, and want to scream out my humiliation. I can't repress the anger I feel, or silence the awful noises in my head. The best I can say is that her conduct leaves me terribly ashamed and confused. As you know, infidelity and betrayal are terrible sins. But incest is in a league of its own."

"Serena, it's very wrong of you to focus solely on your mother's wicked ways. She has committed many good deeds to balance against her wrongdoing. *You* especially should be the first to be aware of that. "

"Dad, the truth is I don't want to think about her at all, yet I can't stop myself. When I consider that her initial incestuous act led to her father's murder, and her mother's suicide, I want to crawl under a rock in shame and hide myself from so revolting a monster. And I realize that you and I, although innocent, have no way of defending ourselves against the scalding slander that will severely scar and perhaps destroy the reputation of the family. Dad, how could I not feel tainted to have come from such a dual abomination?"

"I find your criticism nothing short of vitriolic! You should always remember that your mother loves you and is suffering severely from the rift between the two of you."

"Dad, at the moment, I can't face her. So, I've thought it best to stay away."

"What do you mean? Where will you go?"

"I plan to use the waiting period for Canada's grant of landed immigrant status, to go and live with Joe and Sally."

"Who are Joe and Sally?"

"Both are ESL teachers that Stephen met and befriended on the bus from Seoul. But since I haven't talked to them, my plans are not yet finalized."

"Suppose they don't agree?"

"I think they'll agree since I have a few suggestions that might interest them."

"With two teachers, you'll be able to progress far more quickly in English grammar and fluency," was all he could think of saying. But he didn't say he would miss her was all he was thinking.

Chapter 48

"Dad, I cannot help thinking that before and after I leave Korea, the heavy fallout from the scandal will descend upon you like acid rain. With that in mind, I find it hard to accept the stern and stupid watchword of our small town: 'Caesar's wife must be virtuous.' I worry about how you will weather that cruel storm."

"No doubt, vicious rumors will circulate about your mother and me, as they have in the past. And as in the past, we will ignore what is said and live through the scandal. After all, they are only cruel words whispered in secret. Besides gossips are never sure if what they say is true."

"Dad, it's so unfair that the innocent should be vilified and suffer for the guilty," Serena told him sadly.

"My dear, you are learning that the world we live in doesn't always play fair."

On reading Stephen's email, Serena felt that a great weight was lifted from her shoulders. The relief was enormous. Stephen's attitude allayed her secret fears of being alone in Korea with an estranged husband living abroad. She emailed him at once expressing her relief, her feelings of gratitude and ended by sending him her love.

Stephen sent her the address and phone number of Joe and Sally who lived in the city of Jeonju, some 80 kilometers north west of Hamyang. Serena phoned, inviting them to spend a day at the farm where she would explain to them what she had in mind. The couple accepted the invitation, arriving early on Saturday morning as Serena had requested. They went through all the niceties of Korean protocol before having a hearty breakfast. Serena then conducted them to her father's study where she unveiled her plan:

"When Stephen and Serena marry, he departing Korea resuming Canada job. Serena waiting here, while Canada granting landed immigration status. While waiting, Serena wanting in-depth study of the English, learning grammar, increasing fluency. She wanting you two teaching her." Her words, like those of her father, were spoken in bursts of word groups, scattered like sprays of water sinking into fertile soil.

The couple looked at each other in astonishment and after a moment, nodded their heads in agreement.

"Sally and I are willing to teach you. Maybe you can visit us on evenings and weekends for lessons, if that is convenient to you. We live in Jeonju, quite some distant from here." Joe replied.

"Thanks, but Serena offering different proposition. She coming live you house. As 'guest,' she paying both living and study expenses. Otherwise, Serena not accepting lessons." Needless to say, the couple was completely taken by surprise, not having had the slightest inkling of Serena's plan.

"Why do you want to live with us?" Joe asked. "We live in a humble two bedroom rental apartment, nothing as luxurious as your beautiful home."

"Serena much interested at improving the English. Not important, luxury."

"Very well then," said Sally, "we agree to accept you as a paying guest, but we'll decide on the payment for living expenses after we see how much you eat." They all laughed until Serena asked: "It okay starting lessons right now?" Once again Joe and Sally were caught off guard by Serena's impulsive nature. They noted as well, her eagerness to improve her speech. It took only a moment's thought for Joe to reply:

"Serena, for someone who doesn't speak the language fluently, you have a very large vocabulary and communicate your ideas fairly clearly." Pausing, he added: "But you assassinate language, abuse word order, annihilate and torture sentence structure and demolish grammar. You avoid pronouns and prepositions like the plague, and strangle verbs using only their present participles." Joe's forthrightness drew a burst of laughter from Serena who carefully covered her mouth with her hand as protocol demanded. Tears of hilarity filled her eyes when Sally sugar coated her husband's critique by adding: "In spite of what Joe says Serena, your speech is a marvel of linguistic engineering." Everyone laughed again and the couple was pleased to learn that Serena had a sense of humor.

"Okay, Serena. Let's begin with work on personal and other pronouns and verbs in the present tense. We'll tackle past tenses and prepositions later," Joe said as he went to her father's desk, took up two books, one of which he gave to Serena. He then told her to mimic each of his gestures and to repeat exactly what he said. "My book," Joe stated, clasping the book to his chest and patting it each time he repeated the pronoun, 'my.' Serena did as he asked. Then, pointing at Serena's book while she pointed at his, he stated: "Your book." She followed his lead, repeating the word 'your,' each time she pointed. Next, Joe pointed to the photograph of her father on the desk and stated: "his book," then at Sally, "her book." With a circular gesture including all of them, Joe stated: "our book." Finally, pointing to the group photograph of Serena and family on the desk, Joe said: "their book." Each gesture and statement was repeated a number of times. Serena followed all Joe's gestures and with repetition quickly got the hang of the exercise. The repetition continued until Sally took over.

Following Joe's lead, she used a variety of the different objects in the room to reinforce what Serena had already learnt. Using the appropriate gestures, Sally stated: "my desk, our chair, your picture, his letter, their clothes." She put her student through her paces, over and over, then made Serena assume the role of teacher with Sally as student. Pointing to different objects, the new teacher stated the correct pronoun making Sally repeat what she said before each object or person she indicated. After more than two hours of repetition, the teachers, considering that Serena had been drilled enough with personal, and later, reflexive pronouns, suggested they take a well-deserved break. Clearly, they didn't know Serena who believed, like her Sensei, that breaks should be brief. So after only a short breather, she asked them to begin teaching her the verbs. Her enthusiasm made Joe and Sally realize that they had their work cut out for them in the coming weeks and months. They would definitely earn their fees.

Once Serena moved into the couple's apartment, Joe and Sally alternated as teachers using the same pointing method of teaching the three personal pronouns, singular and plural that went with each verb. I go, you go, he, she or it goes, followed by the plural forms. The lessons continued each evening during the week after work, either teacher using different verbs before progressing from the present to the simple past and finally to the future tenses.

The couple realized that Serena was a gifted student and over the next months would make rapid progress in both grammar and fluency.

An added advantage to Joe and Sally was the surprise that met them each evening of the week when they returned from work. After completing the written assignments set by her hosts the previous evening, Serena first did the house cleaning needed—the couple had kept the apartment spotlessly clean–before cooking supper. She had become a fairly decent cook through the coaching of Tina, her mother's part-time help, whose limited repertoire had been greatly enhanced by her mother. Serena's hosts really enjoyed her surprises, and on weekends Sally returned the compliment taking turns at the stove. She offered some of her favorite Japanese dishes: *karagi* chicken, *tempura* dishes of prawns, carrots, egg plant, yam and onions, or *sashimi*, thinly sliced tuna smothered in a variety of sauces. One of her favorites was *yakitori*, Bar BQ'D chicken and Bell peppers smothered in Teriyaki sauce. *Wasabi,* (hot radish) slivers of ginger and *miso* soup were always on the menu. Sometimes she presented them with savory tidbits like *ebi, unagi,* or *onago* and *California rolls* or *sunomuno* salad garnished with shrimp or crab. Of course, some form of *kimshi* was always present. However, it was Serena who got the greatest and most delightful surprise whenever Joe did the cooking. He introduced her to a sumptuous array of African dishes: rice pilaf with stewed chicken and potatoes in brown gravy; okra slush, ripe plantain sliced lengthwise then fried and sprinkled with granulated sugar; sliced avocados, small taro roots boiled, buttered and rubbed with lime, broiled yams, and roasted turnips. He also curried prawns or dredged them in egg, dipped them in flour and then fried them. He also diced chicken breast or fried filets of fish heavily dusted with a mixture of curry powder and flour and served with rice or pasta. At first, Serena remained glued to the side of both her hosts while they cooked. Afterwards, she busily copied the recipes for each of the dishes which she later helped Joe and Sally prepare. Finally, they both helped her to practice the new culinary skills so she could surprise Stephen in Canada.

The salacious rumors that were circulating about the Ahn family, and more particularly about her own depravity, had reached Leesa and they were, as expected, especially cruel. As she knelt in the confessional to unburden herself, she couldn't withhold tears of shame.

"Father," she sobbed, "my own daughter hates me so much that she excluded me from witnessing her wedding ceremony. Can you believe that?"

"Yes, yes I know. But she did reunite with you after the wedding. So you're wrong. I know she doesn't hate you. She needed time to get used to the negative things she has just learnt about you. She was no doubt waiting for the time when the horrid rumors that were flying around subsided." His compassion goaded him into softening the ugly truth.

"But I don't have time. She's gone to live with ESL teachers while she waits for her landed immigration status from Canada to arrive. She told my husband that she couldn't face me now, when she considers the terrible things I've done."

"Under deep stress people often say things that they don't really mean." He said, trying to comfort her.

"She meant every word, Father. I can still hear the venom expressed in the words she used to me, her mother: "Love Mama, you don't understand the meaning of the word. Love is a free giving of oneself. Your love doesn't give. It's a taking, a selfish grasping; a possession.""

"In anger, people say things they don't mean," he repeated, trying to soften the hurt that was evident in her voice. But what was your reply?"

"Reply? I was so stunned. All I could do was to beg her forgiveness because I knew what she said was true. Father, you no doubt remember that, as a youth, I behaved as though my father was my personal possession and I was especially rebellious towards my mother."

"Some children develop clinging bonds with either one of their parents. Later, it can turn out to be a normal relationship," the priest said. He was again trying to console his deeply distressed penitent.

"Not when that bond poisons your mind against the other parent and turns you into a willful and rebellious child."

"You may have started on the wrong foot, but your many acts of generosity on my behalf and on behalf of the farming community show that you have a good heart, an innate fund of goodness and of generosity, my child."

"Goodness and generosity, Father? Ha! Those are not the words my daughter would use." She repeated Serena's words that were scorched into the fabric of her memory: "Mama, what you call love is venomous. It poisons your mind. You contaminate, Mama, you kill."

"When she spoke those words Serena was overwrought. You shouldn't take what she said as the truth."

"No Father, what she said was true! The hatred I nurtured for my parents had driven me to destroy them both by the incestuous act I committed. I can only try to imagine the disastrous effect that had on my husband, my grand-mother, my mother, and now, on my own daughter?"

"Leesa, that was in the distant past. It's over. You have to let it go."

"No, Father. I haven't changed. Recently, the love I had for my daughter also expressed itself in the form of a possession. My lying to Serena about Stephen's words was purely selfish. It was a means of holding on to her. I com-pletely overlooked her feelings, only thought about my own. I'm still as selfish as ever."

"Mothers always feel a wrench in the gut at the prospect of losing a beloved child. But, you did go further than most in trying to separate the young couple," he said as gently as he could.

"Yes. I almost destroyed the love they felt for each other; their happiness and Serena's exciting challenge of starting a new life in a foreign country. My selfishness encouraged me to do all that."

"Leesa, listen to me. From what you've said I can see that you're in a state of deep distress and depression. But, you mustn't give in to those negative thoughts. You mustn't let the evil one tempt you or lead you to despair. Lean on your faith. Remember all the good things you've done for the farming com-munity, for me and especially for your daughter. Never stop praying my child, and the dark night of this calamity will pass. Leesa, I can never forget that without a word from me, you came to my rescue in my travail. Thanks to you I now have a life. Even if I were not a priest I'll be there for you whenever you need me."

But Leesa had stopped listening to the priest. The peace she had expected to find in prayer and confession was an illusion. Having been unwelcome at the ceremony of her daughter's marriage, and cast adrift from her company forever, she was bowed down with the heavy weight of despair. She would pay for her wickedness by a life of estrangement from the person she loved most. It was just one more installment of punishment from her Maker. From that moment on, she felt that life held nothing in store for her but the punishment of profound regret, sorrow and distress. What an irony! She thought since the calamity was self made. She had been her own worst enemy.

Serena's life with Joe and Sally had taken on a new dimension. Apart from the normal conversation of their daily lives, she was constantly learning a multitude of little things about the Western way of life that her hosts followed. She learnt the laying of the table with either a full table cloth or a place mat for each person. For breakfast, lunch or dinner, a large plate sat in the center of each place setting flanked by fork on its left and knife on its right, cutting edge to the plate. Tea cups and saucers with tea spoons on the top right of each setting for breakfast, were replaced with a water and wine glass for supper. The Western way was totally different from the situation at her home. There, everyone sat on a cushion around a low table serving himself from a variety of dishes, their turn always dictated by rank. At Joe and Sally's home, everyone sat at the same time, and Sally either served everyone, always beginning with her guest, as politeness dictated. Sometimes, the dishes were passed around for everyone to serve himself. In Western tradition, Korean protocol was often turned upside down.

Through repetition, she learnt the English names for each item of clothing that men and women wear, for the different cooking utensils, and for the different methods of cooking–frying, poaching, boiling, baking, stewing, sautéing. Visiting the supermarkets or groceries was always a treat. There, she learnt the English names of the meats and the location in the animal that each cut came from. Then, there were the various sea foods and the seasonings used in each recipe and of course the vegetables and other edible produce they used in the home. At the department stores she learnt the names of the furniture used in bedroom, bathroom, living room, dining room and kitchen as well as the names of each appliance used there. The continuous challenge of learning never seemed to stop, but she absorbed it all like an incredibly thick and thirsty sponge. The continuous grind of the memory work helped to keep her mind from dwelling on the hardship of life away from her husband.

A homework assignment that she particularly enjoyed was the single paragraph essay. Her teachers would give her a list of nouns and verb infinitives that centered on a simple topic: a day at the beach, a walk into the mountains, a visit to a farm or to the cinema, a burglary in a home. She'd have to write an essay using the list, on which she could expand using her own words. Joe and Sally would correct the essay then ask her simple questions based on what she had written. After answering questions using the correct pronouns first with the present tense and later with the simple past, she would then assume the role of teacher. She'd have to question Joe and Sally on the text using both tenses. Finally, she would have to give a verbal account of the topic again using both tenses. She found it an excellent natural method of learning a language. She didn't have to undergo the grinding routine of memorizing the meaning of each noun, verb, adjective and preposition over and over. Their teaching method eliminated the mind-numbing process of repetition that drove students crazy with its monotony.

Serena decided to give Joe and Sally a surprise. Since a host of 'old' but very popular Korean movies was again showing in Seoul and Serena had learnt that her hosts were avid movie fans, she invited them to accompany her to the capital for the week end. They would see some of those films that had outsold Hollywood box office hits like Star Wars, The Matrix, and Harry Potter. It was unusual to have so many Korean movies showing at the same cinema and at the same time. The government limits the showing of foreign films to no more than 40%, thus mandating 60% of their shows to be Korean. She paid for their tickets on the Bullet train, as well as their hotel accommodation. Joe and Sally bought all their movie tickets, and Serena paid for their meals. They found *Shiri* exciting, as was *Joint Security Area*, *My Sassy Girl*, and *Friend*. All were low budget stories of romance, jealousy and violence. Very little sex is permitted in Korean films. They thoroughly discussed each film for its interesting stories, the down-to-earth characters and the fantastic cinematography. Later on, Joe and Sally used each of the films as a topic for English discussion and conversation focusing on the simplest story line as well as the characterization. The trip turned out to afford Serena excellent practice in the accumulation of new vocabulary and in her fluency.

After the movies, they headed down to Myeong-dong's Chinatown to have *jangmyeon*, a bowl of noodles covered in a sweet black bean sauce, pan fried prawns on a bed of onions and *yang chow* fried rice. They also did a little shopping. All agreed that their sojourn in Seoul was a most enjoyable interlude after the routine of studying for weeks on end.

Dearest Stephen,

I hope my email shows that I'm making progress in my writing, as in my speech. Joe and Sally are excellent teachers whose methods have eliminated the monotony of learning by rote. We all went to Seoul and had an enjoyable break from our weekly routine, traveled on the Bullet train, stayed at a comfortable hotel, and saw some interesting movies. In spite of the fun, I kept wishing that you were here to share my enjoyment.

I've been learning to cook some of my hosts' recipes of foreign dishes with which I plan to surprise you. I keep in touch with dad to let him know of my progress in both the language and the 'nouvelle cuisine.' He feels sad about my absence and the way mama is suffering. But I've told him that I still can't face her. Although I'm ashamed of myself for the way I have acted towards her, the truth is that I wouldn't know how to behave, what to say or even how to look at her now that her past is an open book.

It's almost ten months since you left and every day I watch for the mailman hoping that he has news for me. But he's brought me nothing. So I wait impatiently, while pining away for my absent husband. I miss you my dearest and send you all my love.

Serena

While missing his wife, Stephen often thought about his promise to her after he had learned of her violation and proposed marriage. He repeated that all she needed to heal her emotional wounds was his patience, tenderness and devotion. However, he noted that Serena was far from convinced, although his admission warmed her heart. She had permitted him to kiss and caress her, but had never allowed him to go any further. The patience and control she forced him to exercise had caused him tremendous frustration and annoyance. As he thought about the situation, he began to believe in Serena's prediction. The seven month separation would give her all the time she needed to recover. He couldn't wait for the time when she would fulfill *all* the functions of a wife.

However, he felt that as her husband, it seemed to him natural for her to crave intimacy with the man whom she loved and married. He thought of collecting articles extolling the bonds of unity that intimacy created between husband and wife. He'd post them to her for her to learn the delights of the marriage bed they were both missing. But the new Stephen would not dare to stoop so low. The virtue of honesty would not be at all easy to adopt or follow, he realized, not for the first time.

Finally, the papers giving Serena landed immigration status in Canada had arrived. She had to give a stool sample to her doctor and get the certified results as well as injections against Yellow fever before packing her bags. She was sad to leave her new friends, and thanked them for their considerable help with her English. She suggested that they too should immigrate to Canada and promised to write. She then gave them a painting of a black and tan Doberman, alert with bright eyes, pointed ears, sleek head and muscular body. The gift would help to curb Sally's yearning for a dog, since pets were forbidden in the apartment. She thanked Serena as they said their goodbyes. She had another sad parting at dad's office, for he begged her again to forgive her mother before leaving Korea.

"Dad, I love you dearly, and wish only the best for you and mama, but I don't think I can face her. Let me try to explain the way I feel: With betrayal and infidelity, you abandon your principles. With incest, you abandon your soul." She then said: "Dad, tell mama I love her and would like her to continue my poultry farming. Her donations will boost her self esteem by putting the needs of others before her own. Maybe then, her guilt and shame will evaporate. It will also help her to atone for what she's done." Her father told her she would do well to take her own advice. He then replied:

"Why don't you give her that message yourself?"

"Good bye Dad, I love you," she said as she hugged and kissed him before leaving.

She then immediately went to visit Mr. Sing.

"You have been such a good friend, collaborated with me on all my projects, often at your own expense. Then you counseled me so well and so often that I had to come and thank you for your generosity and to say good bye. If mama doesn't continue to help the farmers, will you act on my behalf? I'd like to think that their welfare is in good hands."

"I'll do my best, Miss. I wish you the very best for the future, knowing that you have a generous soul and will accomplish great things for others. Good bye good friend and God speed!"

They hugged.

Part 3

Victoria, British Columbia, Canada

Chapter 49

Serena was very excited as she boarded the plane for Canada. She kept hearing in her mind the strains of Sinatra's *Come fly with me* as she thought of finally reuniting with Stephen. Since she knew the long flight would be boring, she managed to sleep for a few hours before their final descent. When later she stepped off the plane at Victoria International Airport, she was trembling; overcome with anxiety. Finally, she would be with the man she loved and in the country about which she had heard so much. As she descended the roll-away staircase from the aircraft to the tarmac, she got her first surprise. She caught a whiff of the salt fresh air that was an unfamiliar scent. To her, it was so fresh and clean that it added a whole new dimension to the air. Her second surprise came from the weather. It was early February and she expected to be greeted by freezing cold. She thought she would see a thick blanket of snow covering the landscape, exactly as when she had left home. But on landing, she was greeted with sunshine, balmy weather and lush green lawns. She couldn't believe that the only signs of winter were the small pockets of snow that remained in sheltered areas or collected in piles as though it had been swept there. A passenger, leaving on the next flight, was collecting snippets of green grass from the lawn. She was carrying proof to her relations back east that Victoria was really the Garden City and Canada's 'banana belt.' By the time she entered the air-conditioned airport the clean fresh smell she had first encountered had vanished.

Her third and biggest surprise was Stephen's tight bear hug at their meeting, and the long, soulful kisses he pressed upon her. She blushed scarlet, since it was unthinkable for her to display such intimate emotions in public. She could see that Stephen was taken aback by her lack of enthusiasm. However, she managed to bring her emotions under control as she answered his questions about the trip and her parents, while concealing the fear that had emerged from his overheated greeting.

What floored her was the realization that her old fears, involving male intimacy, had not disappeared. She immediately recalled the rush of novel and stirring sensations throughout her body that Stephen's kisses had aroused in Korea. She therefore couldn't understand why after nearly a year, she was still so overwhelmed by his male presence. How was it possible after all that time that she had not fully healed? She now knew that while kissing and caressing was the same as before, going any further was still out of the question. Of course, she didn't dare confess her growing fears to Stephen. Not yet, anyway.

On looking around, she could see many of the other passengers greeting their loved ones and friends. Men and women embraced effusively with the same excessive hugging and kissing, often soulfully on the lips. What seemed quite natural to them made her feel very uncomfortable. Men even embraced each other tightly in greeting, often with both hands clasped around each other, ending with a slap or two on the back. People waved goodbye lifting their hands, palm forward, moving them from left to right, instead of up and down as they did at home. A few were even wiping away tears with fingers or handkerchiefs. She was not used to seeing such naked emotion expressed so publicly. By comparison, Koreans were an introverted people, and thanks to their protocol, far more circumspect.

She told Stephen that he looked well, needing small talk to cover her fears. She asked about their new home, how far it was from the airport and whether he found it comfortable. But despite the small talk, she couldn't keep her fears from surfacing. The sincerity of her relationship with Stephen would not permit her to conceal, for any length of time, the fact that she was still incapable of being intimate. She had had almost a full year to recover fully, so how could she now confess her inability to be a complete wife? How could she make him believe her without causing him frustration, disappointment and perhaps anger? Once again, she needed to put her immediate fears aside and resort to some means of distracting herself from the problem. Unwittingly, Stephen provided the solution.

"Darling, I note that you're frowning and looking uncomfortable. Is something the matter?"

"Well, at home a few hours ago, I was a single unit of the Korean majority. One plane trip later, and suddenly the shoe is on the other foot. I've become a single unit of the Canadian minority; an Asiatic among Caucasians. I feel like the ugly duckling among swans."

"So now you can imagine how I felt in Korea. Everywhere I went, I stood out like a sore thumb. But I didn't mind being stared at. I knew I was much bigger than most of the people around me, and being good looking gave a boost to my ego."

She couldn't ignore the conceit Stephen expressed and thought of saying: When are you going to stop being so modest. But thought better of saying something that would hurt someone she loved. "With me it's different," she said. "At home, I took being one of the many for granted. It made me comfortable in my skin. But as a single Asiatic with evident differences, I stand out like a plucked turkey in a flock of chickens. The slightest glance directed at me makes me feel that I'm some kind of a target and I get hot under the collar. I can't help it Stephen. I find it intrusive and rude."

"Darling, I must compliment you on your English. You've improved beyond my wildest dreams. I know it must have involved a hell of a lot of work."

"Thanks Stephen. It was hard but interesting work, and Joe and Sally were excellent teachers who soon became close friends."

 "Don't pay attention to people staring at you. It's your beauty that fascinates them."

Stephen said, making her smile. He then added: "You keep looking around with lifted eyebrows in surprise. What's the matter now?"

"Stephen, please don't scold! As a new arrival I can't help making comparisons with what I see here that would be abnormal in Korea."

"What's so abnormal here?"

"Well, at home, all the menial tasks at the airport are done by Koreans. Caucasians are either well-heeled tourists or hold executive positions in large firms and corporations. Here, it's surprising to see white men and women using vacuum cleaners, collecting garbage, working as porters ferrying luggage on their carts or with mops cleaning bathrooms. Stranger still is the number of colorful turban-headed East Indian taxi cab drivers chatting together beside their bright yellow cabs."

"I guess you'll find a number of things here that are different, though not necessarily better or worse."

"In this brochure, for example, there are some facts about the airport that I find especially noteworthy. The extensive use of blues and greens in carpets and walls were chosen to reflect the colors of the natural environment in forest, sea and sky. The huge beautifully varnished wooden beams that spider web the ceiling were used to showcase BC's extensive forests. I also admire the slowly revolving structure above the foyer. It surely indicates a clever bit of whimsy."

"It won't take you long to become familiar with the new order of things," Stephen said in a momentary burst of enthusiasm. It made her wonder how long it would take him to become familiar with the new order of things, after she broke the bad news.

While at the carousel awaiting the arrival of her suitcases, she noticed a couple of police patrolling the airport. Their uniforms fitted them smartly, but the weaponry on their belts–a revolver, heavy baton, handcuffs and other items she didn't recognize–stood out. It struck her that the police in BC were on the 'qui vive' for the protection of passengers or any criminal activity that might arise. Stephen then talked about the selling of his former car before buying his new blue Honda Civic. He reminded her of her father's generosity. But since her father hadn't said a word to her about the checks and the new house she hadn't been able to thank him. Finally, they collected her suitcases, placed them on the luggage cart that surprisingly was free of charge. Once outside the airport building on their way to the car, Serena again caught the scent of the fresh salt-scented air. On the highway going home, she suddenly caught sight of the ocean through the car window. Since she lived deep in the country far from the sea, the fresh and clean salt tang of the ocean was not really familiar to her although on one occasion she had visited the port of In-chon with her parents. But she loved the scent since it represented to her the healthy open air of the outdoors. Besides, it gave her the impression of spend-ing a day at the beach. She was pleased to realize that it would be with her every day as long as she lived in Victoria. On their drive home Serena was anxious to see the area in which they would live and to explore their new home and its surroundings.

She noted that there were double and sometimes triple carriageways on either side of the expressway near the airport. They seemed very narrow in comparison with the 12 lane dual carriageways of Korean highways. Incredibly, there were traffic lights forcing vehicles to stop and wait for other vehicles to cross the highway at various points. She thought that flyovers would be more efficient for traffic to cross or merge without stopping. She was fascinated with the green vegetation surrounding her on all sides. There were patches of pine and spruce, open stretches of green fields and large acres of farmland growing various kinds of vegetables. She found it quite natural to record these differences in her mind, but she didn't think it wise to mention all her comparisons to Stephen. That would sound too much like criticism or boasting.

"Stephen, why are their floral decorations and crosses all around that lamp post?"

"Someone had an accident and died nearby, so their loved ones and friends mark it as a sort of shrine. You'll see a few of them along the roads or at dangerous corners and crossings." As they entered the Gordon Head district where their home was located, Serena asked why so many people were selling their garages. With a chuckle Stephen had to explain. "On week ends people collect things they no longer need stack them in front of their homes and advertise 'Garage Sales.' Customers come in droves to check out their items and buy whatever interests them."

Stephen then began his spiel as a tour guide: "The province enjoys a temperate climate, but quite naturally, there is snow higher up in the mountains." Serena mentioned the lady picking handfuls of grass at the airport, and asked about the province's "rich mixture of cultures, including citizens of Aboriginal, European, and Asian descent. She told him she had read that there were also minor ethnic groups from countries belonging to the British Commonwealth and asked about them.

Stephen explained that there were minorities from New Zealand, Australia, Africa, India, Pakistan and the West Indies. These Commonwealth people have introduced the game of cricket to Victorians that their teams play against each other on week ends at Beacon Hill Park.

She was also eager to see the way the province was bustling with energy preparing for the Vancouver 2010 Olympics and Paralympics Winter Games. Stephen pointed out the narrow lanes reserved for cyclists marked with white lines on the outer edge of main thoroughfares. These were designated with painted bicycles on the tarmac. Serena considered herself fortunate to live in a country that could boast of its indoor sports, its outdoor adventure, world-class exhibitions, cosmopolitan culture, uptown shopping and mouth watering cuisine. It excited her to discover that in BC she had the option of not only choosing what to do, but how she would manage to do it all.

She noticed that during the last minutes of their drive, Stephen had retired into himself, silently brooding. When he turned the car into a very short driveway, compared to hers in Korea, she realized they were home and thought it wise to stall any probing questions Stephen might ask by distracting him.

"Are you going to lift your bride over the threshold as Westerners are supposed to do?"

"If that is your wish, my dear," he said, though his voice was devoid of endearment. Once he had carried her up the stairs, opened the patio door and deposited her, none too gently, on the living room sofa, she knew it was time to broach the dreaded subject. Instead of asking to be shown over the house to give herself time to think of how to break the bad news she remained silent, looked at Stephen expectantly, and asked:

"What's bothering you?"

"I noticed that you were less than enthusiastic in your response to my greeting at the Airport. After waiting so long to have my wife with me, it was a serious blow. That isn't the way I expected you to react. I'm your husband now not a stranger on vacation in Korea." She noted immediately that this was the new Stephen, being honest and forthright instead of hiding his thoughts and his innate feelings. Thus, she felt comfortable speaking honestly as she always did.

"I'm glad you mentioned Korea, Stephen. I was brought up there to believe that emotional outbursts ought not to be paraded in the public eye. Korean protocol has drilled into me that such effusive and intimate bear hugs and especially such soulful kissing should be done in private. I'm sorry, Stephen. I didn't mean to upset you. Now, will you show me the rest of the house?" In trepidation, she was postponing her confession, not knowing what to say or how to break the bad news.

"Stephen conducted her in silence through the rest of the house. She noticed the furniture and the carpets he had chosen for each room were all dark shades of brown that created an atmosphere of gloom. The linoleum in the kitchen and bath were grey blah to match the equally blah grey of cupboards and walls. Everything was practical, colorless and coldly utilitarian, evoking a totally masculine landscape that shouted: 'Decor doesn't matter.' She made no comment, deciding to spruce up the place with a feminine touch, using lace curtains perhaps and lighter colored carpets with ceramic tiled kitchen and bathrooms, and of course, vases with flowers; many vases with flowers. She would include some of the work of local artists on the walls that highlighted her decorative choices. It would be a start and give her something to do while Stephen was at work every week day.

She thought it would be wise as well as honest to break the bad news that threatened to create their first quarrel. Uncomfortably, she bit the bullet.

"Stephen, please sit down a moment, I have something very difficult to say." He looked at her silently and sat down without a word. Again, that was unlike Stephen. She couldn't help but recognize the change.

"When you hugged and kissed me at the airport, my reluctance to respond was not only a result of my upbringing. I recoiled involuntarily at the sexual advance of a male."

"I'm not any male. I'm your husband; the male that you married."

"I know that, and I wish I could change my feelings, but I can't."

"What exactly are you telling me?" He asked.

"I'm saying that after all this time I'm still no good to you as a wife. But since our marriage is unconsummated, we can have it annulled immediately and I'll go home to let you get on with your life." Stephen was so shocked that he remained silent in thought for a long moment, grappling with the bombshell he just heard, but unwilling to accept the full consequences of its meaning. He was thinking of his life without Serena, how he had missed her while she remained in Korea waiting for admission to Canada. Oh God, he didn't want to go through that again. When he spoke, his words surprised both Serena and himself.

"Serena, I haven't waited all this time to send home the wife I love without first trying to solve our problem. It's unlikely that more time is what you need. So, what do *you* propose?"

"You're showing great restraint, Stephen, and certainly living up to your promise to be honest and sincere." She didn't add that he was not thinking only of himself as he was once prone to do. "But you need to think further ahead. If as a wife, I was useless to you while away, won't my presence here, as a useless wife, be even worse? So, think Stephen before you respond. I want you to be absolutely certain that you want me to stay and try to work out our problem?"

"I don't have to think. I'm sure. I want you to stay."

"Well, the only thing I can think of to solve our problem is therapy. Do you think that might help?"

"I really don't know, but it's worth a try. I'll take you to see my doctor. We can explain the problem to him and he will probably recommend you to a therapist. In the meantime, I'll try to behave myself and keep my distance, if that is what's worrying you."

"Stephen, I want you to be sure that you can live with me as a 'non-wife' while I go through therapy. Then, there's the wait for recovery. You realize that we won't be able to sleep in the same bed. It will only create complications for me, and temptation for you."

"You're right about that. I'll try not to pressure you in any way."

"Stephen, I want you to be sure you really want me to stay. Take a few days to see if you can bear to have me around knowing that I'm your wife in name only. When you decide, you can tell me to go home, or you can again ask me to stay, okay?"

"Okay."

On the following day, Stephen was as good as his word. He took her to his doctor. Serena explained her problem and he agreed to recommend her to a psychiatrist who would call to give her an appointment. She waited impatiently while Stephen worked during the week. He gave her a ride to her TD Bank where she introduced herself to the Manager and collected a few blank checks from him. He called her a taxi which she directed to the Honda dealership in Victoria. There she bought a new Honda Civic, bought a map of Victoria at a gas station and busied herself shopping at the Sears department store to begin redecorating the house. All the while she worried about whether or not the therapy would be helpful.

During those first few weeks, Stephen tried his best to make her comfortable in her new country. They lived in Gordon Head, one of the pretty residential areas of the city, and he promised to show her those areas of Victoria and the province that he thought she would find interesting.

However, with Stephen at work five days a week, she was continually left alone in a strange house, surrounded by strange decor in a strange city. There were times when a wave of nostalgia would overwhelm her as the feeling of being an outsider struck her with renewed force. Strangers confronted her every time she left the house and everywhere she went to brighten the décor of her home. The multiplicity of buildings crammed so closely together around her home, so different from the spacious vistas surrounding their farm in Korea, seemed to suffocate her and squeeze the breath from her body.

As the days merged into weeks, she found that the noise of traffic–tires trundling over tarmac, the frequent blowing of horns, vehicles playing very loud music, engines starting, stopping or revving loudly, the occasional wail of a siren and even the loud ringing of the telephone gave her a start. The constant noise and clatter of urban life was an unwelcome intrusion into her existence. It had an effect that she found alien and intimidating, accustomed as she was to the blessed silence that had insulated her whole previous life. How she longed for the tranquility of her farm! How she missed the wide expanse of open fields stretching in unbroken succession towards the foothills of the mountains! But more than anything else, she missed the constant love and devotion of the parents she had taken for granted. Brooding over her losses, she tried vainly to count the miles, continents and oceans that separated her from the things and people she so dearly loved. Only then, did she begin to fully understand her unconscionable betrayal of both her parents; her refusal to obey her father or to reunite with her mother. She sank into the depths of misery that, like a mirror, reflected the full extent of her cruelty and ingratitude.

Isolated from others on their farm, Serena was unaccustomed to having neighboring houses hemming her in with their proximity on all sides. She felt as though they were purposely crowding her, making her feel like a prisoner in her own home. She began to feel detached from her past, disconnected from everyone she knew and loved; everything that seemed to matter. She longed for letters from home, but no one wrote to her. There was no news to break the disconnect she felt in her alien world. She cursed those who were ignorant of the fact that news from home nourishes the soul of those abroad, keeping the absentee alive. She yearned for the familiar situations associated with her home in Korea. Oh God, how she craved to be with her parents, to beg her mother's forgiveness, to help her in the kitchen teaching her the new recipes she had learnt from Joe and Sally. She wanted so badly to feel free, wandering the familiar paths of her farm, feeding her animals, driving her red mustang for miles and miles, taking her pigeons on long and longer flights. She yearned to mount on Will's back, and with her father, canter up to their mountain hideaway. But more than anything else, she wanted to beg her mother's forgiveness and experience once again all the love and warmth she had squandered upon Serena in their home.

Instead, as was the case during her recovery from the assault, she felt shut off, isolated, unbearably and terrifyingly alone. At such times, the ghosts of her beloved past would emerge to haunt her. The guilt she felt over her attitude towards her mother and the shame of her invisible rift between her husband and herself would flare. The truth was that with so much time on her hands, she wallowed in self-recrimination. Why, she asked herself for the hundredth time, hadn't she obeyed her father and made peace with her mother? When she thought of all her mother had done for her, it shouldn't have been difficult to be compassionate and forgiving. Worse still, why hadn't she invited her mother to the wedding ceremony? That had been a willful hurt that she had wanted to inflict. But when she did, she felt no gratification that derived from her selfish and cruel act. Some of the things she'd done were so unforgivable that only shame and guilt allowed her to live with herself. With those two sharp knives whittling away at her self esteem, she knew that only the soul's sorrow could permit her to live with herself. She then began racking her brain, wondering what she could do to rectify the situation. But no quick solution came to mind. Finally, she couldn't prevent herself from wondering whether her marriage to Stephen and her departure from Korea had been the right choices. The warning then rose in her mind: "Be careful what you wish for…"

The choices she had made tormented her to such an extent that her mind was often in turmoil, her brain choked with outrageous thoughts. Did she desert her parents as she had begun to think, or had they deserted her? She began behaving with the egotism and arrogance of Shakespeare's Coriolanus who, banished into exile by Rome, declared to the Roman authorities at his departure: "I banish you." Had they in fact sent her into exile for her egotism and intransigence or was her conscience playing tricks on her, forcing her to wallow in self-appointed grief? At such times she would use her grief as a weapon, flogging herself with the thought that the choices she had made had cost her the loss of family, of country, of culture, indeed of everything that defined the person she was. But, no matter how far she ran in her nostalgia, she could never outdistance herself.

Finally, the psychiatrist's receptionist called, told her there was a cancellation and gave her an appointment for the following day. She went to the Medical Building on Fort Street, and entered the office. The doctor introduced himself:

"I am Dr. Jim Jones," he said, "and you must be my newest patient, Serena." He held out his hand, which she took and told him he was correct. He motioned her to a seat while he looked her over as she studied him. He was tall and slim with a face much younger than the proliferation of white hair on his head, eyebrows and chin seemed to testify. His gray-green eyes were bright and far apart while his unusually wide smile seemed to stretch from ear to ear. That, together with his warmth and pleasant voice put her at ease right away. It wasn't only charm he exuded, it was also genuine concern. Then too, he seemed to be a no-nonsense guy since he got down immediately to the business at hand. He asked her to describe her assault as briefly as possible, in the present tense, so that he could tape it for her to take home. She was to practice listening to the tape using techniques that he would be teaching her.

"I am returning home from a movie through abandoned woodland and nearby park. Then, Scarface and his basketball team confronts me. They prevent me from crossing the park to my home. Although I am a karate Black Belt and can usually take care of myself, I begin to feel uncomfortable because I am alone and not sure that I can defeat *five* muscular adults. I can cope with maybe three or perhaps four. Anyway, my heartbeat quickens as does my breathing and my fear grows as Scarface orders one of his men to grab me. I quickly get rid of him. My fears and anxiety grows when he orders a second and later a third thug to immobilize me. When I eliminate them, Scarface himself grabs me from behind and orders his other team members to join him. The leader then exacts his revenge by cuffing and kicking me to the ground where I lie for a moment, half conscious, while the team rips off most of my clothes. Scarface unzips his pants to expose his erection. Somehow, I scramble to my feet trying to escape, backing away half-naked from the five males ogling and advancing on me. They quickly restrain me, rip off the rest of my clothes, grab my arms and spread my legs. The men I whipped start kicking me while Scarface begins his assault. I am shocked, terrified and angry at what is happening to me until a sharp boot to my head envelopes me in blackness. I remain in a coma. When I awake my body is ablaze with pain and as the drugs begin to wear off I have anxiety attacks. I feel guilty, angry and ashamed. My brutalized body feels dirty and I begin to have flashbacks of fighting and of my violation. I have nightmares accompanied by heavy sweating. Later, I learn that I am in the crisis center of a hospital and that I was gang raped."

Gazing through the windows of her new home, Serena was amazed to see that children on their way to school were casually dressed in jeans and shirts, thick sweaters and jackets. No one wore a uniform as was the custom in Korea. The fashion of the "hoodie" had just emerged in BC and both boys and girls wore it proudly in various bright colors. What she also considered novel were the adult Crossing Guards. They waited at the nearby pedestrian crossings before and after school, wearing a blaze-orange top with a huge white neon "x" on front and back. Their outfit made them easily identifiable to chauffeurs. They exercised strict control over all vehicle traffic creating a safe passage for its students to and from school. Teen and even preteen school kids, wearing Crossing Guard attire, often acted in the place of their adult guardians. She found it amazing that chauffeurs stopped at their signals, waiting patiently for kids to cross, treating each child Crossing Guard as the official arm of the law.

"Serena, I want you to listen to the list of questions I've compiled on this handout and give me your reaction after each one I read. Okay?"

"Okay."

"Did you feel alone and deeply depressed after your violation?"

"Yes. I felt sad, distressed and helpless. I sometimes felt that life was not worth living; that I wish I were dead."

"Did your view of sex change after what happened?"

"Yes. I was unable to trust anyone where sex was concerned, even my husband."

"Would you say that you felt responsible for the violation?"

"Yes. I felt that the clothes I wore, revealing tank top and mini-skirt, and the expensive perfume signaling sophistication, made me vulnerable. I also thought that I should have screamed louder, fought harder. I then chose to cross secluded woodland and park all alone as dusk was approaching. My best friend told me I got what I deserved for my stupidity."

"Did your assault alter your vision of yourself?"

"Yes. I feel guilty and ashamed at having been forced to do things that I wouldn't have done otherwise. My self esteem suffered enormously"

"What would you say were the immediate effects of your violation?"

"I have panic attacks that immobilize me whenever some thought, situation, object or smell triggers a memory of the assault. I also have terrifying nightmares."

"Did your attackers make you feel angry towards them and towards others?"

"Yes. My attackers brutalized me, causing me physical and mental pain. They stole something precious from me. I was also angry at family members for not protecting me; for not coming to my rescue."

"As a result of what happened, do you feel that the world is an evil place?"

"Yes. I've installed a light above my door. I keep checking my locks, refuse to go out at night and become easily terrified at a world gone mad."

"Do you tend to avoid situations and thoughts that remind you of what happened?"

"Yes. I try to avoid any thoughts or situations that remind me of the assault."

"Do you often feel that your safety is compromised?"

"Yes. I feel as though I am never safe and can be assaulted at any time and in any place."

"Serena, the questions that I have asked and that you have answered are fairly common to rape victims. Now, take the handout and read it at home over and over. I think you'll find that as the experience grows more and more familiar your terror will gradually erode away. My receptionist will give you the date and time of your next appointment."

Chapter 50

There is a park around the corner from Serena's home and every day, from morning till night, rain or shine, dog owners pass on the street with their pets to exercise them in the park. It surprised her to see that most owners were armed with a plastic bag to collect their dog's 'calling cards.' She was also amazed at the affection that owners showed to their pets. They often stooped, hugged and cuddled with them; sometimes the women owners even kissed them. Koreans have had quite a different relationship with dogs. They were often seen as food for the table. Lately however, a new craze among rich and fashion conscious women has developed. They have big open-top carry-all bags from which one can see the heads of small dogs. They carry them around like human babies to be fussed over and admired.

"Serena, from the violations you described and their related symptoms-the sweating, the panic attacks, the heavy breathing, the racing heartbeat, the flash-backs, the nightmares that numb and exhaust you emotionally, all indicate that you have been afflicted with a case of Post Traumatic Stress Disorder or PTSD."

"Is this disorder curable?"

"It is. But a great deal will depend on your response to the treatment I have in mind."

"Can you explain the treatment?"

"It has been established by the research of psychologists that it is not only the event–in your case, the gang rape–that has caused your fear of the pain associated with rape, penetration and intercourse. It is also the way you think and feel about the circumstances leading up to and surrounding the event. If we can change your perception of these circumstances, then..." Serena cut him off.

"Are you saying that you can change the way I think and feel about those circumstances and about the gang rape itself?"

"No, no." He stated quickly. "It is *you* who will need to change the way you think and feel; *your* perception of those events. If you can do that, it is possible to make a complete recovery."

"You make the solution to my problem sound like a walk in the park."

"That is certainly not my intention. I was merely trying to make you understand the thinking behind Cognitive-Behavioral Therapy, or CBT that we will put to use in your case."

"Doctor, can you explain CBT?"

"It emphasizes the vital role that thought plays in how we feel and what we do."

"And how do you propose to put that theory into practice?"

"My job is to list a series of questions that will act as a guide to help you analyze every aspect of the situations leading up to the assault and the assault itself. Answering those questions can lead to the achievement of your goal –in this case-the removal of fears that cause your panic attacks and especially your belief that you deserved to be raped. If you succeed in doing that, you may be able to have a normal and healthy sexual relationship with your husband."

"What is my job?"

"To do the homework assignments that I give you so that you implement what you've learnt." His answer came as a complete surprise.

"Are you saying that this is an exercise in learning through homework assignments?" Serena asked in amazement.

"Yes. Have you been practicing the exercises I've given you?"

"Yes! I've been working on them until I can call them up naturally."

"And has that been helping you to get rid of the fear and anxiety?"

"In some cases yes, but very slowly, in other cases, not at all."

"Well, perhaps we can change that for the better."

The severe bouts of Serena's home sickness became so physically and emotionally debilitating that instead of dwelling on the past she had to focus on something that would absorb her interest. She began to spend hours at the library reading and making comparisons between the histories of her two countries. She came to realize that in the same way Canada had been conquered and colonized by the British, and French, so South Korea had been conquered and colonized by the Japanese. Whereas Korea became independent by the treaties initiated by the West's Allied Forces at the end of World War 11, independence came to Canada through a series of treaties at the end of her war with Britain. Just as South Koreans were afraid of being one day overrun by North Korea, the country to their north, so Canadians were concerned with one day being swallowed up by the US, the country to their south. Then, in the same way that there was serious tension in South Korea over the possibility of their assimilation by the North, so there was considerable tension in Quebec over the possibility of being assimilated by the rest of Canada. Quebeckers insisted, and like South Korea, finally gained recognition as a "distinct society." She found the similarities and differences in the histories of her two countries quite intriguing.

Although she learnt that there were two official languages in Canada, English and French, she found certain signs awkward to read. Seeing English at the top and French at the bottom of the same road sign, she thought, often led to confusion rather than to clarity. It also puzzled her to learn that in a modern nation like Canada, although the Governor General was a woman, the second female in that post representing the British Crown, "women were still fighting for equality in pay and power" in the same way as at home. However, Canada was much further advanced than Korea in that area.

Stephen saw Serena as an extraordinary individual defiled by the events of place and time. In Korea, he thought of her as a diamond set in the dung of her farmyard. In Victoria, he would flush away the filth. Unfortunately, her being a nonwife put a severe strain on the marriage. He knew that the old Stephen would have found a way to coerce his wife into having his way. After all, weren't they in love and married? Hadn't he restrained himself from all sexual activity during all those months until the arrival of his bride? Wasn't he a worthy husband to have ignored her corrupt family background and to have waited almost a year for the consummation of the marriage? Who could blame him for demanding what he considered the most fundamental rights of a husband?

However, the new Stephen could not allow himself to resume the selfish actions of his past. Doing so, he thought, would be to dishonor himself in the eyes of a bride who had made him an honorable man. He had to take the highroad and agree to live amicably with Serena while she underwent therapy. However, he requested that they set a date for their union three months from the day of her arrival. Both spouses agreed that the waiting period was generous in its length. How could she not agree? Yet, Serena couldn't help thinking: suppose I still feel the same way at that point, what then?

As the days and weeks ground slowly by, Stephen began to have misgivings about his promise to Serena to wait patiently until the appointed day before going to their marriage bed. He believed that if she truly loved him, his mere presence would eventually break down her defenses. However, when weeks went by and she still balked whenever their kissing and fondling seemed to be getting beyond his control, he began to feel even more deeply frustrated and angry. With the pressure building, he began to wonder if Serena was putting him on trial, to see if he would live up to his word as an honorable man. Then, his frustration led him to believe that she was fully healed and just stalling for time. However, on reflection, he realized that Serena would never stoop to such underhand behavior. It was his growing paranoia, he told himself, that led him to think such unworthy thoughts. Yet, the restriction Serena imposed upon him was driving him crazy. He had been a sexually active male all through his college years, he kept telling himself, and now that he was married, he couldn't miss the irony of not being able to have intercourse with his own wife.

What, he kept asking her, was she waiting for? She was a spirited young woman, obviously in the full bloom of her health and was married to a not unattractive male whom she loved. It was natural, he kept repeating to her, for their honeymoon to follow. More and more, he began to bombard her with the arguments that sexual intimacy with him would be a liberating experience for her, and that she had nothing to fear. He was her husband, someone who loved her dearly. He would be gentle and protective and would never hurt her. He produced so many arguments about the physical and spiritual bonding that intercourse creates between husband and wife that Serena began to feel she was being coerced into doing something against her will.

"Stephen, I'm so sorry to be such a disappointment, darling. But you did make me a promise to wait for three months, and I've been here for half that time only. However, if my being here is too much of a problem for you, I'll keep my promise and go home. You only have to say the word. But I want you to know that I am equally frustrated and ashamed of being less than a wife".

The sadness was palpable in her voice. "So my darling, the decision is yours. What will you have me do?"

"Frankly, I don't know. The only thing I do know is that I don't want you to leave. Being with you is damn hard, but being without you is even harder. So, I guess I want you to stay."

"Thank you Stephen. I admire you for sticking to your principles. You *are* a changed man," she said, knowing that such a compliment would help to bolster his resolve.

However, as time wore on and Serena's attitude remained unchanged, Stephen's frustrations increased as did his anger. Over and over he kept reminding himself that he had been a regular Don Juan during his college years. Indeed, his success with women was such that his college buddies had referred to him as the 'leopard' since, like that predator, he was especially cruel and ruthless in his treatment of the women he hunted. Consequently, it was a serious blow to his ego to be married and forced to forego the delights of the marriage bed. For the first time in his life, he reflected, he was a seducer unable to seduce, a predator at the mercy of his prey. He had to do something to change the situation. While he waited, he needed to suppress both his frustration and his escalating anger.

Serena recognized that as Stephen's wife, she had a duty to perform and forced herself to indulge in the limited intimacy she allowed Stephen. He made it clear that these intimacies were no longer enveloped in the innocence of his earlier kisses. Since their marriage, Serena had learnt that in Stephen's mind, a kiss and cuddle was an automatic guarantee of complete intimacy. But since she just couldn't go all the way, she took pains to explain that the very thought of penetration and intercourse brought back the faces of her assailants, the terror and humiliation of her violation. If her feelings seemed like a flimsy excuse to him, it was because he hadn't gone through her experience. In describing how she felt, Stephen could see the sadness on her face and hear it in her voice.

"Serena, I want you to know that I've had numerous patients suffering from an assault like yours. In my experience with the different strategies used to combat the resulting symptoms, I have found that 'Treating the Trauma of Rape using Cognitive–Behavioral Therapy,' the incisive manual by Edna Foa, and Barbara Rothaum, is by far the most simple and the most effective. I will use their theories and their methodology exclusively. Today I'll introduce you to a Measurement Chart of theirs and ask you to give a rating on the scale of 0—10 of how scared you were in each particular situation during and after the rape. Zero indicates no anxiety or fear; ten indicates the extreme fear and anxiety you felt.

Measurement Chart

Situation	Rating after rape
1. Fear of meeting a stranger.	10
2. Talking to a stranger about the assault.	10
3. Going to a movie alone.	10
4. Walking through woodland and park alone.	10
5. Having a nightmare or flashback.	10
6. Meeting your Nazi pursuers.	10
7. Meeting Scarface and his team.	10
8. Wearing the outfit you wore when violated.	10
9. Having sexual contact with Stephen.	10

"Later on, when Serena was far more familiar with Canadian customs, she witnessed conduct that surprised her. She found it difficult to accept the Canadian habit of using Christian names without first being given permission to do so. At first, whenever it happened, she would automatically recoil, feeling as though she had been slapped. If her reaction was noticed, she would then apologize and explain her reaction. It also disturbed her to see women shaking hands with men. That she thought, she'd never get used to. Then, when guests were welcomed into a home for dinner or for a party, they usually brought a gift of flowers or alcohol that was immediately accepted by their host with thanks, as though expected. In Korea, the host would resist accepting such gifts until the guest insisted that he do so and never before the third offer. Whenever she witnessed such an occurrence, she couldn't help feeling embarrassed at the shabby conduct of the host or hostess.

It was a common occurrence in Korea to see most young and adult women friends holding hands while out walking in malls or on sidewalks. Canadian young women kept their hands to themselves as though such marks of friendship and affection were frowned upon in public. Yet, ironically, these same teenagers and adult women thought nothing of embracing their boyfriends or spouses and kissing them soulfully in public. A similar public display of emotions in South Korea would be regarded as exhibitionist, certainly flamboyant, and of course, unthinkable. Their rigid protocol made it almost impossible for her to understand how by Korean standards Canadians were considered extroverted while by US standards they were regarded as shy, polite and even introverted.

"Serena, I note that you hated meeting or talking to a stranger about your assault, yet, when your parents invited a stranger into your home, you gradually got comfortable with him. In fact, you ended up enjoying his kisses and finally accepted his marriage proposal. Your repeated meeting and becoming familiar with the stranger changed your perspective radically; changed the way you had previously thought about the situation. So now, let us again assess your rating of those situations that caused you so much discomfort and anxiety. How would you now rate meeting a stranger and talking to him about your assault after repeated confrontation?

"Zero, I think."

"Good! Now relax and explain why you didn't want to tell Stephen about your rape."

"I was ashamed to reveal the assault. It was so personally demeaning that I thought he would despise me for what had happened. Besides, all strange males brought back memories of the assault."

"Yet, you told him about your gang rape and even showed him pictures that you had painted of it. What was his response?"

"He was sad that it happened, but still wanted to marry me."

"So, you were mistaken in your initial interpretation and Stephen's response changed your assessment of the event! What is your present rating of the event?"

"Again zero!"

"You're doing fine, Serena. Now, about the tank top, mini skirt you refuse to wear because they would bring back memories of the assault. I'm sure you'll agree that there's really nothing about those items of clothing that can hurt or upset you. What rating would you give wearing those clothes now?"

"Another zero."

It was interesting to learn that in BC there were public toilets at all gas stations in many supermarkets, every restaurant, cinema, museum and most public places. They were open for use by patrons of the establishment. In many cases one simply obtained a key from an employee. All had modern flush toilets that were kept remarkably clean and sanitary. In Korea too, there are public toilets everywhere, in bus and train stations, in restaurants and department stores, cinemas and museums. However, few are modern flush toilets. The majority are the tiled holes in the ground which are usually clean. Koreans are used to squatting and have no problem doing so while relieving themselves. Serena had to agree with Stephen: the threat of overbalancing, especially for older folk, made squatting difficult, risky and dangerous. There was always a risk involved.

"I want you to go home and do exercises dealing with the places that cause you anxiety and tension. Since you are afraid to walk through woodland and parks alone, my instructions are to take along with you someone trustworthy who will guarantee your safety and comfort while you visit such a place. On your first attempt you'll both walk in close contact with each other. On the next visit, you'll follow your 'guardian angel' walking well ahead of you but always in sight. On the third visit, your guardian is out of sight, but remains in contact with you by phone to assure you of her presence as you are about to start your visit. You'll continue the routine until finally you can do so alone. We'll discuss your feelings at your next appointment.

It was disappointing to recognize that in Canada, youth accords no special respect, and certainly no veneration, for the elderly as they do in Korea. She was amazed to learn that subordinates in Canada could be forward enough to offer suggestions or advice to a superior without fear of embarrassing him or being considered out of line. Foreign countries sure have strange customs, she though.

On TV, she noted that it was becoming more and more prevalent for networks to raise their ratings by digging into the dirt unearthed by celebrities. As with the O.J. Simpson case, TV juries and audiences are assembled to weigh in on prominent criminal trials. There are also programs dealing with the pregnancies of teen or adult celebrities that occur out of wedlock, broken marriages, nasty divorces, brushes with the law, quick-change dating by movie stars and all sorts of similar celebrity scandals. The media had so hyped up such salacious programming that viewers have become addicted to watching them. They prefer to watch footage of Britney Spears, Lindsay Lohan or Charlie Sheen falling apart rather than see history unfold in the struggle for democracy in the Middle East.

It made Serena proud to read in the "Times Colonist" the high regard in which her new country is held for its ethical conduct in the eyes of the world. "Transparency International" announced that "Canada is viewed as the least corrupt country in the Americas and is an inspiration to its neighbors," according to the September 2008 index released by a Berlin-based watchdog. The country "earned a score of 8.7 out of 10."

Stephen waited impatiently for Serena to overcome the sexual barrier she had erected between them. His frustration and paranoia kept growing, prodding him to question himself: was Serena really in love with him or was she using him in order to escape the slanderous tongues at home? Did she marry him only to get a chance at a new life abroad? Such questions began playing in his head like annoying non-stop recordings. Why the hell was *she* waiting? How much longer did *he* have to wait? On those occasions when Stephen failed to convince her to become a real wife, she could see the frustration in his demeanor and body language blossoming into full-blown anger. But the thought that the date they had set for the consummation of their union would soon be upon them made him repress his anger. He knew that Serena would then be forced to keep her word, no matter what.

While Stephen waited for her to signal her readiness to become a 'true wife,' he had to occupy himself with something to keep his mind from fixating upon that longed-for prize. It was difficult for him, since he was used to women fawning over him and having his way with them. As he thought about the thorny situation, it occurred to him that it would be to his advantage to find some undertaking which he could share with his wife. Since he had considered himself a city man before his Korean vacation, he had seldom traveled beyond the limits of Victoria to explore the natural outdoors existing there. Being well aware of Serena's love for the outdoors Stephen believed that his becoming familiar with the natural world outside the cities of Victoria and Vancouver, would permit him to share a common interest with her.

Chapter 51

He therefore made an effort to acquaint his wife with the wide diversity of the island's landscapes. He had promised to showcase for her the attractions of the province and took her to the North West tip of the island to Cape Scott Park where they planned to set up their tent. Although she had read about the long sandy beaches, bluffs, rocky outcrops, the nearby islands and the old growth temperate rain forest located along the North West coast, it was nothing compared to being there, seeing them for herself and experiencing the reality of it all.

When they got there, she stood with Stephen on the headland overlooking the ocean gazing at the gigantic rollers careening towards the coast, listening to their roar and inhaling the overwhelmingly fresh salt-laden breath of the sea. A howling southwesterly gale had powered those rollers all the way from Japan so that they raced across the Pacific in the serried ranks of an army. A deep valley divided each mountainous mass from its follower. As the continental shelf approaching the New World rose from the depths and the sea grew shallower, the rollers reared up gathering themselves into even greater size and speed. They forced shoals of migrant whales and schools of salmon to flee a collision course with the coastline. Like bunched fists, they pounded against the West Coast, each one sucking in the powerful backwash of the previous wave before crashing majestically against the shoreline. It was quite a spectacle for someone like her who, in Korea, lived so far from the ocean.

They pitched their tent with her anxiety mounting to experience her first entry into a Temperate Rain Forest. On entry, she cautioned Stephen to remain silent and to follow her lead. They spent hours exploring the virgin forest with its fresh scents and its myriad sounds, while she taught him the basics of woodcraft. They marveled at the mysterious silences broken from time to time by the screeching of cicadas, the drumming of grouse or the sudden slap of a beaver tail on the surface of a lake. Amidst the dark green shadows and the shafts of dappled green light piercing the canopy, they inhaled deeply, savoring the pine-scented air. Their steps were silent on the thick cushion of pine needles, cones, ferns and mosses between the great stands of Douglas firs, and pines scattered liberally among the Sitka spruce, Western hemlock and cedars. As they stood still, bathed in that green half-light and screened by the creeping swatches of mist, their forest world took on a surreal appearance.

They followed the almost invisible animal trails, and much to her surprise, Stephen was an admirable student. Not only was he taking a new interest in his surroundings, but he also seemed to enjoy concealing himself like her and gazing silently at each passing animal. What surprised her was that he kept silent and didn't keep twitching about, unable to keep still like most first-timers. With the wind in their faces, they sat so still that their presence spooked none of the deer that moved noiselessly within sight and slipped silently into the thick tangle of underbrush and blow downs. It was astonishing that huge does and bull elk with their tall spiked antlers could so noiselessly move through the thick foliage and vanish like wraiths leaving behind nothing but their tracks and droppings. The couple crawled in the direction of the beaver they had heard and came to a lake beyond a stand of firs. Clumps of cattails sprouted around its shores.

They hunkered down quickly and noiselessly, flattening themselves to the ground on hearing the sound of a heavy body moving through the underbrush some distance away. The movement stopped and they saw the giant bulk of a black bear's head and shoulders poke out suddenly from among the trees on the edge of the lakeshore. It sniffed the air, pointing its nose in different directions, ears erect to catch the slightest enemy scent that would send it bounding away. It then exited the trees, once satisfied that no danger lurked, and lay down, leaning its head and back against a huge rock. It then grunted loudly and at the signal, two cubs shot out of the forest chasing each other rambunctiously all over the lakeshore. Another grunt from the sow brought both cubs rushing to begin suckling. She raised her two arms around them in a protective embrace of maternal concern surprising the observers with its resemblance to the behavior of human mothers.

Several does entered a clearing on the distant side of the lake. They were skittish in their movements no doubt scenting the presence of the predator. After they slid noiselessly into the trees, a buck, with gleaming tips on its multi-spiked antlers, made his slow stately entrance, stealthily sniffing the air. It swiveled its ears, turning his head slowly from side to side surveying the scene and scenting the air alert to any trace of danger. Its bunched muscles were flexed, ready to flee. It stood a long moment, immobile and majestic, before settling down into its bed and vanishing from sight amid the thick underbrush. The eyes of Serena and Stephen switched to a cougar crouched on a rock shelf perched almost directly above and beyond the spot where the buck had bedded down. The buck was unaware of its enemy since it was upwind of the cat. The predator kept eyeing its prey's every movement, and was just about ready to pounce. Its iron grey fur blended perfectly with the rock shelf where it lay motionless. From its open jaws and lips drawn back in a silent snarl, the pink tongue made its huge fangs stand out like wicked enameled stilettos. Coiled tightly, the cougar suddenly pounced, hurling itself down through the air its paws reaching forward, its claws already extended. But some sound, scent or instinct must have warned the buck, for in one swift movement it sprung upwards from its bed. With head bent and antlers aloft, it rammed itself into the cat butting the cougar in midair. The sharply pointed tines of its antlers ripped into the soft underbelly of the airborne cat, hurling it upwards. With a roar of distress, the cat was flung away, scrambling and righting itself in midair to land on its paws. It limped away badly wounded, with red blood staining its ivory underbelly. The attack had happened in a blur, leaving the spectators stunned.

The wild, magnificent scenery and wildlife of the rain forest taught Serena why nature lovers from around the world come to sample the enjoyment that the Park offers to campers and canoers, hikers and surfers, fishermen, kayakers and nature lovers of all kinds. Stephen was amazed that he had enjoyed himself as much he thought, as any 'outdoors-man.' At night they lay in their separate sleeping bags and Stephen kept his word making no sexual advances on his wife.

When the doctor said: "that's enough for today," Serena wanted to tell him about the date she had set with Stephen for their sexual union. She needed to ask him if it was the correct thing to do while she was still in therapy or would it be harmful and worsen the situation. She then asked herself: how could the situation be worse? The question led to confuse her further.

"By the way," the doctor said, breaking into her reverie.

"I'll be attending a couple of learned conferences in Europe, and won't be returning to Canada until the end of next month. My secretary will call to give you an appointment." Serena's confusion as to whether or not she should tell him her concerns led to further procrastination. Before she could voice her thoughts, she was already out the door and on her way home without having broached the subject.

"With her therapist abroad, the date of her promised intimacy with Stephen had arrived. By then, he had produced numerous arguments trying to break down his wife's resistance. He had almost convinced her that his skilled fingers and tongue would whip her up into a frenzy of arousal. She would lose control," he said, "squirming in excitement and anticipation." He almost had her believing that after they became one, she'd be transformed into a panic-crazed woman screaming out in the delightful agony of climax.

Left to herself, she couldn't decide whether or not to believe what he said. True she was making some headway in therapy but she knew that she wasn't completely cured or ready for intimacy as he kept arguing. Could he really initiate her into that blinding experience? Was the sexual bliss he had described really the common experience of most married women or was he using lies to gain his objective? Had he reverted to the selfish con man he once was, using any argument to get his way? After all, hadn't he almost convinced her that she had nothing to fear? Hadn't she begun to dream of her honeymoon, longing to experience the gentle foreplay, the holding and kissing, the very intimate fondling that would precede and prolong the ritualized sexual dance? She wanted so badly to believe him, but her confusion and fear made her realize that she was not ready.

The sun disappeared, the wind rose and darkness fell. It was a blackness that admitted no light. The storm tossed night was one of turbulence with the freezing rain lashing against the roof and window panes. Serena remained deaf, refusing to respond to Stephen's repeated calls from the bedroom. The appointed day had finally arrived, and an uncanny feeling stole over her. The obscene darkness seeped into her flesh, flooding her mind, controlling her thoughts. An icy sheet wrapped around her, its biting cold freezing her limbs.

She had to struggle desperately against the growing hatred she suddenly began to feel towards her husband. She stayed downstairs, remaining purposely deaf to his calls; trying to repress her terror of what was to come.

Despite Stephen's arguments, she remained apprehensive about what he wanted her to do. Wasn't it too soon to be having intercourse? Wouldn't penetration followed by the sexual act bring back the terrible experience of her violation? Wouldn't the panic attacks, the horrible nightmares return; nightmares that could destroy her sleeping and waking hours? Didn't her fear and reluctance tell her that she wasn't ready? Procrastinating, she lingered as long as possible before willing herself towards the bottom of the stairs. Eventually, she began mounting the staircase, silently, leaden feet unwilling to move, step by slow step. She kept battling against a growing anger aimed at Stephen for forcing her against her will to undertake her long delayed duty.

With one slow step at a time she approached their bedroom door. She was slow-hunting, with herself as the prey. She moved like someone on the way to the gallows with terror dominating her thoughts. This, the night of her honeymoon, should have been the most exciting night of her life, she thought, but here she was, shivering, in a cold sweat of terror, hating the man she had vowed before God to love. She lingered outside the bedroom door while the darkness around her intensified, stealing furtively into her, filling her interior. The beckoning image of herself lying safely in her own bed at home, with her parents just a few feet away, brought tears to her eyes. Her body tensed as she struggled against the control of some force outside herself, manipulating her.

She gritted her teeth, clenched her fists, willing thoughts into her mind that would expel her feelings of hatred towards Stephen. She needed every ounce of her strength to push herself forward towards that dreaded ordeal. She resorted to reason, being reluctant and terrified. She told herself that in dealing with pain, she had come to a compromise. Since it didn't kill her, that meant she could bear it. Therefore, it really couldn't be so bad after all. She stiffened her body, balled her hands into fists and shut her eyes tightly. Only then could she enter the dreaded bedroom that had become as dark as her soul. She then willed herself to confront the battlefield of her bed.

"Darling, I need you so," Stephen whispered after he heard her enter. She undressed slowly in the darkness, as the freezing rain pounded against the roof, siding and windowpanes. She was intent on postponing, for as long as possible, the disaster she knew was sure to follow. Yet, Stephen was so patient, so considerate. He had put on a recording of one of her favorite songs and began whispering tender words of endearment that would have been seductive to anyone else. He pulled her gently down making room for her on the bed. He then turned on his side to face her so he could embrace her naked body as he proceeded to hold, kiss and caress her ever so slowly, ever so gently, hoping desperately for the slightest sign of excitement that would signal the beginning of her arousal. Since terror prevented any such response from his wife, he sought to arouse her by starting the seduction slowly with caresses and kisses. He then switched to fondling one brown nipple with his fingers and sucking gently on the other. Serena forced her mind to focus on the love she had initially felt for Stephen, but the dark storm rioting within her nullified any feeling of tenderness or affection. Only panic and anger remained.

She made a desperate effort and began a series of moves that would become a routine. With eyes squeezed tightly shut, she forced her arms around Stephen's body and again balled her hands into fists. She willed herself to accept his sexual embrace, but no matter how hard she tried, she couldn't resist the feelings controlling her. When Stephen's fingers crept below her waist and tip toed further down destined for the silky bush between her legs, he mistook the whisper of panic his wife uttered for the sexual response he so fiercely sought. But what had caused her outcry was the thought of her husband's penetration that brought back the vision of Scarface and his crew and the numbing terror of her rape. Slowly, seductively Stephen penetrated her, but having waited so long to claim his marital privilege he instantly became more aggressive, more enthusiastic in his lovemaking. He thrust harder and harder into her inert body. During her gang rape, wracked with the pain of her torn, bleeding body, she had become an unconscious rag-doll while the ordeal raged within her. With Stephen there was no such release or escape. As she remained frozen in immobility, her husband's ardor increased. Unconsciously, a louder cry of mingled terror and frustration broke from Serena's lips; terror at being forced to relive her pain-ridden past; frustration at the suffering that her husband was thrusting upon her. Then, on hearing her second outcry of agony that he could not possibly mistake for arousal, he became sick with frustration and anger. A blinding rage overwhelmed him and the fury in his eyes revealed his hostility.

Stephen's struggle towards the ecstasy of love had ended in a paroxysm of hatred. He saw his wife as a frigid doll from which he would never get the impassioned sexual response he sought. In frustration and anger after his long wait, he struck out fiercely, trying to force his way past her deathlike indifference. His first slaps landed on her cheeks and temple. The next flurry of blows struck her on both temples, her mouth and nose. In a blinding fit of indignation he pushed her off the bed. She landed on the floor, her face a bloody mess as Stephen stalked from the room in anger and frustration.

Serena's head spun, stars flashed out of a blackened sky and her lips were crushed against her teeth. Blood was dripping from her nose and its salt taste was in her mouth. She was badly hurt, yet her uppermost feelings were not focused on the pain. The shame of having failed her husband and disgust at her shortcomings as a wife filled her. In consequence, she accepted Stephen's battering without retaliation or complaint. That night, she lay in bed, softly sobbing herself to sleep, in a welter of pain and disgust, her body violated by the man she had loved and married. She felt dirty, as though she had been mounted by a lust-crazed madman, then clobbered and discarded like a useless object.

Stephen's 'intimacies' became a permanent and dreaded feature of her marriage and before long, she became pregnant. Since Stephen's sexual assaults always inspired terror, she could never become lubricated or sexually aroused. Each such attack also involved a painful bruising and battering of her genitals. When she finally screamed out her torment, her husband's frustration transformed him into a raging maniac. She soon learned to clamp her hands over her face and head to protect herself from the blows that so often rained down upon her and ended many of their intimacies. The bruising, swelling and discoloration of her face and body forced her to remain indoors in shame and embarrassment until she could conceal the damage with cosmetics and over-sized sunshades covering her eyes.

Stephen booked tickets for them to go whale watching, his motive no doubt to pacify his wife after their most recent debacle in the bedroom. She could tell he was ashamed of his behavior in the way he kept his distance. The hiss of the waves against the inflated hull of the Zodiac was almost drowned out by the twin Mercury outboards roaring their power. She was wrapped warn in her blood-red jumpsuit like all the other watchers in the *Prince of Whales*. The fact that she was three months pregnant did noting to detract from her curiosity or excitement. While the guide pointed to gulls, harbor seals, sea lions, dolphins and a pair of eagles to hold the watchers' interest, Stephen, though some seats behind his wife, had eyes only for her.

Since he refused to believe in his wife's traumatized state, he kept fantasizing about the riotous lovemaking he had in store for her on their return home. Since the date of their agreed-upon intimacy was long past, she could no longer prevent him from going all the way. He was thankful to be clad in his baggy jump-suit, since it concealed the erection prompted by his thoughts.

Suddenly, the spotting network pinpointed the position of a pod of Orcas and, thanks to the Zodiac's hydro-phone, the watchers could hear the explosive blasts of their exhalations. The deep guttural snorts gave an accurate idea of the size and power of the beasts even before they were sighted. When Serena looked back at Stephen, she found him gazing at her with such lust in his eyes that it made her blush in confusion. Knowing he couldn't be trusted even in public, she kept her distance.

Serena found that she pronounced certain words differently from Canadians. This was evidently due to the fact that Joe, her tutor, had learnt the language from Englishmen and women teaching in Africa, and Sally had learnt the language from him. Thus, she rhymed words like "pool" and "school" with "rule," one single syllable. Canadians pronounce those words as though they had two syllables: "poo-ul" and "schoo-ul," though of course not as exaggerated. There were quite a few other differences she noticed. Joe taught her that "drawer," where knives and forks are kept, rhymed with "four." Canadians rhymed drawer more closely with "far," and while she rhymed "egg" with "leg," they rhymed it with "haig." Another word in which their pronunciation differed was "idea." For her, it has two syllables: "i-dear." They elongate it into three: "i-dee-ah." She pronounced the word "address" with the accent on the last syllable: they put the accent on the first. Of course these were only a few of the differences she noticed.

She learnt that the Gordon Head district where she lived was previously farming country in which a number of hobby farms still existed. Most of their owners grow flowers, fruit and vegetables, while a few offer free-range eggs. Each of these items, with their price tags, was often on sale from an untended stall located outside their gate. There was a slit in the stall's counter where the buyer's money was to be deposited for the item bought. She was amazed that such a quaint honor system still existed with no one present to monitor purchases. That the system still remains in use today is a tribute to the honesty of most Victorians.

Her farm in Hamyang is very far from the sea, thus she was surprised to see so many boats on trailers, in garages and driveways all over the city. Even more astonishing were the many marinas crowded with sail and power boats representing hundreds of millions of dollars. The scene testifies to the affluence of BC's citizens, since the boats are all pleasure craft. Serena learnt that many of the province's lakes are annually stocked with numerous varieties of fish, particularly trout, bass, walleye, perch, Kokanee, (landlocked salmon), Arctic grayling and pike. Though fresh and salt water anglers must buy a fresh or salt water license, she considered it a small price to pay for the pleasure of casting a line. In Korea, rice is grown in terraced paddies that are also large, shallow ponds. Farmers often stock them with carp which they harvest at the end of autumn. However, there is no stocking of fish by any governing body for the pleasure of its citizen/anglers.

Outside the bedroom, Serena believed that Stephen was ashamed of his aggression towards her. He tried to make up for his cruelty by showcasing the attractions of the Province he knew she would enjoy. Whenever he looked at her, "blossoming in the radiance of pregnancy," as he had described her appearance, he admitted to her that he couldn't help being aroused. He kept repeating that their lives could be so happy if only she would open her inner self to him. How, she asked herself and him, could he not be aware of the emotional damage that his many violations had prolonged? How could he not know that she was broken inside? Was he so dumb that he didn't realize his repeated violations and battering had made it impossible for them to have a normal sexual relationship? If he were not aware, why would his guilt and shame be stamped so unmistakably on his face?

Chapter 52

The boat shot forward on a parallel course overtaking the whales, gliding well ahead with its motors shut off. The guide explained that Orcas lived in pods or family groups. He made Serena blush by adding: "unlike so many married couples who fight constantly, they live together in harmonious cooperation, hunting, feeding and mating without aggression or serious conflict. In contrast to the whales, Stephen kept breaking his promise to refrain from striking his wife each time his penetration produced an agonized scream that sometimes brought an abrupt halt to their lovemaking. The feeling of rejection that accompanied each such failure sent an angry rush of blood to his brain, and his fists automatically struck out at his unresponsive wife.

"The advancing whales seemed not so much to swim, but rather to part the water effortlessly out of their way with the power of their flukes and their tremendous bulk. Whenever they surfaced snorting from their blowholes, their dorsal fins, like huge black scimitars, cleaved the water leaving a V-shaped wake of ripples trailing behind. The sun glinted off their black bodies and the sea slipped like oil from their gleaming backs. Each time they broke the surface, they shot powerful puffs of moisture-laden spray into the air and their deep guttural snorts raised goose bumps among the watchers. Stephen scrambled forward awkwardly and put his arms around his wife. Although she felt uncomfortable with his clinging presence, she thought his move was a silent attempt to ask forgiveness for his earlier brutality. She squeezed his hand to show that she had forgiven him. But when he began kissing her neck and she felt his penis sticking into her back, she pulled away roughly and moved to an empty seat, embarrassed by his public display of lust. Crimson with humiliation, she lowered her head to avoid the scrutiny of the other watchers.

On weekends, Serena noticed that "Garage," "Yard," and "Moving Sales" had become a phenomenon in Victoria. On Fridays, addresses of these sales would suddenly appear on lamp posts, at street corners and in the local newspapers. These sales, with items very reasonably priced, drew flocks of customers. Front yards and driveways became open-air markets where visitors could see and buy furniture, toys, books, clothes, jewelry, cutlery, crockery, appliances, TV's, microwave ovens, computers, desks, chairs, fishing equipment, small boats and a long list of camping equipment. Although the phenomenon is absent in Korea, she thought its citizens would do well to emulate the custom. She was surprised by another of the habits of Victorians. They know that students at the university are often strapped for money and that many indigenous folk are also in need. In order to help them both, Victorians often put sofas, mattresses, chairs, tables, desks, older appliances, TV's, Microwaves and other household items on their front lawns. Each item is labeled: FREE.

The whales performed a beautiful water ballet, leaping out of the water, dragging gallons of ocean into the air and showing off their gleaming white patches on both their flukes, and undersides. During their performance, Serena kept her distance from Stephen. Every time the whales flopped back joyfully into the sea, they splashed the water crazily. Each of the flying droplets caught the sunlight, dazzling the eye with hundreds of rainbows that hung in the air before disappearing.

Serena felt a close affinity with these magnificent creatures. They were mammals like her, and originally, had been land dwellers, like her. They breathed the same air as she did and nursed their offspring with milk from mammary glands, just as she would do. Again like her, they would spare no effort in tending and protecting their babies during the most vulnerable years of their lives. And though they did not marry, couples forged bonds of affection that lasted a lifetime. She was enjoying herself so much that she wanted to thank Stephen for the outing, but being afraid of his reaction, she decided to wait until they got home and out of the public eye.

Stephen, totally unfazed by the incident on the Zodiac, chatted with Serena on the drive home as though he hadn't misbehaved and embarrassed her on the tour: "In February each year," he began, "while the majority of Canadians back east are shoveling snow and being punished by hoary winter, Victorians are in their gardens, smugly collating their daily total of blossoms. Each gardener passes his "flower count" to the media that relay them to the rest of ice-bound Canada. It's a gentle boast to their fellow citizens that Victorians inhabit a banana belt." Serena didn't miss the pride Stephen took in the statement. Then, trying to placate her for his latest brutality, he came up with a surprise. One minute, he was parking the car in downtown Victoria, and the next, they had entered the gloom of a pine scented Temperate Rain Forest. The atmosphere was so saturated, they had the impression that moisture was actually dripping from the leaves and moss-covered bark of the massive Douglas firs, pines and occasional Blue spruce in the forest.

The scratching sound of a huge grizzly bear rooting in a dry streambed had carried on the wind. The noise startled a bull elk, with head stretched upward, its ears swiveled towards the sound, its nose scenting the air for danger. Focused on the sound, and on high alert, it was unaware of a cougar crouching just yards away. The big cat, at the end of its stalk, was hidden motionless behind a thick clump of ferns. Its muscles were bunched like a coiled spring, ready to pounce. But, like the frozen figures on that magnificent *Grecian Urn*, the creatures in this forest would remain immobile in their respective poses for eternity. She and Stephen were gazing at an exhibit in the Royal British Columbia Museum.

There, they admired the culture of First Nations' peoples who expressed their art in the carving of Totem poles, sculpture, paintings, weaving and a myriad of other artifacts. Much of their work had its origin in the abundant variety of wildlife that inhabited the sea, air, forests, lakes, rivers and surrounding areas where these native people lived. From their artwork, it was evident that wildlife was the central hub around which they built their whole existence. The truth is that it gave them their identity as hunters and fishermen, provided them with flesh for food, bone and sinew for tools and weapons, oil for light, hides for moccasins and clothes for warmth during the winter.

The art forms of these tribal people made it evident that they fully recognized their dependence on wildlife for their survival. Many examples of their art displayed either one or more animals. Their subjects excited Serena since she thought they sprang from the same roots as her painting. However, unlike her subjects, the eagles, ravens, whales and walruses drawn from their real world were often deified. Their shapes were wedded to the Gods of the mythical world of these Northwest Coastal Indians. It was evident that the deification of the animals that fueled their creative process emphasized their intense spirituality.

The couple saw many other impressive exhibits. One displayed the history of flight in a silent movie backed up with authentic examples of early aircraft suspended from the ceiling. Another portrayed the cobbled street of an early frontier town with a glass storefront displaying the goods and services that offered the observer a glimpse into the lifestyle of that bygone era. They then stood in a miniature train station of the past, listening in awe to the roar of an approaching but invisible locomotive drawing ever closer. The walls vibrated, and the floor shook violently under their feet as the invisible train rattled loudly past their station, seeming to sweep them along in its roar that diminished with distance.

The excellent full-life exhibit of a wooly mammoth transfixed Serena as it stood in regal detachment amidst its vast and barren landscape of stunted shrubs, snow and ice. The long thick and grizzled rust colored hair trailing from its body and trunk formed a thick skirt-like outer covering that swept the ground in places. Beneath its outer coat, a much shorter and thicker one covered every inch of its body. Their density provided crucial protection against its glacial environment of isolation. But it was the dual tusks, brandished like a pair of massive curved scimitars thrusting from the animal's jaws that riveted their attention. Suddenly, blinding flashes of lightening dazzled their eyes followed by terrifying rolls of thunder. The brilliance of the light and the crashes of thunder being unexpected were so scary that mothers petitioned the museum to discontinue the light and soundtrack since the combination terrified their kids and made them cry.

A new exhibit of huge prehistoric dinosaur skeletons had been brought from China, entitled: "Dragon Bones." Since some of these huge animals were carnivores, the couple tried to imagine the precautions their ancestors might have taken against their attack. Stephen–thinking of the Masai warriors who, as a rite of passage into manhood, faced a charging lion armed with only a spear–stated that anyone crazy enough to confront those dragons would be not merely courageous, but also incredibly heroic. Serena disagreed. Facing such monsters was neither. It was sheer stupidity, for the outcome was too heavily weighted in favor of the dragon. He argued with her, making her laugh, by suggesting that the real monster was the man. His race, he pointed out, was still flourishing while the dragons were now all extinct. Only their bones remained.

Elsewhere, there was a series of windows depicting the evolutionary stages of man. Each window displayed a separate portrait starting with Neanderthal man that moved the viewer to Cro-Magnon, Homo erectus, and finally to Homo sapiens. In this last window, Serena was expecting another portrait, but was suddenly startled to see her own face reflected in a mirror. She thought the idea especially clever and creative.

The Museum presented the couple with a vivid panorama of the present and the past, the living and the dead, for the IMAX Theater is located in the same building. On a screen that is 6 stories tall, bellowing 12,000 watts of digital surround-sound, it reels off for the viewer images of innovative film magic. She and Stephen visited the Arctic, hobnobbing with polar bears, penguins, seals, walruses and whales. A few minutes later, the terrifying roar of the Kalahari lions immobilized them with shock. Their roar was so deep and guttural, so primal in its power that it inspired a visceral shiver of terror in the pit of their stomachs. Serena trembled along with the rest of the onlookers in the theater. The hair rose on her neck and she felt the frigid finger of fear inching its way along her spine.

"I knew you'd enjoy the displays," Stephen boasted, still keeping his distance. Serena refused to reply being still mad at him for his cruelty. Yet, each time she looked at him, she couldn't fail to note the guilt mingled with shame stamped on his face. The fact that he slunk shamefacedly into the background brought a sharp sense of sorrow to her at the awareness of their marital discord. In an attempt to heal the rift between them, she gently took his hands and raised them to her lips, the light of forgiveness shining in her eyes. After all, she thought, it was Stephen who afforded her the delight of these visits. She could at least show her gratitude.

Chapter 53

Serena could count on receiving both a violation followed by a battering as her reward for the courage and willpower she exerted each time Stephen called her to his bed. She believed that she deserved his violent outbursts since as his wife she hadn't done what all wives were supposed to guarantee–pleasing their husbands in bed. Stephen never ceased to point out her glaring failure as a wife. The criticism made her feel so ashamed that at first she actually begged his forgiveness and promised to try harder next time. She no longer had to wonder whether what she realized was true. It wasn't just her imagination. Stephen had reverted to his old dishonorable self? He couldn't care less about hurting her.

The anger and disgust smoldering in his narrowed eyes and tightened features made her recall her mother's advice: "a good wife makes a conscious effort to please her husband in bed. That's the way to a successful marriage." It was the advice that made her decide that whenever Stephen wanted her, she would do whatever it took to give him pleasure. She would try her damndest to suppress her terror at the graphic images of her gang rape brought on by his sexual aggression. So it was that she opened herself up to intimacy with Stephen, forcing her mind to stop whirling in terror and confusion after permitting him to undress her.

As he slipped off her blouse then unhooked her bra with the touch of an expert, she fought against the cold shiver of fear that shook her body. When he unzipped her jeans, removed them and expertly slipped off her underwear, she concentrated fiercely, allowing him to begin caressing her. She let him cup one breast while his other hand roamed freely over her body. But when he began kissing her stomach before slipping a finger inside her, a rush of images from her rape assaulted her and she could no longer control the terror or the violent fit of trembling that shook her. Though trying as hard as she could, she was unable to dismiss the foul images that stormed into her mind and took control of her body. When regardless of her evident distress, Stephen bored into her and began thrusting, slowly at first, and then with increased fervor, she felt her gorge rise. The imminent threat of vomiting all over Stephen forced her to push him away violently and rush to the bathroom to relieve herself. Stephen chased after her, furious at her aggressive rejection. Kneeling on the floor with the toilet clasped in her arms she kept retching until she began disgorging her dinner. Suddenly, she felt the first of his cuffs on either side of her head followed by a series of stinging slaps. As though maddened, he didn't stop until he saw blood redden the water in the toilet. His heavy blows left her with an aching head and neck while her ears kept ringing for days afterwards. Much later that night, with aching head, bleeding nose and ringing ears, she lay in bed, boiling with rage at her husband's savagery. Tears of anger, shame and frustration filled her eyes at the thought that she was powerless to change her situation against the bully she had married. Yet, she was determined to find a way. When the fears her parents had expressed about marriage to a man she hardly knew entered her mind, she banished them immediately ashamed of having ignored their reasonable arguments.

As though what she had to endure was not enough, Stephen began to snipe at the attention she gave to her interest in photography and painting.

"Your sorties on photographic safaris to gather subjects for your painting were bad enough. But now, added to that, are your renewed efforts at painting. As a wife, you should be organizing your life to spend more time with me instead of resuming projects that keep us apart. If your painting was good enough to sell, then at least it wouldn't be time wasted." She thanked him for his "brilliant critical insight," and for once again "belittling her creative efforts."

"But Stephen, I paint when you're at work, or when insomnia keeps me awake while you are asleep."

"That's not the point," he said.

"What's the point?"

"Whatever you do that keeps you away from me is time wasted. When I'm at home, I expect you to keep me company. I need to discuss the problems I have at work so that you understand what I have to go through each day. I don't want to hear about the problems you face on the particular subject you've chosen to paint. I'm tired of listening to you prattle about photography and painting."

"Stephen, your repeated use of the words I, I, and I, shows your conceit, arrogance and selfishness. How unreasonable can you be! You want me to discuss your problems, but you refuse to discuss mine. What kind of a husband are you? The truth of the matter is that we aren't joined at the hip. Regardless of what *you* want, *I* need time for myself."

"If your work was good enough to sell, then I'd agree you should be allowed time to paint."

"Allowed? Stephen, allowed? What you have to understand is that you don't own me nor will I let you dictate what I can and can't do in my spare time. You're making the same kind of demands that your father used to dictate to your mother, and acting with the same kind of arrogance and stupidity. She didn't put up with it and neither will I." The ultimatum reminded him of his earlier fears that he might live to regret having a dominant wife who was more intelligent. Now that he was being faced with the reality, he felt humiliated, again hearing his father's laughter ringing in his ears. Such was his anger at being compared to his father that his face turned purple with rage. Serena's outright rejection of the half-baked ploys he had thought up to dominate and control her made him feel humiliated, impotent and outmaneuvered. Serena left the room to end the quarrel.

"That's right! Stephen shouted. "Go and begin painting another canvas." Shades of his father's behavior, she thought.

In Stephen's mind, nothing she did was of any value. It was breath wasted to point out that she painted while he was at work or late at night when she couldn't sleep. He was blind to the fact that whatever she enjoyed doing was a vital part of who she was. Like her interest in photography or the environment, her painting was a vital part of her personality. Each of these interests was a means of expressing herself. Bereft of any of these parts, she would be less than whole.

As she deliberated on her earliest meetings with Stephen, she recalled the different personalities he assumed. Sometimes he used a shy, reluctant approach with diffident smile and self-pitying voice that, in an instant, could blaze into anger when he failed to gain his objective. There was his dictatorial attitude and hostility that, when confronted would, in the blink of an eye, change to pleading. There was his impatience with views he didn't share and the insulting questions that followed when proven wrong. Finally, she remembered the arrogant curl of lip and the look of disdain that reflected his air of superiority. How had she managed to overlook these facets of his personality she had known so well? Perhaps she had been blinded by love. More important, how could she not see that he had broken the promise he made to become an honorable man, and had reverted to his dishonorable self? After their last quarrel, Stephen' words eventually made his thinking quite clear.

"Listen woman, I've saved you from the slaughter of gossips. I've given you a fresh start in a sophisticated world. It is more than your farmyard could offer." Since Stephen had convinced himself that she owed him big time for having saved her and her reputation from ruin, he considered that she was beholden to him, and should rush to fulfill his every wish.

"Really Stephen! Instead of what you've just said, I remember you vowing, on more than one occasion, that you were in love with me and wanted to protect me for the rest of my life. So the fact is your protestations of love were all lies?" He continued to make his demands as though she hadn't spoken, hoping through the force of his domination and bluff to regain some of the ground he had lost in arguments with her.

"Since I've been good enough to give you a new life, I expect you to give up your other interests. While I'm present, you must devote yourself wholly to me. I expect you to cook my meals, wash and iron my clothes, clean my house and offer a viewpoint on the subjects I choose to discuss."

"Good God Stephen, you're even worse than your father! You married an equal, not a slave or 'the weaker female of the species.' Since I haven't been a complete wife, I have accepted your violations and your blows without comment, but I will no longer subject myself to your selfish demands! If you want a servant to cook, wash and iron, then you can hire one. But don't you dare forget this is my home. If anyone has to leave it will be you." The truth is that she wanted to shame Stephen for the way he was behaving. His next words almost bowled her over and led her to see clearly behind the mask he wore.

If he pushed even harder, he thought, he just might get his way. "Listen woman, marriage is a melding of two lives in which both partners must focus their efforts on catering to their spouse's welfare. What I said earlier about your hobbies should indicate what I expect you to give up to make our marriage a success."

"You must be insane! While quick to point out the interests I have to give up, you've never said a word about anything you are prepared to abandon. So let me advise you, dear. I have no intention whatever of giving in to your demands."

"We'll see about that!"

"I must point out once again that you've reverted to your dishonorable past." Needing to humiliate him, she added: "You've broken your word displaying your untrustworthiness, your arrogance, your egotism and of course your lack of intelligence. Those virtues you stated that had changed you into an honorable man have all disappeared. In fact, they have always been well beyond your reach. The truth is that you spend your time thinking up new strategies for getting your way. They won't work! If you want to gain the respect of others, you have to earn it and you certainly haven't done that. In fact, you have behaved so dishonorably that you need to change your attitude if you want to remain in this house. I hope you'll give a great deal of thought to what I've said."

"How about a visit to the Butchart Gardens?" Stephen offered a few days later, then added: "That is, if your advanced pregnancy doesn't tire you too much." Suddenly he was all angelic, hoping to conceal the devil behind his mask. Serena wasn't taken in and answered:

"The fact is that I've heard so much about them that I'd love to go. Besides, I'm sure there are seats where I can rest. My pregnancy won't be a bother." She knew that whatever else he was planning, Stephen was ashamed of his behavior and was perhaps trying to atone for his latest arrogant stance. Besides, she knew he didn't want to be thrown out of her house. He'd be forced to find a place of his own and live alone. In Serena's home he lived rent free. If he lived elsewhere he would have to pay and he knew as well that isolation would be no kinder to him than to anyone else.

"Well, there's quite a lot to see, and visiting it all requires a lot of walking. But you're right, there are places where we can sit and you can rest while gazing for as long as you like," he replied. How could he make such an about face and sound so affable after his obnoxious behavior, she asked herself.

It was late spring, and from their car, Serena stared in admiration at the pink and white blossoming Cherry trees that bordered both sides of the road leading to the gardens. Their blossoms grew in bunches resembling colorful snowflakes ready to drop from the branches. Beneath each tree a circle of beautiful blossoms that had fallen there lay on the ground mimicking those above.

Serena's bosom swelled with pride when she caught sight of the South Korean flag flying from the rooftop above the entrance amidst those of many other nations.

"The Butchart Gardens," Stephen gushed, "were created out of a limestone quarry." In assuming the role of tour guide, he was unashamedly parroting the garden's history from the popular book, "The Butchart Gardens," written by Colin Fiddler.

"Serena was delighted with the flowers of every imaginable kind and color that she saw as they began their tour. She was especially taken with the genus, Pelargonium. They had light mauve, white and pink petals with dark magenta smudges like scarified markings on their flower faces. She feasted her eyes on bunches of petunias, in mauve, pink, and white interspersed with bursts of the red blossoms peeping from among green leaves tinged with a light brown veneer. Next to them, bright begonias bloomed in creamy yellows, pinks and reds. There were banks of impatiens, red and white, yellow and pink in beds, pots and baskets. Elsewhere, brick-red tiger lilies exploded alongside white stargazers displaying crimson speckled petals. The erect 'whiskers' sprouting from amidst the petals with a blob of color on their ends gave the impression of deliberate whimsy. She believed that such staggering beauty could only have come from the Creator Himself.

"Clumps of dark blue irises sprouted together with green ferns like tiny bouquets on the lawns surrounding a lake. A raft of green lily pads floated on its surface pierced by the jets of a fountain. Its spray formed lofty curves in the air that created intricate patterns of droplets. In the bright sunshine they stood out like diamonds against the emerald greenery of pines, spruce and firs. Serena sat on a step overlooking the Sunken Garden gazing down on the flagstone walkway bordered by green lawns and tiny hedges encircling flower islands of dazzling colors. Their myriad shades of green leaves highlighted the masses upon masses of low lying annuals–reds and whites, shocking pinks and yellows–forming a quilted blanket alongside thousands of red, yellow, pink and black tulips. Like a real life picture postcard, they filled her heart with pleasure as they danced in the breeze like Wordworth's daffodils.

Brilliantly blooming white, red, purple and pink azalea shrubs and rhododendron bushes highlighted the green ground-cover of the Japanese Garden. Their dazzling colors were set against a variety of green ferns and mosses. The maples in the background stood like blazing sentinels sandwiched between evergreen pines, firs, spruce and copper beeches. They created an air of tranquility and seclusion brooding silently over the pool. The rare and delicate Tibetan Blue Poppy presided there in its tall and slender elegance.

Serena gazed at the soft green lawns encircling colorful flowerbeds and marveled at the gorgeous collaboration between man and nature. Since she became more than a little breathless from her walking, Stephen guided her to a secluded bench in the shade of a man-made bower flanked by thousands of colorful blossoms. The profusion of colors was overwhelming. It quickened her heartbeat, brightening her day. She breathed deeply to inhale the captivating fragrance of the extraordinary bouquet of beauty surrounding her. She gazed at an archway on which rambling roses vied with each other in beauty and color as they twined around poles and arches. Colors clashed and blended with colors to form so rich and diverse a tapestry that her eyes ached in response. Everywhere she went the scented blossoms wafted her into a fantasy land of enchantment.

"You seem to be enjoying yourself," Stephen exclaimed, breaking into her reverie as he saw that she was lost in another world. Since the pleasure she was experiencing was due entirely to Stephen, she put her arms around him, kissing him chastely on the cheek in a gesture of gratitude. In fact, she was just about to thank him for his generosity when he seized her by placing his hands on either side of her face. He then pressed his lips to hers and shot his tongue into her mouth. His kiss, both urgent and demanding, took her breath away. Before she could recover her senses, she felt his hand creeping under the elastic of her underwear. At just that moment, a crowd of tourists rounded the corner and their loud whistles and giggles at Stephen's unrestrained behavior made her blush crimson in embarrassment and humiliation. She sprang from her seat as though pursued by a devil. Rushing away, she hissed:

"Good God, Stephen! You behave like an animal in rut. Can't you control yourself, even in public?"

"There was no one around," he answered lamely. She couldn't prevent herself from asking: Was he really ready to jump my bones in public? She kept her distance making sure he couldn't repeat the incident.

The gardens with their galaxy of blooms appeared to her like a multicolored mosaic of gemstones carefully set in backgrounds of contrast that threw their radiance into focus. Such a profusion of colors, patterns and designs should never have blended harmoniously with each other, but miraculously, they did. She considered that their gardens in Korea, though beautiful, were no match for the acres of loveliness on display before her.

Yet, as she thought about the gardens, it struck her that man's attempts to imitate nature always seemed somewhat manufactured. She believed that in his attempt to equal the natural world he imposed so great a discipline upon it that it seemed artificial.

And in the gathering dusk of a late spring evening, as the last glimmer of the sun stained the clouds a glowing crimson, she and her contrite husband waited with a huge audience for the final event–a fireworks display with musical accompaniment. Eventually, a musical jingle came over the public address system to alert the audience that the entertainment was about to begin. It was so well known and lighthearted a frolic that it encouraged the audience, already in gay mood, to sing along. The experience was as unexpected and as enjoyable as the following fireworks display was spectacular. She couldn't help thinking, with a sense of deep sorrow and regret, the unblemished joy the visit would have afforded her, if only her marriage were not unraveling.

That night, as she lay in bed, she recalled the numerous times she had forgiven Stephen for his aggressive battering. And as her mind switched and lingered on the idea of forgiveness, a thought drifted into her consciousness shattering her peace of mind. It suddenly occurred to her that while she had voluntarily forgiven her husband over and over, she had never showed the same compassion, sympathy and understanding towards her mother, nor had she forgiven her, even after both she and her father had pleaded with her to do so. This truth came as a complete surprise since her uselessness as a wife had made her feel deserving of Stephen's aggression. With her mother it was different. Being the victim, Serena had felt so self-righteous that she had walked out in angry silence knowing the deep hurt that her act would inflict.

Afterwards, she had excused her conduct by telling herself that her mother's betrayal was an ignominious sin. It had dominated her mind since her best friend, Mona, her schoolmates and her teachers had committed the same treachery. The addition of her mother's duplicity made her conduct doubly difficult to accept. She had refused to invite her to the wedding in a deliberate act to make her suffer. By leaving Korea without offering her forgiveness to her mother, Serena had intensified her mother's suffering. And suddenly, she realized the enormity of her own sin. She was guilty of judging her mother, condemning and sentencing her for her crimes. In doing so, Serena realized that it was she who had committed the sin of pride; it was she who was guilty of playing God; it was she who had judged and condemned another human being.

She realized too late that her treachery had been a greater crime than her mother's. She was the one who had betrayed her by her conduct. She had excused her own wickedness certain that her parents would never accuse her, never voice their disapproval. Yet, she could be certain of the sorrow and grief her conduct had occasioned. Selfishly, she had made the clean break with her parents that she'd wanted and realized, far too late, how spiteful and cruel she had been.

Oh God, she wondered. How could she have been so blind, and so vindictive? She had extended a forgiving hand to Stephen, over and over again although he had broken his marriage vows; had violated her then beaten her to a pulp. Her other sin was in forgiving Mona, while turning her back on her mother every time she begged her forgiveness. Recalling her father's words shamed her: "must you be so stubborn and vindictive in bearing a grudge, Serena? Can't you feel the least bit of compassion? It's your mother you're punishing." His voice had trailed off in defeat and shame at her intransigence.

She had set out to hurt her mother on purpose and, at the time, was glad that she had succeeded. She had then justified her leaving by pretending that cutting off her parents would, in time, lessen their suffering. She hadn't given a single thought to their pain. Her only concern had been what was best for her. When she recalled her mother's selflessness in offering her love and support all through her illness and recovery, she was deeply ashamed of herself.

She wondered what she could do to make amends. She rose from her bed and, with arms folded, began frantically pacing the room. When she confided her feelings to Stephen, he said she was creating a mountain out of a molehill.

"There comes a time," he stated, "when parents have to learn to free their offspring; let go of their children." He was sure that her parents would "recognize that viewpoint and move on with their lives." However, Serena knew better. What might be true for Stephen and his family was not true for her. Korean families live a very closely knit lifestyle, and she knew her parents would grieve deeply over her selfish conduct. She also knew that refusing to invite her mother to the wedding and leaving Korea without forgiving her was a far greater betrayal than her mother's transgressions. She finally admitted to herself what she had known inwardly all along. Her mother had tried to shield her from her rash and impulsive self. She also wanted to have her nearby simply because she loved her daughter. Yes, her mother had acted out of love. On the other hand, Serena had acted out of anger and spitefulness. She became miserable, wondering what she could do to heal the wounds she had caused to the people she loved.

Eventually, she returned to her bed, tossing and turning until finally, a solution presented itself. She would phone home and beg her mother's forgiveness for being so selfish and ungrateful. She considered that inviting both parents to Canada to be present at the birth of their grandchild would heal all wounds. The truth was that in her present marital situation, she was too ashamed to tell her mother that her warning had been accurate and that she longed for her presence and advice. She hoped that her phone call would allow her to mend fences and offer both parents the joyful news that they were about to become grandparents. By the time her decision was made, it was nearly dawn and she rang and rang with beating heart but couldn't get through to either to them. The first thing she did on waking later was to try again and again, unable to understand why she kept getting the reply that their numbers were out of service. Since her phone calls failed, she wrote a letter begging her mother's forgiveness and included the invitation to Canada. Only after posting it did she feel a sense of peace.

Chapter 54

During their last quarrel, she had attacked Stephen by emphasizing his aggressive and repugnant behavior. "Although you've promised over and over to await my full recovery before making sexual demands on me, you've broken your promise again and again." His response was swift.

"How dare you accuse me of my shortcomings when you've never stopped being a useless wife?" He knew how to hurt her by striking at her vulnerability, so she tried to hit back.

"Stephen, you keep breaking your promises because you're untrustworthy. The truth of the matter is that nobody can depend on you. You have no core principles that you live by. Worse still, you can't control your urges. Given half a chance you would jump my bones in public. Any normal person would be ashamed of such glaring defects."

"As an abnormal wife, *you're* pointing the finger at abnormality?" He asked ironically.

"Normal people exercise control over their impulses. But from our first meeting your hands were always in your pocket. In my naïveté I took it as a compliment to my charms. But with maturity, I've learnt how wrong I was. My charms had nothing to do with the real target you had in mind."

"Listen wife, your sexual incompetence makes me so mad and frustrated that I feel compelled to strike out. If you participated fully in our intimacy, I would never have to resort to blows. *You* and you alone, are the root cause of my 'repugnant' behavior. The full blame for your battering falls on your own shoulders. So don't try to blame me for your shortcomings."

"I've always accepted my part of the blame, that's why I have never complained or retaliated before. But Stephen, your reasoning is as flawed and as ridiculous as your conduct. Listening to you would suggest that you had nothing whatever to do with the blows with which you batter me. According to your logic, I batter myself. How could I have failed to see not only the bully but the idiot you are? Besides, honorable men don't strike women. There is no excuse whatever for such cowardly behavior." Although the heavy blows hit home, he felt he had to come up with an answer and replied:

"It is you that have made me sick with shame and guilt, forcing me to behave dishonorably. If you behaved yourself like a true wife, I would never have cause to strike you."

"Me behave myself? Stephen, you astonish me with your twisted and self-serving reasoning. What a weasel you turned out to be! The truth of the matter is that unable to control yourself, you behave like an animal, and you know it! What you have to understand is that I make you feel less than the honorable man you want so desperately to be, and you hate me for it. You promised to wait until I was fully healed and you didn't. You vowed before God to love and honor me and you didn't. You also promised to protect me, and again you broke your promise. Instead, you've made me suffer repeatedly with forced intimacy, and then repaid me with blows for my failure to gratify your animal lust."

Stephen wilted under the attack for he knew that Serena's words were true. From his first meetings with her, his hands were always in his pockets, his libido on high alert. Her arguments made him aware that his feelings for her were born of lust rather than love since he was always more concerned with his own needs than with hers. He hated himself for this weakness in his character, the speed at which he, an experienced lover, became aroused by just looking at Serena or even being near her. There was also the suffering he inflicted on her. He knew that he should have exercised control over his urges, especially in public. Yet, although he had tried, he had failed in every attempt to do so. She was right. He had reverted to his old dishonorable self, but he didn't have to share these views with her. He thought it best to keep them to himself.

"Stephen, as a useless wife nearing the end of my third trimester, I'll be sleeping in the nursery from now on." She knew that Stephen hated that kind of ultimatum, and he immediately became enraged, looking for the flimsiest excuse to prevent her leaving his bed.

"I won't hear of it! I'm accustomed to having your warmth and your closeness for me to sleep peacefully."

"As usual, you're thinking only of yourself. What you have to understand Stephen is that I am the one who is pregnant. The truth is that in my condition, I'm uncomfortable all the time and keep having to turn constantly. I also have to get up often to relieve myself and don't wish to disturb you. Besides, being next to you in bed will be a temptation for you, and bearing your heavy burden on my swollen stomach is painful to me and dangerous to the unborn child."

"The doctor says that if we are careful we can still have intercourse." She was tempted to tell him to go and have intercourse with the doctor, but resisted. Instead, she replied:

"After all the reasons I've given, it's still you, you, you, with your needs alone taken into account. Don't you ever listen to another point of view? Must everything turn on you and your needs? Well, for once I'm going to take care of my needs. Besides, did you tell that doctor that intimacy with you involves your wife's violation and her battering?" Stephen was furious at her refusal to bend to his will and ended by threatening blows. She again called him a bully and a coward who could only take advantage of a pregnant and defenseless woman. His face flushed crimson with shame and he left her alone. Seeing his reaction, she wondered why she had never before criticized him so viciously for his cruelty. Standing up to Stephen bolstered her self image. Nothing he said afterwards would change her mind. A surge of relief washed over her, and she vowed she would no longer respond to Stephen's sexual demands.

She believed that Stephen's conduct, like his conclusions, was often irrational and she saw this as another glaring weakness in his character. Whenever his own feelings or desires were concerned, he could not be relied upon for a reasonable response. He also changed his stance with a new argument whenever cornered. There were no firmly rooted principles guiding his thoughts or actions. Then, although his striking figure and handsome face turned out to be his greatest assets, especially where women were concerned, they were also his most serious flaws. They deluded him into the belief of his self-importance; inspired in him the assurance of his singularity. She knew that he saw himself as a superior being standing above the level of lesser mortals. However, she also knew that his self-inflated ego was really an attempt to conceal his glaring insecurities.

Her stay in the nursery ran into weeks and whenever Stephen argued that she should return to his bed, she refused. "If I did return," she told him, "you would be disappointed in our sexual bonding and I would end up being battered. My first and only priority is the baby. Sex with you is out of the question."

Stephen boiled with rage at his wife's ultimatum and kept thinking of what he could do to force her return. Very unusual for him, he put himself in her place trying to find a solution. Only then did he fully realize the torment he had caused her. Had he been in her place, he wouldn't have just left the marriage bed. He'd have left the marriage. Once again, he kept this view to himself.

After her son's birth, Serena went through the anxieties of mothers whose children first attend pre-school, but, she needn't have bothered. Calvin was a happy child who enjoyed finger painting, and group activities. After listening to the stories read to them, the kids competed eagerly to answer simple questions. They learnt nursery rhymes in the morning, and each one got a turn to recite them. After lunch, they had play activities before taking a nap later on. Serena picked Calvin up at three thirty each week day.

"Stephen, please stop harping on the same subject. I cannot be sexually intimate with you while I have my son to take care of. I'm feeding him every two hours so I'm hardly getting any sleep."

"I can't see how a little love would interfere with your taking care of your baby."

"If it were love that would certainly be different. But Stephen, you don't know the meaning of that word. Besides, after feeding Calvin every two hours I'm completely wrung out both physically and emotionally. My fatigue and lack of energy robs me of the mood for sex. It's the furthest thing from my mind."

"You're wrung out emotionally and have no energy for sex because you're so fixated on your son. You keep worrying about him sleeping or awake. You're letting your son keep you away from me."

"Stephen, your reasoning is as skewed as ever. The truth is that I am the one keeping myself away from you, not the baby. The reality of it is that I won't sleep in your bed. I won't have sex with you. I don't want your violation or your battering. What you need to understand is that I'm preoccupied with my new-born son and it's all I can do at present. I refuse to continue this discussion."

"And I refuse to accept your ultimatum," he shouted. "The very thought that you are dictating to me drives me crazy. I'll have to do something about that," he promised, but since she had called him a coward and told him off, he seemed reluctant to confront her aggressively. He didn't want to admit that he was less sure of himself, and if truth be told, not only ashamed, but perhaps even afraid.

Calvin was just as happy in elementary school as he had been in preschool. He loved the enthusiasm of his teachers in the presentation of their subject and got thoroughly involved in the learning process. Although he spent time with friends, Serena taught him that education was vital in making a success of his life and he was content to devote much of his spare time to his projects. During these early years, she supervised his homework, making sure that it was done neatly and correctly. Later on, she took him to the branch of the Nellie Mc Clung library on Mackenzie Avenue where a librarian there made him familiar with the encyclopedias and works of background information that he would find helpful in his projects at Lambrick Park Middle School, located less than a block away from his home.

Since Stephen was an expert with the computer, it was the one time he got involved with his son. He bought him an upgraded machine to start him off, taught him the basics of "Microsoft Word," of using the internet, and bought him the teaching tool: "Computers for Dummies."

Calvin practiced long and hard. Serena believed that he wanted to surprise and win his father's admiration for the competence he displayed in using the gift. The new skill also proved to boost his grades since he learnt to access some of the information he needed for his projects by consulting search engines like Google, Yahoo, Amazon and MSN. It was evident that he hoped his wizardry in using the computer would make his dad proud.

"Do you find the work at High School challenging Calvin?"

"Mom, most teachers give an excellent grade to anyone whose projects are well researched, well written and turned in on time."

"In my day, teachers gave special credit to students who could reproduce the teacher's views but used their own words to do so," Serena stated smiling. "But what sort of marks are you getting?"

"Like you, I tend to remember the teachers' views, using my own words. But since they give additional marks for creativity, I've been checking out encyclopedias and various search engines on the internet. A good deal of my 'creativity' comes from there. My marks are quite high."

Calvin was not a first rate team player in any sport, although he took an active part in the intramural sports between the different Houses to which each student belonged. However, he made up for this deficiency by becoming accomplished with both the guitar and keyboard and often soloed in the school's band-concerts. The latter always drew a solid crowd of parents who donated generously to the school's Musical Instrument Fund after hearing the stirring music of the school's band, and Calvin's rendition of songs by Sinatra.

"Stephen, you are going to your son's concert tonight, aren't you?" My God, Stephen thought, not again. "I'm sorry dear. But I have some work to catch up on, so I won't be able to attend."

"You don't have to go anywhere to attend, dear. He's giving this concert for us, right here, in our living room. I hope you won't disappoint him again. On both occasions he offered to play for us, you were busy." Only when Stephen saw that he was cornered and couldn't very well refuse, did he agree to be present. Calvin had learnt the songs of his three favorite singers not for his school, but mainly to make his dad proud of him for the talent he displayed. With singular performances on guitar and keyboard, he imitated the antics of his favorite singer, belting out his songs.

"What a performance! Serena stated, loudly clapping her hands after each of Calvin's renditions.

"Stephen, wouldn't you agree that our son has a natural talent for music?" Serena stated with rapture in her voice trying to encourage Stephen to praise his son. And when Stephen only shook his head remaining silent, she chided:

"Good God, say something! Show some enthusiasm!" she whispered. "Calvin is dying to make you proud of him."

"Well, I suppose he's quite a good imitator," Stephen replied unenthusiastically. It wasn't that he didn't recognize Calvin's extraordinary musical talent. It was his unwillingness or inability to praise either Calvin or Serena, and perhaps to let his emotions show. The truth was that Calvin, who longed to make his dad proud of him, was deeply disappointed at his father's apathetic response. It hurt him to think that his father never attended his games, never displayed enthusiasm over his scholastic talent, never even bothered to attend his graduation. Although his mother's reactions were ecstatic, they never quite made up for his father's indifference.

Stephen, you seem to have forgotten that as a husband and father, you have a sacred duty towards your wife and son." Stephen merely glared silently at his wife.

"Despite your vows to support and sustain me "in sickness and in health," your promise to be a companion and helpmate, you have followed in your father's footsteps preferring to be autocratic rather than sympathetic. Worse, you refuse to show Calvin the affection and praise for which he longs."

"My dear," Stephen stated, without the slightest hint of endearment, "I've told you a thousand times to curb your over-enthusiastic praise of Calvin for his musical, as for his academic performances. By rhapsodizing over them, you'll only turn the boy's head, make him conceited. Surely you can see such effusive praise of his ability encourages arrogance and conceit."

"I suppose you'd prefer me to ignore his every attempt to please you, as you always do? Well, I can never be as cold, aloof and unresponsive as you are. And I'm sure that Calvin resents your unspoken indifference. I firmly believe that it amounts to cruelty. As a father, it's something you need to keep in mind."

"When I need your opinion on how I should respond towards my son, I'll let you know. In the meantime I'll like to remind you who is the head of this household." Stephen's determination to be the dominant member in their relationship, to be always in charge, was a facet of his character that Serena remembered from his earlier behavior in Korea. Thanks to this obsession, instead of being a helpmate, he had become his wife's aggressor.

It was Stephen's compulsion to dominate others that prevented him from showing Calvin the love, affection and companionship for which his son yearned. Derelict in this sacred duty, Stephen trampled upon the love of a son for his father, refusing to let it pierce the impervious carapace of his egotism. All through his youth and adolescence, Calvin tried to win his father's respect and admiration without success. Perhaps it was the deep disappointment that Calvin felt at his father's callous detachment that made him behave with such cold indifference towards his mother. It was ironic that while Stephen never exercised any control over his passion towards his wife, he was particularly adept at controlling those same emotions towards his son.

A number of universities accepted Calvin because of his high GPA, but he decided to go to the University of Victoria that was nearby. He still secretly hoped to make his dad proud but nothing he did succeeded–not his musical talent, not his academic achievement, not his acceptance at the better universities, not even the full scholarships he was offered. Stephen behaved like an absentee landlord in his household–pretending interest, but always maintaining a great distance from its occupants. After a while, Calvin decided to treat his father with the same cold detachment he had received. At the end of his first year, without discussing his choices, he decided to read for a double major in English Literature and Intelligence Technology.

Stephen was proud of Calvin. But he was never able to voice the pride he felt at his son's successes. Although he lived under the same roof as his wife and son, he seemed to inhabit a darkened world of his own, aloof from them both. Perhaps he couldn't forget his belief that his new born had kept his wife away from him. Of late, a dark cloud always seemed to be settled around him, goading him to anger. He couldn't understand why his mind was always in turmoil, why his thoughts were constantly clouded by a dense fog of gloom, or why he always seemed so deeply depressed. He knew it stemmed partly from his inability to break into his wife's inner sanctum, but there was something more that he couldn't quite put his finger on. Then, there was that sudden cold that took him by surprise. Finally, the distance between himself and Serena seemed to sap him of the emotional energy he needed to draw closer to his wife and son. But if Calvin felt the neglect, like his dad, he never let his feelings show. He was obedient and respectful to Stephen, though never affectionate. However, Stephen couldn't miss the fact that Calvin kept distancing himself from his mother in the same way as from him.

The specter of his father battering his mother made Calvin hate his father and drove him wild with fury. It also robbed him of his concentration when he tried to study. A violent father and a too-compliant mother made him mad at both parents. The discord between them was making his life a misery. He cursed the fates for their unfairness at his being ignored by the father he worshipped.

Serena tried to make Stephen aware of the adverse effects their volatile relationship was having upon Calvin. "Stephen, I would be willing to put up with your violence in bed if you showed Calvin the paternal affection and concern that he craves."

"So now you're trying to bribe me with sex and dictate how I should behave?"

"I don't want to see you hurt Calvin more than you already have. You can at least balance your failure as a husband by being a success as a father."

"Don't preach to me about my failure as a husband while you continue to be a failure as a wife."

"You violate me again and again, batter me after having your way, then when I give you a son, you have the gall to call me a failure as a wife?" Stephen hated to lose an argument with Serena. It made him feel totally inadequate as a man. In his mind, he heard his father's laughter, ringing down through the years, ridiculing him. His face flushed in humiliation. What could he do, he kept asking himself, to impose a stricter control over this damned woman?

And so the stinging blows to his pride always made their quarrels escalate, constantly deepening the divide that already existed between husband and wife.

It became clear to Serena that marriage had soured her life. In desperation, she had given in to her husband's sexual appetite to tell herself that she was being a "good wife." She later understood that she had been punishing herself for her failure as a spouse. She had been in denial, unwilling to admit that she had made a mistake in her choice of husband. The truth is that with hindsight, she saw that her continual attempts at pleasing him stemmed in part from the memory of their courtship. He had been so compassionate and sympathetic on learning of her gang rape that her heart had melted. Keeping his promise of marriage had inspired in her such devotion that she couldn't believe the monster she now knew was the same man.

How could he have changed so radically? As she lay in bed, cold and alone, while he slept in the other room, she wished she was at home riding into the hills with her father. Had she been so wrong in trying to find happiness with her husband in this beautiful land where the outdoors always promised the joy and excitement of adventure? The pent up anger from the pain of each sexual encounter and the battering that followed had, over time, kept pushing her towards deep depression and further away from Stephen. The evident truth was that a dark cloud of fury kept building inside her until the pressure was such that she could stand it no longer. That was the main reason she had abandoned the attempt at being a "good wife." That was the reason that she had left her husband's bed, even before the birth of Calvin.

Chapter 55

"Department of English, hello?"

"May I speak with Calvin Ahn please?"

"One moment please." Her hand over the mouthpiece, the secretary at the university called to her boss.

"Doris, it's that bothersome Korean woman again for her son, Calvin."

"Tell her not to call her son at this number," Doris replied in annoyance.

"I've already told her at least once." Lifting her hand off the mouthpiece, the secretary told her caller:

"Mrs. Ahn please hang up. Calvin will call you back on another line." She emphasized the last three words.

"Mom?"

"Hello Hwang Yong darling." In a burst of Korean she asks:

"How did you know it was me?"

"The name is Calvin, Mom. Speak English or I'll put the phone down." His manner was abrupt, his voice stern, his tone uncompromising.

"Oh Calvin," she said in despair. "You are not a respectful son. You no longer obey your mother."

"You're in a new country Mom, so stop speaking Korean. Speak English and help to make me feel Canadian," he pleaded, already guilty at the tough attitude he had adopted.

"You're ashamed of your Korean heritage, huh? You've turned your back on Korea? Bad boy!"

"No Mom. Korea is the past. Our present and future are in Canada now. You know that Mom," he said in exasperation.

"The truth is that you're a new Canadian, but an old, old Korean. Don't forget Hwang Yong!"

"Calvin, Mom, Calvin! Stop splitting me in two. It's hard enough just trying to be a single individual."

"Two different halves belong to the same person. That's not hard Calvin! I'm one person. One half is Canadian, the other half Korean."

"Is that why you speak Korean, always walk a couple of steps behind your husband, keep advising me not to trust white girls and to find a nice Korean girl to marry?"

"That's my Korean half."

"What's your Canadian half?"

"I've cut myself off from my Korea, live my life in Canada, eat Canadian food, learn English, use Canadian dress and habits, and never speak Korean. I work as a hostess at a restaurant, serving Canadian food. You don't understand. For me, these things are major changes in my life, Hwang Yong."

"Calvin Mom, last chance before I hang up." Annoyed at her son's lack of respect, at his refusal to obey and re-bond with his culture, Serena burst into a frenzy of Korean only to be cut short again.

"I'm not listening Mom. I'm hanging up."

Angrily, Serena capitulated by spitting out her son's Canadian name through clenched teeth, as though poisoning his ear with venom. Mentally, Calvin gave up. Another lost argument with his mother.

"Anyway Mom, what's so important? I told you not to call me at lunchtime every day, and *never* at the Department's number. What's so important?" Calvin listened to the long silence and heavy breathing of maternal rebuke until she forced him to ask:

"Mom, Mom, are you there?"

"I'm here. I called to learn what present you'd like for your birthday."

The question is meant to cripple her son's already stricken conscience for his disrespect and ingratitude. He gets the message and his guilt flares within him.

"Anything you give me will be fine, you know that," he said, plagued by guilt that kept growing by the minute."

Whenever Calvin thought about his feelings towards his mother, he felt ashamed of himself. The way she always kowtowed towards his father embarrassed him. Then, she behaved as though she were ignorant of the equality of the sexes in her new country, opening doors for him to precede her and helping him on with his coat. He never understood how she could respect a man who slapped, cuffed and shoved her around and wondered how she could condone his violence.

"Your father's not a bad man," she would explain to Calvin. The truth is that he's "just a frustrated one."

"Well, the way he cuffs you around, you'd think he was a prize fighter and you were his punching bag."

"Hey, you're a high school student, not a prosecuting attorney," Serena replied, stifling a chuckle. What she said about Stephen was true. Apart from his dissatisfaction with the sexual aspect of his marriage, Stephen had become frustrated by the way Serena showered her love upon Calvin. Stephen seemed to have forgotten Serena's brutal honesty. She couldn't hide her feelings. Although embarrassed to do so, she had used graphic paintings, to show him exactly what had happened to her, and how she felt. Further, when he proposed marriage, she had again described how terrified she became whenever an adult male encroached on her space. Besides, she couldn't tell him how ashamed she was at being intimidated by the man whom she married. Yet, she could never let herself forget that he had married her despite her paralyzed emotional state. Finally, he had brought her to Canada firmly believing that the only therapy she needed to blossom forth sexually was his "love, tenderness and patience." The reality was that she had to give him credit for his conduct then; perhaps more credit than he deserved.

While he had given her neither the patience nor the protection he had promised, yet her accumulated guilt at being less than adequate as a wife weighed heavily on her conscience. It broke her heart to think of the disintegration of their marriage that she had worked so hard to preserve; had sacrificed so much to save. The fact is that the thought of her family, farm, culture, language and country that she had traded for a life with Stephen left her cold. She had come to a strange new land whose customs were foreign to her. In consequence, despite her fluency in English, she had to accept the role of second class citizen, and worse still, the mental and emotional abuse of the marriage bed. She was willing to accept those losses with the sole purpose of making her marriage work. And she had to be realistic. It was not working.

The accumulation of her problems made her wish for her mother's presence and advice. For quite some time she had begun talking to her and confiding in her as though she were present:

Mama, my life is in shambles. I am a battered housewife, my husband and I are enemies and my marriage is in ruins. I am alone and bitterly unhappy. The fact of the matter is that you warned me, but I was too pigheaded to listen. I feel sure that Stephen is contemplating leaving me just as I have been thinking of leaving him. I firmly believe that you and Dad have cut me off for my cold-bloodedness, my disobedience, my lack of compassion and my ingratitude. If that wasn't enough, my son considers me an idiot and has erected a barrier between us. Since all the people I love have turned away from me, I can only conclude that I must be an evil person indeed. Although I've tried to keep the memories of Korea from my mind, I can't help feeling the vast, aching emptiness and sorrow that echoes my loneliness at being away from you. And there she was, floating on a sea of self-loathing and isolation, deeply distressed and feeling like a storm-battered and rudderless derelict.

Despite Serena's growing antipathy towards Stephen, there were times when she felt a deep sorrow for him. She could never forget the way his neck and cheeks had become flushed, burning with shame and humiliation, as he confessed to her the brutal criticisms of his father. She knew too that he could never forget the stern face or the disdain with which his father's eyes measured and mocked him. From his earliest youth he remembered the name calling—a "spoilt cry-baby" who "peed his pants"–every chance he got. Then, as a teenager, Stephen had grown into a "spineless wonder." Finally, as an adult, he had become "a loser, unfit for the tough world" that didn't tolerate 'weak-kneed whiners.'"

"One day," Stephen confessed, after his father's usual abuse, he had attempted to be sarcastic to him:

"I thanked him for his accolades and inquired whether he had any further compliments to bestow. His response was swift: I was "a smart-ass," and had "a head start on all the jackasses of the world.""

These revelations made Serena wonder at the disastrous effect that such scathing criticism would have on a youth and growing adolescent. She considered that the traumatized childhood of those early years would have robbed Stephen of his self esteem, stunting him emotionally. The guilt he felt at the fierce tug-of-war between his parents that he thought he was responsible for creating, did not help matters. Indeed, having tried vainly to win his father's approval and attempting to be upright and honest, he made a point of turning in the opposite direction. He learnt to have a thorough going disregard for authority. And since he could never expect justice from anyone, he learned to bend the rules and become a law unto himself, a rebel. It would explain his dishonesty in dealing with his mother, with the essay contestants, with Shellie, with his uncle's presents, with "the weaker female of the species," and of course with Serena.

At the same time, his powerful body and handsome face together with his success with women, gave him a false sense of his own worth. His criminal conduct was probably a response to his father's forecast that he would be "a failure in every undertaking." His father's treatment had doubtless fueled his appetite for dominance; his obsession with being in charge. Both could certainly be traced to his low self esteem that needed constant boosting and his unconscious attempt to ape his father's conduct. Finally, the cruelty of his father in so fiercely criticizing his son's weaknesses, would have created a severely twisted mind; an unbalanced personality. These features, Serena knew, were definite aspects of Stephen's character. Yet, despite his faults, Serena hated quarreling with him. Of course, she detested even more the physical battering she received from the man she married. The truth is that she promised herself never to retaliate, never to strike back. But with time, she also promised herself that should the battering continue she would have no alternative but to break that promise.

It was Jim, her psychologist, who had impressed upon Serena that her body belonged to her, and she alone had the right to withhold her sexual favors from anyone, including her husband. When the doctor saw her hesitation in accepting his advice, he kept insisting that Serena was in sole charge of making that decision until he was sure she got the message. Until then, she had felt guilty, convinced that leaving Stephen's bed had been a desertion, a dereliction of her duty as his wife. The doctor's statement cured her of that erroneous belief, but his curiosity got the better of him and he asked: "how did you manage to cope for such a long time with the succession of violations and battering Stephen forced upon you?"

"I suppose the repetition must have taught me somehow to short circuit the synapses in my brain so that I was able to disengage my mind from the physical experience of my body. How else could I have survived?"

Freed from any sense of guilt, she was able to put her sexuality on permanent hold by continuing to refuse Stephen her sexual favors. Thanks to the doctor's advice, she had taken a well-deserved vacation from the painful and humiliating experience. By eliminating sex from her life, she had expelled as well the apprehension and fear that it generated. By the same process, she had begun to release the accumulated anger that had raged within her.

For the first time since her marriage, she felt free to relax both mentally and physically. Encouraged by the doctor's advice, she had also begun to indulge in healthy sexual fantasies that, in turn, led to the practice of feeling and touching herself. The reality was that in doing so, she again learnt that her body responded with amazing sensitivity to her touch. Equipped with this new awareness, she shed the idea of her body as tainted, seeing it instead as an incredibly sensitive instrument, capable of taking her on orgasmic journeys of the purest pleasure. Gradually, she was able to abandon the idea of intercourse as a loathsome and degrading act, as she had seen it through the jaded eyes of a traumatized rape victim.

Darkness had invaded the household as Stephen confronted Serena. The wind kept howling and the night's blizzard froze the earlier rain.

"You keep ignoring me, giving all your attention to that...that child of yours," he hissed through clenched teeth. "You've deserted me, left my bed. I cannot ignore such neglect, not even from a useless wife," he raged. "You accuse me of being a fool rather than an intelligent man."

"Well, the way you behave, I often get confused between the two choices." The sting of her irony angered him even more and, as the darkness overwhelmed the household and its occupants, he decided to teach her a lesson.

"I won't put up with your neglect," he shouted. "I refuse to be ignored, especially by an illiterate farm girl." Serena could see that he had whipped himself up into frenzy and knew that at any moment he would explode and strike her.

Her body stiffened as fear and anger rooted through her. For the first time, instead of flinching, she stood her ground. Such a cowardly threat from the man she married injected a flood of rage and hatred into her bloodstream. Without realizing it, she kept grinding her teeth and balling her fists. Stephen was surprised at her challenging stance since, tiny woman that she was, she had never before dared to flout his physical authority. In his mind, his blows would be paying her back for deserting his bed and making him feel like a fool. Suddenly, in a blur of motion, he struck the first flurry of blows.

She took the punches from the bully she married without complaint or retaliation. Then, a powerful blow to her stomach sent the air rushing out of her body. She felt as though a vacuum had been created within her, and losing her balance, she almost collapsed as a hot rush of nausea scalded the back of her throat. She bent double, actually saw stars bursting against the blackness clouding her vision. She began gasping, sucking air back into her oxygen-starved lungs. When Stephen saw the suffering he had caused, he halted his attack momentarily.

That was his first mistake.

Anger made her nerve endings sizzle like meat on a grill. Her fury flared at the memory of all the blows she had taken over the years. Her face flushed with intense rage at her husband's cruelty. She knew that for him, the blows were just another series of links in the chain of beatings he had administered to a wife in name only. He was merely teaching her the error of her ways. But for her, these blows were very different. She was no longer the naïve young bride accepting Stephen's view of her as less than a wife. The fury bottled up inside her over the years exploded. She grabbed the nearby broom with its thick wooden handle, rushed forward and attacked Stephen like a wildcat, mad with rage. She struck such terrific blows on his head and body that he crouched with aching ribs and head before rushing her to grab the broom away.

That was his second mistake.

He realized this too late when she reversed her weapon, using its point to jolt him hard in the stomach. It knocked the wind out of him and, as he bent double to catch his breath, she whacked him so mercilessly on his head and body that he ran to escape through the door in fear for his life. But such was her rage that she followed him raining a series of heavy blows on his head. Her fury and aggression surprised her almost as much as it had astonished Stephen. Although neither of them had uttered a single word during the fight, they both knew immediately that the incident forecast the end of their marriage.

The fight took only a few moments, but it brought her years of maturity, making her see clearly who Stephen really was, and that she wanted him out of her life. She turned to rest on the windowsill staring out at the leafless branches on the trees that appeared dormant. They were covered with a layer of frost from the night's blizzard. Like her, they were frozen on the outside; empty on the inside. Like them, she waited anxiously to kick-start her dormant life. No more tears, she told herself. No more time wasted on the bully she married. It was time to discard the baggage and move on.

As spring approached, Serena got into her car and drove into the Sooke hills to divert her mind from her problems. She climbed up the trail after leaving her car at the side of a logging road. It was cold but sunny and she saw a shadow zooming past her on the trail she was following. At the top of a steep incline, she looked upwards to see a hawk patrolling the sky in wide circles, seeking out its prey. Down in the valley, a doe and its fawn were contentedly cropping grass on the edge of a riverbank, and somewhere nearby, a grouse was drumming noisily. On days like this, she felt more at home in this wild country than anywhere else. She thought of slow hunting down in the valley, feeling the wind in her face and the warm sun on her shoulders or climbing among the stands of fir, spruce and alder with nothing to cloud her mind or depress her spirits. It was nearing the end of a magnificent day, and she was embedded deeply in her mountain wilderness. She smelled the cool air, the damp earth, the rotting leaves and decaying plant life under the canopy. Suddenly, a breeze brought a breath of the pine-scented air that flowed into her lungs, became absorbed into her bloodstream refreshing her. At once, she felt engulfed by nature, calmed and mystified. There were times like this on her farm when she felt the call of the wilderness that encouraged her to discard inconsequential things that led nowhere. The truth was that she hadn't come here to still hunt, or to be serene in meditation. She jerked her thoughts away from the wilderness and its wonders. She had come to the mountains as a means of escaping to a place where the silence, stillness and the total isolation encouraged deep thought. She needed to think deeply; to take stock of her life.

She had been raped, she had recovered somewhat, she had painted, and she had married. She had then been raped and battered again and again in her marriage. Now, she had a son and her husband had left her. She felt the need to compare her accomplishments with those of her father. While he had cared for hundreds of his workers and their families, bringing them comfort and contentment, she had done absolutely nothing with her life so far. Hers was a clean and shamefully empty slate. Her life was a fat zero, holding no meaning for her or for anyone else. She suspected that her father's Christian faith combined with Confucian ethics was the guiding principle urging him to treat others with the kindness and generosity he would expect for himself. His attitude made her believe that she should make a serious commitment to helping her fellows. The French writer, Voltaire made a similar statement centuries earlier:

"il faut cultiver votre jardin," he repeated in his novella, *Candide;* he meant that each one of us must do our duty to protect, nurture and, like a gardener, 'cultivate' and help those 'plants' and 'flowers' in the 'garden' of our vicinity to thrive. His view made Serena recall the simple statement she had made to her father so long ago: "I want to help others." Returning to Victoria, she vowed to make that goal her first priority.

Chapter 56

There were times when Serena thought about the hostility she had unleashed against her mother, and the sorrow, regret and ingratitude bottled up within her, choked her with shame. Children so often take their parents for granted, especially when growing into adulthood, intent on seeking their independence. She had wanted so badly to make her own decisions in spite of the tremendous confusion she felt. She had wanted so badly for her mother to agree with her choices, whether or not they were right, to boost her confidence and tell her how right she was. But that hadn't happened. Yet, the truth was that she wished she hadn't caused her mother so much pain and heartache. How she wished that she had been a better daughter!

Whenever her guilt popped up its ugly head, it took great effort to repress it; to make it disappear. She mopped and cleaned, washed not only the dishes and the clothes, but also the cushion covers and even the curtains. She painted and painted until she had used up far too many canvases with little to show for the effort. Finally, she paced up and down her bedroom with her arms folded tightly across her bosom. But at the end of the day, if truth be told, the burden of her guilt and shame had not decreased one single iota.

She talked aloud to herself whenever she felt the need for her mother's presence. "Mama," she asked, "what do you do when you stop loving the man you married? What do you do after he violates you and batters you into next week? Should you retaliate with blows or not at all? Should you stick with him because of the vows you made and the fact that you have a son together? Should that make you stay with him or leave him? But if I were to leave Mama, where would I go in this country where I'm still a foreigner? I've felt so empty throughout my whole marriage, weary of the daily loneliness and the nightly trials; of the terrible life I've brought on myself. If I didn't have the love I feel towards my son to sustain me, I'd go raving mad. I'd have to be certified and locked away. And Mama, my son doesn't feel towards me the way I do about him. I've thought of giving up, washing my hands of the whole squalid affair. But then I remembered the biblical figure that washed his hands and I knew it was not the example I should follow. I'm so confused and unhappy Mama that I don't know what to do. Can you tell me what I should do, Mama? Can you?"

Unfortunately, her questions were all rhetorical since she could only confide in her mother mentally. She felt too ashamed of her undaughterly conduct to reveal to her or to her father the disintegration of her marriage. Her conscience was too stricken since she had argued heatedly with them, ignoring their advice and their warnings. Unable to get through on the phone, she assumed that both parents were so mad at her, so ashamed of her behavior that they had cut her off completely. She believed they now had an unlisted number and had refused to respond to her letter.

Previously, Stephen had considered Serena a punching bag, far too accepting, far too compliant. On the one hand, his dominant attitude was an attempt to control his wife and son. On the other, his battering resulted from the frustration he felt at his vain attempt to make contact with his wife's interior self. However, the fight and its outcome had caused a radical change in his thinking. He knew that in his household he would never again have the upper hand. On an overcast day, with storm clouds gathering and the imminent threat of a frigid unearthly darkness, Serena's aggression forced him to resign himself to his fate. He decided to respond positively to her ultimatum. He again arranged for her to see the therapist and also felt it was time to take his leave.

With Stephen away, there was no one to quarrel with her about how she spent her time. She set about badgering the Internet to get the information she needed. In doing so, she learnt that "philanthropy often begins when hardship follows calamity, forcing people to come together to help each other." This need usually culminates in an effort to undertake projects like building schools and churches, fighting fires or starting libraries; projects that work towards the common good. She had no desire to be like those providing opportunities for others eagerly seeking success. One single goal dominated her mind; helping rape victim to recover.

Although with time, she was glad of Stephen's departure, she felt sad at emptying herself of the dreams of happiness that she had so secretly built and nurtured. The fact was that she had imagined him as the loving husband in whose happiness she would share. She had fantasized about the sexual fulfillment they would both enjoy after which they would discuss plans for the precious child they would love and raise together. Instead, she had to resign herself to loss on all these levels. She believed that once more she was sentenced to a life of isolation, one shorn of illusion. For the third time in her life, she felt like a rag-doll, so badly torn and tattered that it had to be abandoned.

She returned to her therapist and he listened patiently as she reminded him of the details of her life with Stephen in Korea, her love and enjoyment of painting, the following of her mother's advice after her violation in that country and the progress she had made in her recovery. She then related their arrival in Canada, their disastrous sexual relationship, her failure as a wife and the battering that had begun to destroy their marriage and ruin their lives. About a year later, their son, Calvin, was born. During the next session, the doctor asked her whether she had practiced the Re-breathing exercise drawing out the cue word t-r-a-n-q-u-i-l with each exhalation of breath as he had instructed. Not only had she done so, but she had also practiced the deep muscle relaxation exercises, using all the muscle groups that he had given her. It had helped her to withstand the violation and battering that had eventually destroyed her marriage.

"Since I saw you last, your husband's violations have thrust you back into trauma. But, if I remember correctly you had first overcome the fear and anxiety of meeting a strange male and eventually of talking to him about your assault. Is that correct?"

"Yes doctor. That is quite correct. I had also followed your instruction and used a coach to get rid of my fears of going to a movie and of walking through an abandoned woodland and park alone."

"We also used reason to point out that wearing the clothes you wore during the assault could bring you no harm. Remember?"

"Yes doctor, I do remember that. Now all that's left is overcoming the fear generated by meeting Scarface and his thugs, and worst of all, having sexual contact with my husband."

"Okay, since you've done all the practicing with breathing and muscle relaxation, we'll begin today with the process of repeated confrontation but from a different angle. We'll help you to reduce your fears and anxieties by a technique known as *Imaginal Exposure*. We realize that in thinking about the rape, you still experience extreme anxiety and other negative feelings, including shame, guilt and anger. Since the assault was a terrifying experience you tend to push it away, to put it out of your mind, to forget it. But, no matter how hard you try, the memory comes back to haunt you through flashbacks and nightmares. This part of our treatment is a part of the technique stated in the manual: "Treating the trauma of Rape: Cognitive Behavioral Therapy for PTSD by authors Edna B. Foa, Barbara Olasof Rothbaum. It will help you to process the memories connected with the assault, rather than running away from them. By having you stay with the memories for an extended period of time, knowing that they are imaginary only and cannot hurt you, we'll help you to decrease the fear and anxieties, the guilt and shame associated with them. We begin by asking you to relate your confrontation with Scarface using the present tense. I'll be making a tape of what you say. Begin!"

"I enter the park and am confronted by Scarface and his gang. My heart-beat quickens and so does my breathing because I know I am in trouble when he refuses to let me through. I force myself to breathe normally and to exhale slowly while drawing out the word 't-r-a-n-q-u-i-l.' I pause before my next breath and inhale normally. The muscles in my jaw tighten and so do those in my stomach. I relax them both repeating the breathing exercise ending in the long drawn out word 't-r-a-n-q-u-i-l.' I then decide to walk around the team members and after passing them, I feel tension in the muscles of my neck, and back since I can no longer see them. My anxiety rises because the team is behind me and at that moment, I'm afraid to look back. I then realize that I'm the one in control since the situation is wholly imagined. I continue my breathing and the relaxation of the muscles in my neck and back. My fear subsides slowly and I begin to feel okay. Suddenly, I have a flashback. Scarface shouts: stop! And he begins walking towards me. I begin to feel anxious, nauseous and faint. My heart rate and breathing accelerates. I begin to think he is again intent on raping me then I stop to question myself. What proof do I have that this is true? And I respond: None, because this is an imagined situation. Besides, Scarface and his buddies are in Korea, perhaps in jail, and I am here in Canada. He and his gang cannot hurt me, can cause me no harm. I will myself to continue my breathing exercise and the relaxation of my muscles. I also know that repeated exposure to confrontation will eventually habituate me to conquer these demons. My fear and anxiety decreases somewhat. I begin to feel okay."

"You have accomplished that first practice very well. Let's use your Measurement Chart to see the rating you give your meeting with Scarface and his gang at the various intervals after each exposure?

This is a Chart measuring your anxiety rating at the start, then after each exposure to Scarface and his gang in your imagination.

Start time	Anxiety rating after each exposure
10 A.M.	8
10 minutes later	8
20 minutes later	7
30 minutes later	7
40 minutes later	6
50 minutes later	6
60 minutes later	5

"Serena, you've done very well! You can see the improvement you've made in the chart. I think that's enough for today. Here's the tape of your narrative and some blank handouts of your measurement chart. Your homework assignment is to listen to the tape several times a day and to enter your ratings after each narration. When we meet for your next session, I trust you will have improved even more. Don't worry if your progress is slow."

Serena knew from experience that the most pressing emotional and physical needs of rape victims were compassionate help, counseling and support. She volunteered on a hot line, began talking to rape victims knowing it was only a first step. Their disturbed and confused emotional state made her aware that talk was not enough. Her forays on the Internet reinforced her realization that she had to have specialized knowledge and skills to do the work that was needed. She therefore advertized in the local newspaper, "The Times Colonist," for volunteers with knowledge, dedication and a passion for helping in the recovery of rape victims. They were to call the phone number she gave. She heard nothing for the first week, and began to believe that her plan was doomed to failure. Then, to her great surprise and delight, within the next couple of weeks the response was enormous. She learned that Victoria was the major city in which Canadians choose to retire mainly because its climate is far milder than the rest of the country. Among her volunteers there were doctors, lawyers, university professors, nurses, teachers and a number of trained personnel with various types of experience. They all enthusiastically offered their services. She thanked them for their interest, made a list of their names, phone numbers and addresses and explained that she'd get back to them as soon as possible.

On her return, the doctor surprised her with the news that Stephen had already had a couple of sessions with him, and had been loud in his complaints about the problems she had caused in their marriage. Having listened patiently to both spouses, the doctor thought that he had a fairly accurate picture of their fractured relationship. He felt sure that he could pinpoint some of the major problems creating their marital discord and began with Stephen's erroneous belief that he related to her sexual problem.

"He believes that if you accidentally fall off a horse, you must get quickly into the saddle again, to overcome the fear of riding. I explained that his horse-riding analogy did not extend to sexual abuse. Forcing a rape victim to have sex before she is fully healed, I insisted, only increased the victim's trauma. Since Stephen didn't accept my explanation, I emphasized the point again and again, determined to make him understand.

"Your wife becomes terrified rather than aroused because of her experience of being raped and the pain she associates with penetration and intercourse. Each time you make sexual demands on her, you terrorize her with the pain she knows is only moments away. Worse, her panic attack freezes her insides. This inhibits her arousal, preventing her from becoming lubricated. Since she is dry, your penetration and subsequent thrusting causes her excruciating pain. Each of your intimacies recreates the terror and pain she experienced in her earlier assault. Thus, your conduct reinforces her suffering and increases her terror of intimacy."

"What was his reaction?" Serena asked, but the doctor ignored the question continuing to explain what he said to Stephen.

"Your demands," I warned him, "are really a succession of rapes, each of which deepens your wife's trauma." Hearing this detached observer dismiss her long trial of suffering in a single short sentence was too much for her. The tears streamed down her cheeks as she thought of what she had endured. The doctor watched her in silence before continuing.

"He complained that the excessive emotional bond you created with your son prevented him from having a normal relationship with either of you."

"Doctor, Stephen is an immature and jealous man who wants me to neglect my son in order to have an obsessive relationship with him, and him alone." He stipulated that I cannot do photography or paint even when he's out or asleep. Further, I must drop everything I'm doing and be ready to discuss his problems but he refuses to discuss mine. Finally, he refuses to compliment his son for any of his successes and didn't even make time to attend his graduation. His lame excuse is that too much interest or praise would turn his son's head. The doctor, recognizing the truth of her statements, continued without comment.

"The suffering Stephen caused you had destroyed the earlier progress you had made in the healing process, so you found it impossible to forgive him. With twisted logic, you blamed him for the loss of family, friends, farm and country, since he took you away from everyone and everything that you loved. Finally, he brought you to a country where your ignorance of language and customs made you a minority and thus automatically, a second class citizen. Are you with me so far?" He asked. As she was too shocked and embarrassed by his accusations, she hesitated to reply. He continued, clearly unfazed by her reaction of surprise.

"Stephen's rapes made you again see yourself as a ruined woman, unworthy of true love, as you saw yourself in your confession to him after your assault. Apart from the sexual trauma and the battering, you also despised Stephen for falling in love with, and marrying the person whom you yourself considered to be 'a ruined woman, unfit for marriage.' In your deep distress, you decided to take revenge."

"Take revenge?" She echoed the doctor's words, scandalized by the insult. "What are you saying, doctor?"

"Unconsciously, you saw Stephen as the cause of all your woes and you retaliated." She realized with annoyance that the doctor seemed to be enjoying himself. He was evidently proud of his analytical skill and especially the way his assessment had surprised and shocked her.

"Doctor," she said angrily, "your diagnosis is perhaps accurate, but you can't really think that I set out to hurt Stephen on purpose?"

"Stephen complained that too many things went wrong for them to be all coincidence."

"What things?"

"It seems you often forgot to cook his meals. When he reminded you, you burned quite a few of them. True?" The doctor asked.

"True," she whispered in embarrassment, "but it wasn't deliberate."

"What about not putting gas or oil in his car after you used it so that it stalled on him a number of times?"

"That happened, but only when mine was being serviced. But again, it wasn't deliberate."

"Did you count how many of his shirts you burnt while ironing them?" Serena's eyes filled with tears, and her voice broke.

"Doctor, I didn't do any of those things on purpose. I'm not a wicked person."

"I'm not here to judge you, Serena, only to present you with a clear picture of your conduct as I have been doing with Stephen. With your problems exposed, it should be easier now for you and Stephen to find solutions."

She couldn't stand the thought that the doctor believed she had deliberately taken revenge on Stephen.

"Doctor," she said, "I didn't hurt Stephen on purpose. I'm not the criminal you and Stephen think."

"Serena, when people are deeply traumatized their survival instincts take over and program them to fight back. You'd be surprised at how far some people go in such self-sabotage."

"Self-sabotage?" She enquired, puzzled.

"When you take revenge on people, even inadvertently, they have a habit of striking back. When the action you take recoils on you adversely, that's self-sabotage." After a moment, he asked:

"Since he had been abusing you all through your marriage, why didn't you leave him?"

"The truth is that the house we live in belongs to me. Besides, I'm a stranger in your country, where would I go?" she replied, in confusion. After thinking a moment she added:

"Perhaps the reality of it is that I remained because he kept telling me that I was inadequate as a wife. It being true, I had to stay, if only to prove him wrong. Since I failed, I have to shoulder a lot of the blame."

"Did you ever fight back?" The doctor asked.

"Verbally yes, but I fought back physically only once. Following your advice I refused to sleep with him. The ultimatum angered him and he began to batter me. I was so enraged after all the blows I had taken that I attacked him. Previously, I had accepted his blows believing that I deserved his punishment since I hadn't fulfilled my duty as a wife."

"You chose to be a victim!" He stated incredulously. Her confusion was such that for a moment she remained silent, then mumbled: "The fact is that I was so ashamed, so confused, it certainly seems that way."

"However, you finally retaliated with blows, and you are here now, Serena. You've finally refused to accept the role of victim." His patient felt somewhat mollified.

Serena called a meeting of the volunteers in a rented school gymnasium, welcomed them heartily and thanked them for coming. "My name is Serena, and I am a woman who was raped. I've had a long struggle towards recovery and now, like many of you here, I want to help women who have had the same experience." Without more ado, she cut to the chase and provided some cold hard facts:

"I work on a rape crisis hotline that is grossly overworked and understaffed. Over the last two decades, sexual assault against women on Vancouver Island has increased alarmingly. Thus, there is a great need for volunteers to take care of rape survivors." She went on to suggest that those in her audience with medical backgrounds and experience in this area should form themselves into a team of doctors, nurses and hospital personnel capable and willing to administer medical attention to rape survivors. A show of hands got her attention and she learnt that at least three of the volunteers had been fully trained in rape survival advocacy. At her suggestion they were willing to train a team of hospital veterans from among their group, herself included. They began training three evenings a week and their team of doctors, nurses and trained advocacy personnel were ready after a six week period.

From her personal experience, she though it would be helpful to find out from the remaining volunteers those willing to undertake non-medical positions: receptionists, chauffeurs, cooks, chambermaids and so on.

"How is Stephen behaving?" The doctor asked.

"I don't know. I think he has left me but you never can tell with Stephen."

"Before we do anything else I'll give you time to finish your exercises with Scarface and his gang. Then, in case Stephen returns, we'll have to confront your fear of sexual contact with him.

"Remember," Serena told the remaining volunteers, putting her recent training to work: "you should remember that it is the duty of everyone to advise survivors that they should be tested for HIV/ AIDS, sexually transmitted diseases, internal injury and for the prevention of pregnancy. Remember too that you are to advise patients on the importance of taking the forensic examination. Any saliva, semen, hair, nails and particles from the attacker's clothes should be collected. If possible, you should also get a written description of the perpetrator. If the victim has injuries it is important to take photographs of them." She then explained that traumatized victims often refuse to take the forensic examinations thinking that the additional stress might be too much to bear. You are to make them aware that the evidence collected is of crucial importance. You should also advise them that they are not to eat, drink, shower or change clothing since it might destroy valuable evidence. Serena ended her talk by distributing printouts of what she had said for her volunteers to memorize.

"Serena, can you explain why you accepted the role of victim?" The doctor again asked during her following appointment.

"Don't you therapists refer to such conduct as the "Stockholm syndrome?" She replied acidly. "The victim allies herself with the aggressor in the hope that the closer relationship will avert or at least reduce further victimization." The doctor was impressed and overlooked the acid as he recognized her anger and distress. But Serena felt his curiosity was intrusive.

"Serena, you've been venting your pent up anger for all your problems on the person closest to you, Stephen. True, he is responsible for many of your problems, but once both of you understand how hurtful your behavior is to each other, you can put a stop to it." She remained silent.

"Further," he continued, deciding to switch topics, "Sex provides some of the most pleasurable sensations that all living beings experience. Rejecting it would be to deny you the physical and spiritual bonding between man and wife that is a vital component for love, trust, communication and a happy marriage."

"You make our problems sound simple, but before intimacy can take place, don't I need time to heal?"

"Your problems seem simpler than they really are. And yes, you do need time to heal. But in the meantime, you and Stephen must understand that both of you harbor concealed anger and resentment against each other. Once both of you accept the fact that you've been hurting each other the anger and resentment you feel towards each other should gradually diminish and finally disappear."

"In short, if we stopped the hurt, the anger would go away."

"Absolutely! It would be a giant step forward. But, you can only release your anger when you no longer feel threatened." There was a moment's silence before he again changed topics.

"You do love Stephen, don't you?"

"He's a good man in many ways."

"You won't continue to see him as a threat?" The doctor asked, noting that she had not answered his question.

"If he listens to his doctor and changes his behavior, then I'll listen to him."

"If you both do that your relationship will improve."

The doctor's speculation was to prove useless. Stephen had no intention of returning to a disastrous marriage. Refusing to listen to his psychiatrist, he convinced himself that he was the only wronged party in his marriage. He also convinced himself that he had suffered severely from a neglectful wife, who had isolated him in their home. He had given Serena all his patience, all his generosity, all his love and she had never once responded. Enough was enough! Finally, he was ready to accept her view of herself as a "ruined woman, unworthy of being loved." This belief suited his macho image. It encouraged him to see his wife as sexually damaged goods. His new sense of self would no longer allow him to take the leavings of other men. Deeply hurt at the way he had been wronged, he resolved to abandon all responsibility for a seriously flawed woman. It was characteristic of Stephen that while accepting the doctor's opinion of Serena's shortcomings, he rejected the medic's views about his own.

At first, Stephen's desertion was like the absence of an amputated limb. It was painful and life threatening, but necessary for her to make a clean break between the past and the future. Her therapist would help her to find solutions for healing, and she would have to solve the problems of living as a single parent and of supporting herself and her son. The separation also severed the connection between her past with Stephen and her future with Calvin.

Serena had kept practicing the therapy exercises at home and had reduced her anxiety and fear of Scarface and his attackers to zero. However, she was extremely anxious to overcome the one remaining obstacle preventing her from becoming whole again. She had to regain her sexuality. With this in mind, she returned to therapy. Jim used the same technique of *imaginal exposure* for Serena to confront the last of her demons.

"Serena, close your eyes and narrate how you feel while Stephen is making sexual advances to you. I'll tape it for your use as a homework assignment."

"My bedroom is in darkness and I am not yet asleep. Since I left his bed, Stephen sleeps in an adjacent bedroom. I hear his footsteps outside my door. Because of our repeated kissing and caressing, I am not as uncomfortable as I used to be in Korea. There, I enjoyed his kisses and caresses knowing that I would not permit him to go any further. However, now that I am his wife, I know that he always expects me to go all the way. I know too that every sexual encounter I have with Stephen has triggered the image of Scarface and the trauma that follows. Therefore, when he enters my bedroom, I feel anxiety and fear creeping up on me. My heartbeat and breathing quickens. That's when I begin my breathing exercise as my jaw and stomach muscles have become tense. I also begin my muscle relaxation exercises. Stephen sidles into bed next to me. When he gently begins to caress my arms and showers gentle kisses on my face and neck, my anxiety and fear grows. I clench my fists tighter and press my head backwards deep into my pillow, continuing my exercises. When one of his hands encircles my waist and the other begins to caress my breasts, my anxiety and fear increases. I realize that at any moment he will force my legs apart, get astride my body, penetrate me and begin thrusting. His frustration and anger at his failure to experience climax would normally end in a brutal battering for me. Before that can happen, I ask myself: what rationale do I have for believing that my fears are justified? There is none! I quickly remind myself that Stephen has left me. Since I am involved in an exercise of imaginal exposure, the truth is that Stephen is far away. In his absence there can be no caressing; no thrusting of my legs apart; no getting astride me and neither penetration nor thrusting. There can also be no battering. Immediately, my anxiety level begins to drop, as does the tension in my jaw and stomach. With a deep sense of relief, I continue my exercises convinced that Stephen is not in bed with me and thus cannot harm me. I therefore have nothing to fear."

"Serena, you have again acquitted yourself very well. Now we'll again use the measurement chart before repeating the exercise.

Chart measuring your anxiety level after each exposure to Stephen's sexual encounter.

Time	Rating
10 A.M.	6
10 minutes later	6
20 minutes later	5
30 minutes later	5
40 minutes later	4
50 minutes later	4
60 minutes later	3

"You again did that very well. Next time we'll replay the tape and repeat the exercise. Before you leave today you'll get the tape for your homework assignment and blank handouts of the measurement chart for you to fill in, okay?"

"Okay doctor." Serena began to feel a great sense of relief.

In an attempt to forget her marital problems temporarily, Serena decided to visit the wild north of the province that she had heard about only in her father's stories, and seen only from the passenger seat of Stephen's car. She hired an outfitter, Jack Horton, and drove up to the Alaska Highway in the north of the province where Jack lived. Upon her arrival after her many hours on the road, the outfitter realized that she was both hungry and tired. He introduced himself to Serena, then his visitor to his wife, Heather, a middle aged blue-eyed blond with the lilting voice of Wales.

"You must be famished after such a long drive. Serena, you have just enough time to freshen up as supper is almost ready. Jack will take your bag up and show you to your room. There are towels there and the bathroom is across the hall." Serena was indeed famished and reappeared in quick time to enjoy what turned out to be a delightful supper.

Before leaving Victoria, Serena had made arrangements for those volunteers interested in mentoring, or in working on the hot line, to receive specialized training at the "Rape Relief and Women's Shelter" in Vancouver. When their training is completed, all will work in conjunction with the two Victoria hospitals, the *Royal Jubilee*, and the *Victoria General*. Either hospital will contact her whenever a rape victim is admitted. She or one of her trained mentors will be the first to meet the survivor to provide counseling and assistance in dealing with their most pressing emotional and physical needs.

Mentors will be trained to recognize that a violated person feels degraded, having suffered a loss of self-esteem and trust in everyone. The mentor's first priority is to help the survivor to regain her dignity, respect and trust by encouraging her to talk about her experience and by listening carefully to what is being said with patience and sympathy. Victims had experienced shock, disbelief, shame, anxiety, fear and anger. They need to talk about their experience *repeatedly*. Venting their distress permits them to enter the first stage of dealing with the after effects of the assault. Mentors need to be especially sensitive and supportive.

Chapter 57

On the morning after her arrival at Jack's home, Serena surprised herself by eating a lumberjack breakfast. She first demolished hot cereal, followed by pancakes sprinkled with cinnamon and dripping with maple syrup. She then made short work of a generous helping of scrambled eggs embedded with nuggets of ham and sausage chunks and sprinkled with finely chopped green peppers, spring onions and parsley. She was so full that she could only nibble at the dessert of mixed fresh fruit: grapes, diced pineapple, papaya and watermelon.

"This is the first time we've had a lone young lady wanting to tramp into the mountains all by herself," Heather told her. "And you say that you aren't a hunter and you haven't brought a camera. Yet, you have come from far Victoria way up north just to gaze at mountains. I hope you don't mind if I ask why."

"I don't mind. You see, to me they aren't 'just mountains.' The forested mountains represent some of the most vital parts of the planet."

"I agree they are important, but isn't your statement somewhat of an exaggeration?"

"Well, follow my lead and we'll see."

"Don't misunderstand me. I'm glad you love the outdoors. I was beginning to think that I was the only woman who enjoyed their splendor."

"The truth is that I *am* a lover of the outdoors, but especially the mountain wilderness. And it isn't only on account of their splendor. As a result of their proximity to the sun, the melt water from their snow-capped peaks and glaziers brings live-giving water to the planet. Mountains also block the moisture laden prevailing winds from the ocean force them upwards so that condensation takes place. The slopes and valleys collect the resulting rain and channel it into rivers, lakes and springs. With sunlight and through the process of photosynthesis, the forested mountains rid the air of carbon dioxide and replenish the oxygen in the atmosphere that all life needs for survival. Then, every year the mountain wilderness brings millions of tourists to take advantage of the myriad recreational opportunities it offers in both summer and winter. In doing so they strengthen the economy by the numerous industries and jobs they create and by the mineral deposits they possess. In BC alone, the lumber, coal, fishing, hunting, tourist and recreation industries, together with the deposits of gold, silver, lead, tungsten and molybdenum, provide jobs for millions. Then there's BC's mountainous topography that is especially suited to the generation of hydro-electricity. And BC Hydro is the main electric distributor serving nearly all the province's industrial and household needs from hydro-electric dams on the Columbia and Peace rivers. But you probably know everything I've stated. What you may not be aware of is the presence of monasteries in mountainous areas. In fact, monasteries are almost synonymous with mountains since the majority of them, their temples and other such places of pilgrimage are mainly located in mountain retreats. They are centers of worship and learning where monks and nuns live and teach. They and their disciples have chosen such secluded locations to seek a time of silence for meditation and prayer. Most people associate monasteries with far Eastern countries like India, Tibet, China, Burma, Indonesia, Korea and Japan. Few people know that there are monasteries like Birken Forest Buddhist Monastery, Queen of Peace and Westminster Abbey all located right here in the forested highlands of BC."

"I must admit I did not know that," Heather stated.

"Well Heather, like the disciples of monasteries, I sometimes feel the need for such seclusion. I need to cut myself off from worldly affairs the better to meditate and realize God. That's why I think of forested mountains as my cathedral, since like Holy Communion they refresh and revivify both my spirits and my soul."

"I notice you haven't mentioned the wildlife," Jack stated.

"When I climb a mountain, I often conceal myself on my way up lying absolutely still at different elevations. I then use my binoculars to spy on the surrounding wilderness. I hope to catch sight of a herd of elk grazing leisurely on an alpine meadow or watch pesky marmots play the deadly game of hide and seek among boulders that a grizzly bear keeps tearing apart hunting them.

A mountain goat and her kid might stroll from behind a rock, their white coats gleaming in the sunlight, as the mother teaches its youngster the edible grasses and shrubs or a magnificent, dark-coated big horn ram might outline itself on a ridge with only the blue sky at its back."

"Your enthusiasm tells me that you have a strong bond with all wildlife. Perhaps you are looking for some favorite animal?"

"I have no favorites. But I do have a close affinity with the dwellers of these forested mountains. If I'm lucky, I may see a bevy of spruce grouse in their smart black attire and fiery red combs practicing their mating rituals on an elevated plateau or gaze at an airborne pair of golden eagles, talons locked together, and spinning as they fall performing their aerial acrobatics. So, yes Heather! I come to the mountain wilderness as I'm especially attracted to wildlife because to me they represent freedom, wildness and of course beauty. Then, there's the beauty of mountains themselves in each of the seasons. When I see a pure white snow-covered mountain ridge against a crimson sunset in winter; the forested mountains dressed in their autumn foliage of green leaves highlighted by red, yellow, brown and gold or an alpine meadow dotted with the red, purple, yellow and blue springtime wildflowers, my heartbeat quickens. I live for those magical moments when the mountain wilderness and its creatures makes me feel at one with the universe. Like majestic sentinels, they stand guard offering their bounties to power the life of the planet."

"Then you must be very disappointed at the devastation that is taking place there," Jack remarked.

"If you are referring to the grand scale of deforestation with its attendant clear cutting; the ripping out of roads through those forests with the consequent destruction of habitat, yes. If you also mean the spread of population with the consequent loss of wildlife habitat, and the widespread extinction of animal species, again yes. What we all have to realize is that the building of family dwellings that goes hand in hand with the world's population growth-7 billion and counting-the extension of farms to feed that growth, is a reality we have to confront. We also have to face the necessity to create reservoirs and to dig for irrigation, with the attendant fouling of land and river systems by pollutants that take a serious toll on the environment." Serena replied. "Those kinds of devastation are evils over which the rest of us have little control."

"Those responsible permit the dazzle of greed to blind them to the fact that forests provide essential habitat for an abundance of creatures that have lived there for millennia and can live nowhere else," Jack stated.

"Yes, the fact is that many people regard the environment only as a storehouse of raw materials for economic development, the harvesting of timber, the mining of coal, precious stones and metals, the reservoirs of oil and gas, the provision of huge government revenues creating direct and indirect jobs, plus a variety of products that are a part of our everyday lives. The reality of it is that they tend to ignore the fact that these forests are complete ecosystems as well. There's so little concern with the protection of species, of fish and wildlife habitat and of other vital resources like water and recreation."

"Yes, there is a need to find a balance between environmental sustainability and the economic benefits created by the forest and other industries," Jack replied.

"But how do we do that while killing forests that help to reduce the amount of pollutants and prevent the build up of carbon dioxide. As the amount of Carbon dioxide in the atmosphere increases, it acts like a blanket preventing the sun's heat from radiating back into space. What really cause the destruction of the ozone layer are the chlorofluro carbons that have since been banned worldwide from use in refrigeration, air conditioning and as a propellant in some aerosol cans." In stating these views, Serena's voice held a note of resignation. "The truth is that unless we curb these global-warming emissions, the pack ice of the Arctic and the Antarctic will melt faster than they're already doing. In the north, this would put at risk Polar bears, whales, walruses, seals, porpoises, penguins and many other creatures that depend for their existence on the rich food source of these regions."

"You're absolutely right, Serena! But excuse me while I go outside to get the gear and everything else ready to roll," Jack said as he disappeared.

"How does the melting of pack ice affect the food of these creatures?" Heather, who had been listening intently, asked.

"Well, the pack ice is like a floating dais underneath which green algae grow. Algae are the food source of krill, a small shrimp-like creature. Although tiny, they exist in such tremendous abundance that, like grass for herbivores, they form the basis of the food chain for seals, dolphins, whales and walruses. The ice is also the platform on which the polar bear is able to hunt seals that keep breathing holes open in the ice to pull themselves through, rest and have their pups. Without the ice that would be impossible. And since the ice bear is too slow a swimmer to catch the seal in the water, this apex predator would have no platform on which to hunt. It would soon become extinct."

"That, I can understand. But Serena, Jack and his buddies talk constantly about ecosystems, biodiversity, global warming and a number of things about the environment that I've never quite understood. Can you throw some light on them for me?"

"I can certainly try. The fact is that the mountain wilderness surrounding us with its divers plants and trees, its predator and prey animals, its clean air and its river system that empties into the sea, forms an ecosystem."

"Can you explain how?" Heather asked.

"Well, if we begin at the ocean end, we would see that the dead marine organisms that fall to the ocean bottom would accumulate over the years except for the upwelling from the cold deep ocean. "

"Why is there an upwelling?"

"Off-shore winds and ocean currents together with the coriolis effect of the earth's rotation thrusts the surface water out to sea. This process causes an upwelling of cold, nutrient-rich water from the continental shelf to replace the displaced surface water, okay?"

"Okay. That's easy to understand."

"Thanks. Now, what you also need to understand is that the same huge mass of water from the depths is the carrier of nutrients that kick off first, an abundance of surface blooms of phytoplankton (plants) followed by a massive amount of zooplankton (animals). Once these organisms come closer to the surface and into contact with the sun's rays, photosynthesis takes place. This process in turn produces so massive a quantity of plant and animal life that they form the basis of the food chain. The small animals prey upon the even smaller herbivores in this chain and they are in turn preyed upon by krill, arctic cod, and the five varieties of salmon.

"Again your explanation is simple and easy to understand. But, what do these marine creatures have to do with our ecosystem?"

"Well the salmon form an integral part of the ecosystem of our mountain wilderness."

"Please explain how you arrive at that conclusion."

"When the salmon surge upriver to breed and produce a new generation, they embody rich nutrients absorbed from the ocean and provide food for bears, eagles, seagulls, owls, crows, wolves and many other creatures that live in the river and in the adjacent forests. As you know, the whole generation of adult salmon dies after spawning. They rot in the rivers, on their banks and in the forests where the bears and other creatures have left the half eaten bodies.

The rotting carcasses in the river have brought the nutrients from the ocean and produce a host of microorganisms that feed the newly-hatched salmon offspring. Those on the banks and in the forests provide food for other creatures. Right?"

"Right!" Replied Heather and continued. "Now, I do know that the predators you mentioned scatter their partially-eaten fish throughout the forest. They do the same with the leftover carcasses of their herbivore prey–deer, elk, moose, sheep, mountain goat and other creatures. While the deserted carcasses provide food for a host of other smaller creatures, their decaying bodies also transfer rich nutrients into the soil and like the salmon, ultimately feed the trees in the forest."

"Exactly! The decomposition produces microorganisms that fertilize the forest and promote healthy growth of the trees and root systems. The latter is important since they serve to protect the soil from being denuded by wind and rain."

"What you are saying is that the whole web of life linking all these strands together is termed bio diversity. Have I got that right?" Heather inquired.

"Let's look at it this way. Bio diversity refers to the number of species of plants and animals in a particular area and not to the processes that drive ecosystems."

"One last question. How is global warming a menace? Heather asked.

"As you probably know, the trees in a forest absorb the build up of carbon dioxide in the air. While this gas is necessary for photosynthesis to take place, an overproduction would act as a barrier shielding the earth from the sun's harmful ultra violet rays. Without this barrier, the sun's radiation would overheat the planet. Global warming would accelerate the speed of the melting glaciers and threaten the world with flooding. Rising ocean levels would obliterate coastal communities all over the world. On land, pollutants of all kinds would further contaminate the water table resulting in widespread disease. In fact, global warming has already destroyed some plants and animals while many more are threatened and in jeopardy."

"How is deforestation an evil?" Heather questioned just as Jack returned.

"Darling we have to go. Serena will perhaps explain that when we return."

"I'll be happy to explain it now since it will only take a minute." Serena replied. "The root systems of trees in a forest retain in the earth much of the water that falls as rain. When deforestation occurs their root systems die. The subsequent rain water, instead of draining into the earth and supplying springs, rivers and lakes, would erode the rich top soil and permit large volumes of the surface water to be lost through evaporation. The water table would drop, with rivers and wells drying up. Severe drought would result turning vast areas into deserts and dust bowls. Then, since forests breathe in carbon dioxide and release oxygen into the air through the process of photosynthesis, they thus reduce air pollution and keep our atmosphere healthy."

"It follows then that deforestation creates a series of problems with grave negative effects for both man and his environment," Heather interjected.

"Exactly! We have to listen to the scientists who forecast that if warmer climates were to continue there would be a giant extinction of those animals and plants that have been acclimatized to cooler weather. We need to realize that the environment can exercise the power of life and death over all species on the planet."

"Serena, perhaps we should get going before the wilderness we are hoping to invade disappears before our very eyes." Jack said chuckling. Serena thanked Heather for their hearty breakfast and their interesting conversation. She then followed Jack outside.

While Jim's analytical skills repaired the marital damage of his patients at the office, he was unable to mend the discord of his own marriage at home. He rubbed his temples and eyes to dispel the blinding headache that kept building as he reflected on the most recent quarrel he had had with Sarah, his wife. A sudden evil fog of darkness had prompted his violent mood swing just before he began to question Sarah. It had him bristling, ready for a fight. Though he shook his head to dispel the dark cloud and the cold that accompanied it, both stubbornly hovered and surrounded him.

"You're going out again? But you've only just come in," he said with growing anger in his voice.

"You, of all people, are objecting to my going out?" Sarah asked her voice loaded with acrimony. She too couldn't understand why she was constantly bothered by the darkness and the cold and always eager to claw and savage her husband.

"Well, you never seem to be home so we can spend time together," said Jim.

"*I* never seem to be home? *You* missed your daughter's last birthday party, her soccer game last week and her school's band concert last night." Her voice kept rising angrily.

"Well you know the vicious schedule I have at the office," Jim replied, trying to head off the storm that seemed about to break. But the angry darkness kept growing in intensity.

"Even when you're here," Sarah continued, "you're unreachable, as remote as the man in the fucking moon." Now that she was married, Jim noticed that of late, Sarah was displaying her verbal vulgarity more often. Yet, he knew what she said was true.

"Look Sarah," he said wearily, "I'm sorry if I'm sometimes remote, but I've been swamped with work." His old half-hearted apology goaded Sarah to fury, making her determined to hurt him.

"You've been ignoring me in the bedroom for so long that I've been forced to take care of my needs elsewhere." She then added: "With you as a husband, I might as well be married to a eunuch." The jibe was too vicious a blow for him to remain passive. He lashed back at her.

"In order to begin our work," Serena told her meeting of volunteers, there are a few things that still need to be done. I have had extra phone lines and computer outlets installed in my home where the hot line will be located for the present. The truth is that I've also approached the Victoria School Board and they've been kind enough to donate a few of their older desks and computers that I have had upgraded. I also need to make a list of those capable and willing to do data entry of the survivors with their names, addresses and phone numbers. These will be passed on to the leader of the medical team and to the mentors who will be expected to meet the victims at their home or in hospital. Over the week end, my son, Calvin, and I will install the computers and desks in our living room.

On Monday morning, I will meet with the medical team leader to draw up provisional rosters for team members. In the meantime, we'll be waiting on the return of the personnel who have elected to be trained in Vancouver before we make a start. As you know, ours is a small operation, but I am sure that once we get going and iron out those problems that are bound to confront any new organization, we will be very well equipped to deal efficiently and compassionately with survivors. I consider that there are other victims' needs that we'll have to address in the future, but let us begin by getting the experience necessary to familiarize ourselves with the basic work needed to be done. May God bless us all and help us to cope efficiently with the work we are about to undertake, and may He bless especially those survivors who seek our help."

To Serena's surprise, there was a horse-drawn cart outside Jack's home that took them down into steep-sided ravines, across small valleys and over stunted hills. As they crossed numerous shallow creeks, she marveled that in spite of the loud squealing of the cart's wheels, and the way she had been buffeted around by the cart's being jolted over the rough terrain, they managed to reach their destination in one piece. Jack drew up at a small clearing in the forest where his huge tent was already pitched.

"This is my base camp that I use to accommodate my hunting clients. You are the first non-hunter to be here."

"You're nothing but a fucking whore." Jim shouted back at Sarah. He was deeply stung at being called a eunuch while feeling guilty of having yet another fight with his wife. In his exhaustion from his marathon session at the office, Jim's blackened mood goaded him to fling another threat at his wife. "And," he shouted, "your clandestine meetings may just get you your bloody wish."

"What the hell does that mean?" Sarah challenged, rushing after him as he stalked from the room in disgust. Jim, already past the door, turned around and slammed it in her face. Sarah noted that their fights were escalating to danger point. It always seemed to materialize, she recalled, with a headache that swooped down upon her whenever that evil darkness clouded her vision and that god-awful smell seemed to emerge suddenly from nowhere.

Janine, their teen aged daughter, was weeping bitterly at another of her parents' fights and could actually feel the atmosphere vibrate with the shafts of hatred they had hurled at each other. Though her door was ajar, the sound of her weeping remained unheard.

During the first few weeks of the rape crisis operation, Serena's team dealt with a slow trickle of victims. The small number was a godsend, for with each new arrival volunteers grew more familiar with what survivors needed and were able to sort out the bugs in their operation. Instead of waiting for hospital notification, Serena set up a roster of trained volunteers to be at each hospital every day. That way, each survivor would immediately meet a volunteer on entering either hospital. The abused victim would no longer have to sit and wait alone for advice, comfort or medical attention.

"What do you do for a living?" Jack asked Serena as they set about unpacking the cart.

"I spend most of my time running a volunteer organization helping rape survivors."

"How is it doing?"

"The first few weeks were difficult, if truth be told. There was some confusion as we tried to get everyone trained and everything organized. But we've also spent a lot of time eliminating the bugs. Everything is now up and running more smoothly. The fact is that the work fills up most of my day. But, I also paint wildlife whenever I can find the time."

"Is that the main reason you're here, to take photographs and to paint?"

"Yes and no. I left my camera behind this time as I have more than enough photographs of the subjects I usually paint. This time, I'll record in my sketchbook or in my mind whatever I want to paint. I really came here to take a breather; to escape from the complexities of life."

"I got the distinct impression in our round-table discussion that the environment is very precious to you?"

"Yes, I firmly believe that it is the key to our planet's survival!"

"I like to think that I chose hunting and outfitting as my vocation since I feel a deep concern for the wilderness and its wildlife."

"How can you say that when your livelihood depends on guiding your clients to kill innocent animals?" Serena asked, shocking him with her honesty.

"Well," he said, "as you know, in any habitat like ours where there are goat, sheep, caribou, deer, elk, moose, wolves, bears and wolverines, there are only a few mature boars, bucks, bulls or rams in their prime" These male animals service their females to pass on the strongest and most productive genes for the survival of future generations. I do not permit my clients to shoot any animal, male or female, in their prime. Young animals too are sacred and never to be targeted. I permit my clients to kill only dry cows–those no longer breeding–or the elderly, boars, bucks, bulls and rams that have passed their prime. Since industry and population growth tends to destroy and reduce animal habitat, my work contributes towards the survival of the fittest." Serena apologized immediately.

"Sorry Jack, I stand corrected." Jack merely bowed.

"What draws you to painting?"

"A long time ago I tried to explain to my husband my interest in painting but he didn't understand. He was blind to everything but the sick zoo animals that were only a small part of my subjects."

"Perhaps you can explain your focus on the animals and what else you depict in your work." The sincerity of his words moved her to open up to him.

"You make me want to confess what I've never felt comfortable revealing to anyone. The truth is quite simple. Forests, rivers, mountains, and the wildlife that live in their vicinity, have always held a fascination for me. You have to understand that the animals I paint represent the wilderness that produced them. The truth is that I portray them and their habitat as they were in the time of Adam and Eve; as though everything on my canvases were untouched by the contaminating hand of man. I try to make my wilderness appear to have been washed by a divine rain. Of course, I don't always succeed. Can you understand that?"

"Your work then is infused with deep spiritual significance, and your words imply that you view your fellow man with a huge dollop of distaste."

"Not everyone! Simply those who despoil the environment, like the big oil and logging companies, those industrialists who drill for minerals, produce hazardous wastes, ravage the areas where they work, and commit the unforgivable sin of polluting with impunity. The fact is that there are also those greedy hunters and fishermen who are constantly driven by some evil genius to surpass their quota."

"I understand your attitude perfectly since my clients and I share those very feelings. But as you know, it's the guilty few who give a bad name to the many."

Jim's problem started when, as a young intern, overworked and underpaid, he often visited "The Golden Palace" where he became friendly with Sarah, a pretty young waitress. His internship all but finished, he mentioned to Sarah his offer of double his salary at a new job and noted with satisfaction the enthusiasm with which she greeted the information. Her response was:

"We have a lot in common being both young, good looking, hard working and intelligent." Jim was often drawn to the Palace for the cozy friendship that was developing between them.

Chapter 58

"You no doubt have realized Jack, from my conversation with your wife, that mountains fascinate me. First, it is in their loftiest recesses that their ice caps and glaciers give birth to rivers. Those are also the areas nearest to the sun. Heat, water, sunlight, the earth-clad mountains, forests and wildlife are the main elements that provide all our basic needs. Thus, in my view mountains are the very source of life." Serena told the outfitter. "Then, the truth is that I can't explain why the pine-scented forests, the mountain wilderness, nestled in broken silences, hold such a compelling attraction for me. I have no idea why standing on a mountain top gazing at the distant horizon or watching wild animals from concealment should quicken the heart and race the blood. Such spectacles awaken in me a sense of freedom and give me an adrenaline rush of the purest pleasure. I firmly believe that the wilderness is in my blood, passed on, perhaps by the genetic legacy of my forbears. If truth be told, I feel as thought I am a part of it as it is a part of me. Such statements may seem foolish to others, but those are the reasons I choose to go on "safari" again and again. Indeed, gazing at the mountain wilderness uplifts my spirits and eliminates the problems that plague me, especially after the betrayal and desertion of those I've loved. I need the catharsis the wilderness offers. In its midst, I feel as though I've received a benediction, even a communion. That's why I sometimes think of them as my cathedral."

Sarah invited Jim to her apartment that he interpreted as an invitation to her bed. He was sure that she would offer her sexual favors in the hope of marriage to the exalted doctor that he thought he was. He argued that while she, a lowly waitress, would struggle to make ends meet, her alliance with him would guarantee her an affluent lifestyle and elevated social status. She would guarantee him a beautiful face and body and an especially healthy dose of lovemaking.

Since she took care that their conversation at her apartment centered on him, his work and his career goals, he translated this as evidence of her curiosity and intelligence, and thoroughly enjoyed himself. She offered him music, drinks, dinner and dessert, but not herself. Later, when he propositioned her, she turned him down flat; scandalized that he could think of her as "that kind of girl." Somewhat later, he heard himself proposing marriage to her. It wouldn't be the last time that a young man asked for his lady's hand when he really wanted her body.

Jack led Serena up through the foothills of the mountain. "Watch out for grizzlies," he warned. They will eat you if given half a chance. Inside your backpack I've put a bell that you should hook on to your belt. Its tinkling, as you walk, should make animals steer clear of the sound they associate with humans. Are you a good actor?" He suddenly asked.

"Why?"

"If you do come face to face with a grizzly, you need to play the role of a dead person really well. Lie on your stomach, keep your head down, and protect your face and neck with your arms and hands. Now, it's okay for you to change your mind. Instead of going alone, I'll gladly accompany you. That's what you've already paid me for." He waited for her reply.

"Thank you Jack, but I'd rather go alone," she replied. He then informed her that apart from the bell, he had put "a huge package of ham sandwiches, chocolate bars, two apples and matches in her backpack. There's also your thick, hard-covered sketchbook and a small pillow, just in case you feel like a nap. It's a long and grueling hike to the top of the ridge and the trail sometimes disappears."

"Thank you, I'll manage," she said, then set off.

A precocious preteen, Sarah had begun to fondle herself whenever she felt unable to resist the dark sensation of arousal that set her body ablaze. She had seduced all the neighborhood adolescent males into sampling her wares. During intimacy, she recognized that her perverse sexuality was the most powerful weapon in her arsenal.

Jim heard Sarah retching violently into the toilet and tried to comfort her. He saw a pregnancy test kit on the edge of the bathtub as she screamed at him: "Look at what you've done!"

"M-me?" he stammered, shocked at her ferocity. "But you yourself admitted that I hadn't touched you in months!"

"That's right! It's your bloody fault that I've had to satisfy myself elsewhere." Glaring at him with her full, red lips and her narrowed eyes spitting blue fire, Sarah's face was cold, cruel and inhuman. She shot her venom at Jim with such fury that he felt certain her rage was directed at herself rather than at him. Her enormous vanity drove her to punish her body at the gym, while pampering it at home. The image of herself bloated in pregnancy must have terrified her.

The sound of their daughter's weeping carried into the corridor, unheard.

Late fall comes early in BC's vast north. Serena went up the narrow trail that, at first, was easy to ascend but quickly grew steeper. Toiling upwards, she forced her way up the steep golden carpet of pine needles and cones, using the stunted trees in the undergrowth and their low-lying branches to pull herself upward. It was hard work and soon she was puffing. The cold morning chill had given way to the warmth of Indian summer and she rested a moment to recover her breath. She was fascinated with the wilderness in its vastness, its brooding intermittent silences, and its mysterious solitude. She heard falling water in the distance and later crossed a stream rushing over rocks that formed a natural bridge. She then kept climbing upwards before stopping for a short rest.

Gazing below, she saw a herd of elk crossing the valley, its calves frolicking and play-fighting with each other on the river bank. The sight warmed her heart. When she looked upwards, she saw the top of the ridge she was climbing towering above her. She kept climbing, heard the scream of a hawk and witnessed its dodging tactics as two irate ravens kept buzzing it, loudly squawking their rage. She filled her lungs with the fresh pine-scented air while listening to the forest sounds of coyote, cicadas and squirrel making evident their annoyance at her intrusion. On climbing further, she took heart on seeing that there was only one more shelf to climb.

Once the word began to spread, the earlier trickle of assaulted women gradually increased to become a small stream. The majority came from Victoria, others, from the north and west of the island. Serena needed to expand her operation to accommodate out-of-towners needing overnight accommodation. At first, she and her volunteers scrambled among themselves to provide what shelter they could. Later, they thought it better to rent a half-way house. Serena realized that they needed something permanent and called a meeting of executives and trained personnel to outline her plans for expansion.

"To outfit our newly rented shelter, I have already gone to the 'Salvation Army,' 'Women In Need Resale Shops,' 'St. Vincent de Paul,' 'Great Finds' and other thrift shops as well as to the public. Once they learnt about our mission, they all offered donations. We now have beds, sheets, pillows, duvets, cutlery, crockery, kettles, electric irons, women's clothes, shoes, mops, brooms and cleaning materials. We have almost everything needed to outfit the shelter. I share this with you to underscore the generosity I met with from our fellow citizens and especially our local shops in Victoria.

"However, there is further need for advocacy personnel who can assist survivors to turn their lives around–by problem solving, writing resumes, teaching job-searching skills, raising self-esteem, decision making, job readiness, preparation for interviews and especially the basic use of computers. We also need motivational speakers to set up workshops on a number of self-help projects. I'll now distribute the computer printouts I've made outlining the needs I've just mentioned. You can offer ideas about how these and other goals can be met at our next meeting."

Serena used hand and footholds to scale a rock wall that blocked off a small grassy plateau at the top of the ridge. Once there, she realized sadly that she'd only have a couple hours of light before beginning her descent if she were to return to camp in time for supper. She knew too that it is far more dangerous to descend a steep mountain than to climb one. Yet, for her, being in the mountains was akin to a religious experience. Huge accumulations of last winter's snow had remained in various rock caverns and sheltered crevasses in the adjacent ridges. The air was so pure and clear that she felt as though she could reach out and touch the clouds. While it seemed to her that the horizon was only a couple of steps away, she felt, in gazing at it, that she was staring at the edges of eternity. Since she was alone and high up almost amidst the clouds, with the heavens seeming only a short distance away, she had a mystical feeling that set her body a-tingle. Her communion with the simple and serene beauty of nature invigorated her and renewed her spirits. She even felt safer since in her mind she was closer to God. She didn't think that her feelings were in conflict with her religious faith, for didn't He love the universe and all the things He created?

The mountain peak before her was badly scarred. She could see the evidence of volcanic activity in places where the underlying rocks were exposed. Several layers of different types of rock lying on top of each other were folded and twisted into enormous curves and wrinkles. Then, during the fiery hot summers when temperatures soared, and the freezing winters during which the mercury plummeted, the continual expansion and contraction eventually fractured and fragmented the rock. Giant slides had occurred leaving steep cliffs and huge gouges in the rock face whose deep pockets were filled with snow. Over the millennia, thunderstorms, lightening bolts and avalanches had assaulted the rock face setting acres of trees ablaze. Swift-flowing streams had then carved and chiseled the mountain leaving huge fissures and ravines that cut deeply into the limestone, feldspar and granite. A few of these had the remnants of winter's snow. Wherever limestone occurred, the rock face was deeply pockmarked with caverns, caves and crevasses. Yet, despite the depredations of time and weather, the steel backbone of the mountain had resisted, refusing to bow to the harsh blows belted out by the elements. Through it all, it had stood firm and unyielding, towering majestically in its silence, resilience and isolation."

Serena remembered expressing these thoughts to the doctor in praise of the mountain on her return to Victoria. His reply had astonished her.

"Serena," he said, "you are a replica of that mountain. You've had more than your share of hard knocks. You've been raped then struck down by an illness that took you to death's door. You've been betrayed and ostracized by your closest friends. In marriage, you've been again violated, battered and finally deserted by your husband. Through it all, you've refused to bow to life's evil battering. I can't think of anyone who would have reacted to such misfortune with their grace, dignity and endurance intact. I'm very proud of you! And you should be very proud of yourself."

Serena was blushing scarlet.

Sarah, who found she wasn't pregnant, terminated her clandestine outings in favor of making her marriage work. Like a jungle cat in heat, she marked her territory by leaving a trail of her sexual mementos at strategic points of her boudoir-habitat. When Jim took no notice, she grew more desperate. Whenever he approached, she worked her parted knees like the lens and shutters of a camera. Each time she flashed her underwear, Jim felt as though she had snapped his picture. Still, he ignored her weird antics.

Serena congratulated her volunteers, telling them that their operation was running smoothly as a result of their efficiency and dedication. Through newspaper ads and word of mouth, they were becoming known to a greater number of victims. Those whom they had assisted had begun calling in to thank them for the compassionate help and advice they had received. After the applause of her volunteers died down, she asked for any ideas that might help to achieve the goal of expansion she had outlined at their last meeting. She was delighted when it was agreed that they would need a building to house their headquarters. A few very affluent doctors, university professors and business women, offered fairly large gifts of money and one businessman even went so far as to donate a blank check. She thanked them for their generosity and immediately formed a committee to collect the donations, oversee their needs and to respond to them as they saw fit.

Jim was a psychologist with the ability to delve into the minds of his patients and ascertain the way they thought and acted. Yet, he had underestimated the character of his wife and the evil of which she was capable. His indifference to her sexual magnetism was the worst insult he could have leveled at her pride. Like the evil and cold-hearted predator she was, she immediately set about planning to ambush her prey and visited the Palace to set in motion the plan she had devised. There, she whispered to her waitress pal and co-conspirator, Jane, the plan she needed her to carry out.

Not long afterwards, a slim, and well-shaped, blue-eyed blonde came to Jim explaining that she had abandoned her husband after a marriage of a few months only. Her eyes brimming with tears, she explained further:

"My husband complained that during intimacy I was frigid and incapable of arousal; that I was like a statue, cold, rigid and detached." Jim found himself attracted to the woman, drawn as much by her sadness and vulnerability as by her strong resemblance to his blond and blue-eyed wife. Surprisingly, she welcomed his advances. Passion swept them off their feet and Jim was so delighted with his new patient that he doubled her weekly sessions.

The sunlit river looked like a sinuous silver mirror hemmed in by forest green at the bottom of the valley below Serena. The tree trunks groaned under the pressure of the fierce wind as they filtered the dying rays of sunlight through their branches. With the scent of warm earth and rotting leaves in her nostrils, she listened to the baying of wolves in the distance. The colors of her surroundings stood out–the silver river heightened the deep green of the forested lower slopes that in turn made the cobalt blue of the sky so much bluer. The yellow slashes of sulphur bleeding from deep crevices heightened the dark brown granite rock face exposed by mud slides. Then, there were the white flashes of snow-bound crevasses and limestone rocks that threw everything into prominence. Yet, nothing she saw could rival the crimson and golden majesty of the sunset wreathed in purple clouds and patches of the still blue sky.

Once again, the sense of mystery that the forested mountains exude captured and exhilarated her. That green untamed wilderness, stretching into oblivion, brought the same rush of joy she had experienced at her Korean cave. The scenery unfurling to the horizon had again worked its magic. Like an antidote to venom, it had overwhelmed the bitterness and sorrow corroding her spirit. At such times, the wild panorama seemed somehow to be embedded in her flesh, dyed in her blood. She couldn't explain how it managed to rejuvenate her body and mind or to refresh her soul. She never tired of wondering whether that innate feeling of being rooted in the wildness, had been transmitted to her through the genes of her ancestors. She knew that her father too had felt the same fascination with high, wild and lonely places. Yet, she still could not fathom why such places haunted the canyons of her mind, and why in the fresh new presence of this isolated mountain, she suddenly felt invigorated and free. Gazing at the mountains, she believed that she was looking at the pillars of the earth, beetling upwards like church steeples, grasping and clutching at the heavens for light. And the thought entered her mind that, like human beings, they too were hungry for the benediction and enlightenment from above. At that precise moment, a question surfaced in her mind, coming out of nowhere, and taking her by surprise: how could she lose faith while standing in the glare of His presence?

Sarah's promiscuity had driven Jim to make a tough decision. He thought of her as the female embodiment of a hurricane. When she came, she'd be hot and wet; when she left, she'd take house, land, car and all his possessions. Jim thus decided to excise her from his life, in the same way that he would cauterize a malignant tumor from his body. He would still be able to enjoy a very comfortable lifestyle on what remained of his earnings since he had a very lucrative practice. But he had grossly underestimated his wife's cunning or the depths of evil and spitefulness to which she could sink. Although Sarah could not abide a husband who was blind to her sexuality, she was sure that there were others with sharper eyesight. She then called on her waitress pal, Jane, to alert her when next she would be 'entertaining' Jim on his couch.

The river below was chock-a-block with spawning sockeye salmon, turning a whole section of the river ablaze. What a sight! Serena marveled at the kinship between artists and the Almighty in their obsession with the dramatic use of color and creativity. A grizzly bear kept chasing the fish towards a low bank onto which they leapt stranding themselves. The huge animal, like a picky gourmet, batted away the males selecting only the females. It gorged upon their golden eggs, protein-rich skin and brains. Serena was reluctant to resume her descent of the mountain for fear of alerting the monster.

Once Sarah got the call, she waited awhile before stepping into Jim's office, her camera at the ready. Jim and his paramour were wrapped in a passionate embrace. Sarah snapped a number of photos before the lovers were aware of her presence. She then slammed the door to draw their attention, while she remained inside the office. She made sure Jim saw her camera before she left them scrambling to dress themselves. Sarah filed for divorce, demanding not half, but three-quarters of Jim's assets on condition that he didn't contest the suit. In exchange, no word or photograph of his misconduct would be leaked to the College of Physicians and Surgeons. On his desk there was an unopened letter from the attorneys of his blond and blue-eyed acrobat. It informed him that Jane too was bringing charges of misconduct against him. Their lawyers would bleed him dry before reporting him to the College of Physicians and Surgeons. He knew then that his beloved wife had brought his career to an end.

On reading the letter, Jim thought of the incongruity of the situation. Wasn't life ironical! His peers would revile, ridicule and condemn him as a sexual predator. But, to so many other couples, he was the trusted and respected physician who had helped to rebuild their shattered marital relationships. An angel to the second, he had become a devil to the first. His thoughts took him back in time to those precious years following his graduation as a doctor of medicine. How proud he had been to continue caring for those patients who couldn't afford to pay him. Sarah immediately put a stop to such insane conduct. Her demands for a life of luxury goaded him to enlarge his practice rather than to care for the dispossessed members of society. She used her lovemaking skills to convince Jim that new clothes, jewelry and late model cars for her, would win for him a continued diet of her unflagging sexual innovation.

Yet, after having swallowed Jim's ultimate insult: indifference, Sarah couldn't resist taunting him with having outmaneuvered him in the 'marriage sweepstakes.' Then, she humiliated him further by confessing that she had plotted his destruction and that of his career with the help of her waitress friend, Jane, his blond and blue-eyed acrobat. Sarah had Jim wondering from what sewer of evil his wife had sprung. He was astonished that any one person could embody such malice.

Serena thought it unwise to move down slope while the grizzly was engrossed in its banquet. But it was getting late and she had to get back before dark. She waited while the bear seemed intent on depleting the river of fish. During its next assault, Serena took off swiftly but had forgotten the bell on her belt that tinkled loudly. The bear immediately looked upward in her direction. She darted forward to get behind a huge rock half way between herself and the enemy and found herself immediately in a quandary. She kept wondering whether to keep hiding or to run.

Jim kept frowning in despair as he watched his lucrative career about to go up in flames. A dark fog of hatred filled his breast at the precise moment that Serena walked into his office. He sniffed as his nostrils dilated with the scent of something rank, unearthly. His brain, suddenly fouled by darkness, goaded him to indulge in thoughts that would otherwise be foreign to his mind. Why, he wondered were these damn women dumping their husbands because of their own sexual inadequacy? Why did they always bring calamity down on the men in their lives? He decided then and there that he would teach one of those bitches the error of her ways.

"Hello Serena," he said, with a wolfish grin, contemplating his prey with wicked thoughts.

"Hello doctor," she replied with a radiant smile, before asking if Stephen had been receptive to any of the doctor's suggestions.

"Stephen refused to accept his own shortcomings and blamed you for putting the marriage at risk. He expected you to benefit from the rich variety of Canada's multinational culture so different from your xenophobic and insular farmyard world; er, his words."

Serena stared at him, speechless. She couldn't believer that Stephen had unleashed such venom!

"Doctor," she said her voice tight, dry and chilly. "You suck the secrets from your patients like those foul bats that suck the blood of their victims." The insult made the doctor resumed his attack.

"Stephen sees your paintings of animals degrading, though consistent with your rustic upbringing." Serena's face turned purple with humiliation, and rage.

"Doctor," she replied. "You embarrass and insult me with your impertinence. Since I am your patient, it means that you are being deliberately abusive and grossly unprofessional." Her accurate assessment prodded the doctor into further attack mode. But she beat him to the punch.

For a moment only, the rock blocked the bear from seeing Serena, and Serena from seeing the bear. During the brief interlude, she armed herself with two huge rocks deciding to go down fighting. As the bear appeared rushing towards her, she remembered Jack's warning to play the passive role of a corpse. But, being tired of the role of victim, she refused to passively accept whatever an alien fate decided was in store for her. It was time to assert herself and to fight back, just as she had with Stephen. The enemy offered little time for decision making. It covered the distance between them in the blink of an eye. When only a few yards away, it stood upright to sniff and stare at its intended prey. It was then that she hurled the first rock with all her strength at the animal's head.

Chapter 59

"I believe that you enjoy prying into the psyche of your patients like a degenerate peeping tom, then rummaging through the secrets you unearth, dissecting your victims like cadavers. You tell yourself that words are gentler than scalpels. But you're wrong, doctor. The truth is that your words are sharper, far more painful and destructive."

The doctor felt compelled to reply with venom:

"Stephen refused to believe his lovemaking forced you back into trauma. He thinks that your failure to enjoy sex with him shows that you never really loved him. He is convinced that you are frigid."

Serena's quickened breathing and blood-drained features clearly conveyed her pain and distress. The doctor dug the knife deeper:

"He believes you used him as a means of leaving behind your ruined reputation; that you married him only to make a new life for yourself. Wouldn't you agree his judgment is accurate?"

Serena was shocked at the doctor's impertinence. Her face was still corpse-like, the muscles of her jaw rigid, her stomach tense. She wanted to get up and leave, but her feet seemed to be glued to the floor and her bottom to the chair. After a moment, she reacted.

"You should be careful of playing a cruel God, hurling your accusations at your patients like thunderbolts!" The sting of Serena's words struck the doctor forcibly and he replied.

"You are wrong, Serena! We do scrutinize our patients' behavior, since the blink of an eye, the tic of a facial muscle, or the limp handshake, can help to separate truth from falsehood. We are not magicians, but there are problems of the mind that we can diagnose and treat." Having made his point, he hadn't expected Serena's challenging reply.

"The fact of the matter is that your assessments are open to more than one interpretation. So, you are likely to be wrong in many of your conclusions. With that in mind, you should be far more careful in assuming the role of the Almighty." The doctor's flushed face revealed that Serena's response had struck a raw nerve. When he rose to speak, she again halted his reply.

There was a loud thwack as the stone bounced off the bear's rock-hard cranium. It stood immobile a moment, giving Serena the chance to aim her second missile. With all her might, she flung the stone scoring another direct hit and had the satisfaction of hearing the sharp contact with bone. But the bear showed more surprise than distress and rushed straight at her. She stood rooted to the spot, astonished that a 1600 pound mountain of muscle could move with such speed. She had begun turning away when the bear roared and swatted her with a ham-like forepaw. The blow knocked her flying and she fell face-down onto the rock shelf, thrusting the breath from her body. Fortunately, her sturdy backpack, stuffed with pillow, hard-covered sketchbook and sandwiches, took the brunt of the blow and was torn from her back. Although numb, but still conscious and remembering Jack's words, she covered her face and neck with her arms and hands remaining absolutely still.

"As you know, doctor, Stephen is prone to embellish, exaggerate and tell outright lies whenever it suits his purpose. The truth is that it puzzles me to hear you insist that your criticisms are really Stephen's views. Yet, in all the years of our marriage, he never used some of the accusations you've leveled against me. I firmly believe that you and you alone, are the author of that venom." As the doctor stood to reply, Serena again spoke.

"I have no idea why a doctor, whose duty is to heal, would deliberately launch such an underhand, mean-spirited and unprofessional attack upon his own patient. It's enough to recognize that you suddenly detest me, and that said, I have no business being here." Without another word, Serena unstuck her bottom from the chair, forced herself upright, and in evident distress as she made her way shakily to the door, stumbled and fell. Her head hit the edge of a chair, and she uttered a shriek of pain before blacking out.

The doctor, seeing the anguish he had caused, felt a surge of guilt and shame for taking unfair advantage of his patient. Whatever spell had held him prisoner was broken. He couldn't have said why he had used Serena as a target. On reviewing his unprofessional conduct, his guilt and shame intensified. He was thankful that the bump on her head was no more than a mild concussion. While lifting her to his couch, he cursed himself silently, wondering what had made him act so cruelly. After icing the swelling that was followed by Serena's recovery, the doctor stated:

"I'm so glad that you've recovered so quickly, Serena. But, despite the sincerity of his voice, she gave him such an icy stare that made him abandon small talk. He then blurted out what he had in mind.

"Serena, I don't know what got into me to make me so belligerent, especially to you, my star patient." He felt compelled to atone for his vicious behavior and shouted as she ignored him and stood about to leave.

"Wait Serena, please wait! I apologize for my unprofessional conduct. Perhaps it's my marital problems that made me act so outrageously. Please forgive me," he pleaded."

Chapter 60

Serena lay motionless on the rock pretending to be dead with the mountain of muscle towering over her. She hoped she was convincing enough, otherwise she'd surely become the bear's supper. Oh God! She thought. How horrible it would be to be eaten by an animal while you were still alive. Almost paralyzed with fear she made her body as small as possible, wondering: how long it would take her to die. She waited in a violent fit of trembling knowing somehow that bears usually immobilize their prey with a head bite. Would she hear the cracking of her own bones as the monster sunk its teeth into her skull? Her mouth was dry, coated with fear. With hands covering her face and eyes, she couldn't see where the bear was or what it was doing. Suddenly, she felt it bat her backpack with a forepaw. The blow was partly absorbed by her heavily coated shoulder, but she'd have serious bruising for a week or more. When the animal rushed away roaring, she lifted her head in time to see the predator sniffing at a sandwich that had fallen out of the package onto the slope below. Her backpack with the other sandwiches must have tumbled down the slope, for the bear wolfed down the fallen sandwich then galloped downhill after the rest of the booty.

Serena had no intention whatever of paying attention to the therapist until she heard his apology. The sincerity and urgency with which his plea was uttered stopped her in her tracks. She stated:

"You know doctor I really came to tell you that I've been practicing my breathing and muscle relaxation techniques while listening to the Scarface and the Stephen tapes. I thought you'd like to know that on the measurement chart I've reduced my anxiety and fears to 2, again and again. Although they seem to be stuck at that figure, I'm feeling much better about myself."

"That's so good to hear, Serena. No one deserves it more than you! I hope I hear from you again. Please forgive my bad manners and intemperate behavior." He didn't again mention his broken marriage but that was the main reason that Serena had stayed to listen.

"Yes, this is Serena Ahn."

"Serena, this is Father Murphy."

"Father Murphy?" She repeated her voice rising in evident surprise. "Where are you Father?"

"I'm here in Victoria. When can I come to see you?"

"The truth is right away, if that's convenient. Do you have my address?"

"Yes, I got it from your dad?"

"How are Mama and dad?"

"I'll tell you when I get there. It shouldn't take me long as I'm not far away."

"I can't wait to see you Father, so please hurry."

Serena recognized the doctor's falsehood in his insistence that he was merely voicing Stephen's views. But still, she couldn't understand why he had suddenly attacked her with such vehemence. Since she didn't trust his interpretation, she attempted to analyze the accusations herself. She had gone through her marriage blaming herself for Stephen's cruelty. Since she wasn't a complete wife, she thought that she deserved to be punished. But the doctor's advice that the choice of having intercourse or not, was hers and hers alone, had removed the guilt she felt at vacating Stephen's bed. She hadn't withheld her favors to spite Stephen as the doctor tried to make her believe. It was Stephen's repeated rapes and battering that drove her away from him. The blame for their broken marriage should not fall solely upon her. Both spouses should share the blame.

While the doctor's advice freed her from guilt, she still had difficulty getting him to accept what she thought really mattered. The truth is that when you truly love someone, you treat that person with tenderness and affection. You don't resort to blows to solve a problem. If you do, it reveals your true character; the control freak you really are. The fact is that she had been trying to save her marriage to a man who didn't really love her, and who had married her for the wrong reasons. Yet, it was the doctor's most vicious accusation that kept driving her to distraction.

Oh God, she kept asking herself, was she naturally frigid or was the terror she experienced at Stephen's sexual approach a result of her many violations? And how was it that a man who swore he loved her could so abruptly switch off her sexual current? She raged up and down, pacing the rooms of her home, wondering if her frigidity was only a temporary curse that would disappear with time and healing. She continued pacing, mourning the loss of her sexuality whose pleasures had so far eluded her.

Although Serena was troubled by the doctor's cruelty, she was more disturbed by the far greater cruelty of her husband. She realized for the first time the true extent of Stephen's hurt and fury after the spiteful views about her, her country and her countrymen that Stephen had divulged to the doctor. The virulence of his attack, his lies that the doctor had further twisted, had been dictated by Stephen's frustration, anger and hatred. The revelation goaded her into a deeper analysis of their relationship.

At first, she had dearly loved Stephen. She had been drawn to him because he was kind and considerate during their courtship, and yes, good looking. She felt bound to admit that since her arrival in Canada, he had spent considerable time and effort showcasing the flora and fauna of his province to her evident delight. However, she questioned whether his generosity was meant to assuage his guilt for battering her, or to win the prize he sought? With hindsight, it was hard to believe that it was because of his love for her or his desire to make her happy.

Together with the zero she graded him as a husband she had to add another zero for his grade as a father. She considered that indifference and cruelty were not the values of a loving father. Then, returning to her assessment of his attitude towards her, she believed that no husband who could so savagely rape, batter and vindictively ill-speak his wife, could truly love her. When you loved a woman, you treated her with respect, consideration and affection. You didn't bash out her brains. But then Stephen always let his emotions dictate his actions, except when it concerned being complimentary to his immediate family. Only then did he use his will or reason to exercise strict control over expressing his true feelings. Otherwise, he surrendered to impulse, freeing his hormones to dictate his conduct.

It was slow going and took longer than she figured to reach that point in the trail down the mountain where she eventually met Jack. She was so glad to see him that racing downhill she almost fell into his arms. He hurriedly explained:

"I came higher up the trail to meet you and since you were late, I was afraid that a bear might have attacked you."

"I did have a strange encounter with Bruin," she replied, feeling foolish for having attacked a grizzly with rocks. What the hell was she thinking? Wasn't it her attempt to prevent the bear from eating her?

"I was on my way up to meet you about an hour ago when I saw a huge grizzly nosing a broken package of ham sandwiches lying in the undergrowth. I recognized the package as the one I had placed in your backpack and immediately shot the bear thinking it had harmed or wounded you."

After she told Jack her story, he advised:

"It's very unusual to antagonize a grizzly and live to get off unscathed. You were very lucky that he preferred ham to human otherwise he would surely have eaten you for his supper." Then he added: "but from what you said, he was already far too stuffed with salmon to pay you more than a cursory attention."

"I have to admit that facing that enraged creature was a terrifying experience," she told Jack, "it swatted me down like a troublesome housefly and I thought it would eat me for sure. So what will you do with the carcass?"

"He'll make a nice trophy stuffed and mounted at the local taxidermist." Serena took a good long look at the animal.

"My God, it's huge! The size of its head alone is almost as big as a Smart car!"

"Forget its head! Look at those six inch canines and the length of its claws. Then, the girth of its paws is as thick as a tree trunk, and as solid! A single blow from one of them can stove in the skull of a moose. You were very lucky. Can you imagine Bruin's 'tree trunk' colliding with your head or having those canines crushing into your skull? You wouldn't last a minute."

"I don't have to imagine any such thing. Having him swat me and breathe down my neck was quite enough. I thought for sure that he'd eat me alive."

"Thank you for coming Serena. Although you do have an appointment, I didn't expect you."

"Doctor, as I told you last time, the exercises I've been doing helped to diminish the fear, anxiety, guilt and shame that I've always felt before and during intercourse with Stephen."

"Well, you need to continue the exercises even though you have reduced the negative feelings that have haunted you. But your new perspective should help considerably, over time, to eliminate the pain and fear you have regarding intimacy and penetration. After your experience with rapists, and later with Stephen, your choice of a partner for intimacy should be someone who wins your approval through his sincerity, kindness and affection."

"Your statement, that I'll be choosing a partner for intimacy, implies that I'm not the same person you accused of being frigid?"

"Please overlook my anger and spitefulness, Serena. You can't be frigid since you genuinely enjoyed kissing and cuddling with Stephen on many occasions." The doctor then continued. "It stands to reason that you're unlikely to choose an emotional relationship with an aggressive and violent type like the rapists. But you should give yourself time, and gradually let yourself get ready. Your mind and body will tell you when."

"Thank you doctor. You've lifted a great burden from my shoulders."

"Keep repeating the exercises and give your new perspective time to sink in. The combination of your mind and body will help you to decide when you are fully healed and ready."

Serena was so weary after her exhausting climb up and down the mountain and so frightened at her close brush with death that she was trembling. Jack noticed but said nothing. Instead, he promised her a hearty supper with his mouth-watering recipe of pork chops to take her mind off the hellish experience. On arrival at his home Serena had enough time to shower and change before joining her host and hostess for a glass of wine before the meal.

"Jack keeps a small cellar of the Island's wines in the basement for his clients. He finds the pinot noir and pinot gris quite impressive like the connoisseurs who have tasted them. These wines come from the Averill Creek Vineyard in Duncan's winegrowing country just north of Victoria. How do you find the pinot noir, Serena?"

"I'm afraid that I know very little about wine. All I can say is that I thought I was really hungry after my mountain adventure but I find that the wine has sharpened my appetite considerably."

"So let's go to the table and satisfy our hunger before we all die of starvation." Jack stated. While waiting for Heather to serve the meal, Serena regaled Jack with a whimsical twist to her adventure entitled: "My meeting with a grizzly bear."

"On huffing and puffing to reach the high plateau, I then looked down and was deeply impressed by the sight below me. In a river chock full of spawning salmon, a huge grizzly bear was fishing. His method was both uniquely individual and highly skillful. Ignoring rod, reel, hook or line he charged the salmon chasing them towards a low level bank upon which the fish leapt and stranded themselves. Like a macho Don Juan, the gentleman bear batted aside all male competition. He then selected only the females with well developed brains, flawless skin and egg filled stomachs to satisfy his needs and have his way. When I tried to escape his notice, the bell I wore rang and alerted him to my presence. No doubt delighted to meet me he sprinted up the slope. In greeting he stuck out his paw inadvertently knocking me to the ground. I was so overwhelmed by his charismatic presence that I lay there as immobile as a tasty entrée. To my utter dismay, he ignored me in favor of my ham sandwiches. I was deeply disappointed to realize that he preferred ham to human."

Jack thought my story would make an interesting conversation piece but said it needed a fitting ending which he promised to supply after the meal.

By the time she was served Serena was so hungry that she wolfed down the pork chops and only nibbled at the new potatoes, green peas and cabbage covered in thick brown gravy. It didn't take long for Heather to notice that Serena's pork chops had disappeared. She offered Serena a second helping. The chops were so tender and succulent that they melted in her mouth and were the best she had ever tasted. She had gorged on so many and was so full at the end of the meal that she had to refuse the home made custard offered for dessert.

"If you are finished," John stated, "I can provide you with a fitting end to your story. I think it could do with a sting in the tail."

"I can't wait to hear what you have to say."

"Do you remember how I warned you about your possible meeting with a grizzly just before you began climbing? I gave you the bell to keep all dangerous animals away. I then explained how you should be a good actor and skillfully play the role of a corpse to prevent the bear from eating you?"

"How could I forget?"

"Well, you turned the tables on the grizzly."

"Turned the tables? What do you mean?"

"Instead of the grizzly eating you for supper Serena, you just ate the grizzly."

"Serena looked stricken as she stated: "I hope you are joking Jack."

He did not respond.

Serena thought of the way Stephen said she affected him; that her sight, scent or touch could so arouse him in an instant that he was ready to make amorous advances, even in public. The realization prompted her to recall his words about the way he saw her: with its "seductive curves," her body was "as sinuous as a cobra," and its effect on him, "just as dangerous." She had to admit that those words had made his naive, teenage wife blush with pleasure at the supposed compliment. The truth is that with hindsight and greater maturity, she recognized that his feelings were simply born of lust. She couldn't forget how, from their very first meeting, his hands were always thrust into his pocket to conceal his erections. She now believed that it just suited his ego to convince himself he was in love with her. The reality of it was that his repeated cruelty could not have been born of love. She finally understood that she had married a control freak. As a naïve and innocent teenager, she had loved Stephen as far as she was capable. But his cruelty towards her had created a great gulf between them. Through close analysis she was able to see clearly the true character of the man she had married.

After she put her suitcase in her car Serena planned to resume work at her rape survivor organization when she got back to Victoria. At the same time, she was wondering what she could do to overcome the mental block that kept preventing her from painting the eagle in attack mode.

Serena knew that she could always turn to her painting as to a trusted friend in whom she could confide, and she was surprised to find more than enough wildlife in British Columbia to pose as her subjects. This aspect of her new country fascinated her, as she saw rabbits, squirrels and deer often in yards, fields or on pavements. She also saw ducks, geese, pigeons, seagulls or crows in flight or at rest whenever she ventured outdoors. Birds abounded in trees and parks, congregated in vacant fields, settled in rafts on lakes and seemed to prefer empty school grounds and golf courses. Early in the morning and late at night, wildlife was a common sight in the city's suburbs like Gordon Head, Oak Bay, Sydney, Langford and Metchosin. The deer and rabbits wandered casually into gardens and orchards, eating flowers and fruit. While a nuisance to gardeners, they were a welcome sight to lovers of wildlife and the outdoors.

On her journey with Stephen into BC's primitive north along the Alaska Highway she had not been prepared for the miles and miles of coniferous forests stretching away from the road towards either horizon. It was only after gazing at the long sweep of the seismographic lines cut parallel to each other and reaching into gray oblivion that she got her first indication of the enormous size of the province. On the trip, she saw mule and white tail deer, moose, grizzly and black bears, the white Dall's, and the dark gray Stone sheep. It surprised her that the white cotton puffballs, standing out against their dark, lofty background, were really mountain goats. But it was in Alberta's National Parks of Jasper and Banff, located just next door to BC, that she was even more amazed to see animals stopping traffic to cross roads. A few rested in undisturbed comfort at the roadside and on street corners. Deer and elk ventured along pavements, wandered into the city's Parks, and like celebrities, posed for the 'paparazzi.' And every year during the late fall, not a few tourists were threatened and chased from the parks by rutting bull elk.

Serena was astonished and inspired as much by Canada's wildlife as by its wildlife artists, and felt compelled to capture the wild animals in their natural habitat to use as her models. She had been planning to portray an eagle in flight for quite some time considering that bird as the embodiment of power, elegance and beauty. It irked her to realize that so far her ideas hadn't seemed to gel. Before attempting to go on a camera safari to get snapshots of the eagle and other animals she wanted to use as her subjects, she considered that it would be prudent to take an evening course in photography. On weekends after her course was completed, she would often go on camera safari to visit Jasper and Banff National Parks to get photographs of the animals she saw. When Calvin was invited to accompany her, he surprised and delighted her by accepting. After the distance he had created between himself and his mother, he thought that it would be helpful to draw closer to her now that his father had deserted them. She noted that he brought along a camera to learn more about his mother's interests. It was evident that his presence on these trips brought them closer together. One evening, while she was practicing her draftsmanship at their hotel, Calvin asked:

"Why are you drawing those bird and animal parts over and over in pencil before painting them?"

"I'm practicing my craft like Michelangelo. He repeatedly drew parts of the human figure before committing them to canvas. When you came in, I had just finished work on the different textures, hair patterns and colors in the coats of deer, elk and moose, as well as their legs, eyes, muscles, musculature and even the veins that protrude from under their skin. Before that I worked on the feathers, beaks, talons, wings and tails of different birds."

"But what's the point; why the repetition? What are you aiming at?"

"The constant practice helps me to hone my skill in draftsmanship. I want my animals and birds to be so real that the viewer will believe they can actually spring or fly off the canvas."

"Well, what you've done looks real enough to me." Calvin's words came as a blessing after she had been crushed so often by his father's criticism of her work."

"Do you have any idea how long you'll be working at it?"

"There's only one more exercise I have to do."

"What's that?"

"I want to capture the sheen on different colored feathers when struck by sunlight."

"How long will that take?"

"Not too long, I hope. I then want to show you what I've done and get you to tell me whether what you see is just fair, good, very good or excellent."

"Okay, but I hope you know that I'll be much tougher than you expect!"

"That's exactly what I want." She became impatient, then anxious and finally apprehensive at the length of time Calvin was taking. He seemed to be scrutinizing every part of every single drawing. Since his face gave no indication of his thoughts, she began to believe that he didn't like what he saw. If that were the case, she would have to begin the whole process again. After minutes that seemed like hours to her, Calvin looked for her and discovered that she had disappeared. He found her brooding in the bathroom deeply depressed at the belief that Calvin was not at all impressed by what he saw.

But he surprised her.

"Mom, you don't have to worry. They are all excellent! What a profound relief it was for her to hear compliments rather than criticism of her work!

The new-found reunion with her son permitted them to visit several art galleries in order for her to study the different techniques of Canada's wildlife artists. She paid special attention to their use of brush strokes that created different textures and to the unique features in the forested background or those weather conditions they used to capture a mood or to give a special character to their subjects. She needed to become familiar with the cobalt blue of the summer skies and their white puffball clouds, as with the sodden, mist-laded winter atmosphere of BC, so saturated that it seemed to drip moisture. She knew that she would need practice in order to establish her individual style as she intended to stamp her own distinct personality on the portrayal of her eagle.

At home again, her thoughts turned morbid. From time to time, she was in the habit of chastising herself for the way she had left Korea. With a heavy heart, she began to dwell on the way she had deserted her parents and the heartrending blow of its impact upon them. In her last year at home, after her assault, it was evident that she had become the air they breathed, the oxygen in their lungs, their very lifeblood. Her father had told Serena and her mother of his decision to retire from business in about six months to spend more time with them. One evening, shortly after the announcement, he had come home with airline tickets and bookings for their first trip abroad—a four week Caribbean vacation to Barbados and Trinidad—a trip that they had discussed endlessly, deciding which of the many shore excursions they would take. The decision she had made to leave Korea would have been no less than a death to both her parents. Once she dropped the bombshell of her departure, she had become aware of their sadness and their silences. She could sense, with a growing degree of shame and sorrow, the way they wept outside her presence, and the unmistakable glint of grief that appeared in the emptiness of their eyes. Although she had been aware of their sadness the recognition had not changed her decision.

"Come in, come in Father Murphy. How are Mama and dad?" Serena asked, her anxiety for news of her parents trumping good manners, but she quickly recovered. Taking his coat, she added: "How are you? I'm so glad you're finally here."

"My being here is both a pleasure and a duty," he said, as she took his coat to the closet.

"I understand the pleasure, but what's all this about duty? Let me get you something to drink. Would you like some tea?" She suddenly gave her visitor a long searching look and then observed: "Forgive me Father for stating the truth and breaking Korean protocol, but you have a very unhealthy pallor, you've lost a lot of weight and you're almost skeletal in appearance. There's more than a slight tremor in your voice. It's not as firm as I remember it." Serena stated this with raised eyebrows of concern. She then asked:

You've been very ill, haven't you?"

"Yes Serena, I'd like some tea, please. And yes, I've been quite ill. As you can see, I'm still not one hundred percent recovered."

"I hope you're not put out by my honesty," she called from the kitchen busying herself with the tea. "Since you helped care for me in my illness, I'd really like to return the compliment. We have a vacant apartment downstairs and you're welcome to use it for as long as you like. You can have your meals with my son, Calvin, and me. That way, we can both take care of you."

"Thanks for your generous offer Serena, but I'm staying with my friend, Father Simon. I'm very comfortable there." As she served the tea, Serena renewed her question:

"How are my parents and how is your visit a duty?"

"Well, when I left your mother was not at all well. After you left Korea, she grieved, waiting for months on your call. When it didn't come, one day in a fit of rage, she ripped out the phones. As her illness got worse, your father retired from business to be at her side. Your parents then suddenly withdrew from the world."

"So that's why I could never get through to her. Father, the fact is that I phoned for days on end to beg Mama's forgiveness and to invite her and dad to come to Canada for the birth of their grandson. I concluded that they were annoyed with me and had cut me off completely."

"No, they were certainly deeply hurt, but never cut you off. The years flew by during which your parents never came to church. Then, one Sunday they surprised me by attending High Mass. I considered it a miracle after your mother's vow never to leave the house. When I made a point of welcoming them back, your mother told me the strangest story that had prompted her presence. It became a story that I was to hear over and over from my other parishioners.

"I can't wait to hear it."

"You must come to Sunday Mass to hear what she and others told me," he said rising to leave.

Chapter 61

Hamyang, Korea

"John," the word burst from Leesa's lips, "I don't know if I can continue to live without our daughter," she confessed soon after Serena's departure. "I've been wicked, as you know, and God is punishing me for my sins."

"My darling, I too am suffering from Serena's absence. Not only has it destroyed my peace of mind, but the fact of the matter is that it has left a great emptiness in my life."

"Ah, but you are strong, John, and with your God to sustain you, you'll endure." As she looked at her husband, her breath caught in her throat and her eyes welled with tears. How could anyone gaze with such love in his eyes? She wondered. "Oh darling, I'm so sorry to heap my own pain upon you as I know you're suffering too." John listened, sidled closer to her on the bed, smoothing her hair, caressing her cheek, pressing her palm to his lips like a mother displaying her tenderness and love for her ailing firstborn. But, he didn't contradict her, overcome as he was by the tone of distress in her voice. He was aware that her paranoia had got worse since she saw every problem as divine retribution for her past crimes.

"With me it's different." She said, noting that he was again biting his nails. "He has forsaken me and I don't have the strength to stand alone, without either Serena or His support. Don't you see John?" She knew that her confession would hurt her husband deeply for leaving him out of the equation, but before she could continue, he replied.

"Why is it different for you? You know that I'm right here beside you and you also know I'll never leave."

"I was hoping that you wouldn't take my love for her as any failing in my love for you, my darling. Nothing could be further from the truth," she lied, failing to make eye contact. While she couldn't tell him the truth, she could at least cushion the blow.

"I can't survive her leaving, John. Her presence helped me to endure the long years of my trial, and my love for her sustained me through that terrible period of turmoil and isolation. I can't imagine my life without her." The sobbing that followed shook her body so violently that she resembled a fragile and delicate glass vessel about to shatter. Quickly, John stopped worrying his nails and enfolded her in his arms.

In the same way as with her mother, Serena's problems arose from a conscience troubled by deep-seated guilt. She had known at the outset that her actions in marrying Stephen had been far from pure. The cloying love of her parents, her unhealthy adolescent attachment to the farm and to her pets, had seemed to cast a wicked spell upon her, holding her in thrall. While they made her happy as a youth and adolescent, she was intelligent enough to realize that these ties had become a barrier to any serious future that she might envisage for herself. It was unlikely that she could earn a livelihood either as the prized daughter of devoted parents, as a volunteer farmhand or as a keeper of pets.

In one horrible sense, the rape had done her a favor by bringing matters to a head. During the more lucid moments of her convalescence, she had grown more and more agitated, realizing that she had to do something to break the spell of a too-comfortable lifestyle that was leading nowhere. While it had previously offered her an ocean of contentment, it was an ocean in which she was slowly drowning. All through the lucid moments of her recovery, she had dreamed of starting afresh. Prior to the rape, she had secretly planned to make the break after graduation, by doing something she considered worthwhile, to start a new phase of her life. However, the rape and its aftermath had derailed her plans.

She had planned to make her move after graduation. Then, like an ill wind, Stephen had blown in out of nowhere. No doubt, she had seen him as a second chance. If she could make him fall in love with her, and propose marriage, she would then have a valid excuse to leave home without censure. Yet, she knew instinctively that her departure would be like a death sentence, dealing her parents a mortal blow. However, since she was on the threshold of adulthood, she told herself that she had to think of her own future. If her parents had their way, she would never leave home. She had calculated that a proposal of marriage from Stephen would help to solve the thorny problem of breaking away from her home and parents. It would permit her to make a fresh start, begin a new life, and have a second chance. The decision she felt obliged to make would devastate her as much as it would her parents, but she convinced herself that she had no other choice. Further, she thought, making a clean break would have the effect of forcing her parents to familiarize themselves to a life without their daughter. She consoled herself with the belief that time would heal any wounds that her departure would inflict on her parents.

Then suddenly, as she thought about the chaotic feelings of shame and guilt that her decision to leave had caused, a blazing anger arose within her towards her parents. Wasn't it natural for a daughter approaching adulthood to feel compelled to leave home? Wasn't it a given that she would want to assert her independence? Why were her parents being so unreasonable in their unwillingness to let her go? Why were they making her feel guilty about following so natural an instinct? Did every parent impose so heavy a burden of guilt and shame upon their children? She could understand their sense of loss, but wasn't that loss nullified by the advantage of their daughter starting a new life and getting a second chance? Oh God, she moaned, how could parents impose such a heavy guilt-trip upon their offspring?

As Serena thought over the doctor's words with the calm that time imposed, she finally had to admit that in many respects he had been accurate in his assessment of her motives. The truths he had unearthed and spat out were in part, the cause of her shame and guilt. She had indeed been selfish in the way she had used Stephen, having very gently but firmly manipulated him to suit her own secret desires for a new opportunity at a future. True, she had been flattered by his attentions and would be eternally grateful for all he had afforded her, but had she ever really loved him? Did she, as an unworldly teenager, really know the true meaning of love? She wasn't at all sure. All she could say was that she had made a conscious effort to be a good wife for a long, long time. And, she felt forced to add, she had paid her dues in pain and suffering. That, she convinced herself, had to count for something.

In considering her behavior, she came to the conclusion that like most people, she was neither wholly good, nor wholly bad. She had had her personal agenda and it had dictated her actions. She had then salved her conscience with the fact that she had done the only thing possible in the circumstances, and said sternly to herself: having made her bed, she had no alternative but to lie in it. Then, conscious of the way she had ill treated and manipulated Stephen, she knew that she would have to criticize him less and less while blaming herself more and more. The fact was that despite her decision, she felt a sense of uneasiness, an unknown but nagging fear that some kind of retribution lay waiting in ambush for her.

What she saw as her sins had made her feel ripe for punishment. Then, for the thousandth time, she couldn't understand why she hadn't phoned earlier; why she had waited so long before writing the letter of invitation to her parents. God, she felt sure, was bound to punish her for her devious conduct of manipulating Stephen, her selfish and wicked choice of deserting her parents and exposing them to the slander and humiliation of wagging tongues. Father Murphy had cleared up why she couldn't get through on the phone. But she couldn't believe that her letter had not arrived either. The guilt and shame she felt at her parents' rejection of her; her distress at the dissolution of her marriage were only the first installments of her punishment. She wondered what other disasters could strike. Perhaps she would contract some terminal disease, like cancer. She rushed to strip before the mirror examining her breasts and body, looking for lumps. Almost disappointed at finding nothing, she began checking further for moles or warts.

Her fear for Calvin's safety made her try to become more protective, more affectionate and loving towards him, but she only made him feel more irritated and distressed at her sudden flood of affection. She could see him wondering what had come over her that she should begin doting over him as though he were a baby. It annoyed him to such an extent that he began to stay away from home, studying, he said, at the library. It hurt her that he should again be keeping his distance, answering her questions in strained monosyllables or unintelligible grunts. Yet, his silences were worse. She would have enjoyed their conversations so much if only he understood her need to break her solitude through a closer relationship with him, or with anyone. How she longed for the past when he watched over her, her photography and her painting like a guardian angel!

Led by the choir, Serena and the congregation sang the offertory hymn before Father Murphy ascended the steps of the pulpit. He gazed around at the unfamiliar church, took in the well-dressed, affluent men and women of this Victoria congregation so markedly different in dress and appearance from the poverty-stricken farmers of his parish in Hamyang. He began...

"Your parish priest, Father Simon, has invited me to speak to you from my heart. He is my spiritual brother and dear friend, with whom I trained as a young man in the seminary. He knew me then in the peak of health, slim but solidly built, with sinuous and wiry muscles, weighing at least one hundred and seventy-five pounds. I mention my health and appearance, only because less than a week ago, one of my former Korean parishioners now living in Victoria met me. Sadness dripping from her voice, she scolded:

"Father, don't be offended if I speak the truth, but you have a very unhealthy pallor! You've lost so much weight that your cassock is hanging on you and makes you look positively skeletal. Then, your voice is not as firm as I remember it. You should take better care of yourself, she chided. You've been very ill, haven't you?"

I admitted that what she said was true. My doctors in Korea had accused me of overwork and advised that I get far away from my parish, to a place where I could rest and recover. That's when I thought of my old friend, Father Simon. But, you see, the doctors were wrong. My present ill health and skeletal appearance has nothing to do with overwork. The way I look is because I've become sick at heart over the spectacle of evil that keeps hammering at our doors, throttling the families of every parish. I'm convinced that there is a malignancy on the wind. Swollen with vice and corruption, it sweeps across the continents and oceans, pouring out its corruption upon the population of the planet. With its passage, violence, rape, incest, prostitution and murder erupt in our cities and invade our homes. Day after day, week after week, I weary of hearing the confessions of my parishioners, their lies and deceit, their broken marriages, child abuse, molestations and every kind of depravity that they keep committing.

At home in Korea, the problem grew worse when a number of families approached, begging me to conduct exorcisms of their homes. In the height of summer, with a bright sun overhead, their homes were engulfed in deep gloom and the atmosphere inside was icy. Closed doors would slam, the flames of oil lamps would suddenly flare up, go out, then, after a long moment of darkness, would suddenly flare up again. Many, plagued by the noisesome scent of putrefaction in their homes, complained of feeling that they were not alone, sensing an unwelcome presence there. I conducted the exorcisms, and observed that the strange manifestations they reported were true. However, the exorcisms I carried out changed nothing.

Feeling a stomach-wrenching despair, I went so far as to consult my bishop on the subject. He pointed out that the Catholic Church has long been aware of these unearthly manifestations. They believe that the profusion of evil is not local at all. It is global in proportion. He himself, many of his priests and his brother bishops abroad, has been approached to perform exorcisms, always without result. Everyone is convinced that the perpetrator is Satan. After the Almighty had debased him in punishment by 'casting him into outer darkness,' he immediately declared war on the Creation. He is keeping his vow of exacting his vengeance upon mankind." Pausing abruptly, the priest stated:

"I shall speak to you again on this subject when I'm feeling better."

When the letter arrived, she was deep in concentration, wrestling with the multitude of problems posed by the demands of the bald eagle she had chosen as her subject. Should she paint it as still life or in action? What should be the location, what the perspective? In what pose should she present her subject on the canvas? What mixture of colors should she use to capture the full reality of the feathers, the beak, the talons, and the eye? These were only a few of the decisions she'd have to make before fusing the elements into a composite whole. Solving these problems would seem to be a monumental headache to others. Yet to her, painting was being at peace, warding off worldly care as, one by one, she worked out the shapes, the sheen created by the light striking the feathers, the steely glint in the eye, the sharp hook in the beak and the awful power in the talons. The truth was that hers was a chaotic peace, for artistic creation confronted each artist with a multiplicity of headaches.

Since the eagle was an ambush predator, she'd have to determine the camouflage it would use in its natural habitat, while dealing with its distinguishing characteristics. She would be preoccupied with all these aspects of her eagle, while doing the same with the prey animal it was pursuing. Solving these problems would take time, research, effort, skill and imagination.

For her, the process of artistic creation blocked out reality to such an extent that she lost awareness of everything else in her other life. Engrossing her mind in the act of painting allowed her to escape into her fantasy world. Worry, guilt, shame and fear evaporated as if by magic. Painting wrapped her in a warm cocoon of oblivion separating her from everyday problems and bringing her a temporary respite. It was her means of refusing to dwell on the dark side of her nature, putting her fears to rest instead of brooding over whatever punishment lay in store for her.

And when the images in her mind began to take shape on the canvas, she became ecstatic, exhilarated at the miracle. Her gift of creation could only have come from the Creator Himself. At such times, she was both exhausted and enthralled, caught in a web of pure joy, at one with the world. Painting, like her faith, had become one of the links that transported her into the world of the spirit. But she had to confess that although she had been planning the painting of the eagle for a long time, some kind of blockage kept preventing her from putting paint on canvas and beginning the portrait. A sudden pounding on the front door broke the spell of her brooding over the problem.

The contents of a letter from her parents' lawyers exploded her fantasy world. The attorneys informed her that both her parents had died in mysterious circumstances that began when her mother called in her priest with the strangest of requests. She needed him to exorcize some abnormal presence that had invaded her home. A gush of cold air greeted the priest who entered her home, and though it was a hot midsummer's day, the interior of the house was clouded in gloom. The priest concluded that something was indeed wrong when he caught scent of the pungent odor of decay permeating the frigid atmosphere. He knew that the nauseating smell couldn't have come from mold because the house had been recently built. Besides, no mold could be found after an exhaustive search and examination of the house.

Although the priest recited the prayers to exorcize the presence of evil that he said was palpable, it did nothing to dispel the foul scented darkness or the bone-chilling cold. The lawyers then pointed out that her mother, whom her doctor stated was stricken with paranoia, kept repeating that God was punishing her for some unnamed crimes she had committed. She was overwhelmed by a grave sorrow and kept repeating that she had nothing to live for. Nothing her husband said could dispel her grief or calm her stricken nerves. He kept telling her that she should stop obsessing on being alone. *He* would never leave her. Despite this insistence, his words had little effect.

Inexplicably, it wasn't long before her husband, witnessing the rapid deterioration of his wife, fell into a steep decline. Their doctor considered that they were both grieving, suffering from some unnamed sorrow, and in a state of deep depression. He prescribed tranquilizing drugs to pry them out of their downward spiral, but either they didn't take the medication or it didn't work. Their decline continued and nothing the doctor prescribed was able to reverse the situation.

Both parents had lost all interest in life and stopped taking care of themselves. From their serious weight loss, the doctor concluded that their depression had turned to despair, and their wasted bodies indicated that they had stopped eating regularly. The lawyers explained further that her parents had instructed them to put both the farm and their business empire up for sale. They had taken their percentage of the transaction, and as instructed, had put the considerable remaining sum in an account to be drawn upon solely by their daughter, Serena. They ended by pointing out that it had taken quite some time to complete the sale of all the businesses and the properties they owned and have the will probated. By the time she received their notification, her parents would have been cremated long ago.

The death of Serena's parents devastated her and the terrible news magnified her already acute sense of guilt and shame. She sat on her bed feeling light-headed, and when her eyes burned, her stomach lurched and her throat constricted. She had to bend double in trying to rid herself of the nausea. She was engulfed in sorrow, with her face bloodless and eyes tightly shut. She felt as though someone had seized her vital organs in an iron grip and kept trying to rip them out of her body. The constriction in her throat made her feel as though she were being garroted. She fought to recover her breath, opened her mouth to take great gulps of air into her lungs as wave upon wave of agony swept over her.

With the passage of time and the gradual recovery of her senses, she wished herself mutilated, pulverized, dead. She couldn't bear to remain a part of the rotten world where life took the form of a sledge-hammer that pounded away at each individual. It was far better to be dead. Then, she could at least spare herself the endless suffering that life had to offer.

"Oh God," she wailed, "strike me down and let me die. I can't bear this pain any longer." Hot tears rolled down her cheeks and a soft keening rose from her lips. Finally, her body took over its own display of deep sorrow, and she found herself swaying backward and forward in the slow rhythm of mourning.

The following day, in a state of near hysteria, she began to question life's sense of timing and indulged in a series of morbid 'what ifs.' What if her mother had not surrendered to the evil urge to commit incest with her father? Would that have prevented her grandmother from murdering her husband? What if her father had been waiting to pick her up after the movie? Wouldn't that have saved her from being raped? What if Stephen had not arrived at the exact time that he had? Wouldn't she have gone to the big city and begun a new life there? What if Stephen had not fallen in love with her? Wouldn't she have stayed in Korea, and wouldn't her life have been different? What if Stephen had been patient enough to let her fully recover instead of forcing her back into trauma with his sexual demands? Wouldn't her marriage have been a success? And most important of all—what if she had not left Korea? Wouldn't her parents still be alive? Yet, even in her deep sorrow, she realized that nothing could change the past. Therefore, indulging in 'what ifs' was a futile and maudlin exercise that revealed the instability of an overwrought brain.

Father Murphy mounted the steps to the pulpit shakily and began:

"Some Sundays ago, I spoke to you about the upsurge of evil in my parish of Hamyang in Korea, and of its disastrous effect upon my health. Even today, I still feel very weak; not at all myself." Decidedly pale and wan, he continued:

"I began to have terrifying nightmares with the same grizzly scenes recurring again and again. In a landscape enveloped in icy darkness, I kept stumbling against what I later learnt were bodies lying at my feet." In a long moment of silence, the priest, sweating profusely kept mopping his brow. He then held on to the pulpit rail to steady himself. "The bodies were scattered throughout a vast wasteland and after a while their agonized cries for help soon made me aware that some were still alive. The realization took me back to the Front where, as a chaplain during the Gulf War, I was also surrounded by the dead and the dying, but those were soldiers. In my nightmare, whenever the moon appeared from behind a cloud, its light would fall on some of the faces around me. I recognized the faces of quite a few members of my parish in Hamyang. Others were the faces of strangers I had never seen. However, during the past weeks since I've been here among you, I now know that the faces I didn't recognize belonged to some of the members of this congregation." The priest stopped suddenly, seemed to stagger for a moment, and then whispered hesitantly:

"As you can see, I'm still not at all well so, if I'm able, I'll continue my message when we meet again."

Although Stephen had rejected the criticism of his wife and doctor, he admitted grudgingly that every quarrel had two sides. The suffering he had experienced at his separation from Serena, had prodded him into a search for answers. The soul searching he had done over the last few months had made him realize that he had been wrong in believing that Serena should shoulder *all* the blame for their broken marriage. He had ignored the doctor's advice that his repeated carnal possession of her and the succession of beatings had been the major factors in destroying their marriage. Still, he had to admit that despite her trauma, Serena had borne the torture countless times in silence until he had climaxed. Otherwise, he reasoned, she could not have become pregnant. With hindsight, he reluctantly had to admit that he should at least share as much of the blame as Serena. Had he waited until she was fully healed, as he had promised to do, he and Serena would probably be a happy couple today.

He then thought of his promise to himself and to Serena that he would change into an honorable human being. He hadn't and thus had only himself to blame for his many broken promises. It was no doubt the sick feeling of isolation that kept torturing him during the last few months that had led him to analyze his conduct and to reach these conclusions. Suddenly, he remembered the stories that Joe and Sally had related about their own exile from home and family. However, he had to admit that there was a vast difference in the two situations. They had been exiled by others. He had exiled himself. For the first time, he began to experience the torment of isolation as a soul-shattering experience that could destroy the peace of an individual at any point in his life. The question that occurred to him was: could he do anything about it?

For the millionth time Serena tortured herself for having lost the people and things that were most private and precious to her—her simplicity and innocence, her husband, her marriage, her country, her farm and now, her parents. And these losses had all resulted from her brilliant decision to marry Stephen, the 'oversexed battering-ram.' It drove her wild to realize that she had abandoned her parents for a cruel and unscrupulous charlatan. Everyone would have to agree that like Stephen, she too was a cruel, selfish bitch.

She knew instinctively that she was due for severe punishment. Then, the voice of her conscience shrieked: *but haven't you been punished enough? Haven't you been gang raped and battered by strangers, and almost to death? Haven't you been cursed with an empty, sterile marriage? Haven't you been betrayed by your best friends and your mother? Haven't you been sexually violated and battered over and over by the man you chose to love and marry, and hasn't he deserted you? Haven't you been sent to Coventry by your son? And now that you'd learnt that you'd had a hand in the death of your parents, wasn't that enough punishment for any single human being?* A loud wail then broke from Serena's lips:

"Good God, what more do you want from me?" She howled the question in her despair and desperation, as she marched like a madwoman from room to room, hugging herself tightly as though to prevent herself from exploding.

While Serena knew she deserved to be punished, she couldn't help asking herself: why did God's punishments have to be so harsh? Since Stephen had left and Calvin didn't know his grandparents, there was no one to whom she could turn to vent her grief, or even to understand her heart-wrenching loss. Once again, as had happened so often before, she was alone against the world. As tears of self recrimination, sorrow and bitterness slid down her cheeks, she kept chastising herself that her selfish decision to leave Korea was the direct cause of all her problems. Thus, she had only herself to blame.

Although she suddenly had more money than she could use in many lifetimes, her guilt at how she had inherited it weighed so heavily upon her that she saw it as 'blood money.' The betrayal of her parents, the loss of her self esteem goaded her to compare herself with the treacherous Judas of the Bible. As he had betrayed his Master, she had betrayed hers, and in both cases the betrayal had sealed the fate of the betrayed. But while Judas' betrayal had been the direct cause of one death, hers had sent two people to the grave. Following the conduct of her accursed role model, she wouldn't dare touch her 'thirty pieces of silver.'

Shame and guilt violated her. Mourning the death of her parents was like having the blood drain from her body and being helpless to stop it. On Calvin's return home, he was deeply moved at witnessing her grief-stricken condition. Since she refused to speak, he didn't understand the cause of her sorrow until he had read the discarded letter. Immediately, he began trying to ease her suffering in the age-old way that men give comfort to women. He hugged her tightly, silently pressing her cheek against his heart. The shuddering of her body and the sound of her weeping made his eyes start. When, moments later, she felt his warm tears on her face, she stopped feeling sorry for herself and her heart almost burst with compassion and love for her son.

Chapter 62

Stephen rang Serena after more soul-searching and debate with his conscience. When she heard his voice she was tempted to hang up, but instead, decided to listen to what she thought would be another twisted assessment of their situation; another series of barbed missiles aimed at her. Stephen surprised her.

"Darling," he began, "in spite of what you might think, I love you very much. Being away from you has been hell. I miss you and think of you so much that I can't keep my mind on my job. Since my work has been suffering, I've taken some time off to recover." His voice was so soft, warm and sincere that Serena could not believe this was the same man who had violated and battered her for years. Could this be the same man who had deserted her after vowing to love, honor and protect her for the rest of her life? Could this be the same man who had 'bad-mouthed' her and her country to their psychiatrist? She remained in silent shock so long that Stephen had to ask if she was still on the line.

"Stephen, I have to admit that your words and manner have taken me by surprise. The truth is that they make you sound like a very different person, but if you are suggesting that we get back together, I have to tell you right away that it won't work."

"Why not," he pleaded. "We could at least try, couldn't we?"

"Oh Calvin," Serena moaned. "I'm so sorry I behaved so selfishly. I wish I'd been a better daughter." The remorse and sorrow in her voice struck Calvin forcibly, making a deep impression on him. He became aware of what was most precious in life—a sense of belonging; a sacred bond stemming from the love of parents, family members and friends. Few people had it, but she did, in spades. It was all so simple, he suddenly realized. A profound sense of shame and sorrow swept over him when he thought of the resentment he had felt; the callous attitude he had previously adopted towards his mother. He vowed that in future he would change; how could he have been so selfish? And thinking of his mother's words, he said out loud: "I whish I had been a better son."

Following up on his vow, Calvin accompanied his mother to the Victoria Hospice where she visited those whom she called 'my family.' He immediately recognized the effect her visits brought to those unfortunates who had been diagnosed with terminal diseases. Although Serena only brought with her the quiet assurance of her sincerity, her patients greeted her like a dearly beloved family member. Calvin was deeply surprised to see the immediate change that her presence at their bedside occasioned. Glum faces grew animated, dead eyes sparkled, firmly closed lips stretched into smiles as his mother held hands and resumed chatting about the particular topic they had been discussing on her last visit. Many patients behaved as though Serena had never left their bedside.

When finally she introduced Calvin, he was further surprised that each patient had already known who he was and even about his college career. They seemed genuinely interested, asking questions about his choice of subjects, what he intended to do later on and what his other interests were. Some patients had a son, daughter, niece or nephew who was an undergraduate or a graduate of his college. Many talked about the 2008 US Presidential election and forecast a run-away victory for Hillary Clinton, it being still early in the campaign. Only a few thought it would be prudent to keep an eye on Obama. McCain had only just surfaced as the Republican nominee. It struck Calvin that a few patients might not be there to witness the election's outcome.

Some patients mentioned his musical accomplishments, making him realize that they could only have heard about it from his mother. When a number of them said that they would be delighted to see and hear him perform, he reasoned that his mother must be very proud of him to have mentioned him and his talent to her patients. The reception that he and his mother received each time they visited never failed to astonish him. With this in mind, he began to consider seriously the repeated requests for him to perform. It struck him that unlike his mother, he had been occupied solely with his own concerns. It had never occurred to him that so small an effort on his part could bring enjoyment to so many.

"Why won't it work Serena?" Stephen again pleaded. "We could at least try, don't you think?"

"No Stephen. You are a man whose ideas and opinions are set in concrete. You are unable to accept or even respect the views of others. You're an egotist who looks down on women. Like your father, you regard us as "the weaker female of the species." In your mind, we are not your equal, but rather some kind of strange mutation present mainly to satisfy your sexual urges, to look after your needs and work around the house."

"Are you finished maligning me or do you have more venom to disgorge?" He asked surprising Serena since there was distress and discouragement rather than anger in his voice. It even sounded as though he agreed with her assessment.

"No Stephen, I haven't finished. You're a bully, a coward, a rapist and a wife beater. Together with all those refined qualifications you're selfish to the core, pleased only when you get your way, regardless of the hurt you cause in getting it."

"Dear wife, I've come to those conclusions myself." Serena was amazed to hear Stephen's acceptance of such stinging criticism. Surely this was not the Stephen she knew. However, she felt that she had to make sure he understood.

"Stephen, I'd like you to understand it's not venom that I'm spewing, and I'm not saying these things to hurt you. I'm merely explaining why trying to give our marriage a second chance wouldn't work. If you examine your conscience you'll see that I'm right."

"When I read the assignment on the professor's handout, I couldn't believe my eyes," said John, voicing his opinion to two of his buddies as they sat in the cafeteria.

"I must admit," replied Tom, "the verse he gave us to analyze is ridiculous, especially since we've spent so much time and effort making critical assessments of the classics of English and French literature."

"Yeah," John chimed in. "We have done a lot more analysis and criticism of writers like Eliot, Shakespeare and Naipaul, Baudelaire, Balzac, Keats and Wordsworth than anyone might have expected."

"Maybe we're being too hasty," Calvin suggested, having remained silent until then.

"Hasty?" Tom queried. "He should be certified. Imagine giving us a nursery rhyme to analyze and assess. That's for putting toddlers to sleep."

"How do you begin to assess something so insignificant?" John asked.

"And, would you believe," said Tom, "that he restricts us to using our own viewpoint, after all the time we've spent reading the opinions of the world's most brilliant writers and critics?"

Calvin listened to the remarks of his fellow students but said nothing more. He acknowledged that their views were reasonable. The poem for analysis seemed like an insult to their intelligence, yet the professor, a very demanding teacher, must have a reason. Calvin then offered a suggestion:

"Perhaps the assignment is a challenge. He's forcing us to use our own critical faculties; testing us to see what we've learnt. Since the assignment counts for sixty percent of the final exam mark, isn't that a distinct possibility?"

No one agreed. Instead they all remained silent in response. After a pause Tom thought that the professor was "adding insult to injury" by stating that the analysis had to be divided under specific headings. Yet, despite their disparaging remarks, the students all knew they would have to give serious thought to the assignment.

"In spite of what you say Serena, it sounds as though you're thoroughly enjoying yourself criticizing me." Serena noted that there was a tone of defeat in his voice.

"As usual Stephen, you refuse to consider any viewpoint other than your own. I wish you'd try to understand. I'm tired to death of trying to make our marriage work by giving in to your urges. All I've ever got was more violations and battering as my reward."

"Anyway Serena, before you resume your attack and remove yourself from my life..." Serena cut him off.

"You see what I mean Stephen it was you who deserted us. Your conclusions are always twisted and self-serving." He ignored the comment and continued.

"I was about to say that there are some things I'd like you to know before we part forever. I've carefully retraced again and again the pattern of my behavior towards you and Calvin, and I know that in many instances what you say is true. I agree with the doctor's assessment that I've behaved abominably. But I want you to believe that throughout our lives together, I really made an effort to change. My earliest decision to visit your home was to use my association with the CEO of a wealthy corporation to gain some profit, monetary or otherwise, for myself. But that changed immediately after I met you. I really fell in love. I was ready to show the world that a leopard could change its spots."

"Stephen, I can't believe this is really you admitting your own shortcomings? You sound like a different person. I have to admit that I'm shocked!"

"Yes, it's me. You may find it hard to believe, but I did try to change on so many occasions." He emphasized the last three words. But I found it so very hard especially as you bested me in our many arguments here, just as you did in Korea. I never thought I could forgive you for the humiliation you caused me. Your habit of belittling me always brought back my father's ridicule. On occasion, it made me hate the very sight of you."

"I knew there were times when you hated me, but I never imagined that belittling you was the cause. You must realize that flogging you verbally was my only means of retaliation for your constant physical battering."

"You and your mouth made me feel less than the man I though I was. Yet, every time I took you on an outing that I knew you'd enjoy, I was trying to make up for the many wrongs I'd done; trying to turn the page and revert to the man I had hoped to become. I began to realize that you never interpreted my intentions in the way I had hoped you would. That was not surprising since I'd never been able to keep doing the right thing for very long."

"Stephen, that's correct. You had instilled such terror in me that I never saw those outings as a serious effort on your part to change. I interpreted them as an attempt to assuage your guilt, and to salve your conscience for your earlier brutality. The truth of the matter is that I also saw them as bribes to win the prize you sought."

"You may well be right, but you didn't give me much encouragement, did you! I suppose I deserved that. But Serena, believe me, I'll never forgive myself for the wrongs I've done–as a thoughtless and unkind husband, and as a neglectful, indifferent father. I want you to know that I really do love both you and Cal, and I was always proud of his many accomplishments. But, you know my weakness: I've always had difficulty voicing my true feelings, especially where praising others was concerned. I suppose I have to thank my father for that."

"Stephen, I never thought that I'd hear those words from you, and I'm sure Cal would be equally surprised and delighted. He tried so hard to make you proud of him."

"Tell him that I've always been proud of him, and loved him but I was never able to voice my true feelings or show them." After a moment's silence, he added: "I don't want you to worry, I'll continue to help with his education, but I won't be able to support you both and myself at the same time."

"Thank you Stephen. I appreciate your generosity and I know so will Cal. I've already begun to look for a job."

"I hope you succeed," he paused. "Since there's no chance of repairing our marriage, I'll take the job I've been offered in another province. I send you and Cal all my love and wish you both the very best."

"Wait," she said, wanting to return his good wishes, but she heard the click of the receiver as he disconnected. She knew that his admission was one of those rare occasions when his better nature had surfaced. He was being sincere, wanting to show her, and certainly himself, the person he had always been struggling to become. She also thought it ironic that the only time he used his son's name with affection was not to Calvin himself.

On their way home after visiting the hospice, Serena noted that Calvin was deep in thought. She was glad that he had accompanied her on her visits over the past months and especially proud that joining her had been his decision. "Why are you frowning so deeply?" She asked.

"I can't understand how the folks you visit talk about such inconsequential things while the evil worm inside them keeps eating away at their flesh. My God, their lives must be hell!"

"I too have always found that an insoluble mystery, but what would you have them do?"

"I suppose they have so much time to dwell on the darkness destroying them that your visits are looked upon as a godsend. You bring light into their darkened world."

"Our visits Cal, *our* visits bring light into their darkened world! I believe that we do give them a brief respite from the terrifying catastrophe that must haunt every moment of their days and nights."

"Before joining you and seeing for myself the actual enthusiasm and enjoyment that our visits bring them, I sincerely believed that you were wasting your time. But isn't there anything more we can do, Mom?" Serena was touched by being called "Mom" with such warmth, and at the interest her son was showing beyond a concern for himself.

"I'm busily wrapped up in organizing my rape center for the rehabilitation of assaulted women and struggling to navigate around the obstacles that hamper me from beginning my eagle. So the real question is Cal: what can *you* do?"

"Well, so many of them ask me to perform that I've been giving it serious thought."

"Oh Cal, that's a wonderful idea! When you do, I want to be there. You'll make me so proud!" Serena spoke with such enthusiasm that Calvin had to state: "Mom relax, I haven't done anything yet."

"Cal, just the thought of doing something for others is a very bright beginning, believe me!"

Serena had saved enough to survive from her father's wedding gift. Free from Stephen's demands, she had spent most of her time doing the demanding work of running her volunteer organization. She had used what remained from her father's wedding gift to buy supplies for her rape victims. She then got a job as waitress/hostess in a posh restaurant where she worked the evening shift. Her paycheck was more than enough to make ends meet, but tips from patrons for her friendly and efficient service more than doubled her earnings.

In her mid-thirties, Serena wore her raven-black hair severely pulled back in a bun. Though she was elfin in size, her bust, behind, well-formed figure and legs were still eye-catching. Her face, with its high cheekbones and slanted eyes, added to her air of mystery and femininity. The proprietor noted her elegance and poise that made her one of his most exotic hostesses. Serena was surprised to learn that men still found her attractive since a number of them propositioned her. She never accepted their invitations.

She refused Calvin's offer to assist with the rent and the groceries from his student loan, wanting him to realize that she was in charge. "Serena is responsible for running the household, Calvin for his studies." But Calvin saw that his mother's sacrifice to support them both, volunteering on a rape hotline, visiting the hospice, running her rape clinic while doing all the household chores, was quite a strain. So, he began buying the basic groceries each week– eggs, bread, milk, sugar and vegetables. He did the laundry, vacuumed the carpets, stacked the dishwasher each night, and each morning tidied his room. With his thoughtfulness he lightened his mother's burden of those responsibilities she would otherwise have had to shoulder.

He made sure to leave enough time to focus on his studies since his mother had drummed into his head that it was only through a thorough education that he could achieve success in life. Calvin wanted to do something that would make his mother proud. While his father had never seemed to care, his mother had always applauded his scholastic and musical efforts. For her part, Serena wanted him to know that he need never worry about survival without a father. And again she thought, only in dire need would she consider using the 'blood money.'

"Since your father left, you've been devoting nearly all your spare time to your studies. I consider that you should take a break, relax a little."

"Now that he's gone, I don't have to worry about his pushing you around and can finally concentrate fully when I study." He then added: "Why did he distance himself from us and never attend any of my intramural games?" His question reminded Serena of how deeply Stephen's indifference had hurt their son.

"Well, don't forget he often took us on outings that were enjoyable."

"How do you enjoy being with someone so preoccupied with his own thoughts that he might as well be absent."

"True. His remoteness was awkward. But the fact is that he sometimes took us both to the cinema or to a play."

"And then he'd soon fall asleep."

"But his being asleep didn't prevent your enjoyment of the show, did it? At least give him credit for trying!"

"His cruelty towards you, and the distance he placed between us made me stop trying to get close to him or to win his praise for any of my successes."

Once Calvin decided to perform at the hospice, he turned to the Internet to learn the popular songs and their lyrics that his elderly audience had listened to while growing up. He was fascinated to learn that the internet provided short videos of singers performing their most memorable songs from both the present and decades past. He also calculated that the age of the patients in the hospice was between 75 and 85 with a very few younger and older ones. He therefore thought that during their early and middle years, when Frank Sinatra was in his prime as the world's most popular crooner, many of them would have witnessed his fame as both singer and actor. Some might have attended one of his concerts and formed part of the generation that hero-worshipped him. A few of the ladies might have, as teenaged 'bobby soxers,' given in to hysteria, fainted in his presence and perhaps even thrown their undergarments on stage. Indeed, he was idolized not only for his singing but also envied for being regarded as the ultimate lady's man. The fact that he married and hob-nobbed with some of the world's most beautiful women and that he won an

Oscar award for his role in the film "From here to Eternity" couldn't have hurt his reputation. But it was the attitude of lover he adopted, the deeply nostalgic situations he conjured up between himself and the beloved, the high compliments he paid to his lady that would have plucked at the heartstrings of his female listeners and made deeply-committed fans of them. Calvin also knew that Sinatra was very popular with men through his 'he-man' image as leader of the 'Rat Pack.' They were a clan of highly-acclaimed singers like Sammy Davis Jr., Dean Martin, and film stars like Peter Lawford, Shirley Mc Lain, and other well-known performers like Joey Bishop. Then, many of his mates, like Calvin himself, conducted their studies with Sinatra songs playing softly in the background. Finally, the 'bad-boy' image that rumor created of his link to the Mob, and the inclusion of "My way" in his repertoire emphasized the 'macho' aspect of his character. Both made Sinatra even more popular with the male members of his generation. Therefore, when Calvin told the Matron of the hospice, Mrs. Drew, that many of the patients had invited him to perform and he explained his view of Sinatra to her, she agreed to his request to entitle his performance: "The Sinatra Concert." However, she asked that he include at least one song by Al Jolson and one by Elvis Presley who, with Sinatra, were her favorite singers. He could not possibly object.

Once he had got Matron to set a date, Calvin then took considerable time and effort to learn the melodies and lyrics, while copying the body language of the three singers. He rehearsed before the mirror until he was comfortable with each performance.

Chapter 63

When the day finally arrived, Calvin saw that a piano had been rolled into the auditorium. He also noticed that patients, nurses, interns, volunteers, a few doctors and even members of the cleaning staff were crowded in from other wards–a few in wheelchairs–to enlarge his audience. Mrs. Drew introduced him to the assembly.

"This is Mr. Calvin Ahn. He's here in response to your kind invitation for him to perform. I feel sure that he won't disappoint you with what you see and hear." There was some applause, laughter, and a noisy screech of whistles from some of the younger male and female nurses, the interns and the numerous volunteers.

Calvin began by singing Jolson's "My Mammy." During his rendition, he saw many in the audience mouthing the lyrics. When he got to the lines: "The sun shines east, the sun shines west, // I know where the sun shines best," he could actually hear their accompaniment as it grew increasingly louder. Then, when he got down on his knees, as Jolson sometimes did, and began: "How I love you, how I love you, my dear old Mammy, // I'll walk a million miles for one of your smiles, my Mah-ah-ha-mie."// He could hear the audience singing along with him, almost drowning him out. At the end of the song, there was loud applause, and a number of encores. Not a sound could be heard when he began tugging at their heartstrings with the words of his next number by Elvis Presley:

"Are you lonesome tonight, do you miss me tonight, are you sorry we've drifted apart?" He saw that members of the audience were wiping their eyes. And when he finally sang: "Does your heart fill with pain, Shall I come back again, // tell me dear, are you lonesome tonight?" While some members of the audience again sang along many were so taken with the memories of their youth the words evoked, that he thought there wasn't a dry eye in the house. Another burst of applause signaled the enjoyment of the audience at the end of the song. But many were sobbing openly as though the singer had cut out their hearts. Many of them, Calvin realized, were at death's door, so being frail and fragile, they could hardly applaud with gusto. But their nurses, interns, volunteers, doctors and the cleaning staff made up for the shortfall.

Having complied with Matron's request, Calvin encouraged his listeners to continue walking down memory lane through Sinatra's lyrics that, he knew, echoed the romantic episodes of their past. He also encouraged them to sing along to Sinatra's "*You go to my head.*" After Calvin sang he told his audience: "I trust you noted how the singer uses words to create a romantic situation and capture a nostalgic mood. He then describes how the irresistible charms of his beloved haunt him and compares his state with the ravaging effects that strong alcohol inflicts on his brain. He confesses that her smile alone is capable of raising his temperature while just the mention of her name is enough to disqualify him from competing with his rivals in the "crazy romance."

After a pause he began to sing: "*Someone to watch over me.*" Again, when the applause died he stated: "The lyrics remind us of that imaginary someone we think and dream about whom we long to meet. He or she, we surely hope, will "carry the key" to fulfill all our romantic fantasies. Since there was some spontaneous clapping after his words, Calvin believed his audience was really listening to, and perhaps liking, what he said.

His next song was "*Blue Moon.*" Once more Calvin followed the song with his remarks: "When through a rare miracle Mr. or Miss Right comes along to break into the numbing loneliness that we all experience without love in our lives, we tend to celebrate the miracle that we do have "a love of our own."

My next song is "*Laura.*" When it was over, Calvin commented: "The lyrics brilliantly recreate the mystery surrounding the dream woman (or man) whose face you imagine, whose footsteps you hear and who rewarded you with "your very first kiss." Sinatra cleverly shares his romantic dreams with his listeners by often using the word "you."

At the end of his next song: "*Over the Rainbow,*" Calvin pointed out that Sinatra succeeds to evoke in his lyrics an imaginary paradise where the skies are forever blue, impossible dreams come true and all troubles evaporate. The singer wishes, like his listeners, to join the "blue birds" as they fly to that magic and mysterious land beyond the rainbow where all their problems will evaporate.

Since Calvin heard a number of requests for Sinatra's "*My Way*," he decided to make it his last song. This time, he made his comments before he sang. "Sinatra captures in his lyrics the high and low points of a life that is at once personal and universal since we can all identify with the mistakes he confesses and the successes he achieved. Above all, he emphasizes the fact that he remains true to his principles: "I did it my way." The audience sang along as usual and the deafening noise of their applause, their shouts and their whistles indicated that the song and the concert was a resounding success.

On his way out of the auditorium he was accosted by a listener who pointed out that Calvin ascribed to Sinatra the situations, ideas and beliefs that belonged to the composer rather than the singer. Calvin replied that while the criticism was true, it was also true that, in the minds of his listeners, Sinatra embraced whole-heartedly and identified completely with the lyrics of his song writers. Finally, he reminded the critic that many of the composers wrote their songs expressly for Sinatra and thus kept his personality in mind when composing. His critic agreed but only half-heartedly.

For days following the event, Calvin's performance was the main topic of conversation at the hospice. Many of his audience hadn't heard their "favorite songs in decades," and congratulated him for "performing them so well and for bringing back some of their most cherished memories." When he visited again with his mother and she listened to the patients begging him to repeat the concert, her face beamed with pride and delight at her exceptionally talented son. Calvin blushed with pleasure on seeing her face. A few days after the performance, Matron took him aside, congratulated him on his performance and told him how delighted she was for the eagerness, energy and enjoyment he had injected into the daily lives of her patients. She made arrangements for him to give his concerts once a week and offered him a fee of one hundred dollars for each performance. He thanked her knowing immediately that he had made a good friend.

Serena was especially touched when Calvin brought her the "proceeds," telling her the money was to be used for the extra medication she often provided for her 'patients.' Then, a sprightly old lady, a member of his audience, approached him and asked that he add *"Abide with Me"* to *''Over the rainbow''* at the end of his repertoire. He agreed but had such a puzzled look on his face that the perky grandmother explained:

"With His abiding presence, we envisage our souls taking flight to that mysterious and colorful land beyond the rainbow. In company with Him and the blue birds, we'll have a couple of aces in the hole to comfort us when the "darkness deepens" to bring our misery to an end." Her remarks brought a blush to Calvin's cheeks and tears to his eyes.

The evident delight that Calvin's musical talent brought to the patients at the hospice had an enormous influence on him. It prodded him to consider what their life was like, in comparison to his own. They were all afflicted with the terminal diseases brought about by ageing, and haunted by the specter of death that would end their sorrow-filled lives. He, on the other hand, was a young man on the threshold of life, bursting with health and energy and looking forward to an array of fascinating possibilities that life had to offer. He marveled at the fact that his petty talent had so thrilled them that for days it eclipsed all their morbid thoughts. They kept complimenting him and could talk of nothing else. Modestly, Calvin often tried to change the subject by suggesting that Obama would make history if he won the US Presidential election.

"His chance of beating Hillary is as likely as that of a sardine eating a whale," one of his listeners responded. "His name Obama is almost the same as Osama (Bin Laden), the world's most wanted gangster another patient stated. How could he possibly win? A number of listeners cackled uproariously, shaking their heads in agreement.

Many patients asked how he came to choose the songs he sang and where he was able to find the lyrics that many of them knew by heart. Their obvious enjoyment was such that he felt humbled. How could so little an effort on the part of one person bring such brightness into the lives of so many? He again asked himself. The repeated praise made him think of expanding the range of his concerts.

"We have spent two terms reading and analyzing the texts of some of the world's greatest poets and prose writers." The professor paused before he continued speaking to his undergraduate class. "I was anxious to see whether you had grasped the techniques they used to make their work stand out. So last week, I gave you what appears on the surface to be an inconsequential verse to analyze, challenging you to assess the work, relying on your opinions alone, and basing your conclusions solely on evidence from the text. I also realized that you would not be able to get any help from the internet or anywhere else."

After a short pause he stated: "Encouraging students to think for themselves is one of the most important goals of a university education." He paused again before continuing. "I further asked you to divide your analysis into three sections under the headings: Content, Manner and Conclusion." He paused again. "I am very pleased to mention that quite a number of the papers I read were interesting. A few were quite imaginative. I should like you to listen to one that I found most impressive."

To activate his plan for extending his concert series, Calvin made a list of Victoria's Retirement Homes with their phone numbers, being careful to choose only those that offered "independent living" suites. He wanted to ensure that many members of his audience would be in full possession of their faculties since he knew that seniors at an advanced stage of ageing, with diseases like Parkinson's, Alzheimer's or Dementia, would also be part of his audience, but unable to enjoy fully the entertainment he provided.

After weeks of rejection by the numerous seniors' homes in Victoria, Calvin felt emotionally wrung out. Being constantly turned down was a humiliating experience that almost made him abandon his plan. Wasn't he happy enough performing for the patients at the hospice? Wasn't it enough that they enjoyed his performances? He then decided that the next call would be his last. He'd had enough rejection to last him a lifetime.

He took a taxi to the West Retirement Residence, an elegant home, "designed with the independent senior in mind." He had made an appointment to see the manageress who would be free later that afternoon. On his arrival, she welcomed him into her elegant office.

"I am Alison Brown," she said, extending her hand, and adding: "Please have a seat, Mr.?"

"Calvin Ahn, Mrs. Brown."

"Ah, you must be the young man who called. What can I do for you, Mr. Ahn?" She was middle-aged, tall, slim, and well dressed. Her blond hair hung down to her shoulders and although her blue eyes twinkled brightly she seemed to be all business.

"In the past two months, I've been giving concerts, that is, playing the guitar, the keyboard and singing for the patients at the Victoria Hospice..." Mrs. Brown cut him off abruptly.

"Say no more Mr. Ahn," she said, looking at him for a moment in silence. "I take it you would like to entertain our seniors?" She asked with such stern features and blue unblinking eyes that Calvin knew immediately that this was another rejection. Well, he thought, he had at least tried. He began to rise from his seat.

"Yes," he answered dejectedly, about to thank the matron for her time.

"Mr. Ahn, the Matron, Mrs. Drew at the Victoria Hospice, spoke very highly of you. She stated that your performance brightened the lives of her patients considerably for quite a number of days. If you would like to do the same here, would you be able to give us one concert a week?"

"Why yes Mrs. Brown," he answered in surprise, "I would be delighted to have such an opportunity." Calvin speedily resumed his seat.

"Now, Mr. Ahn, we can't afford to pay you the two hundred dollars per concert that Matron tells me is your fee at the hospice. But since we have another Residence here in Victoria, if you agreed to play at both our homes once a week, I feel sure you would agree to a fee of one hundred and fifty dollars per performance."

"Mrs. Brown," Calvin said rising, "Thank you very much for your consideration. It's been a pleasure doing business with you."

"One thing," she pointed out, "if you fail 'to brighten the lives of *my* patients,' all bets are off!"

"Agreed!" Calvin quickly replied and shook her hand before leaving.

After a moment the professor called out: "Mr. Ahn, will you please come to the lectern and read your assignment to the class." Although Calvin had worked long and hard on the assignment, he had no idea that it would garner special praise from his professor, and was shocked to be called upon to read it to his class. It was with ill-concealed trepidation and his heart a-flutter with nervous excitement that he made his way to the lectern to read the poem that the professor had selected for analysis. In a loud if shaky voice he began:

"Twinkle, twinkle little star // How I wonder what you are. // Up above the world so high, // Like a diamond in the sky." Calvin felt as though he were in a vacuum. His nervousness increased for the lecture room was as quiet as a tomb.

"Content: Gazing heavenward at a star and studying it, the unknown poet wonders at its nature, its habit of twinkling, its distance from the earth and its resemblance to a rare gem. He uses a single verse to encapsulate his study.

"Manner: The repetition of the first word emphasizes the star's sparkling nature, while the second line questions the aura of mystery surrounding it. His wondering suggests that there may be other questions involved. Why is it twinkling? How should he interpret its incalculable distance from his world? How is it possible for this heavenly body to hang suspended in space? Its great distance from the earth distorts its size making the poet describe it as "little," when common knowledge indicates the very reverse. These questions underscore the mystery that the poet expresses to the reader without mention of the operative word 'mystery.'

"In the final line, the simple "diamond" image, registers the extraordinary value of the gemstone to a race of people who salivate over its worth. At the same time, its incalculable value captures the extent to which the stone has inspired the poet. The diamond expresses as well his intense sense of wonder-expressed in the earlier lines-conveyed through the tremendous value of the gem and the brilliance of the image. The repetition of the first two words, the simplicity of the vocabulary–most of the words are of a single syllable and none are more than two–together with the four short lines and the strong jingling nature of the rhyme scheme,—'star' with 'are' and 'high' with 'sky,'–is particularly pleasing to the ear. These musical qualities and its simplicity suggests that the poem may be a nursery rhyme emphasizing as they do the appeal to the ear of an infant for whom repetition and mimicry are important aspects of the learning process. While appearing simple in words and meaning, this poem, not unlike great art, is open to interpretations on a number of different levels some of which are by no means simple. The diamond image, with its shimmering correspondence to the twinkling of the star, is both appropriate and appealing since it expands the meaning of the poem on a number of levels."

With the permission of Mrs. Brown, Calvin consulted a number of patients and found their tastes covered a fairly broad spectrum of music. However, he thought that a repetition of the concert he had given at the Victoria Hospice with a couple of others would suffice since he only had a few days before the date of his next concert. In future, he would have the time to add more songs to his repertoire.

Calvin finally came to his Conclusion and read the remainder of his essay:
"Since stars appear mainly at night, the background of darkness (left to the reader's imagination) throws into prominent relief the shimmering light of the gemstone, and this image of brilliance reinforces that of the twinkling star. Further, its illumination emphasizes the mystery of the star's suspension in the darkness above the earth. The image of light, mysteriously pulsating

from the darkened heavens, may be seen as a symbol of enlightenment, calling to mind the enigma of the Creation. Its throbbing brilliance seems to mimic God's words: "let there be light." In this context, the star can be interpreted as an image transmitting His message of enlightenment that reflects for us the miraculous work of the Creator. In so doing, the poet seems to be setting his reader on a path of admiration for and worship of the Divine Presence in our universe.

"The continuous twinkling, the poet implies, unravels one of the great mysteries of the universe. Set in motion by the miraculous hand of God, the light attracts the eye of mankind, forces his gaze heavenward and the repetition keeps prodding his mind to probe, and so to unlock some of the most profound secrets of the universe. By doing so, he may eventually discover the Creator and ruler of himself and the universe.

"The reader should note as well the poet as creator. Although his little world reveals his simple yet superb imaginative creativity, it is at best a petty microcosm, exposing the pitiful limitation of mortal man in comparison with the infinite sweep of the Creator's handiwork.

"Focusing his thoughts on a star, the poet embarks on a quest to unravel a universal mystery. He reveals that the shimmering world, high in the heavens, reflects the miraculous hand of God. By communicating this divine message, he fulfills his God-given role as poet, preacher and prophet."

There was a long moment's silence when Calvin stopped reading and looked up to indicate that he had finished. Then, a roar broke from the class as a crimson-faced Calvin stumbled back to his seat trying vainly to suppress a nervous giggle of excitement.

Serena worked hard at her job. Thanks to her appearance, her politeness, her slight foreign accent and her efficiency, she had developed a small but persistent clientele that frequented the restaurant on her shifts. She devoted her spare time to painting and being with Calvin. Like any doting mother with an only son, she plied him with questions. Previously, Calvin had found her too clinging and thought of her persistent questions as an inquisition based on curiosity rather than an interest based on love. They had irked him considerably and he had often replied with a single word, a grunt or not at all. But since his continued visits to the hospice with his mother a change had come over him. Thus, when Serena persisted with her questions about the progress he was making in his studies, whether or not he was meeting new friends or any "nice Korean girls," he replied with patience, affection and humor. When she asked whether he enjoyed the special lunches she rose early each day to prepare, he actually thanked her for the trouble she took and let her know how much he appreciated her sacrifice. He also told her how much he enjoyed them.

On getting such positive responses from her son, she bombarded him with more questions and he surprised her by answering them all. Although she knew she was spoiling him, she excused her behavior by telling herself that the world was a harsh place and indulging her son while she still had the chance would do little harm. She thought with a twinge of guilt that those who truly love always find reasons to justify their overindulgence.

Calvin was no longer irritated by his mother's attention. He regarded with pleasure her vain attempts to shield him from any duty that might take him away from his studies. He knew that she was helping him to achieve the success she insisted that "only came with a first-class education." Whenever the occasion arose, she delighted in the 'quality time' she spent with him. Knowing that she had his welfare at heart, he no longer tried to deflect her questions and genuinely enjoyed the time he spent with her.

It took some time for Calvin to copy the new music and lyrics from the computer and commit them to memory. While his mother was absent, busy with her work on the 'hot line,' he practiced the songs over and over on both his instruments until he was comfortable with the new material. He then casually invited his mother to join him for a concert at the Victoria Hospice. When Calvin drew up at a different location, she became puzzled.

"Cal, this is the West Retirement Residence, not the Victoria Hospice that we visit."

"You think they'll let me play for them?" Calvin asked, getting out of the car with his instruments.

"Calvin, be serious! You can't just walk into a new place and begin to perform without permission."

"Mom," he said, "just watch me!" He wanted to surprise his mother while she hung back as Mrs. Brown came out to meet Calvin and ushered him on to the dais of a large assembly gathered in their auditorium. Mrs. Drew, from the hospice, had accompanied Mrs. Brown and hastily called a reluctant Serena to sit with her at the back of the auditorium.

"Serena," she said, "Calvin is going to perform here and at the other West Residence weekly. But he has to be excellent, otherwise he loses the contract."

"He never said a word about it," Serena confided, suddenly nervous and hoping that Calvin would perform well.

Calvin was then introduced by Mrs. Brown:

"Today, I have a surprise for you. Mr. Calvin Ahn is going to give his first concert here and if you enjoy it, there will be many more. Enjoy!" She said, deserting Calvin. He needed no further incentive and began by singing Elvis's "Are you lonesome tonight, do you miss me tonight, are you sorry we've drifted apart?" He expected the audience would be singing along with him as it had done at the Hospice. Instead, there was almost complete silence in the auditorium and it struck him that something was definitely wrong. By the time he had got to: "Does your heart fill with pain // shall I come back again? // tell me dear are you lonesome tonight?" Mingled with a smattering of applause, there was the soft sound of weeping. Many members of the audience were overcome with grief by the gilded memories of their past that the words of the song evoked. The lyrics contrasted so markedly with their present situation. In a flash, Mrs. Brown was next to him on the stage. She whispered: "Play something more lively!" So he immediately broke into "Over the rainbow." It allowed his listeners time to compose themselves and soon they began to sing along, softly at first, then gradually growing louder. Suddenly, he rose from his seat and slipped the guitar-strap over his shoulder. While he kept strumming to the melody but without singing a note he whirled across the stage in a series of spins leaps and bounds of well rehearsed steps. His "River Dance" footwork took the audience by storm as they applauded loudly. His Jolson and Sinatra songs also generated loud applause and a number of 'encores' with shouts and whistles from the nurses, the volunteers, the doctors and the cleaning staff. Calvin then continued to stun his audience, the two matrons and his mother with a display of his imitative brilliance. He brought down the house with each Sinatra song and the many encores he received sealed his contract. Afterwards, he introduced Mrs. Brown to his mother. While she congratulated Serena on Calvin's ability, he took Mrs. Drew aside.

"I can't thank you enough for your recommending me to Mrs. Brown and getting me a higher fee. I owe you a big one."

"Oh," Matron replied, "the West Organization runs efficient and affluent Residences on the island. They have an excellent reputation, and more important, they can easily afford it. With the rousing performance you gave, there's no possibility of losing the contract."

"But Matron, you did me a great favor so I owe you *big time*. The next concert I give at your hospice will be free of charge."

"Oh no Calvin, I won't hear of it! From now on, your fee at the hospice will remain as is. Now go along young man, your mother is dying to congratulate you."

During the period of his father's remoteness, Calvin had become more surly than ever. He distanced himself from both parents. Then, the combined success of his being on the Honors Roll, his acceptance at numerous colleges, the offer of many scholarships together with his musical ability, had prodded Calvin to get somewhat ahead of himself. When a classmate had ridiculed him for his clumsiness on the basketball and tennis courts, Calvin's response had been:

"Yeah, but I can always kick your ass in academics." The truth was that Calvin had become a bit conceited. The classmate took his revenge by writing on the blackboard: 'Calvin Ahn is an asshole." As the time grew closer to the professor's arrival there was growing anxiety among the students. Their professor had a well-earned reputation for being a volatile wit, so everyone waited eagerly to hear the divinely inspired response of the great man after he entered the classroom and read his blackboard. On arrival, he read what was written, stared at Calvin and proclaimed:

'Ahn, you are boasting again.'"

It was at this time that Calvin had seemed to despise his mother even more for the way she kowtowed towards her husband, treating him like a superior being in a country where there was equality between the genders. He couldn't understand why she often walked a few steps behind him, helped him on with his coat or allowed him to batter her without complaint or retaliation. Besides, he couldn't respect a person who tore him in two over the duality of his culture and embarrassed him by phoning him again and again at the Department office? By keeping his distance, he thought she would see that it irked him to have anything to do with her. He knew she wasn't stupid, so how could she not see that her questions were annoying? How could she not recognize his refusal to show her any affection?

Chapter 64

Serena had translated Calvin's uncivil attitude towards her as a result of his father's cruelty. She believed that he was taking out his hurt and frustration on her. By the time he had begun his college career, she was convinced that he despised her. The recognition that the two people whom she loved and cared for most in Canada hated her guts was a terrible ordeal that made her feel not only unloved and alienated, but also well deserved for her wrongdoing towards her mother. Yet, while she obsessed over being despised by those whom she loved, she busied herself with her rape crisis organization, and continued her visits to the Victoria Hospice.

It wasn't long before her work included counseling, for she understood far better than many of her co-workers, the problems her callers were facing. She knew that she could pass on vital information that would help to ease the emotional pain and suffering of survivors. Perhaps, without realizing it, Serena's motivation to help others was an attempt to atone for the sins of her past. However, she knew that her understanding and sympathy would help to relieve the anguished dislocation that so many victims faced. Without her knowledge and sound advice, they would be incapable of discarding the disgust and shame they inflicted on themselves. To help those traumatized patients to get relief she taught them the breathing and muscle relaxing exercises.

On their way home from the West concert, Serena sat quietly thinking. "Why didn't you tell me about your new contract?" She finally asked.

"I wasn't sure I would be good enough for it to last. Besides, I wanted to surprise you."

"Well, you certainly did. But did you arrange everything by yourself?"

"I set up an interview with Mrs. Brown to get her permission for me to perform there. It turned out that Matron had already spoken to her about me and the way my concerts had given a lift to her patients. She then told Mrs. Brown that my fee was double the amount it really is. As a result, Mrs. Brown offered me one hundred and fifty dollars for a single concert at two of their facilities, which reminds me that I can now offer you more money for housekeeping and the patient's medication fund."

"Oh thank you Cal, but I think you've already done more than your share. Three concerts a week? That's quite a heavy schedule! Will that leave ample time for your studies?"

"Mom, I've already accepted the new contract. I'll do the three performances on Mondays, Wednesdays and Fridays. Besides, I've already done all the hard work memorizing the music and lyrics. This means I'll still have lots of time to study. So please don't argue. I'll be donating half the concert proceeds to you for housekeeping and your Medication Fund."

"Oh no Calvin, I won't accept that! You'll be working too hard. I would prefer you to keep the housekeeping donation for yourself."

"Mom, I'll feel better making up for my less than friendly past behavior towards you. So please consider this discussion over."

Serena began putting her personal medical experience into practice, so that survivors could begin calming their fears and anxieties with the breathing and muscle relaxing exercises she had learnt. She had begun her adventure in volunteering realizing that as a rape survivor herself, she could reduce her own mental anguish, her sense of guilt and shame, by first alleviating the anguish, guilt and shame of others. She also learnt that she could only begin to accept herself as worthwhile after witnessing the progress survivors had made because of the help she had given them. Then, hearing their expressions of gratitude was, she felt, one of the best ways to ensure feeling better about herself. She came to recognize that volunteering was a vital part of her own recovery and rehabilitation process.

It was through the hours she spent volunteering and the encouragement she received from her benefactors that the remnants of her shame and guilt gradually evaporated. While she learnt that "giving back" was indispensable for reclaiming her self-esteem and dignity, she soon found that it was also indispensable for recovering her independence. If truth be told, she lived for the rush of exhilaration that thrilled through her whenever a victim complimented her for breaking through their web of despair.

Calvin never skipped lectures and continued to work tirelessly at his studies. He spent most of his free time and his nights working at home or in the library. As a result, he was very successful in his studies. He had just written the final exams, having read for a double major in English Literature and Intelligence Technology. He thought he had done well since he had answered thoroughly many of the questions he had prepared in advance. With his exams over, he had considerable free time, and kept wondering whether he should keep his promise to himself to draw even closer to his mother by joining her on her visits to the Hospice. The building was very old, the last and only section of the old hospital that had not been rebuilt or renovated. It was a tall three-story building that had been recently painted. Its white coat of paint and blue roof gleamed in the mid-morning sunshine. The red terrazzo steps leading up to the glass door entrance was sandwiched between two beds with an array of colorful annuals. Their pleasing scent and bright colors shimmered in the wind and created an air of liveliness and gaiety that clashed with the building's atmosphere once Serena had crossed the threshold. The unpleasant hospital smell of the old, the sick and the dying mingled with the nauseating scent of soiled sheets and unwashed bodies stopped her in her tracts as though an invisible barrier had sprung up before her. The inside walls of the building had been painted white at some long ago date. With time the white had faded to a dirty grey and together with the peeling plaster and stained ceiling seemed to mimic the derelict state of its patients. The swift and sprightly movement of the male and female staff members gave a sense of liveliness to the atmosphere that contrasted sharply with the paralysis of those who were bedridden and immobilized.

Calvin was still in two minds about accompanying his mother on her visits to the Hospice. He thought it was a waste of time for Serena to visit strangers who only had a limited stay in this world. He thought she could spend her time far more profitably in painting since one day she might be paid for her canvases. However, since he had promised himself to be a better son he decided reluctantly to keep his promise. He was glad that he did for his visits taught him quickly how wrong he had been in his thinking. Each time Serena sat at the bedside of a patient Calvin was amazed to see the instant animation on a face that had been glum and morbid only a moment before. The sudden brightening of dull lackluster eyes and the grim mouth whose lips stretched into a wide smile left him speechless. Then, apart from their animated appearance, Calvin noted that there was a definite change in their attitude. Before Serena got to their bedside, most of the patients seemed to be almost comatose. Their eyes stared into space as though they were hypnotized by the silent and relentless approach of a nemesis against which they had no protection. They lay in their beds immobilized in the saddest state of hopelessness that one could imagine.

Calvin needed to get better acquainted with the terminally ill patients Serena visited. He also continued his weekly concerts that seemed to bring such pleasure to those facing death. Thanks to her increased Medication Fund, Serena was now able to take small gifts for each member of 'her extended family.' Many who had no other relatives, or few visitors, felt so isolated and alone that they considered Serena a kind of ministering angel. The knowledge made Calvin see the relationship between each patient and his mother in a completely new perspective. He also became aware of how crass and selfish his earlier indifference towards her and the patients had been. He noticed that each patient had a story to tell and didn't miss the rapt attention with which Serena listened to the tale of loss, wrongdoing or defeat.

It became evident that however courageous they had been during the earliest stages of their illness, however positive, they had eventually been worn down by the catastrophe they found impossible to overcome. Each patient who had resisted heroically at first had surrendered to the inevitable by the time they had entered the Hospice. It was worse than being on death row. At least the prisoner had a slim chance of a reprieve. For the patient there would be none. Calvin who sat next to his mother noticed that while each patient began by talking about the mundane affairs of everyday life—the food they were served, the boredom of life's sameness, the inane TV shows they couldn't seem to get into, their personal preference among the doctors and nurses—all without exception, finally ended by relating their personal life story. Each story was interesting. All were extremely sad, but one or two were so extraordinary that he found them deeply tragic.

It wasn't surprising that Serena was drawn to Lisa whose name, though spelled differently, was pronounced like that of her mother, Leesa. She was the strong one, brimming with self confidence and completely capable of taking care of herself. Lisa looked you straight in the eye and told her story with unswerving directness and complete honesty. There was no attempt to embellish or to avoid criticism. Lisa had a twin sister, Lina whom she said she loved dearly. Lina was a delicate and gentle soul the very antithesis of Lisa. While lovable because of her defenseless nature, she was totally lacking in that aggressive streak and the self sufficiency that every individual needs to take care of himself. In short, she was weak. The sisters had grown up loving each other and Lisa had always taken care of her younger sibling. She had supervised her homework assignments and when vulnerable during her teenage and adolescent years, Lisa had protected her against the bullies at school. As an adult, it was Lisa who had approved of Lina's fiancé then, when he proposed, had chosen and bought her bridal gown. She had dressed Lina and stood as bridesmaid at her marriage to David, a young, handsome priest. Though pretty and sweet, Lina lacked the gumption to stand up for herself. It soon turned out after the marriage that Lina became pregnant. While she became more and more bloated in childbirth, David grew less and less interested in his wife. At the same time he became more and more taken with Lisa.

"Now," Lisa told Serena: "I want to give you my personal reaction to the situation. David was young and attractive and ill with her morning sickness, Lina spent a great deal of time in bed. It was therefore natural that David and I spent a lot of time together. It so happened that I fell in love with him and he with me. Later on, when I began sharing his bed, David and I relegated Lina to the guest room while he and I took over the master bedroom. When David and I drove together, I sat with David in the front as though I were his wife while we dismissed Lina to the back seat."

"Did Lina know what had happened?" Serena asked.

"Yes she did." Lisa stated.

"How did she react?"

"She looked at us as though we were devils with a blend of jealousy, anger and sadness in her eyes. But since she said neither word of rebuke nor accusation, the situation went on unchanged for more than a year. But I did love my sister and seeing how deeply hurt she was, I invited her, with David's approval, to return to her husband's bed on the condition that I too would continue to sleep with David."

"Did Lina agree?" Serena asked.

"No! She rejected my 'solution' out of hand. She soon became seriously distressed and began brooding. Later, she went from being melancholy to being morose. Evidently, she was in great emotional and physical pain. She stopped eating regularly, lost weight and became frail, old and gaunt overnight. She had stopped speaking to me for months until the day she came to me. She said that my betrayal and infidelity had completely destroyed her happiness and her life. She said she had nothing further to live for and vowed to end her life. Before turning her back on me she stated:

"You've always said you loved me but you really don't know the true meaning of love. One day you will pay dearly for your cruelty."

Knowing her lack of willpower, I paid no attention to her vow, but she kept her word and committed suicide.

On that same day I was diagnosed with incurable ovarian cancer."

On hearing the story, Serena thought: Does yet another story of betrayal and infidelity hold any special meaning for me and my life? Have I been confronted with it for some reason? Like her mother she was always on the look out for divine retribution. She assured herself that she had never been unfaithful. But what about betrayal, she wondered. I'm really not sure. Anyway, what do you say to the narrator of such a tragic story? It seemed to both Calvin and Serena that Lisa needed to rid her conscience of this heavy burden because her next question was:

"Do you think that Lina was right about my cancer being the result of divine retribution?"

"I do not think that God awards punishment to sinners. I prefer to believe that our Father in heaven would rather choose the path of forgiveness."

"Thank you Serena for your sympathy and understanding, but I beg to differ. I know that my betrayal made the life of my sister a living hell. For such cruelty I deserve to be punished. Lina was also right about the true meaning of love. It is no good to say that I loved my sister yet betrayed her in the cruelest way. Since I knew all along that true love is a total giving of oneself, a complete surrender of one's being, what I felt for Lina couldn't have been true love. So I repeat; what I did made me ripe for punishment. If you believe as I do that God is absolute love, then to sin against love is to sin against God. I know that what I did was wrong. I also know that I am being punished for it because all I feel inside me is darkness, emptiness and despair. I have begun to embrace my cancer seeing it as the expiation I must pay for the grievous sins I have committed." Lisa remained silent for a moment before she spat out her belief:

"When that bitch temptation sucks at your soul, which of us is strong enough to resist its overpowering seduction?" Although Lisa kept smiling there were tears in her eyes. Serena and Calvin couldn't control their emotions either.

When later on Calvin discussed Lisa's story with his mother, he noted that she had taken pains to avoid being judgmental with her answers. However, when he asked about her reaction to the story, she was reminded of her doctor and her mother. She believed that Lisa had sinned against both her sister and David by coveting another woman's husband and committing adultery with him. But in agreeing with Lisa's words, she couldn't help but remember those of the defeated doctor:

"We mortals are so weak and flawed with imperfection" that when *'that bitch temptation sucks at your soul, which of us is strong enough to resist its overpowering seduction?'*

Calvin spent most mornings at college translating Korean history for a professor. Most evenings were spent at one of the homes for the elderly. During a concert at the West home he noticed that a bed had been rolled into the auditorium. He couldn't see the person in it although he stood on a dais above floor level. Each time he looked for the bed he found that a row of onlookers blocked his view. The situation became a mystery that he was determined to solve. After the concert, at his request, Mrs. Brown explained that a preteen, who had been severely injured, occupied the bed. The girl was "both mysterious and extraordinary," she said.

"What was the nature of her injury?" Calvin asked.

"That's part of the mystery. At her initial hospitalization, her doctors were unable to determine her illness. She was in an accident in which her parents' car skidded off a steep hill in wintry weather. It plunged over a cliff and ended in a ditch. The police were notified by a driver who saw the car skid off the road. Both her parents were killed and she broke both her arms and legs. They are all mended now that she has been here for almost a year, but she's an amnesiac with complete memory loss."

"I can understand the mystery that surrounds her, but how is she extraordinary?"

"Well there are a number of things that will strike you when you visit her. Go in, this is her room. I can't stay. I have some chores to do."

On entering, Calvin was surprised to see that the room resembled a tiny study rather than a hospital cubicle. There were bookshelves crammed with books— novels, literature, anthologies of poetry and a few on philosophy. "Hello," he said, "I'm Calvin Ahn."

"Yes I know. I've seen you perform. I think you're quite talented."

"Thank you. What shall I call you?"

"Nobody."

"Why should I call you nobody?" Calvin chuckled.

"Well everybody I know has a name and a past. I have neither so clearly I don't exist. Therefore, I must be nobody."

"Matron didn't tell me that you had an acute sense of humor or a sharp wit."

"Did she say horrid things about me?"

"No, she didn't. In fact, she thinks you're an enigma."

"Isn't that another way of saying I'm crackers?"

"No. She thinks that your knowledge is far greater than one would expect from someone your age."

"Since I know nothing of my past and neither my name nor my age, she must have a solid basis on which to form her conclusion, don't you think?"

"She didn't say you used sarcasm and irony in your everyday conversation. But excuse me, I have an appointment and must leave you now. I'd like to come and visit you again if that's okay."

"Are you coming to seduce me with your music and song?"

"If that's what you want, I'll willingly oblige." he said, tongue in cheek.

"No, just come."

He couldn't tell if there was a double entendre in her response.

When Serena heard Calvin complain about the wasted time waiting for the bus and on the rides to and from the campus, she began to scrimp and save secretly to buy a used car for him. She put aside all her tips, stopped taking the bus to work, walking the mile and a half instead. She told herself that she needed the exercise. Not satisfied with their slow growth she further increased her savings with the grocery money she had used to enjoy having breakfasts and lunches at home. For weeks on end she ate only buttered toast for breakfast waiting until dinnertime when she would get a free meal at the restaurant. She lost weight. Yet, still dissatisfied at taking so long to reach her goal, she determined to find a remedy. She was motivated in her conduct by the words of her mother:

"The measure of worthy parents is the lengths to which they will go to seek the welfare of their children." Serena twisted this maxim to include her own belief: The measure of a worthy individual is the length to which he will go to seek the welfare of others.

Serena listened with curiosity whenever the other hostesses at the restaurant talked about the invitations they got from some of their customers. She was shocked to learn that some of her colleagues moonlighted as call girls to put themselves through college, or to help support their children whose fathers had deserted them. Others did it for the excitement, but all did it for the money. They taught her that inviting a response and later a proposition from a diner posed no problem whatever since "men were always on the make" and "so easy to seduce." One hostess expressed the situation somewhat more crudely:

"Their eyes probe into every woman's crotch with their cocks itching to follow." The most inane personal remark was enough to convince a "John" that a hostess had singled him out for special attention.

"I like a man who can hold his liquor," was one of the more common invitations, and one of the more successful. Brassy, also worked well.

"Hey, you look so lonely, if you need someone to take you home, I get off at midnight." Such statements would start a conversation that would eventually provoke a proposition.

When Calvin entered the cubicle she was sitting at her desk near the bed with her back to him. At his greeting:

"Hi Ms. Nobody," he said trying to be humorous, but he saw the sheet of paper on which she had been writing disappear as she swiftly hid it under her pillow. There was an expression of guilt still on her face when she turned around towards him.

"Hello Calvin, you startled me, creeping up on me so stealthily." There was more than a hint of irritation in her voice.

"If that's the way you compliment all your visitors then I'll leave." There was no trace of sarcasm in his voice.

"No, please don't leave. It's just that you caught me off guard." Calvin decided to take the bull by the horns.

"What mischief were you up to? And to whom were you writing?" He enquired boldly.

"I'm not up to mischief but, as you know, I'm nobody writing to everybody."

"I take it that the nobody is you. And since you were writing to everybody, that includes me. So why bother to hide whatever it is?"

"Well if you must know, I was almost struck dumb by the words of the renowned poet / playwright Oscar Wilde."

"What did he say that dumbfounded you?"

"It seemed to me that in part, the words he chose were aimed at my personal situation, and I was analyzing the quotation trying to come to a logical conclusion."

"Come on, he was writing from a past century, way back in time. He couldn't possibly have been referring to you. After all, you weren't even born yet." Despite his words, the child was so taken by the poet's words that she had committed them to memory and quoted them verbatim from his *De Profundis*:

"'Society, as we have constituted it, will have no place for me, has none to offer. But nature, whose sweet rains fall on the unjust and just alike, will have clefts in the rock where I may hide and secret valleys in whose silence I may weep undisturbed. She will hang the night with stars so that I may walk abroad in the darkness without stumbling and send the wind over my footprints so that none may track me to my hurt. She will cleanse me with sweet waters and with bitter herbs make me whole.'" He had joined her in quoting nature's outlook.

"I see that the words have also appealed to you."

"They have, but I'm not sure where you are going with the quotation."

"I'm trying to show that, in part, the sharp contrast the playwright makes between society and nature implies a condemnation of the former by the praise he heaps on the latter."

"Go on," Calvin stated, you've made a good start."

"By implication, Wilde castigates society for its cruel criticism of those like him who indulge in 'the love that dares not speak its name,' forcing him to suffer the pain of alienation. Instead of shunning unfortunates like him for his 'different brand' of love, Wilde celebrates the virtues of nature for coming to his rescue. He harnesses the powers at her command: she will offer him *clefts in the rocks* and *secret valleys* permitting him to weep in *undisturbed silence*. Her *stars* will light his footsteps through the *darkness* without calamity, and her *winds* will conceal his *footprints* to hide him from his pursuers and detractors. Nature will anoint his wounds with the *bitter herbs* of her medication and finally restore him to wholeness through her charity and forgiveness.

"Well Serena, why the hangdog look and the frown. What's happened to upset you?" The doctor's manner and tone were, she noticed, very different from the impertinent and malicious attitude he had adopted only a couple of weeks ago. Since then, he had reviewed his behavior. Oblivious of the ugly darkness that had descended upon him and blackened his mood, he had been quick to excuse himself for his evil and unprofessional conduct. It was his wife he thought, as well as his blond patient/lover, who had caused his obnoxious behavior. The suits that both had filed against him had raised the specter of his ruined career. It was this, he wrongly concluded, that had brought out his spite and aggression.

In his mind, his ruined career was the equivalent of his ruined life, and this belief had turned him into a cornered and very dangerous beast. He had attacked and vomited his rage upon the first person who happened to be available. Later, on recognizing that as a professional, his conduct had been nothing short of criminal, a savage sense of guilt and shame had assailed him with an almost paralyzing effect. Remembering his patient's profound distress, he promised himself to do his utmost to make amends, and began by listening carefully to Serena's complaint.

"Doctor, you'll be pleased to hear that I've been practicing my homework assignment over and over and have finally reduced my rating on Stephen to zero. However, despite that, I know that I've been visiting you for years. Since I still have to continue these sessions, I cannot help feeling *sick*, *sick*, *sick* since I'm unable to regain complete control over my feelings or my life. I'm fed up and ashamed of myself for having to lean so heavily on someone else all this time."

The doctor spoke softly and was quick to reply:

"Serena, I'm really surprised to hear you talk like this, especially after the progress you've made."

"That's exactly the point, doctor. I still visit you every week, so I ask myself: what progress have I made?"

The doctor translated Serena's outcry about the years of therapy that rape sometimes inflicts upon its victims, as a plea for reassurance. He knew that rape therapy often becomes so long and tedious a burden to bear alone that its victims need comfort and reassurance from someone they trust.

"Serena, I well remember your first visit when I stated that rape therapy was often a long and demanding process. You were so confused and disoriented your reason and judgment so awry, that you were unable to make the simplest decisions that previously guided you in life. Rape robbed you of your virginity and your innocence; deprived you of the thrill of sexual arousal and the ecstasy of climax. You also experienced other painful losses that prolonged and deepened your trauma.

"In coming to Canada, you lost the love and support of your parents; your home on the farm, and its animals that were so dear to you. A terrible loss was the use of your language and Korea's cultural traditions of which you are so proud. In Canada, you endured continual violations and the punishing marathon of a battered housewife. You then lost your husband and finally, your parents. The accumulation of suffering made you realize that such a life was unacceptable. You issued an ultimatum to your husband that eventually brought you to me.

"The realization that the choice of having intercourse or not was yours alone to make, gave you a vacation from sex that ended the physical and mental torture you experienced in marriage. With your new found freedom, you were then able to dominate and release your anger which in turn permitted you to recover your sanity." He paused to ask even more gently:

"Surely you remember learning that far from disgusting you, your body began to afford you many pleasure-filled sensations?" Serena flushed crimson, fidgeted in her seat, clasping and unclasping her hands. Her fingers too were dancing a jig.

"Serena, releasing your anger and your fears means that you've eliminated the negative feelings that the abuse of both the rapists and your husband inflicted upon you. Today, you are far better able to make decisions that shape your life. You've developed a new awareness. You've organized and begun to run your own Crisis Line and a Women's Rape Rehabilitation Center. Those are not easy tasks, and the reports I've heard are that both are efficiently run and well regarded. Your recognition that there's evil in the world has made you take care to have solidly locked doors, well-lit exits and entrances, and never to be out-of-doors alone at night. Of course, you've lost your innocence, that precious something that was essentially you. But you've mourned its loss and moved on. In doing so, you've slain the former naïve person you were by having recognized a greater need for planning and forethought in a world that can be both treacherous and unforgiving.

"Now, both your parents have passed away and you believe that your leaving Korea contributed to their deaths. Further, your husband's desertion has forced you to find a job to support yourself and your son. Is it so surprising Serena, that after all this anguish and turmoil in your life, you need to take time out to grieve over the profound losses you have sustained?

"Bravo!" Calvin said. Your analysis is both astute and logical. You must have given the quotation a lot of thought."

"True. Now do you see where I'm going with my analogy?"

"I'm not sure, since you began your analysis by stating the words 'in part.'"

"The other part is that I can't help viewing the quotation as pointing directly at my personal situation."

"There are some similarities, I would have to agree."

"Although I have committed no crime, I too have been struck down and, as an outcast, have been made to suffer the aching agony of alienation. Then, there's the trauma from the accident, the loss of both my parents together with the physical, mental and emotional scars the doctors say have damaged my psyche. Then, I don't know if I'll ever recover my memory. Therefore, I have to suppose that like Wilde and other sexual deviants (though no deviant myself) I shall have to wait on nature and her benevolent agents to come to my rescue."

"Well, you surprise me by finally going off the rails after so solid and logical a beginning. Most of what you have said is true. Unfortunately, your conclusion is false."

"How is it false?"

"In Wilde's quotation, society is the cruel aggressor and nature the benevolent angel who rehabilitates society's victims."

"Well, what's different in my final analysis?"

"In your case it is society that has come to your rescue through its brand of technology. Its doctors and nurses have healed the wounds of your limbs and their medications have helped considerably in that process. Social services have created a hospital to house and shelter you and provide you with food and all your other necessities while you recover. Finally, you are a ward of the province that will look after your welfare from this day forward. All of this is yours thanks to society's organization. Therefore society, not nature, is your benefactor. You can have no quarrel with it."

"Oh my God you're right. I stand corrected, Calvin. Thank you for caring and listening to my litany of woes. I feel sure that as with me, you'll use your intelligence and compassion to help solve the problems of others."

The doctor lowered his voice to a whisper.

"What you should remember is that the progress you've made can only have been accomplished by the exercise of exceptional courage, strength, will power and resilience." He sat down. "Serena, you must begin to focus on the gains you've made. You've regained your self-esteem, your self-confidence, re-claimed your dignity and independence." He paused to catch his breath. "Your fluency in your new language, your course in photography, your organization of a shelter for rape survivors, your work as a counselor on a telephone rape 'hot line,' and your visiting the terminally ill at the Hospice are all new begin-nings. Then, there's your re-commitment to serious painting. All these changes in your lifestyle testify to the progress you've made. I repeat they can only have been accomplished by the exercise of exceptional courage, strength, and will power." Serena sat listening quietly.

"Most people believe that human beings are creatures of habit, so in-grained in their routine that nothing can effect a change in their conduct. Ser-ena, you've exploded that belief. Your quest to recapture what you had lost has brought you a new awareness, new knowledge and wisdom. You've silently shed your old bad habits." Serena, you must think more positively. Instead of mourning your losses, you should be celebrating your gains. You're winning the battle. You've used your crises as an opportunity to grow. You've paid for your progress with sweat and blood. You've gone through one of the most ag-onizing processes of change that human beings can undertake. The best tribute I can pay you is to say that despite the many knockout blows that life has dealt you, blows that would have hurled many others to the canvas; you have never thrown in the towel. With courage and resilience, you have come out unde-feated and with your dignity intact. What more can I say?"

His soothing words had showered Serena's mind like the spray from a di-vine fountain. He had performed a minor miracle. Serena's hangdog look and frown had become transformed into a radiant smile.

After Serena had left the doctor's office, he thought about the words courage, willpower and especially resilience, that he had used to describe Serena's re-habilitation. It struck him that she didn't fully understand the exacting nature of the process she had undertaken to achieve her goal. Had she really under-stood the courage, willpower and resilience she had summoned to confront her demons? He didn't think so, but he marveled at the steel backbone she possessed to accomplish such a feat. Faced with his own demons, he wasn't at all sure he had that kind of backbone; that kind of courage, will power or re-silience. It would be so much easier just to bow to his fate and surrender.

Chapter 65

Mom, I find myself in the exact situation that you and Dad warned me about. Stephen has left me and I am alone with your grandson, Calvin. Since I have no one to confide in or turn to for advice, I hope you won't mind listening while I confess my worries to you. After enjoying the pleasures of my body, I find that self-stimulation has its limits. The fact is that my desire for sexual bonding with a male partner has begun to grow, and I firmly believe that reclaiming my sexuality will fulfill a far greater need than sex itself. Mom, can you understand, I want to be loved. While I've been violated over and over, I'm convinced that my heart is still virgin territory. I need to feel that close bond with someone who will love me not for what I can give, or what he can take, but just for myself. I need to give myself freely, unhesitatingly and totally to someone who will be eager to do the same. Can you understand that Mom? I have never been overwhelmed with the kind of warmth generosity and love that would make me feel as though I'm drowning in my own blood. I have never experienced what I have so dearly wished for: someone to put his arms around me to make me feel that together, we are a complete unit; a world unto ourselves. I want to find someone who will hold me gently and tell me how much I mean to him. I want to cling to someone to whose heartbeat I can listen, knowing that I alone am responsible for its acceleration. Mom, I want someone who will make me feel that with just my presence, I have given new meaning to his life. I want someone to just need me, to say pretty things to me, rather than making constant demands on my sexuality? I want someone who will warm my heart, make it sing as it overflows with love. I have been married, I have borne a son, yet I have never been fulfilled. It frustrates and saddens me to realize that my heart is still virgin territory and that life is passing me by. Mom, can you understand what I'm trying to say?

Mom, I have also been anxious to learn whether or not intercourse would bring me the pleasure I hope for rather than the pain I dread. Equally important, I want to learn whether or not I am frigid, whether or not I would be permanently refused the feelings that would awaken me to the elation, the joyous rapture of love. Of course, my decision to terminate my hiatus from sex makes me realize that its resumption will pose its own problems. How is it possible to relax and become aroused while harboring the terror of returning to my earlier traumatized state?

Mom, when my virgin heart became such a burden that I could bear my celibacy no longer, I chose a longtime client-admirer whose many invitations had, until then, fallen on deaf ears. I was attracted to him because of his politeness, his friendly smile and youthful vitality. His high cheekbones set off a square masculine jaw and he bore the porcelain coloration of Asia. Although he had begun graying at the temples, his hair was thick, and his dark brown eyes, warm, intelligent and penetrating. He moved smoothly like an athlete and he spoke excellent English with just the faintest trace of an accent. I first made sure that the coast was clear, then, with the broadest of smiles, and in crimson confusion, I challenged him in my most flirtatious voice:

"I believe that you like the food at this restaurant, but I have a feeling that perhaps you prefer the hostesses!"

To my astonishment, he replied to me in Korean.

"You are quite correct. I do prefer a hostess, especially one who is beautiful. I've been asking her to dine with me for the longest while." He spoke the language with the assurance of the well-bred and educated Korean. And, I noticed, he was also polite, since before speaking, he stood and bowed. I found myself as excited by his language and self-confidence as by his looks and accepted his dinner invitation for the following evening. He arranged to pass for me at six-thirty when I knew that Calvin would be working late at the library. Mom, while getting ready, I changed my dress three times and decided on the colored scarf with tiny green slashes to set off my final choice, the jade green dress I bought recently. I coordinated my purse and shoes with the warm reds in the scarf and was as excited as a school-girl about to receive her first kiss.

When John arrived the next evening, I thanked him for the bouquet of red roses he brought, and after arranging them in a vase I went off with him in his car. He took me to a restaurant where he chose a secluded table. Without being asked, he began telling me about himself. Mom, I hope I'm not boring you.

I was amazed at the simple enjoyment of listening to the flow of words pouring from his lips, and was borne along on the current of familiar sound I hadn't heard in years. As my ears attuned themselves to his accent and speech rhythm, I listened to the beautiful music of Korea's voice that I had missed so much these long years. It brought back those images that have haunted me since my departure–dad replacing me in the kitchen to help you prepare the evening meal or my photographs on its four walls, placed so that wherever you turned you'd have your daughter for company.

Can you imagine how I felt, Mom? I journeyed to Korea, my home and my parents on those exhilarating waves of sound. I imagined that I was also visiting my farm, my pigeons, my colt, my riverbank and my mountain cave. I wanted to reminisce at those places where I had dreamed so often of the future and what it might hold. I found that listening to my own language was like hearing waves of music lapping gently against my heart. I never knew that mere sound could carry me away on such a magical carpet of pleasure. John's words filled me with such joy that my eyes began to glisten and finally overflowed. When I'd had a chance to explain, John understood and sympathized. He too had had a similar experience during his early years in Canada.

"I am a businessman whose modest success has allowed me to retire early," John told me.

"What business were you in?" I asked.

"I had a small chain of jewelry stores."

"But if they were successful, why did you retire?"

"Unfortunately, my wife died of cancer even before she had children, and I thought that vacationing in the city where I had graduated would turn my thoughts back into an enjoyable past instead of dwelling on a morbid present."

"I suppose you believed that doing so would help you overcome your grief? Did it?"

"It's too soon to decide. However, now that you know a bit about me, why don't you tell me about yourself?" Serena couldn't prevent herself from pouring out the homesickness she felt or the guilt that plagued her about leaving Korea. She also confessed that her departure was partly responsible for the death of her parents. The confession again brought tears to her eyes.

"All young people are anxious to leave the nest and to try their wings. You went further by journeying to a foreign country, so you've shown tremendous courage." While he was being honest, she knew he was also trying to comfort her. When able to control her emotions, she replied:

"I have a son, Calvin, who has just finished writing his finals at U-Vic."

"Having a son, means you're probably married. By the way, U-Vic's my 'Alma Mater. It's where I trained in Business Administration. So tell me more about yourself."

"Why don't we save that part of my story for another time?" I replied. Mom, the truth was that I didn't want to mention my rape or my marital difficulties, so early in my relationship with John. After a moment's silence on my part, he explained that he had become addicted to salmon fishing during the summers of his university years when he served as a deck-hand to help pay his university fees. He was looking forward to catching some of his favorite fish in the next couple of weeks when the run of Coho, Sockeye and Chinook salmon would be at its height. He didn't force himself on me and his gentle yet enthusiastic manner of speaking made me feel comfortable to be with him. I then heard myself telling him about my life on the farm, about Will, and even about my racing pigeons. I ended by telling him that I was a serious painter but that I had been frustrated for a long time. After accumulating all the details necessary to begin an eagle on the hunt, for some reason that I couldn't understand, I was unable to put a single brush stroke on my canvas. Mom, the inability to paint my eagle is exactly like my inability to make love. Both are heartbreaking Mom, but do you think they might be related? Could love be an ingredient that is essential for completing any task with excellence? Thinking about their possible relationship is tearing me apart, Mom! If I can't paint I might as well die.

John sympathized with me, seeming very interested and asking many questions about my painting, my colt, and even more about my pigeons. For the first time in Canada, I was able to talk with nostalgia about my home and parents, my favorite spot by the river, the mountain cave and my painting. I became so relaxed talking my own language and listening to it that I felt as though I had known John for a lifetime. After he took me home, I was astonished at having enjoyed myself so much that I could hardly remember the name of the restaurant or what I had eaten. Thanks for listening Mom. I can't wait to go out with him again, though he hasn't called in the last few days as promised. Do you think he didn't enjoy my company or that he'll call again?

John had gone to Sooke where he had rented a cabin and hired a boat for a few days at the 'Sunny shores Marina' to fish Becher Bay. He had risen before sunrise with the dew still sparkling on the marina's lawn. The tide was low so the ocean had receded exposing the naked shore. Its potent stench struck him forcibly. The odor was overpowering, as fresh as an unwashed woman, and as foul. Early morning mist hung over the land and had crept upwards encircling the dark green mountains sheltering the village of Sooke. The filtering mist softened the light from the rising sun turning it into liquid gold.

On mornings like this, the salt-saturated atmosphere made John feel alive to all the small nuances of nature. It was the time of day that he enjoyed most since the still silent world encouraged him to let his mind wander lingering upon his innermost thoughts. As he gazed out at the Juan de Fuca Straights before him, he mused about the nature of the sea, with whom he had fallen in love, during those summers he had spent as a deck-hand aboard a commercial trawler. Fishing allowed him to earn a tidy sum of money and taught him to become familiar with the moods of the ocean.

He thought that no one who hadn't made a living off the sea really knew her contrasting moods. Today she was as flat and transparent as a pane of glass, giving the observer a false impression of her purity, her innocence and her calm. Tomorrow, her waves would be pounding against the shoreline and crashing against the rocky outcrops with such aggression that no one would remember her calm and innocent yesterday. At another time her vastness could make him feel so alone, insignificant and abandoned that tears would come to his eyes. Many, he thought, saw the ocean as being always at rest, its quiescent mass dispatching tiny wavelets to caress the shoreline. Then, with an impulsive wind, it could also give the impression of frivolity by playfully lifting her frothy skirts above her knees, and like a capricious woman, exposing the white lace of her underwear for the entire world to see.

As the tide slowed towards the full John set out in his rented boat with two down-riggers, one on either gunwale. A ten-pound lead ball hung from the end of each down-rigger's steel cable clipped to the line on the rod. The lowered cables would take each line into the depths with its anchovy-baited hook trolled behind the boat. John sank one lure to about eighty feet and the other to about a hundred. He then began a slow troll following the pattern of a figure eight on either side of the rocky outcrop nicknamed "The Head." When a fish struck either bait, the line on the rod would become unclipped and the angler would be able to play a fish free of the downrigger.

After about half an hour, one rod tip suddenly went crazy. It kept jerking up and down in its holder and bending almost double as line hissed from the reel. John quickly grabbed the rod out of its holder, before it could snap in two. He quickly loosened the drag on the reel to lessen the tension on the hook. The slackened line would permit the fish to continue making long runs, darting frantically this way and that or lunging again and again into the depths without dislodging the hook. The rod tip kept bowing and buckling, curving and flexing up and down. John had to tighten his grip and hang on as the rod throbbed and pulsated in his fingers, shuddering through his wrist and forearms and then vibrating up to his elbows. His hope that the fish would exhaust itself was short-lived as he realized it was a strong, 'silver-bright' salmon that had just come straight from the open Pacific Ocean. It kept bending and rocking the rod as it surged through the depths dragging out yards and yards of line. Finally, when there was not much line left on the reel, and John thought he would lose the fish; its runs grew somewhat less spirited as it began to exhaust itself and shorten the tug-of-war. Then suddenly, John realized that the fight wasn't done yet. The fish refused to give up the life-and-death struggle diving deeply under the boat or racing in short bursts across the surface dragging the line that cut through the water behind it. Since the fish had finally come to the surface John believed for the second time that the fight was nearing its end. But instead of weakening, the fish seemed to grow stronger with each successive effort. It kept tugging at the line and making frantic runs again and again. John could feel the power generated by each lunge as the fish kept shaking its head trying to throw the hook. Each head-shake was transferred up through the line and rod to John's hands and threatened to rip the quivering rod from his grip. Suddenly, the line went slack and the rod straightened. "Good Christ, I've lost the fish," John shouted aloud. He felt frustrated at losing the battle and was about to put the rod back in its holder when its tip again went crazy and he had to grab the rod and grip it tightly. The line sang a heart-hammering song of excitement as it sizzled from the reel and the rod kept bending, flexing and jerking. This fish has to be a monster, John thought, I don't want to lose it. I should at least see it before it disappears. Just then, the salmon shot through the surface into the air wildly twisting and toppling head over tail all the while shaking its head. It kept thrashing wildly as it fell back into the sea splashing the surface with its tail and sending gallons of water skyward in all directions. John saw it was indeed a huge fish. The hook was deeply embedded in its jaw and blood-stained water dripped from its gills. For an instant, its dark green head and silver-bright flanks flashed in the morning sunlight before it disappeared. It dived deeply, still crazily shaking its head trying repeatedly to free itself from its imprisonment on the hook. As it ripped through the water dragging out more line, John tightened the drag then began lifting his rod tip high in the air then lowering it while reeling desperately to win back the line he had lost. The rod tip kept bowing and the rod itself bending in protest as John kept winding in more and more line and the salmon's maddened rushes grew less and less frantic. Finally, the fish again rose to the surface, made a few half-hearted lunges before slowing down and turning on its side to float upward completely exhausted. John only had to net the fish to end his thrilling battle. His adventure ended after he caught his limit, two Coho and two Chinook salmon. With heart pounding violently, John found the tug-of-war between man and fish every bit as thrilling as it ever had been. Afterwards, he phoned Serena, explained where he was and invited her to join him. When she heard his voice her heart began leaping in her bosom like a Masai warrior on the Serengeti plains.

"Thanks for the invitation. You sound so excited describing what you're doing that I'd really love to be with you. But, I have to decline as there's so much I have to do here."

"I'm looking forward to being with you again, as I enjoyed our last outing together."

"I had a very enjoyable time too, and am so pleased that you called. When do you plan to return to Victoria?"

"I'll be back in a couple of days. Have you made any headway with that eagle of yours?"

"You know, I've set up my easel, primed my brushes and got my palette ready trying to get it started again and again, but I can't seem to come to grips with it. Maddeningly, it continues to elude me. I really can't understand it. This has never happened before."

John heard the bitterness in her voice.

Calvin heard all about John from Serena who explained that he was an educated and good-looking Korean friend whom she had met at the restaurant. Calvin was pleased that his mother had finally found someone to keep her company, a friend who would help to dispel the loneliness of her life. Now, he hoped that she would be happier than she had been. Perhaps, John too would join them in visiting the terminally-ill patients. He was so glad to have finally bridged the divide between himself and his mother.

"Hello."

"Hello, is this Calvin Ahn?"

"Yes."

"Hi Calvin, my name is John, a friend of your mom."

"Yes, she spoke to me about you."

"Can you tell me when she will be away from home for a few hours?" Calvin thought it a strange question, but answered since his mother had said he was a friend.

"Well, she leaves here at about 9 A.M. during the day, to organize a crisis center for rape survivors. Afterwards, she visits terminally ill AIDS, cancer and other patients at the Victoria Hospice, before going to the restaurant to begin her evening shift."

"Thanks Calvin, I'll see you tomorrow after she leaves."

True to his word, John arrived the next day with a couple of workmen and materials after Serena had left home. He set them to work with instructions to call him when they were done. They did, and he arrived to inspect their work and to pay them. When Serena returned home she was amazed at what she saw. Standing in her back yard was a newly built loft with three pairs of homing pigeons.

"Hello, John Yuk See here."

"Hello John, this is Serena. I'm calling to thank you for the delightful surprise of your pigeon loft and the birds. I'm overwhelmed by your thoughtfulness and generosity."

"I'm so glad you approve. The birds are the offspring from thoroughbred racing parents. They're to help you get over your recent bereavement and homesickness. I know how hard both can hit."

"I'll have to think of something to return your kind gesture. It isn't every day that I receive such thoughtful gifts." After hanging up, she couldn't decide how far she should go. On one level, it seemed to be the perfect opportunity to offer the gift of herself? However, she wasn't at all sure that she wanted to go that far. After giving it much thought, she finally decided that she'd continue to date John and see where the relationship led. Although sexually excited by his company, she finally decided that she was no longer in a hurry to go to bed with anyone.

John took her by ferry to Vancouver, where, at the Queen Elizabeth Theater, "The Phantom of the Opera" was being performed. The Phantom, an especially gifted musician, was so terribly disfigured that unable to face society, he hid himself, living in the sewers beneath the Paris Opera House. He fell in love with the singing of a girl, Christine, whom he kidnapped, taking the terrified girl into his labyrinthine lair. There, he taught his "angel of beauty" to sing praises to the forces of darkness. Both John and Serena were overwhelmed by the dark frisson of evil that was the dominant theme of both the music and lyrics. John felt deep compassion for an exceptionally talented man who was so damaged in appearance that he felt obliged to take refuge in the isolation of the sewers under the theater. Worse, John considered it a scathing indictment of the society that had forced the disfigured Phantom to live in abandonment. Like so many other isolated outcasts, he took his revenge on society. In his deep despair, he turned his back on the Almighty and enlisted instead the aid of the Prince of darkness.

Serena was enchanted by the romantic notion that anyone could love so deeply that he would kidnap his beloved against her will. She teased John with the suggestion that any man who became so besotted by a woman that he felt forced to kidnap her, was demented anyway. John pointed out that there were certain women who had such a devastating effect on men that it would make them crazy enough to possess such women. Just as he had expected, Serena was both delighted and scandalized at the viewpoint and blushed crimson at the veiled compliment.

They attended Victoria's Annual Jazz Festival where they were entertained by some of the great musicians of the twenty-first century. John criticized the way some musicians suddenly abandoned the well-established path of a traditional melody to wander aimlessly into a 'no man's land.' He considered that their 'interlude' clashed with and destroyed the beautifully ordered pattern of the music. Musicians, he felt, should guard against veering off into 'uncharted territory,' since their 'insertions' forced them to stumble back gracelessly to resume the well-designed pattern of the melody. He couldn't believe "that such idiots didn't hear the way their egotistic input savaged the beautifully ordered composition!"

Serena argued heatedly that "leaving the traditional pattern" was the whole point of the exercise. It allowed musicians to create and introduce, often on the spur of the moment, their own individual composition that acted as a brilliant counterpoint to the melody. While she considered that each musical deviation was "an innovative showcasing of individuality," he accused the musicians of "immodestly trumpeting their ego."

It seemed inevitable for John and Serena to have heated discussions about everything they saw and heard. More often than not, they disagreed with each other, each valiantly defending the view he or she espoused, taking pleasure in opposing the other's opinion, just for the hell of it. Since both expressed a point of view that the other found novel, each considered the exchanges clever, and therefore their relationship, stimulating.

Being a man of the world, John recognized Serena's reluctance to let him get too close. Since she hadn't let him kiss her, he was experienced enough to realize that some incident in her past had made her ultra cautious. He determined not to frighten her away by moving too fast and forcing himself on her. Since he missed having his wife around and found Serena so exciting to be with, he continued to date her every chance he got. Serena too was delighted with his company and companionship without having to worry about his sexual advances.

Serena could not have known it, but the repeated violations she had experienced had ruptured something vital inside her. Not only had they defiled her, but the constant battering she received from the rapists and the man she loved had in some way trampled upon and obliterated her capacity to love. Evidently, some barrier or impediment had blocked the channels, obstructing those pathways through which the passion of love flows to and from the heart. She couldn't be sure, but in some inexplicable way, the repeated violations had polluted her essence, preventing her from the enjoyment of sexual bonding, thus making her unable to love. In thinking more deeply about her condition she realized that her ideas, while appearing relevant, were far too scattered. She needed to impose a unity upon them and decided that could only be done by somehow linking love with creativity. As she thought of the problem, the words of Lisa from the hospice came back to her: "God is love, so a sin against love is a sin against God." But Serena thought, God is also the Creator, so that love and creativity are inextricably linked. While that is true on the immortal level she would then check to see if it were also true on the human level.

Love, she began, is a total giving of the self. The sexual act is the purest form of love since in coupling both participants give themselves to each other without reservation. Since the end result of the love act of ten leads to creation, then, on the human level love and creativity are also inextricably bound. It follows then that a violation of love is also a violation of creativity. Serena felt she was now closer to the truth. Her repeated defilement in the act of love had indeed destroyed something vital inside her. The corruption, in some way, blocked the creative process from taking place thereby impeding her ability to paint, not merely with her brush, but also from her heart. She had been trying for the longest while to paint a bald eagle and her incapacity frustrated every effort she made to do so. The truth suddenly dawned upon her. Love was an essential ingredient in the creative process.

Wow! Her conscience interrupted: it seems to me that you've been comparing yourself with God. Wouldn't that be the height of egotism and arrogance?

Not at all! I've been merely examining the possibilities and trying to unearth what exactly might be responsible for my inability to paint the eagle. But your thoughts seem to make more sense than mine. The 'logic' that I've conjured up might well be a gross and dangerous overreaching on my part.

On analyzing and assessing the canvases she had completed after her violations, it depressed Serena to realize that although well done, they were inferior to her earlier work, failing to portray exactly the end result she had envisaged. They all lacked the inspiration and creativity; the vigorous life force that had informed her earlier work. The latter displayed qualities that were difficult to define. It was as though an enchanted spell had been cast upon her earlier subjects and injected them with a special radiance, a loving glow.

One night, as John took Serena home, he embraced her just as she was about to slip inside the front door, and turned her towards him. He kissed her lightly on her forehead, then on her cheek and finally, full on her mouth. The last kiss was especially passionate and demanding. It lingered smoldering on her lips, forcing her to feel his need. It was a thrilling moment for both of them. Serena, still not sure of what she wanted, stammered her thanks for a wonderful evening and quickly slipped into the safety of her home. Once inside, she remonstrated with herself, accusing herself of being a muddle-headed idiot who couldn't decide what she wanted. Even when she knew, she was too cowardly to take the opportunity when it was offered. Next, she blamed the muddle-headed idiot for being too prone to criticize her every action. She then consoled herself with the thought that the idiot was doing the right thing though she admitted that she didn't know what the right thing was. Finally, she decided that her mind was too full of contradictions for her to arrive at any logical conclusion. There, she let the matter rest.

In dating John, she disapproved of their outings since technically she was still Stephen's wife. Then, her motives to be with John were selfish, since she had dated him mainly to test the level of her sexual recovery. On reviewing her conduct, she first saw herself as an unfaithful wife, then as a shameless mother. Finally, she was revolted at the spectacle of herself as a depraved woman eager to whore herself. She wandered around her home, hugging herself, plagued by guilt. In a daze, she convinced herself that nothing   she did could save her from the beckoning arms of Satan and the terrors of hell. Yet, such was her delight in John's company that she continued, what she considered, her "steep descent into immorality." Her twin fingers were whirling like dervishes.

In striving to refrain from having intercourse with John, she put up a desperate fight. Whenever his kisses aroused her and she began to feel carried away, she exerted her considerable willpower to fight against her mounting desire. For quite some time she succeeded, but then, at last passion and need overwhelmed her. Ironically, it was she who had begun the process that encouraged John to make his move.

Aware of the invisible barrier that Serena had erected against intercourse with him, John didn't press his suit. Instead, he enjoyed her kisses, waiting patiently until she was ready. Then, one evening on returning from an outing with him, she was going up the concrete walkway to her front door when she slipped, fell and must have hurt herself, for she stayed where she was, apparently in pain or shock.

John rushed to help her up, deep concern on his face, as he lifted her to her feet.

"Are you hurt?" He asked.

"No," she replied embracing John tightly for support, "but I need a moment to catch my breath."

"What happened?" He asked supporting her in his arms.

"I don't know," she whispered moving her lips a breath away from his mouth. "I must have stepped on a pebble."

"You must be more careful," he said. "You must know I don't want anything to happen to you."

"No, I didn't..." She began... Suddenly John's mouth was clamped against hers and she thanked God for that non-existent pebble. Previously, whenever John tried to kiss her, her breath would clog in her throat, her heart would begin to hammer against her ribs and she would always resist before finally giving in. But this time, such was her enjoyment of the hot kisses John was planting on her mouth that she put up no resistance whatever. Instead, she eagerly returned his kisses.

"I've been dying to taste your kisses for ages," she told him, and John needed no further encouragement. He lifted her in his arms showering kisses on her face and neck while taking her inside to her bed. There, he undressed her, gazing lovingly at her nakedness. He told her how beautiful she was, punctuating his words with kisses and caresses on her cheeks, neck and shoulders. The slow erotic swirl of John's tongue caressed one dark brown nipple that stood erect while his fingers teased the other. Serena's body smoldered with the heated shockwaves of passion rocketing through it. As her breathing quickened and her body tensed, she uttered a low moan that testified to the sweetness of his touch and the skill of his technique. Moments later she felt the butterfly kisses assaulting her navel and the slow descent of his mouth towards the apex of her thighs where they stopped abruptly at the springy bush nestled there. Her whole body began twisting in the throes of expectancy for his next move. Then, as he did nothing but inhale the heady perfume of her femininity, she couldn't stop herself from pressing his head down to maneuver his mouth into the cradle of her thighs. While his fingers toyed with her nipples now gently, now firmly, his tongue delved into the secret well of her womanhood alternately massaging its folds then sucking at its juices. He then turned his attention to her clitoris and began stroking it gently then firmly with the tip of his tongue. Her heart pounded against her ribs. Her blood rushed crazily through its vessels as wave after wave of passion swept through her. Her back arched and a series of blinding spasms rocked through her body. Still not satisfied, she wanted more and he climbed astride her coming face to face. When his mouth claimed one nipple and his fingers another, her legs spread themselves wide as if by magic. Her fingers then clasped his erection and guided it directly into the very heart of her secret center. It slid in like a well-oiled dagger into its sheath.

Before marriage, she had tried to anticipate how she would feel during foreplay, but what she had imagined could never compare with the convulsive tremors of excitement that had her shuddering with passion and delight. She felt like a cello string too tightly strung as the heat of arousal thrummed through her veins and arteries. All thought and reason fled as she was locked against John in the tumultuous rhythm of passionate exchange. Only then did she experience the powerful bond of intimacy that sexual union brought. John's ardor increased to fever pitch, and suddenly, Serena's body slipped from her control. Without her permission, her fingernails dug into John's hips, dragging him closer. Her body began writhing, squirming and bucking, ablaze with sensations that she had never known. It was then that John heard the soft animal sounds escaping from her throat, a moment before her pelvic muscles contracted tightly around his member. He uttered a series of deep groans and his thrusting accelerated as the couple continued their erotic dance. "Wait for me, darling," John whispered. She did and in a moment they erupted in the delightful agony of climax. He poured himself into her, and a ragged shriek marked the end of her spasm. She savaged John's mouth with kisses of pure joy for the wild ride he had given her before they both collapsed exhausted in the glorious afterglow of sex.

During their intimacy, each time her passion seemed to flag and John guessed she was being distracted by some past memory he kissed her lips, caressed her body and talked to her. Keeping her attention firmly focused upon him, he made her aware that it was John, who was making love to her in the present, and so succeeded to block out any of her demons from the past. Suddenly she began to cry.

"Was I so incompetent that you shed tears of frustration?" John asked gently.

"No, no! Not at all! I'm sorry," she replied through tears and confusion. Yet, her sobbing increased, followed by a series of loud moans. John became thoroughly alarmed as he tried to comfort her. He pleaded with her to calm down, to tell him what was wrong. When the emotional storm passed, she was surprised to hear herself confessing to John the most intimate details of her rape, her disastrous marriage, Stephen's abandonment and her feelings of guilt whenever she was in John's company.

"My failure to forgive my mother," she then told him, "coupled with the fact that I was in part to blame for the death of my parents, made me aware that I was a wicked woman who has no right to such happiness." Then, blushing in confusion, she explained that intimacy with him was the first she had ever thoroughly enjoyed. She further confessed that her emotional outburst was motivated by a mixture of joy and shame. In the past, she had been an innocent victim, attacked and overcome by superior strength and numbers. Tonight, the fact that she had initiated the seduction, made her feel guilty. She tried to excuse her confusion and tears by saying that she couldn't help how she felt; she just couldn't.

Deeply moved by Serena's chain of misfortunes, her overwhelming and irrational feelings of guilt, and certainly as much by his delight in their lovemaking, John soothed her with kisses and caresses. He pointed out how sad and lonely he had been since the passing of his wife, and how much he had enjoyed being with her. He insisted on emphasizing the joy she had brought into his life. Above all, he confessed, it was she who had helped him to overcome his grief. Finally, he stated what she had been longing to hear.

"Darling Serena, you're a pretty extraordinary person, you know?" The warmth of his words suffused her body and he caressed her face as she cuddled closer to him. Holding her tightly, he continued: "I've fallen in love with you, and it seems evident that you've fallen in love with me. Otherwise," he pointed out with reason, "you would never have given yourself to me with such passionate abandonment." His mention of her enthusiasm made her blush, but, as John took care to hug, kiss and caress her while explaining his feelings and thoughts, she beamed with secret pleasure. After he whispered his logic and tender endearments into her ear, they soon found their way into her heart, and his expressions of love brought about an outpouring of her tenderness towards him.

"I do not know if what I felt was love, but the fact is that I experienced a sense of completeness, of being ushered into a new realm beyond that which was purely physical. This astonished me since I never imagined that physical passion could lift me into a state of spiritual ecstasy. How else could I describe the sensation of exaltation, of being pulled beyond my bone, flesh and skin to merge with the world around me in such complete and utter joy? By some miracle, my body and soul seems to have soared into the stratosphere and I felt at peace with the whole wide world around me. Yet, such was my confusion that my feelings warred with each other. On the one hand, I was like a bomb ready to explode. On the other, I felt as pure and chaste as though I had received a benediction." Returning to the memories of her childhood to show the extent of her love for John, she stretched her arms on either side of her body as far as she could reach, in the way she had so often done to show her mother the full extent of her love.

After John left, Serena felt such happiness that she couldn't help but ask herself: Oh John, how did you manage to wrap your heart so completely around mine? How did you manage to crawl into my soul? The thought made her light-headed and so happy that she began humming a tune. She then danced slowly as she selected the paints, brushes and palette to begin painting. She felt sure that the powerful current of love overflowing from John's heart into hers had burst the dam; destroyed the blockage preventing her from painting her eagle. Until the moment of ecstasy that she had experienced in John's arms, she had not fully recovered; had not been completely whole. Having reclaimed her sexuality, she knew that she was not frigid. At last, love had blessed her, flooding her heart with its magic. From that moment, it had ceased to be virgin territory. She was no longer like the 'Tin Man' in "The Wizard of Oz," cursed with the inability to love. Completing the eagle would tell her whether or not she was right in thinking that without love, human beings are incomplete. In the meantime, she couldn't help believing that John's love was the catalyst that had helped to make her whole.

Chapter 66

Before she began painting, she decided to do her household chores while singing softly to herself and even giving way to a dance-step or two as she listened to the music in her heart. Again and again she would suddenly stop, her face flaming in embarrassment whenever she remembered how her hands and body had behaved in such shameless and wanton abandonment. When the music in her heart started, she again began to dance then suddenly stopped. Her face then flushed scarlet when she turned to see Calvin staring at her in amazement. She was convinced that the whole episode with John was stamped on her face. Thank God, Calvin just smiled and said nothing. Evidently, he was glad to see that at last, she was happy.

"What are you doing here Serena?" said the doctor, surprised and ashamed at being caught cleaning out his desk. "I thought we'd already had our last session."

"After the fierceness with which you attacked me on that one previous occasion, I've though a great deal about your conduct," she replied. The doctor didn't respond. "Since then, I've tried to determine what motivated you into being so aggressive, so vicious. I could think of nothing I had done or said that could have made you treat me with such cruelty, not after the way you had been so helpful in the past." The doctor again stared at Serena without comment.

"I finally gave up trying to understand your behavior until I heard about your trouble. Only then did the penny drop. I realized then that you must have condemned me as just another one of those vicious wives constantly at war with their husbands. Since I happened to be present, you took the opportunity to teach me a lesson."

Every so often while Serena began preparing her canvas, thoughts of her delightful and erotic intimacy with John kept stealing into her mind. A smile would form on her lips and she would become enchantingly distracted. As she used her brush to transfer her penciled sketches and photographs to canvas, one thing became immediately noticeable about the figures she painted. Her subjects were not fettered with the sense of panic or frustration that had haunted the eyes and appearance of the captive animals she had painted after her violations in Korea and Canada. In contrast, her subjects were free, wild and alert, since she was able once more to capture and convey the vitality of creatures that were exuberant and intensely alive. John's love had filled her heart and it was no longer virgin. She was finally whole and able to imbue her painting with the same delightful radiance evident in her best work. She couldn't help believing it was the taint of evil that had robbed her of the creative process.

The doctor sat at his desk for the last time brooding over his past mistakes. As a young man, he had been one of those idealists who regarded infidelity between marriage partners as a cardinal sin, one of the worst forms of betrayal. At that time, the powerful surge of passion that could inflame the body, confound reason and short-circuit the brain had been unknown to him. His own affair had given him a different take on the subject. It had taught him that when passion erupts, it often takes the form of a tidal wave that few barriers can contain. He recognized that like him, many highly placed dignitaries and officials had come to grief through the overwhelming sweep that passion exerts over reason. The words of Hamlet came to mind: "Give me that man that is not passion's slave."

With Calvin's birthday only a week away, Serena took the day off to surprise her son with the gift of a used car that she was able to buy with her savings. She planned to spend a day with him, taking the ferry from the island to Vancouver and visiting the Stanley Park Zoo and Aquarium. Perhaps they would go to a movie or do wherever he wanted. When she told him there was a surprise waiting for him with his lunch, she was as excited at seeing his reaction as a teenager on her first date. She had ordered his favorite pizza, bought him an iced cake with twenty-two candles and set the table carefully. There was a new lace tablecloth, candles, a chilled bottle of champagne and a small floral bouquet. After parking the car next door, Serena placed the key in a little blue envelope with a tiny bow at Calvin's place setting.

"Congratulations on your insightful assessment," the doctor said dryly. "Okay Serena, so you've heard about my trouble and you've come to gloat."

"No, no! I heard you're leaving, and if so, I've come to tell you a few things in case I don't see you again." After the way he had treated her, the words she used sounded ominous. He braced himself for a verbal attack.

"First," she said, "I'll really miss you. You've been my brilliant counselor, my mentor, and although you may not know it, one of my dearest friends. I've come to thank you for your counseling, and even more, for babysitting me over the years. I'm here also to tell you how sorry I am to learn of your trouble." Tears sprang to the doctor's eyes but with an effort he controlled his emotions.

"Well thank you Serena. That's very kind of you." He seemed relieved that he had just escaped a well-deserved tongue-lashing. "And how are things going with you? Have you managed to recapture your lost loves?" She noticed that his voice was neutral carrying no hint of sarcasm.

"That's a question I've thought about a lot," she replied. "When I first came to Canada, my eyes were tightly shut and my mind focused solely on what I'd left behind."

"That's quite normal for those who have left behind the people and things that are familiar and beloved."

"Very true, Doctor! I could only dwell on the fact that I'd lost contact with my parents, my country, my language and culture. Then, my husband's violence and my failing marriage drove me to obsess on my losses, making me wallow in self-pity."

"I remember your constant complaint that your husband's conduct, your grief and homesickness had made your presence in Canada a life of anguish."

"But then you opened my eyes, Doctor. You are the person who made me realize that I should focus on my gains. Once I began to consider what you taught me, the losses on which I had been focusing were no longer as glaring and became less and less so."

"You no longer miss Korea and all that it meant to you?" The doctor asked with surprise.

"Yes and no. Once I learned of the loss of my family there, I had no reason to return. And since I've started our clinic for assaulted women here, that and my Hospice visits take up most of my time."

"I've heard very good reports of your clinic."

"I'm pleased to hear that. As I was saying, on meeting some of my countrymen from the Victoria Inter Cultural Association, I've made some very close friends. We visit and cook Korean and Canadian dishes for each other, go to movies together, and pack quantities of food to picnic sites. While we Bar-B-Q Canadian style, their kids play with each other and we adults continue our endless discussions about the love-hate relationship we have with Korea and Canada."

"Love-hate relationship? I don't understand. Explain that to me."

"We love to go back to Korea but hate to leave Canada. We never stop arguing heatedly about the advantages and disadvantages of life here."

"So finally, you're actually beginning to think of Canada as home?" The doctor asked in amazement.

"You know, doctor, Canada has been an extraordinarily generous host to all of us. No other country that we know of goes so far out of its way to help its 'new citizens.' We can't begin to count the blessings, directly or indirectly, that Canada has given us." After a pause, she said: "But enough about me. What about you doctor, how will *you* manage?"

"Before we get into that, tell me about your farm, its animals, and the whole environment that you identified with so strongly?"

"Oh, I'll miss them Doctor, but only a blind person could fail to notice that BC is one of the most prolific wildlife reserves that exists anywhere. It is the very epitome of what the environment is all about. I've come to realize that the term, "supernatural" so often used to describe BC, is not hype. It is reality itself. That's why people come here in droves to experience eco-tourism in all its richness and diversity. Those who haven't yet visited have no idea what they're missing."

"You've always managed to surprise me, Serena. I'm so pleased to learn that you've re-entered the mainstream of life becoming intensely involved all over again."

"Yes, and I owe it all to you."

"Ah! Thank you Serena, for your kindness, but that's not at all true. You are the one who did all the hard work. You are the one who struggled and fought throughout those tough years to accomplish an almost total 'make over' of yourself and your character. That's not at all easy, Serena. In fact, it's so difficult that few people accomplish it!"

"But Doctor, we keep getting off the point. My visit is really about you. What will you do now?"

"I haven't yet decided," he paused as though making a decision, then whispered: "You know, my women and my peers have stripped me of everything." His voice broke, and tears sprang to his eyes as he struggled to control his emotions. "And," he continued after a moment, "When in your hour of need you turn to those you've loved and helped, it's heartbreaking to find that they've all abandoned you. Serena," he said, "when you are in need and become fortunate enough to be the beneficiary of someone's generosity, you owe that benefactor a huge debt. This is especially true when that benefactor has extended many acts of kindness to you. Any refusal on your part to respond with equal kindness would be the equivalent of outrageous ingratitude. That's why I consider that ingratitude ranks with pride as one of the most deadly sins." He paused for a moment, seeming to concentrate. He then changed the subject.

"Serena, do you know what it feels like to be completely alone, ostracized by everyone? Your abandonment, because of a serious transgression, forces you to obsess on your corruption. Your shame and humiliation becomes so overwhelming that you lose all hope of ever feeling clean again. You begin to hate yourself and feel unfit for the company of your friends. Yet, you're dying inside to be surrounded by those same friends you've loved and lost. Every moment of your life is consumed with self-loathing. You've become a lost wayfarer, and life an ache too painful to endure. There's darkness; darkness and emptiness all around." Shamefully, he wiped the tears from his eyes.

"Oh, I too have tasted the bitter gall of abandonment," Serena replied, tears stinging her eyes as she saw the evident distress of the doctor and recalled the memory of her own experience. She remembered her own wretched heartache at the betrayal of those close to her, and her compassion went out to him. "If you'd like, you can come and stay with Calvin and me. We have a free bedroom in our apartment that you can have for as long as you like. As I said, you've done so much for me that I consider you my dearest friend in Canada."

"Thank you so much Serena, but I've made other arrangements. You know," he said turning philosophic, "it occurs to me that when you behave dishonorably, life has a way of turning viciously upon you. But we humans are so frail and scarred with imperfection, so easily led astray by our passion, that I believe we all deserve a second chance. Unfortunately, we seldom get one. I believe that if we did, many of us would straighten up and fly right." Serena immediately thought of Mona, Stephen, Lisa, her mother and herself.

The doctor then turned maudlin. His heart was heavy with the sense of defeat at the imminent ruin of his reputation, his career and his life. He added, "as a result of this business, I've begun to feel a numbing cold creeping into both my body and mind. It's as though a kind of darkness has gathered around me, and from time to time I get a whiff of an unearthly odor, as of something putrefying. It makes me feel so dark and empty inside. I don't really know how to describe it. Can you make any sense of that?"

"Oh, I think so, but I'm not sure if what I felt is the same as what you describe," she replied. "You see, just before my assault, an uncanny pall of darkness, similar to what you describe, hung about me and an unworldly scent made me choke. Since then, I've recognized that rape too is a kind of death. It surely kills the person you were. Then, you burn in hell throughout the whole long process of guilt, shame and recovery during the years that follow. But, if you are determined, and lucky enough to get good counseling," she looked at him with a winning smile, "a new person can emerge from the ashes."

"Serena," he said smiling, in spite of the emptiness of despair that had sucked the fight out of him, "are you that phoenix?"

"I hope so, doctor. I sincerely hope so." And she added with a wistful smile. "So what can I do to assist the old friend who steered me so unerringly towards the goal of reclaiming my sexuality?" His face brightened at his patient's words evidently catching their full meaning. He then spoke in the saddest of voices:

"I have a small, secret spot where I'll be going. But, get on with your life, Serena and be happy. You've made an excellent start." His words had the finality of a farewell, and he rose from his chair, as he always did, to signal the end of their meeting.

Serena took the cue, surprised him with a quick hug, a peck on the cheek and left.

A few days later, she was heartbroken to hear the news of his suicide. Regardless of his transgression, he had been a good man, responsible for successfully bringing her out of the darkness and exposing her to the light. There must have been many others like her whom he had helped in the healing process. She felt bound to agree with his statement that "we humans are so frail and scarred with imperfection, so easily led astray by our passions that we all deserve a second chance." Once again Serena thought of Grandma Kim, Mona, and Stephen, her mother and herself.

On the news, she heard the announcer mention the note the doctor had left behind. She read it with the detachment that only stone-hearted newscasters manage successfully:

"You could have given me a second chance," was all it said. Stone-heart explained: "the 'you' in the suicide note referred to his poor wife who had left him because of his infidelity with her best friend." However, Serena interpreted the message as an indictment of society as a whole and of the doctor's women and peers in particular. Thinking of the words he had used at their last meeting, she realized that he had already chosen his "small, secret spot." Poor, poor man! She thought. He had done so much for her that she hung her head in sorrow. How many others would be there with her to mourn his passing? She wondered. She found out where and when he would be buried and took a white rose of forgiveness to rest on his coffin. She and the priest were his only mourners.

Calvin tried to repress his excitement all through his morning translation of Korean history for the professor who had hired him after his final exams. His impatience to see his birthday present made him lose his focus and he was unable to concentrate on his work. Then, as midday approached, he began to experience some difficulty with his sight. His vision became clouded. By the time he had put away the books in the library, it had got worse. When he walked out into brilliant sunshine, there was a veil-like fog over his eyes and he moved in semi-obscurity. He felt as though someone had covered his eyes with a translucent blindfold through which he could barely orient himself. He kept wiping his eyes and shaking his head but the semi-darkness remained stubbornly in place. There was nothing he could do to clear his vision and he thanked God that the bus stop was just across the street. Then, his skin began to crawl, the hair on the back of his neck stood up as a repugnant scent filled his nostrils. The sudden sensation disoriented him and he began to feel that he was not alone. However, since he experienced no pain, he kept hoping that his feelings were some sort of temporary aberration. Although confused and unable to see clearly, he suddenly experienced an impulse to quicken his pace; to rush. He became so excited to see his birthday gift that he raced across the street to the bus stop just as the traffic light began to change. An impatient motorist plowed into him. The collision knocked his legs out from under him and he somersaulted backwards through the air crashing headfirst into the windshield of the car.

In hospital, Serena found Calvin unconscious with both his legs in casts and the upper part of his head wrapped in bandages. The doctor told her that he had lost the sight in both his eyes and his two legs were broken. They had to insert an intra-medullar nail in the tibia with fixation screws in both legs. He also needed additional screws for both medial mallebolar fractures. She asked the doctor to translate the medical jargon into simple English. They had inserted steel pins in the realigned bones to strengthen them while they healed and became fused together. Serena was so overwhelmed by the news that she went into shock and had to be sedated.

On awakening, she found that the nightmare was real. However, the only good news was that Calvin's legs would heal without problems. As for his eyes, only time would tell. Serena had to use her considerable willpower to restrain herself from baring her teeth and shaking a threatening fist at God, but shamefacedly she then considered that blasphemy was beneath her. To suppress the violent urge possessing her to blame someone, she found some solace in cursing Dame Fortune for the fate of her son.

Judy's nursing friends, who kept her informed about new and unusual cases, told her about their most recent patient. He was an only son who had just finished writing his final exams for an honors degree. As it was his birthday, he was rushing home to see the surprise his mom had promised. A car ran him down, broke his legs, blinding him in both eyes. The young man was so traumatized by his condition that although conscious, he refused to speak to his nurse, his doctor, or even his mother, who remained in a state of deep depression consumed with grief and guilt. She was convinced that she was the cause of his accident and sat weeping inconsolably at his bedside.

Intrigued, Judy decided to visit the patient. She saw Calvin's body stiffen as he fought the pain in his legs and head. In his suffering, he looked so helpless and lost that she was drawn to him from the first moment she saw him. Although his eyes were bandaged, she thought his face had to be pleasing, what she could see of it through the shape of the bandages. Like most Orientals, his cheekbones were high, but unlike them, his nose was more prominent than flat, and his nostrils did not flare. The hair protruding from his bandages was curly and black. His skin was baby smooth with the neutral color of porcelain. There was a masculine cast to his features with a hard and stubborn jaw line. What she liked most about him were his lips. They were full and generous, making her smile involuntarily thinking that they invited kisses.

Judy hadn't seen one of her nursing buddies in an opposite cubicle looking quizzically at her while she gazed at Calvin. "I'll never forget what I saw when she first visited the patient," the buddy told a friend. "Her neutral stance suddenly stiffened, the bright expression on her face became sad then what looked like surprise, compassion and affection stamped themselves on her features. Her whole frame reacted as though an electric shock had zapped her body making it stiffen. The change that came over her took me by surprise. I would never have believed that 'no-nonsense Judy Cuchulain' would react in that way to any patient since she's visited and helped any number of male patients here before."

Since Judy had a wealth of experience in dealing with those suffering from vision loss, she knew that it would take some time before Calvin could recover from his nightmare world and begin the long, slow climb back from the darkness. He was evidently in pain and she knew that, like others in his situation, he was feeling completely disoriented and alone. As the pulse at his throat kept up its feeble throbbing, it seemed that his life was hanging by the slenderest thread. Judy's instincts were such that she could almost feel his pain. Her heart quickened and a rush of compassion overwhelmed her. Calvin soon became exhausted from flexing his muscles to fight against the waves of pain that kept sweeping over him. Once the anesthetic had worn off the pain kept growing. He began to twist his body from side to side in an attempt to lessen its intensity. Judy gazed at his body for a long moment in rapt concentration. Suddenly, she felt a change in the rhythm of his pain. It began to subside and his body went limp. He then slid off into merciful sleep.

Serena gave John the news about Calvin when he rang to take her to dinner. He immediately asked if he could visit him with her the next day. Although it was thoughtful and considerate of him, she didn't think it was a good idea, not in Calvin's present state of mind. She thanked John for his concern but decided she would let him know when Calvin was feeling up to having visitors.

When Calvin awoke he found himself in a wintry world devoid of feeling. It was as though a cold blast of Arctic air had frozen his body into a block of ice. Much later, after he emerged from winter's paralysis his anger escalated into a steaming rage directed at the world. He refused to be civil, communicating with neither nurse doctor nor mother. Life had dealt him a resounding blow that had frozen the well of compassion within him and he determined to isolate himself forever.

Calvin's rage gradually relaxed its seizure over mind and body with the passage of time. When this phase was past, he responded to blindness with widespread panic. This shock wave was accompanied by confusion as his mind fought against the terror short-circuiting his brain. Emotion was his sole guide since reason had deserted him. He was incapable of stopping his downward spiral into despair overwhelmed as he was by the darkness and depression that engulfed him. He couldn't help fixating upon what for him was impossible, disoriented by his loss and in a state of complete confusion.

He itemized a list of negatives. He couldn't walk. Movement from one place to another had become a painful process of humiliation. A male nurse had to lift and carry him from his bed to a wheelchair. He visited the toilet by the same process, but he often had an accident on the way and would burn with humiliation. His loss of mobility translated into loss of freedom and worst of all, loss of privacy. He felt ashamed to be treated like a baby and at the mercy of strange hands invading his most private parts. He could no longer see where he was going or the person to whom he was speaking. He couldn't read, watch television, play squash or drive his own car. The simplest pleasures were denied him–gazing at a beautiful sunset or the way dust motes did a slow dance in a shaft of sunlight–the joy of staring at the graceful curves of a beautiful woman and watching in fascination at the fluid sway of her hips as she sashayed along, oblivious of all but the waves she was making.

There were moments, before he was fully awake, when he was unaware of his loss. Pleasant thoughts would assault him momentarily before the realization of his blindness flayed his mind like the lashes from a bullwhip. The fact that his life was in shambles drove him crazy with frustration and self-pity. He yearned for his old life, playing his keyboard or guitar imitating Frank, Paul and Stevie, seeing a great movie, or reading an entertaining novel by Wilbur Smith, Jeffrey Archer, Louis L'amour, Balzac and Bernanos, or the poems of Baudelaire, Shelley, Keats, Wordsworth, Eliot and Longfellow. In his blindness, he felt he had become one of society's outcasts, falling into the pitiful category of the deaf-mute, the paraplegic and the amputee. He was the kind of person that forced others to avert their eyes. Worst of all, he'd have to demean himself, begging strangers for help to do the simplest things. In his mind he had ceased to be human, and gradually, solitude, that savage bitch, began to rake his mind with its infected claws.

Early in his hospitalization, Calvin grieved for his lost sight. He wallowed in self- pity, stunned by the reality of having to live the rest of his life in darkness. His rage and resentment imprisoned him in the solitary world of shadows and silence that made him morose and unreachable. When Judy visited and instantly recognized his attitude she wanted to jerk him away from his self-pity to which he clung like bark to a tree. She believed a bright future awaited him, but she also knew that for him any thoughts of the future would be enveloped in gloom. Trying to reason with him in his present mood would be wasted breath, so she didn't try. She left him still clinging to his self-pity, like a suckling newborn to its mother's breast. He sank into the quicksand of his solitude obsessing on what he had lost.

Chapter 67

Serena like Calvin was in a state of shock. She was traumatized with guilt at the belief that it was she who had caused his calamity. Calvin was asleep when she visited him but there was a pretty young nurse at his bedside who explained:

"Calvin is in the initial stages of shock that follows such accidents. He won't be able to reason normally or communicate with anyone for a while. Once the doctors examine the x-rays of his eyes and pinpoint the problem, you should then go to a library to find out as much as you can about his complication. Your findings will help you to determine the next step you need to take."

Serena thanked the nurse and learnt from the doctor that the cornea in both Calvin's eyes had been damaged. She decided to follow the nurse's advice.

As the days went by and Calvin approached the next phase of his recovery, he realized that his greatest loss, after that of sight, was his independence. He would soon learn as well that, in its initial stages, blindness so blankets the mind of its victims that they find it impossible either to listen to reason or to take advice. Their trauma is so deep that they become convinced that nothing can be done to change their situation; that no advice can help.

Serena found that she couldn't concentrate on the pages that she kept reading over and over at the library. Her mind would constantly betray her, returning again and again to relive the accident through the doctor's words. Over and over, she kept seeing the automobile crashing into Calvin, upending him, sending him spinning head over heels through the air. The final head-first crash into the car's windshield and the crumpled body of her son brought tears to her eyes and prevented her from concentrating on her task. Once she got past this phase, she began blaming herself for not waiting to surprise Calvin *after* he was safely home. However, with time and her determination, she was finally able to focus on the project she set herself.

It took her days to read innumerable books on blindness, to gather from each what information she found relevant, and then to translate her notes into a comprehensible form. From the data she had collected up to that point, two possibilities impressed her most—corneal transplants and microsurgery. Her heart leapt when she learned that the two had been successful in restoring either partial or complete vision to other victims. It was too late for her to visit Calvin, so she called John and suggested that he come over to keep her company so his presence would prevent her from obsessing on her son's accident. He agreed, but brought bad news. He had only a week remaining before his visa expired and he had to return to Korea. Serena was heartbroken.

Calvin heard his curtain being drawn around the bed and the trilling voice:

"Hi Calvin, I'm Judy, giving us some privacy. Hey, can I ask you a very personal question?" She thought it might be possible to jolt him out of his negative attitude by asking him an obscene question.

Calvin responded with a grunt, asking:

"Judy who?" The fact that he answered surprised her.

"Judy Cuchulain. I advised your mother to go to the library and learn everything she could about the damage to your eyes. Her voice slow and musical, her tone breezy, she spoke as if it was the most natural question to ask a complete stranger: "Can you show me your testicles?" She knew the question would rattle him, perhaps even jerking him out of his uncommunicative attitude.

"What?" Calvin sputtered, mortified by the question. Unable to believe the impertinence, he finally retaliated: "You surveying the testicles of all blind male patients?"

"No silly! Some people like to express their views about Oriental male equipment. I only want to see if what they say is true." Judy hoped that he'd continue to talk and remained silent, waiting. Despite his fury and embarrassment, Calvin couldn't understand why his mind was focused on the musical lilt of her voice rather than the insolence of her question. He fought hard to overcome his confusion and assume her breezy attitude.

"I thought you wanted to see my balls?"

"Well, try showing me your balls without exposing your penis," she challenged perkily. In a desperate attempt to mimic her matter-of-fact attitude, he tried humor.

"If I show you mine, you'll have to show me yours!"

"Sure, but I have the advantage. Your eyes are bandaged so you won't see anything." It seemed that her strategy might be working. Instead of the silent treatment he had given everyone else, he was at least bandying words with her.

"You haven't noticed? Now, I see with my hands," Calvin replied thinking that would bring her curiosity to a halt.

"Okay," she said. Not one to refuse a dare, Judy hiked up her skirt thinking: the things I do for those in pain! With one hand on her hip as if posing for the camera, she took Calvin's hand and placed it ever so gently, cupping it against the bikini brief covering her most private part. As Calvin felt the soft, warm flesh beneath, his penis rocketed upward creating a bulge in his IV gown. "I think you must be seeing enough," Judy chuckled.

Calvin had never experienced anything like this before. Flushed with confusion and excitement, he remained dumbstruck.

"Okay, now it's your turn," Judy said in an everyday conversational tone.

"Go ahead," he replied awkwardly. "Lift my gown and look."

"Oh no, you don't get off that easily. That's not what I did."

Calvin managed to mumble as he flushed even redder: "You said you wanted to see."

"Yeah, but then you went and changed the rules," Judy told him. At that point, Calvin's erection was rocklike. He put his hand out, took hers and gently placed it where she wanted. Although the room was silent, he felt as though they could hear his heart pounding in Terra del Fuego. Judy gripped his penis hard, holding it as she giggled cheekily.

"Wow!" Was all she exclaimed.

The contact was too much for Calvin. He came with a series of spurts into her hand and turned purple with confusion.

My, my!" Judy said. "And a virgin too!" After washing her hands, she added: "By the way, I'll be back to see you. Ta da," she said and she was gone.

Not fifteen minutes later, Serena visited, introduced John, and mentioned that there was a back up in the OR. His operation had been postponed and he would have to wait for the doctors to reschedule the procedure. Afterwards, John and Serena kept Calvin's company for a while but John saw that his presence made it awkward for both Calvin and Serena. He excused himself, leaving Serena alone with her son. John explained that he would call her later, the thought of which gladdened her heart.

Calvin's next visitor was Judy. After she announced herself, he made a determined effort to greet her humorously:

"Hey lady, you waltz into my room and shatter my already disordered mind and body. What kind of a woman are you?"

"I like giving people pleasure, and I have a feeling I succeeded." She chuckled.

"What pleasure is there in being shown that you're not only blind, but sexually, less than a man?"

"Blind yes, only temporarily, we hope. But Calvin, being a virgin doesn't make you less than a man. The whole world starts off by being virgin." She realized that her ploy had not worked completely. Although he was talking, he was reproaching himself and therefore, still in self-pity mode.

"At my age, it's nothing to be proud of."

"You're wrong in so many things, but you'll learn with time and therapy."

"Time and therapy won't restore my sight."

"You'd be surprised! I see that I'll have to change your thinking, Calvin."

"You talk like some kind of miracle worker. Who the hell are you?"

"Time enough for that when your mind isn't still scrambling through fog, with loneliness and despair as your only companions. But, you intrigue me. The you that's hurting so badly, and especially the idiot who thinks his life is over?"

"You mean I'm not only your "boy-toy?""

"I'm curious to learn what will become of you if you maintain your present dumb attitude."

"Oh, so your curiosity has taken a new turn? Now, it's centered upon my brain instead of my balls. Even so, your kind of curiosity leaves me cold."

"My kind of curiosity? So, you presume to delve into my mind and reveal what I'm thinking?" Here, she thought, was another opportunity to divert his preoccupation with self-pity that can only end in depression. "Calvin," she said, "I can tell by your attitude that you haven't given any thought about the real meaning of curiosity."

"And you're just the person to enlighten me, right?" Calvin responded with a sarcastic grin.

"Have you ever thought, I mean, really thought about curiosity? Do you even know what the word really means?" If she could take him outside himself, maybe that would help to make him a bit more reasonable. She decided that it couldn't hurt to give it the old college try.

"Well," he said cheekily. "It solved your problem, didn't it?"

"I wish you'd stop trying to be glib." She looked at him, paused, and then began her trite tale that she hoped would jolt him into looking outside himself:

"Cal, curiosity is what set us on the path to progress." Her voice dropped and she smiled as she continued. "Of course, it can get us into trouble when our egos get in the way. As you know, it got Adam and Eve kicked out of Paradise." She paused again before continuing. "But curiosity can more often be a force for good. It coerced us into leaving the cave; introduced us to fire and the wheel; inspired us with knowledge of the sea, ship-building, and the ocean routes that led us to the New World and beyond." While speaking, she kept checking his body language to see if her plan was succeeding, or whether her story sounded to him as hackneyed as it did to her. "It prodded us to the discovery of flight, then to the invention of the computer and finally lifted us to the moon." She paused for effect then whispered: "From the cave to the moon Cal. It was curiosity that took us there."

Calvin remained silent, but when Judy looked for his reaction, she saw that he was struggling not to explode with laughter at her dumb lecture. Blushing with humiliation, she realized that 'the old college try' had succeeded, though not in the way she had forecast. At any rate, she told herself, she had made him laugh and that was a good sign. With an effort, she controlled herself and resumed her normal voice and perky attitude before adding: "I'll be coming to visit you again." He heard the grate of the drawn curtain. Then she was gone.

Doggedly, Serena continued her research, trying to find if there was any other important data she might have missed. Yet, she couldn't keep her mind from dwelling on Calvin's accident. She had been relieved to learn from his doctor that the broken bones in his legs were healing nicely. In a couple of days he'd be on crutches and in a few weeks he'd be walking again without them. However, since the doctor had also said that the accident had scarred the cornea in both his eyes, she determined to zero in on the details of what exactly the cornea was, so that she could examine the possibilities of her son's recovery.

She began collecting information that seemed to offer distinct possibilities and suddenly became elated. She wasn't sure that what she had read would convince Calvin to agree to surgery, but it was a start. She had been careful in taking her notes, and then rushed to the hospital where she consulted an ophthalmologist to ascertain whether her facts were accurate. On finding that they were, she then sped to Calvin's bedside.

"Merciful Father, when the bomb shattered my life and my future yawned before me like a black abyss, I turned to you, pleading for a miracle. I remember promising faithfully that if my sight returned, I would dedicate my life to helping those afflicted like me. You gave me back my vision and I kept my word. Now, Calvin has been cursed with the same affliction. He's in the depths of despair, just as I was then. I don't quite know why, but on witnessing his suffering, I experienced what I can only describe as an epiphany. His affliction took me back to my own calamity and I remembered the hopelessness that had overwhelmed me as I contemplated my ruined future. There are moments when his pain is so intense that it radiates from him in waves that I can actually feel as though it were my own. Anyway, I know you can help him to recover in the same way that you helped me. I won't try to bargain with you this time as I know it's wrong, but I plead with you and pray for your help in his recovery."

"Mom, where have you been? You haven't visited in the last four days."

"I've been busy in the library. I've got good news for you."

"Good news, Mom? Do you know Judy?"

"Judy? Judy who?"

"Judy Cuchulain, the volunteer nurse who has been visiting me." Instantly the name rang a bell in Serena's mind.

"Oh my God!" She exclaimed, suddenly remembering the nurse who had advised her to go to the library. The name also made her recall the prophecy her father had related to her about the mysterious Mary Cuchulain in the restaurant. Even before his marriage, she had foretold that Leesa would have a daughter whose son "would get help from one of my kind." What did she say?"

"She said she'd be returning to visit me." Calvin replied.

Oh God! Serena thought to herself. With that name and her prediction of the future, she must be a descendant. How could Mary Cuchulain have known what she told father? But then she was right, wasn't she?

Serena told her son to listen carefully before she began to read her notes:

"The Cornea is the 'window' of the eye, a clear structure on the eyeball's surface, covering the iris and the pupil. While a healthy cornea is very clear, an injured one is cloudy and indicates that one's vision is either seriously affected or completely lost.

"Calvin, you're not listening. Pay attention," Serena pleaded. "With a corneal transplant you'll recover your sight." She repeated, "Calvin please listen, a transplant will make you see again."

When Calvin didn't respond, having ignored what she had read, an exasperated Serena kept trying to make him listen; to recognize the importance of her findings.

"These are the facts, Calvin. The doctor will measure the eye, remove the damaged cornea, and sew the new one in place. The operation is painless. Finally, he will place an eye pad and shield on the eye. The whole procedure will take less than three days in hospital." Serena didn't tell him that what she had explained was part of the American health system and not always available in Canada. She saw no point in creating unnecessary obstacles and had already decided how she would solve any problem that arose. Still, expecting Calvin to be ecstatic about the good news, she concluded on a note of triumph:

"I also managed to find a donor, Calvin. You'll be able to see again." She was almost hysterical with excitement. "Calvin," she repeated, "with the transplant you'll be able to see again."

Calvin finally deigned to answer:

"Mom, why can't you understand? A one-eyed man is a disfigured creature, an outcast. In the eyes of others, he's only one step up from human garbage." Calvin's response was like a whiplash. It immediately destroyed Serena's jubilant mood. Like a sucker punch in the stomach, it drove all the air from her body, leaving her gasping for breath. Her eyes burnt, tears started. Deeply disappointed and appalled by Calvin's negative response, Serena kept trying to persuade him to accept the donation.

"Calvin," she begged, "please listen; don't pass up this opportunity. You are so lucky to have found a donor when there are no other corneas available for love or money. Try to understand, darling. Recovering your sight will make all the difference to your life and your career." Over and over, Serena repeated her plea, refusing to accept her son's stubborn attitude, but her appeal was in vain.

In fact, Calvin was not even listening to her. His thoughts were far away, wrestling with the mystery of Judy's breezy, upbeat voice, the perfume she brought into his cubicle and the image of youth and beauty that he conjured up in his imagination. Realizing that Calvin was ignoring her, after she had spent so much time and effort on his behalf, Serena's temper flared and she shrieked:

"Calvin! You damn ungrateful son! You don't know how lucky you are to get a cornea! Only a jackass would refuse the opportunity to see again!"

Shocked by the angry outburst–his mother never swore in his presence–and moved by her sobbing, Calvin felt ashamed of the additional suffering he had caused her. But her swearing had its effect, shocking him into rethinking his decision.

Judy visited Calvin's home and noted that he was using his crutches adeptly. She told him:

"I need you to use your hands and the walls to orient yourself. They will prevent you from knocking over obstacles or knocking yourself out," she chuckled. She then showed him how to label drawers, cupboards, doors and appliances with rough plastic tape so that he could "feel" his way around, substituting touch for sight. She taught him to listen more carefully, finally getting him to find an object that she had dropped, using only his sense of sound. He realized that she was using her know-how to ease his transition from sighted individual to one with vision loss.

Each time Judy left him, Calvin felt intensely depressed. It humbled him, forcing him to see himself as a loser. He recalled his earlier egotism, derived from the successes he had achieved in high school and college: acing his exams, being singled out for praise by teachers and professors, making the honors list, and being praised for his musical talent. The accolades had set him dreaming of dominating the big world outside just as he had dominated the little worlds of school and college. He had grown arrogant, thinking himself superior, until his father's continued indifference and final desertion had taught him a lesson in humiliation. Adversity had a way of bringing you down to earth, of humbling you, making you realize that you were definitely not in charge. Evidently, he hadn't yet learnt the lesson life had been teaching him.

After his successes at college, he had again got ahead of himself. Although awaiting his results, he knew that he had distinguished himself since he had answered all the questions thoroughly. Arrogantly believing that with the excellent qualifications he'd receive, he was once more in the driver's seat and could map out any career he chose. No one would halt *his* forward march. No one would block his path to the summit. I and I alone will decide how far I'll go! He kept saying to himself. Clearly, he still hadn't learnt life's lesson. After his performance of a Sinatra song that had brought the house down, he found himself fishing for compliments by stating to a buddy:

"You'll have to admit, my song was the breakout performance of the night! Right?"

"Right! But you'll be especially remembered for your modesty."

The satirical retort struck home, and the ridicule implied made him realize that he had reverted to his earlier egotism and arrogance. He had believed that he could snigger in the face of life, since he was once again 'in charge.' His new darkened world reminded him forcefully that he had again begun to take himself far too seriously. The fact that life was the one laughing in his face was another painful lesson in humility. If that wasn't enough to add to his distress, Judy had turned her back on him.

Why are you feeling so depressed? Has it anything to do with Judy's absence? His conscience asked.

Mind your own bloody business!

Any one can see that her departures always send you spiraling down into a blackened mood.

So how the hell does that concern you?

I watch you dying for the phone to ring so you can hear her voice. Although you'd never admit it, you can't wait for her visits.

Well, if you must know, I find her sunny disposition, her humor and upbeat nature especially appealing. The last time she was here she pointed out that one of my shoes was black and the other brown. In her perky and melodious voice, she then asked if that was my latest fashion statement.

I suppose you know that whenever she urges you to make an extra effort, it's because she knows that each act you accomplish by yourself will increase your self-esteem.

I hadn't thought of that, but she does act as a thoughtful friend. I remember too that after I abandoned my crutches, she often called for me to accompany her on a ride to the lake.

What did she do once you got there?

She'd take care to ask questions that would test my senses other than that of sight.

Waves of disillusion engulfed him and he felt overwhelmed by despair. He felt impotent, frozen in confusion and frustrated by his lack of experience with women. He would give everything he owned to know what he should say and do to bring Judy closer to him.

Chapter 68

Calvin didn't know that whenever he was with Judy, she could read him like a book. She noticed his nervous pacing, the effort he made to repress his true feelings and to appear calm. Yet, the more he tried to rein himself in, seeming awkward in his speech and body language, the more his uneasiness and agitation showed. Judy pretended not to notice his awkwardness in her presence, recognizing that he had probably never been alone with a girl before. Yet, the situation pursued them although it was unstated; an irksome presence that neither dared to address.

"Expose all your senses Calvin," Judy would say: "Take a deep breath," then pausing, she would challenge: "Name the fragrance coming to you from across the lake?"

"Cherry blossoms," he replied in a flash. As his senses grew sharper, her questions became more difficult.

"What can you hear?"

"Apart from the cries of gulls, the chatter of a squirrel and the quacking of ducks, I can just make out the lapping of the wavelets against the lakeshore."

She would ask what he felt about the weather when the sky was overcast and the sun absent or she'd seek his response when she made him touch with his index finger alone, a rose petal, a corroded metal fence or the smooth bark of a sapling.

On one occasion, Judy woke Calvin early telling him only that they were going on a drive.

"Keep your wits about you," she warned as she helped him into her car. Less than an hour later, she turned off the highway on to Anderson road that after a mile or two left the asphalt. It thinned out onto a logging road that climbed steeply upward until they came to a sudden stop. She helped him out of the car before leading him to a secluded spot that was heavily forested. They were surrounded by tall Douglas firs, Pines, the occasional Spruce and Western Red Cedar. She led Calvin to a fallen tree trunk, sat next to him and challenged him to "take the pulse of the landscape."

Calvin had been aware of the length of the drive. On leaving the smooth highway, he felt the sharp right turn of the car that forced him to lean against his seat belt to the left. He noted the sudden roughness of the road surface and heard pebbles rattling on the underside of the car. He reasoned that they had left the smooth asphalt highway turning into more rugged terrain that was perhaps a logging road. The steep incline and the lower gear needed to push the car over the last eight to ten miles told him they had been climbing steadily. Once he left the car, he could feel a definite drop in temperature although he was wearing a sweater. Then, the wind blowing on his face had a salt tang and he could hear the long-drawn-out mournful grunt of the foghorn warning sea Captains to be on the alert. He also made out the bark of a startled deer, the chatter of a squirrel and the shrill song of cicada.

"It must be a deeply overcast day, with thick fog over the sea" he said, "and we are in a densely forested area high up in the Sooke Mountains. He knew there were few mountains less than an hour's drive from Victoria where you were close to the sea and could hear a foghorn. From time to time when the wind was right, he could hear the distant fall of water. Being high up in the Sooke Mountains not far from a stream, he told her: "we are surrounded by huge Douglas firs, Pines, some Cedar and Hemlock." He then accurately pointed out that "the cool, moisture-laden air would favor the growth of some Sitka Spruce and along the banks of the stream there would certainly be stands of Alder. Judy had to grade him with an 'A +' for the use of his senses and his knowledge of the environment.

Calvin's new sensitivity to the world around him made him feel somewhat more alive. Though blind, he began to feel more comfortable in his darkened world, something that was new to him. And he had to admit, he owed it all to Judy for taking such pains to hone his other senses. He knew too that it was his determination to please her that had speeded up his progress. At times, when she thought she'd asked enough questions, she'd simply describe the scene:

"Today we have a strangely sad sunset seeping through a heavy, overcast sky. It reflects the image of a tired and disgruntled Creator."

On another occasion, she painted the scene for him.

"The heavens are radiant with starlight and moon-glow." Since the words reminded her of a favorite poem, she stopped for a moment to recite it and then held his hand to lead him on a moonlight stroll. Walking hand in hand with the girl he loved, he racked his brain, trying to understand why she would choose to recite a poem about love to him of all people. The possibility of the answer made him more terrified than ever, lest he never escape from the silence and darkness that engulfed him. With the passage of time and a thousand questions, he was able to answer Judy with more and more accuracy until one day he startled her with a question of his own: "Judy, can you feel the trembling rhythm of life in the earth under your feet?" She knew then that she had accomplished a part of her mission: to begin the process of making Calvin feel whole again.

Evidently Calvin enjoyed being with Judy. Although he couldn't see her, he had learnt to absorb her presence by scent and sound. She gave off the aroma of faint cologne, fragrant soap and when she talked her breath was clean and fresh. Her voice was accented with a musical quality, but there were times, when talking to him, it could be slow, thick and rich like molasses. He wondered what that huskiness in her voice could mean. He knew she wore a charm bracelet for he could hear the charms click against each other when she spoke and gestured with her hands. Those scents, sounds and especially her laughter, affected him physically, viscerally. His heart would pound, his blood race, and her feminine presence would cloud his senses turning him into a muddled-headed idiot. He would force himself to remain silent; struggling to suppress his impulsive nature, lest he voice some inanity that would make Judy recognize the bumbling idiot he was. No matter what, he couldn't show his true feelings, afraid that he might say or do something that would irritate her and spoil their relationship. He would keep his fantasizing for later, when she was at a safe distance away from him.

He had also learnt to absorb Judy's presence by her touch. She, being a tactile person, often held his hand to guide him on their walks, to help him sit or stand; to touch him often as she spoke. And whenever she touched him it was all he could do to prevent himself from following his urges. Oh God! how he yearned to hold her in his arms and blurt out his love and longing for her. Although he always managed to hold himself in check, it wasn't at all easy.

He listened enraptured to her voice, but seldom spoke other than to answer her questions. However, on returning home he always thanked her for her help and her thoughtfulness. She understood that he had never before been alone with a girl and realized that he was confused by the amount of time she spent with him. Worse, he was still embarrassed and humiliated by his dependence on others, and especially on her.

Calvin was alarmed by his feelings for Judy and couldn't fool himself. Her patience, thoughtfulness and generosity impressed him deeply. He admired her breezy, matter-of-fact attitude and her sense of humor. Above all, he loved her touch, her voice and in fact, everything about her. He had to admit that he was badly smitten. In the clear light of day Calvin knew that the sensible thing, the sane thing would be to accept the fact that he had no chance of an emotional relationship with her. He had nothing to recommend him, he told himself. He was blind, with the frightening probability of never recovering his sight. He had no experience in the world outside the university, no job and no prospects of getting one.

In his sightless world, it would be a long time before he even thought of putting his computer skills to use. Since he couldn't even support himself, how could he hope to support a wife? Abruptly, he checked his thoughts, realizing that he had strayed way beyond the possibility of an emotional relationship and had been arrogant enough to be contemplating not only love, but marriage. It made him more than ever aware of the hopelessness of his situation. He concluded that a person with such a lively, ebullient nature could never be interested in a loser like him. It was not the kind of thinking that would brighten his dark world.

Calvin heard the scrape of the curtain around his bed being drawn aside and asked eagerly: "Is that you Judy?"

"No it's Judy's mother, Mrs. Johnson." The voice was cold, stern and hostile. "The way Judy spoke to me about you, I had to come to see you for myself." This time the voice was colder, sterner, and even more hostile.

Uncertainly, Calvin asked:

"What did Judy say about me?"

"She said you were a man who had a terrible accident, went blind and had both his legs broken. But there was something in her voice that alerted me to her feelings. I thought I'd come and speak to you about how things stand."

Recognizing the hostility of the speaker, Calvin inquired:

"And how do things stand, Mrs. Johnson?"

"My daughter has a very promising career and life ahead of her. As her mother, I don't want her future jeopardized by an emotional entanglement with anyone having so bleak a future as yours; a blind, half-caste, non-Caucasian foreigner." Calvin was about to answer when Serena entered the cubicle.

"I caught those wicked remarks of yours," she said, confronting Mrs. Johnson. "How dare you spew your venom on my ailing son?"

"He will explain," Mrs. Johnson said icily as she turned her back on Serena and stalked out.

After Calvin's explanation, Serena felt cold inside. She didn't want Calvin faced with any problem that might interfere with his recovery. And she certainly didn't expect him to have to deal with racism, especially in his condition. So Serena questioned: "Who is this Judy?"

"She's the volunteer nurse who's been very helpful...and, and friendly."

"I see! And is she emotionally drawn to you as her mother seems to think?" Serena asked.

"Mom, what woman would be drawn to a blind man without a future?" His mother heard the distress and deep hurt in his voice.

"Cal darling, don't torture yourself so!" That was all she said.

"Mom, Judy said with a chuckle of delight. "At last, Cal is just about getting over his trauma and I've been teaching him the use of his other senses." Her mother noticed the shortening of Calvin's name and was put out by the dreamy way in which her daughter spoke, and what it could mean.

"Is that the guy you told me about? The foreigner, who had an accident, went blind and broke both his legs? I don't know why you show interest in such people, or spend so much time with them." There was exasperation and not a little acid in her voice. It was as though she had tasted something unclean.

"Mom, you know very well that Cal is Canadian. I told you he was born here, in this country."

"Yes dear. So you did. But his mother is Korean and his skin color, and close resemblance to her, makes him as much of a foreigner as she is."

"Aha! So you've met them!"

"Yes dear. And from the excessive warmth and affection you've shown in describing your many outings together, I got the distinct impression that he was more than just another patient. So, to prevent my impulsive daughter from doing anything that might compromise her future, I visited him at the hospital. His mother entered just as I was leaving."

"Mom, you've never visited any of my male patients before. Why now?"

"Judy, you've never spent so much time or spoken with such affection about any male patient before. I know how impulsive and headstrong you can be. As your mother, I have to look after your best interests, haven't I?"

"What you're doing is not looking after my best interests! You've been prying Mom, and I don't like it!

"Don't you see Judy; you'd never get so worked up over a patient if your interests weren't more than just sympathetic and affectionate!"

"So what if my interests are more than sympathetic and affectionate? Is that a crime?"

"No, but I have to curb your impulsive nature. So let me spell it out for you just as I did for Calvin. I told him that you have a very bright future ahead of you and I didn't want you emotionally entangled with a non-white, half-caste foreigner; especially one who is blind, with broken legs and no chance whatever of having a successful career."

"Mom, you've never displayed such a horrible racial attitude before. You displease, disappoint and sadden me with your racial slurs, your lack of compassion and your unscrupulous behavior. You should be ashamed of yourself for such ugly conduct."

"If you're talking about what I said to Calvin, what's so wrong with protecting my daughter's welfare?"

"Is that what you were doing? Well excuse me. I thought that you were taking advantage of a blind man, lying in a hospital bed with two broken legs. Worse, I'm horrified to learn that my mother stooped to the conduct and vocabulary of a common fishwife."

"I had to behave like a fishwife to make sure that I got my point across to Calvin and to you!"

"Well, congratulations Mom, for being so protective of your daughter's welfare. But you've forgotten something very important. You can suggest, advise and even order me. But I make my own decisions. So stop prying!" Her mother could hear the anger in Judy's voice, and her message was loud and clear.

Judy knocked on the door of Calvin's home and Serena quickly put aside her paints and shut the door of her sewing room studio. Opened, it faced the front door and she didn't want any visitor to see her work. She opened the front door asking: "Who's there?"

"It's Judy, Mrs. Ahn."

"Judy? The same nurse Judy Cuchulain who advised me to go to the library and who's been visiting my son, Calvin?"

"Yes, I'm a friend of his."

"You're pregnant?"

"No Mrs. Ahn. Whatever gave you that idea?

"I smell alcohol. Have you been drinking?"

"No!" Judy blushed. "That must be my cologne. It has an alcohol base."

"The truth is that naughty girls try to tempt poor Calvin." Serena thought she was being clever to test her visitor's mettle. "Why do you want to talk to me?"

"I just want to help Calvin, Mrs. Ahn." So, Serena said to herself, the prophecy must be true.

"Well, what can you do to help?"

"Maybe I can persuade him to accept the eye donation a nursing friend of mine heard your offer to him and his refusal.

"Why do you want to help Calvin? You must have another motive?" Serena questioned.

"Without your permission, I'd be interfering in a matter you might consider is no concern of mine. But really, I only want to help Cal see again. But excuse me. May I use your wash room?"

"Certainly, follow me." Serena said.

"When Judy was finished she mistakenly opened the wrong door and was confronted by the incredibly lifelike painting of an eagle darting down on a pheasant. The portrait was huge and the room full of finished canvases all containing different species of wildlife as their subject. She quickly left the studio and returned to the living room without a word to Serena about what she had discovered. Serena resumed the conversation:

"It's very thoughtful of you to take an interest in…er, Cal. Go right ahead. If you can persuade him to have the operation you'll be performing a miracle. And thank you for your interest."

"Oh, by the way," Judy replied, "I'd like to apologize for my mother and hope you can overlook her rudeness and hostility towards Calvin. I'll be bringing her over to apologize personally. Judy then slipped out the door.

"Mom thanks a lot for telling Judy you have a blind son."

"Not only blind, but a stubborn, idiot son who refuses to obey his only parent. What did the pretty girl say?"

"She said I'm too deep in self-pity to think clearly."

"Didn't she say you were lucky too?"

"Yeah, like all blind people."

"Anyway, Judy seems like a very sensible girl. And she likes you a lot."

"Mom, you've never been in favor of Canadian girls. Why the sudden change?"

"All Canadian girls are not like Judy. She's very different; pretty and intelligent too; that's a rare combination."

"How would you know?"

"She's interested in you, isn't she?"

"What makes her different? Is it because she pities me?"

"No Calvin. It isn't pity. Perhaps it's sympathy or compassion. Maybe even love, but definitely not pity."

"Okay, I'll ask her to marry me. That's what you want, right?"

"No my stubborn idiot son, I only want you to accept the operation."

"Mom, I told you how people feel about a one-eyed man."

"See Judy! Change your mind! Accept the eye, idiot child!"

Chapter 69

Judy arrived unexpectedly, and as always, in a rush. Calvin was so surprised and delighted at her presence that his face was split in two with the widest and most sparkling of smiles. He looked forward to having her to himself for as long as he could stall her. Today was his lucky day, he thought.

"Calvin, I'm here to speak bluntly," she said. Her new voice was harsh, ominous. "Your belief that blind people are doomed to a useless existence stems from ignorance. I thought that your prolonged practice honing your other senses had cured you of such stupidity." There was a steely toughness in her voice that sounded like a Master Sergeant, angrily training a platoon of spoiled civilian recruits. She was all business.

"Now that you're out of your cave, take note of what I say." Calvin's initial reaction to this side of Judy was like receiving a stinging slap across his face with an ice pack. She had suddenly turned from intimate friend to aggressive enemy. She ignored his tortured body language and proceeded in an even sterner manner. Her voice had lost all trace of music.

"Stop obsessing on your loss. Your eyes no longer function? Well, damn it! You have many other senses. Use them! You've already been taught how. Another thing, self-pity is wasted energy. Accept your mother's offer." Her practiced speech done, she gritted her teeth as tears stung her eyes. For once, she was grateful that Calvin couldn't see and she managed to mumble, "I've got to go," before covering her nose and mouth with her hand to stifle the sound of her sobs.

Oh God, she really believes I'm a shit, Calvin thought. I wanted her to stay so badly. Her very presence makes me feel how precious, joyful and confusing life can be just being near the person you love. But, when she comes across like this, she frightens and frustrates me to such an extent that I want to go wild and destroy everything in sight. So saying, he grabbed one of his crutches and hurled it against the wall muttering great oaths that made his blood boil. He then yanked the pillows and sheet from the bed and hurled them from him. But nothing he did could assuage his deep distress and disappointment. "At times like this, she makes me feel as though I'm dealing with a savage lioness; one with a teddy-bear complex."

When Serena again introduced the topic of eye donation, Calvin had had time to absorb the harsh truths of the tongue-lashing he had got from both his mother and Judy. As a result, he had become cautiously optimistic at the possibility of seeing again. And once the idea of escaping from his blackened world began to taken hold, the urge to regain his sight gripped him with stunning intensity. The possibility and the changes for the better it entailed, provoked an overwhelming desire in him.

He had fantasized in secret about regaining his sight, thinking of all the things he couldn't do now and just might be able to do again. The myriad of possibilities gave him a tremendous boost of hope: he might be able to lead a full life and even have a chance of getting Judy to fall in love with him. Such thoughts aroused feelings of intoxication. Then, the possibility of the transplant failing immediately destroyed such fanciful beliefs.

He blessed the tough attitudes of the two women in his life, and cursed himself for his stupidity and stubbornness. In reply to Serena's question about the eye operation when she next visited him, Calvin blurted out:

"Mom, Mom, I'll accept that donation right now, right now." Serena was so astonished and relieved, that she burst into tears. Calvin tried to calm her:

"Don't cry Mom. Everything will be all right, you'll see." And he thought, who knows, maybe so will I.

After she consulted the doctors, Serena told Calvin the day on which the operation was re-scheduled. In the meantime, he again began to fantasize about regaining his sight, his looks, and being able to live a full life like Judy. He knew that he had fallen head over heels in love with her but dared not express his feelings as long as he was blind. If he recovered his sight, if his head wounds did not disfigure him too badly, and if he could find a way to support himself, he toyed with the remote possibility of Judy falling in love with him. But he had to admit those were a lot of ifs. He coupled the hope of seeing Judy again with that of winning her love, and the uncertainty of both drove him out of his mind. He cursed the reality of not knowing and agonized in his misery. The belief that her angry advice might have been her parting shot set him grieving at the thought of never seeing her again.

"Mrs. Ahn, what you are considering is a terribly risky business."

"Doctor, just tell me. Is it possible?"

"Yes, it is. But there could be serious complications."

"Complications don't worry me."

"They should."

"Doctor, when would you need me?"

"I'll have to let you know."

"Please make it soon."

"I'll get in touch."

Whenever faced with a problem, Serena often turned to her art to temporarily banish the distress such problems caused. She had decided to paint a bald eagle in flight, rocketing down in its stoup upon an unsuspecting quarry. Although she had made some headway with the knowledge of her subject, she was still working out in her mind the background against which she wanted to portray the raptor. Apart from using close up photographs of the creature, she had visited taxidermy shops and museums with her camera and scrapbook to get the exact size of the bird, the shape of head and body, the color of eye, feathers, the hook of the beak and talons. The research on its background had revealed its habits, the habitat it frequented, its strength and fitness for the chase. The information would be vital to help her organize the dissident parts of her painting into a harmonious whole that would lend verisimilitude to the work.

"Hi Cal, I hear you had a very hostile visitor." Judy stated.

"Yes. Your mom was kind enough to give me an earful, and a reality check. She let me know exactly how things stand between you and me."

"Cal, she told me what she said in a discussion we had at home about the incident. She thought she was protecting my interests, but she needn't have been so bellicose, mean-spirited or racist. Cal, don't let either her vulgarity or her hostility get you down. Your first priority is to get well. Don't let anything and anybody stand in the way of your recovery."

"He then asked the question that had been plaguing him since Jan's attack:

"What caused your mom to tell me off with such venom?"

"Do you remember viciously criticizing a one-eyed man? It was your reply when your mother tried to convince you to accept the eye donation and the procedure that would make you see again?"

"Now that you've reminded me, yes I do. But, I make no apology Judy. I still maintain that such a handicap is a giant barrier to a successful future."

"Then I don't suppose you can blame my mother from sharing your opinion. Can you?"

"I suppose not," Calvin replied, realizing how deftly Judy had sidestepped the real question: was she or wasn't she 'emotionally involved' with him, as her mother had implied? Unfortunately, in his present circumstances, it was a question he dared not ask.

Serena was impressed that the bald eagle was perhaps nature's most lethal raptor. Not only had it established a fearsome reputation as an airborne killer, but its eyes, the sharpest in the animal kingdom, had a visual field of 120 degrees that made it able to spot its prey from a distance of over three kilometers. While the tail gave it great maneuverability, and the powerful muscles and seven-foot wingspan propelled it swiftly through the air, the breakneck speed of its stoup allowed it easily to overtake its quarry. Its crushing talons that could snatch its victims in midair, from trees and even from under the surface of lake, river or ocean, were perhaps its greatest assets. Those claw-like talons were capable of tearing flesh apart, and the hooked beak, with needle-sharp tip, could easily puncture and rip flesh from bone.

"Mom," Judy said, "you've been so deeply worried during the past few days. I hope you're not still obsessing on the Calvin issue."

"No darling, it's something far more important."

"What could be more important than Calvin's future?"

"Ours!" Her mother replied.

"Why don't you tell me what's really worrying you?" Jan was furious at herself for forgetting that Judy would be able to ferret out her secret fear with a confession. But how could she tell Judy what she had done? Or would she already know? She thought that she had better get right to the point.

"Darling I've gambled a fair-sized chunk of our finances trying to make a killing. Instead, the stocks I bought have plummeted and we've taken a serious loss. The thing is, I've done it so often in the past and been successful. I still don't understand how it could have failed." Jan was wringing her hands in despair. "Was I so greedy that I overlooked the obvious risks? Did I need you to know what a brilliant investor I am?" At that point in her self-recrimination, Judy broke in.

"Mom please tell me the whole truth! I've just been to the bank. The anger in her voice made her mother tremble.

"What do you mean," her mother replied, pretending she didn't understand her daughter's words.

"*We* haven't taken a huge loss, Mom. *I* have. You gambled with my investments while making sure yours remained safe. Mom, how could you do such a thing? How could you be so underhand, and selfish?"

"You checked with the bankers behind my back? I suppose," Jan replied in a huff.

"Mom, this is the second time in a few weeks that you've made me so ashamed of you. I couldn't believe the gross fishwife act you put on with Calvin, and now this."

"Oh Judy, I'm so sorry for being nasty to Calvin. I didn't really know that you were smitten with him," she lied.

"That's just it Mom. I do enjoy his company a lot, and he is the kind of man I could easily fall for, but I don't think I'm smitten, at least not yet!"

"I'm really sorry Judy. Please forgive me. You know, I thought I was protecting your future."

"Okay, apology accepted! Mom, I know how much time and effort you put into taking care of our finances. I know too that it's a full time job and that you've always tried to protect me and to look after our investments with an eagle eye. So I know that you've done a terrific job. Don't worry about the loss. There are ways to make it up. Now the next vital question is: what do you propose to do about Calvin?"

"Anything at all that you would have me do."

"What do you think you *should* do?"

"Would it be acceptable if I apologized to both Calvin and his mother?"

"It would, but your casual attitude suggests that you don't realize how mean, contemptible and vulgar you were! I'd want to be there to make sure you do it right."

"Come along then."

Judy had disappeared and Calvin had no idea where she was. He wasn't sure if his stupidity was the cause of her disappearance, though he gradually convinced himself that it was. Every morning he awoke with the knife of guilt plunged deeply into his heart. Every night before sleep, he pleaded with her image to forgive him. During those days and nights the absence of his beloved so sorely grieved him that his heart became a gravestone in the cemetery of his chest.

Since the eagle is an ambush predator, Serena was still struggling over the decision of how best to make it remain invisible to its prey. So far however, both the predator and its prey were so clearly depicted in her mind and on the canvas; the shapes and colors so accurately reproduced that she could easily believe she was looking through a window at reality. However, she still had failed to decide on a centralizing artistic design. After rejecting a number of other possibilities, she finally decided to use the ploy of camouflage as the predator's technique to remain invisible to its prey. Indeed, Serena the artist had become a predator with a difference. She experienced the thrill of the hunt and the exhilaration of the chase, but stopped short at seizing the quarry itself. Her only concern was capturing its image on canvas.

You have no one else to blame but yourself, Calvin's conscience chided. *It's no use chastising yourself and wallowing in self pity. You've chased her away by stubbornly acting like a jackass. Now add that loss to your list of grievances.*

I suppose you're right. Two whole bloody weeks have passed and I haven't seen her. I'd hate to think that I won't ever see her again.

By the end of the first week, he had begun to feel acute disappointment, and by the end of the second, he had given way to despair. Serena could see that something was seriously wrong, but Calvin refused to say what was depressing him. By the end of the third week, when he still hadn't heard from her, his sense of depression was bordering on melancholia.

Since meeting Judy, your life has been divided into two extremes.

You know me well. When she's with me, it's pure delight. She's so thoughtful, energetic and considerate that she makes me feel alive. She's a shot of adrenaline directly into my bloodstream. I want to do things that I've never done before, seek challenges that I've never considered. I want to make her proud of me. But my blindness is always there, a wall between us; a giant obstacle impossible to surmount.

Yeah, in her presence, you become so excited, so full of joy and confusion that you act like a frightened rabbit. It's as though something has happened to you that you've never experienced before.

That's true. The sound of her voice sets my pulses racing, my heart pounding against my ribs. Tears fill my eyes, my nose begins to run, and I begin to tremble. When that happens, I quickly turn from her, trying to conceal my feelings, grabbing a handful of tissues. I don't want her to know how her presence affects me. Yet, like an idiot, I give myself away by swiping at my bandaged eyes, blowing my nose and clearing my constricted throat.

I've been watching you closely. There are times when you feel so euphoric that you need to exert all your willpower to hold yourself in check, to rein in the drunken ecstasy that overwhelms you. Away from her, your life is abject misery, and since her tongue-lashing, you've been behaving like a man without a soul, left to sicken and wither in your solitude.

For the first time, Judy felt ill at ease on being away from home. She had postponed her visit to Calvin with her mother when her nursing network had alerted her that a young American woman had given up the will to live after the trauma of vision loss. The void of icy blackness with its cold, otherworldly scent that she inhabited had so terrified her that she had tried to destroy herself with sleeping pills. In her disordered mind, death was preferable to a life sentence of darkness and isolation without a future.

The victim's mother, horrified by her daughter's reaction, had relayed an urgent appeal to Judy after hearing through the 'nursing grapevine' about the 'miracles' Judy had worked on people in similar situations. Judy had rushed to the scene as she usually did in any emergency, and in her own personal style, had begun working to pry the young woman out of her traumatized condition. She told her patient, Anne, that it was her negative attitude, not her blindness that was denying her any chance of a positive future. But it had taken quite some time to convince Anne that her attitude needed changing. Judy had had to open a miniature window into her darkened world before the light had come pouring through to transform Anne's despair into hope. But that's not how it all began.

"With Judy out of the country, Jan worked out a plan and went to visit Serena. Impatiently, she quickly pressed the bell numerous times as though summoning a subordinate. Serena was engrossed in her painting and on hearing the uncivil person at the front door, rushed from her studio, closing the door behind her. She was surprised and suspicious at seeing Jan on her doorstep.

"Serena," Jan began ..." but Serena cut her off.

"What do you want?" Serena asked, with both venom and suspicion in her voice.

"I want to make you a proposition."

"I can't think of anything you have that I want." She made her voice sound as cold and unfriendly as she could.

"Serena, please listen to what I have to say."

"Go ahead!"

"You work as a waitress. As a single mother, it must be a tremendous financial struggle to support yourself and Calvin, especially with the fees for his college education. I appeal to you as a mother seeking the welfare of her only daughter with a bright future. Judy seems to think that she's in love with Calvin. I believe that because of his severe injuries, he can only be a serious setback in her life."

"Go on, I don't know what you're getting at, but I'm sure you have more to say." Serena said sternly.

"I would like you to take Calvin away to some distant part of the province so he won't be present to complicate Judy's life or jeopardize her future. I want the best for my daughter just as I'm sure you want the best for your son."

"Are you done?" Serena enquired.

"No! I'm willing to offer you ten thousand dollars. But you'll have to move immediately."

"I can't believe what I'm hearing. You think that Judy is in love with Calvin, yet you want to destroy that love. Is that looking after her welfare? Isn't that the worst form of betrayal?" Not having expected the question or the rebuke, Jan remained silent. "Then," Serena continued, "If I do as you ask, do you think Judy will treat your betrayal as looking after her best interests?"

"Serena, I don't care what you think of me or of my behavior. Believe it or not, I am concerned with Judy's future. My offer is twenty thousand dollars." Jan said with conviction, believing that Serena was negotiating for a higher offer. "Do you accept?"

"You still don't understand, do you? You're trying to decide the future of two individual human beings. Where do you get such arrogance? You're guilty of playing God! And no! I don't want your money, even if you doubled the offer. Now, please leave."

"Serena, I'll give you a few days to think over my offer," Jan said as she turned to go, but the conviction had gone out of her voice.

"Hello Anne, I'm Judy," she told her patient. "I lost my sight in both eyes just like you."

"Mama said you're here to help. What's your plan?" The tone was unfriendly, the voice radiating denial and hostility.

"Well, the doctors said it's possible for you to see again, like me."

"How did they make you see again?" Her voice was stern and challenging, her disbelief evident.

"After the scars on my eyes healed, the doctors used microsurgery and a corneal transplant. Thanks to their procedures, I recovered my sight."

"Are you saying this to make me feel better?"

"No, I'm telling the truth, so you should feel better."

"Are you saying that they can do for me what they did for you?"

"I feel sure that they can. But you'll still have to wait a while until your scars heal."

"How can you talk with such bloody certainty?" Anger sharpened her voice. I know you can't tell the future." Anne's torment convinced her that no cure for her blindness existed. Judy could imagine the fierce scowl and the angry face under her bandages.

"I know they can because you have almost the exact damage as I did."

"You're a bloody fraud! Don't you know that deceiving people with false hope is cruel?"

"Calm down! I'll prove what I said."

"How the hell can you do that?" The anger in her voice echoed her disgust and disbelief.

"I'm afraid you'll just have to wait for that to happen."

"I knew you were a bloody fraud." Anne's voice was angry and jubilant with Judy standing at her bedside.

"So, you play the piano, sing your own compositions, and even write the lyrics," Judy stated a few days later. Hearing Judy's voice, Anne apologized profusely before asking: "You went to LA and returned so quickly?"

"I didn't go anywhere. A phone call to your boss was all I needed to learn that you're a gifted teacher. So smarten up! I believe you have a bright future ahead of you. Now I must go and convince others of the same thing."

"Excuse me if I sound ungrateful, but in my isolated limbo, your 'prediction' seemed impossible."

Thanks to Judy's prediction Anne's terror had evaporated and she had begun to improve. The same could not be said of Judy's depression. Although Judy had begun packing for home, she kept experiencing a sense of unease, even a sharp feeling of dejection instead of the joy or the simple relief that the success of such an undertaking normally brought. She tried to remonstrate with herself to define her dissatisfaction; to dispel her darkened mood.

She had a solid financial base that would permit her to continue her work while affording her a lifestyle that went well beyond comfortable. The cruelty of fate would always provide a continuous flow of patients. Yet, there was a chasm in her life. She needed something more tangible than either money or career satisfaction to complete her. Her heart was heavy. A simple joy was missing from her life.

She paced her hotel room with loneliness like an ache in her gut, thinking of the many hotel rooms she had slept in alone, the many mornings she had awakened with no one but strangers for company. Why did she feel so miserable, cut off from the warmth of the world and its human companionship? Why was her heart hurting so? The help she gave to others was gratifying, but the calamities to which she was drawn inspired sympathy, anxiety and compassion rather than joy or gaiety. While the human call of distress was the turmoil into whose familiarity she fitted comfortably, she felt as though her heart would break in its emptiness. Was that because it was still virgin territory?

She became so engrossed in the sick sense of despair surrounding each patient that her own feelings never surfaced. But once her ministrations were finished, the dreaded torment returned. A 'drowsy numbness' froze her senses although she had drunk no 'opiate' that would inspire the emptiness and isolation she experienced. She felt divorced from the world, a forbidding darkness overcame her, and her mood turned angry and sad. She felt heartbroken, but couldn't say against whom or what her anger was targeted.

There was a time, she recalled, when being alone was exactly what she had wanted, indeed what she had prized. After all, she was self-sufficient. It was only recently that the satisfaction generated by her work had begun to evaporate. What had happened to change the mission of solitude that had so delighted her previously? How could she recapture that sense of contentment? How could the emptiness of a heart weigh so heavily on the soul? No answer came to reassure her. But suddenly the image of Calvin's bandaged head flickered upon the screen of her mind.

Chapter 70

]s Calvin the man whom I can trust to help carry on my work? Judy wondered. Is he the one to whom I can cling for warmth and comfort during those long, lonely nights? Will I be able to confide in him and together discuss our personal goals? I do care for him, but if I did fall in love with him, would he return my love? Later on, would he be willing to start a family? She couldn't be sure that Calvin could provide the answers to her flurry of questions. But later, when she was in an aircraft flying home, she was surprised to find that the same bandaged head kept invading her thoughts.

By the time another week had passed, Calvin was convinced that his stupidity had caused Judy to disappear and he would never see her again. He couldn't sleep, lost his appetite, felt the heavy weight of the world on his shoulders. It was then that the soothing voice of Sinatra arose in his mind to rescue him from the depth of his depression.

With each day, Calvin grew even more morose and uncommunicative. Neither nurses, doctors nor his mother could account for his mood of profound despair. And then, out of the blue, Judy phoned.

"I was called away unexpectedly to the US to care for a young woman with serious eye injuries," she said. "Anne, a graduate teaching assistant, was conducting an experiment in the lab. A test tube exploded in her face and blinded her on the eve of her wedding. Her weasel of a fiancé took off, leaving a note behind saying: "Sorry Anne, I can't spend the rest of my life looking after a blind wife."

By the time Judy had rattled off the explanation of her absence, and asked how he was feeling Calvin was so overcome with surprise and delight that he remained speechless. Her voice had struck him like an unexpected body blow. He staggered as a rush of emotion, a tight blend of love, hope and delight, wrapped themselves into a closed fist and pounded into his solar plexus. The blow left him so choked up with emotion that he began to cry helplessly into the phone.

"Hey! Cal? What's wrong?" Judy's voice rose in alarm as she heard his sobs and she shouted into the phone, sounding both stunned and terrified:

"Cal, tell me! What's wrong?" Still choked up, Calvin could only sob in response.

"Cal," she whispered, "whatever it is, don't you worry. I'll be there as soon as I can."

Judy's early return caught Jan off-guard. Judy knew that something was very wrong when she saw the worried frown on her mother's face. She immediately told Jan that after going to see Calvin, she would go to the bank to check on her finances.

"You've never done that before," Jan said. "All you need is to ask me."

"Well, why don't you tell me what you've done that has made you so ashamed of yourself?"

"You don't already know?"

"I would like you to tell me what mischief you've been up to. Please, can you do that?"

"I withdrew twenty thousand dollars from our investments to finance a project."

"Mom, I'm waiting for you to tell me the whole truth."

"Okay damn it! I took the full sum from your investments to make a proposition to Serena. I offered her twenty thousand dollars to spirit herself and Calvin away so he wouldn't be here to complicate your life on your return." Jan had the grace to hang her head and blush.

"And I suppose you were using *my* money to look after *my* welfare?" Judy asked with scathing sarcasm. Mom, that's a betrayal of my trust in you. How can you be so mean, deceitful and underhand? In these last weeks you've lost all vestige of morality and you're getting more corrupt by the minute. You then keep justifying your conduct by telling yourself that you're looking after *my* welfare. Well, it has to stop, and at once!"

"Judy I do love you as my very dearest daughter. Everything I've done is out of my love for you. Now, you need to understand this. Whenever I risk your money on an investment, if it fails, I always take the sum I risked from my account and deposit it into yours. I've already done that, so if Serena accepts, I'll be the loser, not you. But since what I've done obviously hurts you, I'm really sorry. Can you forgive me darling? Can you?"

"Yes, of course I forgive you. You're my mother and I can't hold a grudge against you after all you've done for me. But you'll have to pay a price," Judy told her with a loud chuckle.

"What's so funny?" Jan asked, as Judy's chuckle ended in loud girlish laughter.

"I think you'll find it funny and perhaps humiliating when I tell you what you've done."

"So tell me."

"You offered to buy off Serena with a measly twenty thousand dollars when she has more money than you and I can spend in three lifetimes. My friend at her bank, a fearsome gossip, heard about Calvin's accident and tipped me off about his mother's wealth. I find that really funny, and I'm sure Serena must be laughing her head off. But you deserve her ridicule and your own humiliation for your behavior, don't you think?" Jan was at once so astonished and embarrassed that she didn't know what to say.

"Calvin, Jan offered me twenty thousand dollars for us to move away so you wouldn't jeopardize Judy's bright future. She's also given me a few days to think over her offer." Before a shocked Calvin could reply, Serena added:

"Of course, I won't accept her money, but moving might be a good idea to get out of the clutches of such cruel and unscrupulous people. Don't you agree, Cal?" She knew that Calvin was in love with Judy but was anxiously testing him to hear how he would respond.

"Mom, as you must know, I'm in love with Judy. I've never mentioned it to her, given my condition and all. She's the most wonderful human being that has come into my life. And don't you dare group her with that horrible mother of hers. Judy is the most generous and ethical person I know."

"So you don't think moving would be a good idea?" She asked with a broad smile.

"It's a terrible idea!"

I'm so glad you think so Cal! I didn't want to uproot us after the promising start we've made."

When the doorbell rang, Serena was surprised to see Jan standing on her doorstep.

"I suppose you've come to renew your attack on my son and me?"

"You're wrong Serena. I know I made a mess with the harsh things I said, and by offering you money to move. May I come in so that I can do what I promised myself and Judy?"

"Come in, I'll go and call Calvin." A moment later, Calvin appeared looking as though he had been crying. "Calvin and Serena," Jan said, "I've come to apologize to you both for my shameless conduct. I thought Judy was smitten with you, Calvin, and if it were true, you would destroy her successful career. I am not racist, but I had to play the foul-tongued fishwife to make my attack sound authentic. Please forgive me for my vulgar conduct. I was genuinely seeking my daughter's welfare."

Serena and Calvin stood stock still in dumb amazement.

Calvin managed to stop his tears but not his trembling in nervous anticipation of Judy's arrival. Suddenly, the door burst open Judy rushed into the room, stopped abruptly at seeing Calvin with Jan and Serena. Jan and Serena quickly retired to leave the young couple alone. Judy then leapt forward wrapping her arms tightly around Calvin clinging to him. She then pleaded in a whisper:

"Oh Cal! Cal darling, tell me. What's wrong?" Calvin felt her hot tears on his cheek, and as he embraced her he felt her warm lips on his, kissing him tenderly, lovingly. Before she knew it, Calvin was returning her kisses.

Opening the front door a week later, Serena was surprised to see Judy with a stranger.

"I dropped by Serena, to bring a good friend to meet you. Jerry Dalton, this is Serena Ahn about whom I spoke. Serena, this is Jerry Dalton, a close friend of mine and a prominent art critic," Judy stated.

"Hello, may I call you Serena?" Jerry stuck out his hand and Serena, hesitating somewhat, shook it.

"Certainly Jerry, please come in." Serena said, wondering about the art critic bit.

"Judy mentioned that you're a devoted wildlife painter, Serena. We'd like to see your work."

"Judy? You want to see my work?" Completely puzzled, Serena replied:

"I've never shown my paintings to anyone. How could Judy know about my work?"

"Please Serena may we see your work?" Judy asked. Still puzzled, Serena led the visitors to her studio, but before entering, asked:

"Why do you want to see my paintings?"

"I'm an art collector and critic. My specialty of interest is wildlife. Judy told me that's also your specialty and that you're working on a bald eagle."

The statement jolted Serena. Completely puzzled, she tried to understand how Judy could know that she was a painter, and who could have told her about a canvas that she had never shown to anyone. She ushered her two visitors into her studio puzzling over the mystery.

Chapter 71

On entering the studio Jerry and Serena were confronted by the canvas of a bald eagle swooping down on its prey. The canvas, its base sitting on the floor, blocked out the entire far wall, dominating the whole room. Serena had greatly exaggerated the eagle's size in proportion to its prey, a ring-necked pheasant just breaking from ground cover. The sight struck the two observers like a jolt of electricity. Its impact was immediate and visceral. They both drew in a sharp breath and held it as though struck by a sharp blow. Their stomachs lurched. Above the brownish green of stubble and stunted bushes dotting a drab field in the lower foreground, the fiery reds and gold of the pheasant's feathers glittered while the iridescent sheen of the head gleamed. Below the pure white ring encircling its neck, the black stitching parallel to the lower edge of its golden wings ended in the green up-sweep of a forked tail. The somber colors of both the eagle above and the landscape below highlighted the brilliant colors of the pheasant. Serena could actually witness the visible excitement of the effect on Judy and her friend. Both were holding their breath, momentarily speechless.

The raptor was set against a granite mountain background broken by wisps of early morning mist. The shadow lighting was so cleverly arranged that the very dark wings and body of the bird merged almost seamlessly with the darker grey of the granite rock. The eagle's white head and tail blended with patches of mist making it invisible to its prey. With wings folded back and tendrils of mist trailing from its wings and tail, the raptor streaked down on the pheasant in what appeared to be a dazzling display of speed.

Judy stood entranced. She could almost hear the high-pitched scream from the eagle's partly opened beak. Jerry watched its extended talons, like grappling hooks, already moving forward to rip into its quarry. Like Judy, he too was captivated. His eyes were glued to the single shaft of sunlight that fell on the iridescent green of the pheasant's head and neck lighting up the canvas with their radiance. Finally, still in amazement, Jerry turned towards the other paintings that decorated the two other walls, and what he saw captivated him further.

"Oh my God Serena! Your eagle painting is dramatic in its grandeur. The figures teem with life and display your excellent draftsmanship in the way they're so accurately drawn. The blend of light and shade allows your eagle to merge so naturally into its background that the viewer witnesses the cunning of the ambush predator as well as the skill of the artist. You've captured their realism while displaying your individuality in their treatment. Then, there's the visual excitement in the dramatic tug of war you've created with the disproportion in the sizes between predator and prey. In my mind, your painting is a magnificent work of art." Serena was too excited to respond.

"I don't use those words lightly," Jerry said. "Your canvas captures many of the qualities that critics consider indispensable to great art. Simplicity and realism are of paramount importance. Drawn from the natural world, your scene is both simple and real. Equally important is the fact that great art magnifies its message and meaning. Your work lends itself to interpretation on several different levels. While it portrays the advantage of the strong, it also depicts the handicap of the weak. On the one hand, it expresses imminent death in action and on the other, the tragedy of life about to occur. The powerful figure of the eagle may accurately be termed the nemesis that heralds disaster, or even the inexplicable hand of Fate. While the colorful portrait of the pheasant's imminent death may be seen as the transience of beauty, the portrait also depicts the survival of the fittest.

"What about triumph and tragedy, or ambush predator," Judy chimed in.

"They will certainly do," Jerry replied. "But equally remarkable is that each of the versions to which your canvas lays claim, lifts that interpretation to a universal plain through its symbolism. Although using an image from the natural world, the title of the painting, *Deliver us from Evil*, comes from a prayer that is known worldwide. This title magnifies the meaning of the painting to include an appeal from the human race to its Creator. In meeting these requirements, and of course there are others, your canvas must be considered a true work of art."

Serena was so elated with the compliments that she didn't know what to say. Therefore, she remained silent but a crimson flush of delight suffused her neck and face.

"Oh, I see," Jerry continued after a short silence, "you've made your subjects evolve out of their natural habitat, using their sense of camouflage, their cunning, to capture their wildness, their instinctive bond with nature, their freedom. Oh my God, Serena," he whispered as though in church: "You've made them fresh, rich and alive as on the very first day of creation."

After the shock of Judy's first kiss, Calvin's body had tensed in arousal and as he felt the shiver of pleasure that swept through her, he had slipped his tongue into her mouth hungrily, impatiently demanding more. She realized with a jolt of desire that he was trying to press his advantage with hungry kisses, and although she couldn't suppress the joy of being wanted, she drew away gently from him. She was definitely looking forward to exploring the passion of his embrace, but she'd leave that for some future date. Both recovered somewhat awkwardly. Calvin then asked in a voice husky with desire:

"Why did you call?"

"I wanted you to go with me to the lake. The weather is so beautiful and I have some explaining to do." What she said about the weather was true. March had sashayed in on tiptoe like a ballet dancer. Her breath was warm, her movements smooth and graceful. After the restraints that winter's gales, snow, freezing cold and overcast skies, had imposed on Victorians, they felt good to be alive. The weather, unseasonably warm and fragrant with spring's blossoms, had begun greening the trees. Nature had taken the birds by surprise, throwing them off balance for a while, and then prodding them gently into their mating rituals.

In the car Calvin began:

"How do you know about things before they happen?"

"That's difficult to explain."

"Try me."

"I can't. I don't know how."

"Why are you being so mysterious?"

"Because it's a mystery I don't understand. But Cal, I'm really sorry about my harsh words to you. Sometimes I just get cranky. But what I said must have helped, because you accepted your mom's offer."

"She told you?"

"She didn't have to."

"How do you know?"

"Like I said, the knowledge comes of its own accord." She answered the ring on her cell-phone before telling him. "There's been an emergency Cal, a casualty from another accident needs my help. I'm sorry, but I'll drop you off at home as I have to leave at once." She paused a moment before adding:

"By the way, your mom's on her way here and has news about the operation. See you Cal." She left, after taking him into the house and giving him a quick peck on the cheek.

When Serena told Calvin she had learned from the doctors that the operation was scheduled for a week later than promised, as there was a backup of procedures in the OR, Calvin was deeply disappointed that he would have to live a week longer in his dark world.

"Oh Mom," Calvin said, "I just remembered, there was a phone call from a mystery man. He said he had to see me, knew it was inconvenient, but said it was important. He stammers badly."

"What did he want?"

"He'll tell me when he comes."

"When is he coming?"

"Later this evening."

Jerry returned with Judy to Serena's home a few days later to make a slow study of her other paintings that were stacked along the walls and in a corner. He wanted to see if they were of the same quality as the ones exposed. Incredibly, he found that they were.

"Serena" he said, "I've been thinking about those qualities that are so evident in your eagle portrait–the grandeur of dominance, its simplicity, individuality and realism, the accuracy of anatomical draftsmanship, the dramatic tension of opposition, and the universal quality of its symbolism. It strikes me that each of these elements is a major facet of the Renaissance school of art. Although you've incorporated these elements into your work, you've taken care to maintain your own style and individuality. I can't remember seeing these qualities so well depicted by any other wildlife artist."

"Thank you Jerry." Serena said, again blushing scarlet.

"Don't show anyone else your paintings. Promise me. Okay?" He frowned in thought for a moment before he again spoke:

"Serena, listen to me a moment. Please don't take offense at what I'm about to say. Do you promise?"

"I don't know what you're about to say, Jerry, so you have me at a disadvantage."

"Okay. Judy told me that right now you're working as a hostess in a restaurant."

"That's true," Judy said. "I also told him about your Hospice visits and your rape crisis line."

"You're squandering a great deal of time on visiting the sick and the dying, counseling rape victims, organizing and running a shelter for rape survivors. I don't mean to state that these aren't very worthy causes. They are, but only for ordinary people. Let me repeat that Serena so that you fully understand what I'm about to say. What you are doing can be done by any ordinary person. But the talent you have excludes you from that category. Has it ever occurred to you that you're neglecting the one major talent you possess that makes you extraordinary?"

"Jerry, you have a habit of scaring me and making me blush. Besides, I'm not sure what you mean. I can't stop working. How else would I support myself and Calvin? And I can't stop volunteering," she added silently; how else would I be able to atone for, and hopefully expiate my past wrongdoing?

"Serena, you have a God-given talent. It's a special gift that's very, very rare. Evidently you don't realize it, but that gift does not belong to you alone. What you have is meant to be shared with others, to delight and inspire those of us less-gifted mortals. At present, you're frittering away precious time in your other pursuits. You should realize that people with exceptional gifts like yours are a national treasure."

"Jerry, you're scaring me again with such highfalutin praise. You know what they say? "When God lifts you out of obscurity by shining His light on you, you should beware! He has chosen a really tough assignment for you. If that's true, it terrifies me that I might not be able to cope. Now Jerry, what in the world would you have me do?"

"Drop everything! Cut out everything that uses up your time! Devote every second, every minute, every day that you can to painting. I'll buy the painting of the eagle from you right now. My offer will be generous enough to free you financially from doing anything else. You'll then be able to devote all your time to painting."

"Just you wait a minute, Mr. Jerry Dalton," Judy cut in sharply. "I brought you here to assess and offer a fair evaluation of Serena's work. With that in mind, I intended to buy both the eagle and some of her other canvases so she could spend her time painting and painting alone. So," Judy continued. "Jerry, what do you estimate that canvas of the bald eagle is worth?"

"There's a lot of very good wildlife painting coming out of BC and Canada at present, and collectors have been buying them up. However, few of the works are of the caliber of Serena's. None that I know of is of the size and grandeur. None possesses so many of the other qualities that elevate and enhance the quality of her work. If the eagle were shown at any upscale gallery, unframed, it would fetch somewhere between one and two hundred thousand dollars. Professionally framed, it would perhaps go for a great deal more. I have kept my assessment lower than it should be because as an artist, Serena is completely unknown to the art world."

"But Jerry, her being unknown is hardly the point. It's the rare quality of the work that counts," Judy replied. Serena couldn't believe what she was hearing. Judy and an art critic were arguing with each other about buying one of her paintings and the figures mentioned were astronomical. But they were both behaving as though she were absent. She thought it time to assert herself.

"Judy, thank you so much for bringing Jerry over to assess my work. And thank you Jerry for your assessment. But you must be joking. Do you really think my work is good enough to sell, and in that lofty price range?" Serena asked with awe in her voice.

"Why else would Judy and I both be offering to buy your canvases?" Jerry replied.

"Anyway, thank you, Jerry and Judy for your compliments about my work. You couldn't begin to understand the encouragement it gives me. Then, thank you both for your generous offers. But what you're asking is impossible."

"Why impossible?" Judy asked. "Because you think that volunteering is more important?"

"If I stopped my charity work, and devoted myself solely to painting, I'd be guilty of promoting my own welfare and ignoring the needs of others. That would be the height of selfishness. Believe me Judy, I've traveled that road before and found it a very corrupting influence. I hope I've learnt my lesson." She paused, and Judy replied.

"Serena, as a volunteer myself, I can fully understand and sympathize with the way you feel, since I too am drawn towards some of the world's unfortunates. So, go ahead, continue doing what you feel you must do, but at the same time, use every moment of your free time to paint. And I still want to buy a number of your canvases beginning with the bald eagle. How about it, do you agree?" Before she could answer, Jerry piped up. "I'm willing to buy some of your other canvases too, Serena."

Serena thought the offers were too good to refuse, but she also felt that the prices mentioned were exorbitant. "Will you both give me a few days to think over your offers?" She asked. Both Judy and Jerry agreed, and then Jerry added. "Serena, the offer is not at all unrealistic. As a critic, I can tell you that once other collectors see your work, the prices will skyrocket. So my estimate is not at all too high. You should also know that if we decided to sell later on, we'd make a nice profit."

"Okay," Serena replied, "then it's settled. Give me a few days to think over what you have in mind and I'll get in touch with you."

"Just don't show your work to anyone else while you decide, Jerry reminded her."

In retrospect, Serena knew she had no intention of cutting down on her volunteering. However, she would give up her job at the restaurant immediately and postpone everything else for the present. But Jerry's compliments had given a much-needed boost to her sagging self-esteem. The more she thought about his later words, the more enthusiastic she became about his advice. Those words provided the inspiration she needed to set her working like a slave under the whip. She kept obsessing on Jerry's words, repeating them over and over until she could actually taste their sweetness:

"Your work will jolt the viewer into seeing the supernatural beauty of our province with new eyes. They'll view our mountains, rivers, forests and wildlife as though for the first time, and with sharpened vision." Then, he continued, "You've brought out the grace and beauty of your wild beasts as though each one were emerging from its primal habitat for the first time. Your work," he said finally, "will inspire in the observer an admiration that approaches veneration." Some compliments! Serena thought. His words had brought a soothing balm to her parched artistic soul inciting her with a compelling urge to paint that amounted to an obsession. Immediately, she had begun to sleep less and less and to paint more and more. The habit grew so that she would paint without sleep for so long that only the chafing of her eyeballs would stop her. She would then fall into bed exhausted.

Chapter 72

In reply to Calvin's question, Judy said:

Well, that's exactly what dad would have suggested: "Pass on the good deed to others in need. It was dad's favorite message. But you didn't need his advice. You volunteered to give your mother half the proceeds from your concerts."

Standing close enough so that he could smell her perfume, Calvin drew her gently towards him and began raining kisses on her lips with greater and greater urgency. Her lips almost smoking from the contact and her body growing hot with the excitement of arousal, Judy needed to exert all her control to neatly draw herself away. It was so stimulating, so absolutely fantastic to feel desired by someone you cared for.

Serena answered a knock on the door, opened it and saw a highly-polished Mercedes in front of her gate and a well-dressed man on her doorstep. He looked deeply embarrassed and stammered:

"I've c-come to s-see Mr. Ahn."

"I'm Calvin's mother, Serena. You're?"

"Mr. B-Brown," he said, with even greater embarrassment.

"Come in please and have a seat." Serena called out to her son that he had a visitor and they both looked up as a door opened and Calvin stood there. He then groped his way into the room with his bandaged head and his mouth in a grim line. He first held on to the doorknob, and then to the wall. From there, he scrambled unsteadily to a chair. Guiding himself clumsily, he sat down as the visitor sprang to his feet, a look that blended guilt, shame and sadness on his face.

"Mr. A-Ahn," he stuttered, "I-I drove the c-car that r-ran you down." The statement shocked both his listeners so visibly that Mr. Brown began to weep softly. He took out a handkerchief, wiped his eyes and it was some time before he managed to control himself.

"You s-see," he began, "I had a s-son like you who just disappeared one day. Since t-then I d-drive around l-looking for him ev-everywhere. Just before the ac-accident, I had t-trouble with my eye-eyesight. Things w-went suddenly d-dark as a kind of f-fog blocked my vi-vision. I-I felt really c-cold and couldn't see c-clearly. Then, just be-before the c-crash, I had a com-complete blackout." Mr. Brown sighed. "Since I've c-caused you so much p-pain, and c-changed your life f-for the worse, I must m-make it up t-to you. I've written a c-check with the same f-figure as that of the in-insurance com-company." He placed a check on the side table, saying: "I'm s-so sorry for the p-pain I c-caused you b-both." He then hurriedly withdrew, holding the damp handkerchief to his eyes. Calvin was left feeling almost sorrier for Mr. Brown than for himself.

It took some time for Calvin to remember that he too had had a similar experience of blurred vision, a kind of darkness that blinded him just before his accident. He wondered if there was some mysterious coincidence between the two events. After a few moments' consideration, he dismissed the thought as nothing more than a curious coincidence.

Judy pulled into the driveway of her home and led Calvin to the front door where her mother met them.

"Judy, I didn't expect you, or you Calvin."

"Calvin stammered, taken by surprise. "Hello Mrs. ..."

"Johnson, but call me Jan. I hope you've forgiven me for my unconscionable behavior, Calvin. Judy seems to be fascinated with you and talks about you all the time."

"Mom, don't embarrass me, please. But, excuse me. I'll be back in a jiffy."

"I hear you've just finished your final exams," Jan said, helping him to a chair. "Were they tough?"

"I was well prepared, so they weren't that tough. But, tell me about yourself. What keeps you busy besides taking care of Judy, though that must be a full time job," he joked.

"My dear, Judy takes care of me. But I'm busy keeping a watchful eye on the family's finances. Investments take a great deal of time and effort."

"You sound as though you have no confidence in brokerage firms. Aren't they supposed to be financial wizards?"

"I wish they were. Instead, they are the ones you have to keep on a short leash. But enough talk about investments. I also travel to a lot of countries where I dance with my former partners."

"You're a professional dancer? Then you must love music. What's your favorite for dancing?"

"I love the Latin beat, especially the Argentine tango, and the 'pas a doble.' By the way," she added without missing a breath, "you know Judy is very fond of you..."

"Mom, how could you?" Judy said, reappearing just then and sounding exasperated. "Don't say another word please."

"Okay, but I just thought he should know."

"Cal, don't pay any attention to Jan. She just enjoys trying to make me squirm. Anyway Mom darling, we've got to rush." In the car, Calvin said:

"You told me your name was Judy Cuchulain, but your Mom said her name is Johnson. How is that?"

"My Mom kept her maiden name, Johnson that she used as a professional dancer. Cuchulain was my father's name. It is said to date back to a time even before the birth of Christ and belonged to a heroic Gaelic family of the Druid religion. They were supposed to hold extraordinary powers. The legendary background seems to be accurate, for the Druids were renowned for their knowledge, their sorcery and especially the gift of prophecy. But who really knows? I believe that even historians tend to embroider the past."

"Did you get your information from your father?"

"Yes. But Dad was reluctant to talk about his family history. I also did some digging on the Internet and got information from there as well. Now, I know you're bursting to ask questions. Before you do, give me your hand." When he did, she placed it just under her left eye and instructed: "Now, touch my eyeball very gently." He moved his fingertip gingerly over her eyelashes, and then pressed it very gently on her eyeball. It was as smooth as marble, and as hard.

"Oh my God! Why didn't you tell me?" he exploded in astonishment.

"Isn't that what I'm doing now?" she asked, feigning innocence.

"Why are you driving a different car? I can feel the luxurious leather and there's that new car smell. The engine also sounds more powerful though much smoother."

"Congratulations, you're using your other senses. The Toyota was almost out of gas."

"So which car is this?"

"It's the Mercedes."

"You have two cars?"

"Three."

Having learned that Judy was wealthy, Calvin switched to the subject of her artificial eye.

"You were like me?"

"Yes I was. But let me get you home. As soon as they were in the door, she said:

"I've got to leave now Cal, but I'll see you later."

"Hey lady, you're always rushing off just when there's so much about you I need to know. Can't you stay awhile?"

"No I've got to go."

"Please stay a bit longer. There's so much I want to know about you."

"Look," she said, "Dad did a great deal to help accident victims. He was setting an example, teaching me that my gift would draw me towards those in pain. It would be worthwhile only when used on behalf of such people. He repeated that those of us who have more of this world's bounties also have more of its responsibility for helping those who have less. His words filled me with a passion to follow his example. Each time my effort succeeds I feel as though I've been placed on the planet for a reason; I'm making a difference. With each success I get a tremendous rush of exhilaration, a sense of fulfillment that I wouldn't give up for the world. I'm sorry Cal darling, but try to understand. It's not that I love you less. It's that those who are suffering need me more."

Chapter 73

Calvin considered Judy's motive for showing him her artificial eye. Her intention, he thought, was to make him realize that she, like him and others, had experienced the trauma of vision loss. She too had journeyed through the dark night of hell, and had had to conquer her own demons. In doing so, she had learned to depend on her other senses. She was showing him that she had been struck down by calamity, but instead of buckling under, she had used the crisis as a step towards new growth, new development, even a new identity. He recalled how she had described, "giving back" to him:

"After climbing out of the abyss, I embarked on a new and fulfilling life. Whenever my struggle to help others is successful; whenever a patient compliments me for her recovery, I experience a feeling akin to rapture. It's a sensation of fulfillment I never expected, one I never want to forget. It makes me believe that I was born into the world for a purpose and that I'm fulfilling that role. Besides, it offers solid evidence to prove something that I've always thought: that good *can* blossom from evil. Don't you agree?"

"Since your conclusion is supported by personal experience, I have to agree." But he wondered: is she trying to tell me something about my future?

"Previously, I had always thought that the concept of evil was too complicated for us poor mortals to examine, analyze or fathom. Yet, I've noticed in the past few months that there has been an acceleration in the number of cases I've had. Since most of those have turned out successfully, I feel that my conclusion is valid." After a moment she added:

"Cal, your misfortune may also turn out to prove my point."

However, in Calvin's mind, their situations were very different. It was all very well for Judy to assume that goodness and beauty can blossom from evil. Owing to the generosity of a victim, and a successful operation, she had recovered her sight. He couldn't possibly adopt her viewpoint, yet. If his operation failed, he would live in perpetual darkness. Nothing good would have come out of his calamity. Yet, he couldn't help thinking of the outpouring of goodness and generosity that had followed the evil of 9/11, as well as calamities like the tsunami of South East Asia and Katrina.

On Judy's next visit, Calvin complained that she'd had so much to tell him, yet had left him to agonize over not knowing how she had lost her eye. He sounded hurt when asking her how it happened.

"Take a guess," she said playfully, trying to mollify him.

"I'm out of guesses."

"It's really very simple. I had an accident like you."

"You were hit by a car and lost an eye?"

"No not exactly! It was around midday, and I was having lunch with a friend in a restaurant. I began rubbing my eyes because suddenly I could hardly see. A dark screen seemed to be blocking my view. I wiped my eyes thinking that the problem was temporary. I shook my head, hoping it would go away. It didn't and that puzzled me until I suddenly felt cold, and then a putrid odor assaulted me out of nowhere. It was then that I sensed the presence of evil all around me. I knew that something horrible was about to happen. A moment later, there was a terrific explosion..."

Calvin broke in before she could continue.

"Oh my God! Was the blockage a kind of dark fog surrounding you that blurred your vision? Did you feel as though you were suddenly plunged into semi-darkness? Did the icy feeling and the foul odor come later?"

"That's exactly what happened. How did you know?" Judy asked puzzled.

"The same thing happened to me before my accident." He kept silent for a moment, thinking back. Suddenly he exploded: "Oh shit!"

"What? What?" Judy cried impatiently. "Tell me!"

"I just remembered. Mr. Brown, the driver who ran me over, said the same thing happened to him just before his car collided with me. Since he and I had similar experiences, I thought that we might have shared an odd coincidence. But it's no longer a coincidence when the same thing happened three times, to three different people and each one just before a dreadful accident."

"And mine was on another continent," Judy reminded him.

"The repetition seems to offer solid proof that the darkness clouding our vision, the cold and the foul odor were not coincidence. And you say that during the incident you felt the presence of evil?" Calvin asked.

"Yes. It was the sense of evil that convinced me something horrible was about to happen. And it did. So I was right. But what does it mean?" Judy asked.

"I'm not sure," Calvin replied. "Perhaps we need to consult someone who understands what is taking place when darkness, cold and the odor of putrefaction inflicts themselves on an individual?"

"Look, it's evident that darkness clouds the vision and cold numbs the senses. When both assaulted us in conjunction with the putrid odor, we were both unable to prevent the calamity that followed. Just a few moments after they happened a suicide bomber blew herself up and the place erupted. I lost the vision in both my eyes, and a number of people were killed. Since you, Mr. Brown and I had similar experiences, it all seems to fit."

"Oh my God! Did you have other injuries? Were you the only one who survived?" Calvin's surprise and distress were evident in his voice, the taut line of his lips and his body language.

"No, I was far from the bomb, but eight people were killed and a number of others, badly wounded."

"So if you lost vision in both eyes, how come you can see again?"

"It happened through a combination of luck and technology. The mother of a girl who died in the blast donated a cornea from her dead daughter. Then, for me to recover my sight, the doctors used microsurgery and a corneal transplant."

"But don't suicide bombings happen mostly in places like the Middle East?"

"Yes, I was in Israel, working with a kid who had been blinded in one of the Palestinian raids."

"My God, if it happened to you way over there, then these symptoms of evil aren't local. They must manifest themselves all over the world, don't you see?"

"What?"

"Let me think about it," he said before changing the topic. "Your life must be really interesting, traveling the world helping people in distress."

"Except I always have to deal with a calamity that causes suffering and pain. But Cal, I hope I've made you realize there's a full life after blindness.

Now I've got to make others realize that too. So long darling, I'll see you soon, I promise."

"Hello Judy, I see you've brought Jan as arranged. Hello Jan, come in both of you and have a seat."

"Judy, you arranged this meeting with Serena without telling me?" Jan asked, puzzled.

"Don't you remember I promised you a surprise? Well Jan, Serena is a wildlife painter, and Serena, Jan is a critic and collector of wildlife art. I've brought her here to see your work."

"Why didn't you tell me that Serena was a painter of wildlife?"

"Isn't that's what I'm doing now? But wait until you see her work," Judy said smiling mischievously.

On entering the studio, Jan was confronted by the huge canvas dominating the room's space as its subject, the eagle, swooped down on the pheasant. Unprepared for what she saw, she was shocked by its powerful impact. The hair rose up on her arms and back like the quills on an angry porcupine. Despite her years as a critic and her assessment of many wildlife canvases, no painting had impacted her with such power. She knew that all art tells a story, but only great art does so on several different levels at the same time and in the simplest of terms. Instead of capturing the predator as a still life in a single moment of immobility, Serena had arranged its position and the surrounding elements in such a way it seemed that more than one action was taking place. The painter had juxtaposed a series of images permitting the viewer to see what was happening and what was about to happen. The almost vertical incline of the eagle's body in its dive, and the wisps of mist trailing in its wake, conveyed a breathless sense of its speed that was intensified by its swept-back wings. The scene brought to Jan's mind the image of a jet aircraft with flowing contrail roaring down on its target. The tactic that the raptor used to blend into its background was a tribute to the bird's cunning as to the painter's imagination and skill. Catching sight of its nemesis, the pheasant, newly flushed from ground cover, was in the act of diving to conceal itself in the bushes. Witnessing the break-neck speed of the raptor's stoop, Jan could almost hear the dull thud of its collision with the quarry, as talons ripped through flesh and cracked bone on impact. There was no doubt whatever about the outcome of the episode. Jan immediately saw a chance to recoup the losses she had sustained in the risk she had taken using Judy's finances. "I would like to buy your bald eagle." Jan said to Serena. "I would place its worth at about $150.000. You might get a higher price at auction, but you'd also lose more than a quarter of that figure to the auctioneers.

"I'm sorry. It doesn't belong to her any more." Judy answered. "It's already been sold."

"What about the other canvases on the walls?"

"They too have already been sold," Judy again replied.

"How do you know?" Jan asked. "You seem to know a lot about Serena's paintings."

"I do, because Jerry and I bought them all."

"All? And you never mentioned a word to me about Serena's work when you know that collecting wildlife art is a special love of mine. Besides, works like these will skyrocket in value as word gets out about their brilliance."

"Well Mom, I promised that you'd have to pay dearly for your horrible treatment of Calvin and Serena. I conferred with her and we decided that you won't be permitted to buy any of her works. That, we feel sure, will be punishment enough for your disgraceful behavior."

"Well, now that you've both made your point, you won't mind if I leave," Jan said as she walked out the door in a huff, blushing in anger and humiliation.

"Don't pay any attention to her," Judy told Serena. "She knows that she acted despicably. Anyway she has a good heart and won't stay angry for very long."

"How is Calvin getting on?" Judy asked.

"I think that we both convinced him to accept the eye, and he's doing as well as can be expected. The doctors said that the bones in both his legs healed cleanly. The truth of the matter is that I'm still surprised to see him walking almost as though the accident never happened. His head wounds needed special care but are healing well. Those above the hairline were more severe and have more healing to do, but they'll be covered by the re-growth of his hair."

"I'm so glad to know he won't be disfigured." Judy told her.

Calvin hastened to tell Serena that before her accident Judy had suffered the same experience of semi-blindness and cold followed by the rank scent of evil just as he and Mr. Brown had done. He explained further that her accident had taken place abroad, in Israel. The realization indicated that all three happenings couldn't possibly be coincidence. Serena reacted with astonishment at his words and he became alarmed when she suddenly recoiled as though struck. Her face had turned into a pallid mask, the skin pulled tightly over her cheekbones. He had never seen her look so terrified when she turned abruptly, and without a word, rushed out of the house.

Serena ran half stumbling to the church. She could never forget the icy darkness that had engulfed her and the pungent scent of evil that had filled her lungs and overwhelmed her prior to and during her gang rape. Then, she could still hear her psychiatrist telling her that he too, had experienced similar sensations before the violent quarrels with his wife. He later confided that he had had the same experience just before he had launched his verbal attack upon her. Finally, Serena recalled that the letter from her parents' lawyers had mentioned the same menacing darkness, the cold and the revolting smell that had invaded her parents' home. It had induced her mother to summon the parish priest to exorcize the evil presence.

Once in the confessional, Serena related to Father Murphy the sinister events that had taken place in each of the isolated incidents and asked him if he could explain what it all meant.

"My child," he replied, "we in the Church are aware that darkness, cold and the odor of decay, often strike together. It seems evident that they signify the presence of evil and Satan. In fact, it is on record that tragedy almost always follows these mysterious occurrences. I've recently learnt that the Church has long been aware that this contagion, eating at the heart of humanity, is orchestrated by none other than the evil one. The calamity that follows fits in perfectly with his propensity for wreaking havoc on the human race." For a moment, the priest seemed to be in deep thought, before he added:

"You should remember that the prayers and suffering of each individual does not go unrewarded." He again thought deeply before adding:

"It shouldn't surprise you to learn that our prayers and especially our suffering helps us to share in the agony of Christ on the cross. In doing so, we participate with Him in atonement for the sins of mankind and thus in our own and each other's redemption. Every starving beggar, every haunted sinner, every suffering human-being like every priest, is a foot soldier in God's invincible army—the Communion of the Saints. So, calm your fears, my child. There are always others praying, suffering and interceding on your behalf and that of the rest of the world. But your own input is important. You must never cease to pray."

The priest then stated an often-overlooked truth:

"It was the French poet, Baudelaire who pointed out that the power wielded by Satan over the human race resides in the fact that he chose to make himself invisible. By masking his presence, he induces human beings to believe that he no longer exists. Ignored or overlooked by mankind, the adversary is more easily able to tempt, seduce, terrorize and dispatch the myriad members of a race who remain for the most part oblivious to his presence. However, we should all remember that while it is true that the archfiend is a formidable foe, it is also true that God is a far more formidable ally."

Serena thanked the priest and immediately went to kneel and pray for the protection of Calvin, Judy, Jan and herself. She hurried home and rushed inside trembling, blurting out the priest's explanation and advice to Calvin. She reminded him that the same infernal darkness, foul odor and cold had induced his grandmother and others to call on their priest for an exorcism of their homes. She cautioned him about the high risk they had both run as victims of the archfiend. Her words and even more, her reactions scared the life out of Calvin and he thought it prudent to follow the priest's advice.

Chapter 74

Jan visited Calvin at home ostensibly to learn how he was getting on, but really to mend fences. She again offered a heartfelt apology for the way she had acted and the things she had said. Calvin remained aloof, though civil in his responses. She asked if Serena were present and Calvin replied that his mother was out. He then mentioned the ominous sensations of vision impairment, stench and cold that Serena, Judy, Calvin and Mr. Brown had all shared before their accidents. Jan considered the information not only scary but especially weird. She didn't know what to make of it.

While waiting, Jan learnt that Serena was checking with the doctors to ensure that the date and time of Calvin's procedure hadn't changed. She felt so positive that the operation would restore his sight that she was bubbling with excitement. "Anyone can tell how happy she really is. The excitement in her voice and her constant chatter tells you that she's on cloud nine. She's even started to hum and while doing the housework she actually adds a dance-step or two. Can you imagine?" Calvin asked. "I've never heard her humming before or seen her dancing."

"And it's all on your account," Jan pointed out. "She must love you a lot."

Calvin felt too guilty to answer.

On Judy's next visit, Calvin was upset. "You know that I don't want to pry," he told her, "but there are things I'd like to know about you."

"Ask away," she replied, smiling.

"Well, how come you're so wealthy?"

"How do you know I'm wealthy? Since you can't see, you must have the 'gift,' of prophecy she said, toying with him.

"Well, you bought half of mom's paintings at impossible prices, and you live in a mansion in the Uplands. That's Victoria's number one residential area that only the very well-heeled can afford. Then, you change cars like dresses, and there's your and Jan's investments that take up so much of her time. If that wasn't enough, both you and your mother have globe-trotting lifestyles. It follows that you're not exactly living from hand to mouth."

"Cal, you'd make a first-class detective even with your eyes bandaged," she told him laughing. "Mom and I inherited our money from dad. It's more than enough to keep us quite comfortably."

"So with all your money, how come you work for a volunteer group?"

"I don't work for, nor do I belong to any group, volunteer or otherwise," she replied with a chuckle. "I do volunteer my services but only to those whom I consider to be in dire financial or emotional need. Those patients who wish to contribute to my services do so of their own accord. My network of nurses and friends keep me in touch here, and so do others abroad."

"So you and your dad robbed all the casinos, or was it the banks?"

"No-o idiot," she said laughing. "He was an officer in Desert Storm, but he never talked about the war; never said how he got his money. His life as a soldier remains a mystery. But his buddies, who attended his funeral, told a story that his lawyers corroborated. Both make it sound logical."

"I'm all ears."

"One wet, cold and very dark evening, he, his grunts and a number of men from another division, suddenly found themselves trapped in a minefield. After one man panicked, moved and was blown to bits, more than a hundred others just stood there, immobilized with terror. Dad, who was furthest ahead, found his way out, making a line in the sand behind him with his bayonet. From safety, he shouted to those stranded that he would rescue them all if they didn't move. He then followed the exit route he had marked, and reentered the minefield going to his original spot. From there, he traced another line behind him to each of the stranded men who were able to follow the lines drawn in the sand to safety. Dad's courage and self-sacrifice in rescuing his men left them in such awe that, in gratitude, they contributed a huge sum to 'The Savior's fund.' This, his lawyers claimed, he invested in the South East Asian market when it was paying hefty dividends. He got out before the crash and salted it all away in a Swiss numbered account that he bequeathed to Mom and me."

"How did your dad manage to save all his buddies without being killed?"

"Take a wild guess."

"Okay, he had the gift."

"You are right. He took me to a casino on my first winning spree. Gosh! It was so exciting! But his constant advice was that I should use my gift to help others." Judy's voice was wistful.

"You sound as though you miss him terribly."

"I do, but I didn't realize how much until I started talking about him." Calvin didn't miss the tone of adulation that had crept into her voice.

"Your dad must have been an extraordinary human-being."

"With his gentleness, his understanding and love, he was my first real hero."

On Calvin's arrival for surgery, the nurse administered eye drops after he had been knocked out by the doctor's anesthetic. He remained unconscious during the period when the ophthalmologist measured his eye, carefully removed the damaged cornea and sewed the clear donor cornea in place. After he placed an eye pad and an eye shield over the eye and bandaged it securely, he left, instructing the nurse to call him when the patient awoke. She did so while Calvin was emerging from his tranquillized sleep. When he was fully awake, she asked: "How do you feel?"

"Oh God!" he wailed, "I'm still blind. All I can see is the same blackness. Oh God, the operation failed!" At that moment, someone knocked on the door. The nurse opened it and then whispered to the doctor who nodded. Serena, leaning on Judy for support, entered the room and both sat, waiting.

"Don't panic Calvin! You can't see because your bandages are still in place." It took Calvin a moment to understand the doctor's words.

"Jesus! You all scared the life out of me," he said. "I've become so accustomed to the bandages, that I completely forgot they were there. I was terrified that the operation had failed and I would be blind for the rest of my life."

"The operation went as well as could be expected," the doctor told Calvin. The nurse then turned off the lights and drew the curtains. However, light still penetrated the room from the sunlit day outside. The nurse then seated Calvin before a wall mirror. In slow motion, the doctor began removing the bandages.

"Calvin," he said, "your head wounds are almost completely healed and there is no scarring; none at all." He took a long moment carefully examining each of the scars before moving on to the next one. After what to Calvin seemed like an hour, but in reality took only a few minutes, he stated:

"Yes, the scars are all healing nicely. You're lucky. Despite that awful accident, your legs and your head wounds will be totally healed. You'll have your good looks back in no time."

Serena told Judy that since she had taken the trouble to get her critic friend to assess the value of her paintings, she couldn't in all conscience sell them to her for the price mentioned. Judy refused to budge from their earlier agreement.

"The paintings I bought are very valuable, and will help me to recover the recent losses I've had in my investments. Then too, with your agreement, Jan has created a website on the internet. The canvases she put there–with her own critiques and Jerry's on each work–have already generated quite a bit of interest. We've had a number of callers wanting to buy the limited editions. Jan took their names and phone numbers and is waiting to ensure that both you and your work are better known before any sale price is agreed upon. She has already contacted the editors of leading newspapers in Vancouver, Toronto, Montreal, Edmonton and Halifax. She also sent photographs and critiques to them in order to publicize your work. A few have replied showing interest and she believes that once they begin to publish your paintings, your reputation will spread. Soon you'll be a house-hold name, at least in Canada. Jan thinks that the publication in newspapers will also spark interest in the US. I think she is trying to make up for her offensive behavior to Calvin and to you."

"Thanks to your advice, I've been devoting much more time to my painting and have a number of new works. Then, because of Jan's website, I too have had a number of calls from prospective buyers. I'm so thankful to Jan for her expertise and all she has done to help sell my work that I wonder whether she'd be willing to act as my agent."

"That's a wonderful idea, Serena. I know she'd love it."

Jan's assessment turned out to be accurate. Once the newspapers, private collectors and art dealers in Canada and the US saw the display of new and innovative wildlife paintings, they were eager to buy the originals. But with the passage of time, there was a far greater demand for the many limited edition prints of each work, and as Serena's agent, Jan would keep a percentage of each sale. Over the next months, she was inundated with requests from buyers representing museums, art galleries, collectors and private citizens anxious to own one or more of Serena's canvases, before their prices soared into the stratosphere.

Calvin was aching for the doctor to shut up. He was so excited at the prospect of seeing again that he was trembling with impatience. He felt like screaming at the doctor to get on with the job, but exercising tremendous restraint, he kept gripping the arms of his chair, and taking only shallow breaths to hold himself in check and keep strict control over his temper and his tongue.

The doctor carefully removed the eye shield, but so slowly and methodically that Calvin, in his impatience and anxiety, barely managed to prevent himself from shouting at him to hurry. Finally, holding the eye pad in place, the doctor instructed: "Calvin, when I remove this pad, the light will hurt your eye if you open it at once. Keep it closed for as long as you need until it has had a chance to adjust. If all went well, we'll see what happens."

"Do you ever dream of having an exhibition of your work to sell your paintings," Jan asked.

"Yes. It's been a long-held goal of mine, especially after all the negative criticism I've received from my former husband."

"Well Serena, how would you like to turn your dream into reality?" Jan asked.

"You know, there's a scary and unnerving side to showing your work and selling it," Serena stated.

"Why should the obvious admiration of people scare you?" Judy asked.

"You know, every artistic work expresses a great deal of the artist's persona. Each work is therefore a partial display; an 'expose' of oneself. It makes me feel like a stripper displaying her wares and demanding payment for the striptease."

"You make art sound like a gross display of personal nakedness of both body and soul. In that perspective it might seem shameful. But that's not what art is," Jan replied.

"Well, I can't help the way I feel about showing my work. But painting is what I love and since stopping would be the equivalent of a death sentence, I'll keep on whether or not people are willing to buy my work."

"Now we've settled that Serena, I can now forecast, after the calls I've had about your work that you'll never again have to do anything else but paint." Serena couldn't believe Jan's words. But from her knowledge of the art world Jan forecast that Serena's works would soon be breaking records. "You need never do another day's hosting in your life. In fact you can confine yourself wholly and solely to painting. Except for Serena's charity work, Jan's prediction proved to be accurate.

Since Calvin was about to have the procedure done, Serena was in seventh heaven and seemed to be walking on air. In a state of euphoria, she felt convinced that nobody had a right to such happiness. As everything was coming up roses for her, she reversed her vicious attack on Dame Fortune, and in an attempt at atonement, prayed feverishly for the welfare of the Lady.

On the eve of the big day, Serena told Judy that she wasn't feeling well and that her doctor had arranged to run some tests. She asked Judy to drive Cal to the hospital for the procedure. "Don't worry," she said. "I'll be there for the removal of the bandages." Judy immediately felt that Serena was hiding something.

On the way to the hospital, Cal wondered at Serena's absence.

"Where's Serena?" He inquired with surprise and disappointment in his voice.

"She asked me to drive you to the hospital as she was feeling unwell. Her doctor decided to run some tests so she too had to go to the hospital. Didn't she tell you that?" Judy asked in a puzzled voice.

"She never said a word."

"I'm sure she didn't want to upset you, especially just before the operation," Judy said to dispel his anxiety, certain now that something was amiss. But she held her tongue.

"That's not like Serena. She could have said something."

"You needn't worry, she promised to be there for the removal of the bandages." Judy's words should have dispelled Calvin's fears. Instead, they had the reverse effect. The ideas that kept worrying Calvin suddenly surfaced. It was Serena who had set in motion the procedure he had to undergo. It was she who had spent long days at the library researching the facts that a corneal transplant and microsurgery might make him see again. It was Serena too who had then checked with the ophthalmologist to verify that her findings were accurate. Finally, it was she who had found a corneal donor when none was otherwise available. She had then rushed to the hospital to harangue him into reconsidering his earlier negative attitude. The obvious question leapt into his mind. "Why wasn't she here to witness the result of all her hard work?" At that moment, the nurse whispered that his mother and Judy had just arrived and he immediately felt a great sense of relief.

Calvin felt the light stab into his tightly closed eye when the doctor had nearly removed all the bandages. While his eye stung from the pain, he forced himself to keep it shut although dying to open it to learn if he could see again. Gradually, by maddeningly slow degrees, the piercing pain grew less and less intense. Only when it had almost completely disappeared did he dare to open his eye very slowly. However, a blaze of light kept dazzling the open eye while his heart pounded like a sledgehammer and his brain whirled in anxiety, fear and excitement. Then very gradually, like something emerging out of the mists of a blurred Polaroid photograph, in the mirror before him a hazy image appeared.

"I must be hallucinating," was his first thought. He had become so used to darkness that at first he didn't recognize the image in front of him. It took him a long moment for his brain to interpret and then convince him what it was that had materialized in the mirror. He finally recognized his face.

"Oh Jesus Christ!" He suddenly shouted. "I can see! Judy, Mom, Doctor, I can really see!" In a burst of exuberance and triumphant relief, he turned from the mirror to share his joy with Serena and Judy. What he saw froze his insides to the core. Serena sat, with her head heavily bandaged, leaning on Judy's shoulder. What he could see of her face was as white as an iceberg. The strained smile she was trying to fix on her lips was closer to a grimace. She had only one eye.

The doctor watched Serena's pallid features and noted her inability to stand without Judy's support. He realized immediately that she was exhausted from her recent procedure. He scolded her gently for being out of bed, instructed the nurse to give her a sedative, and ordered Serena to stay in bed until she recovered sufficiently to be taken home.

Calvin's first sight of Judy's beauty struck him with almost the same euphoria as the restoration of his sight. "My God," he said, "you're even more beautiful than I imagined." Judy blushed at the compliment and she too was ecstatic that her prayer had been answered. The man she loved had regained his sight. When they got to his home she thought it was high time to show him her true feelings.

"There's something I've been meaning to ask you," Judy said, as she took his hand and preceded him into his bedroom. "There's a vacancy in my outfit for someone to join me in helping those who have had experiences like ours?"

She walked him backwards to the bed and getting in with him began raining kisses on his lips and into his mouth. He immediately stiffened in arousal, and before she knew it, his arms were around her and he was returning her kisses. Although he felt an infinite number of emotions rocketing through his body, he suddenly remembered having read somewhere that a vital part of foreplay involved suppressing his own urges to give his partner enough time to become thoroughly aroused. Women, he heard, took longer than men to reach their peak. It clearly meant that he had to prolong the period of foreplay. Since this situation was a first for him he didn't want to botch the job and would have to make a superhuman effort to hold himself in abeyance. He lay on his side facing her and when she closed her eyes he began by nibbling on an ear. He then sprayed tender kisses along her jaw line moving his lips ever so slowly back towards her mouth. On again tasting Judy's lips and tongue he had to fight against his violent urge to get to first base and begin his assault. With enormous restraint he somehow managed to repress his compelling hunger. Judy's eager embrace, probing tongue and feminine scent almost unmanned him. They sent his pulse racing with uncontrollable delight. Clumsily, they then took time out to help each other disrobe and when they again embraced, both were naked.

The brutal eagerness of his lips, the taste of his tongue and his deep gasps for air made Judy groan in her need. And when their mouths and bodies were clamped together, she maneuvered his head to one breast while his fingers had already begun to caress the other. Calvin felt delightfully consumed as their tongues twisted and curled around each other and delved into every niche and corner of their mouths. Calvin's busy ministrations at Judy's breasts made her nipples rise and stiffen and she felt shockwaves of excitement spiraling down through her torso towards the apex of her womanhood. She couldn't help but conclude that Cal's fingers and tongue were both skilled and demanding. Calvin's head swam as sexual electricity charged through his body and poured into his groin. She directed one of his hands to the bush between her legs and this was the moment, he realized, that he needed to force himself to fondle the golden nest for quite a spell in order to goad his partner towards fever pitch before he took the plunge. Judy's impatience for Calvin's next move kept growing and her pelvis began thrusting against him. Only when she uttered a series of moans from the depths of her throat did Calvin permit his fingers to delve into the satin folds of her feminine center. Immediately, her hips began to jerk against his finger following its rhythmic movement, now in, now out.

With pressure from her hand, Calvin moved his head down to replace his finger. Her legs opened wider and after clamping his mouth to her like a leach, he claimed her nub with his tongue and began licking it gently then slashing at it more firmly. Jolts of passion shot through her setting her body ablaze. As her spasms began to build, her moaning grew louder and louder until Calvin felt her stiffen and utter a long, low moan as she came in an overpowering burst of ecstasy. But she was not satisfied. Greedily, she wanted more of Calvin and sensing this he clambered up her body until they were face to face. She rewarded him for being a gifted student and taking hold of his hard erection inserted its full length into her. Since she was hot, wet and ready, it glided in. Slowly at first he began to thrust into her. But slow was not the rhythm she craved. Immediately, she began urging him to quicken his pace. He did and she kept up with his rhythm. He locked onto her mouth with lips and tongue as both his hands caressed her erect nipples. All the while he kept thrusting deeply into her and withdrawing working himself up into such bliss as he had never known. He was almost out of control when her back arched and she felt as though her body were about to explode. She gripped him in a powerful embrace thrusting her hips violently upwards against him again and again. Whispering his name she groaned in the agony of climax and came with a rush.

After the marathon of restraint Calvin too could no longer hold his impulses in check since he had reached the edge of release. At that moment Judy swiftly withdrew from him and clasped his penis in an iron grip. The shock restrained him as it was meant to do. She then took him again into herself, whimpering at the pleasure she derived from feeling him inside her. Clamped together, flesh against trembling flesh, they rode each other and the heightened feeling of arousal peaked with a whirling of their senses. Each of his thrusts sent a shudder of delight crashing through her. A soft sobbing bubbled from her throat as she locked herself into his rhythm, slow thrust for slow thrust accelerating in intensity. The delight they experienced grew like a rising tide that kept building until to stop would have caused them an ocean of loss. They soaked up greedily the sensations rioting through their bodies until the pleasure was too great to endure. Flexing her pelvic muscles, she felt them contract in a vice-like grip around his penis. The tight fit made Calvin's head spin. Together, they climbed higher and higher until they came together in an outpouring of sheer joy.

When it was over, they lay gasping from the effort. Their bodies, slack with exhaustion, gloried in the afterglow of sexual satisfaction. While his fingers were still knotted in her hair, and she kept nuzzling his chest with her lips, Calvin thought it was the moment for which he had dreamt so often. "My darling," he began. "I've been hopelessly in love with you ever since you first visited me in hospital. Every time you were with me, I had to struggle against my impulse to tell you how much I loved you. But the thought that I might never recover my sight always prevented me from expressing my feelings. Now that I've regained my sight, I shouldn't find it difficult to get a good job. So, once that happens, will you marry me, my darling?"

"Yes oh yes, Calvin! I'll marry you in a heartbeat. I've been so miserable and frustrated during these last weeks, deeply distressed that I had no one with whom to share my love and my life. I felt as though my heart were empty. And suddenly, while flying home, the image of your bandaged head kept intruding into my thoughts. Your marriage proposal makes me so happy, I feel as though you've insinuated yourself into my flesh and blood. Darling Calvin, your love has managed to fill my virgin heart."

"Shall I take that as a yes? Or are you slyly bargaining for more of what you've just had?" Since they were still in each other's arms, she grabbed his penis demanding that he take back the insult. He quickly agreed, coming alive and alert in her hand like a predator about to pounce. Judy marveled at the resilience of the beast.

While Judy remained silent, Calvin kept thinking about his situation. Stupid men, he thought, often congratulate themselves on their conquests. Others marvel at their good fortune. He truly believed that only a miracle could have caused his path to cross with Judy's. An errant thought then crossed his mind. When people say that good can blossom from evil that is perhaps what they mean. Judy then told him the news after reading the letter in her hand. "Hey," she said with enthusiasm, "congratulations darling, you've passed your final exams with the distinction "cum laude." She hugged and kissed him tenderly.

"Thanks Jude. You know, I still can't believe the long, tedious process of studying for a degree is finally over. It seems that life is just one long succession of trials."

"Tell me about it," she mused, and then smiling, shot him a question.

Calvin was so taken aback that he remained silent, puzzled as to what was going on in her head.

"Well," she repeated, "do you know Prufrock?"

"That's a hell of a question! Why are you focusing on poetry at this special moment?"

"Well, if you must know, I love literature and poetry is a favorite of mine. Since we've been spending so much time together, I'd like to be able to discuss the things I enjoy with you. So far, our conversation has been limited to things dealing with your recovery. I have more than enough of that with my other patients. Besides, I've often wondered about your interest in literature." She became defensive. "Do you have any objections?"

"None whatever! In *The Love song of J. Alfred Prufrock*, the latter is as ridiculous as his love song. I should point out that I find T. S. Elliot's poem presents the bitter satire of a ridiculous man rather than "a drama of literary anguish," which is the view of many critics. Calvin heard Judy's swift intake of breath, a reaction of surprise, pleasure or both. He couldn't be sure.

"I'd like to hear why you find him ridiculous."

"Prufrock, representing twentieth-century man, has fallen in love and has decided to leave his home to propose to his lady. However, he reneges on his decision almost immediately and never leaves home. His fear of rejection that fuels his indecision is cowardly and his failure to act, after deciding to do so, makes him a flip flopper. His indecision and his inability to act makes him a comic figure."

"His rival is Michelangelo, the brilliant Renaissance man. Since the sole topic of his lady's conversation is also the poem's refrain:

'In the room the women come and go // talking of Michelangelo //'–it seems that Prufrock's fear of rejection is justified."

"His fear inspires sympathy and compassion, not ridicule." Judy stated, waiting for his reply.

"One of the poem's main themes is the satire of Prufrock's comic figure."

"Prove it." Judy challenged, with a smile on her lips and pleasure in her voice.

"The poem's title, "The Love song of J. Alfred Prufrock," expresses his desire to propose to his lady. Yet, in the first line, 'Let us go then you and I' he is alone, holding a debate with himself. Since he never leaves home, never proposes, his 'love song' is never sung. This thus reduces the lover to a ridiculous figure of farce."

"Go ahead," she said with sarcasm, "I gather you have more to say."

"The 'you and I,' both referring to himself, suggests a schizoid personality, a divided character. He is a being struggling against himself. Not only is he afraid of rejection but also of making a serious commitment."

Doesn't the split personality offer a tragic view of modern man too burdened with the fear of rejection to commit? Isn't such a pessimistic figure also
sympathetic?" Judy suggested.

"No! Fear of rejection is cowardice, and together with indecision, depicts
an absurd anti-hero. Then, 'frock,' the second syllable of his name, is a synonym
for a dress. It is reasonable to conclude that any male associated with cross-
dressing is ridiculous. The same syllable also suggests the word 'unfrocked,'
and applies to either priest or monk dismissed from his profession in disgrace.
The merging of both terms depicts Prufrock as a disgraced person; a ridiculous
object of mockery; a clown." Suddenly, a thought occurred to Calvin. It was
the second time that Judy had broached the subject of a love poem while with
him. Had she been trying to tell him something all this time? If that were true,
then he was an even less sensitive idiot than he imagined. Perhaps it was his
blindness that stood in the way, he thought, trying to justify his insensitivity.

"Prufrock's beloved and her friends consider Michelangelo the heroic role
model, the man of action, the genius. In comparison, Prufrock is presented in
association with the evening: 'the patient etherized upon a table.' He is thus
the sick and paralyzed man, for whom any action is a 'presumption.' He is a
person who has 'measured out (his) life with coffee spoons.' In short, he is a
coffee-drinking procrastinator; the dreamer rather than the man of action like
the great painter.

"Calvin, doesn't a paralyzed person elicit sympathy and compassion rather
than ridicule?" Judy pointed out with a note of triumph in her voice.

"There is certainly a tragic note, but in my mind, this element highlights
what is comic by the use of juxtaposition," Calvin replied. "You should remember that Prufrock is also compared to Hamlet, focusing, not on his more
princely qualities, but solely on his indecision and procrastination. His constant repetition of:

'There will be time..,'" and his belief that his most trivial risk will "Disturb
the universe" depicts him as a coward making him far more ridiculous than
tragic!" Calvin spoke with even more conviction and triumph in his voice.

Judy stated that "Prufrock's shoddy character stems from the ghetto-like
urban wasteland where he lives. There, you wear a mask to "shamefully face
your hundred indecisions and revisions." Such a patient arouses more sympathy than ridicule." The triumph in Judy's voice was unmistakable.

"Ah, but you should remember that besides the emphasis on his shameful indecisions, his cowardice and his procrastination, Prufrock sees himself as an insect, "pinned and wriggling on the wall," and later as a crab, "a pair of ragged claws scuttling across the floors of silent seas." As a bug, he is the lowest form of life, a creature you crush without a thought. As a crab, he is an invertebrate, a spineless creature. Living on the ocean bottom, Prufrock, as both insect and crab, is excluded from the world of men and buried deeply in a nether world. Certainly, the humor is black, but it is humor nonetheless. And there," he said, "I rest my case."

Judy, radiant with her youth and beauty, was congratulating herself on the success of her hidden agenda. If she could provoke Calvin into so stimulating a discussion on such an abstract topic, she thought that he would certainly be a worthy partner in marriage.

Calvin too was congratulating himself in the belief that he had won the argument. However, Judy saw the poem as being devoid of hope. Further, the portrait of modern man was too deeply pessimistic for the main character to be dismissed as ridiculous or comic. But her joyous heart made her gracious, and she thought it prudent to concede that the black humor gave the poem artistic balance.

Chapter 75

"Now that your procedure has been successful, I've been looking for someone to share my work and my life. Since I consider you have all the qualities needed–warmth, compassion, solid principles and dedication, and you're exceptionally bright, Mr. Cum Laude," she said with the widest of smiles, "would you be willing to help me carry on both my work and my life?"

"My darling, nothing would give me greater pleasure. Besides, how could I refuse you after all you've done for me?"

"I hope you don't think that the sky's the limit with regard to wages and perks just because I'd be your wife and your employer," she stated with the widest of grins.

"Don't worry! You won't have to pay me a cent. I'll be quite willing to accept payment in kind," he replied, as he again began to caress her while she luxuriated in the warmth of his embrace. Now that he could see, as the flood of arousal thrilled through his body, he conceded that there might indeed be a bright future ahead for him.

After their joyous union, Judy took it upon herself to fill in the blanks about Serena's doings to a still-baffled Calvin. "What Serena read to you about the corneas and their availability was really a statement about the American health system. It was your suffering and despair that led her to the desperate step she took. When she learnt that in Canada there were no corneas available for donation, she decided that she would replace what she had taken away. She had

convinced herself that she alone had been responsible for your vision loss."
Judy paused, and Calvin commented:

"I owe her my sight and my life!"

Judy continued her explanation. "She was so sick with worry, so tormented with what she had done, that she decided to give you *both* her corneas."

"Both? She couldn't do that. It would have made her blind."

"Exactly, her insistence was such that I had to get the doctors' help to prevent her. They refused to take both corneas. But they hadn't reckoned with Serena's willpower. Their refusal didn't change her mind. She simply decided to go elsewhere to get the procedure done."

"I can't believe what you're telling me. Why would Serena give up both her corneas knowing she'd then be blind?" Calvin asked. "It meant that she would never be able to paint again which would be as good as a death sentence."

After great debate with herself, Serena realized that instead of letting her "blood money" remain in the bank doing nothing, she could put her parents' huge legacy to excellent use. With such an enormous sum, she began mentally planning for her next mega project. Once she and Calvin had fully recovered from their glass eye implants, she discussed her idea with him to get his input on the matter. She explained that prior to her departure from Korea, her dad, the corporate head of a fairly successful business empire, had corrected her belief that business was run solely to make a profit for the employer at the expense of his employees."

"Mom, even I know that such a belief is really naïve," Calvin stated.

"Well, dad was aghast at my ignorance of business affairs. It goaded him into explaining the length to which his corporation went to help his employees and their families enjoy a decent lifestyle. Through small wage deductions, he enabled them to purchase healthy food, clothes, furniture, appliances and even vacations at discount prices. The corporation also used its influence to place their children into better schools and helped pay the tuition of those who needed it. The best workers were even encouraged to buy shares in the corporation. In short, thanks to your grandfather, hundreds of families were able to maintain quite a comfortable lifestyle. He treated them and theirs like extended family.

"Cal, what I'm trying to say is that his generosity had a very powerful influence on me, so that when he asked what I wanted to do with my life, I quickly replied that I would like to help people in the same way that he was doing. But at that moment I didn't know in what capacity I would make that contribution. He made me promise to call on him when I decided, as he wanted very much to help. Unfortunately, he passed away before I knew what I wanted to do, but he left an enormous sum of money for me. I want you to help me make the best possible use of it."

"Gran-dad must have been quite a man," Calvin replied.

"He was! I wish you could have known him." Serena said. "He would have been so proud of you."

"Well, let me know what you have in mind and I'll set about helping in any way I can."

Serena gave Calvin the job of collating the information she needed to set her plan in motion. He began with intense research into building construction methods and the most modern materials used. When, after weeks of research, he was satisfied that he had compiled the information needed, he made an appointment with one of the island's architects, David Simpson, who specialized in designing energy-efficient buildings.

Simpson welcomed Calvin into his spacious office, one complete glass wall of which showed a very impressive view of the ocean between Victoria's shoreline and the Olympic Mountains across the Straights of Juan de Fuca. In his late forties, Simpson was tall and balding with his stomach just beginning to sag over his belt. He wore a well trimmed mustache and he gazed at Calvin with shrewd grey eyes from a smiling face.

"What brings you here Mr. Ahn?"

"We need you to build a shelter for women survivors of rape. You are to use the latest design and construction methods requiring a minimum amount of energy for heating and cooling the building. While being comfortable and healthy, the building must be a complete "thermal envelope.""

"Mr. Ahn, you've obviously done your homework since you've stipulated a design concept that I think is well suited to your needs. But excuse me if I state that you seem very young for such a tall order. What you have in mind will be quite expensive."

"My mother and I will see to it that the project is adequately funded, Mr. Simpson. Your fee will be deposited into an account at our bankers and once your design is agreed upon, we'll issue a check to you after each stage of the building program–excavation, footings, foundations, framing and so on–is complete and inspected. Is that acceptable?"

"That is perfectly acceptable! But first, I'll need to know your requirements for the interior of the building so that I can incorporate them into my design."

"I'm not a builder, but I've done quite a bit of research to find what I'll need. When I tell you what I have in mind, you'll tell me what you think and make whatever inclusions you might think necessary," Calvin said. Simpson then called his secretary on his speaker phone and instructed her to listen in, make notes and list the requirements stipulated.

"I can only tell you what happened, Calvin. No matter what argument I used in trying to stop Serena from donating both corneas, she found it impossible to dispel the guilt-ridden thoughts that had invaded her mind. Don't you understand that?"

"No! That still doesn't explain why she'd make herself blind," Calvin replied stubbornly.

"Cal, she told herself that she was the direct cause of your blindness, since it was **she** who had encouraged you to rush home. No one could convince her that she was not to blame for your accident. Wasn't it she who telephoned you at college to peak your curiosity?"

"Yes."

"Well, she blamed herself for not having waited to surprise you *after* you had returned home."

"But Judy, we know that it wasn't Serena's fault, it was the cloud of darkness blinding Mr. Brown and me that caused the accident."

"Nevertheless, Serena thought she had robbed you of the worthwhile future she knew you would have carved out for yourself. You know how stubborn she can be when she gets an idea into her head. Besides, there were two other reasons that drove her obsession."

"I can't think of any reasons more persuasive than the doctors' words?"

"She firmly believed one of her mother's maxims that had burned themselves into her consciousness: "the worth of parents is measured by the sacrifice they are willing to make for the welfare of their children." It was this chilling doctrine that drove her to reach the one conclusion that, she believed, would rectify the wrong she had done—the donation of both her eyes."

"Have you chosen a site for your shelter?" Simpson asked Calvin at their next meeting.

"Not yet. After we decide on the design, I thought you might be able to help in that decision. I'd also like you to recommend a firm of contractors with whom you've worked and consider experienced, reliable and cost effective."

"I can recommend the very best. Now, I'm anxious to hear your needs for the building, Mr. Ahn."

"I envisage something simple: a fairly long rectangular building with small bedrooms on either side of a central corridor on both the first and second floors. Reception will be inside the main entrance to the building's center, facing the street. Each bedroom will hold two single beds, a built-in dressing table with mirror and chest of drawers, a cupboard and a medicine cabinet above a wash basin. On one side half way down the corridor, a bank of shower stalls will occupy the ground floor next to a cluster of toilets. There will also be an infirmary, a large comfortable lounge and cafeteria. How am I doing?"

"You're doing very well!"

"On the lower floor we'll need a large laundry room capable of holding industrial washers and dryers plus a couple of ironing boards that fold into the wall and a table for folding clothes. There'll be large separate cupboards for sheets, pillows, pillow cases and blankets with enough shelves for holding detergents, bleach, fabric softeners and other cleaning materials. We'll also need broom cupboards with space for industrial use vacuum cleaners, mops and brooms. I've left the heating of the building for last," Calvin stated. "For that, I'll want you to use solar energy in conjunction with traditional gas heating."

"You're very thorough, but we can certainly do what you ask. We'll design a south facing roof with an array of solar panels that will capture the direct rays of the sun, both morning and afternoon. This will reduce the cost of your gas powered furnaces. We can also install efficient wind driven fans to minimize the cost of air conditioning in the summer," Simpson replied.

"The upper floor, reached by a staircase set in the middle of the ground floor, will have a similar floor plan to the lower floor with bedrooms, bathrooms and toilets but no lounge, cafeteria or infirmary."

"What you state sounds both efficient and thorough. But now that we've settled the needs of the occupants, what thoughts do you have about the specifications for the construction of the building itself?"

"To shield the building from the weather, I'd want you to use insulating concrete forms, two layers of extruded form board with steel reinforced centers, inside and outside the building."

"That's sensible. It will save heating and cooling costs in the long run."

"I'll also want R-30 to insulate the wall foundations and R-70 for the ceiling and wall cavities." Calvin stated. "I know it's more than the normal level required, but it will help to minimize water vapor condensation that can cause serious deterioration in the structure of a building."

"I agree. That's very important!"

"I'd like you to install airtight drywall and gypsum board on the interior of the building and sealed form board on the exterior. This will reduce air moisture filtration and solve the possible problem of deterioration."

"We can use heat recovery ventilators to eliminate those possibilities," Simpson stated.

"For the basement, floors and lower walls I would like you to use filtrated cement slabs. Being water resistant, they'll eliminate the need for moisture barriers. I would also like you to seal the edges around the exterior windows and doors using air/vapor diffusion retarder. For the roof, 25 year guaranteed shingles should suffice."

"Let me congratulate you, Mr. Ahn. You've done some very thorough research!"

"Thank you. Using the best materials will be a bit more costly, but will minimize energy costs later on," won't it?"

"It surely will," Simpson agreed.

After the architect had submitted the preliminary design and won the approval of Serena and Calvin, the hard lined plans were then passed by the Municipality of Saanich. Simpson found them a couple of vacant lots on which the building could be located. Calvin then chose the larger one and arranged its purchase through their lawyers. Serena and Calvin examined the proposed cost of each phase, and checked it out with Green, their contractor to verify that there were no useless inclusions. Finally, they signed a contract with Simpson and gave him the green light to begin the project. It was estimated that the building would be completed within a three to four month period. Calvin breathed a sigh of relief.

As he was being shown out of Simpson's office, his secretary told her boss that a caller, who refused to give his name, had been trying to get in touch with him every fifteen minutes for the last two hours. Calvin saw what seemed to be a look of guilt flit across the architect's face that set him wondering.

"If he calls again, tell him I'm busy with a project and won't be able to see him anytime this week," Simpson replied. Since his own business with the architect was finished for the day, Calvin thought it strange that Simpson should be turning away a possible client. He was certainly free to take a call. Calvin found the situation puzzling, but decided that it was none of his business.

"I can't believe that the doctors failed to convince Serena that her decision to donate both corneas was hopelessly wrong." Calvin told Judy. "I feel sure that I'd have been able to change her mind," he continued. "But didn't you say that there were two reasons?"

"Yes. It drives me wild to think that you were the cause of that reason."

"Me? Calvin barked in surprise. What could I have done that would force Serena to blind herself?"

"It isn't what you did, it's what you said. Don't you remember that really moronic statement you repeated over and over to your mother?"

"No! I don't remember saying anything that would force Serena to blind herself," he said heatedly.

"Think back, Calvin. Think back to your first idiotic reaction to Serena's attempt to persuade you to accept the corneal donation and the surgical procedure."

"Judy, for Christ sake, will you just tell me what I said?"

"Calvin, how could you forget repeating that 'a one-eyed man is one step up from human garbage?" The shock of recalling his stupidity coupled with the stern rebuke in Judy's attitude staggered Calvin. He remained silent with shame. On recovering, he remonstrated with himself:

"Oh God," he said aloud, "how could I have been such a moron! But Judy, I hope you're aware that I had no idea that my statement, uttered in a moment of despair, could possibly lead to Serena's decision?"

"Yes dear, I do. And that's why you're forgiven."

"Thank you, Judy. Now, how did you succeed in changing her mind?"

"Well, that was another tough problem. I though and thought until finally, I came to believe that there was only one possibility that would convince Serena to change her mind."

"What was that?" Calvin asked, shame and guilt still evident in his face and voice.

"I had to lie."

"If the doctors couldn't persuade her, what lie could you use to change her mind?"

"It wasn't easy. I had to give the idea a lot of thought before I came up with the only fabrication powerful enough to convince her."

"Stop stalling! I can't possibly imagine what that lie could be!"

"I told her that if she blinded herself by giving you both her eyes, you would feel forced not only to take care of her, but also to have her live with you for the rest of your life."

Calvin remained silent before stating: "But that's not a lie. If she became blind, I would have made her live with me. Besides, how would that change her mind?"

"It was then that I resorted to the lie, Calvin. Every time you saw her," I said, "she'd remind you of a debt that you would find impossible to repay. Pretty soon, you'd begin to hate the very sight of her for forcing you into a lifestyle that you could never change."

That was a real whopper, was all Calvin could think of saying. Instead, he remained silent more ashamed and guilty than ever.

"Well, it did the trick," Judy said.

Once the building of the shelter had begun, Calvin went to the site each morning to keep track of its progress. He met with Green, the contractor, and noted that Simpson only came in from time to time. He oversaw the excavation and the many layers of gravel at its bottom to ensure proper drainage, the piping that had to be installed to bring in electricity, gas, and water and to take away waste. Later, this last pipeline would be hooked up to the city's underground drainage and sewer systems. Green and Calvin then supervised the building of the plywood forms to hold the cement for the footings, the steel rods to strengthen the cement and the pouring of the cement itself.

Calvin found it interesting to see the efficiency with which the professionals did their work with a minimum of effort. Once the cement was dry the framers began erecting the skeleton of the outer walls, fastening on the extruded form board with steel reinforced centers, and framing in the areas for the windows, doors and cupboards with studs on sixteen inch centers. The carpenters then began to section off the main divisions of the various rooms and cupboards before framing in the staircase.

Once that was done, the pre-fabricated trusses for the roof were trucked in with a crane to lift them into place. They were bolted to the rafters on either side of the outer perimeter of the building and joined to each other at the top to frame the roof. The carpenters then nailed 3/4 inch ply to the trusses that they covered with tar paper before installing the shingles. Following tradition, builder and workmen celebrated the completion of the roof at a local pub.

Meanwhile, workers sealed the outer walls with tar paper and wire to support the stucco that would form the outer coat. Once this was dry, they began the plastering. Inside the building, they fitted insulation in between the studs, stapled in the vapor barriers before installing the dry wall-board to create the inner walls. The windows were then brought in and installed. Calvin was pleased that Simpson dropped in to see that the workers were following his plans step by step and using the exact materials stipulated in the contract. Indeed, everything was progressing so smoothly that Calvin sang the praises of the combined teamwork of architect, contractor and their workmen to his mother.

"I'd like to congratulate you on the excellent job you did in first researching the project, finding the right architect, and then using your knowledge to organize the construction of my new rape survival facility," Serena told Calvin while Judy listened smiling proudly. "Simpson got in touch with me as you arranged, and was high in his praise of your knowledge and suggestions for constructing a thermal envelope..."

"Well, thank you Mom," Calvin replied, before adding: "I too have good news. I've asked Mrs. Johnson for her daughter's hand in marriage, and she gave me her blessing. I'd like you to know that Judy and I have wedding plans for the near future."

"I wish you both the heartiest congratulations, Cal and Judy. That's wonderful news! But I too have plans for you both. As I just mentioned Judy, Calvin and I are building a center for rape survivors that will be completed, we hope in about four months."

"Yes, I know. Calvin mentioned the work he was doing for you, Serena."

"I want you both to visit our present rental shelter and compile a detailed inventory of the items we'll need for the new shelter. When it opens, I'm offering you both the job of heading the organization and acting in a supervisory capacity for running the two shelters with me. Both are too big a job for me to do alone. I have been commissioned to do a number of paintings that will take up much of my time. Your jobs, if you accept, will be to interview and then hire a full time staff, beginning with a well-qualified Matron, who will help you choose the qualified staff needed–beyond those we'll transfer from our present rental facility–to run the institution. Those patients still present in our rental facility will occupy the new one, and then new staff will be needed to replace those vacancies created by the staff transfers. The present manageress, untrained workers and volunteers will continue working at our rental facility that will be converted to serve in the future as a shelter for battered women.

I'm afraid the job I'm offering you is far bigger than it sounds. Besides the hiring of new staff, you'll have to make arrangements for their monthly payment as well as the purchasing of all the furnishings and appliances needed for the new shelter. You'll have to evaluate each item needed for its carpeted bedrooms and living room, tiled kitchen, toilet facilities, and shower stalls. I want the best of everything, from beds and mattresses, through industrial vacuum cleaners, right down to brooms, mops and cleaning materials. I realize that this comes as quite a surprise, so I'll give you a week to think it over and decide. If you accept, we'll discuss wages and perks, which will be generous..." Judy cut her off.

"Serena, your offer is very kind and I can tell you now that I'll be happy to help run your organizations. The only problem is whether you'll allow both Calvin and me to continue working with my patients afflicted with vision loss. You see, he's already in my employ as husband-to-be and co-worker," Judy said with a grin.

"Of course I'll allow you to continue your work Judy. And there'll always be bed space at the new facility for any of your patients who may need it. Also we're quite near both hospitals so the commute, should they need it, will be easy."

"Thank you Serena, that's very generous of you."

"Mom, I fully agree with Judy," Calvin chimed in. "We don't need time to think it over."

"I'm glad to hear that. You'll have to look over the design of the new center to determine all your needs. Just tell me when you would like to start so I can put you both on the payroll."

"Mom, we'll start right away," Calvin chimed in. "I'll hire Mrs. Drew as the new Matron, okay?

"That's a matter for you and Judy to decide."

Calvin found that he had spoken too quickly about the progress of their new shelter. After he and Green had supervised the pouring of the concrete, the purchase of the lumber, the framing of the walls and the completion of the roofing, Green told Calvin the bad news. Simpson had disappeared, and his phones, both at home and at the office, were disconnected. Worse, he had drawn on the last phase of the work and had left without paying the plumber and electrician for their time. There was more bad news. Many of the laborers had fled to find new jobs where their pay would be assured. Worse still, the plumbing and wiring, though finished, had not been inspected.

"Would we be able to rehire the workers?" Calvin asked Green.

"That's very unlikely. They've been hired under duress. Deserting their new employer would ruin their reputation for reliability," Green replied.

Calvin cursed himself for the problems realizing the truth of the maxim: 'nothing is easy.'

"What do you propose?" Calvin asked.

"The laborers still here can bring the unused materials into the building, and then secure the entrances and exits against theft. We'll shut down the project until we find a new crew to finish the job."

"Good! I'll inform the previous workers to collect their pay after work on Friday. Calvin realized that few workmen were available because of Victoria's building boom. He'd therefore spent the next days seeking workers outside the municipalities of Victoria. In a nearby suburb, View Royal, the Builders Association steered him towards a project that was due for completion in a week's time. He immediately hired workers to finish the job. Finally, since the unpaid plumber and electrician had put liens on the property, he would have to solve that problem as well.

"Mom, the rebuilding will begin in a week. In the meantime, I'll get the last phases inspected.

"The contract clearly states that payment can be drawn only *after* it is inspected and passed," Serena said sternly. "How did Simpson manage to draw on the account *before* the inspections?"

"Green trusted him as they had worked together before. But, the police informed me that Simpson's quite a slippery fellow. When I reported the incident they said that he had broken an earlier contract, was in serious financial difficulty and under investigation. They think he slipped away somewhere."

"That still doesn't answer the question." Serena repeated sternly.

"When Simpson told Green that he had "arranged for the inspectors to be here any day soon," Green believed him, so he and I signed off on the draw expecting the inspectors to show up. They never did. So, it's really my fault for not keeping a sharper eye on things." Serena did not contradict him, seeing it as a lesson he wouldn't forget. To make up for his lapse in judgment, Calvin used some of his insurance money to repay the workers without mentioning it to his mother. He then went to the municipality, explained the situation and requested that inspectors come to the site to inspect the plumbing and wiring–phases that had been completed but not inspected. Calvin, having learnt his lesson, accompanied Green to the site while the inspection was being done. Once it was completed, he thanked the inspectors for their cooperation.

By aiding rape survivors as well as battered women, Serena felt that at last she was on the way to realizing the promise she had made to her dad and to herself. But she considered what she had done was just a beginning. She called Calvin and Judy to join her and the three put their heads together to discuss plans for their next project. At the end of the meeting her heart took wing and began to soar.

Chapter 76

Calvin experienced a tremendous sense of relief once the inspections were complete. Together, he and Green selected and purchased the rest of the materials needed to complete the work yet to be done. Green then directed the new crew to finish the interior of the building, before calling in the new electrician and plumber to check that those two phases were indeed efficiently completed. The carpenters would complete work on the doors, cupboards, cabinetry, and framing in the baths, toilets and the infirmary. Once the interior was completed, the painting would begin, and the tiles and carpets would be laid. Finally, the landscapers would be brought in. Serena was happy to hear that the new shelter for rape survivors would soon be finished. Afterwards, Calvin and Green would both be on hand for another week to tie up loose ends and to solve whatever problems remained.

There was still the serious problem of the unpaid plumber and electrician who had put liens on the property. Calvin thought long and hard trying to find a solution before meeting with the two journeymen to explain what he had in mind. "Like you," he told them, "I too have been shafted by Simpson. The latter has absconded with our money for jobs that have been paid for but not inspected. If I pay you your full wages, I'll be paying a second time for the same work. Then, I'll still have the hassle of getting the inspectors and the two phases passed. Seen in that perspective, I'm the only one who's being completely screwed. Do you follow me?"

"Yes we do. But why should we be the ones who get screwed?" The electrician answered.

"That's certainly not what I have in mind." Calvin stated. "Wouldn't it be fairer if we both shared the loss? You see, the only way that you can make a claim on your liens is when the building is sold. That won't be in my lifetime..." He let his words hang in the air.

"So, rather than have to wait forever, you are willing to pay us half what is owed?"

"That's exactly what I had in mind!" Calvin thought that he had them over a barrel."

"We'll settle for sixty percent of our wages," the electrician said.

"How about accepting fifty-five percent?" Calvin suggested.

"No, sixty is what we'll accept."

They shook hands and Calvin paid them.

The completed shelter was solidly built and practical for its purpose. Once the paint was dry, Judy and Calvin bought the furnishings, and hired the Matron, Mrs. Drew. Together, the three of them determined the number of qualified and unqualified staff needed, and then worked out, with Matron's help, the wages of the new employees. After the furnishings were installed and the smell of the paint had evaporated, Serena called in Father Murphy to bless the premises and the survivors who had already been moved into the new facility. The priest was happy to comply with Serena's request. Then, the police informed Calvin that Simpson had been caught in Mexico. He had confessed and would be deported to Canada for trial. All's well that ends well, Serena thought.

On the following Sunday, Father Murphy, again in Church, felt a stomach wrenching need to pray for his flock. He was in despair at the way in which corruption was devastating his and the world's parishes. Such was the depth of his disillusion that he buried his face in his hands instead of clasping them in prayer. He saw the world mired in filth and felt helpless to stop it slipping over the edge of an infernal abyss. He had spent his whole life fighting against the forces of evil and it galled him to recognize that he was being defeated. For the second time in his life he cried out in anguish and despair: "If You knew that I would lose the battle, why did You urge me to choose this vocation?"

Cal and Judy, I'd like to thank you both for the great work you've done in getting the new shelter ready for its occupants," Serena said. "I know it's been hard work with especially long hours. To show my appreciation, the three of us can start looking for a present that would be appropriate. What do you think?"

"Two incredible offers coming one after the other. Wow! We're infinitely lucky. Thank you so much Serena, I don't know what else to say." Both Calvin and Judy were blushing, elated at the news.

With time, Serena grew stronger and, as with Calvin, it was impossible to tell that one of their eyes was artificial. Her facial expression remained unchanged, and although as beautiful as before, she was plagued with another problem. Would she be able to paint as well with only one eye? She began by first drawing, and then painting a series of animal parts: eyes, tails, wing feathers and heads to judge whether there was any difference between these and her earlier work. She painted and painted, making many comparisons, but still couldn't tell if there were any differences. With only one eye, she felt sure that she had lost the ability to assess and judge her work competently. What she needed was an unbiased critical eye to do the assessment.

"Calvin, how does beauty affect you?" Judy asked, blindsiding him with the question. Calvin, caught off guard, needed time to collect his thoughts before he could come up with a worthwhile answer.

"Well, if you mean the beauty of a painting, or of an incredible performance, or the natural beauty of a star-studded night-sky with the full moon presiding, I'd say that they all give a jolt to the viewer's senses, inspiring astonishment, shock and even awe. The power of the impact can make the stomach lurch, cause hair on the arms, neck and shoulders to bristle, and even take one's breath away. On occasion, the power of the impact can even bring tears to the eyes." He thought for a long moment before adding: "there are some who believe that the contemplation of beauty can make the viewer a better person. Such people think like this: since beauty approaches perfection, those who gaze upon it wish to mimic it and ape its perfection. Their thinking is akin to the inspiration that role models exert upon their followers or the influence that mentors wield over their disciples.

"I'd like you to be more specific?" Judy pressed, making Calvin wonder why she was being so insistent, before he replied:

"Well, a beautiful painting or a brilliant performance also communicates a special message to the viewer. While he enjoys the spectacle, both also force him to recognize the exceptional genius of the painter or the performer plus the message he's trying to convey. At the same time, they inspire the viewer with a sense of joy or awe that can be overwhelming. Of course, natural beauty falls into a completely different category. A beautiful moonlit night or a stunning sunset also inspires the observer with an inordinate sense of joy. But they also compel the observer to recognize the extraordinary message of the author. And since no mere mortal can orchestrate such an event, the message signals that the spectacle can only have been created by the hand of the Almighty. Does that answer your question?"

"I would have tried to answer it in similar fashion, though I doubt that my reply would have been quite as eloquent. There's hope for your pedestrian soul yet, Cal." Judy concluded with a chuckle, a broad smile of satisfaction and a loud smack on his cheek.

"Hello, Hwang Yong!" There was glee in Serena's voice. I find your face is as beautiful as ever."

"Mom, I prefer you to call me Calvin," he said mildly. "And please stop trying to embarrass me."

"I like to remind you of your Korean heritage," she said mischievously, knowing that after her sacrifice, Calvin would not dare to disobey her. Cracking the whip of her newfound authority, she barked out her orders like a staff sergeant to his new recruits. Her eye was filled with mischief, and there was a broad smile on her face to show she was kidding. "Hwang Yong, be ready at 9 hours sharp tomorrow. I'll be taking you and Judy on the shopping spree I promised! There's a beautiful house I want you to look at."

"Wow, Mom, what a fantastic treat! Both Judy and I would be delighted."

"I also cooked a special dinner to introduce Judy to Korean cuisine this evening." Hearing the jovial tone in her voice, Calvin responded with an immediate salute and an:

"Aye, aye Sir," followed by: "What time Sir?"

"Come at nineteen hours sharp, and not a minute later!" Serena said in stentorian tones. With a maternal smile, her eye still sparkling with mischief, Serena began humming softly as she went to prepare dinner.

Serena had spent the last weeks painting various parts of the anatomy of different animals and birds. She was obsessed with trying to judge whether or not the loss of sight in her one eye had adversely affected her ability to paint. A phone call interrupted her.

"Hello," she said. "Serena here."

"Hello Serena, there's a Korean lady in Victoria that I can't seem to get out of my system. I've been wondering whether or not I should come and live there. Do you think she'd be agreeable?" Delighted at hearing John's voice, she teased:

"I'll have to ask and see what the lady says."

"If I say that I'm dying to set her body on fire all over again, do you think she'll agree?"

"Shush!" Serena whispered as though the world were listening. "She says that her body can't wait for the fire to start."

"Now that I know how she feels, tell her I won't be coming at all." It was his turn to tease.

"She says that if you don't arrive soon, when you do, she'll probably be busy with someone else." Oh John," she thought but didn't say: how did you manage to wrap yourself around my heart so tightly and crawl into my soul?

"My darling, I'm at a downtown hotel, and I'll be over in time to chase away any rivals."

"She'd surely be agreeable to that, she paused before adding: and anything else."

When Serena heard the knock, she rushed to the door and was surprised to find Jan, not John. She hid her disappointment and bravely said:

"Come in Jan, you're just the person I wanted to see."

"Serena, I came to see how you were doing."

"I need you to look at the work I've just finished. You've got to tell me if my painting is any different from the work I did before my corneal donation."

"You ought to be in bed resting, not working already," Jan scolded.

"Painting is not work for me, Jan. If I couldn't paint, I'd shrivel up and die."

"What nonsense!" Jan began, as Serena dragged her by the arm to the studio showing her the body parts of the animals she had recently done. Jan made a long and detailed study of each one. She frowned in concentration and it looked as though her face became grave and her breathing seemed to stop as she took her time scrutinizing each one of the many animal parts. Sometimes, she seemed to be lost in concentration for so long that Serena was convinced her work had deteriorated. The terrible blow was so hard for her to accept that she fled from the room to hide her bitter disappointment. In confusion, with tears almost blinding her, she hugged herself tightly and began to pace wondering what she could possibly do to rectify the situation. Jan was astonished to find herself alone in the studio when ready to deliver her verdict. She found Serena in tears, pacing up and down her bedroom like a madwoman.

"Serena," Jan began...Sternly, Serena cut her off.

"Don't you dare lie to me Jan. That deep frown I saw on your face reflected your opinion perfectly."

"Well Serena, since you've read my mind, I suppose there's nothing more to add."

"Do you think that in time my work will improve? I mean after I get used to painting with only one eye?" The pleading tone of her voice made Jan stop her teasing.

"Perhaps you should let me tell you what I think, Serena."

"I already know what you think. Just answer my question," she replied rudely.

"In comparing your recent work with the past, there's not a shred of difference." Jan said.

"Please don't lie just to make me feel better."

"It's the truth, Serena! If I put those paintings on the market, they'll sell just as they are."

"Really!" Serena replied, unable to believe what her ears had been longing to hear. She was already rejoicing. Her eye was bright and shining with pleasure. There was an interruption when Calvin and Judy knocked and entered holding hands and smiling shyly at each other and at their parents. The two mothers kissed and congratulated them, then immediately set about making plans for the wedding date they had set.

Chapter 77

Some months ago, I spoke to you about the onslaught of evil that was invading the parishes of the world, and told you that the Church was convinced the instigator was Satan. He was the serpent that brought sin into the world through his corruption of Eve and Adam. He too, on being punished by God, had vowed to take his revenge. But, being helpless against the Almighty, he had declared war on His Creation, and thus on mankind. Like many of my brother priests, I believe that Satan and evil are synonymous. When I spoke to you last, I promised to provide further proof of the global crisis that has been taking place. Since then, my nightmares have returned together with a debilitating illness, forcing me to remain bedridden and unable to keep my promise to you until now. Today, I am here to express the thoughts that have occurred to me; thoughts that I consider it my duty to convey to you.

For a long time, it seemed to me that the worm of evil wriggles unseen into the hearts of man, inciting him to mock the virtues of a Christian life. The evil worm goads him into temptation that he is powerless to resist. Of late, it has been especially active, boring deeply into the hearts of the families of this and other congregations across the globe. In consequence, wrongdoing has escalated considerably and family members have become more and more immoral, more and more depraved. I am deeply saddened at the preponderance of deceit, malice, betrayal, cruelty and evil of every sort that is taking place in the heart of every parish, every city and every nation. A few priests like me, have been so ashamed of our own depravity that we have tried to destroy ourselves.

Of late, my nightmares have been more terrifying than ever, though my doctors believe that I am overworked and deeply disturbed. They think that I have slipped back into my past illness when I was hospitalized after my tours of duty during the Gulf war. They state that I am delusional, as I was then, but have not used the term. I agree that I am deeply disturbed, but I repeat, it is not from overwork. Lately, I see myself stumbling through the darkness of a wasteland. As I told you, it is strewn with the corpses of my flock, struck down for their disobedience and their wickedness. Because the images of these night-mare-massacres have been repeating themselves over and over, I've interpret them as divine warnings of God's savage vengeance that will descend upon us." The priest took a long pause, appearing to be exhausted before he continued.

"Even before my attempted suicide, I had preached these warnings to my parishioners in Korea. Today, I repeat them. Although I am neither prophet nor soothsayer, the warnings seem to be an obvious conclusion to my recurring nightmares." In a trembling voice he suddenly said: "Forgive me, I'm not feel-ing well. I have to stop."

As he climbed down slowly from the pulpit bent almost double and breathing deeply, he looked exhausted as if he had just run a marathon. When rested, the priest remembered that his Korean congregation hadn't believed him then. Why would this one believe him now, especially after he had humiliated himself and scandalized Mother Church by his attempted suicide? Yet, he couldn't help feeling that if he had held his tongue, it would have been a dereliction of his duty.

After lying down and resting some more he recovered somewhat. In des-peration, he turned to the Internet to learn what the great minds of the 21st century thought about evil. He was dumbfounded by what he read. Using sta-tistics, those intellectuals stated that with the downward trend of criminal ac-tivity all over the globe, the world "appears to be a friendlier place." In short, the great minds thought that evil was on the decline.

However, the black angel knew differently. As the embodiment of corruption, his stock in trade was disease. So it was that he laid waste the planet with bubonic plague, smallpox, leprosy, cholera, typhus, TB and cancer. Proud of his achievement, he also lashed out at mankind with polio, MS, Parkinson's, Alzheimer's and a slew of venereal diseases. Still not satisfied, in recent years, he added some choice variations to the mix–AIDS, SARS, the Ebola and West Nile virus, E. coli, and not a few incompetent physicians and surgeons.

With his attention focused on Europe, Asia and North America, the demon targeted livestock. He spawned diseases like Mad Cow, Hoof and Mouth, Swine Fever and various forms of avian 'flu, dealing a crippling blow to the world's meat industry. Yet, the monotony of attack without visible retaliation soon bored him and he transferred his perverse attention to the Dark Continent where heat, light and moisture promoted the germination, growth and proliferation of corruption. There he spawned the tsetse fly so that sleeping sickness, malaria, rinderpest, canine distemper and rabies, dispatched big and small game together with human beings in the tens of thousands.

"In their conclusion that evil is on the decline, the High Priests of the Internet have ignored the recent history lesson on the subject that the demon was bent on teaching," the priest told his congregation at their next meeting. "Today, August 6th is the sixtieth anniversary of the Holocaust, the unspeakable crimes committed by the Nazis of Germany's Third Reich. Entitled the "Final Solution," it was the systematic annihilation of six million Jews during the Nazi genocide. Although the event is well documented, it is not easy to put a singular face on the sheer barbarity of those responsible for the slaughter of so many innocent men, women and children. Some would say it was Adolph Hitler, since he was the political leader of Germany at the time. Others would say it was Adolph Eichmann, since it was he who organized the atrocity. But, others who believe that evil is not a singular entity, prefer to see it as resembling an octopus with a contagious cancer, each one of its many tentacles being venomous. It seems then, that the prize should be shared with a physician, Dr. Josef Mengele chiefly because he was the most venomous tentacle that devastated the numerous human beings whom it caressed.

Doctor Mengele, a Nazi German SS officer and leading physician in the concentration camp at Auschwitz-Birkenau, was in charge of the train loads of Jewish prisoners from Hungary. He divided incoming prisoners into right and left lines, separating families and condemning to death hundreds of thousands of fathers, mothers, and children, including babies, adolescent girls and grandparents. He shot a mother who refused to be separated from her teenaged daughter. As punishment for daring to flout his authority, he sent to the gas chamber all those who had the misfortune of sharing the vehicle that transported her. When one block of the prison was infected with lice, he gassed all 750 women in it. He drew a line on a wall of the children's prison, 5 feet 2inches above the floor and sent to the gas chamber all the children whose heads didn't reach the line. He "routinely tossed babies into ovens alive," and ordered pregnant women to lie on their backs, then stamped on their stomachs until they aborted.

Dr. Mengele and his team of doctors put prisoners into pressure chambers then raised the simulated altitudes. Severe burns from mustard gas were inflicted on prisoners; others were forced to remain for hours in tanks of ice water; still others were infected with diseases like malaria and typhus or injected with various poisons. All these experiments were carried out to test the most efficient means of treating various diseases. Of course the few who didn't die suffered excruciating pain and injury.

Dr. Mengele was fascinated with experimentation on twins. On one occasion he injected chloroform into the heart of 28 gipsy twins. After their death, he casually set about dissecting them. He also experimented on no less than 3000 twins killing all but 400. He was especially keen on bleeding identical twins to death. He was known to perform vivisections on pregnant women before dispatching them to the gas ovens. Very few of the victims on whom he operated ever survived. He gave shock treatment to inmates, injected chemicals into children's eyes seeking to change their eye color, and conducted amputations of limbs and internal organs without anesthetics. It is easy to understand why Doctor Mengele was called 'the Angel of death.' Yet, the world knows that no one should dare use the name Mengele and angel in the same sentence.

Just three years later, during the final stages of that same war, the United States dropped an atomic bomb on two Japanese cities, Hiroshima and Nagasaki. The bombs named "little boy," and "fat man," annihilated hundreds of thousands of civilians, innocent men, women and children. The shame of the attack must fall squarely on the shoulders of the administration of the United States of America. This abomination was regarded as "the most sinister development in warfare in the 20th century." Both these events took place at the end of World War 11, when leaders of the free world vowed that they would never again sit idly by and permit such an atrocity to recur. Of course, they were referring to the holocaust. But if you asked them why, they would say: "that was the war to end all wars."

Some years later in 1964, after the division of Cambodia into the communist North and the US backed, South Vietnam, civil war broke out between the two sides. In this case, the world points the finger at the villains: US B-2 bombers, using napalm and carpet bombs, killed some 750,000 Cambodian men, women and children. Then, the Khmer Rouge, a guerilla group under the command of Pol Pot, imposed a program to reconstruct Cambodia. Men, women and children were ordered to leave their homes in villages, towns and cities to work on one huge collective labor farm. The young, the old, the disabled were all made to work or die. Factories, schools, universities and hospitals were shut down. Professional men and women, doctors, lawyers, engineers, teachers, and scientists were all killed together with their extended families. All Buddhist monks were put to death and their temples destroyed. Laughing, crying, knowing a foreign language or wearing glasses was enough to get you killed. Racism was rife, with all minorities slaughtered–Chinese, Vietnamese, Thai, half the Muslim population and 800,000 Christians.

"Not content with the depredation he had unleashed on the planet, Satan focused on man's greed by tempting hunter and poacher into escalating their slaughter. The first, shot every animal within range, the second, slaughtered every living thing to promote the illegal sale of flesh, bone, horns, hides, feathers, claws and even internal organs. His insatiable cravings still unsatisfied, the demon seduced industrialists into desecrating the environment. They destroyed future generations of salmon by crossing streams with heavy equipment silting up the spawning sections of river beds, and secretly dumping their toxic wastes into waterways. He goaded fishermen to multiply their catch a thousand-fold. Thanks to his meticulous attention to detail creatures like the polar bear, tiger, gorilla, cod and others are bound for the same exit as the mammoth, the passenger pigeon, the dinosaur and the dodo bird.

Unwilling to rest on his laurels, the rebel angel guided man's hands in the indiscriminate use of fire, axe and chainsaw, making the world's temperate and tropical forests disappear with alarming speed." "Painting for you a picture of the accumulation of mankind's corruption is for me an undertaking that is as painful and as distasteful as it is demoralizing," the priest told his parishioners. "I have no doubt that my illness is a result of this contagion. But ill or not, I shall try to bring you up to date on the matter when we meet again next Sunday."

After a long fit of coughing a very shaky Father Murphy mounted to the pulpit and told his congregation:

"Today I shall continue where I left off last Sunday, again using historical fact from the Internet to pinpoint the sinfulness and iniquity that has been, and is still devastating the population of the planet." This time, he didn't mention that his doctor had diagnosed that he was showing symptoms of his earlier illness, and that there were times when he was definitely delusional. "During the break up of the former country, Yugoslavia, Slobodan Milosevic inflamed the hatred already existing between the Serbs, Croats and Muslims. When in 1991 Slovenia and Croatia declared independence from Yugoslavia, Serbian guerillas under Milosevic invaded the city of Vukovac. They used daggers, axes, sledgehammers, iron bars, flame throwers and explosives to kill their Muslim enemies, before mutilating and then roasting their corpses." The priest drank some water holding the glass with trembling fingers and continued with a quivering voice, determined to finish his message. He couldn't tell whether he was addressing his congregation or whether the people to whom he was speaking were all in his imagination, but he brushed aside the thought and continued:

"Between 1992 and 1995, in response to Bosnia's declaration of independence, Serbian forces attacked Sarajevo and organized the mass murder of 8,000 men and boys. They terrorized Muslim families using rape as a weapon against women and girls. After the war, the Serbs shocked the leaders of the free world by terming the slaughter of 200,000 Muslims, "ethnic cleansing." At this point the priest, although gasping and in evident pain and distress, forced himself to continue.

"In the region of the Sudan, the conflict in Darfur has been an ongoing battle since 2003. The Hutu dominated Sudanese Muslim military and the Janjaweed, a government-sponsored group, used rape, mass murder and organized starvation, to slaughter more than 400,000 Tutsis, besides displacing two and a half million of them into refugee camps.

The immortal beast was teaching the world another lesson. He would not allow his evil handiwork to be stamped out by mere mortals.

Apart from ignoring the genocides of the past seventy years, during the past decade, the Internet scholars had also overlooked the 9/11 destruction of the World Trade Center and the Pentagon, the laying waste of Afghanistan by US carpet bombing, the suicide bombings of the Middle East, and the slaughter of thousands of US troops, Iraqi and Afghan insurgents and civilians. During the same period, terrorists had killed both military and civilian personnel in Sri Lanka, Nepal, Israel, England, Ireland, Scotland, Indonesia, Morocco,

Spain, France, Germany, Norway, Sweden, Turkey, Africa and India. Such an accumulation of senseless killing testifies to the falsehood of the conclusions drawn by Internet scholars.

Today, the countries of the Middle East are involved in the turmoil of revolution, and their earth is stained with the flow of innocent blood. Refusing to bow any longer to their corrupt and tyrannical dictators, the people of Tunisia, Egypt, Libya, Yemen, Bahrain, Syria and Iran have risen up in revolt against their dictatorial regimes. All are in the process of demanding their freedom with a thunderous roar for democracy. Tunisia's President Zine El Abidine Ben Ali has already been exiled, and Egypt's President Mubarak has stepped aside. The world is waiting to see what will happen to those other states embroiled in the turmoil of revolution. .

"During the twentieth, and at the start of the twenty-first century, evil had stamped its boot so thunderously upon the earth that the planet shook itself in disgust." Father Murphy kept speaking out. He was in a quandary, unable to tell whether he was talking to himself or preaching to his congregation. Nevertheless, he pressed on with his message. "Although the Almighty was outraged at the havoc evil had wrought in His Creation, He had had all eternity to practice the virtue of patience, and so, He waited. But when the accumulated scent of blood, corruption and death had assaulted His nostrils, the priest believed that He was sorely vexed to see that man had disobeyed his Ten Commandments. He had expressly laid these down as a guide for man's conduct. Further, He noted that man had failed to use his conscience and his choice of free will–with which he had been specially endowed–to help him cleave to that which is good and eschew that which is evil. Finally, the Father noted that man had ignored the supreme sacrifice He had made of His son, to teach the vital lesson of love. Disobeying His will, man had wallowed in sin." The priest firmly believed that as their shepherd, he was doing his duty in warning his parishioners. He continued his sermon:

"The Almighty could not believe that human beings had forgotten the catastrophe that could befall them when His anger was aroused. Had they forgotten the Flood, when He had saved all the animals, and ignored all human beings except Noah and his family? Had they forgotten that He had completely destroyed Sodom and Gomorrah for their sinful, disobedient ways? Did they not remember that He had bedeviled Egypt with plagues of vermin and disease before finally slaying the entire firstborn of Egypt's children and animals? Did they dare forget the scourge He had put upon Pharaoh's world for his refusal to let His people go? The King had finally got the message, but clearly, modern man had not.

"Was it possible that human beings had fixated solely on His miracles, remembering that He had raised the dead, fed the hungry, healed the sick, restored sight to the blind and made the lame walk? Had their focus on His benevolent nature made them ignore His terrifying boast?" Once again in the pulpit, the priest decided he would finish his message by reminding his parishioners of God's words:

"I the Lord thy God am a jealous God," who "visits the sins of the fathers upon the children..." for countless generations. To protect his people he firmly believed that they needed to be reminded that: "the wrath of God (cometh) upon the children of disobedience."

"And the LORD said, "I will destroy man whom I have created; "And, behold, I, even I, (will) bring a flood of water upon the earth, and every thing that is in the earth shall die."

Through the dizziness of delirium the priest would swear that he actually saw the index finger of the Almighty thrust itself through the inky curtain of clouds shrouding the heavens. He watched in awe as its shadow stretched over the continents and oceans, shutting out the midday sun. Darkness enveloped the planet and a rushing wind howled over the earth, terrifying all life upon it. Flashes of lightening splintered the darkness and resounding thunderclaps roared His rage. Thunderbolts leapt from His fingertip plunged into the depths of the world's oceans and smashed against the massive tectonic plates at the earth's core. The resulting collisions discharged enormous pressure buckling the seabed. Submarine volcanoes erupted hurling millions of tons of water to the oceans' surfaces. A series of volcanic islands were born as did a series of deadly tsunamis. They headed towards the coasts of all the world's continents."

"Oh my God!" The priest shouted in alarm," is what I am seeing truth or falsehood? Have I lost the battle against evil that I have been fighting all these years?" In awe, he looked at the panorama unfolding before him through closed eyes:

Traveling at breakneck speed, the gargantuan waves roared across the surface of the world's oceans. Like giant fists of steel, they smote against the hulls of ocean liners, oil tankers, container carriers, fishing fleets and vessels of every description. The blows stove in their hulls hurling them, their passengers and cargoes reeling into the depths, drowning all aboard. The giant rollers raced towards the shores of the continents, crashed into the fleets of vessels anchored in ports and marinas, ripping them from their moorings, and scattering their debris together with hundreds of thousands of fish, men, women, children, animals and debris miles and miles inland.

Screams of anguish, shrieks of horror were quickly drowned by the rushing water. Deluge upon deluge swept over the shorelines engulfing whole cities, towns, ports, buildings, churches, hospitals, schools, jails and their inhabitants. The fierce assault of the successive waves hammered away at the outer shell of the continents, raping and ravaging the land mass, uprooting trees, smashing roads and bridges, hurling the splintered remains of ships, cars, buses and trains far inland, destroying everything and everyone in their path.

The mountainous waves swept away the protective walls of Nuclear Plants rupturing the reactor vessels and exposing their graphite rods. Ignited, they released highly toxic radioactive material into the atmosphere that snuffed out all life over extensive areas. The mammoth waves demolished coastal oil farms. Fireballs erupted amidst their flammable petroleum products and spread fan-wise over the landscape, burning urban and rural areas that blazed for weeks on end leaving everything behind them in cinders.

Bolts of lightening struck the firmament incinerating buildings and trees that exploded like bombshells. Their flames spread further and further afield until a red inferno gradually engulfed the earth. Ashes of the millions upon millions of the incinerated dead were strewn about everywhere. The extent of the catastrophe and the number of the dead was so vast as to be incalculable. The stench of corruption circulated in the air for months, and without clean water, food or medicine, any would-be survivors died from cholera, typhoid, malaria, dysentery or starvation.

"And all flesh died that moved upon the earth."

The only living humans left were those who had taken refuge by launching their boats into inland seas, lakes, rivers and waterways far from the assault of the oceans. Sickened by the evil smell, Father Murphy gazed in shock and terror at the nightmare scene of devastation. He didn't miss the irony that the water which had brought death and destruction to so many, had become the saving grace of the survivors. Like the latter, the priest remained terrified, wearied and chastened. He reminded those who would listen: that "God spoke to the remnants of the earth saying: "Bring forth every living thing..., that they may breed abundantly...and be fruitful and multiply..."

Both priest and survivors were overcome at witnessing the world-wide terror spread by the catastrophe. They dropped to their knees and prayed for forgiveness; begged for divine mercy.

"Deliver us from evil," the priest intoned, and the awestruck congregations repeated the words over and over: "Deliver us from evil; oh God, deliver us from evil."

Once the cataclysm was past, it seemed to Father Murphy that the Almighty poured His benevolence upon the earth, and he reminded mankind of John's words:

"In him was life; and the life was the light of men. And the light shineth in darkness; and the darkness comprehended it not." Gradually, the miracle of enlightenment pierced the hearts of men, sweeping away the darkness harbored there. A great hush fell upon the planet and men held their collective breath. Miraculously, the scales fell from their eyes, and filled with joy, they awoke to a new day. The power of love flowed from their hearts to herald a new beginning. It was the moment for which the priest had always hoped and prayed. He wanted to give thanks, but still wasn't sure if what he had witnessed was reality or a figment of his overwrought imagination.

As God's benevolence hovered over the planet and funneled its way into men's hearts, Satan was shocked out of his self-satisfied musing. He knew instantly the full extent of God's miracle and the spectacle of His power curdled his immortal blood. For the first time since his attack on the Creation, his arrogance deserted him. An authority far greater than his had wrested power from his hands. Reeling in shock and confusion, he retired in humiliation to the darkness of the noisome bog over which he ruled.

His dejection gave way to deep despair as he noted with alarm mankind's new obsession—rushing to the help and care of those in need. Dominated by these motives, men and women of every nation formed themselves into groups, cooperatives, organizations and foundations. The fever of their commitment spread and a multiplicity of charitable institutions sprang up.

They raised an army, drawing recruits from every nation; every walk of life, crossing the boundaries of class, race, religion and color. With a genuine love for their fellows and a passion for self-sacrifice, they fixated on a single objective–ministering to those in need. Recruits employed different methods to attain their goal. Some used their celebrity status, others their special talents, and still others, their boundless energy, personal charisma and drive. Their commitment is so compelling, their cause so sacred, that they infuse new meaning into old words. Philanthropy, altruism, civic duty, simple charity and compassion have caught fire in their hearts and minds. As a result, governments and corporations, churches and charitable organizations, banks, businesses, educational institutions, hospitals, families and of course, individuals have all become acutely conscious of their most sacred responsibility—investing their time, effort and money in people.

In every corner of the modern world, God's international horde of beggars stands with outstretched hands at the entrance to shopping mall, bank, grocery, department and liquor store and every other kind of business. They knock on doors, ring doorbells, and make phone calls enlisting help on behalf of all sorts of victims. They organize concerts, banquets, and elite social occasions. They raffle appliances, automobiles, houses, boats and airplanes. They sell poppies, chocolates and lemonade; organize car washes, garage sales, marathons, walkathons and bottle drives. Never satisfied, they fleece their benefactors of anything and everything of value with the sole aim of funding worthy causes.

An international gang of these crusaders struggles bravely to salvage what's left of everything that has been blasted. This rag tag horde is extraordinary in that it puts the idea of service before that of personal gain. Educators teach passionately to share knowledge; healers labor incessantly to relieve suffering while environmentalists toil to preserve what's left of the wilderness. People before profit is their watchword and the citizens of every nation have adopted this unique brand of service. They attain fulfillment by sacrificing personal interests to brighten the lives of others. Others expend their energy to bring relief to the disabled the elderly and those at risk. Their dedication has met with overwhelming success throughout the world. This passion to benefit the downtrodden is based on their compassion, a virtue preached by Christ himself in the parable of the Publican who rescued and ministered to the needs of a fallen stranger that all others avoided. Shelters, clinics and halfway houses have sprung up for the battered, the abused and the abandoned. Rehab centers and missions have mushroomed to care for the addicted, and the homeless.

A multiplicity of well known international societies like the Red Cross, the Salvation Army, the United Nations, Amnesty International and the Blue Cross has sprung into action. They form a part of every nation, raising awareness and funds to solve problems on almost every issue imaginable. They help to eliminate poverty, housing shortages, and hunger. They sponsor children, adopt orphans and provide medical and financial aid to some of the poorest people in the developing world. They rebuild churches, clinics and homes that have been bombed or razed, rally against the abuse of drugs, alcohol, porn and prostitution. They bombard governments, crusade against the death penalty and torture. They urge countries like China, North Korea, Iran, Zimbabwe, Pakistan and others to enact laws that prevent the violation of human rights.

They stop violence against women and children, exert pressure against the unregulated global trade in arms that sponsor war and cause misery, murder, rape and property loss. Some campaign against corporate corruption, and fraud in the marketplace. Others use their funding to improve humanitarian causes like education, the welfare of children and animals. Still others travel the world offering medical assistance like "doctors without borders," or "a fresh pair of eyes," and the essentials of life–clean water, food, security and health care. They also provide the tools to fight the pandemic of AIDS and other contagious diseases.

These charities are about people helping people, creating groups, corporations and foundations that bring together entire communities. They magnify a shared vision of caring to impact the issues that matter most. Through them, the words "giving back" have become an international mantra, and no job application is complete without some form of community service completed by the hopeful applicant. Such widespread rehabilitation has strengthened the physical and moral fabric of society since it permits its unproductive members to rejoin the social structure that aids unfortunates. Recruits act as a safety net that catches those who fall between the cracks and fulfill their purpose by keeping alive the dreams of the disadvantaged. Together, they have formed themselves into an invincible horde that launched the world's most powerful crusade against the forces of darkness. This army marches under the proud banner: VOLUNTEERS.

Satan noted with alarm the swift growth and strength of God's Volunteers that had already begun to erode the successes he had achieved He swore a great oath in his anger and consternation at seeing so much of his evil unraveling and realized that once again he was losing the battle against his arch enemy. Yet, despite everything he saw, he vowed that no mortal army could defeat an immortal like him.

On hearing this absurd boast, the Almighty realized that Satan's egomania had affected his brain. Those afflicted with the disease, He knew, begin by being dissatisfied with their station in life. In their arrogance, they elevate themselves to the status of deities attempting to replace God and to usurp His power, His authority. They yearn to be in charge, believing that the lies they tell themselves about their superiority become true in the telling. Not surprisingly, they overestimate their ability by setting themselves tasks that are well beyond their capability. In doing so, they orchestrate their own failure. In the same way that puny mortals like Hitler, Attila the Hun, Alexander the Great, Napoleon and Joseph Stalin, the immortal Prince of darkness was doomed to fail in his personal vendetta–to destroy God's Creation. That same egotism and flawed reasoning that had incited him to lead a rebellion against heaven; those same defects of character that had caused his defeat then, would lead to a similar result in his war against mankind.

Epilogue

Such was the compassion and mercy of the Almighty that over the centuries He had given serious consideration to forgive Satan his wrongdoing and perhaps even to restore him to his former post. It was a tacit admission that He missed the constant upheaval caused in His kingdom by this flamboyant rascal whom He considered both colorful and brilliant. Why else would He have chosen Lucifer, the bright angel of light, to be the leader of His heavenly host, if not for his superlative qualities, even perhaps, his genius?

However, the archfiend's egotism and vaulting ambition had created such instability in the Almighty's kingdom that he often turned out to be a pain in the heavenly butt. It was this thorn that had made Satan both aggravating and unbearable. Yet, the Almighty actually missed confrontation with so gifted, stimulating and resourceful an adversary. He thought it almost a blasphemy to admit, but wouldn't Satan keep Him on His celestial toes?

It was a matter to which the Almighty would have to give serious thought before making a decision that even He might regret. But time was on His side. And so again, He waited.

The End

References

Axtell, Roger E.   *The Do's and Taboos of Body Language around the World*, John Wiley & Sons, Inc. Toronto, 1999

The World of Business: Explanatory Notes, Dialogues pp 50–74

Engel, Beverly   *The Emotionally Abused Woman*, Radom House Publishing Group, New York, 1990

Fiddler, Colin   *The Buchart Gardens*, Buchart Gardens Publishing Co.

Foa, Edna and   *Treating the trauma of Rape using Cognitive Behavioral*
Rathaum, Barbara   *therapy*, The Guilford Press.

Storey, Robert   *Korea*, Lonely Planet Publications, 1997.

Covell, Jon Carter   *Korea's Cultural Roots*, Hollym International Corp. 1983.

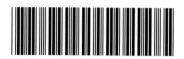